JEAN LARTÉGUY (b. Jean Pierre Lucien Osty) was born in Maisons-Alfort, a small town just southeast of Paris. In March 1942, he escaped occupied France for Spain, where he spent time in prison before joining the Free French Forces. He served seven years of military service in North Africa and Korea, during which he earned various military awards. After being wounded by a grenade, Lartéguy turned to writing, working as a journalist and war correspondent. He covered conflicts in eastern Europe, the Middle East, southeast Asia, and North Africa, primarily for the magazine *Paris Match*. In 1955, he earned the Albert Londres Prize for his reporting in Indochina. A prolific writer, Lartéguy's body of work includes more than thirty works of fiction and nonfiction, most of which focus on the consequences of war and decolonization in the twentieth century. He is best remembered for his Algerian War trilogy, consisting of *The Mercenaries* (1954), *The Centurions* (1960), and *The Praetorians* (1961). *The Centurions*, an overnight sensation and bestseller in France, became a film titled *Lost Command*, starring Anthony Quinn, in 1966. Though he died in 2011, his significance as a chronicler of irregular warfare continues to rise with the proliferation of modern guerrilla warfare and counterinsurgency tactics.

ROBERT D. KAPLAN is the author of many acclaimed books on the military, foreign affairs, and travel, including *Imperial Grunts: The American Military on the Ground, Hog Pilots, Blue Water Grunts: The American Military in the Air, at Sea, and on the Ground, The Coming Anarchy,* and *The Revenge of Geography: What the Map Tells Us About Coming Conflict and the Battle Against Fate.* He is a contributing editor to *The Atlantic* and a senior fellow at the Center for a New American Security. He served on the Defense Policy Board and was named by *Foreign Policy* magazine as one of the world's Top 100 Global Thinkers in both 2011 and 2012.

ALEXANDER (XAN) WALLACE FIELDING was a British author and translator. He served as a Special Operations executive
in the British Army in Crete, France, and the Far East. The author of several books of his own, he also translated works by
Pierre Boulle, Jean Lartéguy, and others from French into English. He died in Paris in 1991.

JEAN LARTÉGUY

The Centurions

Translated by
XAN FIELDING

Foreword by
ROBERT D. KAPLAN

PENGUIN BOOKS

PENGUIN BOOKS

Published by the Penguin Group
Penguin Group (USA) LLC
375 Hudson Street
New York, New York 10014

USA | Canada | UK | Ireland | Australia | New Zealand | India | South Africa | China
penguin.com
A Penguin Random House Company

First published in Great Britain by Hutchinson & Co. (Publishers) Ltd. 1961
First published in the United States of America by E. P. Dutton & Co., Inc. 1962
This edition with a foreword by Robert D. Kaplan published in Penguin Books 2015

Originally published in French as *Les Centurions* by Presses de la Cite

Robert D. Kaplan's foreword is a revised version of his article "Rereading Vietnam"
which appeared online in *The Atlantic* in 2007.

ISBN 978-0-14-310744-6

Printed in the United States of America

Set in Sabon LT Std

To Jean Pouget

Contents

in his own person encapsulates the divide between a professional warrior class that lives by these enduring, historical truths and a civilian home front alienated from them. Lartéguy inhabits the very soul of the U.S. Special Operations community, alienating not only civilian readers but members of the conventional military in the process.

Throughout my years observing the Special Operations community close up, I witnessed several editions of Lartéguy's *The Centurions* (1960) passing through the hands of those about whom I reported. Green Berets recommended to me not only Lartéguy's *The Centurions* but also *The Praetorians* (1961): books about French paratroopers in Vietnam and Algeria in the 1950s that resonated with their own experiences in Afghanistan and Iraq. And it wasn't just Green Berets who found Lartéguy essential. Alistair Horne, the renowned historian of the Algerian War, uses Lartéguy for epigrams in *A Savage War of Peace* (1977). Some years back, Gen. David Petraeus—then the future commander of U.S. ground forces in Iraq—pulled *The Centurions* off a shelf at his quarters in Fort Leavenworth, Kansas, and gave me a disquisition about the small-unit leadership principles exemplified by one of the book's characters.

More than half a century ago, this Frenchman was obsessed about a home front that had no context for a hot, irregular war; about a professional warrior class alienated from its civilian compatriots as much as from its own conventional infantry battalions; about the need to engage in both combat and civil affairs in a new form of warfare to follow an age of victory parades and what he called "cinema-heroics"; about an enemy with complete freedom of action, allowed "to do what we didn't dare"; and about the danger of creating a "sect" of singularly brave iron men, whose ideals were so exalted that beyond the battlefield they had a tendency to become woolly-headed. Lartéguy dedicates his book to the memory of centurions who died so that Rome might survive, but he notes in his conclusion that it was these same centurions who destroyed Rome.

Born in 1920, Jean Lartéguy—a pseudonym; his real name was Jean Pierre Lucien Osty—fought with the Free French and afterward became a journalist. Because of his military experience

Foreword

Jean Lartéguy: Decoding the Warrior Ethos

For thousands of years men have fought one another in situations where the battle lines are not fixed and words like *front* and *rear* lines have little meaning—for the war is everywhere, with civilians caught up and brutalized in the conflict. Irregular warfare, guerrilla uprisings, and counterinsurgency are timeless—not merely fads of the moment. Malaya, Vietnam, Somalia, Bosnia, Kosovo, Chechnya, the Congo, Afghanistan, Iraq, and Syria are just some of the datelines in which the twentieth and twenty-first centuries register conflicts whose fundamentals the ancients would have been familiar with. With the collapse of central authority in the Middle East, otherwise known as the "Arab Spring," this situation applies to an even greater degree. For countries like Libya, Yemen, Syria, and Iraq are barely states at this juncture, with tribes, militias, and gangs, divided by territory, sect, and ethnicity, battling for primacy over a confused and violent landscape.

Conventional modern war, which Napoleon did so much to define and institutionalize, with its formalized set-piece battles and vertical chains of command, has mainly been with us for little more than two centuries. Its future, moreover, is uncertain. So while counterinsurgency is presently disparaged, because the results in Iraq and Afghanistan have been so unsatisfying for Americans, the lessons of counterinsurgency—if forgotten—will only have to be relearned on some future morrow. For that is the verdict of history going back to antiquity.

You cannot approach Vietnam and Iraq in particular, or the subject of counterinsurgency in general, without reference to Jean Lartéguy, a French novelist and war correspondent who and Resistance ties, he had nearly unrivaled access to French para-troopers who fought at Dien Bien Phu and in the Battle of Algiers. His empathy for these men, some of whom were torturers, made him especially loathed by the Parisian Left, even though he broke with the paratroopers themselves, out of opposition to their political goals, which he labeled "neofascism."

Lartéguy eventually found his military ideal in Israel, where he became revered by paratroopers who translated *The Centurions* into Hebrew to read at their training centers. He called these Jewish soldiers "the most remarkable of all of war's servants, superior even to the Viet, who at the same time detests war the most." By the mid-1970s, though, he became disillusioned with the Israel Defense Forces. He said it had ceased to be "a manageable grouping of commandos" and was becoming a "cumbersome machine" too dependent on American-style technology—as if foreseeing some of the problems with the 2006 Lebanon campaign.

I remember walking into the office of a U.S. Army Special Forces colonel in South Korea and noticing a plaque with Lartéguy's famous "two armies" quote. (The translation is by Xan Fielding, a British Special Operations officer who, in addition to rendering Lartéguy's classics into English, was also a close friend of the late British travel writer Patrick Leigh Fermor, to whom Fermor addresses his introduction in his own 1977 classic, *A Time of Gifts*.) In *The Centurions*, one of Lartéguy's paratroopers declares:

> I'd like . . . two armies: one for display, with lovely guns, tanks, little soldiers, fanfares, staffs, distinguished and doddering generals, and dear little regimental officers . . . an army that would be shown for a modest fee on every fairground in the country.
>
> The other would be the real one, composed entirely of young enthusiasts in camouflage battledress, who would not be put on display but from whom . . . all sorts of tricks would be taught. That's the army in which I should like to fight.

But the reply from another character in *The Centurions* to this declaration is swift: "you're heading for a lot of trouble." The exchange telescopes the philosophical dilemma about the measures that need to be taken against enemies who would erect a far worse world than you, but which, nevertheless, are impossible to carry out because of the "remorse" that afflicts soldiers when they violate their own notion of purity of arms—even in situations where such "tricks" might somehow be rationalized. They may win the battle, but will surely lose their souls.

Rather than a roughneck, this Army Special Forces colonel epitomized the soft, indirect approach to unconventional war that is in contrast to "direct action." The message that he and other professional warriors have always taken away from Lartéguy's famous "two armies" quote—rooted in Lartéguy's own Vietnam experience—is that *the mission is everything*, and conventional militaries, by virtue of being vast bureaucratic machines obsessed with rank and privilege, are insufficiently focused on the mission: regardless of whether it is direct action or humanitarian affairs.

Of course, the conventional officer would reply that the special operator's field of sight is so narrow that he can't see anything beyond the mission. "They're dangerous," one of Lartéguy's protagonists says of the paratroopers, "because they go to any lengths . . . beyond the conventional notion of good and evil." For if the warrior's actions contradict his faith, his doubts are easily overcome by belief in the larger cause. Lartéguy writes of one soldier: "He had placed the whole of his life under the sign of Christ who had preached peace, charity, brotherhood . . . and at the same time he had arranged for the delayed-action bombs at the Cat-Bi airfield . . . 'What of it? There's a war on and we can't allow Hanoi to be captured.'"

Vietnam, like Iraq, represented a war of frustrating half measures, fought against an enemy that respected no limits. More than any writer I know, Lartéguy communicates the intensity of such frustrations, which, in turn, create the psychological gulf that separates warriors from both a conscript army and a civilian home front.

The best units, according to Lartéguy, while officially built on high ideals, are, in fact, products of such deep bonds of brotherhood and familiarity that the world outside requires a dose of "cynicism" merely to stomach. As one Green Beret once wrote me, "There are no more cynical soldiers on the planet than the SF [Special Forces] guys I work with, they snort at the platitudes we are expected to parrot, but," he went on, "you will not find anyone who gets the job done better in tough environments like Iraq." In fact, in extreme and difficult situations like Iraq, cynics may actually serve a purpose. For in the regular army there is a tendency to report up the command chain that the mission is succeeding, even if it isn't. Cynics won't buy that, and will say so bluntly. Lartéguy immortalizes such soldiers.

Lartéguy writes that the warrior looks down on the rest of the military as "the profession of the sluggard," men who "get up early to do nothing." Yet as one paratrooper notes in *The Praetorians*:

> In Algeria that type of officer died out. When we came in from operations we had to deal with the police, build sports grounds, attend classes. Regulations? They hadn't provided for anything, even if one tried to make an exegesis of them with the subtlety of a rabbi.

Dirty, badly conceived wars in Vietnam and Algeria had begotten a radicalized French warrior class of noncommissioned officers, able to kill in the morning and build schools in the afternoon, which had a higher regard for its Muslim guerrilla adversaries than for regular officers in its own ranks. Such men would gladly advance toward a machine-gun nest without looking back, and yet were "booed by the crowds" upon returning home: so that they saw the civilian society they were defending as "vile, corrupt and degraded."

The estrangement of soldiers from their own citizenry is somewhat particular to counterinsurgencies and *small wars*, where there are no neat battle lines and thus no easy narrative for the people back home to follow. The frustrations in these wars are great precisely because they are not easily communicated. Lartéguy writes: Imagine an environment where a whole garrison of two thousand troops is "held in check" by a small "band of thugs and murderers." The enemy is able to "know everything: every movement of our troops, the departure times of the convoys . . .

Meanwhile we're rushing about the bare mountains, exhausting our men; we shall never be able to find anything."

Because the enemy is not limited by Western notions of war, the temptation arises among a stymied soldiery to bend its own rules. Following an atrocity carried out by French paratroopers that calms a rural area of Algeria, one soldier rationalizes to another: "'Fear has changed sides, tongues have been loosened . . . We obtained more in a day than in six months fighting, and more with twenty-seven dead than with several hundreds.'" The soldiers comfort themselves further with a quotation from a fourteenth-century Catholic bishop: "When her existence is threatened, the Church is absolved of all moral commandments." It is the purest of them, Lartéguy goes on, who are most likely to commit torture.

Here we enter territory that is unrelated to the individual Americans I covered as a correspondent. It is important to make such distinctions. When Lartéguy writes about bravery and alienation, he understands American warriors; when he writes about political insurrections and torture, some exceptions aside, he is talking about a particular caste of French paratroopers. Yet his discussion is relevant to America's past in Vietnam and Iraq. I don't mean My Lai and Abu Ghraib, both of which aided the enemy rather than ourselves, but the moral gray area that we increasingly inhabit concerning collateral civilian deaths.

In *The Face of War: Reflections on Men and Combat* (1976), Lartéguy writes that contemporary wars are, in particular, made for the side that doesn't care about "the preservation of a good conscience." So he asks, "How do you explain that to save liberty, liberty must first be suppressed?" His answer can only be thus: "In that rests the weakness of democratic regimes, a weakness that is at the same time a credit to them, an honor."

One thing is clear: we have rarely been good at predicting the next war. And given the history of war, not to mention the undeniable, ongoing transformation of the army toward a greater emphasis on Special Operations, the lessons of *The Centurions* will persist. So will the need to nurture a professional warrior class that is determined to preserve its honor, even if that inhibits the mission.

ROBERT D. KAPLAN

We had been told, on leaving our native soil, that we were going to defend the sacred rights conferred on us by so many of our citizens settled overseas, so many years of our presence, so many benefits brought by us to populations in need of our assistance and our civilization.

We were able to verify that all this was true, and, because it was true, we did not hesitate to shed our quota of blood, to sacrifice our youth and our hopes. We regretted nothing, but whereas we over here are inspired by this frame of mind, I am told that in Rome factions and conspiracies are rife, that treachery flourishes, and that many people in their uncertainty and confusion lend a ready ear to the dire temptations of relinquishment and vilify our action.

I cannot believe that all this is true and yet recent wars have shown how pernicious such a state of mind could be and to where it could lead.

Make haste to reassure me, I beg you, and tell me that our fellow-citizens understand us, support us and protect us as we ourselves are protecting the glory of the Empire.

If it should be otherwise, if we should have to leave our bleached bones on these desert sands in vain, then beware of the anger of the Legions!

MARCUS FLAVINIUS,
CENTURION IN THE 2ND COHORT OF THE AUGUSTA LEGION,
TO HIS COUSIN TERTULLUS IN ROME

Author's Note

I knew them well, the centurions of the wars of Indo-China and Algeria. At one time I was one of their number; then, as a journalist, I became their observer and, on occasion, their confidant.

I shall always feel attached to those men, even if I should ever disagree with the course they choose to follow, but I feel in no way bound to give a conventional or idealised picture of them.

This book is first and foremost a novel and the characters in it are imaginary. They might at a pinch, through some feature or incident, recall one or another of my former comrades now famous or dead and forgotten. But there is not one of these characters to whom one could put a name without going astray. On the other hand, the facts, the situations, the scenes of action are almost all taken from real life and I have endeavoured to adhere to the correct dates.

I dedicate this book to the memory of all the centurions who perished so that Rome might survive.

JEAN LARTÉGUY

The Centurions

PART ONE

CAMP ONE

CAPTAIN DE GLATIGNY'S SENSE OF MILITARY HONOUR

Tied up to one another, the prisoners looked like a column of caterpillars on the march. They emerged into a little basin, flanked by their Vietminh guards who kept yelling at them: "*Di-di, mau-len* . . . Keep going, get a move on!" All of them remembered those bicycle-rickshaws they used to take at Hanoi or Saigon only a few weeks or a few months before. They used to shout at the coolies in the same way: "*Mau-len, mau-len* . . . Get a move on, you bastard, there's a pretty little half-caste waiting for me in the Rue Catinat. She's such a slut that if I'm even ten minutes late she'll have found someone else. *Mau-len, mau-len!* Our leave's over, the battalion's been alerted, we probably jump tonight. *Mau-len*, hurry up and get past that bit of garden and that slender beckoning figure in white!"

The basin looked like any other in this part of the country. The trail emerged from the valley, hemmed in between the mountains and the forest, and came out on to a system of rice-fields fitted one into another like inlaid chequer-work. The geometrical pattern of the little mud embankments seemed to separate the colours: the various shades of deep, deep green which are those of paddy-grass.

The village in the middle of the basin had been destroyed. All that remained was a few charred piles rising above the tall elephant-grass. The inhabitants had fled into the forest, but even so the Political Committee were using these piles as propaganda hoardings. There was a crudely drawn poster of a Thai couple in national dress, the woman with her flat hat, close-fitting bodice and flowing skirt, the man with his baggy black trousers and short jacket. They were represented giving an enthusiastic welcome to a *bo-doi*, a victorious soldier of the Democratic Republic of Viet-Nam, with a palm-fibre helmet on his head and a huge yellow star on a red ground pinned to his tunic.

A *bo-doi* similar to the one in the poster, but who was walking barefoot and carrying a submachine-gun, gave a signal for the prisoners to halt. They sank down into the tall grass on the edge of the trail; they could not use their arms, which were tied behind them, and squirmed about like fragments of worms.

A Thai peasant had come out of the bush and sidled up towards the prisoners. The *bo-doi* exhorted him with sharp little phrases which sounded like slogans. Soon there was a whole group of them, all dressed in black, looking at the captured Frenchmen.

This spectacle seemed incredible to them and they could not decide what attitude to adopt. Not knowing what to do, they stood silent and motionless, ready to take flight. Perhaps they would suddenly see the "long noses" break their bonds and knock down their guards.

One of the Thais, by dint of every kind of precaution and expression of courtesy, questioned another *bo-doi* who had just appeared, armed with a heavy Czech rifle which he held in both hands. Very gently, in the protective tone of an elder brother speaking to a younger, the *bo-doi* replied, but his false modesty made his triumph seem all the more unbearable to Lieutenant Pinières. He rolled over towards Lieutenant Merle:

"Don't you think that Viet's got the nasty expression of a Jesuit on his way back from the Sunday auto-da-fé? They burnt the witch at Dien-Bien-Phu and he must be telling them all about it. The witch was us."

Boisfeuras spoke up in his rasping voice, which to Pinières sounded as self-satisfied as the *bo-doi*'s:

"He's telling them that the Vietnamese people have beaten the imperialists and that they're now free."

The Thai had translated this to his companions. He, in his

turn, gave himself airs, assumed a protective manner and lordly demeanour, as though the mere fact of speaking the language of these strange little soldiers, masters of the French, allowed him to participate in their victory.

The Thais gave one or two delighted cries, but not too loud— a few exclamations and smiles, but which they suppressed— and drew closer to the prisoners to have a better look.

The *bo-doi* raised his hand and made a speech.

"Well, Captain Boisfeuras," Pinières inquired sourly, "what are they saying now?"

"The Viet's talking about President Ho's policy of leniency and telling them not to ill-treat the prisoners, which had never even crossed their minds. The Viet would willingly incite them to do so if only for the pleasure of holding them back. He's also telling them that at five o'clock this afternoon the garrison of Dien-Bien-Phu surrendered."

"Long live President Ho!" the *bo-doi* exclaimed at the end of his harangue.

"Long live President Ho!" the group echoed in the toneless, solemn voice of schoolchildren.

Night had fallen with no intervening twilight. Swarms of mosquitoes and other insect pests set upon the arms, legs and bare chests of the Frenchmen. The Viets could at least fan themselves with leafy branches.

By rolling his body forward, which forced his neighbours likewise to shift theirs, Pinières had drawn a little closer to Glatigny who was looking up at the sky and appeared to be lost in thought.

He was the one they had to thank for being tied up together, for he had fallen foul of the Political Commissar. But none of the twenty men shackled to him held it against him, except perhaps Boisfeuras, who had not, however, ventured an opinion on the subject.

"I say, sir, where does this fellow Boisfeuras come from, who speaks their lingo?"

Pinières addressed everyone by the familiar "*tu*," except Glatigny, out of deference, and Boisfeuras, to show him his dislike.

Glatigny seemed to have some difficulty in shaking off his thoughts. He had to make a great effort to reply:

"I've only known him for forty-eight hours. He showed up at the strong-point on the 4th of May, in the evening, and it's a miracle he got through with his convoy of Pims* laden with ammo and supplies. I'd never heard of him until then."

Pinières mumbled something and rubbed his head against a tuft of grass to get rid of the mosquitoes.

Glatigny was anxious to forget the fall of Dien-Bien-Phu, but the events of the last six days, the attacks that had been launched against the strong-point of Marianne II, which he commanded, all these had welded together in a sort of mould so as to form a solid block of weariness and horror.

The height had been three-quarters surrounded. The Vietminh infantry attacked every night and their heavy mortars harassed the position all day. Out of the whole battalion only forty men were left unscathed or lightly wounded. The rest mingled with the mud in the shell-holes.

During the night Glatigny had made a final wireless contact with Raspéguy, who had just been promoted to lieutenant-colonel; there was no one else replying to signals or issuing orders. He was the one to whom Glatigny had sent his S O S:

"I've no more supplies, sir, no more ammo, and they're over-running the position where we're fighting hand to hand."

Raspéguy's voice, slightly grating but still retaining some of the sing-song intonation of the Basque language, reassured him and infused him with warmth, like a glass of wine after a severe strain.

"Stick it out, man. I'll try and get something through to you."

This was the first time the great paratrooper had addressed him by "*tu*." Raspéguy did not take kindly to staff officers or

---

*P.I.M.: literally, *Prisonniers Internés Militaires*; in fact, suspects or even prisoners of war who acted as coolies for the fighting units, to which they soon attached themselves as combatants. One Christmas evening, in the Foreign Legion camp near Hanoi, I actually saw some of these Pims ward off a Vietminh attack with mortar fire. The legionaries were far too drunk that evening to do it themselves. (Author's note.)

anyone else too closely in touch with the generals, and Glatigny had once been aide-de-camp to the commander-in-chief.

Dawn had broken once again and for a moment a silhouette had blocked the rectangle of light which marked the entrance to the shelter.

The silhouette had bent down, then straightened up again. The man in the mud-stained uniform had carefully laid his American carbine down on the table, then taken off the steel helmet which he was wearing on top of his bush hat. He was barefoot and his trousers were rolled up to his knees. When he turned towards Glatigny, the dull light of that rainy morning had brought out the colour of his eyes which were a very pale watery green.

He had introduced himself:

"Captain Boisfeuras. I've got forty Pims and about thirty cases with me."

The two previous convoys had been forced back after trying to cover the three hundred yards which still connected Marianne II to Marianne III by a shapeless communication trench filled with liquid mud which was under fire from the Viets.

Boisfeuras had taken a piece of paper out of his pocket and checked his list:

"Two thousand seven hundred hand-grenades, fifteen thousand rounds; but there are no more mortar shells and I had to leave the ration boxes behind at Marianne III."

"How did you manage to get through?" asked Glatigny who was not counting on any further assistance.

"I persuaded my Pims that they had to keep going."

Glatigny looked at Boisfeuras more closely. He was rather short, five foot seven at the most, with slim hips and broad shoulders. He had about the same build as a native of the Haute Région: strong and at the same time slender. Without his prominent nose and full lips, he could have been taken for a half-caste; his rather grating voice emphasized this impression.

"What's the latest?" Glatigny asked.

"We're going to be attacked tomorrow, at nightfall, by 308

Division, the toughest of the lot; that's why I dumped the ration boxes so as to bring up a little more ammo."

"How do you know this?"

"Before coming up with the convoy, I went for a little stroll
among the Viets and took a prisoner. He was from the 308th
and he told me."

"H.Q. never let me know."

"I forgot to bring the prisoner back—he was a bit of a
nuisance—so they wouldn't believe me."

While he spoke he had wiped his hands on his hat and taken
a cigarette out of Glatigny's packet, which was the last he had
left.

"Got a light? Thanks. Can I move in here?"

"You're not going back to H.Q.?"

"What for? We're done for there, as we are here. The 308th
have been reorganized completely; they're going to go all out
and mop up everything that's still standing."

Glatigny began to feel irritated by the newcomer's complacency and also by that supercilious glint he could see in his
eye. He tried to put him in his place:

"I suppose it was that prisoner of yours who told you all this
as well."

"No, but a couple of weeks ago I went through the base area
of the 308th and I saw the columns of reinforcements arriving."

"So you're in a position to stroll about among the Viets,
are you?"

"Dressed as a *nha-que*, I'm more or less unrecognizable and
I speak Vietnamese pretty well."

"But where have you come from?"

"From the Chinese border. I was running some guerrilla
bands up there. One day I got the order to drop everything and
make for Dien-Bien-Phu. It took me a month."

A Nung partisan dressed in the same uniform as the captain
now came into the strong-point.

"It's Min, my batman," said Boisfeuras. "He was up there
with me."

He began speaking to him in his language. The Nung shook

his head. Then he lowered his eyes, put his carbine down next to his officer's, took off his equipment and went out.

"What did you say to him?" asked Glatigny whose curiosity had got the better of his antipathy.

"I told him to clear out. He's going to try and get to Luang-Prabang through the Nam-Ou valley."

"You could escape as well if you tried . . ."

"Perhaps, but I'm not going to. I don't want to miss an experience which might be extremely interesting."

"Isn't it an officer's duty to try and escape?"

"I haven't been captured yet; nor have you. But after tomorrow we'll both be prisoners . . . or corpses; it's all in the game."

"You could join the guerrillas who are around Dien-Bien-Phu."

"There are no guerrillas around Dien-Bien-Phu, or if there are they're hand in glove with the Viets. There again we failed, like everywhere else . . . because we didn't wage the right sort of war."

"I was still with the C.-in-C. a month ago. He didn't keep anything hidden from me. I took part in the formation of all those bands, and I never heard about any on the Chinese border."

"They didn't always keep to the border; occasionally they even went across into China. I took my orders direct from Paris, from a service attached to the Présidence du Conseil. No one knew of my existence; like that I could always be disowned if anything happened."

"If we're taken prisoner you're liable to get it in the neck from the Viets."

"They don't know anything about me. I was operating against the Chinese, not against the Viets. My war, if you like, was less localized than yours. Whether in the West, the East or the Far East, Communism forms a whole, and it's childish to think that by attacking one of the members of this community you can localize the conflict. A few men in Paris had realized this."

"You don't know me from Adam yet you seem to be trusting

me already to the extent of telling me things that I might have preferred not to know."

"We're going to have to live together, Captain de Glatigny, maybe for a long time. I liked your attitude when you learned that it was all up with Dien-Bien-Phu and left the C.-in-C., a man of your class and your tradition, to get yourself dropped here.

"I interpreted that attitude in a sense which perhaps you had never intended. In my eyes, you had abandoned the moribund establishment to rejoin the soldiers and the common herd, those who do the actual fighting, the foundation-stone of any army."

That was how Glatigny made the acquaintance of Boisfeuras who now lay a few feet away from him, a prisoner like himself.

During the night Boisfeuras shifted closer to Glatigny.

"The age of heroics is over," he said, "at least the age of cinema heroics. The new armies will have neither regimental standards nor military bands. They will have to be first and foremost efficient. That's what we're going to learn and that's the reason I didn't try and escape."

He held his two hands out to Glatigny, and the latter saw that he had slipped out of his fetters. But he had no reaction; he was even rather bored by Boisfeuras. Everything came to him from a great distance, like an echo.

Glatigny was lying like a gun dog, his jutting shoulder bearing the weight of his body.

The crests of the mountains surrounding the basin stood out clearly against the dark background of the night. Clouds drifted across the sky and from time to time the close or distant sound of an aircraft could be heard in the silence.

He felt no particular urge other than a very remote and very vague desire for warmth. His physical exhaustion was such that he had the impression of being withdrawn from the world, pushed beyond his limits and enabled to contemplate himself from outside. Perhaps this was what Le-Thuong meant by Nirvana.

At Saigon the Buddhist monk Le-Thuong had tried to initiate him into the mysteries of fasting.

"The first few days," he had told him, "you think of nothing but food. However fervent your prayers and your longing for union with God, all your spiritual exercises, all your meditations are tainted by material desires. The liberation of the mind occurs between the eighth and the tenth day. In a few hours it detaches itself from the body. Independent of it, it appears in a startling purity which is made up of lucidity, objectivity and penetrating understanding. Between the thirty-fifth and fortieth day, in the midst of this purity, the urge for food occurs again: this is the final alarm signal given by the organism on the point of exhaustion. Beyond this biological limit, metaphysics cease to exist."

Since dawn on 7 May Glatigny had been in this condition. He had the strange feeling of having two separate states of consciousness, one of which was weakening more and more at every moment but still impelled him to give certain orders, make certain gestures, such as tearing off his badges of rank when he had been captured, while the other took refuge in a sort of dull, morose form of contemplation. Until then he had always lived in a world which was concrete, active, friendly or hostile, but logical even in absurdity.

On 6 May, at eleven o'clock at night, the Viets had blown up the summit of the peak with a mine and forthwith thrown in two battalions which had seized almost the whole of the strong-point and, which was worse, the most commanding positions.

The French counter-attack by the forty survivors had thus started from the foot of the slope.

Glatigny recalled the remark Boisfeuras had made: "This is all completely idiotic!" and Pinières's sharp retort:

"If you're nervous about it, sir, there's no need for you to come with us."

But Boisfeuras was without nerves; he had proved this. He simply seemed indifferent to what was happening, as though he was reserving himself entirely for the second part of the drama.

The counter-attack had been feeble and difficult to get under way. Nevertheless, the men had managed to regain the position, dug-out after dug-out, by means of hand-grenades. At four in the morning the last Viet pinned down on the edge of the crater of the mine had been wiped out; but half the men of the small garrison had lost their lives.

A sudden silence ensued, isolating Marianne II like an island in the midst of a sea on fire. To the west of the Song Ma, the Vietminh artillery was pounding away at General de Castries' H.Q. and for a few seconds the glow of the firing alternately spread and faded in the darkness. To the north, Marianne IV, assailed on all sides, was still holding out.

Cergona, the wireless operator, had been killed at Captain Glatigny's side. But his set, a PCR 10, which he carried strapped to his back, was still working and crackled gently in the silence. Suddenly the crackling gave way to the voice of Portes, who was in command of the last reserve company centred on Marianne IV. This unit had been made up of the survivors of the three parachute battalions to come to the assistance of Marianne II:

"Double Blue, I repeat. I am still at the foot of Marianne II. Impossible to break out. The Viets hold the trenches above me and are chucking grenades right on top of us. I've only got nine men left. Over."

"Blue Three, I've told you to counter-attack. Get a move on, for Christ's sake; we're also getting grenades tossed at us. You should have reached the summit by now."

"Double Blue Three, message received. I'll try and advance. Out."

Silence, followed by another voice insistently repeating:

"Double Blue Four, reply. Double Blue Four?"

But Blue could not reply any longer; old Portes had been shot to pieces attempting to gain the summit. His huge frame lay stretched out on a slope and a tiny Viet was going through his pockets.

Glatigny had listened to this strange wireless conversation

with the indifference of a sports professional who has gone into retirement and tunes in to the broadcasts of the matches by sheer force of habit. But this meant that no one now could come to the aid of Marianne II since Marianne III was lost.

Glatigny could not even summon up enough strength to switch off the PCR 10 which went on crackling until its batteries ran out. Cergona lay with his head in the mud, and the set with its aerial looked like some monstrous beetle which was devouring his body.

A recognition light floating slowly down on the end of its parachute cast a livid gleam over the peak. On the reverse slope, Glatigny could make out the Vietminh trenches which stood out as a series of unbroken black lines. They looked calm and utterly inoffensive.

His platoon officers and company commanders began to trickle back one by one to make their report. Ten yards farther off, Boisfeuras sat with his knees drawn up to his chin, looking up into the sky as though seeking a sign from heaven.

Merle was the first to arrive. He looked lankier than ever and kept picking his nose.

"I've only seven men left in the company, sir, and two magazines of ammo. Not a word from Lacade's platoon which has disappeared completely."

The next to turn up was Sergeant-Major Pontin. The stubble on his cheeks was white; he appeared to be on the point of collapse and on the verge of tears.

"So long as he breaks down alone in his dug-out," Glatigny said to himself.

"Five men left, four magazines," said the sergeant-major.

Then he went off to have his break-down.

Pinières was the last to arrive. He was a senior lieutenant and came and sat down next to Glatigny.

"Only eight men left, and nothing to put in the rifles."

The Viets were now broadcasting the Partisan Song on Marianne II's frequency:

Friend, do you hear the black flight of the ravens in the plains,
Friend, do you hear the dull cry of your country in chains . . .

"That's funny," Pinières remarked bitterly, "it really is funny, sir. They've even gone and stolen that from me."

Pinières had undergone his baptism of fire in an F.T.P. maquis group and had been assimilated into the army: he was one of the rare successes to emerge from this operation.

Merle reappeared.

"Better come, sir. They've found the kid and he's dying."

"The kid" was Second-Lieutenant Lacade, who had been posted to the parachute battalion three months before, straight from Saint-Cyr and after only a few weeks in a training school.

Glatigny got up and Boisfeuras followed him, barefoot and with his trousers rolled up to his knees.

Lacade had received some fragments of grenade in the stomach. His fingers dug into the warm, muddy ground. In the half light Glatigny could hardly distinguish his face, but by the sound of his voice he realized he was done for.

Lacade was twenty-one years old. To give himself an air of authority, he had grown a whisp of blond moustache and made his voice sound gruff. It had now become adolescent once more, a hesitant voice in which the high tones alternated with the low. The kid was no longer putting on an act.

"I'm thirsty," he kept saying, "I'm terribly thirsty, sir."

The only answer Glatigny could give was a lie:

"We'll have you taken down to Marianne III; there's an M.O. there."

It was silly to believe that anyone, hampered with a casualty, could get through the Viet position between the two strong-points. Even the kid knew this; but now he was willing to believe in the impossible. He pinned his faith on his captain's promises.

"I'm thirsty," he repeated, "but I can certainly hang on until it's light. You remember, sir, in Hanoi, at the Normandie, those bottles of beer so cold that they were all misted up? It was like touching a piece of ice."

Glatigny had taken his hand. He slid his fingers up his wrist to feel his pulse which was weakening. The kid would not be suffering much longer.

Lacade cried out once or twice again for some beer and muttered a girl's name, Aline, the name of his little fiancée who was waiting for him in her home in the country, the little fiancée of a Saint-Cyr cadet, bright and gay and not at all well off, who had worn the same dress on Sundays for the last two years.

His fingers dug still deeper into the mud.

Boisfeuras sidled up to Glatigny who was still crouching over the body.

"Seven drafts of Saint-Cyr cadets wiped out in Indo-China. It's too much, Glatigny, when the result is a defeat. It will be difficult to recover from this drain on our manpower."

"A boy of twenty," said Glatigny, "twenty years of hope and enthusiasm dead. That's a hell of a capital to throw away, and can't be easily recovered. I wonder what they think about it in Paris."

"They're just coming out of the theatres about now."

At first light the Viets attacked again. The remaining survivors of Marianne II saw them emerging one by one from the openings in their covered trenches. Then the silhouettes started appearing and disappearing, moving swiftly, bounding and rebounding like india-rubber balls. Not a single shot was fired. Glatigny had given orders to reserve what was left of the ammunition for the final assault.

The captain had a Mills bomb in his hand. He plucked out the pin, keeping his palm pressed down on the spring.

"All I need do," he reflected, "is drop it at my feet just as the Viets are on top of me and count up to five; then we'll all leave this world together, them at the same time as me. I shall have died in the true tradition, like Uncle Joseph in 1940, like my father in Morocco, and my grandfather at Chemin des Dames. Claude will go and join the black battalion of officers' widows. She'll be welcome there, she'll be in good company. My sons will go to La Flèche, my daughters to the Légion d'Honneur."

The joints of his fingers clenching the grenade began to ache.

Less than ten yards off, three Viets in single file had just slipped into a dug-out. He could hear them urging each other on before taking the next bound that would bring them right up to him.

"One, two, three . . ."

He hurled the grenade into the dug-out. But he had raised his head and shoulders above the sky-line and drawn several bursts of machine-gun fire. The grenade exploded and lumps of earth and shreds of clothing and flesh came flying through the air.

He lay flat in the mud. Close by, to his right, he heard the suburban accent of Mansard, a sergeant:

"They've got us now, the bastards; there's nothing left to fire back at them."

Glatigny tore off his badges of rank; he could at least try to pass himself off as an O.R. It would be easier to escape . . . when the time came. Then he stretched out on his side in the hole; all he could do now was wait for the experience that Boisfeuras claimed to be so interesting.

The explosion of a grenade in his dug-out made him take leave of the Greco-Latin-Christian civilized world. When he regained consciousness he was on the other side . . . among the Communists.

A voice was shouting out in the darkness:

"You are completely surrounded. Do not fire. We shall do you no harm. Stand up and keep your hands in the air."

This voice uttered each syllable separately, like the sound-track of a badly dubbed cowboy film.

The voice drew closer; it now addressed itself to Glatigny:

"Are you alive? Wounded? We shall take care of you, we have medical supplies. Where are your weapons?"

"I haven't any. I'm not wounded, only stunned."

Glatigny had to make a great effort to speak and was surprised to hear his own voice; he could hardly recognize it, like that time he had listened to the play-back of a talk he had given on Radio Saigon.

"Don't move," the voice went on, "the medical orderly will be coming up soon."

Glatigny came to his senses in a long narrow shelter shaped

like a tunnel. He was sitting on the ground, his bare back resting against the earth wall. Facing him, a *nha-que* squatting on his haunches was smoking some foul tobacco rolled up in a piece of old newspaper.

The tunnel was lit by two candles, but every *nha-que* who went past kept flashing his electric torch on and off. In the same position as himself, leaning against the earth wall, the captain recognized three Vietnamese paratroopers who were at Marianne II. They glanced across at him, then turned away.

The *nha-que* was bare-headed, his upper lip flanked by two symmetrical tufts of two or three long straggly whiskers. He was wearing a khaki uniform without any distinguishing marks and, unlike the other Viets, had no canvas shoes on his feet and his toes wriggled voluptuously in the warm mud of the shelter.

As he puffed at his cigarette he uttered a few words, and a *bo-doi* with the supple and sinuous backbone of a "boy" bent over Glatigny:

"The battaliong commangder asks you where is French major commangding strong-point."

Glatigny's reaction was that of a regular officer; he could not believe that this *nha-que* squatting on his haunches and smoking foul tobacco was, like him, a battalion commander with the same rank and the same responsibilities as his own. He pointed at him:

"Is that your C.O.?"

"That's him," said the Viet, bowing respectfully in the direction of the Vietminh officer.

Glatigny thought that his "opposite number" looked like a peasant from Haute Corrèze, one of whose female ancestors had been raped by a henchman of Attila's. His face was neither cruel nor intelligent but rather sly, patient and attentive. He fancied he saw the *nha-que* smile and the two narrow slits of his eyes screw up with pleasure.

So this was one of the officers of 308 Division, the best unit in the whole People's Army; it was this peasant from the paddy-fields who had beaten him, Glatigny, the descendant of one of the great military dynasties of the West, for whom war was a profession and the only purpose in life.

The *nha-que* emitted three words with a puff of stinking smoke and the interpreter went over to question the Vietnamese paratroopers. Only one of them answered, the sergeant, and with a jerk of his chin he indicated the captain.

"You are Captain Klatigny, commangding Third Parachute Company, but where is major commangding strong-point?"

Glatigny now felt it was stupid to have tried to pass himself off as an O.R. He replied:

"I was in command of the strong-point. There was no major and I was the senior captain."

He looked at the *nha-que* whose eyes kept blinking but whose expression remained inscrutable. They had fought against each other on equal terms; their heavy mortars were just as effective as the French artillery and the air force had never been able to operate over Marianne II.

Of this fierce hand-to-hand fighting, of this position which had changed hands twenty times over, of this struggle to the death, of all these acts of heroism, of this last French attack in which forty men had swept the Vietminh battalion off the summit and had driven them out of the trenches they had won, there remained no sign on this inscrutable face which betrayed neither respect nor interest nor even hatred.

The days when the victorious side presented arms to the vanquished garrison that had fought bravely were over. There was no room left for military chivalry or what remained of it. In the deadly world of Communism the vanquished was a culprit and was reduced to the position of a man condemned by common law.

Up to April 1945 the principles of caste were still in force. Second-Lieutenant Glatigny was then in command of a platoon outside Karlsruhe. He had taken a German major prisoner and brought him back to his squadron commander, de V——, who was also his cousin and belonged to the same military race of squires who were in turn highway robbers, crusaders, constables of the king, marshals of the empire, and generals of the republic.

The squadron commander had established his H.Q. in a forester's cottage. He had come out to greet his prisoner. They had saluted and introduced themselves; the major likewise bore a great name in the Wehrmacht and had fought gallantly.

Glatigny had been struck by the close resemblance between these two men: the same piercing eyes set deep in their sockets, the same elegant formality of manner, the same thin lips and prominent beaky nose.

He did not realize that he himself also resembled them.

It was very early in the morning. Major de V—— invited Glatigny and his prisoner to have breakfast with him.

The German and the Frenchman, completely at ease since they found themselves among people of their own caste, discussed the various places where they might have fought against each other since 1939. To them it was of little consequence that one was the victor and the other the vanquished provided they had observed the rules and had fought bravely. They had a feeling of respect for each other and, what is more, a feeling of friendship.

De V—— had the major driven to the P.O.W. camp in his own Jeep and, before taking leave of him, shook him by the hand. So did Glatigny.

The *nha-que* battalion commander, who had listened to the "boy" interpreter as he translated Glatigny's reply, now gave an order. A *bo-doi* laid down his rifle, came up to the captain and took a long cord of white nylon out of his pocket: a parachute rigging-line. He forced his arms behind his back and tied his elbows and wrists together with infinite care.

Glatigny looked closely at the *nha-que* and it seemed to him that his half-closed eyes were like the slits in a visor through which someone far less master of himself was peering out at him. His triumph made him feel almost drunk. He would not be able to control himself much longer. He would have to burst out laughing or else strike him.

But the slits in the visor closed and the *nha-que* spoke softly. The *bo-doi*, who had picked his rifle up again, motioned to the Frenchman to follow him.

For several hours Glatigny trudged along trenches that were

thigh-deep in mud, moving against the current of the columns of busy, specialist termites. There were soldier-termites, each with his palm-fibre helmet adorned with the yellow star on a red ground, male or female coolie-termites dressed in black who trotted along under their Vietnamese yokes or Thai panniers. At one stage he passed a column carrying hot rice in baskets.

All these termites looked indistinguishable, and their faces betrayed no expression of any sort, not even one of those primitive feelings that sometimes disrupt the inscrutability of Asiatic features: fear, contentment, hate or anger. Nothing. The same sense of urgency impelled them towards a common but mysterious goal which lay beyond the present fighting. This hive of sexless insects seemed to operate by remote control, as though somewhere in the depths of this enclosed world there was a monstrous queen, a kind of central brain which acted as the collective consciousness of the termites.

Glatigny now felt like one of those explorers invented by science-fiction writers, who suddenly find themselves plunged by some sort of time machine into a monstrous bygone age or a still more ghastly world to come.

He could hardly keep his balance in the mud. The sentry escorting him kept repeating: "*Mau-len, mau-len, di-di, di-di.*"

He was brought to a halt at an intersection between two communication trenches. The *bo-doi* had a word with the post commander, a young Vietnamese who wore an American webbing belt and carried a Colt.

He looked at the Frenchman with a smile that was almost friendly and asked:

"Do you know Paris?"

Glatigny began to see the end of his nightmare.

"Of course."

"And the Quartier Latin? I was a law student. I used to feed at Père Louis's in the Rue Descartes and often went to the Capoulade for a drink."

Glatigny heaved a sigh. The time machine had brought him back to the world of today, next to this young Vietnamese who, at a few years' interval, had haunted the same streets and frequented the same cafés as himself.

"Did Gipsy's in the Rue Cujas exist in your day?" the Vietnamese asked him. "I had some wonderful times there. There was a girl who used to dance there . . . and I felt she was dancing for no one but me."

The *bo-doi*, who did not understand a word of this conversation, was getting impatient. The student with the Colt lowered his eyes, then in a different, curt and unpleasant tone said to the Frenchman:

"You've got to move on now."

"Where are they taking me?"

"I don't know."

"Couldn't you tell the *bo-doi* to loosen my fetters; my fingers are all numb."

"No, that can't be done."

Thereupon he turned his back on Glatigny. He had changed back into a termite and went off slithering in the deep mud.

He would never escape from this ant-hill, never again see the Luxembourg Gardens in springtime or the girls with their skirts swirling round their thighs and a handful of books clutched under their arm.

The prisoner and his escort moved on behind Béatrice, the Legion strong-point commanding the north-eastern exit from the Dien-Bien-Phu basin. Béatrice had fallen during the night of 13–14 March and the jungle was already beginning to invade the barbed-wire entanglements and shattered shelters.

As they emerged from the trench, a shell burst behind them. A solitary gun was still in action at General de Castries' H.Q. and it was now trained on them.

Without a pause they entered the dense forest covering the mountains. The path climbed in a straight line up the narrow ravine over which the tops of the giant silk-cotton trees formed a thick canopy.

Shelters had been cut out of the slope on either side of the path. Glatigny caught a glimpse of some 120-calibre mortars drawn up in a neat row. They glistened faintly in the shadows;

they were well oiled and, as a technician, he could not help admiring their maintenance. There were some men lounging about in undress uniform at the entrance to the shelters. They looked far taller than the average Vietnamese and each of them wore a medallion of Mao-Tse-Tung on his breast. This was 350 Division, the heavy division which had been trained in China. The Intelligence Department at Saigon had reported its arrival.

There were smiles from the men as the captain went past. Perhaps they were hardly aware of him since he did not belong to their world.

With his hands tied behind his back, Glatigny could not walk properly and waddled from side to side like a penguin. He felt utterly exhausted and sank to the ground.

The *bo-doi* leant over him:

"*Di-di, mau-len*, keep going, *titi*."

His tone of voice was patient, almost encouraging, but he did not lift a finger to help him.

The soldiers outside the shelters were now succeeded by *nha-ques* dressed in black. In a patch of sunlight just above the path sat an old man eating his morning rice. Glatigny had no sense of hunger, thirst, shame or anger; he was not even conscious of his weariness; he felt at the same time extremely old and as though he had just been born. But the heady smell of the rice unleashed an animal reaction in him. He had not eaten for five days and suddenly felt ravenous and cast a greedy eye on the mess-tin.

"Any to spare?" he asked the old man.

The *nha-que* bared his black teeth in a sort of smile and gave a nod. Glatigny turned round to show him his fetters, whereupon the man rolled some rice up into a ball between his earth-stained fingers, carefully detached a sliver of dried fish and popped the lot into his mouth.

But the soldier gave the captain a push and he had to set off again up the increasingly steep path.

The sun emerged out of the morning mist; the forest was silent, dense and dark, like one of those dead calm lakes in the crater of a volcano.

Glatigny now began to understand why Boisfeuras had not tried to escape, why he wanted the "experience." In his present plight Boisfeuras was the one who kept crossing his mind and not his superiors or his comrades. Like him he wanted to be able to speak Vietnamese, to lean across towards these soldiers and these coolies and ask them various questions:

"Why do you belong to the Vietminh? Are you married? Do you know who the prophet Marx is? Are you happy? What do you hope to get out of it?"

He had recovered his curiosity, he was no longer a prisoner.

Glatigny had reached the top of the hill. Through the trees he could now see the Dien-Bien-Phu basin and, a little to one side, under the eye of a sentry, a small group of figures: the survivors of the strong-point. Boisfeuras was asleep in the ferns; Merle and Pinières were arguing together somewhat heatedly. Pinières was always inclined to be quick-tempered. They called out to him. Boisfeuras woke up and squatted down on his haunches like a *nha-que*.

But the *bo-doi* urged Glatigny on with the butt of his rifle. A short youngish man in a clean uniform stood in front of one of the shelters. He motioned him to come inside. The shelter was comfortable for a change; there was no mud. In the cool shadows, at a child-size table, the officer caught sight of another short young man exactly like the first. He was smoking a cigarette; the packet on the table was almost full. Glatigny longed for a smoke.

"Sit down," said the young man, speaking in the accent of the French Lycée at Hanoi.

But there was no chair. With his foot Glatigny turned over a heavy American steel helmet which happened to be lying there and sat down on it, making himself as comfortable as he could.

"Your name?"

"Glatigny."

The young man entered this in a sort of account book.

"Christian name?"

"Jacques."

"Rank?"

"Captain."

"Unit?"

"I don't know."

The Viet laid his ball-point pen down on the table, and took a deep puff at his cigarette. He looked ever so slightly disconcerted.

"President Ho-Chi-Minh" (he pronounced the "ch" soft, as the French do) "has given orders that all combatants and the civilian population should be lenient" (he laid great stress on this word) "towards prisoners of war. Have you been badly treated?"

Glatigny got up and showed him his fettered wrists. The young man raised his eyebrows in surprise and gave a discreet order. The first little man appeared from behind a bivouac of brightly coloured parachute material. He knelt down behind the captain and his nimble fingers undid the complicated knots. All at once the blood rushed back into his paralysed forearms. The pain was unbearable: Glatigny felt like swearing out loud, but the people in front of him were so well behaved that he controlled himself.

The interrogation went on:

"You were captured at Marianne II. You were in command of the strong-point. How many men did you have with you?"

"I don't know."

"Are you thirsty?"

"No."

"Then you must be hungry. You'll be given something to eat presently."

"I don't feel hungry either."

"Is there anything you need?"

If he had been offered a cigarette, Glatigny would not have been able to refuse, but the Vietminh did not do so.

"I feel sleepy," the captain suddenly said.

"I can understand that. It was a tough fight. Our soldiers are smaller and less strong than yours, but they fought with more spirit than you did because they're willing to lay down their lives for their country.

"You're now a prisoner of war and it's your duty to answer my questions. What was the strength of Marianne II?"

"I've already given you my name, my Christian name, my rank, everything that belongs to me. The rest isn't mine to give and I know of no international convention that obliges officer prisoners to provide the enemy with information while their comrades are still fighting."

Another heavy sigh from the Vietminh. Another deep puff at his cigarette.

"Why do you refuse to answer?"

Why? Glatigny was beginning to wonder himself. There must be some ruling on this matter in military regulations. Every eventuality is provided for in regulations, even what never comes to pass.

"Military regulations forbid a prisoner to give you information."

"So you only fought because military regulations obliged you to do so?"

"Not only for that reason."

"In refusing to talk, then, perhaps you're abiding by your sense of military honour?"

"You can call it that if you like."

"You have an extremely *bourgeois* conception of military honour. This honour of yours allows you to fight for the interests of the bloated colonials and bankers of Saigon, to massacre people whose only desire is peace and independence. You are prepared to wage war in a country which doesn't belong to you, an unjust war, a war of imperialist conquest. Your honour as an officer adjusts itself to this but forbids you to contribute to the cause of peace and progress by giving the information I request."

Glatigny's immediate reaction was typical of his class; he assumed an air of haughtiness. He was remote and disinterested, as though he was not personally involved at all, and slightly disdainful. The Vietminh noticed this; his eyes glinted, his nostrils dilated and his lips curled over his teeth.

"His French education," Glatigny reflected, "must have weakened his perfect control over his facial expression."

The Vietminh had half risen from his seat:

"Answer! Didn't your sense of honour oblige you to defend

the position you held to the last man? Why didn't you die defending the 'peak of your fathers'?"

For the first time in the conversation the Vietminh had used an expression translated directly from Vietnamese into French: the "peak of your fathers" for "your ancestral land." This minor linguistic problem took Glatigny's mind off the question of military honour. But the little man in green persisted:

"Answer! Why didn't you die defending your position?"

Glatigny also wondered why. He could have done, but he had thrown the grenade at the Viets.

"I can tell you," the Vietminh went on. "You saw our soldiers who looked puny and undersized advancing to attack your trenches, in spite of your artillery, your mines, your barbed-wire entanglements and all the arms the Americans had given you. Our men fought to the death because they were serving a just and popular cause, because they knew, as we all know, that we have the Truth, the only Truth, on our side. That is what made our soldiers invincible. And because you didn't have these reasons, here you are alive, standing in front of me, a prisoner and vanquished.

"You *bourgeois* officers belong to a society which is out of date and polluted by the selfish interests of class. You have helped to keep humanity in the dark. You're nothing but obscurantists, mercenaries incapable of explaining what they are fighting for.

"Go on, then, try and explain! You can't, eh?"

"We're fighting, my dear sir, to protect the people of Viet-Nam from Communist slavery."

Later on, when discussing this reply with Esclavier, Boisfeuras, Merle and Pinières, Glatigny was forced to admit that he was not quite sure how it had occurred to him. In actual fact Glatigny was only fighting for France, because the legal government had ordered him to do so. He had never felt he was there to defend the Terres Rouges plantations or the Bank of Indo-China. He obeyed orders, and that was that. But he had suddenly realized that this reason alone could not possibly seem valid to a Communist. A few fleeting thoughts had flashed through his mind, some notions as yet undefined: Europe, the West, Christian civilization. These had occurred to him all at once and then he had had this idea of a crusade.

Glatigny had scored a direct hit. The narrowed eyes, the dilated nostrils, every feature of the funny little man now expressed nothing but pure, relentless hatred, and he had difficulty in speaking:

"I'm not a Communist, but I believe that Communism promises freedom, progress and peace for the masses."

When he had recovered his self-control, he lit another cigarette. It was Chinese tobacco and had a pleasant smell of new-mown hay. The Viet went on in the declamatory tone to which he seemed to be partial:

"Officer in the pay of the colonialists, you are for that very reason a criminal. You deserve to be tried for your crime against humanity and to be given the usual sentence: death."

It was fascinating. Boisfeuras was absolutely right. A new world was being revealed, one of the principles of which was: "Whoever opposes Communism is *ipso facto* a war criminal beyond the pale of humanity: he must be hanged like those who were tried at Nuremberg."

"Are you married?" the Vietminh asked. "Are your parents alive? Any children? A mother?

"Think of their grief when they learn that you have been executed. Because they can't imagine, can they, that the martyred people of Viet-Nam will pardon their torturers? They will mourn their dead husband, their son, their father."

The act was becoming tiresome and in poor taste.

The Vietminh fell silent for a moment to fill his soul with compassion for this poor French family in mourning, then went on:

"But President Ho knows that you are sons of the French people who have been led astray by the American colonialists and imperialists. The French people is our friend and fights by our side in the camp of Peace. President Ho who knows this has asked the civilian population and combatants of Viet-Nam to stifle their righteous anger towards the prisoners and to apply a policy of leniency."

"In the Middle Ages," Glatigny reflected, "they used this same word 'apply,' but in a different context."

"We shall take good care of you; you'll get the same rations as our soldiers. You'll also be taught the Truth. We shall re-educate you by means of manual labour, which will enable you to emend your *bourgeois* education and redeem your life of idleness.

"That is what the people of Viet-Nam will give you as a punishment for your crimes—the Truth. But you must repay this generosity by complying with all our orders."

Glatigny liked the commissar better when he was carried away by his hatred, for by restoring his normal reactions this hatred at least made him human. When he became smarmy and sanctimonious like this, he frightened and at the same time fascinated him. This sad little man, who hovered about like a ghost in clothes several sizes too large for him and who spoke about Truth with the vacant gaze of a prophet, plunged him back into the termite nightmare. He was one of the antennae of the monstrous brain which wanted to reduce the world to a civilization of insects rooted in their certainty and efficiency.

The voice went on:

"Captain Glatigny, how many men did you have with you in your position?"

"I feel sleepy."

"We could easily find out simply by counting the dead and the prisoners, but I would rather you told me."

"I feel sleepy."

Two soldiers came in and one again tied up the captain's arms, elbows, wrists and fingers. They did not forget the running noose round his neck. The political commissar looked at the *bourgeois* officer with disdain. Glatigny—the name reminded him of something. He was suddenly brought back to the Hanoi Lycée. He had read the name somewhere in the history of France. There was a famous war leader called Glatigny, a man of murder, rape and passion, who had been made a constable by the king and who had died for his royal master. The sad young man was not only part of the Vietminh, a cog in an immense machine. All his recollections as a little yellow boy bullied by his white school-fellows flooded back into his mind and brought him out in a sweat. He could now humiliate France right back to her remote past and he was so afraid that this Glatigny might not be a descendant of the constable's, which would balk him of this strange triumph, that he refused to ask him.

"Captain," he declared, "because of your attitude all your colleagues who were taken prisoner with you will likewise be tied up and they'll know that they owe this to you."

The guards dragged Glatigny off to a deep ravine in the heart of the jungle.

There was a hole there, six feet long, two feet wide, three feet deep: a classical fox-hole which could easily serve as a grave. One of the guards checked his fetters, then stood him over the hole. The other loaded his submachine-gun.

"*Di-di, di-di, mau-len.*"

Glatigny took a pace forward and lowered himself into the trench. He lay stretched out on his numb and fettered arms. Above him the sky looked particularly clear through the foliage of the tall trees. He closed his eyes, to die or else to sleep . . .

Next morning they hauled him off and shackled him to his comrades. The man in front of him was Sergeant Mansard who kept repeating:

"We don't hold it against you, you know, sir."

And to reassure him, he began talking through clenched teeth about Boulogne-Billancourt where he was born, about a dance-hall on the banks of the Seine adjoining a gas station. He used to go there every Saturday with girls whom he knew well since he had been brought up with them. But their pretty dresses, their lipstick suddenly gave them fresh confidence, which made him feel shy.

When Glatigny took command of the battalion, Mansard had not thought much of him. In the eyes of the ex-machinist he was nothing but a high-class gent from G.H.Q. Saigon.

Now, with clumsy tact, the N.C.O. tried to make him see that he regarded him as being on his side and that he was proud his captain had not bowed his head before the little apes.

He rolled over towards Mansard and his shoulder brushed the sergeant's. Thinking he was cold, Mansard pressed up against him.

2

CAPTAIN ESCLAVIER'S
SELF-EXAMINATION

Stretched out in the paddy-field, where the mud mingled with the flattened stubble, the ten men huddled close together. Every so often they dozed off, woke up with a start in the damp night, then sank back again into their nightmares.

Esclavier held on to Lieutenant Lescure by his webbing belt. Lescure was raving; he might have got up and started walking straight ahead, giving that yell of his: "They're attacking, they're attacking! Send over some chickens . . . some ducks!"* He would not have obeyed the Vietminh sentry who told him to stop and would have got himself shot.

Lescure was quite calm at the moment; every so often he gave a little whimper, like a puppy.

In the depths of the darkness a Jeep could be heard slithering along the muddy track, its engine labouring, racing and fading in jerks. It sounded rather like a fly in a closed room knocking against the window-panes. The engine stopped, but Esclavier who had woken up waited hopefully for the familiar noise to start up again.

"Di-di, di-di, mau-len."

The sentry's words of command were accompanied by a few mild and "lenient" blows with the butt of his rifle, which set the shapeless mass of prisoners in motion.

But a voice now addressed them in French:

*Code names for calibre 60 and calibre 81 mortar shells, respectively.

"On your feet! Get up! You've got to come and push a Jeep of the Viet-Nam People's Army."

The tone was patient, certain of being obeyed. The words were distinct, the pronunciation surprisingly and at the same time disturbingly perfect. Lacombe struggled to his feet with a sigh and the rest followed suit. Esclavier knew that Lacombe would always be the first to display obedience and eagerness, that he would turn the other flabby, baby-pink cheek to curry favour with the guards. He would be the model prisoner to the point of turning stool-pigeon. He would flatter the Viets to earn a few privileges, but above all because they were now on top and because he always obeyed the stronger side. To excuse his attitude in the eyes of his comrades, he would try to make them believe that he was hoodwinking the gaolers and exploiting them for the common good.

Esclavier had known this type of man only too well in Mathausen camp. All the inmates there had had their individuality steeped in a bath of quicklime, and all that remained was the bare essentials. Those simplified creatures could then be put into one of three categories: the slaves, the wild ones and what Esclavier with a certain amount of scorn called "the fine souls." Esclavier had been a wild one because he was anxious to survive. Lacombe's true character was that of a slave, a "boy" who would not even steal from his master, who would never make a bid for freedom. But he wore the uniform of a French Army captain and he had to be taught how to behave even if it killed him.

A slim figure wearing a fibre helmet towered over Esclavier and the voice, which by dint of being so precise sounded disembodied, made itself heard again:

"Aren't you going to help your comrades push the Jeep?"

"No," Esclavier replied.

"What's your name?"

"Captain Philippe Esclavier, of the French Army. What's yours?"

"I'm an officer of the People's Army. Why do you refuse to carry out my orders?"

It was not so much a reproach as the statement of an inexplicable fact. With the painstaking care of a conscientious but circumscribed schoolmaster the Vietminh officer was trying to understand the attitude of the big child lying at his feet. Yet the method had been drummed into him in the training schools of Communist China. First of all he had to analyse, then explain and finally convince. This method was infallible; it was part and parcel of the huge perfect whole which Communism represents. It had succeeded with all the prisoners of Cao-Bang. The Viet bent over Esclavier and with a touch of condescension explained:

"President Ho-Chi-Minh has given orders for the People's Army of Viet-Nam to apply a policy of leniency towards all prisoners led astray by the imperialist capitalists . . ."

Lescure made as if to wake up and Esclavier took a firmer grip on his belt. The lieutenant did not realize, and perhaps never would, that the French Army had been defeated at Dien-Bien-Phu; if he woke up suddenly he would be capable of strangling the Vietminh.

The *can-bo* went on:

"You have been treated well, you will continue to be, but it's your duty to obey the orders of the Vietnamese people."

In curt, ringing tones, imbued with violence, anger and irony, and seething with revolt, Esclavier replied for all to hear:

"We have been living in the Democratic Republic of Viet-Nam for only a few hours but we are already in a position to appreciate your policy of leniency. Instead of killing us off decently, you're letting us die from exhaustion and cold. And on top of this, you demand that we should be full of gratitude for good old President Ho and the People's Army of Viet-Nam."

"He'll get us all killed, the silly bastard," Lacombe reflected. "It was hard enough persuading him to surrender, and now he's starting all over again. But all I ask is to understand this popular republic of theirs. That's the only line to take, now that it's all over and we can't do a thing about it."

Esclavier did not stop there. This time, fortunately, he spoke for himself:

"I refuse to push the Jeep. You can look upon that as my personal choice. I would rather be killed on the spot than die by slow degrees, demean myself and perhaps become corrupted in your narrow universe. So please be good enough to give the orders to finish me off straightaway."

"That's done it," Lacombe said to himself. "A couple of sentries will force him to his feet with their rifle-butts, drag him off to the nearest ravine and put a bullet through his head That will put an end to Captain Esclavier's insolence."

But the *can-bo* did not lose his temper: he was beyond anger.

"I'm an officer in the People's Army of Viet-Nam. I have to see that President Ho's orders are properly carried out. We are poor; we haven't many medical facilities or clothing or rice. First of all we've got to provide our own combatants with supplies and ammunition. But you will be treated in the same way as the men of our people in spite of your crimes against humanity. President Ho has asked the people of Viet-Nam to forgive you because you have been led astray and I shall give orders to the soldiers guarding you . . ."

This speech was so impersonal, so mechanical, that it suggested the voice of an old priest saying Mass. Lescure, who was once a choir-boy and had just woken up, responded quite naturally: "Amen." Then he burst out into a long strident laugh which ended up in a sort of breathless panting.

"My comrade has gone mad," said Esclavier.

The Vietminh had a primitive horror of madmen, of whom it is said that the *mah-quis** have devoured their brain. The people's democracy and the declarations of President Ho were of no more avail to him. The darkness was suddenly thronged with all the absurd phantoms of his childhood, with that seething populace that inhabits the waters, the earth and the heavens and never leaves man alone and in peace for an instant. The *mah-quis* slip through the mouths of children, they try to steal the souls of the dead.

He was frightened but, so as not to show his fear, he said a few words to one of the sentries and went back to his Jeep. He switched on the engine; the prisoners all round him started to push. The wheels lifted out of the ditch; the engine started

*Evil spirits of Vietnamese legends.

purring; all the *mah-quis* of darkness were exorcized forthwith by the reassuring sound of the machine, that brutal music of Marxist society.

"*Di-di*," said the sentries, as they led the prisoners back, "now you can sleep."

The *mah-quis* had devoured Lescure's brain. During the week before the surrender the lieutenant had not stopped taking maxiton pills, which were included with the rations, and had eaten very little proper food. Lescure had a thin, lanky body, blotchy skin and lacklustre hair. There was nothing to qualify him for an army career. But he was the son of a colonel who had been killed on the Loire in 1940. One of his brothers had been executed by the Germans and another was condemned to a wheelchair ever since receiving a shell burst in the spinal column at Cassino.

Unlike his father and two brothers, all robust military animals, Yves Lescure delighted in a mild form of anarchy. He was fond of music, the companionship of friends, old books with fine bindings. As a token of loyalty to the memory of his father, he had gone to Coetquidan School, and of those two years spent in the damp marshes of Brittany, among somewhat limited but efficient and disciplined creatures, he retained a depressing memory of an endless succession of practical jokes and inordinate physical effort. This had left him with the impression that he would never be equal to a task for which he had such little inclination.

But to please the casualty of Cassino, to enable him to go on living in the war through the medium of himself, he had volunteered for Indo-China and, without any preliminary training, had dropped into Dien-Bien-Phu—a feat that his disabled brother would have longed to perform had he been able. Lieutenant Lescure had derived little pleasure from the experience.

Esclavier had seen him come down on one of those wonderful evenings that occur just before the rainy season, looking like a bundle of bones in his uniform, having forgotten his personal weapon, and with an expression of utter bewilderment on his face.

The heavy Vietminh mortars were pounding away at Véronique II and the clouds drifting low in the overcast sky were fringed with gold like gypsy shawls.

He had reported to Esclavier: "Lieutenant Lescure, sir."

Dropping his haversack at his feet—a haversack containing books but no change of clothing—he had looked up at the sky: "Beautiful, isn't it?"

Esclavier, who had no time for "day-dreamers," had curtly replied:

"Yes, very beautiful indeed. The parachute battalion holding this position, of which I am in command, was six hundred strong a fortnight ago; there are now ninety of us left. Out of twenty-four officers, only seven are still in a condition to fight."

Lescure had apologized at once.

"I know I'm not a paratrooper, I haven't much talent for this sort of warfare, I'm clumsy and inefficient, but I'll try to do my best."

Lescure, who was scared stiff of not being able "to do his best" had taken to maxiton a few days later. He had taken part in every attack and counter-attack, more oblivious than courageous, living in a sort of secondary state of consciousness. One night he had gone off into no-man's-land to rescue a sergeant-major who had been wounded in the legs.

"Why did you do that?" the captain had asked him.

"My brother would have done it, only he can't any longer. By myself, I couldn't even have attempted it."

"Your brother?"

And Lescure had explained quite simply that it was not himself who was at Dien-Bien-Phu, but his brother Paul who was wheeled round Rennes in an invalid chair. His courage was Paul's, but the clumsiness, the sunsets, the fear—those were all his own.

Since then the captain had begun to keep an eye on him, as the N.C.O.s and privates in his company had already done for some time.

For Véronique, as for all the other positions that were still holding out, the "cease-fire" had come into effect at seventeen-hundred hours. It was then Lescure had collapsed, yelling:

"Quick, some ducks, some chickens! They're attacking!"

Esclavier had continued to keep an eye on him.

In the middle of the night they were woken up and had to abandon the half-light of the paddy-field for the pitch-black darkness of the forest. They followed a path through the jungle. Branches kept lashing their faces; the slimy earth slid from under their feet or else suddenly swelled into a hard mound against which they barked their shins. They had the impression they were going round and round in an endless circle.

"*Di-di, mau-len*," the sentries kept shouting.

The darkness began to fade. They emerged at first light into the Muong-Phan basin.

Esclavier recognized the figure of Boisfeuras outside the first hut. They had untied his hands; in a bamboo pipe he was smoking some *thuoc-lao*, a very strong tobacco which was cured in molasses. A sentry had given it to him after he had exchanged a joke or two with him in his own dialect.

"Want some?" Boisfeuras asked in his rasping voice.

Esclavier took a few puffs which were so harsh that they made him cough. Lescure started yelling his war-cry:

"Some chickens, some ducks!"

And he made a rush at a sentry to grab his weapon. Esclavier held him back just in time.

"What's the matter with him?" Boisfeuras asked.

"He's gone off his head."

"And you're acting as his nurse?"

"Sort of . . . Where are you quartered?"

"In the hut with some of the others."

"I'll join you."

Lescure had calmed down and Esclavier held him by the hand like a child.

"I'll bring Lescure with me. I can't leave him on his own. During the last fortnight this choir-boy, this wet rag, has surpassed even himself. He has performed more acts of courage than the rest of us put together—and do you know why? To please a cripple who lives ten thousand miles away and won't ever know a thing about it. Is that good enough for you?"

"And it's to save his skin that you didn't try and escape?"

"There's nothing to stop me now; the others will take care of Lescure. We might have a go at it together. The jungle's your home ground. I remember the lectures you gave us when we were due to be dropped into Laos during the Japanese occupation. You used to say: 'The jungle is not for the strongest, but for the wiliest, the one with most stamina, the man who can keep his head.' And we all knew you said this from personal experience. Have you got any plan in mind?"

"I've all sorts of ideas, but I'm not going to try to escape, at least not yet . . ."

"If I didn't know you, I'd say you were afraid of it. But I've no doubt you're thinking up some wildcat scheme or other in your complicated Chinaman's brain!

"I didn't realize you were at Dien-Bien-Phu. What were you up to there? I thought you would never have anything to do with that sort of pitched battle."

"I had started something up north, on the border of Yunnan. Something that was liable to annoy the Chinese. It misfired . . . I withdrew to Dien-Bien-Phu on foot."

"The same sort of hare-brained wheeze as your pirate-junks in the Baie d'Along, in which you planned to go marauding up the coast of Hainan?"

"This time it was something to do with leper-colonies."

Esclavier burst out laughing. He was glad to have run into Boisfeuras again, barefoot in the mud and surrounded by the *bo-dois*, but as completely at ease as he had been the year before on the rickety bridge of a heavy junk with purple sails, in charge of a band of pirates recruited from the remnants of the armies of Chiang-Kai-Shek.

Another of his "hare-brained schemes" had been to arm the Chin and Naga headhunters of Burma and launch them against the rear of the Japanese Army. Boisfeuras who was then serving in the British Army had been one of the few survivors of this operation and had been awarded the D.S.O.

Boisfeuras was the man he needed to accompany him on his escape. He was full of resource, a good walker, used to the climate, and acquainted with the languages and customs of a good number of the tribes in the Haute Région.

"Come on, let's have a try at it together."

"No, Esclavier; I'm all for waiting. I'd advise you to as well."

"I can't. I once spent two years in a concentration camp and in order to survive I was reduced to do certain things which horrify me every time I think of them. I swore I would never allow myself to be in a position where I would have to do them again."

Esclavier had squatted down at Boisfeuras's feet and with a sliver of bamboo involuntarily began tracing some figures which were the mountains, others which were the rivers, and a long sinuous line running between the rivers and the mountains, which was his proposed escape route.

No, he could not start being a prisoner all over again . . .

The first mission which Esclavier carried out as a cadet had occurred without a hitch. He retained a fond recollection of his parachute jump by night. It was in the month of June and he had had the impression of being buried alive among the tall grass and wild flowers, of sinking deep into the rich scented soil of France.

There were three men waiting for him: Touraine peasants, who conducted him and his wireless operator to a big manor-house. There they settled them into a lumber-room above a barn.

From this hide-out they could keep the main road under observation and instantly report the movements of the German convoys. Runners came in from the neighbourhood of Nantes with messages and information, which had to be encoded and transmitted. Neither Esclavier nor the wireless operator was allowed to leave the house but all the scents of spring were wafted into their attic.

A merry servant girl, a little animal with lively gestures and rosy cheeks, brought them their meals, sometimes a bunch of flowers, and always some delicious fruit.

One afternoon Philippe put his arms round her; she did not

struggle but returned his kisses with clumsy ardour. He arranged to meet her in the barn below; they met. In the heady smell of the hay, with their ears pricked for the slightest noise, like animals lying in wait, they clumsily embraced and were suddenly carried off by the raging torrent of their desire.

From time to time a bat on its darting flight would brush against their intertwined bodies. Philippe could feel the girl's loins tremble beneath his hands and a fresh surge of desire overwhelmed him.

When he climbed back to the lumber-room, limp with fatigue and with the smell of the crushed straw and their love-making fresh in his nostrils, the wireless operator handed him a signal: it was an order for him to liquidate an Abwehr agent, a Belgian passing himself off as a refugee, who had been taken on as an agricultural labourer in a number of farms.

The peasants were chatterboxes; they loved to talk about what they were doing and hinted that their barns were not only used for the purpose of storing hay. Three of them had just been arrested and shot. This they owed to the Belgian in the Abwehr.

The wireless operator was also keen on the servant girl and jealous of Philippe's success. He sniggered:

"All on one day—bloodshed, ecstasy and death!"

The wireless operator was an educated man: a lecturer at Edinburgh University.

The Belgian was working on a neighbouring farm; after supper his employer asked him in for a drink, to give the two other farm-hands time to dig a grave behind the dung-heap.

Philippe waited by the door of the living-room, hugging the wall. He had butterflies in the stomach and his dagger felt slippery in his sweaty palm.

He would never be able to kill the Belgian. How had he managed to get mixed up in this damned business? He should have listened to his father and stayed behind with him, sheltered by his books instead of playing at hired assassins.

The man came stumbling out, impelled by a shove from the owner of the farm. He had his back turned to Philippe, who sprang forward and buried the dagger between his shoulder-blades, as he had been taught during his commando training. But the blow lacked sufficient strength. Philippe had to repeat it several times over while the peasant sat astride the man's waist to prevent him from fighting back. A filthy butchery! They emptied the Belgian's pockets. Orders had been given for his papers to be sent back to London. Then they tipped the body into the hole by the dung-heap.

Philippe went and vomited behind a low wall.

Bloodshed, ecstasy and death . . .

When he got back to the farm he caught the wireless operator in the act of fornicating with the servant girl. In the arms of this ginger-headed runt, she was heaving the same sighs of pleasure as she had with him an hour or two before. At first his feelings were hurt but he resolved to be cynical about it and came to an arrangement with the operator whereby they each made use of the girl in turn.

Philippe Esclavier succeeded on his second mission, which he carried out on his own, but was arrested before he could even embark on his third.

He had been dropped in with Staff-Sergeant Beudin. The Germans, who had got wind of the operation, were waiting for them on the ground. Beudin, who landed in a stream, managed to escape, but Philippe had a pair of handcuffs snapped round his wrists before he was even able to unfasten his parachute harness and draw his revolver.

He was conducted forthwith to the Préfecture at Rennes and brought before the Gestapo. After being tortured, he had been deported to Mathausen camp.

In his barrack-room there was a skinny little Jew without family or country who had sided with the Communists for some sort of protection. That was what had saved him from the gas chamber. His name was Michel Weihl. The Communist organization within the camp had entrusted him with the task of obtaining information on the newcomer.

"He's a Free French agent from London who was dropped in by parachute," Weihl had reported one evening to the man responsible for that particular barrack-room, a certain Fournier.

"Then he may as well be left on the list of the detachment that's leaving for the salt mines."

Weihl had warned the newcomer. Esclavier had then gone to Fournier and told him that he was the son of the Front Populaire professor.

Fournier had been staggered. The name of Esclavier was still held in great repute among the left and extreme-left wing. But so as not to show his surprise, he had replied:

"The Socialists are a soft *bourgeois* lot. If you want us to help you, you'll have to join our ranks, the Communists."

Philippe Esclavier had agreed to this and his name had been taken off the list. But during the whole of his captivity he had continued to serve the Communists who constituted the only efficient hierarchy in the camp.

What they demanded of him sometimes defied all the rules of the accepted moral code. As a Communist, he might have considered himself absolved by reason of the higher interests of the cause for which he was fighting. But he had never been a Communist, he had only cheated in order to survive; all he had been was a dirty bastard.

Boisfeuras's harsh grating voice brought him back to the Muong-Phan basin:

"Day-dreaming, Esclavier? It's not good for a prisoner to take refuge in the past. He loses his grip, goes into a decline. Come on, I'll show you where we hang out."

Esclavier and the new arrivals reached the huts and sank down on to the bamboo bunks. They heaved a sigh of well-being. It was dry, clean and warm.

Glatigny had propped himself up on his elbows as Esclavier came in.

"Hallo," he said to himself, "here's that proud brute without his dagger or his long-barrelled Colt . . . and without Raspéguy for once."

Esclavier had recognized Glatigny. He bowed slightly from the waist with the affected elegance of a man of the world.

"Hallo, it's you, my dear fellow. How's the C.-in-C.? And his daughter, that dear girl Martine?"

Glatigny reflected that some day or another he would have to bash Esclavier's face in, but that this was hardly the moment. He had almost done so one evening in Saigon, when he had prevented Martine, the general's daughter, from going out with the captain. Esclavier would have made her drink too much and maybe taken her to an opium den, then he would have slept with her, and next morning he would have laughed in her face like the big hoodlum he was.

Glatigny fell back on his bunk and Esclavier went and lay down close at hand.

"All the same, I was surprised," the paratrooper went on, "not to say extremely surprised, that you should have come and joined us."

"Meaning what?"

"Meaning that you're not just a G.H.Q. puppet or the duenna of that dear Martine, but also . . ."

"Yes?"

"But also perhaps . . . an officer . . ."

Esclavier sprang to his feet and went to fetch Lescure who was standing stock-still with a vacant expression in his eyes and his arms swinging loosely by his side.

With infinite care, not to say gentleness, Esclavier made him lie down and placed a kitbag under his head.

"He's raving," he said. "He's lucky; he doesn't realize that the French Army has been beaten by a handful of little yellow dwarfs because of the stupidity and inertia of its leaders. And you yourself must have felt this so strongly, Glatigny, that you abandoned them and came and joined us, ready to commit yourself in our company."

Lescure sat up with a start and, stretching out his hand, began burbling:

"Here they come, here they come, all green like caterpillars! They're swarming all over the place, they're going to eat us up! Quick, for Christ's sake—some chickens, some ducks . . . And while you're about it, why not some partridges, also some thrushes, some pheasants and some hares. We've got to let fly with everything we've got, to crush the caterpillars which are going to devour the whole wide world!"

Immediately afterwards he fell asleep and his face was once more the face of the dreamy, immature adolescent who liked Mozart and the symbolist poets. And from the depths of his madness there came to him the opening bars of *Eine Kleine Nachtmusik*.

Daylight had transformed the absurd, hostile world of the previous night and the smell of hot rice rose in the still morning air. The prisoners, who now numbered thirty or so, were gathered round a basket of woven bamboo full of snow-white rice steaming gently in the sun. Some tea had been poured out for them in empty bully-beef tins, but this was simply an infusion of guava leaves. A few mouthfuls of rice sufficed to appease their hunger now that their stomachs had shrunk so much.

The *bo-dois* ate the same rice and drank the same tea. They appeared to have forgotten their victory in order to commune together in this elementary rite. The sun rose higher and higher in the pewter-coloured sky, the glare became painful, the heat suffocating. Somewhere in the distance an aircraft dropped a stick of bombs.

"The war's still on," Pinières remarked with satisfaction.

With his large paw he kept squashing the mosquitoes on his red-tufted chest. He looked at a sentry as though he longed to strangle him; that skinny neck was a temptation . . . The war was still on.

Unconsciously, the *bo-dois* stiffened and resumed their surly attitude; the morning's truce had come to an end.

Lacombe had gone off with a big handful of rice wrapped up in a banana leaf, which he tried to hide. With a nudge of his elbow Esclavier made him drop the rice, which fell in the mud.

"It's my rice, after all," Lacombe began to whine.

"Try and behave yourself in the future."

A sentry had angrily advanced on the paratroop captain, lifting his rifle butt to strike him, then he had held back; the slogan of the policy of leniency had deterred him just in time. He now drew the other soldiers' attention to the spilled rice and jabbered furiously. Esclavier gathered he was saying something about colonialism and the people's rice.

Glatigny could not help admiring his comrade for having tried to impose a certain standard of behaviour on the group.

Then he relapsed into his day-dream and strove to remember: he had been a prisoner for two days, so it was now the 8th of May. What would Claude be doing back in Paris? She loved the smells of the markets and the colour of the fruit. He pictured her stopping for a moment in front of a stall in the Rue de Passy. Marie was with her, because, in the eyes of the old cook, she had never grown up and was still incapable of managing her life by herself. Claude thrust her bottom lip out slightly and in her low distinguished voice politely asked the prices. And Marie buzzed about behind her:

"I've got some money, milady, let me see to it."

Claude turned round towards her:

"But, Marie, supposing I can't pay you back; there's still no news of the captain."

"I'll stay on; I'll take some job or other in a restaurant. For once they'll get some decent food. The children belong to me just as much as to you."

The wart above Marie's lip quivered with indignation.

A newspaper-boy went past shouting out the latest bulletin: "Dien-Bien-Phu fallen; no news of the seven thousand prisoners or three thousand casualties."

The little countess with the doe-like eyes suddenly turned aside and started weeping silently. The passers-by stared at her in astonishment. Marie rounded on them with rage in her heart; she felt like burying her teeth in them and shouting in their faces that at this very moment her captain was dead . . . or perhaps even worse off.

In the afternoon they watched the arrival of the three hundred officers who had been taken prisoner at Dien-Bien-Phu. Those who were on the staff or who had been captured at General de Castries' H.Q. had had time to make a few preparations. They all wore clean uniforms and their haversacks contained a change of clothing and provisions. They gave the impression that their presence there, amongst all the others, was only by mistake.

Suddenly Raspéguy's powerful voice rang out. He had just caught sight of one of his officers, in a dirty vest and with a filthy bandage round his leg, tied up to a tree because he had jostled a sentry of the People's Army.

"You bastards! What about the rules of war? What do you think you're doing, tying my men up like prize pigs being taken to market?"

Raspéguy was suddenly beginning to find some use for the rules of war which he himself had never observed. On occasion he had been known to conclude his orders with the brief injunction: "Don't be too inhuman." In actual fact he always wrote out his directives after the operations were over and exclusively for the benefit of his superiors.

He was followed by General de Castries, downcast because he had not been able to die and pass into the realm of legend.

His cheeks were sunken, his features drawn, and the khaki bush-shirt which hung on his shoulders looked several sizes too big for him. He wore the red forage cap of the Moroccan Spahis and a Third Regiment scarf. Behind him came "Moustache," his batman, a huge Berber whiskered like a Janissary.

The general had reached a little stream of clear water flowing between muddy banks at the foot of the camp. The Vietnamese believed this water could kill. It had needed Communism and war to induce them to venture into these cursed mountains with clear-flowing rivers.

Moustache had seventeen years' service behind him and knew his job. From his haversack he brought out a clean, well-pressed uniform, bush-shirt and trousers, and a leather toilet case.

Castries took off the shirt he was wearing. He heard a noise behind him and turned round. It was Glatigny.

They had known each other for a long time and their families had intermarried at various stages.

The general lisped with great distinction and detachment:

"Ath you thee, old boy, it'th all over. Yethterday, at theventeen hundred hourth, I gave the order to theath fire. Marianne IV fell at nine in the morning. The Vieth were thtrung out along the river to the eatht. There wath nothing left but the thentral strong-pointh with three thousand wounded piling up in the dug-outh, not to mention the corptheth. I reported to Hanoi at thixteen thirty hourth. Navarre had left for Thaigon and I got on to Cogny who told me: 'Whatever happenth, no white flag, but you're at liberty to take any decision you conthider fit. Do you thtill think a break-out's impothible?' It'th crazy. They never realized what wath going on. They must find thome tholution at Geneva. In three months we'll be releathed."

It was curious how this word Geneva seemed suddenly fraught with hope. Glatigny repeated it under his breath and found there was something magical about the very sound.

The general finished shaving. He handed his shaving-brush still covered in lather to Glatigny, who suddenly realized how dirty and stubbly he was and to what extent he had forgotten how important personal appearance is to a cavalry man. In 1914 cavalry officers used to shave before going into action. In modern warfare all those rites were ludicrous; it was not enough to be well-born, smart and clean; first of all you had to win.

"I'll soon be thinking exactly like Raspéguy and Esclavier," the captain said to himself.

But Castries was already passing him his razor and metal shaving-mirror.

"Im! Im!" the sentry behind them yelled. "Silence! Forbidden you speak to general!"

Castries paid no attention to this interruption.

"You see, all the divisions we were containing at Dien-Bien-Phu will now pour down into the delta which is rotten through and through. Hanoi's liable to be surrounded before the rains start."

"Im! Im!" The sentry was getting impatient.

"We'll have to come to terms. The Americans could have intervened before; now it's too late."

Glatigny was enjoying the feel of the lather on his face, the gliding of the razor over his skin. He had the sensation of shedding a mask and being able to resume his own identity at last.

A *can-bo*, an officer or under-officer with the offensive accent of a brothel attendant, brusquely interrupted them:

"No talking with general: you there, rejoin comrades at once, *mau-len*."

Glatigny had finished shaving. Castries handed him his toothbrush and his tube of toothpaste, but he did not have time to use them; urged on by his superior, the sentry gave him a shove. He rejoined his comrades: Boisfeuras, who was eavesdropping on the *bo-dois'* conversation; Esclavier and Raspéguy looking strangely alike, each with the same lean, wiry body and unruffled expression, and the same slight tension in every muscle.

Raspéguy grinned pleasantly:

"So you managed to find one of your own sort again?"

The prisoners remained in the Muong-Phan basin for a couple of weeks. They were split up into separate teams and that was how Captains Glatigny, Esclavier, Boisfeuras and Lacombe, and Lieutenants Merle, Pinières and Lescure found themselves condemned to live together for several months. They were presently joined by another lieutenant, an Algerian called Mahmoudi. Withdrawn and silent, he prayed twice a day facing in the direction of Mecca. Boisfeuras noticed that he made several mistakes and prostrated himself out of time. He therefore inquired:

"Have you always said your prayers?"

Mahmoudi looked at him in astonishment:

"No, not since I was a child. I only began again after being taken prisoner."

Boisfeuras peered at him with his almost colourless eyes.

"I should like to know the reasons for your renewed fervour—a purely personal interest, I assure you."

"If I told you, sir, that I did not know myself, or at least did not know exactly, and that you wouldn't enjoy hearing what I feel . . ."

"I don't mind hearing anything . . ."

"Well, it seems to me that this defeat at Dien-Bien-Phu,

where *you*"—he laid particular emphasis on the "you"—"have been beaten by one of *your* former colonies, will have considerable repercussions in Algeria and will be the blow which will sever the last links between our two countries. Now, Algeria cannot exist apart from France; she has no past, no history, no great men; she has nothing except a different religion from yours. It's through our religion that we shall be able to start giving Algeria a history and a personality."

"And just so as to be able to say 'you Frenchmen,' you prostrate yourself twice a day in prayer which is absolutely meaningless?"

"More or less, I suppose. But I should have liked, even in this defeat, to be able to say 'we Frenchmen.' You people never let me."

"And now?"

"Now it's too late."

Mahmoudi appeared to think the matter over. He had a long narrow head with a determined jaw, a slightly hooked nose and tranquil eyes, and his fringe of black beard trimmed into a point made him look like the popular conception of a Barbary pirate.

"No, perhaps it isn't too late, but something will have to be done quickly—unless of course a miracle occurs."

"You don't believe in miracles?"

"In your schools they made a point of destroying whatever sense of wonder or belief in the impossible I had."

Mahmoudi continued to pray to a God in whom he no longer believed.

Glatigny also fell into the habit of kneeling down and praying twice a day to his God, but he had faith and this was manifestly clear.

Lieutenant-Colonel Raspéguy, who felt ill at ease with the senior officers, came and joined them whenever he could. He was only really in his element among the subalterns, captains and N.C.O.s. He always went barefoot—by way of training, he claimed, with a view to further operations. But he never mentioned what sort of operations. He would sit on the edge

of a bunk and trace mysterious figures on the earth floor with
a sliver of bamboo. Occasionally he would burst out:

"Why the hell did they have to dump us in this damned basin? Christ Almighty, it's unthinkable . . ."

On one occasion Glatigny tried to put forward the High
Command theory that Dien-Bien-Phu was the key to the whole
of South-East Asia and had been from time immemorial.

"Listen," Raspéguy said to him, "you're quite right to stand
up for your lord and master, but now you're with us, on our
side, and you don't owe him anything more. Dien-Bien-Phu
was a foul-up. The proof of it is, we lost."

Sometimes the colonel would go up to Lescure and then
turn round to Esclavier and ask:

"How's your crackpot? Any better?"

He regarded his favourite captain with a certain amount of
distrust and wondered if he was only looking after the madman
the better to prepare his escape, his "midnight flit," without
even letting him know.

At the time of the surrender Raspéguy had wanted to attempt one last break-out; he had been refused permission. He
had then assembled his red berets and told them:

"I'm granting every one of you your liberty. It's every man
for himself from now on. I, Raspéguy, am not prepared to be
in command of prisoners."

Esclavier was facing him at the time and the colonel had
seen that peculiar glint in his eyes:

"So you're giving me my liberty, are you? Well, you'll see if I
don't take advantage of it . . . and all by myself."

If he had had a son, he would have wanted him to be like the
captain: "as tough as they come," prickly and unmanageable,
with a strong sense of comradeship, and so crammed with
medals and feats of arms that if he had not curbed him a little
he would have had even more than himself.

He went up to Esclavier and laid a hand on his shoulder.

"Philippe, don't be a damned fool. The war's not over yet,
not by a long shot, and I'll be needing you."

"It's every man for himself, sir, you said so yourself."

"We'll have a go at it together later on, when we're ready, when everything's right for it."

On the third morning—while the prisoners were still at Muong-Phan—it began to rain. Water began to drip through the thatch on to their bunks.

Lacombe woke up and remarked that he was hungry. Then, turning round, he noticed that Esclavier's place was empty. He felt there was something wrong and opened the haversack in which he had hidden six tins of baked beans. There were three missing. He woke up the others.

"Someone's stolen my rations; I'd put them aside . . . for all of us . . . just in case. Esclavier must have taken them; he's run out on us."

"Pipe down," Boisfeuras quietly said. "He's decided to try his luck. We'll keep his absence concealed as long as we can."

Glatigny had come up to them:

"He didn't take all the tins?"

"Almost all," said Lacombe, whose flabby cheeks were quivering.

"He didn't want to load himself down. Yet I advised him to take the whole haversack."

"But. . . ."

"Didn't you say you put those tins aside for all of us? Well, one of us needed them particularly badly . . ."

Pinières was furious. He turned to Merle:

"Esclavier might have let us know; we could have gone with him. But you know what he's like: absolutely unco-operative, always does things on his own and trusts no one but himself."

Mahmoudi, sitting cross-legged on his bunk, did not budge. He did not even try to get out of the way of the water dripping down on to his neck. Lescure was quietly singing a strange little ditty about a garden in the rain and a boy and a girl who loved each other but did not realize it.

The storm had broken in the middle of the night and it had suddenly turned as black as pitch, while the thunder rolled round the valley like a salvo of artillery. Two or three flashes

of lightning ripped across the sky. Esclavier had leaped to his
feet and crept up to Boisfeuras's bunk.

"Boisfeuras!"

"What?"

"I'm off."

"You're mad."

"I can't stand it any longer. This storm, you see, there was a
storm like this during my journey from Compiègne to Mathausen. There was a moment when I could have jumped out of the
train through a badly fastened window in the carriage, but I
waited in the hope of a more favourable opportunity."

"You're a damned fool. Can I help you in any way?"

"This is my plan: if I head due south I can reach the Méo
village above Bam-Ou-Tio in a couple of nights. I once had a
look round that part of the country, and the Méos were always
friendly. They're related to Tou-Bi, the head man of Xieng-
Kouang. They'll give me a guide. By following the crests of
the mountains I'll be able to reach the Nam-Bac valley in a
fortnight or so and that's where the operational base of the
Crèvecœur column should be. If it isn't there, I'll push on to
Muong-Sai. The Méos between the Na-Mou and Muong-Sai
are all on our side."

"They're not, they're against us."

"You're wrong. Last February they evacuated all the survivors of the 6th Laotian Light Infantry, including the wounded,
right through the 308 Division lines. The Viets may hold the
valleys, but the Méos hold the heights."

"That was in February. Since then the Viets have overrun
the highlands and conscripted the Méos. Your plan's feasible,
but there are the Viets to reckon with, the whole Vietminh
world, Vietminh organization, the Vietminh intelligence service . . ."

"It can't be true. No Méo has ever served any master except
his own fantasy and has never been known to betray a guest."

Glatigny, who had woken up and heard them whispering together, came over and joined them.

"I'm off," Esclavier told him. "I'd be grateful if you would
look after Lescure for me."

"Can I come with you?"

"Impossible. There's only the remotest chance of success, even for one man on his own. Boisfeuras doesn't think I'll get away with it, and he may be right."

"Have you got any provisions?"

"No."

Without a sound Glatigny went and got Lacombe's kit-bag.

"This might come in useful. That fat swine won't ever need it in an attempt to escape."

"Too heavy," said Esclavier.

He only took three tins. Boisfeuras handed him a silver piastre which he carried strapped to his leg by a band of adhesive tape.

"This is the only currency the Méos recognize. You'll either get yourself killed or be recaptured. Good luck."

Esclavier gave him a tap on the shoulder.

"You were chasing her yourself, you old bastard, while pretending to defend her virtue. Just like the Viets. That was the best policy perhaps. Take good care of Lescure, Glatigny. He did something I could never have done—fought and showed courage for someone other than himself."

Esclavier plunged out into the dark and was instantly soaked by the rain. There was a light flickering in the guard-post hut. The guard-post lay to the north; he would therefore have to move in the opposite direction and take cover in the jungle at once.

"Halt!"

The voice came out of the rain and the darkness.

Esclavier replied:

"*Tou-bi*, prisoner, very bad stomach."

This was the password which enabled them to make the most of Vietminh modesty and leave their huts at night, for the "Hygiene Rule," which was one of the four rules of a soldier in the People's Army, decreed that "the natural functions had to be performed in private."

The sentry let him pass and Esclavier clambered up a slope. He was swallowed up at once in the jungle; the creepers were like tentacles that tried to wrap themselves round him; the thorns were like teeth that tried to tear him to shreds. It was impossible for him to maintain a straight course; there was only one idea in his mind—to keep climbing so as to reach the ridge. Once there, he would be able to take his bearings.

Every now and then he almost collapsed from exhaustion; his eyelids felt like lead; he was tempted to lie down for a bit and go to sleep and resume his march a little later. But he remembered the window in the Compiègne train, squared his shoulders and pushed on. He was right not to have waited any longer before escaping. He knew how quickly a man can lose his strength in a camp where the work is hard and the food insufficient, and how quickly he can lose his courage in the demoralizing company of grousers who are more or less resigned to their condition as prisoners.

By daybreak he had reached the ridge and was able to rest. The valley no longer existed; it was lost in the mist. He was in the country of the Méos who live above the level of the clouds.

In the legendary days of the Jade emperors, the masters of the Ten Thousand Mountains, a dragon had come to China and laid waste the country. It had devoured the armies that were sent out against it and also the warriors clothed in their magic armour. The emperor had then made a promise that anyone who rid him of the dragon would be given his daughter's hand in marriage and half the kingdom. The big dog Méo had slain the dragon and came to claim his reward. The emperor was unwilling to keep his promise but he also feared the dog's strength. One of his counsellors had then suggested a subterfuge. Admittedly, he had promised half of his kingdom to whoever slew the dragon, but he had not specified which half. Why not the upper half? As for the daughter, there was no problem. The emperor had a large number of them and spent most of his time begetting even more.

Thus it was that the dog Méo was given the hand of the emperor's daughter in marriage and, as a dowry, all the land in the empire that lay above the level of the clouds. His descendants, the Méos, wore a silver dog-collar in memory of him. They loved animals, lived in the highlands and, because they were after all descendants of the Jade Emperor, looked down on all the other races, especially the Vietnamese of the deltas.

Esclavier was extremely fond of the Méos even though they were so dirty that their squat little bodies, with calves as thick as a Tibetan sherpa's, were always jet black. They never mixed with the lowlanders, the servile and ingratiating Thais, they admitted no social or family organization; some of them even declined all form of communal life. They kept to their mountain ridges, the last anarchists of the world.

The sun blazed down. Esclavier began to feel thirsty. He kept following the ridge of the mountain and in the afternoon a Fleet Air Arm "Corsaire" flew over him very low. He waved at it wildly, but the pilot did not see him. In any case what could he have done? He had to push on, alone and unaided, and the thought of himself, lost in the midst of the elephant grass, his throat parched with thirst, was strangely beguiling.

He bypassed the first Méo village he saw tucked away behind a mountain peak. He felt it was still too close to the Vietminhs and to Dien-Bien-Phu.

After a further three hours' march he came across a *ray*: a section of the forest that had been burned down. In the cinders the Méos had planted some hard rice, vegetables and poppies. There were four women there, dressed in rags, with panniers on their backs, barefoot—their feet looked almost monstrous—with their calves encased in leggings. They were collecting vegetable marrows. Esclavier knew that he ought to push on farther, but he was at his last gasp, he felt terribly thirsty and it would soon be dark.

He went up to the women. They did not look at all scared but uttered little guttural exclamations and turned their broad flat faces towards him. They smelt so dreadful that he was almost sick.

"It must be a question of habit," Esclavier said to himself. "At Véronique II, towards the end, I was hardly conscious of the stench of the corpses."

A male Méo appeared, with his silver collar round his neck and a primitive hunting-bow in his hand. He was barefoot, his hair falling over his eyes, and wore a short jacket and black trousers.

Esclavier did not know how to communicate with him. He showed him the silver piastre and the sullen face came to life. The captain went through the motions of eating, bent down, plucked a marrow and bit into it. It was juicy and full of flavour.

"Tou-Le," he said, "cousin Tou-Bi, village Bam-ou-Tio."

The Méo made a sign that he had understood and walked ahead. They kept going until it was dark. Tireless, the Méo trotted along hair-raising paths which invariably followed the line of the steepest slope. He had to stop and wait for the Frenchman every two hundred yards.

At last they reached the village, a few thatch huts on low piles. The shaggy little mountain ponies, as tireless as their owners, stood with their heads inside the houses where the feeding-troughs were, the rest of their bodies in the open.

Tou-Le was there, indistinguishable from any of the others, a little older perhaps, a little more shrivelled, fossilized by age and opium. He recognized Esclavier at once and bowed low before him in token of his friendship. The captain was saved, he felt like laughing. The Méos and the highlands still belonged to the French. Boisfeuras was wrong, which was only to be expected since he did not know this region very well.

The Méos had killed a suckling-pig; it was roasting over the embers, exuding a delicious smell of grilled meat. The stodgy hot rice was spicy and dished up in little baskets. Esclavier knew the customs of the country; he rolled it into a ball between his fingers and popped it into his mouth after first dipping it in a red sauce.

The flames in the hearth cast flickering shadows on the inside walls of the hut and red glints were reflected in the eyes of the horses as they snorted and shook their chains.

Esclavier picked up a sliver of bamboo and, in the cinders in front of the fireplace, traced out the route he wanted to take to reach the Nam-Bac valley.

Tou-Le miraculously seemed to understand and showed his approval by nodding his head. He then brought out a bottle of *choum.* The two men gulped down the crude rice wine and belched like a couple of Chinese merchants.

Tou-Le suggested a pipe of opium, Esclavier refused with thanks. He was not used to the stuff and he was afraid he might be too tired to walk next day. Everyone said that Méo opium was the best that could be found in South-East Asia. But a paratrooper never indulged in it; that particular vice was the prerogative of naval or staff officers. The Méos all smoked it; for them it took the place of tobacco and appeared to have no harmful effects.

And so, while Tou-Le puffed at his pipe in the flickering light of the oil lamp and contentedly exhaled the thick pungent smoke, Esclavier fell asleep stretched out in front of the hearth.

A line of verse came back to him, a poem of Apollinaire's:

Under Mirabeau bridge flows the Seine . . .

He would one day watch the Seine flow under Mirabeau bridge, as a free man, having escaped from this hell of green caterpillars which continued to haunt Lescure. He would smile at the first pretty girl he met and ask her out to dinner at a little restaurant on the Ile St. Louis . . .

A kindly hand was gently shaking him. With an effort he opened his eyes. A *bo-doi* was leaning over him; all he could see was his ready-made smile, his slit eyes and his helmet.

The impersonal voice started off:

"President Ho wants the French prisoners to rest after their long exertions . . ."

A nightmare had insinuated itself into his dream. The young girl took him gently by the hand; she caressed him and he fancied he saw in her rather sad eyes that she was ready to surrender.

But the *bo-doi* continued to shake him gently:

"President Ho is also anxious that the prisoners should not catch cold. Accept this blanket offered you by a soldier of the Democratic Republic of Viet-Nam so that after a good sleep you may recover the strength which you have wasted in vain."

Esclavier sat up with a start. Tou-Le had disappeared and he saw a sentry standing at the entrance to the hut, his bayonet glinting in the moonlight . . .

Kind-hearted Tou-Le, the free Méo of the highlands, had delivered him into the hands of the little green men of the valleys and the deltas. Esclavier felt too weary; all he wanted was to sleep and let the night find some solution or no solution at all.

In the morning Esclavier followed the Viets outside, spitting on the floor as he left the hut in which a man of the ancient law had failed to observe the sacred rules of hospitality. Tou-Le turned his face away and pretended he had not seen him. This evening he would smoke a few more pipes than usual and would go on doing so until the day came when "for the public good" some political commissar or other would forbid him any more opium. Then he would die; that was what Esclavier hoped.

The four soldiers escorting the captain showed him every consideration and kindness. They were in high spirits; they sang French marching songs to Vietnamese melodies and helped him over the difficult places and slippery monkey-bridges. Like the Cochin-Chinese partisans he had commanded six months earlier in the marshy forest of the Lagna, they were lively and agile; their weapons were well cared for; they could march without making a sound and, when they took off their helmets, they displayed the shock-headed locks of mischievous schoolboys.

At dusk they reached a main trail deeply pitted by the wheels of heavy trucks. Small detachments of soldiers or coolies kept passing them in both directions. They all trotted along with the same rapid jerky gait.

By the side of the trail the *bo-dois* lit a fire and started cooking their evening meal: rice and lentil soup with one or two little chunks of pork floating in it. On a banana leaf they laid out a few pinches of coarse salt and a handful of wild peppers.

They ate in silence, then one of them brought out a packet of Chinese cigarettes made specially for the Vietminh. He offered one to Esclavier.

The little group surrendered themselves to the peace of the night. Their leader was reluctant to drag himself away from the glow of the fire. With an effort he rose to his feet, adjusted his equipment, put his helmet on and resumed the inscrutable mask of a soldier of the Democratic Republic of Viet-Nam. He turned to the prisoner:

"I must now take you to an officer of the division who wishes to interrogate you."

It was an underground shelter with a floor made of gravel, illuminated by an acetylene lamp. At a table sat a man who looked a great deal more distinguished than the majority of his compatriots. His features seemed to be finely chiselled in very old gold; his hands were long and slender and beautifully kept.

"Your name?"

"Captain Philippe Esclavier."

Esclavier had recognized the inimitable voice. The first time he had heard it was in the dark, when it had ordered him to help push the Jeep.

"I wasn't expecting to see you again so soon, Captain. Have you been decently treated since our last conversation in the Muong-Phan basin? It seems, however, that you didn't follow my advice. I'm glad your rather childish escapade has ended without your coming to any harm. You have now been able to see for yourself how deeply united our nation is, how close the bonds are between the mountain people and those of the lowlands and the deltas, and this despite all the efforts that the French colonialists have made to split us for the last fifty years."

The Voice fell silent, gazed at the captain with friendly curiosity and went on pensively:

"What are we going to do about you, Esclavier?"

"I suppose you'll take some sort of disciplinary action against me. This time I agree with you entirely. I'm prepared to pay for my failure. I should like to inform you, however, that it's the duty of every prisoner to escape and that I hope my next attempt will be successful."

This statement of principle sounded slightly absurd; it would not have seemed so, however, had he been dealing with a German, a Spaniard, an American—a member of his own "brotherhood." This word had just occurred to him; he considered it more closely; it did not seem to carry much weight.

"You want to be a martyr, don't you, to be tied to a tree, beaten with rifle-butts, condemned to death and shot? In your eyes that would be a means of endowing your act with an importance which to us it does not possess. We'd like to put that act in its true perspective; as we see it, you're nothing but a spoilt child who has been playing truant."

This time Esclavier was able to classify the person. His studied expressions: "I wasn't expecting to see you again so soon," and "playing truant"—the man was a schoolmaster. He had the condescending mannerisms of a "somebody." He belonged to the race of pedagogues, but to him both men and arms had been entrusted. What a temptation for an intellectual gasbag!

"I had already appreciated your frankness," the Voice went on. "That frankness of yours will be the first condition of your re-education. During your stay in the Democratic Republic of Viet-Nam you will have time to learn how to conduct a self-examination. You will then realize, I hope, the immensity of your errors, your ignorance, your lack of understanding . . . This time no disciplinary measures will be taken against you. You'll be taken back to your comrades. You will merely have to tell them about your attempt to escape. We rely on your frankness to give them an absolutely accurate account of what happened."

"Instruction Period" in the Muong-Phan camp. The officer prisoners, seated on tree-stumps, formed a semicircle round a sort of bamboo platform on which the "pedagogue" stood, commenting on the latest news of the Geneva conference. As he spoke in his somewhat over-elegant, over-elaborate French, his eyes kept darting over his audience. A *mah-qui* of the termite world, he was there to hollow out the brains of all these men, to empty them of their substance and then stuff them full of propaganda rubbish.

"There is immense hope among the people of France . . .
The Vietnamese armistice commission has been able to make
contact with the democratic elements of your country and to
notify your families at last of your fate . . ."

Then he read out an article in *L'Observateur,* fiercely attacking the intransigent policy of Georges Bidault who was
opposed to any concession. The commissar seemed genuinely
distressed by the desperate efforts of this warmonger who was
trying by every means to obstruct the peace and brotherhood
of the masses and, by the same token, the release of the prisoners. But he still had hope; a single individual could never im-
pede the urge of the masses towards progress.

He concluded his lecture and after folding up *L'Observateur,*
with the pointed remark that this was a French paper and by
no means a Communist one, he indicated Esclavier who was
sitting at the foot of the stand:

"Your comrade, Captain Esclavier, returned to our camp
this morning. He will now tell you in his own words the circumstances of his escape and of his recapture."

A low murmur rose from the prisoners when Esclavier, with
an inscrutable expression on his face, took the commissar's
place on the platform. He spoke in short, clipped phrases,
without looking at any of them but only at the sky which was
streaked with a few grey clouds.

"Christ, I hope he doesn't do anything silly," Raspéguy muttered, leaning over to his neighbour, a fat colonel.

"Such as?"

"Such as strangling that little bastard who's forcing him to
behave like a clown. He's one of my men, you know, a real
tough nut who's easily roused."

Esclavier described all the circumstances of his escape and his
capture. He omitted nothing, neither the women's friendliness,
the juicy vegetable marrow, the smell of the meat grilling over the
fire, nor the welcome warmth of the fireside in the Méo hut. As
they listened to him, they all felt a profound nostalgia for their
lost freedom and dreamt of escaping, even the most timid among
them.

"The only thing I regret," Esclavier concluded, "is having

chosen a bad route. I advise you against the mountain ridges which are held by the Méos and also against the valleys which are held by the Thais."

Then he stepped down from the platform with the same inscrutable expression on his face.

Glatigny leaned over towards Boisfeuras:

"He got out of that one nicely. He's given us all a longing to be free. I'm pleasantly surprised."

"Did you think he was just a big hairy-chested brute?"

"Well, there is that side to him."

"Get to know him better; try and win his friendship—which isn't easy—and you'll find that he's intelligent, sensitive, extremely cultured . . . but he doesn't like to show it."

Lieutenant Mahmoudi had shut his eyes and was dreaming of his homeland, of the arid soil, the grey stones, the pungent smells of the Sahara, of the sheep cooked whole on a spit, of the hand that is dipped into the animal's insides and withdrawn dripping with spicy grease. In the deep blue night a shepherd boy was playing a poignant and monotonous melody on a shrill reed pipe. Somewhere in the distance a jackal howled.

"It's very decent of the Vietminh, don't you think?" Captain Lacombe asked him. "They might have taken it out on us for Esclavier's escape and put him in solitary confinement . . ."

"Captain Esclavier is the sort of man we admire in my country, even if we do have to fight him some day."

And Mahmoudi recalled a proverb of the black tents: "The courage of your enemy does you honour." But Esclavier was not his enemy . . . not yet . . .

As he entered the hut, Esclavier declared that he felt hungry, that his escapade and his little session of self-examination had sharpened his appetite. Without another word he took a tin of baked beans out of Lacombe's haversack, opened it and fell to.

He offered the tin to Glatigny:

"Have some?"

Lacombe felt powerless, he was on the point of tears. It was his very life this savage was devouring in his great champing jaws. Everyone else laughed, even Mahmoudi whose face glistened with cruel delight.

Then Esclavier went and lay down on his bunk in front of the fire.

3

LIEUTENANT PINIÈRES'S
REMORSE

In the afternoon of the 15th of May, during the course of an "Instruction Period," the man whom Esclavier called "The Voice" notified the prisoners that they would be leaving next morning for Camp One. They were split up into four groups, the first being made up of the senior officers and the wounded. The stores and equipment—some huge rice urns attached to bamboo poles, a few picks and shovels—were distributed among the junior officers of the three remaining groups. They were also given a three-day ration of rice. But since they had no sacks to carry it in, a number of them sacrificed their trousers which were transformed into sacks by tying the ends of the legs together.

Lacombe wanted them to get rid of the madman and send him on with the first group. But he came up against violent opposition not only from Esclavier and Glatigny but from all the rest. They clung to Lescure as to a sort of fetish; they looked after him, took good care of him and forced him to eat his rice, thus forgetting their own wretchedness.

Lescure's cry of "Chickens! Ducks!" had become a rallying signal; in their own minds it no longer applied to code names for mortar shells, but to actual chickens and ducks which they hoped to scrounge in the process of moving camp.

"For a prisoner, everything is justified," Esclavier had declared, "stealing, lying . . . From the moment they deprive him of his freedom he is given every right."

Boisfeuras had asked him:

"And what if a régime, a political ideology deprived the whole world of its freedom?"

"Then there are no holds barred."

Each team was to elect a leader. Glatigny proposed the "victualling officer" Lacombe. He had made himself his campaign manager.

"Lacombe has all the necessary qualifications," he explained. "He's sly. He knows how to fend for himself and provides for the future . . . Look at those six tins of beans . . ."

Pinières, the former maquisard, had cottoned on at once:

"He's got the ugly face of a quisling, too. He'll play the part of Laval with the Viets . . . and we'll be the Resistance!"

Thus it was that Lacombe was detailed as leader of the team.

A search had taken place after the meeting; it had been extremely thorough. The *bo-dois* had not confined themselves to going through the prisoners' pockets and the hems of their clothes, but had insisted on them stripping stark naked.

Up till then Boisfeuras had managed to conceal his dagger, a thin stiletto which he carried strapped to the inside of his leg with adhesive tape like the silver piastre he had given Esclavier.

Realizing he would be found out, while Merle, who was one in front of him, was in the process of being searched, he had extracted the dagger and brandished it in the face of the N.C.O. in charge, a former Hanoi rickshaw coolie bursting with self-importance:

"Of course I'm keeping it, that's agreed with the boss. He said each team was entitled to a knife for cutting wild herbs."

Recovering from his surprise, the Viet had thought it over for a moment, then given his assent, when he suddenly realized it was a lethal weapon the prisoner was putting back in his pocket:

"No, you no ungderstangd; give me knife."

Glatigny managed to conceal two silver piastres by slipping them into his mouth, and Pinières a little mirror with a dent in the middle which could reflect the sun's rays and thus be used as a ground-to-air signalling lamp.

Then, at first light on 18 May, the team left for Camp One, with its rice urn slung on a bamboo pole, its madman who quietly followed behind like a poodle, Boisfeuras barefoot as

usual, Glatigny and Esclavier, Merle and Pinières, Lacombe
and Mahmoudi.

"The camp has been set up near Dien-Bien-Phu," Lacombe
had told them, "so as not to be too far away from a landing
ground. Once the armistice is signed at Geneva, aircraft will
be able to come and pick us up."

"I don't believe it," Esclavier had replied. "They'll make us
move down towards Hoa-Binh on the edge of the delta and
hand us over in Hanoi. Or maybe we'll have to march as far as
Son-La, and be taken on from there by truck."

"It's much too far," said Pinières. "We're nearly a hundred
miles from Son-La."

Glatigny felt it wiser to say nothing. At Christmas, as a propaganda move, the Vietminh had released four officers who
had been taken prisoner at Cao-Bang in 1950. The C.-in-C.
had made him responsible for their interrogation, and one of
them had told him that Camp One, where the officer prisoners
were held, was situated in the limestone country of the north-
east, in the region of Bac-Kan, that's to say some five hundred
miles from Dien-Bien-Phu.

Most of the prisoners were in a poor state of health and un-
likely to stay the course.

During the first day's march the prisoners covered twenty
miles or so in a north-easterly direction, towards China. The
senior officers and the wounded had passed them in trucks.

Raspéguy was sitting in the back of the last truck, with his
bare feet dangling over the edge. A Vietminh sentry had been
detailed to keep an eye on him. Had not Generalissimo Giap
declared that his capture was the most important of all? Raspéguy and his battalion had repeatedly eluded the two most
powerful Vietminh divisions and on one occasion had even destroyed the command post of one of them.

Raspéguy waved to the team and shouted:

"Conserve your strength; you're in for a long march."

He would have liked to be with them, to encourage them and
make them stick it out; and he would have shown them that,
colonel though he was, he could do better than the youngest
among them.

He cast a friendly glance at the sentry; he would probably be forced to kill him when he made his escape—because he was going to escape and he was going to succeed where Esclavier had failed.

The prisoners were now moving with the main stream of the Vietminh battalions, trucks and coolies. They no longer existed as themselves; they formed part of a vast human tide.

The heat, the exhaustion, the lack of water were beginning to tell. On the third day they reached Tuan-Giao, an intersection of the R.P.* 41 leading from Hanoi to Lai-Chau. The neighbouring forest swarmed with soldiers, coolies and trucks; it was full of supply stores and ammunition dumps. It was the big invisible base of the army which had attacked Dien-Bien-Phu. The prisoners were quartered in a little Thai hamlet half a mile off the road on a hillock surrounded by bamboos. There they were allowed twenty-four hours' rest; they badly needed it.

The team had not yet settled into a cohesive unit. Later on those who belonged to it came to be known as the "W.S." or "Wily Serpents," for they proved to be singularly impervious to every form of propaganda, with a pronounced taste for pilfering and polemics, and a sort of genius for exploiting every weakness of Vietminh organization.

At the time they embarked on their long march they had not yet reached this stage.

Lacombe was more and more obsequious towards the sentries and called them "sir," a form of address which they demanded in vain from the other prisoners.

Esclavier was quick to take offence.

Boisfeuras seemed to live for himself alone. As he ambled effortlessly along the trail, his bare feet with their prehensile toes gripping into the mud, he never gave his comrades the slightest assistance and confined himself to carrying the rice urn when it came to his turn to do so.

Glatigny occasionally gave himself airs. Lieutenant Merle had once asked him to help with some chore or other:

"Will you give me a hand, Glatigny?"

*Route Provinciale, as opposed to R.C.: Route Coloniale.

"My dear sir, I'm accustomed to my subordinates addressing me by my rank and not by the familiar '*tu*,' especially when my uniform consists of a pair of dirty shorts and my prerogatives are reduced to obeying, as you do, a funny little green man who six months ago was a rickshaw coolie."

Mahmoudi did not say much, but more than once his comrades noticed a look of resentment come into his eyes when the food was doled out, as though he thought they were laughing behind his back because he was an Algerian and a Moslem.

To all the prisoners Camp One appeared as a sort of promised land where, in the shade of giant mango trees, they would spend a few days waiting for their release, smoking treacly tobacco, eating rice and dried fish, and dozing through some vague lectures given by "The Voice."

The sky had filled with the heavy black clouds which herald the monsoon. They concealed the mountain peaks behind a dark green blanket which stretched right across the horizon.

One day, towards the end of the afternoon, they heard the drone of aircraft: a large formation of bombers. They dropped their bombs over the mountains and the explosion echoed round the valleys like distant thunder.

The Voice drove up in his Jeep and immediately assembled the prisoners to inform them of the treachery of the French high command:

"Before the fall of Dien-Bien-Phu the Vietnamese delegation to the armistice commission had suggested an aerial truce to the French command to facilitate the evacuation of the wounded and the transport of the prisoners. The French command had agreed to this. But yesterday, without any warning, it broke this truce. The French commander-in-chief, in his palace in Saigon, does not give a damn for the wounded or the prisoners among his troops. All he wants is to prolong the war in the interest of the bloated colonialists and the bankers. Yesterday a column of French prisoners consisting of your N.C.O.s and other ranks was bombed by your aircraft. Several were killed. To avoid this danger we are going to march you across the Méo highlands by night. We shall be leaving at sunset."

"It's a bit thick, I must say," Lacombe declared. "After all we've been through, to go and unload their bombs on us!"

"What have you been through?" Esclavier demanded. "You spent the whole time back at headquarters, stuffing yourself with the rations you were supposed to send up to us."

Glatigny, rather white in the face, broke into the conversation:

"I know the general extremely well. If he saw fit to break this truce and resume aerial bombardments, it could only have been for a very good reason."

But he felt that no one agreed with him and he heard Lieutenant Merle sneer:

"The general's sitting pretty back in Saigon. This evening, more than likely, he'll be having a romp with his 'boy' or his *congai* while we're struggling across the Méo highlands."

Merle was being deliberately offensive and his vulgarity did not ring true.

Pinières then gave his opinion:

"If he'd had the slightest decency, the general would have come along with us or else put a bullet through his brains."

Glatigny felt like shouting out loud:

"But I'm here with you, aren't I? Can't you understand that I'm here because the general couldn't be, just like Lescure who came in the place of his brother?"

Boisfeuras merely observed:

"That's not the point; anyway it's utterly unimportant."

From their quarters the prisoners had a view of the valley and the road which wound through the paddy-fields and the tall grass circling the edge of the forest.

An hour before sunset the dead valley began to come to life. The battalions poured out of the forest and, like tributary rivers, added their volume to the main green stream. Some trucks moved slowly down the middle of this flow, jolting over the pot-holes with engines racing.

A column of black coolies, the Pims of Dien-Bien-Phu, were drawn up by the side of the road. They marched off and were presently swallowed up in the oncoming traffic. The Voice issued his last orders to the assembled prisoners:

"Tonight's march will be fairly strenuous. You must keep going without complaint and promptly obey every word of command. You will be coming across Vietnamese soldiers, your victors at Dien-Bien-Phu. You are not allowed to speak to them and must show them every sign of respect. We may possibly run into a column of those men whom you call Pims, those civilian deportees whom you snatched away from their families and peaceful peasant labours to transform into coolies. They are now free men who are returning to their hearths and homes. The suffering you have inflicted on them is such that they are filled with resentment against you. I advise you to be particularly respectful towards them. We are here to protect you from their righteous indignation, but do not provoke them, for otherwise we cannot hold ourselves responsible."

The sun was setting as the prisoners began to climb the first slope up the pass. The forest covered the flanks of the mountains like mildew and spread right along the ravines. But higher up, well above them, the peaks were bare except for a uniform blanket of *tran*, a tall razor-edged grass as pale as the ears of corn and, like them, swept by the wind into gentle waves.

They came to a halt in the ditch to make way for a double column of *bo-dois* who set off up the slope with the rhythmic trotting gait of the riflemen, only their pace was even faster and more jerky. They were weighed down under their haversacks, their bundles of rice slung over one shoulder, and their weapons. Panting, sweating, suffocating, they somehow managed to emit what passed for a marching song. There was no joy in their drawn features. Many of them carried two weapons: Russian submachine-guns or Skoda automatic rifles, which had belonged to their comrades killed in the battle of the Haute Région. These weapons would come in useful in the delta to arm the waiting recruits.

"There's no point in killing them," Esclavier despondently observed. "They're like worms; you cut them in two and think that's the end of them, but all you've done is double their number, each separate half assuming a life of its own. They are going to multiply in the delta and finish off what's left of the corpse of our Expeditionary Corps."

A long column of Thais followed behind them. The Thais wore their traditional dress. The women, slender as reeds in their long narrow skirts and short bodices, seemed to have lost their indolent charm and sensual gait. Split up into small groups behind the *can-bos*, who looked like ghosts in their outsize greenish uniforms, they joined in the slogans, taking their cue from the *can-bos*; each of them had the blank and riveted gaze of a fanatic.

Glatigny gave Boisfeuras a nudge:

"Look, the termites have swallowed up the carefree people of the valleys and river-land; they have reduced them to slavery; they've conscripted my Thais, of all people!"

"So what?"

"I lived at Lai-Chau for six months when I first came out here. I thought I had found paradise on earth among these friendly, idle, cheerful men and these lovely, gentle women, always ready for pleasure or for love. These women made me appreciate the joys of the body; I've made love to them on little strips of sand by the banks of the Black River, in their houses on stilts . . . and not once, me a Catholic and a bit of a puritan, not once did I have the slightest feeling of sin, because, you see, the Thais, unlike every other race on earth, have no conception of original sin. And now these chaps have infected them with all their filthy claptrap!"

Night fell all at once like a safety curtain. Some bamboo torches were lit which marked out the twists in the road on the black flank of the mountain. Thereupon Lescure burst into a loud guffaw and they all listened to him in holy terror. It was as though some devil, exploiting his madness, had taken possession of him and was speaking through his mouth. The disjointed flow of words gave birth to extravagant visions.

It was the great procession of the damned who were making their way to the seat of the Last Judgement; angels had lit their torches so that no one should escape in the dark. Enthroned high above them sat the god with the huge belly and eyes as round as millstones. In his claw-like hands he grabbed the humans up by the fistful and tore them apart in his teeth, the just and the unjust, the pure and impure, the believers and unbelievers alike. All were acceptable to him, for he hungered after flesh and blood. Every now and then he gave a solemn belch and the angels applauded with a shout: "Long live President Ho!" But he was still ravenous and so he also devoured them; and even as he snapped their bones between his teeth, they kept on shouting: "Long may he live!"

An explosion very close at hand, a sudden blaze of red and the noise of the repercussion, was amplified in echoes right across the mountain.

"Christ Almighty," said Glatigny, "the aircraft have dropped some delayed-action bombs and we've got to go in that direction."

Delayed-action bombs was one of his ideas. In the course of several aerial reconnaissances he had noticed that as soon as the Viets heard the sound of an aircraft they immediately disappeared, abandoning their work on the trail they were building. They did not come back again until it was dark. He had mentioned this to the general, who had given him a free hand. And now fifty per cent of the bombs were equipped with delay fuses of anything between two and ten hours.

The raid had taken place about eleven o'clock in the morning. Most of the bombs would therefore explode, between ten and twelve that night. He looked for his watch on his wrist, forgetting it had been taken from him. All he had now was his wedding-ring. The Viets had also confiscated all wedding-rings, but the prisoners had told them these were religious objects and so they had handed them back. In his case this was true.

He had placed the whole of his life under the sign of Christ who had preached peace, charity, brotherhood . . . and at the same time he had arranged for the delayed-action bombs at the Cat-Bi airfield at Haiphong.

"Something on your mind?" Esclavier asked him kindly. "Are you married?"

"Yes, I've a wife and five children."

"A paragon of a wife and five children at a Jesuit college?"

"No, only three are with the Jesuits, the others are girls."

"That's perfect, your wife will wait patiently for you to come back and make it a round half-dozen."

"Did you hear the bombs?"

"What of it? There's a war on and we can't allow Hanoi to be captured."

The column set off again. Through a gap in the clouds the moon shone down for several minutes on the long file of prisoners straining up hill, their bodies bent forward. Motionless and silent in the middle of the road stood the trucks towing the 105 calibre guns "Made in U.S.A." Glatigny counted them as he went past. There were exactly twenty-four of them; once again the intelligence reports were correct. There they stood in their original covers, towed by short-framed G.M.C.s or Molotovas which were better suited to the mud. The Americans had given these guns to Chiang Kai-Shek; the Communists had either bought them from his generals or else taken them during the big Kuomintang defeat, then sent them to the Vietminh to carry on the same war.

At the head of the convoy a detachment of soldiers illuminated by their smoky bamboo torches were apparently directing the traffic. Farther on the road had been cut.

"*Mau-len, mau-len!*" The cry passed from mouth to mouth, and all the way back again.

The road, which was carved out of the side of the mountain, had caved in over a distance of fifty yards. Some thousand-pound bombs had been responsible for this damage and the Vietminh ant-hill seethed as though it had been stirred up with a stick. The Thai men, women and children with their picks, their baskets and even their bare hands were busily transporting earth to fill in the craters and placing rocks along the outer edge to keep this earth in position. There were about a thousand of them who had come from villages several days' march away. Some *can-bos* were in charge of them; they kept singing patriotic songs and chanting slogans first in Thai and afterwards in Vietnamese. The leader would give them a cue, then they all joined in while carrying on with their work.

"Long live President Ho!"

"Long live General Giap who has led us to victory!"

"Long live the glorious soldiers of the People's Army!"

Lower down, on the edge of a freshly disturbed crater, lay five mangled bodies: victims of a delayed-action bomb. But Glatigny was the only one who saw them; for the coolies, under the spell of the incantations, had forgotten all about them; and the other prisoners, insensible to anything but their own exhaustion, did not bother to look; it was no concern of theirs.

"Dear God . . ."

Glatigny did not know what he wanted God to do; his prayer was vague and confused. He would have liked to be with the coolies, to share their danger. Another bomb exploded in the middle of a mass of women, men and children and the blast bowled the prisoners over. A Thai with a shattered leg started shrieking in the darkness like a wild beast; several bloodstained bodies coated with earth were no longer moving. The chanting had stopped. But all at once it started up again, faintly at first, then louder and louder: *"Ho Chi Tich, Muon Nam . . . Giap, Muon Nam."*

"Mau-len, mau-len!"

By the light of the torches the prisoners filed past the corpses and the wounded who were being tended by medical orderlies with a band of white gauze stretched over their nose and mouth. The chanting pursued them and drove them on.

Glatigny made the sign of the cross and felt the friendly pressure of Esclavier's hand on his shoulder:

"We all suffer from conscience and remorse; that's why we're losing."

In the course of the night there were three further explosions. Each time Glatigny gave a start; each time he felt his friend's hand on his shoulder.

The noise of motor traffic could be heard again below them. The trucks were now able to get through and their roar grew louder at each bend as the convoy gradually gained on the column of prisoners. The Frenchmen were ordered to the side of the road and the black vehicles, like huge clumsy beetles, rattled slowly past them.

The slopes began to get steeper than ever; the men slithered and staggered up the trail, sweat dripping into their eyes. Some of them fell down altogether and their comrades had to help them to their feet again. Mahmoudi, with an arm under Lescure's shoulder, was helping him along as though in a daze. Pinières, with an ugly expression on his face, took over a kit-bag from Lacombe, who was whimpering shamelessly:

"I was never cut out to be a soldier; I wasn't trained for this sort of thing."

"Then what the hell made you go and join the army?" Pinières demanded, pushing him forward.

"I've got two children . . ."

Carrying the rice urn on its bamboo pole, Boisfeuras trudged along with an easy swing of his shoulders, moving like a Vietnamese so as to absorb the jolt at every step. Esclavier, who was on the other end, kept stumbling and cursing; the skin had been rubbed off his shoulder which was bruised and bleeding. Every ten paces or so he shifted the pole from one side to the other and his arms ached right down to his finger-tips.

Glatigny took over from him. Boisfeuras indicated with a gesture that he could carry on. He knew the value of silence during any prolonged effort and sucked a blade of grass to ward off thirst.

Before their departure the Voice had advised the prisoners to fill whatever water containers they had, but these had long ago been drained. Their tongues were parched, their breathing laboured. Word had gone round that anyone falling out by the side of the road would be finished off as a reprisal against the air raids . . . Even the weakest strained to keep going.

The rasping, urgent voice of Boisfeuras came to their ears:

"Pluck some grass and suck it, for Christ's sake, but only the short, thick blades containing moisture: the others will upset your stomach."

At every halt the wind off the summit froze their sweating bodies, and when they started off again their muscles felt so stiff that they could hardly move.

The crest of the mountain seemed a little closer at every

turn. Eventually it was reached, but behind it rose a second peak more lofty and more distant than the sky, then some bare, contorted ridges extending without a break to the far-thest horizon. Beyond lay Son-La, Na-San, Hoa-Binh and Ha-noi with its cafés stocked with ice-cold drinks—the Ritz, the Club, the Normandie—its fast-living, devil-may-care air pi-lots, its reserved and evasive staff officers making announce-ments to the hordes of journalists and being stood round after round of drinks. Back there the Chinese taxi dancers would be dancing together in the middle of the floor, waiting for their clients. It was said that most of them were lesbians and lived together as married couples. On the civilian airport at Gia-Lam the D.C.4 for Paris would be warming up its engines.

Merle, who was at his last gasp and felt he could not take another step, suddenly yelled:

"To hell with them all, the bastards!"

His resentment against those who were not suffering with him gave him strength to carry on a little longer.

The prisoners were anxious to survive, and for that they had to have something to think about, something to believe in. But all they could find in their vacant minds was of no avail. These were peaceful visions: lying in the grass on the bank of a river, with dragon-flies skimming over the water; reading a detective novel by the gentle light of a lamp, with one's wife in the bath-room next door getting ready for bed and the radio playing some insipid little tune dripping with nostalgia . . .

But gradually each one of them was assailed by a more forceful recollection than any other, one which they tried des-perately to suppress: this was their secret and grievous sin. It was to remain with them for the rest of their arduous march, and for the best of them it would give some meaning to their suffering and atonement. The others, those who had nothing, were destined to leave their bones on the roadside.

Pinières was still just behind Lacombe, whom he kept help-ing to his feet, and cursing. He could not forget what the "vict-ualler" had said: "I've got two children."

Pinières's child was dead before it was born; its mother had also died; she had kept the appointment by the Cascade at Dalat; she knew what was in store for her and they had strangled her. That was how the Vietminh punished those who betrayed them. It was shortly after he first arrived in Indo-China, some three years ago. Pinières had joined up as a paratrooper and volunteered for Indo-China in order to break away completely from a past that was political rather than military. That day he had opted for the army against politics. Since then he had had nothing more to do with his former maquis comrades.

He had been posted to the parachute battalion at Lai-Thieu, a village between Saigon and Tu-Dau-Mot. They held the road outside Lai-Thieu and were responsible for controlling the traffic. His second-in-command, an old sergeant-major, was efficient and conscientious and he was thus enabled to go on leave once a week to Saigon. There he would meet some colleagues of his in a bar; they would all go out and dine together at some local eating-house, then drive down by rickshaw to the Rue des Marins at Cholen. They spent the evening wandering from one brothel to another and occasionally broke a window or two. Pinières did not find this particularly amusing, but he made a point of copying his colleagues' mannerisms and behaviour. He came from the maquis, had not been to military college, and was a teacher by profession; all this he was anxious to live down.

His colleagues still displayed a certain reticence towards him, but their reserve was beginning to melt and soon he would really be one of their number. Then he would embark on the life that suited him: membership of that paratroop freemasonry which was in the process of being born.

One morning, as he was driving back from Saigon to Lai-Thieu, in the civilian bus, an old rattletrap consisting of separate parts from a dozen different vehicles, tied together with string and fitted with threadbare tires, the lieutenant had noticed a young Vietnamese girl sitting quietly beside a crate of chickens. Dressed in black trousers, a loose tunic of white silk, with long hair gathered together at the nape of her neck by a clasp like any other female student or schoolgirl in Cochin-China, she had the

pensive and at the same time merry face of a Greco-Buddhist virgin. A mysterious charm compounded of purity and reflective-
ness emanated from her finely drawn features; her waist was so
slender that Pinières could have encircled it in his powerful
hands.

Pinières was fed up with the girls in the brothels and in order to endure them he had had a great deal to drink. With one
blow of his huge paw he sent the crate of chickens flying; a
peasant woman promptly started screaming. Then he sat
down beside the young girl. All he wanted from her was a
smile to blot out the memory of the whores he had just been
paying.

But the girl recoiled from him with a gesture of disgust and
shrank back against the battered side of the bus.

Pinières was no beauty with his ruddy, freckled complexion,
his over-pronounced features and musky smell—but he gave
an impression of elemental power and his eyes were the deep
blue of those of a new-born child.

His personal reports invariably described him as "the sort
of man who was equally capable of the utmost good and the
utmost harm." He had rarely done harm, he had often done
good.

"Don't be frightened," Pinières told her.

But he had never been able to control his voice.

"Leave me alone," she cried, "go away!"

Everyone in the bus had turned round to watch, including
the driver who, in the process, very nearly drove into the ditch.

"I'll tell my father."

Pinières, who was beginning to get annoyed and felt he was
making a fool of himself, rudely retorted:

"To hell with your father."

"My father is Doctor Phu-Tinh, he's a friend of the High
Commissioner, who often asks him in for consultations . . ."

He noticed she had a small diamond fixed into the lobe of
each ear.

The girl's voice had become breathless. She fumbled in
her bag.

"I've got an up-to-date permit—look, you can see for yourself—signed by the High Commissioner. And if it's of any interest to you, I'm actually a French citizen . . ."

"I only wanted to speak to you . . ."

She looked him up and down:

"Your sort only know how to speak with their hands; go and find another seat."

"I'm sorry."

He had complied with her wish, while everyone round him sniggered.

At Lai-Thieu the girl had got off the bus after him. An old *assam* dressed in black was waiting there to carry her books for her.

The lieutenant made inquiries: the girl, whom everyone called "My-Oi,"* was the only daughter of Doctor Phu-Tinh, an officer of the Légion d'Honneur who was said to be a decent chap, very influential and whole-heartedly in favour of the French.

My-Oi had been brought up at Dalat by the nuns of the Couvent des Oiseaux and was now a first-year student at the University of Saigon; as far as it was known, there was no man in her life.

Pinières forgot all about the girl. Terrorist activity was reaching its peak and, while interrogating a prisoner, the sector commander had discovered that most of the arms and explosives found their way to Lai-Thieu by way of the forest, and from there were sent on to Saigon.

Pinières had practised terrorism in France. He only had to draw on his own memories, the methods which he himself used to employ for delivering arms, and on four separate occasions he intercepted supplies being carried by plantation truck-drivers or by coolies trotting along on foot. Hand-grenades were concealed among piles of rice or even in the insides of fish.

It was then he saw My-Oi again. She went past the section post one morning, dressed in white and followed by her black

* "Darling."

assam. He gave her a brisk salute, to which she replied with a mocking smile. That evening he went and had a word with her. Next day he waited for her at the bus stop. The *assam* had not turned up; he saw her home, carrying her books for her.

She asked him about his life; he told her about his schooldays. They both discovered they preferred Lamartine to Victor Hugo. He ventured to ask her out to dinner with him in Saigon; he would drive her home afterwards in his Jeep. She accepted without any fuss. Her father, it seemed, allowed her a great deal of freedom, which was most unusual. But perhaps his French nationality had inclined him towards liberalism.

At the Vieux Moulin, near the Dakao bridge, she was alternately mocking, affectionate, flirtatious, and, on the terrace of the Kim-Long where they went to dance, her slender body clung to his. There were whispers at every table at the sight of the slim Vietnamese girl almost totally engulfed in the arms of the big red-headed barbarian.

On the way back, in the Jeep, she allowed him to kiss her. She pecked him on the lips like a bird eating grain. My-Oi raised no objection to going back with him to his room. Their first embrace was a disappointment. Passive and detached, she lay there without the slightest reaction, giving only a little cry when he was rough with her. He himself felt clumsy and ill at ease; up till then he had associated exclusively with *congais* and had only thought of his own pleasure.

But under the mosquito-net, after she had fallen alseep, he lay musing for a long time over her naked body, as naked as only an Asiatic's can be, and to him this golden girl was like one of those gifts which the Gold Kings in olden times used to offer the barbarian invaders in homage of their power.

My-Oi fell into the habit of meeting the lieutenant in his room every evening and staying there until the morning.

A week later the rainy season began with a violent storm. He caressed her insensible body and his desire was mingled with rage at being so close to this smooth young flesh which never gave so much as a tremor. The cloudburst developed into an absolute downpour, a puff of wind lifted the mosquito-net and all of a sudden he felt My-Oi come to life. Her sharp nails dug into his shoulder; the slender reed of her body tried to escape him, then clung to him all the more closely and she gave a gentle whimper. When it was all over, she still clung to him and for the first time it was she who provoked his desire. In a completely changed voice, in which surprise was mingled with tenderness and timidity, she asked:

"What's your Christian name?"

"Serge."

Up till then she had not bothered to find out.

My-Oi gave up the university and came to live with him. The black-garbed *assam* moved into a house near by and from then on Pinières ceased to have his meals in the mess with his comrades.

During this period, while the number of terrorist outrages increased still further in Saigon, Pinières's section had a run of bad luck and failed to intercept a single convoy of arms. Yet all the intelligence reports agreed: the Vietminh were still using the Lai-Thieu road.

One evening, after dinner, My-Oi said to the lieutenant:

"Serge, I've been given orders to kill you tonight. Don't worry: you know I could never do it now. At one o'clock the post is going to be attacked to enable a truck to get through loaded with explosives, arms and leaflets. Before the attack is launched, I am supposed to eliminate you. For the last two years I've belonged to a Vietminh organization, the Nam-Bo. It's they who gave me the order to go to bed with you; you were too successful at unearthing our arms. I did so and to begin with I hated it. Then there was that night when the rains started . . . Go and warn your men."

The attack took place at exactly one o'clock in the morning. The Vietminh were repulsed with heavy losses and their truck was blown up.

During the whole battle, My-Oi had sat quietly on the edge of the camp-bed without moving, and when her lover came back, drenched with sweat and spattered with her countrymen's blood, the pleasure she indulged in with him was followed by a sense of appeasement more profound than death itself.

Next day Pinières had brought her before the intelligence officer of the zone. She had followed him without a word.

"Now talk," he had told her.

She had told them all she knew without batting an eyelid and had given away the whole terrorist network in Saigon, its leaders, its arms dumps and meeting places. When the captain misspelled a name, she had corrected it in her own hand.

"Good show, Pinières," the intelligence officer had said. "It's the best thing we've pulled off since we came here. I'm being posted back to France, wouldn't you like to take over from me?"

"No, thanks."

To safeguard My-Oi from the vengeance of the Vietminh, Pinières and the captain had decided to send her to Dalat. They found a room for her in the Couvent des Oiseaux where she had been brought up. Once again she had raised no objection.

Every month Pinières used to go up to Dalat with the convoy and My-Oi would come and join him for three days in a tumbledown Chinese hotel where mah-jong players sat up all night over their little pieces of bamboo and ivory.

One day he received a very brief letter from My-Oi:

I didn't dare tell you before, but I'm expecting a baby by you. What do you intend to do about it? We Vietnamese do not attach as much importance as you do to a child that has not yet been born. Afterwards we deal with it better. Whatever you decide will be all right because I love you.

Ever since My-Oi had betrayed the Vietminh terrorist organization, Pinières had often remembered this incident: at the liberation of France he had ordered his men to shave the scalp of a beautiful, rather silly girl who had openly flaunted her liaison with a German officer. While the operation was being performed, she had looked him straight in the eye:

"I loved my German, I'd got him under my skin. I'm only a woman. I don't give a damn about war and politics. He might have been a Negro, an American or a Russian, it would have been all the same to me, and to protect him I would have sold the lot of you, just as I would have fought at your side if I'd happened to fall for one of you. But with mugs like yours, there wasn't much danger of that . . ."

Pinières had slapped her across the face until she sank to her knees and his men had then made free of her. Later on he had looked for the woman to give her back the jewels they had confiscated from her, but she had already left for Germany.

For a whole week he thought the matter over, then he made up his mind. The child would be born. If it was a girl, he would send her to the convent; if a boy, to a forces' school. He would let My-Oi know his decision himself. As for her . . . he would give her some money for her to go away.

What had that German done with his shaven-pated French girl? Had he married her?

The day the convoy he was due to take left for Dalat, Pinières was out on operations. For four days and nights he had been tracking down a band of guerrillas and had set fire to the village which they used as a hide-out. The stench of burning flesh was still in his nostrils. When he came back, not very proud of this enforced task, he made up his mind to marry My-Oi, the "collaborator." It would be too horrible for her to have betrayed her own people only to lose him in the end; besides, he loved her and also the child which was about to be born and which was not going to go either to the convent or to a forces' school.

He took the following convoy and, since he had not been able to notify My-Oi of his arrival in Dalat, he went straight to the Couvent des Oiseaux. Her room was empty, the girl had vanished. On the table he found a letter in Vietnamese, which he asked someone to translate for him.

The Administrative Committee of the Nam-Bo asked "the little sister" to report to the Cascade at Dalat in order to furnish one of their representatives with a few particulars. She was to be there after dark and alone.

Her body was found next morning, she had been strangled with a silk parachute cord.

Lacombe stumbled again and asked Pinières to help him up.

"You can get up by yourself."

"I've got two children."

The bastard had discovered his weak point; he was going to exploit it, take advantage of it. like a whining beggar.

Pinières bent over him, helped him to his feet, and when it came to the captain's turn to carry the rice urn, he took his place.

4

THE PORCELAINS OF THE
SUMMER PALACE

Dawn broke as the column was struggling across the pass. The R.P. 41 was deserted and the prisoners were once more on their own after the chaos and tumult of the night. The roar of the trucks had died away in the whistling of the wind off the summit, and daylight seemed to have sent the Vietminh termites scuttling back into their holes.

The Voice kept walking up and down the column and his smooth cheeks bore hardly a sign of fatigue. Several times over he gave the *bo-dois* orders to quicken the pace, but without success.

At the end of the morning the prisoners, footsore, exhausted and dying of thirst, were halted in a narrow little valley which threaded its way through the middle of the mountains.

In small groups they flopped down in the mud under cover of the brushwood. They spent the rest of the day there, prostrated in their solitude, without being able to go to sleep or enjoy a moment's oblivion and without finding relief for their cramped limbs.

They had reached that stage of utter weariness beyond which there exists only total collapse and death. During all the remainder of the march they were to carry the weight of this immense lassitude.

Night after night the calvary of the lamentable herd, driven on by its grim *bo-dois*, continued in the heavy rain of the monsoon. The prisoners would take a step forward, stumble, take another step without being certain they would have enough strength to take a third, having long since forgotten why they were on the

move or where they were going in this stifling stormy darkness
through which monstrous visions floated like giant jelly-fish.

It was during one of these nightmares that they came across
the Pims of Dien-Bien-Phu.

The column of prisoners had halted by the side of the road
to let them come past. The Pims moved up slowly, a pathetic
Miracle procession with its cripples whose questionable bandages showed faintly white in the darkness, and its lame dragging themselves along on crutches. Their wounds were rotten
with gangrene, their rags were coated in pus and they gave off
a sugary smell of carrion and sour rice. The Viets had treated
them even worse than the French, even though they had "the
same political value" as the soldiers of the People's Army. The
Voice had said so.

The officers gazed in silence at this procession of ghosts.
There were four or five hundred survivors out of the four thousand coolies who had been flown in to Dien-Bien-Phu six months
earlier.

"The Voice wasn't so far wrong," Pinières reflected. "No doubt
they would be only too pleased to rip our guts out if they had the
chance."

Many others had the same thought in mind.

Suddenly one of the Pims recognized Boisfeuras and rushed
up to him:

"Captain, Captain! Me Pim of Fourth Company . . ."

He seized the captain by the hand, taking this opportunity
to slip him a packet of tobacco. He rubbed up against him like
a domestic pet. As they went by, other Pims recognized their
officers in spite of the darkness. They broke ranks, darted
across the road behind a *bo-doi*'s back, and without a word
shook hands with the Frenchmen, slipping them a shapeless
little packet of tobacco or some food from their own meagre
rations or from what they had managed to "scrounge."

Glatigny was given a little molasses wrapped up in a piece of
newspaper, and Pinières a bit of stale vitamin chocolate from a
box of combat rations.

"What a damned waste!" Pinières exclaimed. "All those
men might have been with us. Even without weapons we could

have pushed all these Vietminh bastards over the border into China, just with a few good kicks in the ass."

Boisfeuras questioned his Pim in Vietnamese and learned that they were being taken off to a hard labour re-education camp. They were going to have it forcibly driven into their heads that friendship was forbidden between men of a different race, that a prisoner could not love his master unless that master was a Communist, otherwise it was treason.

Three of these Pims had been awarded the Military Medal for their heroic conduct at Dien-Bien-Phu, but they had disappeared.

The Voice gave the *bo-dois* orders to keep the Pims and the prisoners apart. For the first time the Viets began striking the officers with their rifle butts.

The column of Pims faded out of the nightmare, the Voice floated in. He addressed the Frenchmen:

"I told you to show respect towards your victims, not to provoke them. You refused to listen and we were obliged to save you from their righteous anger."

"The damned bastard," Pinières murmured, clenching his fist.

"Not at all," Boisfeuras replied, "he's being logical. According to Marxist theory, the colonized cannot fraternize with the colonizer. It's dogmatically impossible. But since this fraternization has just taken place, he simply denies the fact."

The tepid downpour continued without a break. One night the prisoners passed a convoy of trucks bogged down in the mud. The coolies swarming round them, while their engines raced and roared, could not manage to shift them from the potholes. The R.P. 41 was out of service at last, the monsoon had proved more effective than the French pilots . . . but too late.

As though in the throes of fever, Glatigny kept wrestling with his phantoms which took the form of staff plans marked in red and blue, reports, confidential signals, urgent, secret, top secret . . .

He had a vision of the large-scale map at Air Force Headquarters, Hanoi, with its red crosses indicating where the road had been cut. Effective for thirty-six hours, effective for forty-eight hours, of no effect at all. This was two months earlier.

The road had never been cut, the termites worked faster than the bombs and Dien-Bien-Phu had fallen. The big black artery swollen with coolies brought the life-blood to Giap's divisions every night.

The road had to be put out of service and, if bombs proved ineffective, rain had to be made to fall instead. But the carbonic ice they had scattered by the plane-load on the heavy ink-black clouds had done nothing. The metereologist who had been sent out from Paris had gone back after making this sibylline report: "The monsoon cycle is so disturbed in the north-east of Indo-China that any forecast of rain must be regarded as contingent."

The metereologist was now safely ensconced in his cosy little flat in Paris, well protected from hunger and fatigue and from the despair and malediction of defeat. Meanwhile the rain poured down every day on the vanquished struggling along in the mud.

"Christ Almighty," Merle swore, stumbling against Glatigny, "if the general had the runs as I have . . . I've got to go again, though I'm absolutely drained. Here, take my bag."

Between one spasm and the next his thoughts flew to the lovely Micheline, with her beauty-spot and eighteenth-century hairstyle. "If you could only see your paratrooper now, my beauty!" Then: "All the same, I'm not going to die by the side of a road like a destitute beggar simply because I wanted to prolong my holiday. It can't happen!"

Olivier Merle had been brought up in Tours among a lot of old people. Everyone in his background was old: his father, his mother, his aunts, his cousins and even his skinny young sister. Olivier had gone off to do his military service. In the army he had discovered youth and gaiety, but he had failed to distinguish between the regular army and the one in which the young civilians served—the last long holiday before life begins in earnest.

In order to prolong his own holiday, little Merle, after finishing his time, had signed on for two years in Indo-China. In Tours this had been considered rather frivolous of him.

Olivier often recalled the secret joy he had felt that time he went home on leave after passing out of Saint-Maixent. Without his parents' knowledge he had been through a parachute course at the school and had then been posted to a southwestern battalion. For the first time his red beret made a bright splash of colour in the old house on the bank of the Loire.

"What does it mean?" his father had asked him.

"It means I've jumped from an aircraft seven times with a parachute strapped to my back and that each time it opened."

"Eccentrics are frowned upon in our profession. A parachuting notary! What will they think in Tours? It won't do us any good."

"If your practice consisted exclusively of labourers, Father, that might well be so, but most of your clients are from the upper-middle and merchant classes."

"Exactly; the working class doesn't mind that sort of nonsense, but the middle does."

"But surely the army, and the paratroops in particular, are the great defenders of the privileges of the middle class?"

"They distrust defenders of that sort even more than their enemies; they could well do without them. You could be a radical or a Communist and all they would say is, 'He'll get over it, it's just a youthful phase.' But a paratrooper . . . ! Let's hope we can keep it dark."

But his sister had fondled his beret with its winged dagger badge. Never before had Olivier seen such a gleam in her eyes.

"I'm glad you joined," she had told him. "You're the first to escape from this rat-hole of ours. One day you must come back and fetch me away."

Olivier Merle had remained in uniform, partly in defiance of his father, partly to please his sister, but most of all to scandalize the *bourgeoisie* of Tours, and in the evening he had gone out with a party of friends to a night-club.

"Is his lordship trying to compete with me?" young Bezegue of the Magasins Réunis had asked him with a sneer.

Bezegue felt slightly put out. He was regarded as the "Bolshy" of the group. One day he had "borrowed" a motor-car for several hours and his lack of moral sense was a byword. But in one fell swoop Olivier had surpassed him and gone infinitely farther.

Olivier was vaguely in love with all the girls he knew, but up till then they had merely used him to make their boy-friends jealous and only went out with him when they had no one else on hand.

During his fortnight's leave Olivier was in great demand. Everyone referred to him as the "Red Devil" and the girls regarded him with secret yearning and fascinated awe, as though he had already assassinated two or three wealthy widows.

He spent a few nights with Micheline, the prettiest of them all, the one who lent a certain tone to the group, for she spoke of life, love and death with the utmost cynicism. She was nineteen and had had a miscarriage in Switzerland, which added somewhat to her aura.

One day Micheline asked him, as though it was the most commonplace thing in the world:

"Have you ever killed anyone?"

She was obviously disappointed by his answer.

Before he left for Indo-China, Micheline had come and spent a week with him at Vannes. She had dyed her hair dead-white and wore a beauty-spot on the corner of her chin, which made her look like an eighteenth-century marquise.

Micheline had notified him, as though it was a matter of no consequence, of her marriage to Bezegue, and Olivier had realized he was no longer in the running as a prospective husband. It was flattering and at the same time disheartening.

Micheline had made a habit of writing to him regularly in Indo-China; she told him about her love-affairs, her little infidelities here and there, her trips to Paris. One day he replied: "I've killed someone and from now on things are different." Then he had stopped writing to her for good.

To his own amazement, Second-Lieutenant (later Lieutenant) Merle, who had no particular bent for a military career, did extremely well and was highly esteemed for his courage and endurance. Among the decorations that had been handed out wholesale to the defenders of Dien-Bien-Phu when it was

known that the garrison was done for, he was awarded the Légion d'Honneur and everyone felt it was well deserved.

Pinières had told him:

"Now you can stay on in the army and become a regular."

But young Merle had not the slightest wish to become a regular and at the moment he was passing blood.

At one of the halts he dragged himself along to the M.O.

"I'm completely drained," he said, "I'm dying of thirst. I can't
go on."

"I've also got dysentery," the M.O. told him, "and I've nothing to take for it. Emetine's what we need but the Viets haven't
even got any for themselves, so they say."

"Well, what's the answer?"

"There's no answer . . . just carry on. It might cure itself,
you can never tell. Try and drink some of the water in which
the rice is cooked, that's an old wives' remedy. It hasn't done
me any good . . . possibly because, as a medical man, I don't
believe in remedies of that sort."

Merle was getting weaker and weaker and his comrades had
to help him along. He kept saying over and over again: "It's no
joke, it's no joke . . ."

Lacombe swam in his own fat which was becoming as fluid
as oil. He kept dreaming of vast platefuls of boiled beef, stewed
mutton and roast veal, and his hunger was sometimes so ob-
sessive that he fancied he was inhaling the savoury smells of
rich cooking.

Lescure, isolated in his madness, ambled along between
Glatigny and Esclavier, a disjointed sightless puppet attached
to life by a few slender threads.

But when they came to Son-La, where they had to ford a
small stream, he refused to step into the water and began struggling.

"I know this place. It's sown with mines and the Viets are in
position on the far bank. We'll have to go round by the mountains."

He grabbed at a terrified *bo-doi*:

"Go and tell the major, *mau-len*. I've some information for
him. The Viets . . ."

"You're mistaken," Esclavier gently corrected him. "It's our partisans who are holding the far bank."

Instantly pacified, Lescure followed his captain into the water.

During the night of 27–28 May they passed through the old entrenched camp of Na-San.

The Voice ordered a halt, which lasted several hours. It had stopped raining; the sky had cleared; it was now luminous and the colour of milk. They were at the foot of a tooth-shaped peak which was still crowned with a few strands of rusty barbed wire and stacks of punctured sandbags.

"I held this strong-point for three months," Esclavier told Glatigny. "It was full of Viet corpses; they reached right up to my dug-out. I thought Na-San was impregnable. I also thought Dien-Bien-Phu was impregnable . . ."

"Everyone thought Dien-Bien-Phu was impregnable," Glatigny replied in a flat voice, "the captains, the colonels, the generals, the ministers, the Americans, the pilots and even the sailors who knew nothing about it. Everyone, do you realize? No one doubted it for a moment. I was in a particularly good position to know."

The calm of the night, the milky night, the memory of the battles at Na-San, which for him had been victories, made Esclavier tolerant for a certain length of time and he forgot his harsh conception of war and his favourite axiom; "the man who loses is guilty and must be executed."

"Why did we foul it up so badly?" he asked dispassionately.

At this point Glatigny felt that by explaining Dien-Bien-Phu he could exorcize his remorse.

Boisfeuras came up and without a word sat down beside them.

"We had to protect Laos," Glatigny explained, "to which France had just committed herself by signing a treaty of defence. Laos was the first country to join the French Union.

"We had to stem the main Vietminh advance on the Tonkinese delta, on Hanoi and Haiphong. So as to gain time we chose Dien-Bien-Phu in order to engage them."

"Five hundred miles from our bases?" Esclavier interjected.

"The Viets were also five hundred miles from theirs and they had no air force. Their only supply line was this secondary road, R.P. 41, this umbilical cord which our pilots claimed they could put out of service at a moment's notice. That's what they never stopped saying, anyway."

"Only it wasn't true and Dien-Bien-Phu was a basin."

"Certainly, but the largest one in South-East Asia—ten miles by five. We could lay down several landing strips for our modern aircraft. The ridges commanding it were farther away than the range of the Vietminh guns. To shell the entrenched camp, the Viets therefore had to site their artillery either on the forward slope or else in the plain. There, we could fight back, destroy it with our superior guns, our planes and our armour . . . But the Viets dug their guns in, they came down to engage us in the plain and in the plain we held the heights. So the Viets then stormed the heights and overran us."

Boisfeuras broke in:

"We were wrong from start to finish because we tried to see the war from the point of view of Saigon, or, at the most, of Paris, by forcing ourselves to believe that it was possible to isolate the Vietnamese peninsula from the rest of the Asiatic and Communist world and that we could calmly embark on our little operation of colonial reconquest. Sheer stupidity! We should have regarded this war through the eyes of Moscow or Peking. Now, Moscow and Peking did not give a damn about Viet-Nam, this cul-de-sac which led nowhere, but they did care about Dien-Bien-Phu, and very much so.

"I know South-East Asia pretty well. It's more or less my country; I've been around here for years; I've fought here against the Japs and the Chinese. I've also read quite a lot of Communist literature. What does Lenin say? 'The future of world revolution lies with the great masses of Asia.' China is Communist, but there still remains India which is closed to China by the Himalayas, to Russia by the Pamirs and the ranges of Afghanistan. The only point of entry is through Bengal and South-East Asia.

"Among the seething races of the Far East which can hardly be numbered, there's only one ethnic group of any historical or

political interest: the Thais. They've got a history, they've built
an empire. They're called Chans and Karens in Burma; they're
also to be found in Thailand and Laos. In the Haute Région
they represent three-fifths of the population and they're also established in Yunnan. The capital of this Thai empire is Dien-
Bien-Phu.

"The Communists decided to work on the Thais so as to
force an entry into India. They set up the Thai majority in
Yunnan as an autonomous people's republic and, I can tell you
now, it was on that business that I was engaged. The Chinese
want to group all the other Thais round their people's republic. Once that is done, all that's needed is a slight nudge for the
whole of South-East Asia to collapse. Then every gateway into
India will be open to them. They therefore could not allow the
historical and geographical capital of the Thais to be held by
western anti-Communists. Mao-Tse-Tung ordered the capture
of Dien-Bien-Phu while Giap was dreaming about the delta."

"Dien-Bien-Phu was the only basin where the big modern
bombers could take off," Glatigny observed, "and the Americans had thought of it with a view to . . ."

"With a view to what?" Boisfeuras inquired.

"With a view to attacking China, perhaps."

"No one ever mentioned that possibility," said Esclavier.

Glatigny was afraid he had spoken too freely: he tried to
correct himself.

"There was a rumour to that effect; I wasn't in the know about
anything connected with secret international negotiations . . ."

But all of a sudden his regard for security seemed absurd.

"Nevertheless," he went on, "the Americans were most insistent that we should choose Dien-Bien-Phu. And Giap had
thirty thousand of his *bo-dois* slaughtered to please the Chinese. But in return he received from them twenty-four 105
mm. guns, eighteen 75 mm., a hundred 12.7 A.A. guns, eighty
37 mm. and all the ammunition he could possibly want."

"And also the promise of volunteers, if necessary," Boisfeu-
ras chipped in. "The Communists are perfectly logical. Dien-
Bien-Phu was something on which their very life depended.
That's what the Americans failed to see.

"It's true that American opinion, which is anti-colonialist by tradition, would have found it difficult to support a conflict, which the whole of their press condemned as colonial, to the extent of going to war. And yet Dien-Bien-Phu was one of those battles which set the two blocs by the ears. Only the French found themselves facing the whole Communist machine on their own."

Glatigny lay back in the damp grass and gazed up at the sky; in the moonlight the clouds sparkled like strings of artificial jewels.

He had flown over this valley in the comfort of the general's aircraft and attended the briefings at which clever staff officers had dissected the war in detail but without grasping it as a whole. In the same aircraft he had accompanied those wretched little ministers who came out from time to time on a tour of inspection. They were ten thousand miles away from hearth and home and could only regard this conflict from the narrow viewpoint of little town councillors. How could they imagine another world in which vast swarms of men were famished, longing for the smallest morsel of food, and crazed with hope?

After this halt and this respite, the Voice subjected the prisoners to a forced march, as though he wanted to make them atone for their victory at Na-San, and many of them, dazed with fatigue, lay down and died by the side of the road.

Merle was getting worse and worse. As a result of some subtle and secret bargaining, Boisfeuras managed to obtain a few tablets of stovarsol from one of the *bo-dois*. He made the lieutenant take them and Merle began to feel better almost immediately.

Later on he asked Boisfeuras:

"It couldn't have been an easy job getting those tablets?"

"No."

"You wouldn't be able to get any more, I suppose?"

"They're finished."

"And what if you or Glatigny or someone else suddenly needs some?"

"We'll have to do without."

The prisoners were now all living in a secondary state of consciousness; they hovered on the brink between nightmare and reality; their will and courage fell apart while their personal characteristics and everything that contributed to their individualities melted away into the uniform grey mass slogging along through the mud.

The Voice behaved like a scientific chemist; he regulated their hunger, their fatigue and their despair so as to reduce them to the exact point at which, broken and deranged, he could at last work on them and drill them against their past by concentrating on what still remained: the elementary reflexes of fear, fatigue and hunger.

He kept assembling them incessantly for "instruction periods." One day he started inveighing against the French command which had just refused to take over the wounded of Dien-Bien-Phu.

As though to confirm his words, the French Air Force came and bombed the road.

After a night march which was even more exhausting than usual, he kept telling them in that smooth, impersonal, relentless voice of his:

"We are obliged to make you march by night to protect you from being bombed by your own aircraft. That is what Capitalism, with its internal contradictions, leads to."

This was more than Pinières could stomach. He turned to Boisfeuras and asked:

"What the hell does he mean by 'the internal contradictions of Capitalism'?"

"Not daring to wage the sort of war that's necessary to defend oneself. Not reorganizing and remodelling oneself so as to carry the war into the enemy camp, shutting oneself up in ivory towers, not fighting by night, employing mercenaries—like us, for instance—instead of hurling into the fray everyone who is anxious for the Capitalist system to survive, using money and technology as a substitute for faith, forgetting that the masses are the mainspring of all endeavour, corrupting them with modern amenities instead of keeping them wiry and alert with the offer of some valid purpose in life . . .

Pale and emaciated, Merle angrily retorted:

"The masses enjoy modern amenities as much as we do. In Europe they discover the refrigerator and television. The Arabs also take to modern amenities, so do the Hindus, the Chinese and the Patagonians. When I get back to France I shall lie back and wallow in all those amenities. I shan't drink anything unless it's iced and I'll only go to bed with nice clean little girls who wash between the legs with disinfectants."

"The civilization of the frigidaire and the bidet," Esclavier sneered.

On the 7th of June Esclavier stole a fork from one of the *bo-dois* and on the 8th they forded a river in spate. There were several hundred coolies at work in the dark, repairing a bridge by the light of bamboo torches, and each gang, by means of slogans and songs, maintained an illusion of feverish activity.

The sound of an aircraft overhead brought them to a standstill; all the torches were instantly extinguished. Complete silence ensued among coolies and prisoners alike.

All of a sudden Lescure burst out into his mad guffaw.

Two officers from the adjacent group tried to make a break for it, but they were brought back a few hours later, knocked senseless with rifle-butts and dragged before their comrades.

The days of leniency appeared to be over and Lacombe, who had stepped aside into the undergrowth in order to relieve himself, was trussed up as though he too had been trying to escape.

He protested his innocence in a sorrowful voice and was beaten up for his pains.

Boisfeuras, who suddenly felt anxious, eavesdropped on the sentries' conversation: the Geneva conference had fallen through. The number of prisoners who were tied up increased every day.

The Haute Région had now given place to the Moyenne. The mosquitoes were voracious and countless; leeches had appeared on the scene; it began to be extremely hot.

The days and nights never varied in their routine. Daylight meant the rice chore and a period of rest in the midst of a cloud

of mosquitoes; as soon as night fell the *bo-dois* lit their torches
and resumed their march through the forest and paddy-fields.

Lacombe, who had his hands tied behind him, kept stumbling, a grotesque Christ with pendulous cheeks like an old
hag's bottom. He did not even beg Pinières to help him along
any more. The injustice of which he was the victim struck him
as being so enormous that he could not bring himself to protest. Something must have gone seriously wrong with the work-
ings of the Almighty if they believed him to be capable of such
incorrect behaviour as escaping! Yet he was prepared to like
the Vietminh and believe in all their nonsense. In the first place
he had always been in favour of universal peace. The commis-
sariat had nothing to do with war; a supplies officer was simply
a grocer at the disposal of the army, and he fully intended,
when he retired, to start a shop at Bergerac where his wife's
family lived.

He felt a hand behind him unfastening his bonds. It was
Mahmoudi taking pity on him.

"They'll see," protested Lacombe, who insisted on enduring
his punishment even though it was unjust, to show he was well
disposed.

"Leave him alone," said Pinières. "Can't you see he's enjoying it? He's loving every moment."

A *bo-doi* walked down the column and Lacombe wriggled
away from Mahmoudi's hands, heaving deep sighs so that the
sentry should hear him and see for himself how much he was
suffering. He kept going, tittupping along the track.

Many of them were worn out by dysentery and were passing
blood. The Voice gave orders for them to be left behind in the
villages through which they passed.

"Our medical service will take care of them," he promised.

Not one of those prisoners was ever seen again. They died
secretly in the corner of some thatch hut, wasted away by dysentery, festering from their wounds.

The march now appeared to be endless; it went on and on,
in the rain and in the mud, among the mosquitoes and the
leeches; it looked as if it might continue all the way to China,
until all the prisoners died of dysentery by the side of the road.

One night, which was less dark than usual, long after the crossing of the Black River by ferry-boat from Tak-Hoa, they noticed that the wild vegetation all round them was being succeeded by a semblance of cultivation. The trail, which was broad and straight but hemmed in by tall grass, led towards a little hummock. On the summit stood the blackened ruins of a large colonial house with its veranda. There were broad open spaces between the rubber-trees and between each coffee bush, and the undergrowth had not yet encroached on these.

"The pitiful stamp of the white man," Boisfeuras said to himself.

Some peasant had come all the way out here from the mountains of Auvergne or the banks of the Garonne, some stubborn peasant with fists like hams. He had cleared the soil and built himself a house, recruited coolies, sometimes with a kick in the ass, but he had stuck to this valley, the only one of his species, like a medieval robber-baron. He had struggled against the climate, against fever, against the jungle which he forced back step by step, also against the men whom he induced to work according to his methods and to live according to his pace.

The French colonial had come out to Indo-China at a time when white men still deserved to be masters of the world by virtue of their courage, their stamina, their energy, their pride in their own race, their sense of their own strength, their superiority, their lack of scruples.

Boisfeuras did not belong to this category, he was a marauder. His type had infested China. He looked back on his youth as a series of flickering images, like an old news-reel accompanied by the burning, thudding rhythm of fever.

Shanghai: the gunboats on the Whampoo, the evenings at the Sporting Club, the lovely Russian refugees from Harbin, and the bandy-legged little Japs worming their way into the concessions and disembarking their troops . . .

His father collected old jade and little Chinese prostitutes, and officially acted as political adviser to the Chamber of Commerce; he delighted in playing the part of a man of mystery. Perhaps it was from him that he inherited his taste for clandestine activity, which alone could account for his presence in the

army of this "secondary" country, among these wretched prisoners.

Chiang Kai-Shek's forces were hammering at the gates of
the City on the Mud Bank. Julien Boisfeuras was ten years old;
his father and a few other old sharks of his sort met the Chinese generalissimo in secret. They convinced him that the
Communists had decided to kill him to get complete control of
the Kuomintang.

Chiang believed them or pretended to. He came to an arrangement: he stuffed his pockets with dollars and his troops
wiped out the Communists and dipped the skinny little students of Canton into boiling cauldrons.

Julien Boisfeuras was eighteen; he had gone to bed with girls
and found it boring, played poker and felt that it was not
worth gambling unless one staked one's whole life and soul.
He made friends with some young Communists and with a
certain Luang who was operating with his group in the territory of the International Concession. He provided them with
information and money, both of which he got hold of at home.

His old man worked under cover and was pleased to instruct his son in the manifold aspects of underground political
activity in China. One night Julien asked him:

"Was it true about that plot against Chiang Kai-Shek?"

Armand Boisfeuras simply replied:

"Where there are Communists, there's always a plot. Chiang
realized that."

"That's not the kind of information we want," Luang told
him. "That's all over and done with and we don't give a damn.
Has your father met the Japanese consul-general; what did
Chiang say to him the day before yesterday? That's the sort of
thing we're after."

On another occasion his father explained:

"The balance of the world depends on the disunity of China.
A united China in the hands of a single group, of a single
party, is liable to set the world ablaze. Communism is the great
danger because only the Communists are capable of uniting
China; they have all the necessary qualifications: inhumanity,
intolerance, single-mindedness, and they're mad . . ."

"The prattlings of your father?" Luang would say. "Not the slightest interest to us. But we shall be needing arms . . . and through him you could get some for us."

Julien was nineteen. His father had summoned him to his office in the Chamber of Commerce; he had heard about his connexion with the Communist Party. The old man did not moralize—that wasn't his way—he cut him off without a penny and turned him out of the house.

"You can come back when you've got over this nonsense."

But Luang dropped Julien. He was no longer living with his father, he was therefore of no further interest. He did not believe in the conversion of the sons of *taipans*. Their fathers had plundered China, their sons thought they could make amends with a show of remorse and a few contributions. That didn't work. Young whites who were well-disposed were to be handled only as long as they were useful, then they were chucked away like a paper napkin. After all, they had much the same colour, consistency and fragility as one.

Julien was twenty. He was reconciled to his father and the old man had sent him to a business college in America. Came the 1940 armistice in France. Julien felt it was unpleasant but was not deeply affected by it. He did not regard himself as a citizen of a small western country but as a white man of the Far East, and to him the internal quarrels of Europe seemed ludicrous.

Came the Japanese attack on Pearl Harbour, which forced him to come to some decision. He had a French passport, he was living in America, his father was in China. He therefore joined up in the British Army.

At the age of twenty-two he had the D.S.O., amoebic dysentery, an abscess of the liver and malaria. Within six months he was patched up in a hospital in New Delhi. His father was then in Chungking, acting as official adviser to Chiang Kai-Shek. He went and joined him.

The old man was still surrounded by his retinue of policemen, intelligence agents, prostitutes, smugglers, bankers and generals. He was like certain mushrooms, he needed all this dung in order to live. The old man was still pursuing his pet ideas, enjoying his pipe of opium and going to bed with younger and younger girls.

He considered that the real enemies of China were the Communists, not the Japanese whom the Americans would soon bring to heel. He urged Chiang to use the arms and equipment provided by the U.S.A. against the troops of Mao-Tse-Tung and Chu-The while these were still badly organized. But at this American sentiment rebelled. Washington could only deal with one war at a time and the crafty *taipan* Boisfeuras was sent into exile.

Julien joined the French Army and was posted to Mission Five at Kung-Ming. He set off for Yunnan, reached the Haute Région of Tonkin and made contact for the first time with the Vietminh guerrillas.

In fulfilment of his mission, he convinced the Communist leaders that he had come as a defender of democracy and not as the vanguard of a colonial reconquest. He already considered the Vietminh efficient and dangerous. He was frequently sent into China. Each time he came back to Indo-China he noticed the Vietminh were organizing and developing according to the self-same methods as the Chinese Communist Party.

When he went down to Saigon, he stayed with the director of the Bank of Indo-China and established close connexions with the big Chinese bankers of Cholon. The American and Chinese services in Formosa repeatedly invited him to work for them, but he was not interested in money. The French intelligence service was better suited to his temperament and to the aim he had in mind. Its disorganization and complexity allowed him a completely free hand.

He had an old score to settle with Luang; for that purpose it was more convenient to be in uniform . . .

His father stayed on in Shanghai when the Communists entered in order to negotiate some commercial agreements with the new régime. He had plenty of guts, the old bastard! His negotiations met with failure; there was no one left to corrupt except the whole régime, and even that could not be done at once. For four years *taipan* Armand Boisfeuras, deprived of his opium and little girls, had remained as a hostage in the hands of the Communists; then he had gone back to France. The Communists had denied him the dung on which he lived; it was a wonder he did not die.

In China the only form of self-indulgence left was the synthetic breeding of sexless ants in chemically pure surroundings.

In the morning one of the *bo-dois* came to fetch Boisfeuras. The Voice watched the captain approaching. There was a strange smile on his face as he offered him a cigarette.

"You don't seem to have suffered much from this arduous march, Captain."

Then all of a sudden he broke into Vietnamese.

"I'm told you speak our language extremely well . . . as only those who have got our blood in their veins can do. You're a half-caste, aren't you, at two or three generations' removed perhaps?"

"I was brought up by a Vietnamese nurse and I learnt your language before my own."

"What were you doing at Dien-Bien-Phu?"

"I was in charge of the Pims because of my knowledge of Vietnamese. I've already told you that."

At a sign from the Voice two *bo-dois* seized the captain. They tied his hands behind his back with a length of wire, pulling his elbows up with a jerk.

"That was a lie, Captain Boisfeuras. You belonged to the G.C.M.A.* organization and you only got to Dien-Bien-Phu during the last few days. Before that you were north of Phong-Tho where you commanded a group of partisans. You were one of those wretches who were trying to raise the mountain minorities against the Vietnamese people."

Boisfeuras had only passed through Phong-Tho. He had gone farther north to deal with the Thais of Yunnan. The Voice was confusing him with a quadroon officer who belonged to that organization and had tried to form a guerrilla group from the mountain people and some Chinese bandits. The officer

---

*Groupe de Commandos Mixtes Autonomes—an organization engaged on creating guerrilla bands behind the Vietminh lines.

had been killed in an ambush laid by his own men: there had
been some fuss over a girl or over money or opium. The Vietminh had had nothing to do with the business.

He saw that it was very much in his interests to be confused
with this half-caste.

"I admit I lied."

"I appreciate your frankness, late though it is. It's my duty
to punish you. You will be tied up for the rest of the march.
You are absolutely forbidden to say a word to the sentries. But
if you are so keen on practising Vietnamese, you can always
come and see me. We could then discuss what you were doing
north of Phong-Tho."

"My mission there was a failure . . ."

"It was bound to be. We shall hold a court of inquiry to see
if you committed any war crimes. Until then you will be under
special surveillance."

Boisfeuras completed the march isolated from his comrades
and under the close watch of three sentries who jabbed the
barrels of their submachine-guns into his ribs as soon as he
opened his mouth. His guards were changed every day.

Tied up between two *bo-dois*, Boisfeuras marched at the
end of the column. The wire had bitten into his wrists; his
swollen, purple hands were paralysed. He had lost his former
agility and stubbed his feet on every obstacle in his path.
Sometimes his ears, buzzing with fever, echoed with the din of
heavy hobnailed boots tramping over delicate porcelain, with
the shrill cries of women being raped and with the noise of
tearing canvas. Then in his mind's eye he saw that lovely painting on silk that used to be in his father's house in Shanghai
and which came from the plunder of the Summer Palace. It
represented three reeds and a corner of a lake by moonlight.

"They smashed everything," his father told him, "with the
toes of their boots or the butts of their rifles, the loveliest and
oldest vases in the world. There was a marine lieutenant with
them who suddenly found he had a taste for Chinese objects.
He only broke what he could not steal; that was your grandfather, my boy."

As Boisfeuras's exhaustion increased, the sound of breaking

porcelain became louder and more ear-shattering until he had to clench his teeth.

He had a vague notion that he was being made to suffer to atone for his grandfather's looting. When he realized this, he felt furious at the thought of being so deeply affected by the Christian or Communist sense of sin—an original sin with the Christians, a class sin with the Communists.

He then applied himself to freeing his hands. After a long and patient endeavour which took him three days, he managed to slip the wire off his wrists. During the few hours they halted he was able to move his cramped fingers and revive the circulation.

When the sentry came to check his bonds in the evening, he had refastened them and they appeared to be as tight as ever.

From then on he no longer heard the sound of smashing porcelain in the Summer Palace.

5

LIEUTENANT MAHMOUDI'S THEFT

After crossing the Red River at Yen-Bay, the prisoners headed in a northerly direction across the Moyenne Région. One night, during a longer lap than usual, they emerged on to the R.C. 2. In the moonlight they could see a signpost: Hanoi 161 kilometres, then another: Hanoi 160 kilometres.

These signposts with their French measures of distance, the good old kilometres of the Ile-de-France, of Normandy, Gascony and Provence, were like lifebuoys to which they could cling for a few precious seconds before being swept back into their nightmare.

Hanoi 157 kilometres. They left the Hanoi road and turned down a side-trail leading towards the Bright River. The surface was corrugated with six-year-old furrows over which ran a winding path for pedestrians and cyclists.

The following night they crossed the Bright River in canoes. The village of Bac-Nhang on the far bank was intact.

The Voice gave orders for the sick to be evacuated to the hospital and Lescure was taken from his comrades; then, as a "measure of leniency" he had the bonds removed from all the officers who had been tied up, with the exception of Boisfeuras.

At daybreak the column did not make its customary halt. By tortuous paths it kept going until it reached a vast open space flanked by a pebbly stream. Several columns of prisoners were drawn up at the edge of the forest, divided according to race: French, North Africans, Blacks. A little to one side stood the group of senior officers from Dien-Bien-Phu who had left Muong-Phan by truck a month earlier.

A small detachment of *bo-dois* had been detailed to keep watch over General de Castries.

The heat was suffocating.

There was a watch-tower near the river. A camera and tripod had been set up on its platform which was shaded by a strip of matting. Beside it stood a white man in a fibre helmet, surrounded by a group of *can-bos*. He was tall and fair, dressed in a bush-shirt, khaki slacks and light jungle boots.

"They're going to film us for the news-reels," said Pinières.

"They just want to kill us off," said Merle, who was dying of fatigue, heat and thirst.

None of them had anything to drink and they were not allowed to draw any water from the river.

"*Im . . . Im . . .*"

The *bo-dois* were getting touchier and nastier. They had smartened themselves up and cleaned their weapons. The Voice was strutting about among the group of *can-bos* surrounding the film-director, while the prisoners stood pressed together, marking time in the full blaze of the sun.

Eventually the *can-bos* returned to their respective groups. They paraded the prisoners on the open ground formed by the deposit of the river and drew them up in one solid column twelve deep, the officers at the head, with General de Castries alone in front.

To give the impression of an endless mass, to create the illusion that the number of prisoners was infinitely greater, the last ranks were tucked away behind a bend in the river, and it looked as though these thousands of men were merely the advance guard of the huge captive armies of the West.

The white man directed the scene, giving his orders in a French which was barely distorted by his Russian accent, and his voice was solemn and melodious:

"Forward . . . slowly."

The massive column staggered forward as he focused his camera.

"Back a few paces . . ."

It was essential not to show the rear ranks.

"Move the head of the column a few paces to the left . . . Forward . . . As you were . . . We'll start again . . ."

This sinister ballet of the vanquished lasted until midday. Esclavier and Glatigny were marching side by side in the centre of one rank, their heads hung in shame, both of them overwhelmed by the same feeling of humiliation.

"The camera to which the vanquished are subjected," said Glatigny. "The modern yoke, but more degrading. We'll be seen under this yoke thousands and thousands of times in every cinema in the world."

"Damned bastards," Esclavier muttered, wild with rage.

The Soviet film-director Karmen, a familiar figure at the Cannes festival and in the bars of Paris, relaxed, professional and smiling, was trifling with the ultimate physical resources of his racial brothers for the sake of political propaganda.

"A dirty traitor," Esclavier hissed. "If I could only get my hands round his neck and slowly choke the life out of him . . ."

He was identifying the Soviet film-director with his brother-in-law, little Weihl-Esclavier with his damp hands, who had robbed him of everything, even his name; it was Weihl he was dreaming of strangling.

"As you were . . . We'll begin again . . . Forward . . ."

That evening three officers died of exhaustion.

One day the limestone formations came into sight and Glatigny knew that he had not been mistaken. They were being taken to join the prisoners of Cao-Bang in the Na-Hang-Na-Koc quadrilateral in which the French Air Force had been ordered not to operate. So as not to land fully laden, a pilot returning from a mission had once jettisoned his bombs on to some huts where he saw some men moving, and without knowing it had killed some of his own comrades. The commanders-in-chief were now on their guard against the trigger-happiness of the air force pilots.

The night marches came to an end.

On 21 June the prisoners were given their rice ration at dawn. The column then set off along a broad, "easy" trail, which climbed a gentle slope in a dead straight line. The rumour spread throughout the column that they were about to arrive and the men derived fresh strength to push on, though they had been ready to drop a few moments before.

The trail now ran past neat little villages with squat Vietnamese hutments. Red flags and banners everywhere lent a gay carnival note to the scene.

A few Chinese merchants, whose wares overflowed into the road, had adorned their shop-fronts with the Chinese Communist flag and a photograph of Mao-Tse-Tung looking fat and self-satisfied.

"Civilians at last," Merle observed gleefully. "We're back in civilization. Where there's a Chinaman, there's hope."

Still tied up, Boisfeuras in his turn filed past the shops. The smell of Cantonese spices, the sight of pig's bladders, the sound of a language which was even more familiar to him than Vietnamese, put new life into him. Boisfeuras loved China and was rather scornful of Viet-Nam.

Greater China was in a period of flux and her flag already floated over Tonkin, the Haute and Moyenne Régions. She would overrun Malaya, Burma, India and the East Indies and one day the tide would turn, perhaps under atomic bombardment. But the flow would gather fresh impetus. China was an ocean bound by cosmic influences and, in spite of their pertinacity, their diligence and cruelty, the contemptible and pretentious masters who thought they could direct her would suffer the same fate as the other invaders before them: the Huns, the Mongols, the Manchus. Because their junks had for a moment or two sailed over this ocean which was the Chinese people, they fondly believed themselves to be the masters of it.

And as he stumbled along between his three sentries, Boisfeuras used the pure Mandarin language of Mao-Tse-Tung to recite this poem by the new master of China:

> Standing on the highest summit of the Six Mountains
> Beneath the red flag waving in the westerly breeze
> With a long rope in my hand, I dream of the day
> When we shall be able to bind the Monster fast . . .

Mao was mistaken. China was not the monster, the dragon "with a hundred thousand mouths and a hundred thousand talons," but this ocean which could not be bound fast with a rope or dominated by force of arms.

The column came to a halt by a thicket where there were some banana trees. Esclavier had got rid of his depression after the crossing of the Bright River at Bac-Nhang and was now seething with energy and revolt.

"We're not dead yet," he said. "I think we've got away with it this time. Now we'll show these dirty little bastards what we're made of. There are some bananas on those trees. Let's have them. Come on, Pinières, Merle, Glatigny."

The officers went and asked a sentry for permission to relieve themselves. The *bo-doi* accompanied them as far as the banana trees but, since he belonged to the puritan republic of Viet-Nam, he turned away as the four men squatted down on their haunches.

"Go!" Esclavier shouted, as though on a parachute jump, and they snaffled the bananas and crammed them into their pockets. But the sentry had turned round and caught Pinières who was slower than the others. Beside himself with rage, the little green dwarf started hammering his fists into the ginger-haired giant, the odious imperialist who had stolen the property of the people.

"For Christ's sake don't hit back," Esclavier shouted out to warn him. "He's only doing his job."

Pinières was quivering with anger; to master his feelings, he stood stiffly to attention while the *bo-doi* went on hammering him with his puny little fists.

"You've still got the bananas?" Esclavier asked him.

"Yes."

"That's the main thing."

Merle gave a couple of small bananas to Lieutenant Mahmoudi who was down in the dumps and racked with fever. But Mahmoudi took umbrage:

"Why are you giving me these bananas?"

Merle shrugged his shoulders:

"You're not in very good shape, you know. Lack of vitamins,

that's the reason for your fever. You're afraid to eat wild herbs as we do, so keep up your strength on bananas. It looks as though we're over the worst and we don't want to see you die."

"Why?"

"Now listen. You're an Algerian and a Moslem; I'm on the reserve and, if anything, anti-militarist. Army people bore me to tears. They're not adult, not properly mature. But that's a minor detail for you and me, as it is for Glatigny and Boisfeuras, for Pinières and Esclavier, and even for Lacombe. We're prisoners, so we're all in the same boat; we've got to survive, our bodies have got to hold out, but our characters have got to survive as well. We must safeguard whatever it is that makes us different individuals, each with his own particular quirk, his spirit of rebellion, his indolence, his taste for alcohol or girls. We've got to protect all this against these insects who are trying to grind it out of us. Esclavier's right, we've got to show them what we're made of.

"When that's done we can settle our own accounts, between us, as people of the same universe."

"There are only two universes," Mahmoudi replied darkly, "that of the oppressors and that of the oppressed, of the colonizers and of the colonized—in Algeria, that of the Arabs and that of the French."

"You're wrong," said little Merle, lifting his finger in a falsely sententious manner. "There are those who believe in mankind and can tear out their own guts without any danger, and those who defy the human species in order to deny the individual. The latter give you leprosy as soon as you touch them."

They went through another village where they had to pass in front of a Chinese shop outside which there was a sort of large jar filled with molasses.

"Mahmoudi, how would you go about it to steal some molasses?"

"Me steal molasses?"

He seemed surprised. This chap Merle was really rather disconcerting with the way he had of jumping abruptly from one subject to the next, of showing after a whole month of cohabitation that he was capable of personal ideas and reflection in spite

of his spoilt child manners. Stealing molasses . . . stealing . . .
The word stirred his memory. It was at Laghouat, a market
day in spring, when the grey and blue-throated doves coo in
the palm trees and the streams run clear and swift like young
colts. They were coming down from the mountains, a band of
barefoot urchins, and in the hoods of their threadbare *jellabas*
they were carrying a few handfuls of dates for the road. On
the square, where the camels of the Black Tent nomads had
their pitch, they gathered round the doughnut merchant. Two
of them made a pretence of fighting and the others knocked
over the stall and made off, their hands sticky with the sug-
ared cakes.

"Merle," said Mahmoudi, "I think I know a way. Let's organize a fight in front of the Chinaman's stall—between you
and me, for instance. You call me a thief, I'll go for you, and
meanwhile the other chaps can pinch the molasses."

"Why should I call you a thief?"

Mahmoudi gave a smile which lent his drawn features a certain mystery and beauty.

"It will remind me . . . of a doughnut merchant!"

They enacted the scene to perfection.

"Dirty thief!" Merle yelled.

Mahmoudi sprang at the lieutenant and both of them tus-
sled together on the ground in front of the shop. The prisoners
had gathered round the two men whom the sentries were trying to separate. The Chinese was jumping up and down, his
arms outstretched, as fat and furious as a turkey.

"*Di-di, mau-len!*"

"Go!" Esclavier shouted.

Empty tins were whipped out of pockets and each member
of the team plunged his into the pot of molasses. At the next
halt Lacombe was elected to distribute the stuff between the
members of the group. He was well qualified for the task.

Notified of the incident, the Voice sent for Mahmoudi.

"I hear," he said, "that one of your comrades insulted you
outrageously and that all the other prisoners, out of racial
spite, took his side. If you will tell me who this comrade was,
he will be severely punished."

Mahmoudi gently shook his head.

"It was a purely personal misunderstanding and racialism did not come into it."

The Voice abruptly dropped his impersonal tone. He became passionate:

"You're a simpleton. With them racialism always exists. They make a show of being your brothers, those friends of yours, of considering you their equals, but if you really want to mix your blood with theirs, marry one of their women, for instance, then they send you packing as though you had committed some sacrilege. Which comrade was it?"

"No."

"You needn't feel any solidarity with them; they're the colonialists who are holding your people in subjection, they're the ones who were beaten at Dien-Bien-Phu. Dien-Bien-Phu is the victory of all the Arab nations which are still under the heel of France. It's your duty to tell me which of them insulted you."

Mahmoudi's lips were dry. He felt a fit of trembling coming on . . .

"Your duty as an Algerian oppressed by French imperialism . . ."

The Voice's finely drawn and handsome features had recovered their hieratic quality and beauty—also their spell, for he was the conqueror of an army which Mahmoudi had always admired.

The eyes in the golden mask opened and closed and the lieutenant felt he was being observed by a creature of infinite patience. To release himself from their spell, he confessed the truth:

"I organized that scuffle, sir, to enable my comrades"—he had stressed this word with a sort of fury which did not escape the Voice—"to steal some molasses from a Chinese merchant."

"You ought to be punished . . . but I shall let you off. Go away."

The Voice watched him as he went. He had avoided making the bad mistake of sending him back with his hands tied behind him. Because of this punishment the Arab would have felt an even stronger solidarity with the other prisoners, and party instructions on this score were explicit: use every means to separate the blacks and North Africans from the French.

Lieutenant Mahmoudi did not have the calm strength of Dia, the black medical officer, with the powerful laugh which rose from his belly. He was more apprehensive, more uncertain. But this imbecile had reopened a secret wound in the Voice's heart.

It was in the days of Admiral Decoux. Pham was then a student at Hanoi and belonged to a youth movement founded by Commander Ducoroy. It was the first time in Indo-China that white youths and young Vietnamese were to be found together in the same camps and under the same organization. Stripped to the waist, in khaki shorts, mingling together like brothers, they saluted the striking of the French flag at sunset, while the whole of the White Man's Asia was crumbling under the blows of the Japanese who already held the aerodromes in Tonkin.

It was there Pham had met Jacques Sellier, one of the group leaders, a lad of nineteen with sturdy calves and close-cropped hair, who wore a scout's badge. Sellier made a cult of leadership, tradition, the Church, personal hygiene, physical fitness and frankness which he called loyalty.

A violent admiration had drawn him towards this prince whom the camp had somehow acquired. There was nothing unusual about this devotion, which they all showed towards him, yellow and white alike.

Jacques Sellier, more by instinct than reasoning, knew how to make his friendship valued.

At his table—a few planks on two trestles set under a big Chinese pine—the food consisted of rice and bully-beef and was served in metal mess-tins. But the boy he had selected to sit on his right because he had shown most stamina on a test march, or because he had constructed a raft of creepers and bamboo with his own hands or had killed a snake without even appealing to his comrades for help—that boy, the Prince's guest, felt his endeavour and courage well rewarded by this distinction.

Pham often sat on Jacques's right. Although he hated physical training, he had become supple and strong. Although he enjoyed sophisticated conversation and improving on reality by means of poetic fancy, he had become down-to-earth and even slightly brusque.

When they left camp Jacques Sellier, the son of a colonial administrator, had invited him home. His life as an impoverished student had been transformed. The Selliers were extremely affable; they considered that their religion gave them certain duties towards others and, like Anglo-Saxon parsons, they were inclined to play a role that was something between a director of conscience and a sports trainer. They had seven children; Jacques's younger sister was called Béatrice. She was not very pretty, but had an indefinable adolescent charm. Every morning Pham and his friend went for a run round the Great Lake; they would come home panting and exhausted.

Béatrice used to say:

"You're like a couple of puppies scampering after the wind and coming back with nothing. Tomorrow I want some flowers . . ."

Pham had brought her some flowers. She had smiled and kissed him on the cheek.

The young Vietnamese had fallen in love with Béatrice and did not hide it from her.

One day Jacques had said:

"Let's not go running today. Come for a stroll round the garden."

Pham still remembered the blaze of the flamboyants, the pale grey colour of the sky and the acid pear-drop flavour of the morning air.

With his hands thrust into the pockets of his shorts, Jacques hung his head and kicked up the sand in the path with the toes of his sandals.

"Pham, my parents have asked me to talk to you about Béatrice. You know, she's only seventeen and nothing but a tomboy . . . and any idea of your marrying her is out of the question."

"Why?"

"We're Catholics and for us everyone, whatever his race, is equal and alike . . . in principle . . . but . . ."

Pham had felt the sort of ice-cold blast that heralds a bout of fever. Jacques had gone on:

"It will be difficult for me to see you again for some time. Oh, come along now, don't take on so. If you could only see your face! It'll work out all right in the end. You'll forget Béatrice, you'll marry a girl from your own country."

Pham had left without a word. His friendship for Jacques and what he believed to be his love for Béatrice had turned into a deep-rooted secret hatred for all whites, especially those who tried to bridge the gap between the two races and then fought shy.

At this juncture he was approached by some of his university friends at Hanoi who belonged to the Indo-Chinese Communist Party. After its suppression in 1940, the Central Committee had been obliged to withdraw to China and the students were getting slightly out of hand. They harboured a sense of injustice and dreamed in a vague way of the independence of their country and of splendid destinies for themselves. Pham had followed them. He had the same feeling of resentment, the same ambition and not a vestige of political education.

But one morning a man had turned up from Tien-Tsin. He had assembled the students and had given them the latest international directives of the Komintern.

"From now on the Communist Party must take the lead in every national liberation movement and unite the maximum number of nationalist and socialist organizations in the struggle against Fascist imperialism."

And Pham was the one whom the Central Committee's envoy had made responsible for initiating his comrades into the Vietminh programme as it had been worked out in the depths of China by a certain Nguyen-Ai-Quoc who was now known by the name of Ho-Chi-Minh.

He could recite the three points of this programme by heart:

"We must get rid of the French and Japanese Fascists and aim at the independence of Viet-Nam.

"We must establish a democratic republic of Viet-Nam.

"We must form an alliance with the democracies which are opposed to Fascism and aggression."

To Pham Fascism had assumed the brawny muscular form of Jacques Sellier.

But Jacques Sellier did not die as a Fascist. At the time of the Japanese advance he and two other scouts had joined a guerrilla band organized by a half-caste lieutenant. He had been wounded and the bandy-legged little soldiers of the Mikado had finished him off. Pham had never forgiven him, either, for meeting such a noble end.

He had already become a true Communist and he felt that outside the Party there could be neither hope nor heroism.

The halt lasted until early in the afternoon. Captain de Glatigny, banana thief and former staff officer, lay stretched out in the grass. He was dreaming vaguely of a number of things, of his comrades and of Lescure who had left them.

On the eve of his departure for hospital Glatigny had sat beside the madman who was teasing a cricket with a blade of grass. The captain had suddenly had the impression that Lescure was re-establishing contact with the real world. He called out to him in a parade-ground voice:

"Lescure! Lieutenant Lescure!"

Lescure went on playing with the cricket and, without raising his head, gently answered:

"To hell with you, captain. I don't want to know anything, I don't want to be told anything and I'm perfectly all right, thank you."

To be like Lescure! To reject all the anxieties, all the problems to which modern life was bound to subject every officer, to adopt the favourite bureaucratic formula: "I don't want to know"—how restful that would be!

The prisoners had to leave the trail to negotiate some slippery little mud embankments which ran between the bright green rectangles of the paddy-fields, past screens of bamboo and clumps of mango, banana and guava trees. Darkness was beginning to fall and lent a limpid crystalline transparency to the atmosphere.

It was then the two men appeared, emerging from behind a screen of trees. They were naked to the waist, clothed only in a cheap *ke-kouan* of uncertain colour and, to prevent themselves from slipping, they walked with their toes spread out like ducks. They were carrying a huge black pig suspended from a bamboo pole and moved extremely fast, trotting along with a loose-limbed gait like all Vietnamese peasants. But they were far taller, and their skin was not the colour of virgin oil but looked greyish and dull. One of them wore a sort of blackish beret on his head, and the other a grotesque hat made of rice straw.

They caught up with the column by a short cut, lowered the pig and the pole to the ground, rounded on a *bo-doi* who tried to make them move on, and watched the pitiful procession of prisoners with profound interest and unmixed pleasure.

"Here, I say, Esclavier," said the one with the beret. "What are you doing here, sausage-face?"

Esclavier recognized that slightly rasping voice and also the expression "sausage-face," but not the man with the translucid complexion, whose skinny body could not have weighed more than 130 pounds. Yet it could be none other than Lieutenant Leroy of the 6th BCP who had been reported missing at Cao-Bang—the athlete who had run away with the army athletics championship in spite of his 200 pounds' weight.

Esclavier ran his tongue over his dry lips.

"Don't tell me it's you, Leroy?"

"It's me all right, and the chap at the other end of the pig is Orsini of the 3rd BEP. We've been expecting you for several days."

"Are we still far from the camp?"

"A mile or two. So long, sausage-face, we'll come and see you this evening What the hell does this damned little *bo-doi* think he's doing, pushing me around? And the peace of the people, what about that, you little monkey? It's your duty to re-educate us, all right, but that doesn't mean you can push us around."

"*Im! Im!*"

Disconcerted by the assurance of the two old hands and the flood of words they let fly at him, the *bo-doi* calmly allowed them to pick up their pig and bamboo pole and move on. With their fast trotting gait they soon left the column behind them and disappeared behind a screen of trees.

A Tho village appeared with its houses raised on stilts among the trees.

"Halt!"

The column came to a standstill. Each group leader was ordered to count his men and then went and reported to the Voice. He was accompanied by another Viet, as squat and bandy-legged as a Japanese. A sort of map-case hung on his skinny buttocks. His name was Trin; he was the general supervisor; the head warder of Camp One. He was ruthless, brutal and efficient, and the Voice knew he could trust him implicitly.

The Voice was sensitive and certain things repelled him; Trin made himself responsible for these. The Voice was the pure conscience of the Vietminh world, Trin was the material element.

The Voice embarked on a speech:

"You have reached your internment camp. It is useless to try and escape. A certain number of your comrades captured at Cao-Bung have tried more than once. Not one of them succeeded and we had to take severe disciplinary measures. Now they have come to their senses and have mended their ways. You are here in order to be re-educated. You must take advantage of this stay in the Democratic Republic of Viet-Nam to instruct yourselves, discover the evil of your errors, repent and become fighters for peace. From now on you will have some of your former comrades as group leaders. We have selected them from the ablest among them."

"Dirty rats," Esclavier muttered through clenched teeth.

"You must obey them, follow their instructions . . . I also have a splendid piece of news to announce. The new French Prime Minister, Mr. Mendès-France, appears to be inspired with the best intentions with a view to signing the armistice."

"Who's this fellow Mendès?" Pinières asked Glatigny.

"An awkward character, who has always been in favour of the evacuation of Indo-China. I personally regard him as a sort of Kerensky, only less beguiling."

"I know him," said Esclavier, "on the strength of having met him once or twice in England, when he was with de Gaulle. He's ugly, brittle and conceited but at least he fought, which is pretty rare for a politician; he's intelligent, which is rarer still, and he's got character, which is exceptional."

"But a man like that won't ever sign the armistice," said Lacombe dejectedly.

"He's a Jew," said Mahmoudi contemptuously, "and a Jew might do anything. There are no Jews here with us."

"You're wrong," said Esclavier, "as a matter of fact there are two: a captain who fought extremely well and who's no different from any of us, and a crackpot lieutenant who dreams of stuffing himself with cakes and being made a librarian at the Nationale so as to be able to spend the rest of his life reading."

Each team was quartered in a hut on stilts. On the far side of a tributary of the Bright River which the last storm had swollen and filled with mud, the prisoners could see the neat lines of huts of Camp One.

The officers taken prisoner at Cao-Bang had been living there for the last four years; ninety of them had survived.

Lacombe lowered himself on to his bunk with a deep sigh:

"Well, we've got here at last: we may as well make the best of it. I really thought I was done for and I'm sure if it hadn't been for Pinières and you others . . ."

"Balls to that," the lieutenant muttered. "Whatever you say, you're part of the army and a comrade and that's why we helped you."

"What's happened to Boisfeuras, I wonder?" Glatigny asked.

"Boisfeuras has got out of tighter spots than this," Esclavier replied. "He was once in the hands of the Japs for three weeks . . . and he came through all right. I once had a brush with the Gestapo, we compared our experience. His was . . . slightly more refined, shall we say?"

Lieutenants Leroy and Orsini turned up shortly afterwards,

still as unconcerned as ever. Out of their pockets tumbled
some bananas and tobacco and an old copy of *l'Humanité*.

"*L'Humanité*'s not for reading," said Orsini, who was short,
thickset and swarthy, "it's for rolling cigarettes."

"How did you come by all this stuff?" Merle asked.

"How do you think? We pinched it, of course!"

"In the interest of reciprocal rights," Orsini explained.

"Now here's the dope," said Leroy. "Your team seems to
have a pretty bad reputation, since the group leader they've
chosen for you is little Marindelle, who couldn't be better at
the job."

"Marindelle!" Orsini said delightedly. "That's someone to
conjure with."

"A bastard, is he?" said Glatigny. "That name seems to ring
a bell."

"A stool-pigeon?" Pinières asked.

"Our best friend," said Leroy. "Officially the number one
collaborator of the camp, but actually he could be called the
head of the Resistance."

"He's got the right idea,"—Orsini scratched round his arm-
pit and brought out a louse which he crushed between his
thumbnails—"to get the best of the Viets you've got to humour them and give them confidence in you. He's a double, a
triple, a quadruple agent. He has got the best of everyone, the
Viets, the Camp Commander, the Meteor, us and perhaps
himself as well."

"You'd better spread it around," Leroy went on. "Potin, another group leader, is a Communist. He turned Communist
here. He believes in it quite sincerely, but he makes a point
of behaving decently and setting a good example. Ménard, on
the other hand, is an absolute bastard, an out-and-out swine."

"This is the difference we draw between them," said Orsini.
"Potin we'll bump off but we'll shake his hand first, and afterwards we'll see to his wife and kids. Ménard we'll do to death
by slow degrees and then dump him in a shit-house.

"Fabert's a chap who doesn't give a damn so long as he's left
in peace and there's no trouble. Trézec's a bible-thumper and a
dreary bore: always preaching, but for his own church, not the

Viets." Geniez is the only pederast in the camp and it's not his fault. So he's a progressive. Most people can't stand him, but I've seen him fight and I know that he's then a lion.

"Ah, here comes that dear little bastard, Marindelle."

They made a face at the new arrival, got up and disappeared.

6

THE VIETMINH

"My name's Marindelle," he said, "Yves Marindelle, a lieutenant in the 3rd Foreign Parachute Battalion . . ."

He was naked to the waist and every rib showed in his skinny chest. He had a tuft of fair hair on the top of his head, which made him look like one of those comic music-hall characters: Tufted Riquet or Cadet Rousselle . . . His beedy little eyes sparkled with intelligence. He squatted down on his haunches in front of the team:

"I've been detailed as your group leader and as such I'm responsible for initiating you into camp regulations and supervising your re-education."

"To hell with you," said Esclavier in measured tones.

In spite of all he had heard about him, he did not take to the lieutenant at all.

"You must never say that to the Vietminh. What you must say is: 'I don't understand and I'd like you to explain.' They love explaining. Your team has made a bit of a name for itself. The Meteor . . ."

"We call him the Voice," said Pinières.

"Well then, the Voice accuses your little group of three attempts to escape, constantly failing to comply with orders, theft and even a racial squabble."

"That was in order to pinch some molasses," said Mahmoudi, "I told him that."

"What's more, you've got a war criminal and a madman with you. The war criminal will be back with you tomorrow after he has made his public self-examination and cleansed himself of his sins by Marxist confession. But where's the madman?"

"In hospital already."

Marindelle scratched his throat:

"He'll be better off there; Dia will look after him. He's a very good doctor and has worked miracles. I've been through his hands myself and his herb soups put me back on my feet. Tomorrow there's an instruction period for the whole camp. You'll meet your old friends from Cao-Bang and be initiated into camp routine. I was given to understand that Captain de Glatigny was with you."

"Yes, I'm Captain de Glatigny."

Marindelle's voice underwent a sudden change; it became apprehensive. He was no longer Cadet Rousselle, but a crumpled adolescent.

"May I have a word with you in private, sir? It's something personal."

Glatigny got up. Pinières noticed that in spite of his rags and exhaustion he still looked as elegant as ever. He wished he could have looked like that himself.

The two officers climbed down the ladder from the hut and went and sat down in the shade of the big banana trees.

"We're vaguely related," said Marindelle, ". . . through your wife. I married Jeanine de Hellian, whose father . . ."

"Now I remember . . . I thought your name sounded familiar."

"I've been without news of my wife for four years. I left for Indo-China three months after we married and then came Cao-Bang."

"I imagine she's waiting for you just as all our wives are waiting for us, bringing up their children, helping one another and visiting the wounded in hospital."

"No. Jeanine isn't waiting for me and I haven't any children."

"It's just come back to me . . . I believe I met her in Paris about a year ago, at my place."

"Is she as lovely as ever?"

"I remember a slender girl with long hair which she twisted into a plait and wore on one side of her head."

"You see, she's gone back to the way she wore her hair before she was married, and yet she knows that I'm alive and a prisoner. She never writes to me."

"My dear chap, you've got no proof and it's simply for the pleasure of torturing yourself that you're letting your imagination run away with you. When you get back to her, all your doubts will seem ridiculous."

"How can you be sure . . ."

"My wife wouldn't have anything to do with a fellow-officer's wife who didn't behave correctly."

"Thank you."

He had recovered his spirits.

"By the way, you'll have a good laugh tomorrow. We're putting on a really splendid knockabout-Marxist turn. A first-class show."

When Jeanine Marindelle entered the drawing-room of the Glatignys' house in the Avenue de Saxe, that little museum dedicated to a whole race of soldiers with its standards, its flags and its arms, Claude had clutched her husband's arm.

"How dare she come here!"

Glatigny could not bear rivalry between women and thought it was an absurd and childish game in which a man was well advised not to meddle. He merely said:

"Oh, well . . ."

He started towards Jeanine, for she had that provocative child-wife beauty that had always attracted him. But Claude held him back:

"Her husband . . . Perhaps you knew him, Lieutenant Marindelle . . . . He's a prisoner of the Vietminh . . . She hasn't been faithful to him."

"How long has he been a prisoner?"

"Three years."

"And she's twenty-one at the most."

"I know, Jacques. I wouldn't do it myself, but I'm not so stupid . . . or unfeeling . . . that I don't understand certain . . . shortcomings. But she's living openly with another man, in his house, and he's a contemptible creature . . . a journalist called Pasfeuro."

"That's her business."

"I don't agree. We women derive our strength, our fidelity,

largely from our cohesion. We're a clan on our own with its own unwritten but nevertheless strict laws. We try and help one another . . . we criticize one another too, and Jeanine Marindelle is my cousin."

Glatigny looked at his wife with her pale shapely face, her large doe eyes which now revealed no tenderness, her set jaw, her nostrils quivering with anger.

He gently freed his arm and went across and kissed Jeanine Marindelle's hand. She said to him:

"Claude isn't very fond of me, Captain."

"I don't know what she's got against you."

"Yes, you do, you know perfectly well."

She had the astonished voice of a hurt child; she played this up perhaps.

"Claude thinks it's a scandal that I'm not making a mystery of it but living quite openly with Pierre Pasfeuro. If we met now and then in some sordid hotel bedroom or between five and seven in his chambers, no one would say a word and I would then be in a position to criticize the other officers' wives."

"You don't love your husband any more?"

"How extraordinary you are, you men! Of course I love him. We were brought up together, we played games together and as children we even shared the same bed. He was the first boy I ever kissed. We married like a brother and sister, so as to go on playing our games. We lived in our own little world with its legends and its taboos. Only a few people were admitted: Judith the old maid, Uncle Joseph who is deaf, and my cousin Pierre Pasfeuro who used to bring us gramophone records.

"When I knew there was very little chance of my ever seeing Yves again, I left his family, whom I didn't like and who were prepared to have me locked up, to kill me like a widow in India. I went and stayed with Pierre. In him I found the man, the stranger in my life. I could hurt him, I'm jealous—which would never even occur to me with Yves. Do you see what I mean, Captain?"

"I think so."

"Then why are they all against me? I used to be very fond of

Claude. She can't understand me, she didn't marry her own brother and then afterwards meet the only man in her life."

"What did she say in her defence?" Claude subsequently asked her husband.

"But she has no defence at all. You don't know how defenceless she is; she's just a poor young girl into whom you're trying to get your cattish old claws. I'd be grateful if you asked her here as often as possible."

A few days later Glatigny had flown out to Saigon.

The instruction and self-examination period took place next day after the afternoon rest. All the officer prisoners were assembled near the river in a large open space that had been cleared on the edge of the forest and was shaded by the big mango trees. In front of them stood a bamboo platform surmounted by the photograph of Ho-Chi-Minh with his straggly beard and the red flag adorned with a yellow star. Some rudimentary benches had been made by the prisoners out of bamboo poles and creepers.

The veterans of Cao-Bang met their comrades from Dien-Bien-Phu again for the first time and some of them recognized one another. They thumped one another on the shoulder, uttered loud exclamations of surprise and delight, but in the end had nothing to say. They belonged to two separate worlds which so far had nothing in common. They stuck to their own respective groups. Marindelle, Orsini and Leroy were about the only ones who sat with the newcomers.

The old hands appeared to look forward to the spectacle with a certain interest and even pleasure. The star performer that day was Lieutenant Millet and they admired his qualities as an actor, his subtle and at the same direct manner, the brutal frankness which enabled him to put over his wopping great lies.

The programme also included the first performance of a newcomer, a certain Boisfeuras whom none of the veterans knew, who was kept isolated in a *canh-na* guarded by three sentries just outside the village. So he could not yet have learnt the rules of the game: an amateur, in other words, but whose story might be interesting all the same.

The appearance of the Voice caused a stir among the prisoners. The show was about to begin. The curtain went up on the big lie of "democracy based on the peace of the masses and reciprocal understanding."

The Voice started off, as usual, by giving a summary of the news, which everyone looked forward to. They knew it was out of date, partly falsified, distorted for the sake of propaganda, and incomplete; but it was the only source of news they had. One day perhaps he would at last announce that the armistice had been signed at Geneva.

But in sorrowful tones the Voice informed them that the Geneva negotiations were dragging on interminably in spite of the good will and efforts of the Vietnamese delegation. After raising everyone's hopes, Mendès-France was revealing his true face, the face of a colonialist more crafty than the others. If he was intent on bringing the war in Indo-China to an end, it was only to repatriate the expeditionary force and send it out again to defend the vast estates that his wife owned in Tunisia.

"I'm beginning to like this Mendès," said Pinières, "only I hope he won't leave us in the lurch."

"His wife's estates are in Egypt," said Esclavier.

The Voice went on:

"Your role later on, as fighters for peace, will be to keep a close watch on those false liberals in the service of the banks, who, while appearing to defend peace, will in fact ally themselves to the warmongers, since they are only prompted by their selfish class interests. Your comrade Millet has prepared a little lecture on the colonial movement in what you used to call Indo-China. It's your duty to listen to him with the utmost attention, for it's a thoroughly objective study."

Lieutenant Millet appeared on the platform. He was all skin and bone, with long cowboy legs. A bullet in the knee made him limp. In his hand he held a piece of paper, bamboo paper of such poor quality that one could only write on it in pencil. His expression was solemn and self-important.

He began by stating some grotesque perversions of the truth, which made no impression on the old hands but dumbfounded the new arrivals.

"Statistics show that the government of Indo-China made a point of lowering the birth-rate . . . Certain districts of North Viet-Nam were systematically starved so that the population might be transported as labourers to swell the slave-camps of the big plantations in Cochin-China. Wives were separated from their husbands to increase their output. In order to restrict the transport of rice to the North, thousands of women, children and old people were exterminated. The coolies were never known to come back from the plantations . . ."

The clan of old hands was well organized—in the first row, the two officers who were Communists or who thought they were; then the progressive group leaders, listening attentively, nodding assent, taking notes; behind them, the "mob" chatting together under their breath, applauding every so often and endlessly discussing what they were going to do with their four years' back-pay which was automatically piling up in their bank accounts. For all these tattered officers were millionaires and kept dreaming, though without much hope, of the cars they would buy and the gargantuan meals they would eat in the big three-star restaurants.

Captain Verdier leaned over towards his neighbour:

"A newcomer told me that Lapérouse is not what it was, that the Tour d'Argent now leads the field. I was planning to take my wife there. Most annoying."

"And what about the Vedette, the new Vedette?" his comrade replied. "Pretty cheesy, it seems, and eats up gas."

"I'll treat myself to wine," said Pestagas in his Bordeaux accent, "nothing but wine seeing as how I haven't had any for four years. I'll have a barrel hung over my bed with a pipe attached to it, and when I can't take any more through my mouth, I'll stuff it up my nostrils and after that damned if I don't take it like an enema!"

There was complete silence as Lieutenant Millet embarked on the interesting part: his own self-examination.

"Comrades," he declared, "the best illustration of the horrors of colonialism in Indo-China is myself. During my first tour of duty, from 1947 to 1949, I held the Minh-Thanh post in the Mekong delta. With my platoon of mercenaries, who hated the workers and the people, for they all came from the wealthy districts of Boulogne-Billancourt and La Villette, we led a life of idleness and, since idleness breeds vice, we were all vicious."

"But Boulogne isn't a wealthy district!" Pinières protested.

"Pipe down," Marindelle replied, giving him a nudge. "The Voice is now convinced that Neuilly and the Seizième are the slums where the workers wallow in misery and that La Villette is next door to the Champs-Élysées."

"Yes, comrades, we oppressed the Vietnamese people and forced them to satisfy our gluttony with ducks, chickens and the young buffaloes they badly needed to cultivate their paddy-fields. We went even further in our misdeeds. To offend the susceptibilities of the Vietnamese people, we bathed stark naked in the middle of the village, while our concubines, whom we scornfully referred to as 'congais,' virtuous young women snatched by force from their families, were made to pour the water over us."

"He's doing well," Orsini exclaimed in admiration.

"Tch . . . tch . . ." Leroy shook his head. "Février was much better."

"One night," Millet went on, "a unit of the People's Army of Viet-Nam, anxious to avenge the oppressed population of Minh-Tanh, attacked our post which would have fallen but for the air support provided by the American imperialists. It was horrible: the bombs wiped out those valiant patriots and fire swept through the hutments.

"I was so misguided that I wanted to avenge the assistance which the patriotic population had given to the People's Army. A parachute battalion came to clear up the district and I myself told them which men to execute. They behaved with their customary brutality and I would rather not tell you all the atrocities they committed.

"It has taken four years of re-education, four years of this policy of leniency which is the Republic of Viet-Nam's reply to our imperialist barbarism, to open my eyes and fill my soul with remorse.

"I ask the Vietnamese people and the soldiers of the People's

Army for forgiveness, and I declare that the rest of my life will be devoted to fighting for peace and the brotherhood of the masses."

There was a round of applause. The newcomers were completely at sea.

"The damned swine," Pinières muttered, "I'll break his jaw for him . . ."

"Go on, clap," Marindelle told him, "clap hard. At that date Millet was in Germany, and anyway he has never set foot in southern Viet-Nam."

"The bastard," Pinières raged.

Lieutenant Millet left the platform, wearing an expression of triumph and remorse. He had high hopes of winning the chicken his comrades had promised for the best self-examination of the month.

After congratulating the lieutenant on his frankness, the Voice remarked that a full assessment of his crimes was an indispensable condition for a prisoner's moral recovery.

He then announced Boisfeuras, one of the most dangerous war criminals captured at Dien-Bien-Phu, who had himself requested this opportunity to explain himself to his comrades.

The sun was shining straight into Boisfeuras's face and he shut his eyes like a nocturnal bird which had suddenly been taken from its lair. He was filthy dirty and caked in dry mud. His voice was more grating than ever:

"Gentlemen," he said, "my misdeeds are infinitely greater than those of my comrade Millet, for they are political. I was born in this part of the world, for over a century my family has exploited the impoverished masses. I learnt the language and customs of Viet-Nam so as to be able to exploit the people all the more. I was one of those who benefited from the war. North of Phon-Tho, among the mountain people, I tried to create a movement of separatism from the people of Viet-Nam. I took advantage of those peasants' credulity; I corrupted them with money; I furnished them with arms. I made them fight against their brothers. But those primitive men, enlightened by an envoy of the Democratic Republic, recovered their patriotism and class consciousness; they kicked me out.

"I refused to see the Truth, and my mercenary's pride impelled me to make for Dien-Bien-Phu in order to continue the fight against the people and defend the selfish interests of my family.

"Today I am beginning to see the light. I repent, and all I ask is to atone for my faults by exemplary conduct in future. I do not deserve the leniency"—he laid his swollen, paralysed hands on the little bamboo lectern in front of him—"which the soldiers of the People's Army have shown towards me."

He climbed down from the platform and the Voice declared that Boisfeuras could go and join his comrades now that he had recognized the error of his ways.

"A serious rival to Millet," Orsini said in admiration.

As a reward for this particularly successful session, the camp commandant, the bandy-legged man who looked like a Japanese and who bore the title of general supervisor as in a college, increased the rations. In addition to their usual ball of rice, the prisoners were given two spoonfuls of molasses—which contributed to the atmosphere of euphoria. Many of them saw in this issue of molasses the hope of a speedy release.

Darkness fell in a few minutes. A fire, which was never allowed to go out, glowed on a patch of bare earth in the centre of the hut. Every so often a hand would rekindle it with a few slivers of dry bamboo. Then it would burst into flame and in the shadows could be seen the faces of Esclavier and Glatigny. Merle was reminded of a scout camp he had once attended in the mountains of Auvergne, Pinières of the long nights he had spent in a farm in Corrèze during the Resistance. Mahmoudi pondered on the affable girls from the Ouled-Nail mountains with their heavy silver jewelry.

Lacombe lay fast asleep on the bare floor under his mosquito net. Mosquito nets had been issued with great ceremony, one for every two prisoners. Since then he never stopped sleeping and from time to time he whimpered in his sleep.

Boisfeuras was sitting next to the fire engaged in an endless conversation with the owner of the house, an old Tho with a wrinkled weather-beaten face. The Tho was optimistic about the future, for his son was head of the village militia which consisted of three men armed with a single shot-gun. He drew the *tou-bi*'s attention to his feet, pitted and deformed by "Hong-Kong foot" or "buffalo's disease," of which he seemed almost proud.

The river babbled gently outside, mingling its noise with the distant echoes of a storm. The air, saturated with heat and humidity, felt as heavy as wool; it seemed to contain no oxygen at all and everyone was suffocating.

Above the grunting of the black pigs that lived under the piles, they heard the sound of voices, then the noise of water dripping on to a flat stone.

Below the hut, at the foot of the ladder, stood a jar of water with a ladle: a wooden *ke-bat*; this water was used to wash the mud off one's feet before coming into the house.

Orsini and Leroy appeared on the threshold. They had come from the veterans' camp and had brought with them a roll of tobacco, tied up like a sausage—a product of their plantation or the result of some mysterious bartering with the Mans of the neighbouring foothills.

They squatted down among the other prisoners, took some home-made pipes out of their pockets and some letters from home which they used as cigarette paper.

Marindelle came and sat down next to Boisfeuras and put a hand on his shoulder.

"They've come to congratulate you. You've got away with it this time. We were rather worried about you. We learnt from one of the *bo-dois* that some chaps who were doing the same job as you—two warrant officers of the Colibri guerrilla gang, a lieutenant of the Tabac gang and Captain Hillarin—had been tried by a people's tribunal and executed a few days after their capture."

"They chopped off Hillarin's head with a hatchet," said Orsini. "He was my instructor at Saint Cyr."

"If they had found out who I was and what I was doing," Boisfeuras calmly replied, "I wouldn't have had a chance of getting away with it. But they would have waited a long time before trying me and perhaps they would have handed me over to my old friends the Chinese. For I was never at Phong-Tho, and I wasn't born in Viet-Nam but in China."

"You took the only course that could save you . . . as though you knew the Viets extremely well."

"I once lived among them—it was in 1945—but they're no longer the same as they were then. You who've been with them for the last four years, could you tell us what the Vietminh is really like?"

Merle clapped his hands:

"Take your seats for another instruction period, only this time everyone will tell the truth."

Imitating the Voice, his impersonal and self-satisfied tone, he began:

"Our veteran comrades, re-educated by four years of a policy of leniency, having reverted, now that night has fallen, to what they have never ceased to be, that's to say vile colonial mercenaries, will now give an objective account of what they think of the psychology and behaviour of that strange, repellant beast, the Vietminh."

"So as to be able," Esclavier interjected, "to show him what we're made of, to pinch his crops and even rape his woman if possible . . ."

"It's not possible," Orsini regretfully observed.

"To beat him in the end," Glatigny concluded with a certain solemnity.

"You kick off, Marindelle," said Leroy.

Marindelle promptly entered into the spirit of the game:

"Comrades, contrary to what you may believe, we are no longer absolutely vile colonial mercenaries, for these repellant people have forced us to learn certain things. The Voice is perhaps not completely wrong when he tells us we must recognize our faults, or rather our 'errors.'"

"Our tactical errors?" Glatigny asked.

"No, our political errors. In the strategy of modern warfare military tactics are a matter of secondary importance, politics will always take precedence."

"Let's discuss the enemy," exclaimed Esclavier, who was irritated by this preamble.

"They're of adverse will, as Clausewitz would say. The Vietminh have been hardened, changed by seven years of fighting. You're right, Boisfeuras, they're no longer the same as they were in 1945. They have created a human type which is repeated indefinitely and cast in the same mould. For example, every year, in every Vietminh division, at the end of the rainy season a recollection is held."

"What's that?" Pinières asked.

"It's a favourite term of the Jesuits. Nothing resembles the Vietminh world as closely as the Jesuits. I know, I was brought up by them. A recollection means a retreat, communal withdrawal, the examination of one's conscience over the period of a year."

"Go on."

"With the Viets it lasts a fortnight and in some units up to ten per cent of the personnel are sometimes shot because they no longer conform to the model laid down. In this process the guilty are their own public prosecutors and demand their punishment themselves."

"Nevertheless," said Glatigny, "in spite of our strokes of audacity and strokes of luck, in spite of our fits of laziness and energy, there was always Vietminh organization, Vietminh pertinacity: an ant-heap for ever active and in the process of reconstruction."

"That's true," said Marindelle. "The Vietminh coolie, soldier, officer and propagandist have always worked relentlessly and with a sense of purpose that is scarcely human. They have built dug-outs, trenches, underground villages . . ."

This reminded them all of the operations in the Delta, of the whole of that landscape remodelled and camouflaged by the human termites.

"We should have dragged them out of their holes one by one," said Esclavier, "like snails out of their shells."

Marindelle went on with undisguised admiration:

"During the day they cultivated their paddy-fields and made war; by night they organized committees, sub-committees and associations of old dodderers and lads of ten. They hardly ever slept; they were under-nourished, they always seemed to be on their last legs, but they still had the strength to carry on. Weren't you struck, as I was, by their physical appearance— their ascetic faces, their feverish eyes, their silent, gliding gait? In their outsize Chinese-style clothes they looked like ghosts . . ."

"I thrashed it all out," said Orsini, "with a Viet from the 304th who spoke French fairly well. He told me something about his life. 'We only moved at night,' he told me, 'in single file and in complete silence. We each used to carry a firefly in a little cage of transparent paper attached to our haversacks. So as not to lose our way, we simply followed these little lights. Some of my comrades made the same firefly last three nights running. So as to avoid being encircled, we often used to march for twenty-five nights at a stretch and our only food was a bowl of rice, a few wild herbs and, occasionally, a little dried fish. In the end I felt my body was a machine which moved, stopped, started up again of its own accord and I myself was outside it, half dreaming, half asleep . . . ' "

"We've all been able to see how the Viets work," Glatigny went on. "All the way along the roads and trails which their convoys used, they had rigged up military shelters under the thick foliage of the jungle. At the mere sound of an aircraft everything, trucks and men, disappeared in a matter of minutes, and there was nothing left but an empty trail. That was all our pilots could see on each of their sorties—empty trails. Just think of the work involved! And it was carried out over hundreds, over thousands of miles, and only by coolies who had nothing but picks, shovels and hatchets and who could only work by night. Meanwhile we were idling away in the brothels and opium dens . . ."

"It's through the coolies they got the better of us," said Boisfeuras, "by means of that vast horde swarming through the elephant grass with their baskets balanced on their shoulders. They used to start off from the Delta with a hundred pounds of rice slung on their poles. They would march three hundred miles over the twisting trails of the Haute Région in order to deliver ten pounds of rice to the *bo-dois*. They had to feed themselves on the way and still keep a pound or two back for the return journey. These thousands and thousands of coolies trotting along the trails were invisible to our aircraft . . . It wasn't only terror that kept them going."

"Propaganda as well?"

"Even that's not enough. Propaganda doesn't work or give such good results unless it touches something deep, something real in a man."

"Such as breaking his solitude," Esclavier solemnly explained.

"It's been a long time since the Viets have known solitude," said Marindelle. "The Viets remind me of those grinds at school, those bookworms who by dint of sheer hard work and perseverance carry off all the prizes at the end of the term. And yet they're the least gifted.

"We soldiers of the expeditionary corps were fairly well off. We had our cars waiting outside as we set off on operations, we had our cases of beer and our rations. Sometimes we felt rather parched, so aircraft would come and drop us some ice. Now and then we carried out some brilliant raids before breakfast, but never bothered to follow them up. Meanwhile the earnest, hardworking grinds carried on with their laborious war. The Vietminh were not better soldiers than we were, especially when you compare their untold strength to our twenty thousand-odd paratroopers and legionaries who were the only ones to face them in pitched battle. Even so they had to be five or ten against one to get the better of us. But then the Viets *all* made war, and without stopping, day and night, whether they were regulars, coolies, Du-Kit guerrillas, women or babes in arms . . . They made any amount of mistakes, they had about as much gumption as an old boot, but they never failed to learn from their mistakes.

"As a result of this sort of warfare, these termite methods," Marindelle went on after a short silence, "the Viets have become pernickety and bureaucratic-minded. They take endless notes, make reports and keep files at every level of command, using tiny little bits of paper, because that's what they're short of, paper."

"For the last four years," said Leroy, "we've been pushed around the whole time by the *can-bos* or the officers. They keep whipping out note-book and pencil, demanding to know our names and why we came to Indo-China, asking a mass of technical questions about weapons and equipment. They solemnly take down anything you can think of, then wander off completely happy."

"That mania of theirs was extremely useful to us," said Glatigny. "They never stopped working their W.T. sets to broadcast the minutest detail. Every evening, at every level, they gave us a full report of their activities. We were able to intercept it all and we knew to the nearest pound what they were getting from China."

"Then why the hell did we come to grief?" Esclavier rudely inquired. "We knew everything to the nearest pound. And the Viet artillery at Dien-Bien-Phu? We knew everything, and that's all; we did nothing about it."

"Without that information we might have been driven out of Indo-China two years earlier."

"Well spoken, my little staff officer!"

Seeing that the discussion was taking a nasty turn, Orsini broke in:

"Here, in the camp, the Viets keep revising the nominal roll over and over again. They jib at an accent, at a comma. They're so bigoted, it makes you sick. You're not allowed to use the word 'Vietminh'; you must always talk about the Democratic Government of Viet-Nam, and say 'sir' to the lowest *bo-doi* besotted by propaganda. But we haven't the right to wear our badges of rank. There's no way of knowing what they think or how they live. You come up against a blank wall and their reply is the same old phonograph record.

"To begin with, during the first year or two, we thought they were wary of us. Then we noticed it was more than that. They simply have nothing to say apart from ready-made phrases, there's nothing personal about them. The Party and the army, that's their whole life. Outside them they have no existence whatever."

"That explains it," said Boisfeuras. "Many of the officers and other ranks have been waging clandestine war for the last seven years. They've lived in bands quartered in out-of-the-way little villages, either in the mountains of Thanh-Hoa or the limestone country of the Day. They had nothing in common with the mountain people who despised them as inhabitants of the Delta. So they were reduced to living among them in this military, intransigent, rigorist and highly organized community . . ."

"That's absolutely true," said Marindelle. "Even the Voice, who's a graduate of Hanoi and quite brilliant, I believe, has ceased to have an original thought or to struggle against his surroundings. All those chaps, just in order to survive, needed all the strength they had. They had to endure night marches, battles to the death, insufficient food. In their leisure hours they were transformed into propaganda machines. They were compelled to reiterate again and again the same slogans that had to be hammered into the thick skulls of the *nah-ques*. They organized all sorts of associations to embrace the civilian population and saw to it that these associations did not come adrift immediately. They had to instruct recruits, conscript coolies, collect money . . . These men didn't have a minute to themselves; their life wasn't their own, and when, utterly exhausted, they found time to sleep for a few hours, they preferred to accept the Communist system wholesale rather than to ponder over it and discuss it."

"You seem to be very fond of them," Esclavier remarked rather nastily.

"I try to understand them, certainly. If I had been a Vietnamese, I don't think I could have held out, I should have sided with them. Imagine the life of a young militant before he is poured into the Vietminh mould which will eventually depersonalize him. He knows the romance of revolution. He slips into a village at night. In the depths of a hut lit by an oil lamp he organizes a meeting. Often it's only a hundred yards or so from a French post. He hears the sentries clearing their throats.

All that is known about him is his pseudonym; he leads a mysterious, fascinating life."

"You've been reading too much Malraux," Boisfeuras gently remarked. "Communism isn't like that at all."

"That doesn't stop these peasants, who have never left their little bit of paddy-field, from talking about China and the U.S.S.R. He lets them think that he has just arrived from those distant countries and they gape at him in admiration. His voice becomes seductive and compelling. He uses words that have a magic ring to them, such as Michourism, Collectivism, which he is mad about himself. He leads a life of adventure and all the girls look at him with yearning as they peck away at their sunflower seeds."

"I'd also be on their side," thought Merle. "And I," thought Mahmoudi, "may soon be obliged to lead that sort of life, but in my case the *canh-nas* will be *mechtas*; China and the U.S.S.R., Egypt and Iraq; Communism, Islam."

"I've known that sort of thing," Pinières reflected.

Marindelle fell silent for a moment or two. The old Tho spat and cleared his throat. Marindelle went on in a calmer tone of voice:

"And after a few years of communal life the result is a man without a soul who is totally inhuman and at the same time ambitious and incredibly naïve, like all those who believe they have found the one and only Truth. On top of that there's the influence of the boy-scout movement, for Ta-Quan-Bau who's in charge of the Vietminh youth is a former scoutmaster and inspector general of the Admiral Decoux schools. The doctrines of national revolution took firm root there and many of the leading Viets have been through those schools. You mustn't overlook doctrinaire intransigence. They're still in the first stage of Communism, that of revolution and single-mindedness. They have a faith untempered by any sense of reality."

"He's a fine speaker is our Marindelle," said Orsini with satisfaction.

"I think I can round off your explanation," said Boisfeuras. "There are times when the Vietminh appear to be solely a section of the Communist Party. Their implementation of the agrarian reforms, their methods, their propaganda system, particularly as addressed towards the women, their soldiers' uniform, their manner of fighting, all these are Chinese. The Chinese Communist armies of Mao-Tse-Tung and Chu-Teh have brought those tactics to a fine art. Yet though this hold that China has on them is strong, it is not as complete as it might appear. Although linked to Peking, the Vietnamese Communist Party has its own contacts with the central organization in Moscow. Most of the Vietminh leaders were groomed in France by French Communists directly responsible to the U.S.S.R. The Vietminh is therefore more orthodox than the Chinese Communist Party. They have decided to apply wholesale Communism without trying to adapt it to the local temperament or climate, as Mao-Tse-Tung and his lot have done on a very big scale.

"Perhaps that's why the Vietminh fight shy of discussion and stick to their catechism. They seem to be afraid, they're not sure of themselves. They haven't the traditions or the intelligence of the Chinese. They've always been a slave nation."

"The Vietminh have become solemn and melancholy and have lost all their spontaneity," Marindelle went on. "That has almost happened before my eyes. You hardly ever see them laugh and if they do it's usually the private soldiers, never the N.C.O.s or officers. They have rapidly lost their youthful virtue, their revolutionary enthusiasm and ardour, and that's why they're so disturbing. They can't stand a joke; they can't even see one."

"What about the girls?" asked Merle.

"The women are now considered equal to the men. They have the same rights, therefore the same duties. They have become officers, propaganda agents, political figures, but they have lost all their personality."

"Vietnamese girls as sweet as mangoes," Pinières involuntarily muttered at the memory of My-Oi.

"Sentimental and even sexual relations are looked upon as useless, worthless and uninteresting. The Vietminh has become a puritan, partly by necessity. His exhausting life leaves him hardly any spare time or energy. He denies all religion, but behaves like the strictest Quaker."

Esclavier sniggered:

"I wouldn't mind having a go at a young militant Viet girl to see if Marxism prevents her from enjoying it . . ."

"That sort of thing," said Leroy, "is strictly forbidden between a *tou-bi* and a girl of the Democratic Republic of Viet-Nam. Anyway camp routine doesn't allow the slightest carnal desire to exist. It's the great sex truce. But if, in spite of everything, the impossible happened, it would mean the immediate liquidation of the *tou-bi* and a concentration camp for the girl, in other words death for both."

"In actual fact, to what use have you put these theories of yours?" Boisfeuras asked. "You seem to have landed on your feet all right in the artificial world of the Vietminh."

"In order to survive," Marindelle explained, "we have found the right balance. This balance we call the 'political fiction' of the camp. It's at the same time a philosophy, an organization and a way of life. It's unexpressed and unacknowledged, but everyone here has assimilated it. It gives us the exact attitude to adopt in order to find the best solution to each problem of our daily life.

"It's time to go to bed. Orsini and Leroy have to get back to their barracks. There's Mass tomorrow. Everyone goes, even those who aren't Catholics, even those who don't believe in anything. For us it's the equivalent of taking up a political and moral stand. That's why, Mahmoudi, I'd be grateful if you would come. You see, it's our church against theirs and you belong to ours."

"I'll see."

"You must come."

"All right then, I'll come."

Glatigny lay awake for a long time. He never imagined this sort of conversation could have been possible among a group of young officers or that they could have been able to analyse the situation with such lucidity. And that child-lieutenant Marindelle, completely at ease in the Marxist world, talking quite naturally about the political fiction of the camp, urging his comrades to go to Mass because it was a question of taking a political stand . . . that child who was more mature than all of them with the possible exception of Boisfeuras and whose sister-wife back in Paris was being unfaithful to him with a certain Pasfeuro who was a journalist . . .

7

LIEUTENANT
MARINDELLE'S VENTRAL

During the first year of their captivity the hundred and twenty
officer prisoners of Camp One had refused to co-operate with
the Vietminh in any way. They attended the instruction periods, but the *bo-dois* had to drive them to the assembly place
with their rifle butts.

There, on a little bamboo platform, the Voice or some other
political commissar entrusted with their re-education would
lecture them on a given theme: the misdeeds of colonialism . . .
the exploitation of man by capitalism . . . But not one of the
prisoners listened to their educators' ponderous phrases, and
when the Voice afterwards questioned them on the lesson they
could never give the right answers.

Faced with this display of ill-will, this refusal to collaborate
in their re-education, the Voice had taken certain measures
and the prisoners had their daily rations reduced to a ball of
rice with a few herbs, but without so much as an ounce of fat
or fish juice.

They had held out a whole year, but thirty of them had died
from exhaustion, beri-beri and vitamin deficiency. It was then the
oldest and highest ranking officer in the camp, Colonel Charton,
had given the order to "play the game" in order to survive.

And so the day came when a lieutenant, young Marindelle,
spoke up and gave the correct answers. The Voice was exultant
and he felt that the secret wound deep inside him was beginning to close.

The rations were improved, the prisoners were given molasses, dried fish and bananas, and they signed manifestoes in favour of peace and against the atomic bomb. They accused themselves of all sorts of crimes, almost always falsely; they shouted their guilt out loud; and in return were allowed a certain amount of medical treatment.

But Potin who had been a Communist, and who could not be trusted to stand by his comrades to resist the Vietminh, was inveigled back into the bosom of the party whose expressions and vocabulary were already familiar to him.

He was like those Christians who, after neglecting their duties for a long time, are restored to the church by some sudden chance in the course of a service. This swarthy little man who wore steel-rimmed spectacles was absolutely honest about it. One day he came up to his comrades and said:

"Look. I was once a Communist. I didn't think I still was but I have become one again, completely and without reservations. So from now on I'm on the side of the Vietminh. I want you to know this and to treat me accordingly. I shall try not to know what you are doing, what escapes you are planning, but please don't tell me about it. Stop trusting me in any way."

From then on he had volunteered for the nastiest, most arduous fatigues; he had refused everything which could have improved his lot.

Even Orsini and Leroy, who were irrepressible and animated by a tenacious and steadfast hatred for the Vietminh, bore him no malice. But they spoke to him as though to a *bo-doi*, which hurt him deeply, for he admired both of the lieutenants for their courage, loyalty and sense of friendship. Marindelle alone showed some understanding, but he was wary of him and his lively intelligence. He was the worm in the Communist apple, the choirboy who served Mass in order to drink the communion wine.

Ménard was also converted, but his reasons were more questionable and when he was thrown out of the army, although he claimed to have played the double game, he found no one to defend him. A few others took to progressivism, either through conviction, cowardice, or to be given extra privileges. Marindelle was one of these, but for another reason. This incurable chatterbox, this cheerful merry andrew had an astonishing capacity for secrecy. This was only realized two years later when he escaped with the whole group of irrepressibles.

There were a number of setbacks which should have enlightened the Vietminh and made them realize that their propaganda had gained a hold upon no more than half a dozen individuals. For instance, the incident of the chickens.

The prisoners had been given permission to keep chickens for their own consumption. Orsini, with many an obscene allusion, applied to have ducks instead but his request was not taken into consideration; each prisoner, with the ardour of a retired suburban, kept two or three birds. There was clucking all over the camp.

During one of his lectures the Voice announced that in token of satisfaction for this praiseworthy endeavour, he would allow the prisoners to put all their chickens into a common pool, which would enable them to recognize the superiority of collectivization to private enterprise. So, as from the next day, a chicken *kolkhoz* was to be established.

The prisoners did put their chickens into a common pool, but in a somewhat unforeseen manner. They killed them all that night and clubbed together to eat them.

At the end of the third year, however, they witnessed a strange conversion due entirely to the influence of Marindelle. The group of irrepressibles, about twelve strong, suddenly gave evidence of unexpected zeal. They hastened to sign every petition condemning war, the use of the atomic bomb and napalm. Given half a chance, they would also have condemned the air-gun and the bow and arrow. They indulged with frenzy in self-examinations, accused themselves violently of every crime they could think of, made a still noisier show of repenting of them, manifested their desire to be instructed in the Marxist religion and made really remarkable progress in dialectics.

Marindelle had to do his utmost to curb their zeal for fear it should appear suspicious.

The Viets are rather like Christians; they welcomed these last-minute converts with open arms, and, having soon become

model fighters for peace, the neophytes occupied every responsible post in the camp.

Not content with their daytime activity, with inventing a
progressivist hymn in which every word had a double meaning, they also met at night, but always among themselves, to
perfect their education under the tutelage of Marindelle.

Marindelle would take a seat in the centre of the circle and
fire questions at them:

"Leroy?"

"Present."

"How much rice did you steal today?"

"Three handfuls. That brings our store up to a hundred
pounds. We'll need four times more than that."

"Millet?"

"I'll get the hatchet tomorrow. The Man wants a litre of
choum and a couple of chickens for it."

"Orsini?"

"I scrounged a pair of trousers; they could be made into a
sack. They belonged to Ménard and he made a fuss. So I
pitched into him and accused him in the presence of a *bo-doi*
of playing a double game and being nothing but an imperialist
in disguise."

"Don't overdo it."

"I," said Maincent, "managed to relieve one of the *bo-dois*
of his tinder lighter."

"Have you prepared your self-examination?"

"I can't think of any more crimes to accuse myself of."

"Use your imagination; you've got to replace Potin as officer
i/c stores before the rainy season begins. I've been working on
the Meteor for the last fortnight, but the supervisor-general is
on his guard. From now on we're going to work in four teams
of three; each team will build its own raft. We'll have the
hatchet in turns."

"I've got a map," said Juves, "or rather, a tracing on a bit of
bum-wad. They let me have a look at a pamphlet on French
atrocities and it contained a map of Tonkin. I made a copy
of it."

"So what?"

"Do you realize, smart guy, what we're letting ourselves in for? Over three hundred miles roped to bamboo rafts; first the river by the camp in full spate, then the Song-Gam with its falls and rapids near Tho-Son. Enough to drown us twenty times over. We meet the Bright River at Binh-Ca, with Viets stationed on all the islets. It's a hundred to one, a thousand to one, against our pulling it off."

"Do you know a better way? Can you see us marching bare-foot through the jungle?"

"No."

"Well, then? Do you want to die here, still performing your Marxist monkey-tricks? Especially as you're not particularly gifted."

Orsini broke in heatedly:

"We've agreed once and for all. Marindelle's the boss and we're sticking to his plan."

"This war is bound to end some day," Juves protested.

"Don't you believe it. Do you think France is going to climb down because of these little bastards? If we stay on here, all that's left for us is to become collaborators like Ménard or, better still, Commies like Potin. I'd rather do myself in."

The following month Maincent succeeded Potin as officer i/c stores. The Communist, who had given ample proof of his integrity, did not protest even though Marindelle had reported him to the camp commandant for stealing rice for himself and his friends. Leroy saw fit to apologize:

"You understand . . ."

"I think I understand," he curtly replied.

He went off, hunching his shoulders. He would have given anything to be one of them, to share in the fresh strength they had suddenly derived from preparing their escape and through which they had made themselves masters of the camp.

That was how the political fiction of the camp came into be-ing. The Vietminh only knew prisoners who were zealous or reluctant, who advanced with faltering steps along the path of re-education or else, on the contrary, made rapid progress. But in the shadows there already existed a sort of clandestine collective government which ascribed the role that each man had to play in the vast charade that had been prepared for the benefit of the Voice and the camp guards.

To begin with, this state of mind was unconscious and unexpressed. It was Marindelle and his group who, in preparing their escape, gave it a cohesive and specific form. After they were recaptured the political fiction became general. With the sly and patient perseverance of prisoners, the officers of Camp One managed to lend a double meaning to every gesture and every word, to ridicule their guards, their ideas and their convictions at every instant, and to trick them all the time while maintaining an air of the utmost gravity.

Discovering laughter again, the prisoners contrived to prize open the mysterious gates of this Kafkaesque hell into which they had been plunged.

They remained captives, admittedly, but the part of them which the Vietminh were so anxious to enslave, all that was not purely physical, had broken free, and this time laughter was more effective than bamboo rafts.

For the escape bid met with total failure.

The rains had started. The level of the river no longer dropped in the interval between two storms and its muddy waters churned with driftwood. The four rafts were ready and, weighted with stones, lay on the river bed. They had been crudely constructed out of bamboo sticks held together with creepers which had already started to rot in the water. These rafts were in fact nothing more than thick logs some fifteen to twenty feet long which the officers planned to sit astride rather like horses. They were pierced by a plank at both ends to prevent them from turning turtle in the water. They had knocked together some clumsy paddles with which to steer them. The rafts, which they had tried out on several occasions, floated almost totally submerged, so that they had to carry their foodstuffs slung round their necks. Each team was equipped with fifty pounds of rice and a bully-beef tin full of salt, which was nowhere near sufficient.

Four copies had been made of Juves's map. Each prisoner

had provided all the information he could on the country to be crossed and this information had been recorded on the maps.

"A suicide operation," Juves maintained.

"It's tonight or never," Marindelle announced one morning. "Tomorrow they're organizing a general search; we'll have to be off before. That s.o.b. of a supervisor-general is beginning to suspect something. He's not straight, that rat. He's a dirty *nha-que* who's impervious to all dialectic."

They attended the instruction period which took place at five every evening. The daily storm broke after supper, towards seven o'clock. The downpour drowned every other noise and isolated the huts. This was the moment they chose for their escape.

Marindelle had previously handed Trézel, "the parson," a letter addressed to the Voice with instructions to leave it outside the camp office but not until the following morning.

"What's it all about?" asked the wary Breton who had never been able to understand Marindelle's complex character.

"Don't ask too many questions. I'm making a break for it . . . but I'm taking certain precautions. In other words, I'm buckling on my ventral."*

The letter was written in pencil on bamboo paper and the Jesuits by whom Marindelle had been brought up in the prison-convent of Saint François de Sales at Evreux would have been proud of their pupil.

> *Democratic Republic of Viet-Nam,*
> *Camp One*

Sir,

When you read these lines I shall have left Camp One in the hope of reaching Hanoi and France. I suppose you will be disappointed and will think that I have relapsed into my former errors. I wish to justify myself in your eyes for I need your moral

---

*The spare parachute which is fastened on to the stomach, while the main parachute, the dorsal, is worn on the back. It is only used in an extreme emergency, when the first parachute fails to open.

support if I am to carry on the struggle for peace. During the thirty months I spent in your camp you made me see not only where my duty lay but also that the title of peace fighter had to be earned. I now feel fully qualified and certain of my aim. I am impatient to engage in this campaign which you are waging throughout the world to wipe out the last traces of a society that is rotten, selfish and damned to eternity.

This campaign I must wage in my own country, among my own people and my own class. If you had released me, I should have appeared suspect to many of my comrades and to my own government. Having escaped, however, I shall be able to operate in complete freedom. Were it otherwise, would I be writing to you now?

My two comrades, Orsini and Leroy, likewise share my views.

I am convinced that one day we shall meet again and that side by side, fraternally united, in Paris, the centre of our communal culture, we shall work together to bring about that world of hope and peace for which you have already sacrificed more than your life.

Allow me, sir, to thank you for having made a new man of me. Thanks to your instruction and your example, I shall in my turn be able to conquer and to triumph.

YVES MARINDELLE,
FIGHTER FOR PEACE

In groups of three they made their way to the river through the undergrowth, took the rice out of its hiding place, and distributed the prepared packets. Some of them dived in and pulled up the rafts. The river was in full spate and flooding the jungle.

"See you in Paris," said Orsini.

"Or in hell," said Juves.

They climbed on to their rafts and with great difficulty reached mid-stream. The current swept them down one after another.

All of a sudden it stopped raining. The darkness cleared, like ink being diluted by water, and the evening star appeared in the sky. They were soaked to the skin and began to shudder with cold.

"Have you got a wife?" Marindelle asked Orsini.

"No, but I'm going to find one, and not only one, a whole mass."

"What about you, Leroy?"

"An old girl-friend down at Béziers."

"My wife's name is Jeanine," Marindelle solemnly announced. "She's very young, very beautiful and it's been a long time for her to wait."

The first night they covered forty miles, but one of the rafts, the one carrying Captain Juves, overturned. The three men managed to swim back to the bank, but at dawn they ran across a Vietminh patrol. They made a dash for it and the *bo-dois* opened fire. One prisoner was killed, another was wounded, and Juves gave himself up. The Viets finished off the wounded man and made Juves kneel down on the muddy bank. The corporal leading the patrol put a bullet through his head and with his foot toppled the body over into the stream which promptly carried it off.

In the Song-Gam rapids the second raft came to grief against a rock. The creepers holding the bamboos together broke. Two prisoners were drowned and the third, Lieutenant Millet, was saved by some fishermen and handed over to the Vietminh. To punish him while waiting for instructions, the local commander had him tied naked to an ant-heap. All night long Millet begged them to put him out of his misery. The following morning he was taken back to camp where a people's tribunal condemned him to nine months' solitary confinement for having betrayed the trust of the Vietnamese people.

The third raft capsized several times. The rice fell into the water. Dying of hunger, the three prisoners gave themselves up to the Communists. They were brought back to camp, tried and condemned to six months' solitary confinement.

The cells were rather like bamboo cages with a trapdoor opening. They were too small for the solitary prisoner to stretch his legs. Once a day a *bo-doi* brought him a minimum amount of food and for the rest of the time he stewed and rotted in the damp heat and solitude, haunted by his memories.

The three lieutenants on the fourth raft held out for a fortnight. They had forgotten the number of times their vessel had turned turtle. Eaten alive by the mosquitoes, obliged to feed on raw rice, shivering with cold and fever, their limbs cramped and aching, they were frequently pushed to the limits of human endurance. But each time, at the last moment, they clung to life, Orsini and Leroy through hatred, Marindelle through love.

Later on Orsini and Leroy were astonished to realize that in this pitiful and admirable endeavour they had still been able, after three years' captivity, to summon sufficient strength and courage to perform one of those impossible deeds that gives man his grandeur, and that at the same time they had been delivered of their hatred.

Marindelle's love for Jeanine had, on the contrary, gathered fresh strength, for he now identified his wife with everything that was best in him: his endurance, his courage, his refusal to give up and die.

It was on the morning of the fifteenth day, as they were floating down the Bright River, that they caught sight of the Duong-Tho post, its square crenellated tower and forecourt of earth and planks.

"We've made it, we're on French-held territory," said Leroy, who had once been garrisoned there for six months.

"It's Duong-Tho," said Marindelle. "We've come down much lower than we thought. Three more days and we should have reached Hanoi. We should merely have had to jump off the raft to go straight to the Normandie for a drink. It's one of those strokes of luck you read about in the papers."

They summoned up enough strength to land, but had to lie stretched out in the grass for over half an hour before being able to move their cramped limbs.

"Where's the French flag?" Marindelle asked with sudden anxiety.

In the grey light, under the leaden sky, he could see nothing unfurled on the tower.

"They haven't raised the colours yet," said Orsini. "The garrison troops are colonials and you know what they're like, not exactly gluttons for work. They're sitting pretty down here, so close to Hanoi; there are no Viets around."

"Let's go," said Leroy. "There's a path leading up to the post round at the back. We'd better take it, they might have laid some mines."

Duong-Tho had just been evacuated and the three prisoners were greeted at the entrance to the post by some *bo-dois*. There were a dozen of them picking through the rubbish left behind by the French, turning over the empty tins and wooden and cardboard cases with their bayonets.

The officers had not enough strength left to double back on their tracks. They sank down against the walls of the fore-court and fell fast asleep. They were much too tired to feel either anger or disappointment.

Some time later, as the sun was beginning to sink behind the river, an officer came and woke them up. He made a note of their names and rank and had them tied up to one another without brutality.

In the morning they were released from their fetters. Orders had arrived during the night to treat them well. They were given the same rations as the soldiers, were allowed to rest, and on the following day they set off under escort on their way back to Camp One.

They ambled along for three weeks; the Viets were soon on good terms with them and seemed to be in no hurry to get back to the camp. They turned a blind eye on the *tou-bis*' pilfering and shared the fruits of their plunder with them.

The prisoners reached Camp One after dark and were promptly locked up in the cells. Next morning Marindelle was sent for. The Voice wanted to have a word with him before taking disciplinary action.

In spite of his cynicism, Marindelle came away from the interview somewhat chastened. The Voice with his fine mask of gold had gently reprimanded him, as a scoutmaster might his favourite cub. He had spoken with disarming naïveté:

"Why didn't you come and see me before trying to escape,

Marindelle? I shouldn't have dissuaded you. You haven't grasped the point of our tuition. Before attempting anything, you should first approach your superiors, for what may strike you as a happy decision may in fact have an adverse effect on the Party of Peace. Furthermore, you have set your comrades a bad example, even though you acted in good faith.

"I shall therefore ask you and your two comrades to make a thorough self-examination, and I think I shall then be able to adopt a lenient attitude. You've still got a lot to learn, Marindelle, but the sincerity of your feelings has always given me grounds for hope."

The three lieutenants had made their self-examination. Even so Orsini and Leroy were confined to the cells for a week before being pardoned, whereas Marindelle, after a few days, was restored to his position of group leader.

For a long time no one in the camp could talk of anything else but this extraordinary act of mercy, which could not be completely accounted for by Marindelle's letter. There was even a suggestion that the Voice harboured an unnatural passion for the lieutenant, and Ménard insinuated that Marindelle had denounced his comrades. This hypothesis was absurd and without foundation but nevertheless gained a certain credence.

Boisfeuras asked Marindelle what had prompted the Voice to act as he had done.

Marindelle gave several reasons: first of all his boy-scout naïveté. Secondly, his incredible vanity as a Communist intellectual convinced of being in possession of the one and only Truth; finally, a certain nostalgic friendliness towards Westerners among whom he had been brought up and whose culture he had assimilated.

Marindelle knew nothing about Commander Ducoroy's youth camps or the boy with the sturdy calves and close-cropped hair who had been the Prince of one of those camps.

For a week Lacombe was a lifeless mass who had to be fed by his comrades. He showed no more interest in life and refused to move from his bunk and go down to the river to wash.

He became mildly delirious. He imagined he was living in a huge grocery, filled with tins of every shape and size, barrels of oil, sacks of rice and flour, cases of biscuits, macaroni and sugar.

He went over his stock again and again, for people kept stealing from it. Sometimes it was Glatigny or Boisfeuras, at other times Esclavier, Merle or Pinières.

The Voice gently pointed out that his accounts did not balance. He would then start all over again:

Three thousand tins of peas; two thousand of string beans; two hundred boned hams, ten barrels of oil . . . there was a barrel of oil missing.

Esclavier came and leant on the counter and sniggered stupidly.

Then everything started to swim before his eyes. The doctor who was sent for shrugged his shoulders. There was nothing to be done. There was no physical ailment he could diagnose, but something had gone wrong. He advised the services of a priest.

One morning Lacombe stopped counting his tins. He was buried in a little clearing on the side of the mountain above Camp One. For a few weeks his grave was marked with a bamboo cross, then it was swallowed up in the jungle.

There were several other officers in the camp who gave up the ghost like this—mostly those who had shown the greatest endurance during the march and had afterwards heaved a profound sigh of relief as they dropped on to their bunks in Camp One.

Esclavier and Glatigny had one mosquito net between them and shared the same blanket which they spread out at night on the bamboo slats of the floor. One night Esclavier, who normally slept like a top, twisted and turned in a fever. After the evening downpour the temperature had dropped abruptly; he started shivering. Glatigny wrapped him up in the blanket with all the tenderness and affection he now felt for this hardened condottiere.

Reveille sounded shortly before dawn. A Viet would hammer on a large bamboo hanging from a branch, slowly at first, then with progressively increasing speed as the sound gradually diminished. This was the great rhythm of Asia, the rhythm of feasts and pagodas, of funerals and births, of the chase and of war. From the distant monasteries of Tibet to vermilion-hued Peking, from the narrow valleys of the Thai countryside to the kampongs of Malaya, all life was geared to the clash of gong and wooden rattle.

The prisoners assembled in teams outside their huts to draw their "breakfast soup," a meagre ration of rice recooked in slightly salted water. They gobbled it up, standing in the fresh invigorating light of dawn before reporting on the parade ground for the daily fatigues.

"Shall I bring up your soup?" asked Glatigny who was worried by his comrade's immobility.

Esclavier lay hunched up under the blanket, bathed in sweat. He muttered weakly:

"No, you can have my share."

This looked serious. No one could afford to miss a meal. Refusing rice was the first symptom of the capitulation which in a few days had brought Lacombe to the little clearing tucked away in the jungle.

"None of that now; you're going to eat up like the rest of us."

Glatigny unhooked the two wooden ladles hanging on the partition above their bed-space and held them for a few seconds over the flames in the hearth to sterilize them. In addition to the bugs and the mosquitoes, rats swarmed through the huts all night in search of the smallest grain of rice. Famished and mangy, they were carriers of a deadly germ, the spirochete; in humans this germ caused a burning fever which reduced the body to a state of mummification. French hospitals had perfected a rigorous and costly treatment and this alone was capable of saving the patients. They were kept alive by intravenous injections of a serum in all four limbs, which enabled them to survive during the ten days it took for the spirochete to develop and die.

In Camp One this treatment was not available and disinfection by fire was the only form of prevention against this illness which was almost always lethal.

Holding a *cai-bat* heaped with rice in one hand, Glatigny

knelt down beside his companion and raised his head with the other:

"Come on, eat up."

Esclavier opened his feverish, bloodshot eyes.

"I can't swallow."

"Eat up, I tell you."

"Give me something to drink."

"Get this down first, then I'll make you some tea. There's nothing left to drink at the moment."

In "the country of water that kills" they first had to boil the liquid to which they added a few leaves of wild tea, guava or bitter orange.

In spite of his reluctance, Glatigny forced his comrade to swallow his "breakfast soup." Esclavier sank back exhausted and brought it all up in a series of shuddering retches.

The others, having folded their blankets and mosquito nets and equipped themselves for the morning fatigues, climbed down the ladder and went off to the parade ground.

"Marindelle," Glatingy called out, "Esclavier's ill. Tell the Voice I'm staying behind to look after him."

He cleaned the soiled blanket, washed the captain's face and chest in cold water, then boiled some tea.

Esclavier seemed a little easier now; his face betrayed enormous strain and in one night had assumed the translucid grey-brown complexion of "the veterans of Cao-Bang." The fever appeared to have abated. He had managed to keep down two large bowls of tea.

"I feel better now. There's no need for you to stay."

Esclavier seemed ashamed of inflicting these nursing duties on his comrade. He knew how keen Glatigny was on his morning fatigue—a ten-mile walk, there and back, to fetch the rice from the depot. He called this "physical culture" and claimed it kept him in shape.

But Glatigny refused to leave him:

"I'm not going out this morning, I'm on barrack fatigue. I'm going to clean up and bring in the water and wood. You had a nice bout of malaria last night."

"My attacks are violent but short, I'll be up and about tomorrow."

In the course of the morning, Captain Evrard, the medical officer on duty that day, came and saw Esclavier. He sounded his stomach, examined his throat, felt his pulse.

"I've got malaria," Esclavier insisted almost angrily.

Glatigny followed Evrard outside and, when they were some distance away from the hut, questioned him:

"What's wrong with him?"

"Fever," said Evrard, "I can't say more than that without being able to make an analysis. I'll put him down for the régime,* but I don't know if Prosper will accept him. Your team has a rather bad name, you know."

"Prosper," an arrogant little Vietnamese who barely concealed his hatred for the whites, bore the pompous title of Camp Doctor. He had been an orderly of sorts at the Gia-Dinh hospital before joining the Vietminh two years earlier. Every morning he presided under this title at a medical inspection in the infirmary where the sick had to come and report in person.

From the sixteen medical officer prisoners he had selected two assistants to whom he had at least conceded the title of male nurse. His assistants examined the patients, which he was incapable of doing himself, made their diagnosis and prescribed a treatment which they recorded in an exercise book. This was eventually submitted to Prosper who made the final decision, without even having seen the patients, according to standards that were utterly alien to medical practice.

Beside Esclavier's name was the note: "malaria, two tablets of nivaquine, three days' régime."

Prosper screwed up his little monkey face. Esclavier and his team were classified as W.S.s (wily serpents). He crossed out "malaria" and wrote in: "fever, relieved of duty for forty-eight

---

*The régime entitled the patient to improved rations consisting of less abundant but richer food: chicken, molasses, tinned sardines (for the most serious cases) and half a banana.

hours," which meant that his team would draw only half a ration of rice for him.

"Thank heavens the little rat doesn't know Molière," Evrard reflected, "otherwise he would have the whole lot bled so as to kill them off the more quickly."

For four days Esclavier's temperature kept rising. He lay without moving under the blankets which his comrades piled on top of him. Glatigny, who never left his side, persuaded him to drink a little boiled water every two hours. More often than not he brought it up, and at night he was delirious.

One evening the old Tho, before smoking his water-pipe, came and squatted down by his head. He looked at the whites of his eyes, lifting the lid with a finger the colour of paddy-field mud, and drew back his lips to examine the gums. He cleared his throat and aimed a long jet of saliva with accuracy through a gap in the floorboards. Then he rejoined Boisfeuras by the fire.

"*Tiet!*" he said, taking out his pipe, "*tou-bi tiet.*"

Boisfeuras questioned him in Tho, but the old man merely shook his head and repeated: "*Tiet.*"

"*Tiet*" meant "death" in Vietnamese. The old man made no further comment, he had no time to waste in gestures and words for a man whom he considered already *tiet*.

Evrard called half a dozen times, bringing with him a different doctor each time. They discussed the case at the bedside of the patient whose skin, stretched over an emaciated frame, had gone a reddish-yellow colour. Glatigny or Marindelle walked back with them to hear their verdict.

"He ought to go to hospital," Evrard declared one morning, "he can't last another week. But Prosper won't hear of it. Yesterday his note in the book was: 'dysentery, diet.' He might just as well have written down 'small-pox, aspirin' . . . if small-pox were a disease which is tolerated by the puritan democratic republic. I'd like to strangle that filthy little politico who dares to assume the title of doctor but can't even give an injection!"

Marindelle persuaded Potin and the doctor to come with him to see the Voice about it. His dialectic, supported by Evrard's technical arguments and Potin's political guarantee, eventually extracted an agreement from the political commissar to move Esclavier to hospital.

The hospital was two days' march away and the patient had to be carried there on a stretcher. The whole team was given permission to join a fatigue party which was going to bring back some salt. Leroy and Orsini volunteered to go with them.

Mahmoudi was worn out but decided to accompany them all the same.

Boisfeuras believed in the old Tho's diagnosis. Esclavier was *tiet*; there was nothing more to be done for him. But he preferred not to say so. Esclavier would end up being carried by his comrades: like a barbarian warrior, he would receive in homage their sweat and their endeavour.

And that was something which could hardly fail to please the strange captain.

8

DIA THE MAGNIFICENT

The Thu-Vat hospital was situated among wooded hills inter-
sected by broad cultivated patches in the vicinity of the Bright
River whose reddish waters were a churning mass of tree-
trunks, driftwood, carrion and tufts of grass. It was the biggest
and best one in the People's Army and consisted of over thirty
Annamite huts built at ground level and scattered through the
forest. They were connected to one another by paths of beaten
earth shaded by huge trees, redwood *saus, lims* as hard as iron,
silk-cotton trees with thick white trunks, and giant *bang-langs*
which are used for making dug-out canoes.

A tangle of creepers draped the hospital in a natural camouflage net which was impenetrable to observation from the air.

From the straight white secondary road between Bac-Nhung
and Chiem-Hoa, which bordered it on the east, there was
nothing to betray its presence except for a few sentries posted
at the near end of the paths which were hidden by thick clumps
of bamboo.

The group of prisoners carrying Esclavier reached the hospital late in the evening. Esclavier was still alive but delirious. His
comrades were exhausted from their efforts. They had hurried
all the way and their legs trembled while a Viet orderly, trying
to impress them by wearing a gauze mask over his mouth,
looked with disgust at the patient they had laid down at his feet.

"*Tiet*," he said. "You may as well take him away."

"He's no more *tiet* than you are."

Dia appeared, wearing nothing but a pair of shorts, with his
muscular ebony torso, his slim waist, his sprinter's legs and his
powerful bass voice booming like a drum.

"What has he been treated for?" he asked Marindelle, as he bent over Esclavier.

"Malaria."

"He's got spirochetosis. My dear colleagues don't know how to use their eyes, they need laboratories and analyses, radio equipment and neatly labelled bottles of medicine. But since all these are lacking, they just throw up their hands in despair. They've stopped being proper doctors. Real doctors should be like wizards who possess the secrets of life and death, of plants, poisons and sex . . . I, Dia, have a number of secrets . . . even for curing spirochetosis."

"What do you use?" Glatigny asked.

"Bromide," Dia calmly replied, shrugging his massive shoulders. "It was a brainwave. There was nothing else available, so I thought of bromide. If I'd had any aspirin, I might have thought of aspirin . . . But above all I believe I inspire those who have thrown in the sponge with a will to live. My dear colleagues have a name for that: psychosomatosis. They give high-falutin names to whatever they don't understand.

"Bring the patient to that hut down there."

Captain Dia of the Medical Corps disappeared into a *canh-na* behind a screen.

"He's a bit of a crackpot, isn't he?" Merle asked Marindelle.

"Most of us owe our lives to his secrets. There are plants that he knows, but above all it's his love for mankind, for all men, and the life and strength he disseminates all round him. He's looking after Lescure . . . he may be able to save Esclavier."

"He has even made an impression on the Viets," said Orsini.

"Haven't they tried to work on him politically?" Boisfeuras asked.

"Dia's not like us," said Marindelle, "fragile and inconstant, uncertain of everything. He's a magnificent and generous life-force. I can't explain it more clearly, but he's neither white, nor Negro, nor a civilian, nor a soldier; he's a sort of benign power. What do you think the sterile, sexless Vietminh termites can do to him? Termites only attack dead trees."

Dia reappeared; he was sweating freely and scratching his crinkly hair.

"We might be able to save him," he said, "if he wants to be saved, but it won't be easy. Is he a new arrival? What's his name, Marindelle?"

"Captain Esclavier."

"Lescure has told me a lot about him—Captain Esclavier, the man who led him by the hand like a small child throughout the march."

"Lescure talks to you?" Glatigny asked.

"Certainly. He's not mad, you know . . . just a little strange. He's taken refuge in a sort of cocoon where he doesn't want to be disturbed by anyone. I'm very fond of him. He stays with me, where I can keep an eye on him."

"Can we see him?"

"Not yet. He's cured all right but he doesn't know it, he's got to get used to the idea. Off you go now, chaps. I'll take good care of Esclavier . . . because I appreciate what he did for Lescure. Marindelle, please tell Evrard that he might have sent him along a little sooner."

"It's Prosper."

"Sometimes," said Dia, "I dream that I've got my hands round his throat and that I'm squeezing, squeezing hard. Then I let go and he drops down dead. Prosper . . . and all his dirty politics which poison man's happiness."

He waved goodbye and went off to join Lescure in a small hut where he lived with him on the edge of the forest.

Lescure was cutting down a tree with a hatchet, humming under his breath as usual.

Dia came and squatted down beside him.

"What's that tune?" he asked.

"A Mozart concerto."

"Go on, I like it . . . Yes, I like it very much, but I couldn't sing it like that, I'd have to alter the beat. Go on, my lad, sing."

He picked up a wooden calabash, turned it upside down and started tapping out a jazz rhythm with the palm of his hand. Lescure sang louder and the marvellous, elegant music seemed to lend itself cheerfully to the big Negro's fanciful improvisation.

"There's something I'd like you to hear," said Dia. "Every now and then it comes back to me. It's music from the Sacred Forest, the music of my people, the Guerzés; it's the Nyomou or fetish song. I couldn't have been more than twelve when I last heard it, but I haven't forgotten it."

He started whistling through his teeth, beating time on the calabash. The sound he produced was plaintive, like the whimpering of a sick animal or an unhappy child, but accompanied by the deep resounding rhythm of the jungle, the rhythm of nature, overwhelming, savage and inexorable and at the same time serene and beguiling. It spread its arms wide to welcome men, beasts and plants alike in its warm embrace, to reduce them to their essential atoms and bring them back to life in the various forms adopted by the "vital force," as the Guerzés of the Sacred Forest called it.

"Your music's lovely," said Lescure, "but it lacks tenderness and sweetness, the sort of friendly gentleness of a human smile . . . What about Esclavier? You'll save him, won't you? You've got no idea how I hated him until I discovered what lay behind those grey eyes of his. Esclavier's rather like your music, your Nyomou song, the part you accompanied on the calabash. He's hard, relentless, tireless, completely unbowed, proud in his animal strength . . . but he's also an utterly pure, subtle and ancient melody . . . friendship and human affection . . . the violins in the 'Autumn' part of Vivaldi's 'Four Seasons.'"

"You express yourself extremely well!"

"All I can do is talk or make music, but I don't know how to fight like Esclavier, or how to cure like you . . ."

"You don't enjoy fighting?"

"No, neither the noise of the guns, nor the whistle of the bullets, nor the mangled corpses, nor the waving flags . . ."

"And you don't want to remember . . ."

"But I don't remember any more."

"Let's have something to eat, then I'll go and see Esclavier. If I can keep him alive for two more days, he's saved."

"Will you speak to him?"

"No, he wouldn't hear me. But I'll be near him, within arm's reach. What he really needs is a woman at his bedside all the time. I'm going to ask for a nurse."

It was comrade nurse Souen-Cuan of the 22nd First Aid Section at Thanh-Hoa who was detailed by the director of the hospital, as much on account of her knowledge of French as by virtue of her sound political education. She was a pure product of the Vinh training establishments. She wore uniform tunic and trousers, both several sizes too big, and a *bo-doi*'s fibre helmet from which two long plaits escaped. In spite of this garb and her abrupt and bossy manner she was beautiful, for her beauty lay in the purity and delicacy of her features and the harmony and elegance of her gestures.

The first task Dia gave her was to cut the patient's hair, shave him, make him drink a mouthful of tea every half-hour and a spoonful of bromide every two hours. But Souen demanded that the Vietminh doctor should confirm this treatment, for it was scarcely to be believed that a man who was not a Communist should know anything about medicine or even have access to any form of knowledge whatsoever.

The Vietminh doctor was extremely flattered; he congratulated "his little sister" but nevertheless asked her to obey the medical officer who, in spite of his primitive methods, sometimes obtained excellent results. In any case she would quickly be relieved of her task, since the prisoner had no more than a few hours to live.

Souen raised Esclavier's head, opened his chapped lips and poured a little tea between his clenched teeth. His face was covered in a heavy growth of beard. His hollow cheeks threw his jaw and cheek-bones into sharp relief. He could scarcely open his burning, bloodshot eyes; racked with fever, he could no longer articulate, while his body, which day by day lost more and more of its substance, was reduced to a sort of skeleton under a tightly stretched, orange-coloured skin.

As she touched him, however, Souen felt a faint indefinable tremor, which she attributed to her fatigue or the heat. This was the first time she had been put in charge of a white man, and she had been warned that this particular one had been an extremely dangerous type before his claws had been blunted by disease.

Esclavier had a sort of spasm which contracted his limbs. With a jerk of his foot he threw back the bedclothes. He was stark naked except for a filthy, stained slip which concealed his private parts. Souen realized how strong and vigorous he must have been. His chest was hairless, his wrists and ankles slender. As she pulled back the bedclothes, she noticed several scars on his chest and thighs. She could not refrain from touching one of these with her finger.

Her sister Ngoc at Hanoi had once had a lover who was a white man like this one. She lived with him in a villa with a garden and when he came back from the war they used to give little parties to which they invited Frenchmen and their wives or their Vietnamese girl-friends. Little Japanese lanterns were hung among the trees; there was music; there were sweet things to eat, preserved ginger and papaw salad.

Ngoc and all her friends were nothing but strumpets. One day the soldiers of the People's Army had killed the major who lived with her sister. Ngoc had been so besotted with him that she had refused to marry the son of the governor of Tonkin and had gone off to live with another white man. She was nothing but a cat in heat, who had no other thought in her head, who mewed in the dark when making love.

Perhaps this man who was lying here and whom she was tending had been to her sister's parties, perhaps he had even held her in his arms . . .

One night in Hanoi the major had introduced her to a swarthy, bandy-legged little lieutenant with an overpowering smell. When he had tried to lay hands on her, Souen had sent him off with a flea in his ear. Then she had packed her few belongings and gone off to Hai-Duong to stay with a girl-friend who belonged to the Vietminh organization. First of all she had done a spell with the Du-Kits and, since she spoke good French, she had been detailed to pick up drunken legionaries and try to buy their arms or induce them to desert. On two occasions she had narrowly missed being raped and one night it was only by a miracle that she escaped from a police patrol. Her partisan comrades also tried to sleep with her and on three or four occasions she had had to give in to them, because they accused her of being an aristocrat and a reactionary and of reserving herself for the caresses and slender hands of a mandarin's son.

She had developed an absolute horror of everything to do with men and sex and it was with profound relief that she had joined the regular army where chastity was the rule.

Souen tried to imagine how Esclavier must have looked before his illness and what she would have done if the major had introduced her to him instead of to the runtish little lieutenant. She dismissed this absurd thought from her mind. He was an enemy of the Vietnamese people, a colonial mercenary, and it was only because President Ho had advocated a policy of leniency that she was looking after him.

On the evening of the ninth day of his illness Esclavier had an internal haemorrhage. Souen was wiping the bunk clean with cold water when Dia, accompanied by the doctor in charge of the hospital, looked in. They were both laughing, because the Negro even managed to make the little Asiatic unbend and made him forget his old resentment as a medical student in Saigon who used to fall asleep over his books from sheer fatigue and as an underpaid doctor on a plantation in Cambodia who was only allowed to look after the coolies. Besides, Dia was a Negro, a member of a race that was exploited by the whites, and the instructions about him were explicit: in spite of the failure they had so far encountered, they were to persevere in their attempts to indoctrinate him in the hope of winning him over to the Communist cause.

Thanks to these many pretexts, Doctor Nguyen-Van-Tach was able to indulge in an occasional display of friendship before resuming the inflexible mask of a Vietminh director.

Dia looked at the bloodstained rags and drew closer to the patient.

"How do you feel this evening?"

In the interval between two bouts of fever it sometimes happened that Esclavier recovered his full lucidity. He would then lie hunched up under the bedclothes, motionless and silent. With an effort the captain would muster all his strength and try to fight the illness. But like those fragile banks of sand that children build on the seashore and which the tide eventually comes and sweeps away, the powerful waves of the fever likewise destroyed his last defences and dragged him back into the furnace in which his memories, his resentments, his hopes and his strength were all consumed in flickering red flames.

Dia put his hand on his forehead, and at once he felt a sense of relief, as though another child had come to help him build his dam. The Negro repeated his question:

"How do you feel?"

What remained of Esclavier made an effort to speak and to smile. He started off by swallowing hard, then managed to utter the words:

"I'm thirsty, I'm always thirsty, but I keep bringing up whatever I drink."

Dia burst into a loud guffaw:

"You'll be better tomorrow."

Souen left the room with the doctor in charge and Dia. The Negro was scratching his head and had become extremely solemn, which gave an innocent and at the same time sly expression to his face.

"He's been passing blood, hasn't he, Miss Souen?"

She felt she should defend her patient:

"This evening was the very first time."

"God Almighty, they brought him here too late. Intestinal haemorrhages are the final symptoms of spirochetosis. I've never seen anyone survive who's reached that stage."

Dia turned to the doctor in charge:

"Miss Souen will have to stay with the patient all night to give him something to drink at regular intervals. She's got a certain way with her."

"Comrade Souen," the Viet replied, "will certainly volunteer for this additional task. She knows her duty as a militant and has pledged herself to our cause body and soul and once and for all."

He delivered this little speech with unconcealed self-satisfaction. He looked to see if it had made any impression, but the big Negro remained impervious, his thoughts elsewhere. He was running over in his mind everything he knew about this illness, every treatment that had been discovered. None of them was available here, and in any case it was now too late. He hung his head and felt the sharp pang that occurred every time death got the better of life and snatched one of his patients from him. He was a Christian at heart but he still vaguely believed in the old animist legends and felt that every creature that died diminished the sum total of the "vital force" of the entire universe. Some of his own strength would be taken from him when Esclavier strained for the last time to expel what life he had left. He would also lose a comrade, and he had an extremely profound sense of solidarity. Between themselves Negroes called one another brother, but Dia also called many white men brother.

In the early hours of the morning Esclavier's temperature went up again and Souen remembered what the black doctor had said . . . The Frenchman was going to die . . . unless . . . But she hadn't the right to think of that.

It was amoebic dysentery the patient had, since he was passing blood; she knew this, she didn't have to be a doctor for that.

In the director's medicine chest there were some of those long brown phials that cure dysentery; they contained emetine. But emetine was in short supply, it was reserved for the soldiers of the People's Army.

Esclavier started moaning again. She wiped the sweat off his forehead with a damp cloth. His features were drawn; he was battling with death all by himself, battling with the big black fisherman of legend who haunted the sunny beaches of Annam with the souls of men in his net. She was there to help him, and she was doing nothing. But she had not the right to do anything, not even to believe in the big fisherman.

Once again she wiped his forehead and tried to force his teeth open to make him swallow a drop of tea.

The emetine was reserved for the soldiers of the People's Army; this was as it should be, for they had to fight without aircraft, without medical facilities against the wealthy soldiers defending imperialism. But President Ho had decreed a policy of leniency . . .

Esclavier gave a sort of violent hiccup; Souen thought he was going to die and she felt overwhelmed with sorrow as though someone very dear to her was about to be snatched away: her father, her mother . . . No, this was different, it was something even stronger. Then the patient recovered his breath.

She tried desperately to find a solution:

"I'll go and see the director; I have done my duty by him, he has confidence in me; I shall ask him, as an exceptional favour, for a phial of emetine. He won't be able to deny me this. Yes, but he's not here; he's asleep, he's tired, I can't wake him up for something so unimportant. I shall report to him tomorrow. Anyway there will soon be peace, and medicines will start arriving from all four corners of the earth."

Souen hurried across to the infirmary; she was blinded by the gusts of rain which twice tore the helmet off her head.

She lit her way by switching her electric torch on and off, as she had been taught, so as not to waste the battery.

When she got back, she had the precious phial clutched in her damp hand. She took a syringe and a needle out of her first-aid box and by the light of a candle-end heated up some water on the open fire.

The water took a long time to boil. She felt like screaming with impatience; the patient was liable to die at any moment. She blew frantically on the embers. Outside, the monsoon burst into a steady downpour.

Eventually she managed to give the injection and Esclavier immediately seemed more comfortable and began to breathe more regularly again.

The downpour had also abated slightly; it had lost its aspect of violence and fury and the myriad drops of rain tapping on the roof of the hut sounded almost friendly. The fire flickered and slowly died down, still throwing off a gleam or two which flared over the thin partitions and over the patient's face, that emaciated mask in which the eyes formed two dark cavities.

Souen felt happy; at the bedside of this man whose very name was unknown to her, this man of an alien race, she experienced a feeling of joy of which she had never before suspected the existence.

With her little wicker fan she slowly swept the thick air

above the prisoner's face and smiled. He was hers, for she had saved him, of that she was certain, little knowing that emetine had no effect at all on spirochetosis. One day peace would come and they would meet again. He would be strong and upstanding again, the finest, strongest white man in the world. Then she would tell him how for his sake she had stolen the precious phial.

Her misgivings returned, but gently, like the sound of the rain, and, like the rain, they seemed to share her secret.

Souen had made the *tou-bi* a gift of her first fault against the Party, almost as though it was her virginity. As a result of this she felt vaguely distressed and at the same time filled with wonder.

When Dia came back the following morning, Esclavier was asleep and still being attended by an exhausted and radiant little Miss Souen. He put a hand on the patient's forehead and felt his pulse. The fever had abated. With a final effort, by summoning up all his strength, Esclavier had managed to reach the threshold of the tenth day.

Dia felt like laughing out loud, singing and dancing. Death had been warded off, humanity was the richer by a man's strength. That night he had prayed to the Lord for Esclavier's soul and all the time the Lord, with a great chuckle, was busy curing the captain. He was immensely pleased.

"He's saved," Dia told the nurse. "I can't get over it. He saved himself all on his own, without my medicine . . ."

"Don't you think . . ."

She stopped short. For the pleasure of scoring over the black man, she had almost revealed her theft of the emetine.

When Dia bent over Esclavier to examine him more closely, she started forward as though intent on defending her patient. Dia looked at the girl and was astonished to see that she was no longer an insect, that there was something warm, triumphant emanating from her, that her eyes sparkled and her nostrils quivered. Life was coursing once more through her veins.

"It can't be possible," Dia said to himself. "She's showing every symptom of being in love!"

In the four years he had been at this hospital he had never seen such a thing: a Vietminh woman falling for a prisoner.

He felt like being very gentle with her, calling her "little sister" and telling her to be extremely careful because she risked death, and Esclavier as well, if anything occurred between them. For the moment Esclavier was quite incapable of doing the least thing, but she, Souen, was aglow with love; it was as visible as a firefly in the dark.

When he went back to Lescure, Dia was singing. He seized the slender lieutenant by the elbows and dandled him in the air like a child:

"Two miracles have happened," he chanted. "Blessed be the Holy Virgin and all the angels and all the demons of hell. Esclavier should have died last night; this morning he's alive, alive and kicking, his fever's almost gone; and that little brute Souen has fallen in love with him and is beaming like a candle. Love has come into the big Vietminh hospital of Thu-Vat for the first time, like a ray of sunshine on the termites. Perhaps they'll all die of it."

By the evening Esclavier was much better. He no longer brought everything up and cheerfully gulped down every cup of tea that Souen made him. Dia brought him a tin of condensed milk which he was keeping for a special occasion. It still bore the label: "Gift of the American Red Cross."

When Souen came back next morning, she found that the captain, while attempting to sit up, had fallen off his bunk. Stark naked, with one elbow resting on an emaciated leg, he looked sheepish and at the same time furious. She could not help laughing.

"Well, well, well," said Esclavier, "that's the first time I've heard you laugh. I thought you all had something cut out of your throats."

She helped him climb back on to his bunk and experienced a fresh tremor as she felt Esclavier's arm round her shoulder. She tried to reason with him:

"That's not very nice of you, Eclapier . . ."

The captain peevishly corrected the pronunciation of his name:

"Esclavier. Captain Philippe Esclavier of the 4th Colonial Parachute Battalion . . ."

"There are no captains here, or paratroops. There are just

tou-bis, prisoners to whom we're applying President Ho's policy of leniency . . ."

"Oh, balls!"

Exhausted, the captain fell asleep. Souen pulled the bedclothes over him and ran her fingers over his forehead. He was called Philippe. She repeated the name: Philippe . . . Philippe . . . He had big grey eyes, as luminous as the sea on certain mornings in the Baie d'Along. For a moment she imagined herself sleeping in his arms, like her sister with the major, then instantly dismissed the idea. Philippe was just a *tou-bi*, an enemy of her people.

That evening Souen attended the political education meeting which was held once a week for the personnel of the hospital under the presidency of the director, Doctor Nguyen-Van-Tach, a member of the Central Committee.

As usual, the meeting began with a collective self-examination undertaken by Nguyen-Van-Tach. He reproached himself in the name of his comrades for the insufficient efficiency of the hospital and emphasized the fact that even if the armistice was signed at Geneva, the struggle would go on until every vestige of capitalism disappeared from the earth.

Some of the participants then accused themselves of minor faults, promised to make amends and made solemn resolutions that were utterly out of proportion to their misdemeanours. The usual routine.

Souen was sitting in the front row and for the first time the doctor noticed how beautiful she was: a butterfly that had just emerged from its chrysalis and was stretching its new wings in the sun.

All the desires he had suppressed since he had joined the People's Army—high-spirited young girls, iced beer, unreserved friendships with men like Dia, the click of mah-jong pieces in Chinese shops—came flooding back like a whiff of magnolia on a June evening in Pnom-Penh. He would have liked to hold Souen tight in his arms and caress her long eyelashes with his lips.

He mastered his emotion and cleared his throat.

"I must congratulate our comrade Souen," he said, "for the great forbearance with which she has looked after a prisoner in spite of the disgust and contempt this mercenary inspired in her . . ."

"No," said Souen.

There was a heavy silence. One never protested when praise was meted out to one but, on the contrary, it was customary to lower one's eyes and assume a modest, startled air of embarrassment.

"No, Comrade Tach, I'm not worthy of your praise. It's my duty to inform you that in the course of this task I committed a serious fault. In your absence, when the *tou-bi* was going to die, I took it on myself to take a phial of emetine and inject him with it. My pride tempted me to put my own interpretation on President Ho's directives on the policy of leniency . . . But today you have made me aware of my fault, for I should have known this medicine was reserved for our valiant combatants. I beg leave to be removed from my post."

Souen had spoken on the spur of the moment, to be relieved of her sin, and she was already regretting it, for she was going to be separated from her *tou-bi*.

Doctor Nguyen scrutinized his audience but no one showed either anger or compassion. They were all waiting for him to give a sign of the one or the other. Souen was really gorgeous, sitting bolt upright, her face raised towards him, offering herself for punishment.

He had some difficulty in assuming the injured tone to suit the occasion:

"Comrade Souen, I must give you a severe reprimand. I see, however, that you recognize the gravity of your fault. Your past record and political background speak for the purity of your intention. I feel partly responsible myself for having allotted you these extra tasks which might have warped your judgement to such an extent that you allowed yourself to put your own interpretation on our beloved leader's decisions. You will remain in your post and deal with the *tou-bis* instead of tending our glorious combatants. That will be your punishment."

Only then did everyone manifest his compassion.

"I shall be seeing Philippe again," Souen said to herself, "I shall be with him every day."

A thrill of delight ran through her.

Next day Dia, for whom the walls of the hospital had ears, heard all about it. He discussed it with Lescure.

"That silly little Souen might have killed Esclavier with her emetine! Emetine jolts the heart; and now she believes she saved him. She's as blindly in love as a schoolgirl. It will turn out badly for her in the end, badly for both of them perhaps. Have you ever been in love, Lescure?"

Lescure bent his head over the piece of bamboo he was carving into a shepherd's flute:

"A cousin of mine. I told her and she started squirming about in her chair as though she was sitting on a packet of pins. And she laughed and laughed . . . After that, only tarts. I was quite popular at the Panier Fleuri in Hanoi. I used to play the piano for them. Esclavier's a lucky dog!"

Dia peeled a banana pensively.

"I'm very fond of you," he said all of a sudden. "I'd like to keep you here with me. We're left in peace, we only talk when we feel like talking. You'll soon be able to play me that flute of yours. But the director of the hospital is beginning to think you're not so very mad. He's talking of sending you back to Camp One."

"But I am mad, Dia. I can show him."

"I'll bring him in for a consultation. We'll arrange a little scene for him."

Next day, when Dr. Nguyen-Van-Tach came into the hut, Lescure pretended to be asleep. He woke up with a start:

"Boy," he shouted, "*mau-len*! Make tea at once, I shout for you the whole time, you good-for-nothing!"

Dia crept up behind the director with a bowl of tea.

"He's very over-excited this evening. Here, hand him the tea, I've put some bromide in it."

"Come on, boy, *mau-len*!"

Nguyen-Van-Tach was furious. Dia gently reasoned with him:

"Come, sir, he's mad, and you're a doctor . . . an excellent doctor, moreover. Hand him this bowl of tea. He doesn't know you have beaten the French Army at Dien-Bien-Phu."

"I'd like you to cure him so that he learns. It's really too easy a position."

"Madness is often an easy solution for those who take refuge in it."

And thus it was that Lescure stayed on at the hospital and was served tea by the director.

Esclavier quickly recovered his strength. His skin lost its strange colour. In addition to his improved "régime" rations, Souen brought him fruit, guavas and slices of fresh pineapple, and enriched his rice with chicken or sometimes little chunks of fat pork cooked in sugar.

Relieved by her confession and by the absolution that had followed, she devoted herself whole-heartedly to her nursing duties, little realizing that her attitude towards the prisoner was that of a *congai* in love. She forgot all her Marxist vocabulary and the "peace of the people" to ask him more personal questions.

"What is Paris like?"

Esclavier tried to think.

"It's very beautiful and very dirty, very rich and very poor, There's a wood on either side of it: Vincennes where the poor go, Boulogne which is for the rich."

"And where did you go?"

"To the Luxembourg, where the students go—who are poor, but who all believe that one day they'll be rich and famous."

"Are French girls pretty?"

"Today's the 18th July, isn't it? The beaches will be crowded with golden-skinned girls, laughing, splashing about in the water, playing with rubber balls, who are in love, or believe they are, or pretend they are. When they come back from the beach, they put on bright-coloured dresses and reflectively sip long iced drinks while pretending to understand a boring boy who talks to them about Sartre but who has gentle eyes. And it's his eyes they look at. Our lovely young French girls don't know there's a war going on."

He suddenly looked at the little Vietnamese girl with her plaits, her collar buttoned up to her chin, in her dull-green uniform:

"But you're also lovely, Souen, you're also golden-skinned . . . and you're at war!"

"I'm at war for my people."

"Our pretty girls dance, drink, eat, play in the sun and make love for the sole pleasure of their selfish bodies."

He was lying on his bunk, propped up on his elbows, with his head resting in his hands; and through his mind scampered the slender girls of his country, the merry, eager girls tasting of sugar and vinegar.

Souen squatted by the head of the bed. Esclavier turned towards her and gently stroked her hair. He felt deep affection and friendship for his little Vietnamese sister in uniform who was suffocating with him in this hut among the blazing limestones, who, like him, had known war and all its horrors and who had been moved by human suffering. To make her ugly, she had been given a helmet and tunic several sizes too big for her, and her magnificent hair had been knotted into two long plaits which hung down to her shoulders. She had been forbidden to be a woman.

Esclavier drew Souen closer to him and her cheek brushed against his. She gave a little sob and shut her eyes. She was trembling from head to foot and she felt as if she was drowning in an emerald-green sea which was warm and cool at one and the same time; then everything seemed as simple as love, as simple as death.

She loved her *tou-bi*; her defences were down. She would do whatever he wished. She would risk death in order to please him; she would steal to get him better food; she would escape with him if he asked her. She would be his little *congai*, like her sister with the major, and if ever he left her she would kill herself.

She ran her damp finger over the captain's brow and the last memory she had of him was his big grey eyes and the desire she fancied she read in them. In fact it was only astonishment.

A *bo-doi* had come to tell Souen that the director wanted her. He had thrust his head through the door of the hut and had seen her with her cheek against the *tou-bi*'s; he had witnessed her treachery against the people when she had caressed him. He had crept away without a sound to notify his superiors.

Souen rose to her feet.

"I'm going to fetch your meal," she said, "I'll be back at once."

"She's a nice little thing," Esclavier said to himself. "When I'm released, I must try and send her a little present."

But it was a *bo-doi* who brought him his meal.

Doctor Nguyen-Van-Tach had called a meeting of the camp vigilance committee to interrogate Souen. They were eight in number, including three women, and the meeting was held in a hut with an armed guard outside the door.

Souen faced them, standing bareheaded and stiffly to attention.

The *bo-doi* who had caught her out delivered his evidence.

Yes, he had seen Comrade Souen pressed amorously against the prisoner; yes, she had certainly stroked his face. Did he think sexual intercourse had previously taken place between them? No, he did not think so. Comrade Souen had her uniform jacket buttoned up and the prisoner just had his arm round her shoulder.

The head nurse rose to her feet.

"Can you state, Comrade Souen, that you have never had the slightest sexual intercourse with the prisoner Esclavier?"

"Yes, I can."

"Yet because of him you stole a phial of emetine?"

"Yes."

"Were you . . ." she hesitated before uttering the horrible, obscene word ". . . in love with him?"

"Yes."

Doctor Nguyen broke in. Once again he was anxious to save the little fool and tried to help her.

"This prisoner, who is classified as a dangerous type, tried to take advantage of you in a moment of weakness, was that it?"

"No. He doesn't come into it, he doesn't even know I love him. I was the one who leant over him, I was the one who caressed him, just as the *bo-doi* told you."

The head nurse broke in again in her icy, insinuating, knowing voice:

"Comrade Souen, think carefully now before answering. Would your waywardness have led you to commit the sexual act with the prisoner?"

Souen dropped her deferential attitude towards this dried-up, hypocritical, ignoble old woman who had always hated her:

"Yes, comrade, I would have done it. I would have lain down beside him and since I am young and pretty he would have made love to me."

"And for that infamous physical contact which is punishable by death . . ."

"It's not an infamous contact, it's love."

"For this infamous contact you were prepared to betray the confidence of your people, and of the Party and the army . . ."

"I wouldn't have betrayed anyone. I love this man; I'm only happy when I'm by his side. If you gave me my freedom I would go back to him. I don't know what's happened, but apart from him nothing else exists . . ."

"Do you repent?" the director asked.

"Repent?"

She looked absolutely amazed.

"But how can a woman repent of being in love?"

Nguyen could do nothing more for her. To have interceded again would have appeared suspicious. He made a proposal that Souen should be expelled from the Party forthwith and sent to a re-education camp for an indefinite period of time. This was tantamount to a death-sentence. No one, man or woman, white or Vietnamese, had ever returned from those forced labour camps. Souen knew this. It was one of those things that were discussed in undertones in the divisions.

The proposal was accepted by the majority. The members of the committee withdrew and for a moment Doctor Tach was left alone with Souen.

"I wanted to help you," he told her, "and avoid such a severe measure being taken against you. But if you mend your ways, in a few months you may be reprieved."

"Doctor Tach, I'd like to see him just once more. He must be asleep now, he won't even notice. Just once more . . ."

"No, that's absolutely out of the question."

"It was nothing to do with him; he mustn't be punished. Promise me you won't take any action against him."

"We shall hold a court of inquiry . . ."

"Promise me, Doctor Tach. I was very fond of you; you're the only one I was fond of in the whole of this camp."

"I promise."

Souen seized his hand and kissed it before he had time to snatch it back. Two sentries came and marched her off.

Nguyen-Van-Tach went on sitting with his head between his hands, trying to sort the matter out in his mind. Souen had made the ancient womanly gesture of submission; she no longer behaved like a Vietminh girl; she had recovered her allure and her beauty. He himself had been aware of her attraction. All this, because she had fallen in love.

It would be difficult to establish Communism completely as long as men and women still existed, with their instincts and their passions, their beauty and their youth. In the old days the Chinese used to bind their women's feet to make them smaller; that was the fashion; it must have had some religious or erotic significance. Now, in the name of Communism, they bound the whole human frame, they frustrated and distorted it.

That also might be nothing but a fashion. Souen had discovered love and kicked everything else overboard, recovering at the same time her freedom of action and speech. A fashion! To kill thousands of creatures in the name of a fashion! To disrupt their lives and habits until one day someone would speak up and declare that Communism was out of fashion!

Nguyen had some difficulty in dismissing these unwelcome thoughts from his mind. He had his job to do as a doctor. He was a good doctor, Dia had said so. He loved his country; even as a child he had dreamt of its independence. That was something positive. That wasn't just a fashion.

On the following day Dia, accompanied by Lescure, came and fetched Esclavier. They helped him to walk to their hut and settled him in.

Dia did not come back until after dark and was a little tipsy when he arrived. He had got hold of a bottle of *choum*, a crude rice spirit produced by the Mans who lived below the hospital, for which he had bartered a few tablets of quinine.

"We must drink," he said, ". . . all three of us . . . Because a little light has gone out in the camp. Drink up, Esclavier, it's because of you, though it's not your fault. Drink up, Lescure, my lad, and play us that flute you made. Play what went on in your head when your little cousin laughed at you because you were in love with her. And I'll sing—I, Dia, the Negro, with all my university degrees. I'll sing like a man of my people to exorcize the evil fetish, the curse that lies on us, because the little light has been snuffed out."

"Dia, what are you talking about?" Esclavier inquired.

"Little Souen—they've sent her to a concentration camp because she was in love with a handsome *tou-bi*. For his sake she had stolen a phial of emetine. A *bo-doi* caught her kissing him and denounced her. But she was so proud of her love that she refused to repent and spat in their faces like an angry cat."

"Dia, I didn't even notice it!"

"Of course not! Drink up, Esclavier. Doctor Tach told me you won't get into trouble. That was her last request before being marched off by the *bo-dois*: that you should be spared. Nguyen would also like to get drunk tonight. But he can't. He daren't admit it even to himself, but he was also in love with Souen. Love is catching, it might have spread through the hospital, then the camp, then the whole Vietminh. So quick, out with that little light!

"When I was a little bush nigger, a bearded missionary came and took me by the hand. He was called Father Teissèdre. I served Mass for him; he taught me to read and write. Then, as he loved the jungle, our customs, our songs, our secrets, he used to come with me and visit the sorcerers and witch-doctors, those who slay the Prince of the Dance with a golden arrow every seven years and those who fasten iron talons to their hands to play at panther-men.

"Before knowing him, as a naked little nigger-boy, I used to tremble with fear. But when he held my little black paw in his great hairy fist, I was no longer scared of the fetishes or poisons. Father Teissèdre was love: the love of the Negroes, of the white men, of the whole world; he was stranger than all the fetishes and witch-doctors and political commissars . . .

"One day he came into an inheritance: a farm in his native Auvergne. He sold it to pay for my education . . . In the name of love, in the name of Father Teissèdre, to hell with the Vietminh!"

He took a great gulp of the rice spirit.

"The Vietminh and all those who deny love and mystery and gods, who block their ears so as not to hear the joyful and bewitching tomtoms of nature, sex and life, all those will be found dead one morning and no one will know why. When they've snuffed out all the lights, they'll fall flat on their backs and die . . ."

And Dia the magnificent, dead drunk, fell flat on his back himself, while there rose in the clammy, stifling darkness the sweet, clear melody of Lescure's shepherd's flute.

9

THE YELLOW INFECTION

After delivering Esclavier at the hospital, the team of stretcher-bearers under the leadership of Marindelle made their way back to Camp One by easy stages.

As soon as they were away from their chiefs, the three *bo-dois* who made up the escort became carefree, cheerful and friendly with the prisoners, from whom they could only be distinguished by the weapons which encumbered them. They merely attended to the evening meal, which they made a point of preparing themselves, for the *tou-bis* were no good at cooking the rice which had to come out of the pot after twenty minutes' simmering, hot, dry and each grain separate. The "newcomers" would have willingly prolonged this holiday-camp existence, but Marindelle, Orsini and Leroy told them they had to be back in camp by 14 July.

"Anyway," said Leroy, "we've only got enough rice to last up to the twelfth."

Parodying the Voice, Marindelle explained:

"The 14th of July is the feast of the liberation and brotherhood of the masses. The French people, our friends, who are fighting by our side in the camp of Peace, were the first to shake off the yoke of tyranny and feudalism on the 14th July 1789. The Bolshevik revolution of 1917 completed this task of liberation. These are the great dates of humanity on the path of progress and in the historical sense . . ."

Marindelle resumed his normal voice:

"Therefore, by way of celebration, on the 14th July 1954 rations will be doubled all round provided we put on a big show with lectures, news bulletins, self-examinations at every level, both national and individual, manifestoes and motions, choirs and orchestras, theatrical productions and I don't know what else . . . A show that's not to be missed, calories to be built up, and perhaps the announcement of our release."

They reached camp on 13 July, shortly before the midday meal.

The parade ground was already decorated with banners in honour of every liberation movement, denouncing every form of constraint and imperialism, and cursing every Bastille and every prison.

Merle, with his hands in the pockets of his shorts, his beret tipped forward over his nose, and his nose sniffing the wind, was on the prowl for "news items." He wanted, he said, to write a full report on the preparations and the event itself for the camp newspaper.

At the slaughter-house he saw four skinny goats fastened to two stakes, some chickens and ducks for those on the "régime," and two pigs whose exact weight he noted down for the sake of accuracy. They had to be weighed on old-fashioned bamboo scales. One came to just over seventy pounds, the other to almost eighty.

He went and interviewed the camp commandant who told him that for 14 July the prisoners would be issued, in addition to their rice in lard and lentils, with a supplementary ration of goat in sauce, rice and molasses, and half an ounce of salt per man.

He exaggerated these items of news as he saw fit, spoke of pigs weighing the best part of three hundred pounds and whole flocks of goats, and hinted that the Viets who had just discovered a store of wine-concentrate were going to dole out a quart to every man in the camp . . .

Merle's article was a great success. He decided that once he was free he would embark on a journalistic career.

Marindelle then assembled his team.

"We must all contribute," he told them, "within the limit of our means and our imagination, to the celebrations organized for the 14th July. The afternoon meeting will be brought to a close by the adoption of a manifesto addressed to the French

people which will be broadcast on the Vietminh radio and reported in France in *l'Humanité*. This manifesto has been
drafted by some of the old hands; I did a certain amount of
work on it myself and you can count on us. There's nothing
missing; we've even made sure of just the right amount of exag-
geration to make anyone with any sense in his head howl with
laughter. Needless to say, all the old hands will be only too eager to sign it, and also a large number of the newcomers."

Marindelle was pacing up and down in front of his comrades who sat squatting on their heels.

"Nevertheless, in order to prove the sincerity of our feelings,
it wouldn't be a bad thing if some of you refused to sign this
manifesto. I therefore propose to distribute the various roles
we have to play. When the Voice calls on you individually for
your official signature, you will all read through the text with
the utmost care and if necessary ask a few judicious questions
before putting your name to the manifesto. Captain Glatigny
who is looked upon as a 'feudalist'—that's written down in his
file, I've seen it—obviously can't be expected to sign. So you'll
declare, sir, if you don't mind, of course:

"'I am an aristocrat and the son of an aristocrat, a pupil of
the Jesuits and a French officer. During the last few weeks,
thanks to the humiliation of defeat, I have become aware that
my heredity, my background and my profession have corrupted the man in me. I now recognize the bestial selfishness
of my class. But I have not yet been completely stripped of my
inheritance of false ideas. If you order me to do it, I am quite
prepared to sign this text with which I heartily agree in so far
as it concerns the peace and brotherhood of the masses. But I
am not convinced by the rest of it and I should feel I was deceiving you if I did not confess what doubts I have on this
score.'

"Assume the proper tone of voice and an air of modesty
combined with a certain forthright endeavour that suggests
your regret at not being able to fall in completely with the
fighters for Peace. After that, confide in the Voice who, with
tears of joy in his eyes, will take the pen out of your hand and

urge you to persevere with your re-education which has started so well. Shall we rehearse it together?"

"No, Marindelle," said Glatigny, "I do not care to lie, not even to an enemy."

Marindelle's voice became as dry as Glatigny's:

"I must remind you, sir, that you are still at war; what I'm asking you to do is an act of war. It's something more subtle but infinitely more realistic than a cavalry charge."

Boisfeuras broke in.

"Marindelle's right, Glatigny. Perhaps this role doesn't appeal to you because in your case there's a certain amount of truth in it?"

Glatigny made an effort to speak in a detached tone but he felt the anger welling up inside him.

"Would you kindly explain exactly what you mean by that, Boisfeuras?"

"You have recognized the failure of your class, the feudalism of generals and staff officers to which you belong. Which makes you so grumpy that you lose all sense of subtlety and self-control."

Glatigny gradually calmed down:

"You must forgive me, Marindelle. You're right, my re-education is still not complete. You ask me to perform an act of war and as such I shall do it . . . to the best of my ability. In my military career I've been required to do a number of unpleasant things, and this is one of them."

"I've been having to do unpleasant things for the last four years," Marindelle gently replied.

"I shan't sign all that crap," Pinières declared.

Orsini took him to task for this, and his voice suddenly betrayed the inflexions of his native Corsica:

"Don't be a nitwit, it's the surest way of letting your family know you're still alive."

"I happen to have worked with the Commies, when I was in the F.T.P. They're not such bloody fools as that; they know what I'm like and they realize I'm hardly likely to take part in their little games again."

"All the more reason," said Marindelle. "Your name on the list will act as a further disclaimer."

"Do you really hate them as much as all that?" Boisfeuras asked Marindelle.

"I sometimes admire their courage and endurance; they're fortunate in having a faith; I've even got a certain weakness for the Voice, I've hoodwinked him so often. I realize that many of their methods are valid and that we ought to adapt ourselves to their form of warfare in order to get the better of them.

"It's difficult to explain exactly, but it's rather like bridge as compared to *belote*. When we make war, we play *belote* with thirty-two cards in the pack. But their game is bridge and they have fifty-two cards: twenty more than we do. Those twenty cards short will always prevent us from getting the better of them. They've got nothing to do with traditional warfare, they're marked with the sign of politics, propaganda, faith, agrarian reform . . .

"What's biting Glatigny?"

"I think he's beginning to realize that we've got to play with fifty-two cards and he doesn't like it at all . . . Those twenty extra cards aren't at all to his liking."

The 14th July festivities were a great success. For several hours the prisoners forgot their circumstances.

There was a civilian in the camp. He had been there for two years. The Vietminh had captured him in the Moyenne Région while he was going round from post to post selling odds and ends. He was about thirty years old, with a little moustache, and was for ever taking his notebook out of his pocket and totting up rows of figures. He was working out all the money he would have earned if, instead of being a poor wretched civilian, he had been a soldier whose pay was accumulating in a post office savings' account.

Sometimes he shyly asked one of the officers:

"The Vietminh have put me in the same camp as you; they therefore regard me as a military prisoner and an officer. On this score I may be entitled to an officer's pay. I've lost everything. I even owe some money to a Chinaman. No? You don't think I'll be considered as an officer? My truck which they burnt was worth 40,000 piastres, the contents 100,000 piastres, and they took all the ready cash I had on me: 60,000 piastres . . ."

The prisoners were hoping that at the evening meeting they would be informed that the war was over. But the Voice made no announcement. The prisoners went back to their *canh-nas*, weighed down with disappointment.

The fortnight that followed was one of the gloomiest periods of their whole captivity. The instruction sessions brought the same old news of the Geneva negotiations which were dragging on interminably. A rumour sometimes spread through the camp in a matter of minutes and brought all the prisoners out of their huts: "American marines have just landed at Haiphong and two units of Chinese volunteers are concentrating on Mon-Kay and Lang-Son . . ."

The old hands discussed the news with a sort of disillusioned philosophical attitude, while the newcomers at once drew dramatic conclusions from it: they were going to be sent to China, they would never be released.

Some of them came and saw Glatigny, hoping he would still know all about the intentions of G.H.Q.

"What do you think?" they would ask the C.-in-C.'s former A.D.C.

Glatigny refused to cheat in order to reassure his comrades.

"The internationalization of the war is a solution which has never been completely excluded. The French in Indo-China are fighting against the entire Communist world. It would thus be logical if the nations of the free world stepped in, as they did in Korea."

"So you believe that the marines have really landed?"

"It would mean that the Geneva conference has broken down."

"In that case we ought to try and escape at the first opportunity," said Pinières. "Who's with me?"

"Don't let them lead you on, though," Marindelle warned them. "That rumour of a marine landing is utter nonsense. I'm pretty certain it was put out by the Voice, the source and medium of every news item. We shall have to undertake your education a little more thoroughly.

"Political re-education has a great deal in common with market-gardening. When you arrived here you were fallow land covered in weeds, thickets and wild flowers. The problem was to make this land yield a good solid Marxist crop."

"So the soil was broken up for tilling," said Orsini, "meaning that you were reduced to the appropriate mental and physical condition by an extremely judicious diet."

"Twenty-five ounces of rice a day in fact," Leroy chipped in.

The three old hands were performing a well-rehearsed turn. They never missed a cue; they each appeared in turn and made their little speech, then disappeared into the wings.

"Yes, twenty-five ounces of rice a day—the minimum vital ration. Within a few hours, as you saw for yourselves, you were dying of hunger; all you could think of was food. Your stomach clamoured for attention and left you no time for any preoccupations of a philosophical, political or even religious nature. Then the instruction periods began."

"That was the seed being sown, the good old Marxist seed. It encountered no resistance in such well-tilled soil . . .

"The next thing was to create a sort of Pavlovian conditioned reflex in you, a politico-stomachic reflex. The prisoners have been enlightened and are making political progress. The minimum vital ration is increased proportionally and the stomach is prepared to think along the right lines . . . On the other hand, any backsliding is punished by a reduction in the diet and the stomach has to suffer the consequences of this mental rebellion."

"But there was still one weed which was particularly tenacious because its roots lay buried deep in the earth: hope—the hope of getting back to France, living as free men once again, seeing our families once more and making love to a girl without committing a political sin."

"It's worse than quack-grass, this hope. No sooner is it pulled up than it grows again and in a trice strangles the tender little shoots of the Marxist crop. It's got to be pulled up all the time. The best method they've found is the false rumour.

Here's what I mean: on the 14th July everyone in camp was filled with hope of a speedy release. The quack-grass was running wild. So the Voice disseminates one of his false rumours by one of his usual means: a piece of paper dropped on the ground, a *bo-doi* who shoots his mouth off: 'The Vietnamese delegation has left Geneva for Prague. The Mendès-France government has just been overthrown; the marines are landing at Haiphong . . .' Hope is abruptly snuffed out. There's no other solution . . . the only way to survive and get away with a whole skin is to become good fighters for Peace."

"And all the time there's the stomach clamouring for its ration, anxious not to have it decreased . . . The conditioned reflex . . . Good night, gentlemen, sleep well. Take it from me, that rumour's all nonsense. But we shouldn't have been able to tell you so with such conviction if we had not ourselves been subjected to this treatment hundreds and hundreds of times."

When the news of the Geneva armistice eventually reached Camp One, no one needed any confirmation to believe it. Truth always has a stronger, more convincing flavour than rumour.

On 21 July, after the siesta in the damp heat of late afternoon, a great clamour rose from the old hands' quarters and spread across the river. Boisfeuras, Glatigny, Merle, Marindelle, Orsini, Mahmoudi and Pinières got up without saying a word. Leroy appeared at the top of the ladder:

"This is it; it's all over; they've signed," he said.

Marindelle had gone quite pale beneath his dull yellow tan and Glatigny had to support him.

"You know, Jacques," he said, "I'd given up all hope. Now I'll be seeing Jeanine again."

Glatigny suddenly felt deep affection for the little lieutenant. He put his arm round his shoulder and made him turn round towards the corner of the hut so that no one should see the tears in the eyes of this aged child who was so weak and so strong, worldly and naïve, cynical and tender.

All the *canh-nas* were disgorging their *tou-bis*, who raced in single file along the mud embankments towards the river to join the old hands.

Prisoners and *bo-dois* intermingled, fell into one another's arms and fraternized and, as God was witness, at that moment there was no one in the whole camp except men who saw their hard time coming to an end.

That evening the Voice, all sugar and spice, informed them that the armistice had been signed some days before* and they would soon be leaving for the release camp. Preparations for the departure began in an atmosphere of enthusiasm and delight.

The Voice called for volunteers to act as stretcher-bearers for the sick and seriously wounded. Every member of Marindelle's team of "wily serpents" offered his services, even Esclavier who had just rejoined his comrades and could still hardly stand upright.

"We'll be free in three days' time," said the optimists. "Trucks will come and fetch us away."

"Nothing's as simple as that in the Communist world," said the old hands.

On the day of the departure from Camp One a certain number of Vietminh officers and N.C.O.s approached their prisoners with paper and pencil. Hiding from one another, they asked the Frenchmen to give them a written testimonial stating that they had treated them decently and had behaved well towards them.

"They're afraid we might come back," Pinières sneered, "so they're taking proper precautions."

"It's not that exactly," said Marindelle. "In a few weeks' time they're all going to undergo a purge; they'll be demoted and a few of them will be shot. They're already preparing their defence without even knowing if they're guilty. Anything may be useful, even a prisoner's testimonial.

"They're the poor wretches, not us, for they have to stay on in prison and haven't a hope of ever getting out."

"Are you getting soft-hearted?" Esclavier asked him in a peculiar tone.

"I went and said goodbye to the Voice. I was almost moved

---

*The armistice was signed in Geneva on 20 July 1954.

by the bastard. I thought he was going to ask me to kiss him, as a man condemned to death might ask his lawyer or the chaplain at the foot of the scaffold.

"And look what he gave me."

He held out his hand to show them a little boy-scout cross.

"There's every sort of type in the Vietminh," Esclavier curtly replied, "pearls and swine included, but it's always the swine who eat the pearls."

"You don't seem to have much to say about your spell in hospital. There was a rumour, however . . ."

"I almost died. Dia, a little Viet nurse and good luck saved me."

The team was given only one sick man to escort. He was an elderly senior officer who had been captured at Cao-Bang. He was on his last legs; but he had sworn that he would not die in the hands of the Viets, so he was infinitely careful in the use he made of what life he had left. He never spoke, he never moved.

Throughout the march the "wily serpents" helped themselves to fruit, molasses and poultry and halted when they felt like it in the huts along the road. They got hold of some *choum* by threatening the peasants that they would denounce them—for it was forbidden to possess any alcohol—and some wads of tobacco by exchanging them for objects which they subsequently took back.

They trotted along like coolies, four of them at a time carrying the stretcher. They would cover three or four miles in an hour, then suddenly declare that they had had enough and doss down just outside a village where, as soon as darkness fell, they would go "scrounging."

All personal differences within the team soon disappeared, while solid bonds of friendship between them began to be forged; they formed a united and unbroken front. What belonged to one belonged to the others. No one gave orders, but they had fallen into the habit of putting their heads together to decide what they were going to do next.

They parodied those meetings of the People's Army at which each *bo-doi* made his self-examination and gave his opinion on the best way to capture Dien-Bien-Phu or look after a rifle.

But, without realizing it, they were developing collective habits in their everyday life and way of thinking; they were no longer merely comrades thrown together by chance and circumstance but an organization with its own rites (based on stealing molasses), a cell whose function was to frustrate another organization.

Three years later, when the military examining magistrate was interrogating Mahmoudi in Cherche-Midi prison, he asked him this question:

"Why, after signing the letter to the President of the Republic, didn't you go the whole hog and join the F.L.N.?"

Mahmoudi looked at the captain from the judge advocate general's branch with his well-cut uniform and gold-rimmed spectacles. He had noticed the bureaucratic self-satisfaction with which he had spread out on the table the carefully documented papers he carried in his brief-case.

"Were you ever out in Indo-China?" he asked.

"No."

"Then it would be difficult for you to understand."

What had held him back was Pinières and Glatigny, the touchy Esclavier with whom a little Vietminh girl had fallen in love, the madman Lescure whom he had protected, and little Merle who longed for civilian life; it was Marindelle and his tuft of tow-coloured hair on the top of his head, and Orsini who once told him: "You silly fool, when you get caught stealing, you must always think up some excuse, otherwise what's the point of dialectics?"; it was Leroy and that old colonel they had carried on the stretcher who was hanging on to life in order to see France again.

It was one of those things you can't discuss with an examining magistrate.

On 30 August, after a fortnight's rest on the banks of the Bright River, the prisoners reached Vietri where the release camp had been installed. It consisted of some big, newly constructed bamboo huts over which fluttered Vietminh flags, banners and Picasso doves of peace.

The prisoners had been issued with cigarettes, new uniforms like those worn by the *bo-dois* and fibre helmets which were not, however, covered in camouflage material, and, one hour before their release, some very poor-quality canvas shoes.

The transit camp was situated on a sort of hill which descended in a gentle slope towards the Red River where the LCTs of the French Navy were now moored.

The evening before, a large detachment of Pims had arrived who were to be released as a reciprocal measure; a group of journalists accompanied the party. The entire population of the neighbouring villages was assembled on the beach, lined up along the barrier in their cone-shaped hats and black trousers under the command of *can-bos* in uniform.

When the first boat lowered its ramp the *can-bos* gave a signal and the crowd gave a loud cheer and waved their hats.

The Pims replied by waving their hands, but without much enthusiasm. At Haiphong they had almost had to be driven on to the vessels by force and some of them had taken flight, so reluctant were they to go back to the Vietminh paradise.

The journalists Pasfeuro and Villèle, who had flown out from France a week earlier, made an incongruous pair on the beach, standing slightly apart from the cohort of accredited pressmen, agency representatives, magazine photographers, news-reel and television cameramen, and foreign correspondents.

In spite of the torrid heat and an uncomfortable night on the LCT, Villèle still looked elegant in his sky-blue tropical suit and tie worn with studied negligence. He had a patrician figure in spite of slightly lop-sided shoulders. With his handsome face, intelligent features and deep-set eyes, he took a well-meaning interest in everything. He invited confidences and his perpetual expression of mild astonishment prompted the people he interviewed to tell him more than they had intended in order to convince him.

They all thought him pleasant, understanding and well-disposed until the moment they read what he had written about them. But by then it was too late and they couldn't even bash his face in, for he had skipped off.

He was thirty-five years old; a few grey strands in his thick well-groomed hair added to his charm and distinction.

No one had ever seen Pasfeuro in anything but baggy trousers and a shirt opened at the neck to reveal a powerful torso. There was always a cigarette dangling from his lips and his uncouthness was proverbial. He had a sulky face and undistinguished features; he was extremely clumsy both with people and inanimate objects, he sweated copiously, had a strong smell and frequently forgot to wash. His heavy square hands were those of a stone-mason or riveter who by some stroke of fate had taken to journalism. He scribbled notes down on odd bits of paper and more often than not mislaid them.

When Pasfeuro smiled a mischievous gleam came into his dark brown eyes; he then looked extremely young. Children, dogs and even his own colleagues were quite fond of him, whereas they could not abide Villèle.

Ten years earlier Villèle was still called Zammit and his parents kept a shop at Saint-Eugène near Algiers. His father was Maltese, his mother a Greek from Alexandria, and the blood of every Mediterranean race flowed through his veins.

Villèle had spent his childhood in the little streets which smelt of rancid butter, grilled skewered meat and *kesra*. He knew every pimp, tart, kif-addict and pickpocket in the Kasbah. He liked to make himself useful to the members of this underworld. But his brothers and comrades, quarrelsome, touchy and ticklish on a point of honour which in general they did not value particularly highly, accused him of lack of virility and referred to him with contempt as a *coulo*.*

He won a scholarship; his father and uncles paid for his passage to France. He shed his accent, invented a suitable family for himself, passed out of college with flying colours and, on joining the weekly *Influence*, became Luc Villèle. It was only an unexpected sense of the ridiculous that prevented him from adding the particle "de" to his assumed name.

Progressivism was all the rage, so he followed the fashion.

Villèle loved discreet luxury, deep arm-chairs, cakes and pastries and very sweet coffee with cream, and delighted in the heady scent of high game that emanated from western civilization in

*Algerian slang for "homosexual."

this decaying city of Paris. He had no political opinion, but his instinct prompted him to rise up at once against anyone who preached courage, endurance, endeavour and heroism. He had a taste for defeat and anarchy.

From time to time a fit of aggressive nationalism prompted him, under the influence of passion or in a spirit of rebellion, to write the opposite of what he generally preached. He was regarded then as suffering from a twinge of conscience, which enabled him in consequence to pass himself off as a journalist torn between two stools, a man of absolute integrity and largely independent of the editorial policy of his paper. Whereupon he would resume his slow undermining activity with increased effectiveness.

He had heard that Phillipe Esclavier might be in the batch of prisoners who were shortly to be released: the poor misguided idiots.

He thought of writing a long article on the return of the captain, heir to one of the greatest names of the French left wing, the son of the late Professor Esclavier, who had been taken prisoner in a colonialist war while fighting against the liberty of the people, whereas back in France his sister and brother-in-law, the Weihl-Esclaviers, were directing the para-Communist movement of the Fighters for Peace.

With an article on these lines he could get everyone's back up and assume the pathetic tone which he exploited only too well to expound on those heroic degenerates who were the last remaining defenders of a condemned civilization.

At the end of the war Pasfeuro had been authorized by a court decision to assume the strange name he had thought out for himself, while serving with the maquis in Savoy, to the exclusion of all his others: Herbert de Mortfault de Puysaignac de Cortelier, Marquis of This and Count of That, all perfectly authentic titles earned in a succession of royal beds. When the daughter of the family wouldn't do, the son was sent in her place. No inhibitions or complexes in that clan—if they failed by the front entrance, they succeeded by the rear! And their success had been brilliant, as all the history books showed. They had played the same game with the Empire and the Republic, with the Jewish bankers and American big business. During the occupation they had carried on in the same way with the Germans. But they did not sleep with any old German, never anyone below the rank of general; so no one had worried about it.

Pasfeuro sometimes wondered who on earth his father might be. Certainly not the old marquis, whose tastes were exclusively unnatural. Perhaps the plumber who happened to call that day. Ever since the Crusades his family had been easy-going in that respect. But what the hell did he care? He was now plain Pasfeuro, a reporter on the *Quotidien*, who earned 150,000 francs a month, plus the fiddles on his expense account.

He loved his job, but he was less talented than Villèle; he did not cheat so much. Pasfeuro was against the war in Indo-China but not against the men taking part in it.

Perhaps he would shortly see Yves Marindelle, Jeanine's husband, coming down the sandy path. It might be slightly embarrassing . . . In this batch there was probably also a distant family relation, that fellow Glatigny who wore an eyeglass and who was allowed to ride horses which were even better bred than he was.

Pasfeuro suddenly noticed a little Vietminh in uniform who earlier on had introduced himself to him as a journalist. He was now on board one of the LCTs and had just handed a piece of paper to one of the Pims.

The latter promptly turned round towards his comrades and gave certain instructions.

*"Ho Chu Tich, Muon Nam!"** the Pim shouted.

His comrades took up the cry, shouting louder and louder, and suddenly, at a sign from the "journalist" who had gone back ashore, they all threw their bush hats into the water.

That wretched dented headgear which was worn by every soldier in the expeditionary corps had suddenly become the symbol of servitude.

The crowd on the banks cheered and waved small flags but there was nothing spontaneous about this manifestation.

***

*"Long live President Ho!"

"Enjoying it?" Pasfeuro asked Villèle. "The whole thing's a put up job."

"Men regaining their liberty, it's always rather moving."

As a Pim passed close by him waving wildly, for it was wiser to be in with the new masters, Villèle recoiled in a squeamish sort of way. Pasfeuro sneered:

"They're quite clean, you know; they were all given a bath before embarking."

A medical orderly or doctor in a white smock, with a surgeon's mask stretched across his mouth, was preparing to deal with the sick and had lined his stretchers up in a row on the bank. Behind him stood his team of nurses, detached and aloof. But the Pims were all perfectly well; they were as plump as could be and bursting with health. The man in the white smock dithered; he had received his instructions and behind him two cameramen were watching him rather reproachfully.

At long last he noticed a victim of sea-sickness who was still somewhat green in the face. He fastened on to him; he was saved; here at last was a victim of colonialist atrocity. The Pim, wondering what was happening to him, tried to get away, but he found himself laid flat on his back, held down on the stretcher, photographed and filmed. Only his legs kept kicking out in a rather ridiculous manner.

"Brain-washing makes me sick," said Pasfeuro, "any form of brain-washing. Propaganda's a filthy business. Are you going to write about this show, Villèle?"

Villèle put his head on one side and in a slightly scornful tone replied:

"It's only a detail. You've got to try and see things as a whole . . ."

Three violins playing out of tune; a drum which couldn't very well do anything else but play in tune; three little pig-tailed Vietminh girls going through the motions of a national dance, and behind them, looking very pale, the French prisoners.

They marched under a triumphal arch of paper and bamboo which proclaimed the brotherhood of the masses, then another, smaller one, which wished them a safe and speedy return to hearth and home.

Pasfeuro could scarcely recognize the emaciated youngster in the front rank as Yves Marindelle. He was no longer the mischievous noisy, truant schoolboy with his pockets stuffed with practical jokes and snares who had flown out to Indo-China four years earlier after entrusting him with his child-bride. This was a cross between an old man and an adolescent.

Yves caught sight of him, rushed up and burst into tears.

"It's you, old man, you've come all the way here. How's Jeanine?"

"She's waiting for you in Paris."

"Why didn't she write . . . through Prague?"

"She tried to . . . several times . . . through the Red Cross."

Glatigny had now come up behind them. He too had changed; he no longer looked like one of his horses.

"Glatigny, let me introduce a cousin of Jeanine's, who now goes by the name of Pasfeuro."

"I know him," said Glatigny. "He's also a cousin of mine."

He gave a slight bow and turned his back on him.

"What's wrong, Herbert? He doesn't seem exactly delighted to see you. Oh, of course, it's because you've changed your name."

"I'd almost forgotten," Pasfeuro was thinking, "I've also got that silly Christian name, Herbert, maybe because my mother slept with a lord . . . or with the butler."

Pasfeuro had promised Jeanine to put Yves in the picture, to tell him it was all over between them, that she wouldn't ever sleep with him again, that she would no longer be his wife but always his sister if he wanted. He couldn't do it: it would have been worse than hitting a cripple. He would stand him a lot of drinks, give him the best meal that money could buy, get hold of a girl for him, the loveliest girl in Saigon . . . and afterwards perhaps he might bring himself to tell him.

After having their names checked, the prisoners filed on to the LCT, still in complete silence. A few journalists followed them aboard. When the ramp was raised behind them a voice rang out, the voice of a former prisoner perched in the bows:

"Off with this filthy crap!"

He hurled his Vietminh helmet into the water. All his comrades followed suit.

Villèle leaned towards Pasfeuro and asked under his breath:

"Who's that savage who's trying to jeopardize our relations with the Vietminh by that idiotic gesture?"

"Captain Phillipe Esclavier."

The helmets now mingled in the Red River with the bush hats and bobbed about in the wake of the boat as it drew away from the shore.

The senior officers were liberated after the subalterns, and General de Castries on the last day.

When a journalist asked him what he was looking forward to most, he replied with an extremely distinguished lisp:

"Thteak and french-fried potatoeth."

Pasfeuro interviewed Raspéguy who was in great form, beaming with health and vigour; he had done two hours' physical culture every day.

"Did you have a very hard time in captivity, Colonel?"

"Not at all. In fact I might even say I found it extremely interesting. I think it taught me a lot—for instance, how to go about it so as not to let those fellows get the upper hand . . . smart fellows, you know. Nowadays you've got to have the people on your side if you want to win a war."

"There's no longer any question of war; the armistice has been signed."

"The armistice! That's just another staff college idea! The armistice! There won't be any now . . . or if there is it'll be a swindle or some sort of racket. You didn't by any chance see a man called Esclavier and his gang of ruffians go through?"

"Yes, three days ago. They're all in the Lannemezan hospital."

"Have you ever done any fighting yourself?"

"Yes, and I can't say I enjoyed it very much."

Raspéguy looked utterly bewildered; he could not understand how anyone could fail to enjoy fighting.

Lescure and Dia were evacuated together, but by helicopter with the seriously sick.

When Colonel V—— who commanded the French detachment saw the Negro doctor, he turned to his second-in-command and said:

"Better keep an eye on that bird: a doctor, therefore an educated black; must have been influenced by Vietminh propaganda; a Communist most likely; make a note of him."

The colonel had a powerful voice; Dia, a sensitive ear; he had heard everything. He turned towards Lescure:

"I suppose we're going to run into bastards like that everywhere!"

Lescure played two or three notes on his flute and shrugged his shoulders.

The former prisoners spent anything between one week and one month in various hospitals in Indo-China. Then they began taking to drink, sleeping with women or smoking opium . . . but hardly any of them seemed to be in a hurry to get back to France.

They were becoming re-acquainted with the pleasures of Vietnamese life; instead of alienating them from "yellow skins"; their captivity had brought them closer. They could be seen arguing with rickshaw coolies and Chinese itinerant vendors. They proved to be amenable and not at all recalcitrant, they reported punctually whenever required and filled in any number of forms, but they appeared to be living outside the Army, in a world of their own; they eschewed the company of white women and of their former comrades who had not been through the same ordeal.

One morning they were quietly herded on to a ship; it was the *Edouard Branly*, a stout old Chargeurs Réunis tub with good food and comfortable cabins. They put into Singapore, where they bought mangoes and Chinese knick-knacks; Colombo, where they made an excursion to Kandy; Djibouti and Port Said; and one day, towards ten-thirty in the evening, they reached Algiers.

It was 11 November 1954.

They were told that the boat would be leaving again at two o'clock in the morning and that they could go ashore.

Mahmoudi left them there. He had been ill during the voyage and an ambulance was waiting to take him to the Maillot hospital. He could hardly bring himself to part from them. In leaving them he seemed afraid he would once more be assailed by all his doubts, uncertainties and contradictions.

The former prisoners of Camp One went ashore and were astonished to find the town as dead as though it was under siege. All the shops in the Rue d'Isly were closed. Patrols tramped the pavements in their hobnailed boots. The steps of the main post office were picketed by a platoon of C.R.S. wearing steel helmets and armed with submachine-guns.

They made for the Kasbah in the hope of finding a night-club or brothel open but came up against barbed-wire entanglements guarded by Zouaves. They did not come across any of their comrades of the parachute units, and at the empty bar of the Aletti Guillaume the barman told them they had all left the evening before for the Aurès.

Not knowing where to go, frightened of finding themselves plunged once again into an atmosphere of war, a fear to which they thought they had become impervious, they fled back to the boat. In the bar Merle had picked up a Paris newspaper, and since his comrades were jostling all round him, he read bits of it out loud.

Seeing this little gathering, Raspéguy promptly joined them, followed by a portly little major of the Algiers garrison wearing the red forage cap of the Zouaves.

Aurès. First major engagement. Entrenched in the caves, the fellaghas are firing on our troops. Thirty rebels captured in Kabylie. Batna, tenth November. The first major engagement in the general mopping-up operations in the Aurès is now taking place in the Djebel Ichmoul two kilometres from Foum-Toub; south of this locality a detachment consisting of two companies of paratroops have made contact with a band of outlaws who have taken refuge in some caves from which they are firing with automatic weapons. The battle was still going on at dawn this morning.

Three paratroopers have been wounded, one seriously. They have been brought back to Batna by helicopter. The bodies of two rebels have been found and one prisoner has been taken; he was armed with a rifle and revolver.

In Kabylie, near Dra-el-Mizan, two policemen have captured thirty rebels who had committed various offences in the area. While they were passing through the village, the population attacked them. In spite of the policemen's intervention, one was killed and another wounded.

In Algiers the police have discovered a store of bombs in the residential quarter of the town. A similar discovery has been made in the department of Oran, at Er Rahel.

At Rio-Salado in the same department, the police have identified eight men who were being sought for terrorist activities and arrested six of them. Twenty pounds of explosive and three rifles were found in their house.

For the last forty-eight hours all civilian aircraft have been grounded. An aeroplane was reported last night, flying with all lights extinguished above the Aurès range, while a number of fires were observed in the mountains; the authorities believe that the rebels, whose supplies are running short since the roads have been cut, may be receiving arms and food by parachute.*

"It's the same old war going on," said Boisfeuras. "The Viets were right."

The little major could not let this pass. All the men arriving from Indo-China had their vision completely distorted by their captivity or engagements against the Vietminh. They had caught some nasty yellow infection of which they would have to be cured, come what may.

"Captain," he said, button-holing Boisfeuras but addressing all the other officers as well, "Algeria is not Indo-China. The Arab is a Moslem and not a Communist. We are dealing with an essentially localized rebellion, a few bands of Chaouia brigands. We have sent in the paratroops, which we should have done some time ago. It will all be over in a week. In Algeria there have always been flare-ups of this kind . . . ever since Bugeaud, and in the same area. Forget Indo-China, you're now in Algeria, only a few hundred miles away from France."

*Paris-Presse, 11 November 1954.

He turned to Raspéguy who, as a senior officer, was surely bound to back him up.

"That's right, isn't it?"

Raspéguy sucked his pipe and cast a glance of inquiry at Esclavier.

"No," he abruptly replied. "I haven't got much book learning and I don't express myself very well, but I feel old Uncle Boisfeuras is right even though he has never set foot in Africa before. Your little flare-up in the Aurès isn't going to be snuffed out just like that."

"I've been out here fifteen years, Colonel, I speak Arabic . . ."

"Maybe you might have done better if you'd gone to Indo-China. Out there they were already *talking* about the next war."

Raspéguy repeated this sentence for his own benefit. He found it striking, but it didn't seem to have much effect on that old sod Esclavier who was reading the paper over Merle's shoulder. He must be doing it on purpose.

Merle did not give a damn about this business in Algeria. It was all over; he was a civilian and he was glancing through the paper to see if there was anything that might interest a genuine civilian like him.

The Socialists had replied to Mendès-France. Herriot had been invited to Moscow. So he was still alive, that old Republican gasbag! Dany Robin liked Picasso. But who the hell was Dany Robin? Hold-up in the Rue d'Avron, a million francs stolen from a cashier. A million wasn't much . . . Floods in Morocco; twenty-three dead. Hossein Fatimi, the former Minister for Foreign Affairs of Iran, had been shot. After the execution, by way of a funeral oration, General Teimour Baktyar had stated that he had more blood than a bull. Another tender-hearted chap! One hundred and eighty eighteenth-century court costumes at the Musée Carnevalet. In the entertainments column Robert Dhery and the Branquignols claimed it was the audience that amused them; and on the book page Kléber Haedens was reviewing the memoirs of a writer who signed himself de Gaulle.

De Gaulle—there was a chap who had soon been forgotten, even by those who wore his insignia, the Free French cross: the

Esclaviers and Boisfeurases of the world. In camp no one had so much as mentioned his name.

"General de Gaulle's book is infinitely superior to the works that are usually written by war leaders and statesmen . . . Men in power, once their strength begins to decline . . ."

The siren of the *Edouard Branly* announced their departure. The docks of Algiers were deserted. One by one the officers went below. It was cold out on deck.

Two days later, at eight o'clock in the morning, a loudspeaker announced that the coast of France was in sight. Still half asleep, they went up on deck. Under the overcast sky the coast looked black. Gulls flew to and fro above the boat, giving their piercing cries.

They were all there, pressed close together, leaning over the rail. The paradise they had dreamt about so often in the prison camps was slowly approaching and already it was losing its appeal.

They were dreaming of another paradise: Indo-China—that was what was uppermost in the thoughts of all of them. They were not sorrowful sons coming home to lick their wounds, they were strangers. Bitterness welled up in them.

In 1950, at Orange, a train full of Far East wounded had been stopped by the Communists who had insulted and struck the men lying on the stretchers. A Paris hospital advertising for blood donors had specified that their contribution would not be used for the wounded from Indo-China. At Marseilles, which could now be seen looming over the horizon, they had refused to disembark the coffins of the dead.

They had been abandoned, like those mercenaries for whom there was suddenly no further use and whom Carthage had therefore massacred so as to avoid having to pay them their due. Cut off from their own country, they had re-created an artificial motherland for themselves in the friendship of the Vietnamese and in the arms of their slant-eyed women.

They were almost horrified to realize that they now had more in common with the Vietminh whom they had hated, with the Voice and his mysterious smile, with the oafish *bo-dois*, than with these people who were waiting for them on the quayside with a wretched little military band and a detachment of soldiers sloppily presenting arms.

"If the war had gone on," Esclavier pensively observed, "if an honourable peace had been made, a real fusion might have come about between us and the Vietnamese and the world might have seen the birth of the first Eurasian race . . ."

Which of them would the child of Souen and Esclavier have taken after?

But he went on furiously:

"No peace is ever honourable for the vanquished."

They had all picked up an insidious infection, the yellow infection. They were bringing it back to France with them and it was a crowd of contaminated men that disembarked on the quayside at Marseilles and kissed their wives, their mothers and their children whom they no longer recognized.

Even the morning air smelled alien to them.

PART TWO

THE COLONEL FROM INDO-CHINA

THE CATS OF MARSEILLES

Boisfeuras had parted from his comrades in Marseilles. On a grey November morning, with a catch in their throats, they had seen his slim figure disappear. With his old cardboard suitcase whose handle was reinforced with string, and his cape which was too long for him and hung down to his heels, he was the perfect picture of the poor soldier back from the wars who has no idea where to go and who will shortly be a human wreck destined for the workhouse.

He had given Florence's address to the taxi which drove him off. The driver had a more pronounced accent than most Marseillais, which made him sound like a stage comedian deliberately overacting:

"So the war's over at last, Captain, eh?"

"Yes, it's over."

"Personally, mind you, I respect everyone's opinion—but Indo-China, we couldn't very well hang on to it since the people who lived out there wanted to see the last of us."

The taxi stopped outside a large modern block of flats in pink stucco built at the foot of Notre-Dame de la Garde. Boisfeuras felt the slight tremor that came over him each time he went to see Florence.

"There we are, sir, home again, with your little wife waiting for you inside. That's better than war now, isn't it? That'll be three hundred and eighty francs. The tip's not included. No offence meant, but some people, after being overseas so long, tend to forget the customs of our fair land of France . . ."

The driver laid particular stress on the last words. Feeling ill at ease, Boisfeuras said to himself:

"Our fair land of France is enough to make one sick."

He paid off the taxi, gave the driver a tip and asked the concierge:

"Miss Florence Mercardier's, please?"

"Third on the left. You can't go wrong, there's always music and a lot of noise."

She spoke in a dry, disagreeable tone; Florence was obviously up to the same old tricks. He went upstairs, dragging the suitcase whose handle had broken yet again, rang the bell and Florence was in his arms, against a background of sugary, insipid music dripping from the radio; the chairs, the tables, the floor itself, were littered with empty bottles, saucers of cigarette-ends and the remnants of a cold supper.

"The maid hasn't come," said the half-caste apologetically.

She was barefoot and wearing an old dressing-gown, but her smooth slender body exuded a faint perfume of vanilla. Contemptuous and disgusted by all this mess, a white tabby cat had taken refuge on a shelf. She yawned, opening her pink throat, and stretched one paw above her ear.

Boisfeuras cleared an arm-chair for himself. Florence came and sat down on his lap; her thick black hair was pressed against his cheek.

"Haven't you paid the maid?"

"She doesn't like me, no one likes me in France."

Florence unbuttoned the captain's jacket, then his shirt, and with her long hand and hard nails began stroking his chest. The unmade bed, which still retained the smell of woman and love-making, soon beckoned them; and with his lovely whore Julien Boisfeuras once again experienced the intense sort of pleasure which she alone knew how to produce.

"Real pleasure is painful and degrading," his father, *taipan* Boisfeuras, used to say. "Otherwise it's little more than an organic function. It must defy all constraint and taboo to be what the Christians call a sin. When you make war, you risk your skin; when you make love, you must risk your soul."

With Florence, the little half-caste who, with parted lips, was now lovingly stroking her stomach and breasts, Julien played with his soul in the same way as a bullfighter manipulates his cape.

"Shall we go out and eat?"

"No."

"I want to go to Alex's. We'll have Chinese soup, fried *nemes* and abalones that come from Hong Kong already tinned; they're very expensive. Then you'll buy me some dresses and we'll go to the cinema and tonight I'll be . . ."

She ran the tip of her tongue over her full, fleshy lips:

". . . very . . . very . . . sweet to you."

He slapped her in the face, deliberately, without anger, and she clung to him, limp and chastened; sobs, which were succeeded by pleasure, made her firm stomach expand and contract.

He thrust her aside and lit a cigarette.

"I'm behaving like a pimp in a film," he said to himself, "but that's the only way to avoid being relegated by Florence to a mere accessory. She spent last night with another man; then, when he went off, shortly before I arrived, she stroked her stomach and breasts in the same manner to thank them for the pleasure they had just given her. And she's already forgotten the accessory which served her purpose. A cruel, selfish, soulless little strumpet! But I'm only interested in her body and my degradation."

Florence took his hand, rubbed it gently against her lips and kissed it. He reacted to this with complete indifference, while the cat with her red-brown eyes stared down at them from her shelf.

Julien heaved the half-caste out of bed:

"Turn off that music and go out and buy something to eat."

Florence looked at herself in the wardrobe glass and twisted round to catch the reflection of her lightly arched loins. She would have liked to be a man so as to adore her body and make love to herself. In a science-fiction novel she had read about a creature which reproduced itself in order to go out and kill people, the fool, instead of giving itself pleasure. There was a faint mark near her eye where Julien had slapped her.

"You've given me a bruise."

She said this simply as a statement of fact. When she saw Maguy, she would tell him that her captain had come back from the war and that for the time being it would be better for her not to do the round of the bars too regularly. Florence was happy that Julien was back, for she was tired of her freedom. The half-caste was bored in Marseilles and missed Saigon, the Dakao quarter and its seething life, its little bars, its "compartments" thronged with amoral, sexual families. Old fathers there sold their daughters, assuming the haughty air of hidalgos. Brothers got a rake-off for introducing their sisters to "friends." The whole quarter wallowed in a warm miasma of sex, *nuoc mam*, and dried shrimps. Then came the war, as fiery as red peppers, which lent an unexpected zest to each fresh embrace. Florence had experienced passion as furtive and brutal as that of wild beasts, pursuits, fights, and murders. One day she had fallen into the hands of the Binh-Xuyens and Julien had saved her. The chief of the arroyo pirates who ran all the gambling-dens in Cholon could not afford to fall out with Captain Boisfeuras who knew the name of the coolie whom he had once killed in order to steal two piastres from him. That was ten years before he became a colonel and a friend of the Emperor.

Florence disappeared into the bath-room and came out again wearing close-fitting leopard-skin trousers, a chunky black sweater and a canary-yellow scarf. She looked common and provocative. Her dull skin and slanting eyes, the sinuous movement of her limbs, gave her the additional tang of some exotic fruit. Boisfeuras lit another cigarette. He surrendered to the clammy but beguiling self-disgust in which his energy and resolution melted away. He had to plumb the depths of this disgust so as to have the necessary purchase for his foot which, with a kick, would send him rising to the surface again.

The captain spent a week with his lovely whore, took her out to the cinema once or twice, ran through several detective novels and smoked enough cigarettes to sear the roof of his mouth.

At the most unusual hours Florence produced a number of

meals in which Vietnamese dishes which she cooked herself were supplemented by poor quality cold cuts from the neighbouring butcher's shop. To drink she bought nothing but sugary aperitifs tasting of chemicals which cloyed palate and stomach alike.

When his disgust almost swept him off his feet like a wave, Julien went out on to the balcony and watched the cats.

At the back of the building there was an empty plot of ground enclosed by a high wooden fence. Hundreds of cats, grey, white and black, romped about in this playground among the bits of corrugated iron, piles of rubble, broken bottles, clumps of nettles and carcasses of old trucks. The darkness sparkled with countless gold and emerald-green eyes.

They reminded Julien of his big game hunts by night in Burma, of the eyes of the animals caught in the headlights, which the rifle shots extinguished like so many candles.

Burton in his sentimental way used to say:

"One gets the feeling one's killing eyes. It's far nastier than shooting animals whose head, limbs and body are visible. Putting out their eyes in the dark is like killing life itself."

Men's eyes do not shine in the dark. During a hunt in the Naga hills they ran into some Japanese and Burton was shot dead.

The cats, Julien noticed, had a recognized leader, a gaunt, lean-ribbed grey beast. Whenever any refuse wrapped up in a piece of newspaper was thrown down from one of the balconies of the building, they all pounced on it, fur bristling, claws bared, and formed a circle round the packet, not daring to advance for fear of being attacked by the others.

At this point the grey cat intervened. He would pick the packet up in his jaws and make off with it. But the newspaper, dragging along the ground, would fall apart, spilling out the old bones, crusts of bread and kitchen refuse, which were snatched up by his pursuers, and the grey cat would find himself on the discarded dustbin which served as his throne with an empty piece of torn paper between his teeth.

The cats disappeared in the afternoon, but in the evening, when the lights began to come on in all the villas scattered over the hill, they would suddenly reappear and embark on their saraband. They clawed and nibbled, squealed with passion, made love and killed one another. The white tabby cat would start trembling, brushing up against the captain's legs and mewing. One night he opened the door for her and she scuttled off to join the free world of cats covered with scabs and mange, ruled by a stupid and short-sighted tyrant.

On the following day Julien Boisfeuras gave Florence her freedom. She too needed to scamper about the wastelands of Marseilles and resume her adventurous love-life; he left her enough money to live on for three months; she pretended to be grieved.

When he left, she cursed him up hill and down dale, burst out laughing when the door closed behind him, shed a few tears shortly afterwards because she was already beginning to miss him, and consoled herself by promptly spending some of the money he had left her on a television set. That evening she went out and met Maguy and her old bar cronies, while the white tabby in the empty plot of ground squalled with love as she let herself be mounted by the stupid king, the big gaunt grey.

Julien Boisfeuras had cured himself of Florence as of a fever which is suddenly brought down. He had needed her out in Indo-China in order not to think about the war. This war had begun to lose its appeal when the flavour of exotic and unusual adventure that it had at the beginning began to fade. By 1952 it was already nothing more than a useless dissipation of heroism, suffering, endeavour and human life, while corruption, the black market and chair-borne warriors were all on the increase.

Boisfeuras had been forced to make false promises to his partisans in the Baie d'Along and on the Chinese border. When he came down to Saigon to ask for arms, rice and money, more often than not he met with a refusal. The money had been spent in the capital to swell the coffers of some political party or other; the arms had been issued to some parade-ground Vietnamese units who neither knew nor wished to learn how to use them. Then, so as to have the courage to deceive his partisans with further lies, he used to go and see Florence in her "compartment" at Dakao and expend all his strength and fury on that smooth, eager, selfish body. There were times when Julien felt he would like to alter the course of history all by himself, to be as puerile as a Don Quixote, who, armed with a spear and encased in a suit of armour, attempts to halt a heavy tank attack. Heroic, stupid, play-acting!

Because he thought the conflict was pointless, he had needed the heady drug which was secreted between his mistress's thighs. Eroticism was the answer to despair.

When Julien thought about that war, all he remembered was a series of disconnected adventures, adventures of the kind that Esclavier called "hare-brained schemes." A big junk prowled up the Chinese coast in the darkness; the wind rose and filled the sails which were reinforced with slivers of bamboo; the tiller creaked at every movement of the vessel. Julien was lying out on deck next to his batman Min. When Vong, the owner of the junk, drew on his water-pipe and made the embers right next to them come to life, his face emerged out of the darkness like a ghost. It was a wrinkled old face with cruel little eyes. Vong may well have betrayed them—but not for political reasons or out of self-interest; he was above anything of that sort. The gamble was all that could make his deadened nerves tingle any longer.

The sea was like a millpond and the stifling salty air seemed to be glued to its surface. Min rolled over to shift his revolver from his hip to his waist; like that he would be able to fire more quickly while lying flat on the deck. He believed in Vong's treachery but had never mentioned it to his captain who had known about it for some time; for Min trod warily, bristling like a cat on guard against dogs.

Vong's head emerged out of the darkness again. He spoke softly:

"The junk's arriving."

The sound of flapping sails and rippling water grew louder. A pin-point of light flashed on and off in the distance. So Vong had not betrayed them. Why not? He hardly knew himself—maybe because this time the stakes were so much higher. He

was gambling with the lives of the whole of his family left behind in China.

Min went down into the hold to rouse the dozen men of the
commando. They came up on deck barefoot and fully armed.
Boisfeuras made them lie down along the scuppers. A machine-
gun had been set up in the bows, concealed behind some sacks
of rice.

Vong put down his water-pipe and began signalling with an
old hurricane lamp.

The little Corsican sergeant in command of the Nung partisans sidled up to Boisfeuras.

"What do you think it's going to be, sir, opium, girls . . . ?"

He might equally well have said gold, rum, spices or pearls.
Andréani and Boisfeuras savoured the deep, savage joy of pi-
racy; this war had granted them an adventure of some bygone
age: a boarding on the China seas.

The junk from Hainan drew closer; there was a sound of
voices. How many were there on board? Were they armed?

Vong embarked on a palaver with the other owner. The wind
had dropped completely and the two vessels now lay side by
side. The machine-gun loosed off three bursts and the dozen
men of the commando sprang to their feet with a yell.

The Chinese put up no defence, but the crew had to be pitched
overboard just the same, for there was nothing else to be done
with them. The junk was loaded with arms and medical supplies for the Vietminh.

No, for all his money, *taipan* Boisfeuras could never have
offered his son sensations of such power and intensity.

Then one day Julien grew tired of these stereotyped roman-
tics and tried to find some purpose in this fighting. Since there
was none that he could discover, he took to Florence who
proved to be a much more potent drug than anything else.

At Dien-Bien-Phu he met officers who claimed to be fighting
simply because they had been ordered to do so. It had needed
the defeat to make them subsequently seek a more or less valid
reason for their having fought and to dismiss from their minds
the myth of discipline which the defeat of 1940, the Resistance
and the liberation had deprived of all its content.

From some incomprehensible sense of shame, however, those officers still would not admit, as he did, that their war had become a mere game for desperate dilettanti.

Boisfeuras had no feeling of nationalism; he was therefore unable to invoke the defence of his country, of "mother France." He needed a more universal cause; like many of his comrades, he believed he had found it in the struggle against Communism. Communism as he had known it in Camp One, deprived of all human substance by the Vietminh, could only result in a universe of sexless insects without contradictions and therefore without genius, without any extension in the infinite and therefore without hope.

Man in his diversity and richness was suddenly menaced, but were not those who wished to take up his defence bound to find themselves harnessed to this mass of rubble which was all that was left of the West, its myths and its beliefs?

Boisfeuras felt it was his duty to take part in this defence of the individual. But he refused to confuse this new form of crusade with the guard mounted by a motionless sentry over the walls of a deserted citadel, the porch of an empty church, or the bars of a museum or library in which no one set foot any longer.

As he made his way towards the Saint-Charles station in his civilian suit which made him look like a workman in his Sunday best, Julien Boisfeuras recalled the hordes of cats in the empty plot of ground, their cruel habits and their king who was as stupid and brutal as an American gang leader.

Still carrying his battered old suitcase, he got into the train for Cannes. Someone had left yesterday's paper behind in the compartment; he glanced through it. The insurrection was spreading through the whole of Algeria. Fresh troops were being sent out. G.H.Q. announced that it would all be over in a matter of weeks.

He thought of Mahmoudi. What would he have done in his place? The finest role is always that of the rebel; books, films and men of goodwill are always on his side. But defending rubble is an ungrateful and demeaning pastime.

What passed through the minds of the Roman centurions

who were left behind in Africa and who, with a few veterans, a few barbarian auxiliaries ever ready to turn traitor, tried to maintain the outposts of the Empire while the people back in Rome were sinking into Christianity, and the Caesars into debauchery?

At Cannes Julien Boisfeuras took the bus which dropped him off at La Serbalière, his father's estate. It stretched all the way from Grasse up the hill towards Cabris and was hidden from the public eye by thick smooth walls like those of a prison. He rang the bell at the gate; an old Chinaman opened a peephole and curtly inquired through the grille:

"What you want?"

Then suddenly he recognized him and a broad smile came over his grumpy face:

"Ong Julien, me velly happy . . ."

He threw the gate wide open to allow Julien's car to drive through, but there was only the young master with his battered suitcase standing there. He snatched the suitcase out of his hand and scrutinized him closely. Ong Julien was mad; perhaps it was the fault of that Vietnamese nurse who had brought him up and used to take him with her every day to burn incense in the pagodas of the Buddha. He had inhaled too much incense, which must have disturbed his mind. He, Lung, was a good Christian, a good Protestant, who preferred the smell of soap. Ong Julien had not changed, he was still dressed like a tramp. Neither large cars, nor fine clothes, nor opium, nor good food, nor, like the old master, pretty little girls—nothing interested him but war and politics . . .

A man appeared outside on the veranda of the house. He had a long narrow head culminating in a mouth that was more like a sucker. His lips were so red that they looked made up; his skin so pale as to be transparent, revealing a blue network of veins and arteries. His emaciated frame was swathed in a sort of monk's cowl.

All round this creature who had just emerged from the dark and was blinking his eyes, splendid beds of flowers blazed in the late autumn light. The breeze brought with it all the scents which are those of Provence, sunshine and life: the scent of thyme, mother-of-thyme, fennel, sweet marjoram and the pungent smell of pine-trees. But the man looked like a corpse in this magnificent garden.

"Ah, there you are at last, Julien!"

"Yes, Father."

"I sent you out an air ticket to the bank at Saigon."

"I preferred to come back by boat with my friends."

"Still refusing to touch a penny of what you look upon as my ill-gotten gains?"

"No, it's simpler than that: I'm ill at ease with money, I feel it keeps me apart from something that is basically essential to me. Anyway, I'm very happy to see you again."

"So am I; come in."

Julien at once noticed the heady, penetrating smell of opium, mingled with a faint effluvium of pharmacy. They went through a big hall with Chinese hangings and lacquer furniture, then entered a dark little room. Two thin rush mats were spread out on the floor. Between them stood all the smoker's paraphernalia: the little oil lamp with its golden flame, the bamboo pipes. The smell of the drug, like leaf-mould after rain, was unmistakable, drowning all the others.

Above the lamp the roll of painted silk which had been looted from the Summer Palace hung like a Japanese *kakemono*.

"I often thought of that painting," said Julien, "especially when I was marching in chains along the tracks of the Moyenne Région. I imagined it much bigger and it's nothing but an old bit of faded silk."

He settled down on the mat facing his father and watched him hold the little pellet of opium over the flame between two long silver pincers.

The old man peered at him with his rheumy eyes:

"Well, what's your opinion of this war we've . . . yes, this war we've just lost."

"It was inevitable we should lose it."

"Not enough arms, enough money . . . ?"

"We had too many arms, too much money. With the money we bought up a lot of puppets, while we let the Vietminh take the arms. We had no valid reason for fighting, apart from preventing the Communists from fanning out into South-East Asia. To succeed in this aim, we needed the support of the Vietnamese people. But how could they give us their support since, at the very outset, we denied them their independence?

"But it was only much later, in the prison camps, that we realized this conflict had overreached itself."

"But you, what part did you have to play in this business?"

"A quick-change music-hall performer, by turns a partisan leader, a political adviser to racial minorities, an intelligence agent; but more often than not I acted as an observer, a witness."

"Care for a pipe of opium?"

"No, thanks."

"Yet opium is the vice of witnesses."

Armand Boisfeuras drew on his pipe. The little pellet bubbled, expanded, and the *taipan* exhaled the smoke.

"Do you want to go and lie down? Your room has been ready for you for over a week."

"No, thanks."

"Go on, then."

"Asia is lost. The Communists have introduced extremely effective and worth-while methods out there. They have transformed China and Northern Viet-Nam into a vast, perfectly organized, perfectly inhuman ant-heap. It will hold out for quite a time . . ."

Old Boisfeuras clapped his hands and Lung came in with some tea.

"It will hold out as long as their police system holds out."

"Supposing a sort of popular tidal wave suddenly wiped out the whole Chinese Communist organization. What would be the result, Father?"

"Anarchy, monstrous, cosmic anarchy on a world-wide scale, a human ocean lashed to fury by the winds and smashing down every breakwater . . ."

Julien again remembered the hordes of cats in Marseilles and their stupid king. Kuomintang China was rather like that, with its war-lords and brigand generals.

"A nasty thought, isn't it, Father? On this over-populated

earth of ours, where distance has been abolished, we can hardly afford an anarchy six hundred million strong."

Armand Boisfeuras emptied the bowl of his pipe, shook out the *dross* which he put aside in a little box, stretched out and laid his head on a small cushion:

"The Communists have either absorbed or liquidated every branch of society that might at a pinch have controlled that anarchy. The world is becoming an extremely disagreeable place, my dear Julien, with more and more insoluble problems presenting themselves every day. I shall soon be of an age to take leave of it, so for me those problems don't exist. Meanwhile I've got this refuge: the smoker's den where the sound and fury of the present age only reach me in the form of a muffled echo, deprived of all hysteria and pathos. You'll be leaving the army, I suppose. I was planning to give you the directorship of our group of insurance companies. You'll have absolutely no work to do; it's the sort of sinecure that only a capitalist world can offer. It will enable you to live on a grand scale, to travel anywhere that takes your fancy, to have, shall we say, a social purpose . . . Stay here for a bit, have a good rest, go to bed with some girls . . . and in the evening, as you used to in Shanghai, come and lie down here with me on the mat. I'm rather bored, but I refuse to live in Paris. I have a horror of big towns in the West. I need warmth, silence and the beauty of flowers. A shark but at the same time an artist, my boy, and also resigned—resigned and weary to the point of not wanting to corrupt anyone any more, not even you. Yes, I'm decidedly bored with this world. Take advantage of its decline and its perversions, Julien, whether as an artist or a moralist, it's much the same thing. You can have as much money as you like. I don't enjoy things any more. What one can do with a woman or even a very young girl is pretty limited in the long run . . . You don't bother about it, Julien? That sort of thing leaves you cold? You're merely obsessed by your lust for power, the longing you have to fasten your name to some historical incident. Beware of the temptation of Communism; you've already experienced it, it might easily come back. In another age you would have been a financial tycoon, but money has lost its power and perhaps that's why you despise it. The masses now represent the only power, and in order to win them over men indulge in the same savage, cynical tussle as the sharks of Wall Street or the City did in the old days.

"Only this new form of capital can't be locked away in the vaults of a bank. This capital lives, eats, suffers, dies and rebels.

"In spite of my ghastly reputation, I believe I'm more human than the whole lot of you. I've only tried to corrupt my fellow man, not to use him as a limited capital. You think I'm off my head, that I've smoked too much opium. No, I've merely realized the absurdity of our condition and the immensity of our vanity . . . Don't bother about the human race, Julien, just eat, drink, make love or listen to music, take drugs, you'll be all the better for it. Why not marry? You'll have children, you'll build yourself a home, you'll bring off a big deal, and one day you'll be old and there'll be nothing left for you but to wait sanctimoniously for the sky to drop on top of you . . . Come on, have a little pipe . . ."

Julien Boisfeuras got up and went to bed. He knew how deeply his father was suffering through having nothing more to do, through rotting away all alone in the sunshine of Provence without being able to contaminate any more continents with his personal gangrene.

Next day Julien Boisfeuras went for a walk through the narrow lanes of Grasse. Washing hung out from every window; round an old fountain some peasant women were selling the flowers and wild herbs from the mountains; hordes of children scampered up and down the steps and threw stones at one another; a beautiful, dark-haired girl with dull skin and a profile of classical purity was enthroned behind a stall of figs and lettuces.

Julien sat down on the damp rim of the fountain and appraised the girl dispassionately as a beautiful object.

"Hallo, Captain."

A heavy hand came to rest on his shoulder. He looked up and recognized the journalist who had attended the prisoners' release at Vietri and who knew Marindelle.

"Hallo."

"Pretty girl, isn't she? She might have been born in a Florentine palace in the Quattrocento. You can see her fingering her jewels. Her page comes in and kneels at her feet, bringing back the dagger with which he has killed her unfaithful lover. She kisses him, keeps him all night in her bed and gives orders for him to be hanged in the morning. She has taken so much out of him that the page doesn't even have the final orgasm which all men who are hanged are said to have . . . I've just been reading the Chronicle of the Cenci, I'm so bored here!"

"Why don't you go away then?"

"You may well ask, Captain. I've got a month's holiday, not a penny to spend, and an old aunt who's putting me up at Grasse. She is extremely well-born and extremely deaf . . . Do you live in these parts?"

"My father does."

"Don't you miss Indo-China?"

"I was born in China, so it's China I should miss if anywhere."

"I believe you know my cousin, Yves Marindelle?"

"Extremely well, we were prisoners together in Camp One."

"For four years all he had to eat was rice. Now that he's back in France, he only takes his wife out to Vietnamese restaurants. He wants to teach her Annamite. Are you free for lunch, Captain?"

Julien had no wish to go back to his father wandering about in his old dressing-gown among the flower-beds, leaving a smell of corpses and pharmacy behind him.

"Why not?"

"We could go up to Cabris. You're sure to have a car. An Aronde or a Vedette, or maybe a Frégate? All the officers back from Indo-China have cars."

"I don't."

"That's odd. Let's take mine, then, if she can manage the climb, she's an old rattletrap. Are you building yourself a house? The few officers who haven't bought cars are building themselves houses."

"I'm not."

During the meal the journalist never stopped drinking and kept ordering bottle after bottle. At one point he even clutched his glass so tightly that it broke in his hand.

"Are you feeling restless?" Boisfeuras asked him. "Bored with your long holiday?"

"You've got an ugly face like myself, Captain, a mug that's enough to turn the milk sour, as the peasants say, and your voice is as grating as a rusty hinge. As for me, I've got about as much grace as an elephant, and when I sweat I stink like an old billy-goat. A girl must be either off her head or completely blind to fall for me. Have you ever been in love?"

"It's never happened to me. I believe in carnal passion, not in love . . . and since I've got an ugly face, as you've just reminded me, I pay for my pleasure, which doesn't in any way detract from carnal passion, rather the reverse in fact."

"I was madly in love with a girl once. I don't know if she ever loved me in return, but at least she was used to me. I brought her husband back for her from Indo-China after stuffing him with hormones and vitamins, beefsteaks and caviar; then I came down to Grasse to get over it."

"Marindelle's wife, I suppose?"

"Yes, Jeanine Marindelle. They hadn't got a flat, so they took mine. They insinuated themselves into my life like a couple of tapeworms."

"Yet you took advantage of the wife when her husband was a prisoner."

"I behaved badly, I realize that, and yet . . . Have a brandy with your coffee, won't you? Do you know Ussel—that's right, in Corrèze? You ought to see that town in the rain: a long black road, flanked as far as the eye can see by horrible middle-class houses with blank façades concealing mysteries which couldn't be anything but sordid. A creeping sense of despair grips your guts and you feel like slipping some arsenic into grandma's cup just for the sake of a laugh.

"Three months after their marriage, Yves Marindelle flew out to Indo-China and Jeanine went to stay with little Yves's parents at Ussel, in one of the dreariest houses on that road. The father made a packet in hardware, wholesale groceries or something of that sort—a radical-socialist, a freemason, though he sends his wife to Mass, and a member of the Rotary Club. The Rotary Club of Ussel! The aunts, a couple of ugly old maids. All of them hated her. Jeanine was young and pretty and when she laughed a dimple appeared in her cheek. She came from a good family, but her parents had lost all their money. To her middle-class in-laws she was the adventuress who had stolen the heart of poor little Yves.

"Come on, have some brandy, Captain Boisfeuras. You were born in China, you wouldn't understand how cruel and narrow-minded the French provincial middle class can be.

"Well, Jeanine made her escape for fear they might kill her by injecting all their poisons into her own life. I was her cousin, I used to buy her sweets when she was a little girl, gramophone records when she grew up. I was the only member of her family who went to the wedding. She was marrying her childhood friend, with whom she used to share the sweets I bought her and to whom she used to play my records.

"For the old house at Ussel, the rain of Ussel, the boredom of Ussel, had unaccountably produced the marvellous youth called Yves who resembled her so closely.

"Jeanine took refuge with me in Paris. She brought with her an entire childhood with all its strange and infinitely varied rites, and I, Captain, had never had a childhood of my own. She used to sing those silly little songs that school-children sing at round-games. She used to weep over a flower, smear her face with chocolate and talk of dying as though it was like going for a stroll round the garden.

"Now this is what I feel: love can't exist unless it's linked to that mysterious power and ritual of childhood. I fell madly in love, I stopped drinking, I found a job on the *Quotidien*.

"One day, while holding Jeanine a little too closely in my arms, I made her my mistress. It wasn't particularly convenient, but it was inevitable.

"After that I experienced both paradise and hell. My pleasure was increased by a sense of sacrilege. There was I, the coarse old dullard, admitted into the fairyland of childhood, and at the same time being granted more pleasure than mortal

man can have. The dragon taking advantage of the fairy princess he has captured! The prince came back, delivered his
princess, and the dragon is now eating his heart out . . .

"Unfortunately it wasn't as simple as all that: it was the
fairy princess who held the dragon captive . . . she had developed a taste for his embraces . . . but it was still the poor old
dragon who went off and fetched back the prince.

"I'm drunk, I'm boring you to tears with this story . . . and
yet I can't talk about anything else. From the moment Jeanine
saw Yves again I ceased to exist for her. Before seeing him, she
wanted to leave him. Now, I could swear she doesn't even remember that she lived a whole year with me."

"Did Yves Marindelle know?"

"He amazed me, that boy. 'Four years is a long time,' he
said, 'and you're handing me back my wife just as she was
when I left her, as though you had kept her under glass, protected from the heat and cold. She hasn't aged, she hasn't
changed at all, and yet she has acquired any amount of new
tastes: the music of Stravinsky and Erik Satie, the poetry of
Desnos, blue jeans and pony-tails. Thank you, Herbert.' For
you didn't know, Captain, did you . . ."

Pasfeuro brought his huge fist down on the table:

"My Christian name is Herbert and I'm more well-born
than the whole of the Polish aristocracy put together."

Julien Boisfeuras took to meeting the journalist fairly frequently. Pasfeuro proved to be a mass of contradictions, with a
taste for the weird and the unusual, mad and generous, cynical
and tender-hearted at one and the same time. He hated all
forms of hierarchy and lumped together the Communists, with
whom he was once in conflict, the Jesuits, with whom he had
been brought up, the police, with whom he had often had a
brush, the middle class, towards whom he felt an aristocrat's
contempt, the military, whom he considered stupid, and all
dried up old maids, members of the educational profession,
clergy, technicians, inspectors of finances, pimps, Corsicans,
people from Auvergne and infant prodigies.

Pasfeuro on his side respected the captain, his contempt for sartorial elegance, that manner he had of being at home anywhere, and his sound political and economic background. He seemed to belong to no particular country, had no national prejudice, attached no importance to money or decorations and was astonished and mystified to find himself in the army.

A slightly grudging friendship sprang up between the two of them. When Pasfeuro was posted as permanent correspondent in Algeria and had to go back to Paris, Boisfeuras decided to go with him. They took the holiday route along the Mediterranean coast as far as Montpellier and then crossed the Cevennes. This brought them one morning to the little Lozère village of Rozier on the edge of the Gorges du Tarn.

The trees had shed their last leaves and winter was beginning to assert its authority under the clear sky, among the quivering skeletons of elms, poplars and beech trees. All the gorges were bathed in a blue mist which the December sun could scarcely penetrate. The cliff of Capluc stood like a barrier at the junction between the black waters of the Joute and the green waters of the Tarn. Near a tumbledown old bridge a peasant pointed out a goat path leading up to the summit.

He was a nice old man in a black drill jacket, corduroy trousers, hobnailed boots and cloth cap. He spoke slowly with a strong accent, taking his time, happy to be alive:

"Up there at Capluc," he said, "at one time there were Templars, as in many other places in the Causses. No one ever knew what they were up to in these parts."

Pasfeuro and Boisfeuras embarked on the ascent. At each step the loose pebbles slipped away from under their feet. Pasfeuro admired the agility of the captain who effortlessly climbed the steepest slopes, swinging his shoulders slightly. The journalist was out of breath and, in spite of the cool breeze fanning his face, he sweated copiously. He thought to himself:

"What an unnatural life I led in Paris—the office, bars, cinemas and theatres to which Jeanine made me take her almost every night. She always seemed anxious to postpone the moment she would be alone with me. Each time we went to bed there was a minute or two of ghastly embarrassment. She would turn out the light and undress in the dark, but as soon as beauty's body and the body of the beast came into contact, she would be overcome with passion. Does she turn out the light with Yves Marindelle, I wonder?"

Pasfeuro sat down on a boulder opposite a wall. He did not notice the splendid view, the ochre-coloured ledges of rock, the pinewoods punctuating the lighter expanses of stone and, far down below, the clear green waters of the Tarn.

The captain's rasping voice broke into his unpleasant daydream, plunging him into this bath of light and colour, and his love resumed its ludicrous dimensions.

"Come on, journalist, one last effort. There's a village behind this rock, and above that the Templars' commandery."

Pasfeuro went on climbing and presently the ruins of a village appeared among the nettles, bushes and broom. Some of the houses were still intact with their dry-stone roofs, walls as thick as fortifications and semi-circular vaults. The Templars' commandery dominated the village; all that remained of it was a vast stretch of wall which threatened to collapse and bury the rest of the ruins.

"It's lovely," said Boisfeuras, "this silence and solitude, these ruins and these gorges bathed in a blue mist, like some parts of the country in the north of China. It's the first time I've come across a place in France where I don't feel a stranger. What made the Templars, those strange warriors who owned most of the wealth of the western world, come and take refuge in this wilderness?"

"Not much is known of their history," Pasfeuro told him. "The East, it's certain, provided the Templars with a certain number of rites which they introduced into their Christianity, the initiation ceremonies among others. Perhaps they came up to these commanderies in the Causses to prepare the fusion between the Islamic East and the Christian West, which was the dream of their Grand Master Simon de Montferrat and which would have been the first step towards the unification of the world.

"The Templars discovered the power of money at a time when money was despised, and in Syria the sect of the Assassins had taught them the power of a dagger wielded by a fanatic, in other words terrorism. They were ready for the conquest of the world."

"The ancestors of the Communists?"

"Perhaps. But the Templars were burnt on the stakes of Philippe le Bel just as the Communists were shot through the head by Stalin's henchmen."

"I'd rather like to rebuild this village and this commandery on this very spot," said Boisfeuras, "bring a few men I know up here and re-create a new sect which might have its assassins but, above all its missionaries, who would attempt to bring about not the fusion of the religions of the East and the West, but of Marxism and what I can only call, for want of a better word, Occidentalism."

"Do you really mean that?"

Boisfeuras gave a cynical sneer:

"Of course not. I'm in my father's hands, I'll soon be the director of an insurance company. Where would I recruit my initiates? Among the agents, clerks and typists? Initiates of that sort are only to be found among the young paratroop officers, who have a sense of brotherhood. They are still sufficiently unspoilt and disinterested to do without comfort. They are ready for any adventure and capable of laying down their lives for any high-minded cause, provided it does not conflict with certain prejudices to which they still cling.

"Can't you see them in this restored village of Capluc, quarrying stones and reading books which they can no longer possibly ignore—Karl Marx, Engels, Mao-Tse-Tung, Sorel, Proudhon . . . ?"

" 'Go through the motions and you will believe,' Pascal said. Go through the motions of the Communists, read their books, and you will become a Communist."

"No. All the officers in my monastery would already be innoculated against Communism by the Vietminh camps."

Boisfeuras gave another cynical laugh.

"But these are just words which are lost in the winds of Lozère, just a senseless dream which can never be realized, isn't it?"

"I don't like dreams of that sort, they culminate in Fascism, Communism, Nazism and unleash those epidemics which people find hard to cure. The Germans aren't cured of Nazism, nor are the French cured of Pétain and the occupation. There's not a single Communist country which has managed to stamp out the blight of Marxism. Don't toy with ideas of that sort, Boisfeuras. Leave the tinder in the hands of the older generation; they're in too much fear of dying not to use it with infinite precaution."

"That's also what my father thinks. He would like me to grow old quickly so as to leave the world in peace."

A thick, soot-laden fog hung over Paris when they got there. It was cold and the city rumbled with a joyful ferocity, crunching and devouring mankind.

Boisfeuras and Pasfeuro were swallowed up in the seething crowd, the former cherishing his "big scheme," the other his love, that darling vulture that was eating out his heart.

2

THE BEAUTIFUL BUILDINGS
OF PARIS

"I firmly believe, sir, and I'm not the only one, that this is the root of all our troubles. De Gaulle should have come to an agreement with Pètain. Decoux would have stayed on in Indo-China and we should never have had this wretched war."

The man was elegantly dressed and smelled of lavender water; greying hair added to his distinction; his double chin quivered above a polka-dot bow tie; and the button-hole of his blue suit was adorned with the narrow ribbon of the Légion d'Honneur.

"Someone who's on to a good racket," Philippe Esclavier immediately concluded. "Not the sort of man to have done any fighting but one who's got a certain pull with the Government . . ."

The Mistral train was going all out up the Rhône valley, belting through the stations, thundering over the points.

It stopped for a moment at Avignon. Philippe got up and peered through the carriage window, as though his father might suddenly appear on the platform with his finely chiselled features, his flowing white hair and that air of calm assurance with which he moved. He was one of those men whom ticket-collectors scarcely dared to approach. Uncle Paul, on the other hand, always gave the impression of not having paid his fare.

The train jerked Philippe back from his memories. His travelling companion was holding forth again in the faintly protective and slightly disillusioned tone of voice affected by the fifty-year-old man who has succeeded in business.

"The war in Indo-China, Captain, is the outcome of a series

of unforgivable mistakes. One of my cousins was under-secretary to the Ministry of Associated States at the time of Dien-Bien-Phu; he always said . . ."

"I'm in France," Esclavier kept telling himself. "I've just passed through Avignon station and I don't feel a thing, no sensation at all, not the slightest urge to cry. I simply sit back in my seat facing this old bore."

"Let me introduce myself: Georges Percenier-Moreau, laboratory director of the Mercure pharmaceutical products. We did a lot of work for the army during the Indo-China War, antibiotics for the most part . . ."

"So you're a chemist, are you?"

Percenier-Moreau gave a start, like a barman in a smart hotel on being addressed as "waiter." He had not noticed the mischievous glint that had come into the captain's grey eyes and said to himself:

"What imbeciles these army people are. Outside their own profession they don't know a thing."

Yet he could not bear the idea of being taken for a pharmacy assistant:

"A chemist, Captain, does not have an annual turnover of several million francs. Let's say that the chemist is the retailer and I'm the manufacturer. I make, I invent the goods that he sells."

"You must forgive my ignorance. So you're by way of being both a research worker and manufacturer."

"That's more like it. Our research department . . ."

He preferred to evade the question. The activities of Mercure laboratories were confined to packaging the products which other firms invented and manufactured.

"But I mustn't bore you with all that. You're a nice young man, I can see"—the tone was now distinctly protective—"would you mind telling me your name?"

"Captain Philippe Esclavier of the Fourth Colonial Parachute Battalion."

"I say, that's interesting. You're not related by any chance to *the* Esclavier, the professor?"

"I'm his son."

"I would never have imagined . . ."

"Nor did he, and he died without understanding it."

"I also know Mr. . . ."

"Yes, a certain Weihl who calls himself Esclavier. My brother-in-law. Weihl is all for the Communist revolution, purges and firing squads. He sends that little shiver down your spine, which makes a pear taste better and your mistress's skin feel softer; he leaves you room to hope, if you do one or two little things that aren't too compromising, that he might, once he's in power, include you among the useful middle class."

"But, Captain . . ."

"Utter nonsense, my dear sir. The Communists, and I think I know them pretty well, will put the Weihls of the world into the same concentration camp as the . . . but what did you say your name was?"

"Percenier-Moreau."

"As the Percenier-Moreaus. Why Moreau, incidentally?"

"That's my wife's name."

"As clear as daylight," Philippe thought to himself, "his father-in-law is the real boss. Percenier-Moreau is a parasite of the Weihl-Esclavier class. My father also ran a laboratory, but for distilling and conditioning ideas. He left it to the retailers— the journalists, schoolmasters and professors—to advertise and sell his wares. Weihl appropriated the trademark and is now living on his reputation."

It was Françoise Percenier-Moreau who had dragged her husband along to the Rue de l'Université. He had been bored to death there: nothing to drink but a sort of tepid, watered-down punch, and dainty little sandwiches. Weihl's attitude to the "Mercure Laboratories" had been somewhat condescending, which had punctured its managing director's vanity. Françoise, meanwhile, wallowed with delight in the swirling mists of abstract discussion and wrinkled her brow as she spoke of the working class.

The captain closed his eyes and put his feet up on the seat.

"Scandalous behaviour," Percenier said to himself. "That's the sort of thing you might expect in the third class, but hardly in the first. Service personnel don't pay any fare, or else only quarter-price; they travel in a manner beyond their means and therefore above their station."

He unfolded his newspaper. Trouble in Algeria. What was the army doing about it? Nothing, and meanwhile the officers lolled about in luxury trains.

Percenier turned over to the entertainments page. In the centre there was a photograph of a new discovery, a slender and at the same time sensual figure with a childish yet somehow provocative mouth: Brigitte Bardot. He thought she looked rather like Mina, a little starlet whom he was keeping. Mina did not cost him much. He managed to provide for her out of the firm's expense account. So long as the Treasury did not get wise to it. But when she went out to dinner she invariably ordered roast duck. He dreamt of a girl who would take her time over the menu and give a sophisticated pout as she dipped her lips into the Lanson 1945.

Drowsed by the swaying motion of the train, Philippe let himself be carried away by the memory of his father, Étienne Esclavier, the man he had loved more, admired more and despised more than anyone else in the world, and this memory was at the same time tender and bitter, provoking anger as much as tears.

A hand was gently shaking Philippe:

"Captain . . . Captain . . . we've arrived in Paris, the City of Lights, the vast forcing-house of exotic flowers. But beware, they're carnivorous! Are you being met? Have you got a car? I'd be delighted to drop you anywhere."

Percenier-Moreau had an umbrella and a pigskin briefcase in his hands, and his jaunty little hat set carefully aslant his greying hair gave him the mocking, insolent appearance of a Parisian pierrot.

The grey Bentley glided noiselessly up the luminous stream of the Champs-Élysées.

"Forgive me for coming this round-about way," said Percenier, "but I've got to drop in and say hallo to a little friend who's waiting for me in a bar . . . just long enough to down a whisky. You're not in a hurry, I hope?"

"No. No one's waiting for me."

Percenier-Moreau was far from displeased at being able to show the captain that a "fifty-year-old chemist" could treat himself to someone like little Mina.

The Brent Bar was down a side street a few yards off the Champs-Élysées. Dark panelling, red plush seats and a long bar adorned with the flags of the nations gave the place the atmosphere of one of those comfortable London clubs where whisky is at its best.

The clients spoke in subdued voices. The men all looked like Percenier-Moreau, most of the women were young and pretty. Mina was enthroned on a stool near the cashier's desk, petulantly nibbling at a straw.

"I might have gone to the cinema," she was telling the cashier, "instead of waiting for him here like a little tart who needs a few thousand francs to see her through till the end of the month."

"Oh, come now, Miss Mina, we don't have any tarts in here."

"What do you call Solange, then? She's never with the same fellow longer than a week."

Mina pouted with infinite charm; she had a hungry mouth, a sensual, womanly body, all curves, and the features of a child.

Percenier rushed up to her with much ado, seized her hand and kissed (or rather, licked) it.

"I'm sorry to have kept you waiting, darling. I'd like you to meet a friend of mine, Captain Philippe Esclavier; he's just back from Indo-China."

Philippe and Mina looked into each other's eyes. They barely shook hands and pretended to disregard each other, but both of them already felt that they were going to spend the night together. The voice of desire was insistent, making their ears tingle; they took great care not to let their hands so much as brush against each other, while Percenier-Moreau kept buzzing round them like a fat old bumble-bee.

He left them for a moment to go and telephone his house. Philippe laid his hand on Mina's—a hard, heavy hand which could hurt.

"Wait for me here; I'll be back."

"And then?"

"Then we'll go and have a drink somewhere else . . ."

"I've never felt *this* so strongly," Mina thought to herself.
"What's this man with the gaunt face and big grey eyes got?
Something, in any case, which Percenier never had. How I can
make old Percenier sweat with my roast duck! The captain has
the famished look of the fairy-tale wolf. Mina, my pet, you'd
better watch your step! *Achtung*, Mina, out-of-bounds; handle
with care. He must have slim hips and a firm, flat stomach.
Not like Albert's little pot-belly, carefully squeezed into a flan-
nel belt!"

Albert Percenier-Moreau came traipsing back.

"We'd better be off, Captain. Darling, I'll ring you up tomorrow morning."

Esclavier asked to be dropped near the Luxembourg, from
where he took a taxi straight back to the Brent Bar. Edouard,
the barman, was aware of his little game. He was pleased with
the trick that was being played on the "chemist" and inwardly
rejoiced. This big fellow who wasted no time on details or subterfuge, who went straight after what he wanted, appealed to
him; and so did Mina, who pretended to be stupid but who
was as crafty as a monkey, full of appetite and sensuality.

Esclavier wanted to settle up for the two whiskies Mina and
he had just drunk in silence.

Edouard refused the money.

"It's on the house."

"Why?"

Edouard leant over the edge of the bar and quietly replied:

"Because I like the look of you both."

All of a sudden Philippe was overwhelmed by the memory
of Souen, the Vietminh girl. He could no longer recall every
detail of her face but tried to reconstruct it mentally round the
slanting eyes. Souen alone was love; all the rest were mere encounters, like Mina, this exciting little tart who was clinging
on to his arm.

Philippe Esclavier was woken by the telephone ringing. He
rolled over on his side, rolled back again, and even stuffed

the pillow over his head to escape the persistent noise pursuing him.

Mina picked up the receiver in the dark:

"Hallo? Oh, it's you, Albert. What do you mean by waking me up at this unearthly hour? It's ten o'clock already? But it's quite dark outside. There's a fog, is there? No, I don't feel like going out. No, you can't come here either. The place is in a dreadful mess and anyway I'm rather tired. What did I think of Captain Esclavier? Oh, nothing to write home about . . ."

She was quietly stroking Philippe's leg and the warm palm of her hand felt gently insistent.

"No, Albert, I don't like those cocksure young types who think every woman's going to fall into their arms. What I need is tenderness and affection, which can only be found in men who have had some experience of life, like you, my dear . . ."

The pressure of her hand increased.

Philippe snuggled up to her, returning her caresses in his usual straightforward manner. Mina's voice changed, becoming deep and guttural, on the verge of a passionate groan, the sort of voice that Percenier-Moreau had rarely had occasion to hear.

"Of course I love you, honeybunch!"

She hung up, uttering a long wail of pleasure.

Mina eventually got up to make breakfast. She drew the curtains; a dim light filtered through the window and presently the smell of coffee and toast began to fill the room. The phonograph played a languid blues in the background.

She came back carrying a large tray. Her auburn hair hung in heavy coils above her white silk dressing-gown. She looked like a greedy, hypocritical virgin.

"How much sugar, darling? I've already buttered the toast. A cigarette? Here, do you want to see the *Figaro*? Albert gave me a subscription to it."

"It's comfortable here," said Philippe. "Your coffee is excellent, you minister to a man's needs, you don't talk too much, and you know how to make love. The perfect concubine for a fat chemist who has made millions out of Indo-China while others were dying of hunger or disease. Do you know how much a Nung, Thai or Méo partisan got for carrying a rifle, fighting and in many cases dying? Twenty-five piastres a month and a few handfuls of rice."

"You hate my chemist, don't you?"

"He's not worth hating. But you do, my beauty, don't you? What about that little telephone conversation just now? Why did you have to lead him on like that?"

"I don't want him to feel uneasy. I know what fat old Albert's like. If he felt uneasy about me, he would drop me without the slightest hesitation. Albert's an old softy who's wrapped up in cotton wool, but if you rub him up the wrong way he gets furious. Every now and then, without his knowing it, if it's not too risky, I treat myself to a handsome young lad who happens to take my fancy."

"And you call Percenier up on the telephone?"

"No, that was the first time."

Mina lay down beside the captain and nestled her head against his shoulder.

"I'd never thought of it before. Perhaps it was you who gave me the idea. I don't know you from Adam, you don't bother your head about niceties, you fling your shoes into one corner of the room, your coat into another. You have a bath and splash the water all over the place . . . and I get up and make you breakfast. All the others, I used to send packing at dawn. Once the show was over, off they went and no harm done. Just because a man knows what a girl's got under her skirt, that doesn't mean he's got any rights over her. But I want to hang on to you . . . maybe because you're like me, because you don't find life so wonderful . . ."

"What do you find wrong with it?"

"Even a little *poule* has her dreams. Do you know which is the loveliest street in Paris?"

"No."

"The Rue de Buci. That's where I was born, among the carrots, cauliflowers and leeks in the market. My mother was a concierge, my father worked in a post office. She was a holy terror, my mother. She gave everyone hell, you should have heard her! I remember one row about a fish that wasn't quite fresh; she pelted the fishmonger with his own whitings and mackerels, screaming it was an 'insult to the working class.' There were two or three other harridans as foul-mouthed as she who promptly rose in support of the 'working class.' It was a regular free-for-all. My mother fought with one half of the neighbourhood and was ready to quarrel with the other. On liberation day she denounced the whole lot of them. Liberation committees were meat and drink to her . . . Life at home was anything but placid; every day was spent in an atmosphere of high drama."

"What did your father do?"

"He smoked his pipe and read his paper with his spectacles slipping off the end of his nose. When I think of all the energy my mother expended just for the sake of putting fifty yards of the Rue de Buci in a state of revolt. I left school and studied shorthand-typing at Pigier Secretarial College. A friend of my father's found me a job with the Mercure Laboratories where I started as a book-keeper. The head of the personnel made it quite clear from the start—either I went to bed with him or I should find myself in trouble. It was common knowledge in the office that the boss was partial to little beginners. I went and complained to Mr. Albert Percenier-Moreau . . . That very evening I became his girl-friend. There was no other way out . . ."

"Are you sure?"

"I could have settled down, of course—home, husband, squalling brats and all the rest of it. But I should still have had to go to bed with the head of the personnel. Thanks to Albert, I've already had my photo in the weeklies."

"To advertise his products?"

"What of it? I've had some small parts in films; one day I might be given a big one. I'm following a course of dramatic art and my teacher says I show promise. I photograph well, my face seems to be expressive."

"So's the rest of you."

"Anyway I'm no longer broke, making do with a cup of

coffee and a couple of croissants for lunch. I can afford a fine young captain when I feel like it, and in linen sheets too; I've every reason to be hopeful. Prince Charmings aren't to be found in a typist's office, but they all go to the cinema."

"What does your mother think about it?"

"She says I'm a traitor to the 'working class' but still accepts my money to buy herself a refrigerator. I see her as little as possible. She enjoys the role of the mother whose daughter has gone to the dogs . . . and since she needs an audience, well, it all takes place in the street. I'm very fond of that street all the same. Over there I'm once again the little Merchut girl, Elizabeth Merchut."

"Whereas here . . . ?"

"Whereas here I'm Mina Lecouvreur. But that's enough about me. What about you? For someone who's just back from Indo-China, you don't seem to be in much of a hurry to get home. Are you married?"

"No, thank heavens."

"Well, then?"

Philippe ran his fingers through Mina's hair.

"I've got a score to settle with a dirty little bastard."

"Are you going to break him?"

"It's not quite as simple as that; the little bastard may not be as much of a bastard as he seems . . ."

"Did he run off with your girl when you were away fighting?"

"No."

With her chin in her hand, Mina voiced her thoughts out loud:

"Worse than that even? He stole your apartment?"

"And everything in it, but I've only myself to blame."

"Take a leaf out of Mother Merchut's book. Start screaming: 'It's an insult to the working class' and then pitch in. We could bring her along with us if you like. She loves meddling in other people's business . . . Only a paratroop officer and the working class don't quite go together. Don't worry, though Nathalie Merchut has always put her taste for squabbling above her political convictions . . . and like her daughter, she's got a weakness for handsome young soldiers . . ."

This time Philippe Esclavier laughed out loud, visualizing his arrival at the Rue de l'Université flanked by Mother Merchut and her daughter, breaking in on the staid meeting of Weihl and his progressivist friends, and shrieking: "It's an insult to the working class." "And nothing could be closer to the truth," he reflected.

"You don't often laugh, Philippe. A pity, because it suits you, you no longer look like an angry old bear. Here, give me a kiss. Do you know anyone in show business?"

"Not a soul. I'm just a brutal and licentious soldier."

"It was too much to expect, I suppose. Have you ever been in love with a girl . . . I mean, really in love?"

Esclavier hung his head and felt the blood rushing to his face.

"Yes, I've been in love . . . I never went to bed with her; I only kissed her once, and then only on the cheek . . ."

"Calf love."

"No, it was . . . three months ago . . ."

"Don't cheat, Esclavier," Dia had told him when they had got drunk together in Marseilles. "The whole thing's too good to be true. Little Souen was all on her own; you had nothing to do with it, you were just a pretext. Lescure probably got closer to her than anyone else, playing his little flute in the dark."

And here he was professing his love for Souen, for the benefit of this little bitch! Yet he could not resist it. He was certainly the son of his father, whose two or three extra-conjugal adventures had given rise to books or rather literary discussions . . .

Intellectuals didn't know how to love; they were always obsessed by their own problems; they listened in raptures to the beating of their heart; anything served as a pretext for them to probe their souls in order to produce a spate of words. He had not yet been able to eradicate this persistent weed, this observant and monstrous egoism.

Like little Mina, he was obsessed by show business; but his show business was exclusively for himself and a few initiates. He suffered but consciously thought of putting his suffering to use, he struggled with himself while pondering on the way in which he could describe his struggle, he loved or pretended to love in the hope of using that love in the form of narrative. This was in his blood, this need to serve as an intermediary between what he experienced and felt, and a public. This obsession with the public was inherited from his father; it was like a thistle that had to be rooted out.

As he felt in his coat pocket for a packet of cigarettes, Philippe found a notebook in which he had jotted down the addresses and telephone numbers of his comrades on leaving them in Marseilles.

Glatigny: Invalides 08–22. He rang him up while Mina lay down on the thick carpet and did some stretching exercises "for the sake of her figure."

A very well-bred, over-bred, deep-throated voice replied:

"Countess Glatigny speaking. You wish to speak to the captain? Who shall I say? Captain Philippe Esclavier. He'll be delighted; he never stops talking about you. I hope we shall meet soon. Just a moment, here he is."

Esclavier gave a little shudder:

"Brr . . . I bet Glatigny doesn't have much fun."

But his comrade's warm voice was already on the other end of the line:

"So you've got to Paris at last. How long did you stay in Marseilles?"

"Four days."

"Where are you? Come and lunch with us. You know the address: 17 Boulevard des Invalides. You haven't got a car . . . Shall I come and fetch you?"

Philippe had no wish to partake of a family meal, to be interrogated on every count, to have to answer questions which ostensibly had no connexion but which would enable the countess to determine his social background and fit his accent and manners to the preconceived idea she would have of him.

"I suggest we lunch together alone, Glatigny. Let's meet at the Brent Bar off the Champs-Élysées. It's in a side street next door to the Colisée."

"I'll see if I can get away."

Philippe heard his comrade's voice more faintly:

"Claude, I shan't be in to lunch. What's that? General de Percenailles's coming? Well, you'll have to make some excuse for me!"

A child shouted in the background, then another, and Glatigny's voice sounded closer:

"Right, Esclavier, see you in your bar at half-past twelve."

Philippe had the impression that his comrade was relieved and delighted with this opportunity he had just been given to escape from his little family hell.

"Take my number as well," said Mina. "If you ever feel low just give me a ring and if Albert isn't about, come over and see me. Just a couple of good pals doing each other a good turn . . . I'd like to take you to the Rue de Buci some day, if only to show my mother and her little crowd that I'm not just an old man's moll."

"Look out, Mina, you're getting sentimental. Very bad for your career."

"You can be so sweet sometimes, just for a few minutes, and then, suddenly, out you come in your true colours . . . the real man, selfish and cruel . . . who takes his pleasure and promptly puts his trousers on again."

"Well I never, you're trying to start a row!"

Mina held her chin in her hand.

"But it's true, you know."

She gave a rather forced little laugh.

Leaning back in her arm-chair, the Comtesse de Glatigny scrutinized the stranger who was sitting in her drawing-room reading the paper, in a pair of old slippers and a grey pullover.

The stranger was her husband, the father of her five children.

"Jacques."

"Yes?"

He looked up; she did not even recognize his face. Was it leanness that exaggerated his features and his square chin, the rather common chin of a boxer or swimming-instructor?

Why had he thought it necessary to parachute into Dien-

Bien-Phu? It was a splendid, dashing gesture, and at the time Jacques had been praised to the skies by everyone she met. Later on there had been a certain reservation. By jumping in he had betrayed his class, for in the army, as in the rest of the country, there were class distinctions which had nothing to do with rank or service. By his action he had publicly repudiated the general staff to which he belonged. Yes, the action of an officer of the line . . . a breach of manners on his part . . . and now this habit he affected of pinning a paratrooper's badge on his uniform! Paratroops were nothing but adventurers disguised as soldiers.

Rather than lunch with General de Percenailles, he preferred to meet this chap Esclavier in a bar. General de Percenailles was a dreary old bore, but he still had useful connexions in the cavalry and played the dual role of arbiter of elegance and chairman of a sort of honorary jury; he it was who decided what was done and what was not done. He was one of those who had condemned Jacques's gesture. This luncheon might have set everything to rights, but Captain de Glatigny, a staff officer who was in the running for the command of a squadron, preferred to meet a big oaf of a paratrooper in a bar.

Since his return Jacques had never stopped talking about this fellow Esclavier and all the tricks he got up to, about a sort of tramp called Boisfeuras, about Pinières and Mahmoudi, an Arab, and a certain Raspéguy, an illiterate who had become a colonel and who at any other time would have remained a warrant-officer for life.

The day after he got back, they had both gone out to dine with Colonel Puysange who was said to wield considerable influence behind the scenes in the army.

General Mélies of the Ministry of National Defence was also there, and in the course of the evening the name of Lieutenant Marindelle had cropped up.

Lowering his eyelids, which gave him a vaguely sphinx-like appearance, Puysange had observed:

"I've had a report on that officer. During his four years' captivity it seems the Communists worked on him pretty thoroughly and he actually became one himself. His parents are well off; we're going to ask him to resign his commission."

Claude de Glatigny had seen her husband go white in the face and raise his voice all of a sudden:

"If you did that, Colonel, it would be a pretty dirty trick apart from being a crime against the army."

"But, Captain, he can be invalided out. We can put it down to malaria; that's been done before you know . . ."

"Lieutenant Marindelle was one of the few of us who understood about revolutionary warfare. His conduct in the camps was above all praise, I can vouch for that . . . He's an exceptional man, Colonel . . ."

Colonel Puysange had been warned that anyone who had been in a Vietminh camp was never quite the same when he came out. But for a Glatigny to have changed to such an extent—this was really astonishing. Yet he could not tolerate such an attitude in one of his subalterns, and at the same time he had to tone down the necessary reprimand and make it sound like a friendly admonition, for the captain belonged to a powerful clan.

"I don't doubt the soundness of your opinion, Jacques, old boy, but perhaps it was distorted by the atmosphere of the camps and the endless propaganda to which you were subjected. The army's one thing, politics are another, and the expression 'revolutionary warfare' is the absolute negation of our traditions."

"All warfare is bound to become political, Colonel, and an officer with no political training will soon prove ineffective. Frequently the word 'tradition' only serves to conceal our laziness."

General Mélies had then chipped in. He had a fine military record and prostate trouble, but it was said he would not have this much longer. His snow-white moustache was set in motion with every word he gobbled.

"We know how much you've suffered, my dear fellow . . . France let you down badly. You were forced to take decisions which were often beyond your capacity. The army has finished with 'operations' of that sort, I think. It must recover its former position, resume its traditions . . . And for that we shall have to separate the sheep from the goats . . ."

Claude had motioned to her husband to let the matter drop. But Jacques had persisted:

"In that case, General, we're all of us goats—all who were in the maquis in France, who served in the First Army or the F.F.L., who took part in the Indo-China campaign, in the fighting units, who died of hunger on the tracks of the Haute Région, all who believe that the army depends on the people just as a fish depends on water. That's what Mao-Tse-Tung wrote, and it's because we ignored his theories on revolutionary warfare that we deserved our crushing defeat. If you get rid of all of us, what will remain of the army?"

Colonel Puysange struck the table-cloth with his knife. Glatigny was even more contaminated than he had thought; he quoted Mao-Tse-Tung, a Communist, therefore he had read Communist books. Oh, if only all those goats weren't needed in order to wage war, how easily this scourge would be wiped out!

He came to the rescue of the general:

"This is just an individual case, the question of Lieutenant Marindelle. A simple disciplinary action against him, I feel . . ."

"I feel any disciplinary action against him would jeopardize the morale of the army and be most unwelcome and unpopular with the friends of Lieutenant Marindelle . . ."

"Of whom you are one."

"Of whom I am one."

Everyone had stopped talking. With difficulty the mistress of the house brought the conversation round to the latest theatrical success. Captain de Glatigny had not opened his mouth again.

After dinner a lieutenant sitting at the end of the table had come up to him and Claude had realized he was congratulating him. The lieutenant had been out in Indo-China.

But Puysange had led the young woman into a corner of the drawing-room.

"My dear Claude, you must curb the captain's tongue; if we hadn't been among friends, among people of the same social standing, the incident might have proved extremely serious and harmful to your husband's career. He must get rid of those ideas of his. You can help there. He seems to have Communist sympathies . . ."

"Jacques a Communist!"

"I won't go so far as that. Solid traditions, a sincere faith, and love of his profession would prevent him from sinking to that, my dear."

In the car, an old Mercedes they had brought back from Germany, Claude asked her husband with horror in her voice:

"Is it true you're a Communist?"

"Puysange said so, I suppose. I shall never be able to understand how a man with such a noble, forthright appearance can be so low-minded or how, with all those decorations of his, he has never heard a shot fired in anger. Do you know what Communism is? No, of course not. And even the Communists in France don't know either. Communism is a country in another planet. Now I don't happen to have any inclination for space travel. Will you please ring up Jeanine Marindelle tomorrow and ask her to dinner with her husband."

"Ring up Jeanine after what she has done!"

"That's Yves Marindelle's business, not ours. But I absolutely insist on having the lieutenant and his wife at our table tomorrow. You'd better ask that windbag Major Gernier as well. Like that everyone will hear about it, including that old fool Puysange."

Now he was referring to his superior officers as fools! This was what Communism meant—lowering one's standards, denying the established order of things—and not that cock-and-bull story about space travel.

During the dinner Claude had felt deeply offended, first of all by the presence of Jeanine, the adulterous wife, all sugar and spice, and by her beauty which was more startling than ever (as though sinning was good for the complexion) and, secondly, by the close relationship that existed between her husband and Marindelle. The lieutenant addressed Jacques by the familiar "*tu*" and talked to him as an equal, forgetting the difference of rank, age and, to put it bluntly, social background.

After all, Captain de Glatigny had served as an aide-de-camp to several generals.

And Jeanine, all smiles and gaiety—that little bitch with the looks of an angel who had given herself to that filthy ginger-headed beast, Pasfeuro!

Jacques chattered and joked with her. Perhaps he was actually after her himself, now that he knew how easy she was to get.

How Jacques had changed! Instead of getting up and shaving, there he was lying back in his arm-chair reading a paper. Since his return he lolled about in bed, spent hours playing with the children or else sat astride a chair in the kitchen, watching Marie peel the vegetables or prepare a stew. Sometimes he even helped her.

The children were getting too familiar with their father, and Marie was inclined to be insubordinate. He no longer kept them at a proper distance, and the results of this were deplorable.

It was a complete stranger who had shared her bed that first evening. He had behaved disgustingly, and she had felt as though she was committing adultery. He had treated her like any casual pick-up, panting and groaning on top of her, while she lay on her back looking up at the crucifix on the wall, at an outraged and reproachful Christ. Then he had thanked her with a clumsy sentimental kiss.

In the indignation which this physical contact caused her, she had plucked up her courage and told him everything.

"Jacques, I think you ought to know . . ."

"Yes?"

He wanted to feel his wife's head nestling on his shoulder, to hold her tight in his arms and tell her how much he had thought about her and the children when he was out there, at Marianne II, and had expected to be killed.

But she drew away, shrinking from the contact of his body.

"Jacques, I decided to use the money you sent me for a rather different purpose than we agreed upon. I had the roof of the Château de Pressinges re-done. It was almost falling in."

Glatigny half sat up in bed.

"You're joking, I suppose . . ."

"No, seriously. It was a little more expensive than I thought: two and a half million . . ."

"You couldn't have been as stupid as that!"

"What do you mean?"

"What I say—as stupid, idiotic and senseless as that. I thought we'd seen the last of that useless, worm-eaten old pile of stones . . ."

"I was born there, and all my family before me, and two of our sons as well, Xavier and Yvon . . ."

"For two months in the year you like to play the lady of the manor, to be solicitous and condescending over the kids of peasants ten times richer than we are, to queen it in your pew in church . . . you're as vain as a pea-hen."

"I never realized you could be so common."

"That money was for the children and, a bit of it, for us. Seaside holidays, two bicycles for Xavier and Yvon, a little pocket money . . . a new car."

"The children will be all right at Pressinges . . ."

"In that damp, icy old castle . . ."

"At least it will make them conscious of their position."

"My dear Claude, all that nonsense is finished and done with."

Claude felt like crying as she thought how much she had loved Jacques when he was at Dien-Bien-Phu, and after that, in the P.O.W. camp; she had loved him so much she would have died for him, and this imitation Jacques had come back to her.

But what had become of the original, the well-mannered, courteous and slightly disdainful Jacques de Glatigny who was proud of his name and made his senior officers feel that he was doing them a favour by obeying them? He used to win horse shows and played bridge perfectly.

And now she had to be content with this vulgar, coarsened counterfeit in the arm-chair. No, it wasn't possible.

Jacques peered at his wife over the top of his newspaper. She still had those doe eyes which had so beguiled him, eyes that were something between yellow and red, in a shapely, finely chiselled face, and a slender equestrienne's figure which child-birth had not thickened.

Claude was small and well bred, indestructible and intransigent; she knew how to entertain, direct a conversation, bring up children, speak to servants; she could recite the Army List by heart and boasted almost as many generals in her family as there were in his. But she was difficult to get on with and not very intelligent.

Their marriage had been celebrated with a great ball in the park of the already tumbledown Château de Pressinges. There had been several hundred guests, including a marshal of France, an archbishop, all the local nobility, and all the officers from the neighbouring garrisons provided they were sufficiently well born. What remained of the Pressinges fortune had been swallowed up in this final display. The bells which rang for their wedding, eight days later sounded the war alarm. Xavier, the eldest of their children, was now fifteen.

Until then Jacques had managed to get along with his wife; he only used to see her long enough to give her a child. After going away in 1939, he was wounded and taken prisoner; then, having escaped, he had spent two years with the maquis in Savoie. Geneviève had been born in a little town in the Black Forest where Dr. Faust was said to have lived. That year of occupation in Germany, the only year the couple had been together, had been extremely pleasant: hunting, balls, regimental dinners and horse shows.

Comtesse de Glatigny, the niece of a commander-in-chief and of a high commissioner of France, related to all the nobility, including the German nobility which was rising again from the ruins, rich for once, possessing a car and servants, fancied she had found the rank and position that were her due.

She had reigned over that wild year and turned the heads of several lieutenants who had married into her family. Since she often entertained the Wehrmacht General Heinrich von Bulöckv, a cousin on her mother's side, she was looked upon as a very great lady who could afford to overlook the prejudices of victor and vanquished. But she knew how to get the best out of victory just the same.

One day von Bulöckv had said to the captain:

"Claude takes pleasure in showing me off, my dear Jacques; I'm her scandal, but a good quality scandal; I plotted against Hitler and I never committed any so-called 'war crimes.' As though it were possible to make war without committing crimes! I come here and sing for my supper by describing my battle in France—I rather enjoy that—and my campaign in Russia—which is somewhat more painful. Sometimes I can't help wondering if your wife isn't a little monster . . . Give me another glass of that excellent brandy . . . I know of a wonderful horse that has managed to survive the war; it's stabled just round the corner. You could requisition it . . . If it leaves Germany, at least it won't be leaving the family."

According to the latest news, the former Panzer General von Bulöckv was in the process of building up one of the largest fortunes in Germany from prefabricated houses which he sold throughout the world.

He had invited Xavier and Geneviève to spend Christmas with him on his country estate near Cologne. He would come over himself to fetch them and would stay in Paris for a day.

Bulöckv had not had any of his old castles rebuilt; on the contrary, he had had what remained of them blown up with dynamite. Then he had built himself a villa equipped with every modern comfort on the banks of the Bodensee. To round everything off, he had just married a mannequin twenty-five years younger than himself.

Over the ruined walls of Pressinges, Claude had had a new roof put on! While he was holding the grenade in his hand, when Marianne had been taken, while he was slogging along the tracks, listening to the Voice and carrying Esclavier on a stretcher, the little money he had earned by the sweat of his brow had been wasted on this vain and anachronistic impulse.

Before his capture Glatigny had found his wife's anxiety to restore the castle quite natural. Like all his family, he had a sense of possession which was very different from that of the middle or merchant classes. For him a castle was still a communal building. In the Middle Ages everyone could find refuge there, today everyone could visit it. The owner of the moment was responsible not only to his own dynasty but also to the nation.

But his evolution which had begun at Camp One now led him to take an aversion to the world in which his wife continued to live and in which the castle stood. Yvon came and sat down on his father's knee. Claude's dry voice chided him:

"Now then, you boys, I've forbidden you to come in here. Yvon, go back to your room."

"Wait a moment," his father gently said. "Claude, look how pale he is. The seaside would have done him a lot of good."

Geneviève came in with Indo-China I and II: Muriel and Olivier, the girl and boy they had engendered on each home leave. The children clustered round him, hanging on his neck, pulling his hair, clutching at his pullover, jostling one another, laughing, screaming, fighting.

"I give up," said Claude. "Since you came back all the manners I've taught them have gone by the board. So it's settled, is it, you're going out to meet Esclavier?"

"Let's not go over that again. What's more, I hope to bring him back here to dinner and also see Marindelle, if I can . . ."

"I shan't be here. If this goes on, we'll have your N.C.O.s and privates invading this drawing-room."

"I wouldn't mind at all if they did, but you see, my dear, they're all dead."

Jacques de Glatigny glanced round the drawing-room with its pictures, suits of armour, standards and coats of arms. On the shelves stood rows of miniature cannons, a complete little military museum.

That stained and tattered old flag had come from Waterloo, and that large sword, which only a giant could wield, had belonged to the Constable. The large crystal chandelier had been looted in Italy, and the sumptuous carpets brought back by General Gardanne, whom Napoleon had sent into Persia to persuade the Shah to side with him against the British. In a glass case hung the starred cloak of a Grand Master of the Knights of Malta, and on a pillar stood the dented breastplate of an officer of the Pontifical Zouaves.

Yes, indeed, what would Bachelier and Bermanju, Moustier and Dupont, Merkilof and Javelle, have said if they had found themselves here, among all these remnants of history? And Cergona with his W.T. set which seemed to be devouring his back? But their bodies were now rotting in the Dien-Bien-Phu basin.

He plucked the children off him as though they were bunches of grapes, and went off to dress. He was going to be late for his meeting with Esclavier. He felt extremely tired. He would have liked to be living alone in a wooden hut in the country, tramping through the forests in hobnailed boots, feeding on bread, wine, raw onions, sardines and eggs . . . in solitude . . . and in prayer . . . searching for the mysterious thread which he needed to guide him through this new existence in which he discovered that generals can be imbeciles and one's own wife a stranger.

Yet he was the first to arrive at the Brent Bar and he almost ordered a whisky, then changed his mind—that was a habit he would have to get rid of. With a captain's pay, a wife with big ideas, five bouncing children and a flat like a military museum, whisky was a forbidden luxury.

"A port, please, barman."

"You're not going to drink that muck," Esclavier exclaimed, rushing in. "Two whiskies, please, barman."

"Good morning, Captain," said Edouard.

The barman gave Philippe Esclavier a conspiratorial smile.

This was the first time Philippe had seen his friend in civilian clothes: he was surprised. Although dressed with the utmost care, Glatigny looked shrunken, thinner and smaller than he really was, in his rather old-fashioned blue suit which smelt faintly of mothballs. He had put his roll-brim hat and gloves down beside him on the bar and sat astride his stool as though it was a saddle. His features were drawn, his smile melancholy. He had a smelly old pipe in his mouth.

Esclavier put his hand on his shoulder, as he had done up there in the Méo highlands.

"Well, Jacques?"

"Well, Philippe?"

"What was it like getting back?"

"I found my children had grown a lot. I behave towards them like a doddering old papa, dripping with affection; I tremble for them, for they'll be forced to live in the termite world which we once knew. My wife has got used to being alone; she has acquired self-reliance, a certain sense of independence. The great tragedy is that in the Vietminh camps we developed on our own, away from our families, our social class, our profession and country. So coming back isn't so easy."

"With the Viets, the problem was over-simple. It boiled down to this: survival. Some of us went a little farther and tried to understand it."

"I've seen Marindelle again."

"Oh yes?"

"He's happy, he's playing at being happy . . . but . . ."

"Yes, he has a gift for theatricals."

"He's being accused of turning Communist."

"Marindelle!"

"I've had to stand up for him, consequently I'm now regarded as a fellow-traveller!"

Esclavier reverted to his dry, scornful tone:

"The army is the biggest collection of dirty dogs and idiots that I've ever come across."

"Well, why are you in it then?"

"It's also where you meet the most unselfish men and most loyal friends."

"Have you been home yet?"

"No. I don't know how to put it, but I can't bear the idea. Two more whiskies, please, Edouard: make them doubles. It's true, we've developed away from our homes . . . and for the first time I feel that we army people are ahead . . . for the first time in centuries. Only, there we are, it's mere chance that has pushed us ahead; we weren't prepared for it. Let's go and eat; I need your help to get me in the proper frame of mind to go home to the Rue de l'Université."

By eight o'clock that evening Glatigny and Esclavier were drunk. They had run into Orsini wandering about the Champs-

Élysées in search of a cinema. He never got up until two in the afternoon and spent his time playing poker all night with his fellow Corsicans. Up to now he had been winning.

"They're handing it to me on a plate," he said. "It's the first time I've ever seen them lose."

All three of them had gone back to the Brent Bar and a fascinated Edouard listened to them, forgetting his other clients.

"As far as I'm concerned," said Glatigny, dipping his nose into his glass, "love boils down to a purely social function; religion to a number of senseless gestures; warfare to a form of technology more or less suited to the purpose. Do you realize, you two, why I fought at Dien-Bien-Phu, why I slogged through those muddy trenches with my hands tied behind my back, rotting with fever in the monsoon, do you realize why we waged that war in Indo-China? Just so that the Comtesse de Glatigny could put a new roof on a pile of old ruins."

"I'm fed up already," said Orsini. "One ought to be able to spend one's leave with a few friends . . . who, like me, have neither wife nor family . . . I've never been so thirsty as this evening. All the thirst I felt at Camp One is parching my throat. What do you say to ringing up Marindelle?"

"Marindelle is living on love," said Esclavier. "I think I'm now at last in a fit state to go home."

He left, with his beret planted firmly on his head and his lips set in a thin, grim line. Glatigny and Orsini went on drinking.

With his hands in the pockets of his raincoat, a cigarette drooping from his lip, his face very pale and thin, Philippe Esclavier stood outside the front door.

His sister Jacqueline opened it and heaved a deep sigh.

"It's you, Philippe. We thought you were dead."

"Thought or hoped?"

She was shivering, for she felt she was looking at a ghost—the ghost of her father, grimly accoutred. The resemblance was overwhelming.

"Please, Philippe. I'm so pleased you've come back."

She tried to kiss him. He let her do so, keeping his hands in his pockets and his cigarette in his mouth, then pushed past her through the door.

The muffled sound of a number of voices came from the drawing-room.

"You've got company, I gather. Is Weihl holding forth as usual?"

"Philippe, don't let's have a row. Our opinions may differ . . ."

"It's not just our opinions . . ."

"Everyone will be delighted to see you, including Michel . . . After all, you were both deported together . . ."

"Not for the same reasons . . ."

"Please, Philippe. I've got out your civilian clothes. Would you like me to go and fetch them. Go and have a wash to freshen yourself up. Then change and . . . come and join us."

"Why change?"

"That uniform you're wearing . . ."

"I might have known it. When I came back from Mathausen, you wanted me to keep on my deportee's uniform. Now that I'm back from Indo-China as an officer . . ."

"A paratroop officer . . . Philippe . . ."

"You want me to disguise myself as a civilian, to slink home in the dark, to kowtow to a dirty little crook and his friends who are mucking up my carpets, to ask forgiveness for failing to get myself killed twenty times over, for miraculously coming out alive after being dumped in a Vietminh hospital. There must be something wrong with you, Jacqueline."

Jacqueline burst into tears.

"You're an utter savage, and you've been drinking, you reek of drink. Our father never used to drink."

Philippe stepped into the drawing-room with his beret still on his head, but he had taken off his raincoat, revealing his parachute badge and decorations.

Michel Weihl-Esclavier was speaking with the scornful detachment, the rather precious insistence on the choice of expression, which enabled him to pose as a sensitive soul and writer of wide culture. He was leaning against the mantelpiece under the big portrait of Étienne Esclavier, and one of his hands, which were his best feature, drooped in an attitude of studied negligence.

Ensconced in an arm-chair, Villèle seemed to be hanging on his lips, but he wasn't listening to him and his thoughts were elsewhere. Villèle hated Weihl and his success; he congratulated him on his books, which he signed Michel W. Esclavier, but said behind his back that they were junk, and never read them. He himself would have liked to live in this apartment where generations of professors, men of law, famous doctors and politicians had amassed their tasteful treasures.

The Fantin-Latour hanging on the opposite wall was a fortune in itself.

Since Weihl was not looking at him, he turned his head slightly and saw the charming profile of Guitte, Goldschmidt's daughter. The old professor was asleep in his chair, his mouth wide open. She was lively and attractive, the little minx. What would she be like in bed? Prudish? Bold? A mixture of the two? It was something worth considering . . .

Nothing else of interest in this group: a few activists with thick ankles and short hair; two or three society women as silly as that Françoise Percenier-Moreau who was said to be Weihl's mistress; some badly dressed, shiny-faced female students . . . barely fit for a roll in the hay in an interval between two self-examination periods.

The men were not much better: university people with an exaggerated idea of themselves; a painter who turned up at every meeting because he had been given to think that he might meet Picasso there. But what no one knew was that the painter carried in his pocket a syringe filled with black paint with which he intended to spray the "mystery-monger who had ruined painting."

He, Villèle, did know and was biding his time . . . One evening he had written a paper, a very good paper, in which he sided with Picasso, of course, but with reservations, extremely subtle reservations. The paper could not appear yet; and perhaps if the incident did occur, the outcome might be entirely different. There was also a stage-manager who was noted for his unnatural tastes. And lastly, a Dominican. There is always a Dominican in the offing.

Not one of the thirty people assembled there found favour in Villèle's eyes, not even the little philosophy mistress from a provincial *lycée* who was blushing with admiration for the master and delightedly dipping the tip of her tongue into a glass of tepid orangeade. How sordid it all was, Weihl and his orangeade!

He caught sight of Philippe Esclavier who had just come in, and recognized him at once. He was the tall captain who at Vietri had given the released prisoners the order to throw away their fibre helmets and canvas boots. Villèle had a photographic memory for faces. He assumed a puzzled expression as a wave of jubilation swept over him. The show-down promised to be a good one.

"Our action in favour of peace," Weihl was saying, "has met with magnificent results. We raised public opinion against the war in Indo-China, and the outcome was the armistice and the victory of our friends of the Democratic Republic of Viet-Nam. Soon they'll be masters of the South, where the puppet set up by the Americans won't be able to hold out for more than a few days."

"Still talking away?"

Philippe's voice chipped in, dry as the crackle of a forest tree on a frosty day. He was leaning against the door-post as though to block the exit through which his prey might try to escape.

"I wonder what our country has done to you for you to think of nothing but destroying it, or my family for you to have come and infected them."

Michel Weihl felt the blood draining from his face, chest and limbs and taking refuge in some mysterious part of his body, a sort of basin into which it always settled as soon as things began to go wrong. He had been expecting this encounter and had prepared for it, but was nevertheless taken by surprise.

The Dominican rose to his feet and tried to make for the

doorway. Philippe's voice brought him to a standstill like a butterfly on a pin.

"Back to your seat, Vicar, and stay there!"

Jacqueline tried to come through the door from the other side. She drummed on him with her bare fists but soon gave up.

"She has gone to her room to have a good cry," Weihl thought to himself. "That's all she's good for—crying like her mother. The Dominican has also sat down again. And that little sod Villèle is secretly laughing his head off! Goldschmidt has woken up at last; he's rubbing his eyes. He's beaming all over his face; he has recognized his little Philippe . . . This is all very interesting. At the moment I am outside the drama, like a spectator, but I am also at the centre of it. This theme would be worth developing, but later, later. I must recover my position on stage, in the centre of the stage. Françoise is trying to look shocked. That won't do any good, my little Françoise; this time it's serious, and Philippe hasn't even noticed your facial contortions. I'm his 'sacrificial beast.'" Michel suddenly recalled this Persian expression to which he had attached a deep significance: "May I be your sacrificial beast."

He noticed that a complete silence had fallen and that most of the audience had got up and were waiting for something to happen. He composed his voice.

"I'm glad to see you again, Philippe."

"I'm not. I'll repeat my question: what has my country done to you for you to think of nothing but destroying it?"

"It's my country as well."

"No, it isn't."

"Because I'm a Jew?"

"No. Goldschmidt's also Jewish, but it's still his country."

"Because I'm a Progressivist?"

"Goldschmidt also claims to be a Progressivist, and it's still his country."

"Then why?"

"Because you're a dirty little shit. You've got an unhealthy liking for misfortune, putrefaction and defeat. You're a born lackey, servile and fawning . . ."

"I saved your life at Mathausen."

"Not you, your masters . . . the Communists. It was Fournier who had my name taken off the list. Fournier and I don't see eye to eye, but at least we respect each other."

"Why are you trying to make a row?"

"I was lucky enough to find you surrounded by a particularly choice bunch of asses, bitches and snobs. I couldn't resist such a pleasure. Tomorrow we'll disinfect the place . . . with D.D.T."

"This is outrageous," the philosophy mistress cried out in a shrill voice.

"This happens to be my house, madame. It's a funny thing, but among all these friends of the people I can't see a single working-class person, and among these Fighters for Peace not a single person capable of handling a rifle. Not a single Commie either. The Communists aren't like us. They're much more intolerant. They guard against contagion, they keep themselves clean and tip their refuse out on to the heads of others. They've filled my drawing-room with it."

"It's not as bad as all that," Weihl said to himself, "as long as he sticks to generalizations. Perhaps he won't talk about Mathausen and the reason why I was deported . . . perhaps . . . because Fournier must certainly have told him all about it. He's a sensitive man, old Philippe. Even though he's a bit of a brute he's frightened of hurting his sister or dishonouring the family name. Deported for black market activities. After all, one had to live, or rather survive. Philippe can't understand that. The Esclaviers have been steeped in honour and fine sentiments for centuries. Now that I have established myself I'm ready to have as many fine sentiments, and even finer, as anyone else!"

"Are you drunk, Philippe?"

He could not resist provoking his brother-in-law. Perhaps Philippe would now strike him, lay him out as he had done in the camp when he caught him stealing someone else's rations. At the time he had experienced a disturbing sensation of well-being; very odd, that sensation.

Philippe's voice sounded distant and remote.

"I'm not yet drunk enough. Weihl, go and fetch some alcohol, for we drink alcohol in my house and not milksop concoctions.

We'll both get blind drunk together. No, everyone will get blind drunk with us, even the vicar. Jump to it, Michel my lad, I'm thirsty. Go on, you know what drinks to choose, don't try and pretend . . ."

This time the illusion was pointed. Weihl had sold the Germans a store of contraband alcohol, that was why he had been sent to Mathausen . . . Philippe was drunk. Villèle was sweating with curiosity. He felt some really juicy secret was about to be revealed.

"Get a move on, Michel."

Weihl slowly unhooked himself from the mantelpiece.

The captain opened the door for him and shoved him outside. Guitte, too, had sprung to her feet, as though the spell which held them all rooted to the spot had been broken. She rubbed her head against Philippe's chest, nibbled him, kissed him, scratched him, laughed, sobbed and stroked his face.

"You've come back at last, Philippe. I'm touching you, kissing you. You're as unshaven as ever this evening."

Panting and puffing, old Goldschmidt had grasped the captain's hand and was holding it against his fat paunch; he was snivelling, which made him look even uglier than usual.

"Why didn't you let us know? We should have come and met you at the station, or at Marseilles . . ."

Villèle lit a cigarette and thought:

"This isn't at all funny, everyone's in tears. It's too trite and yet just now we were very near the moment of truth. Interesting, this captain, very interesting. He's the great love of little Guitte, you can see."

Weihl's guests trooped past, one after another, without daring to look at Philippe who was still standing by the door. On his way the Dominican delivered himself in an unctuous tone:

"May God forgive you, my son."

"I'd like to see you again, Captain," said Villèle. "You remember, I was at Vietri at the time of your release . . . That magnificent gesture, yes, throwing your fibre helmets into the river . . . I'll ring you up . . . in the very near future."

In his surprise Esclavier allowed him to shake the hand which Goldschmidt was not holding.

He suddenly felt tired out, bereft, devoid of anger. Ashamed of himself and of his outburst.

Weihl came back with a bottle of brandy, put it down on the table and disappeared. He had suddenly assumed the smooth manner of a head waiter.

"You went too far, Philippe," Goldschmidt gently observed, forcing the captain to sit down beside him. "It was you alone who allowed Weihl to become the heir to your father and to his thought. Do you know he's got the makings of a great writer? He's an exhibitionist who hates to reveal himself in public though at the same time he can't resist the temptation to do so . . ."

"A mental strip-tease, but he takes good care not to give the reason for his deportation!"

"He will one day . . . because he won't be able to stop himself. Exhibitionists are queer people, and we Jews are all exhibitionists."

"Even the Jews of Israel?" Guitte inquired.

"No, they seem to have escaped the curse. But at the same time they're going to lose their genius, which is a compound of subtlety, restlessness and also fear. In every Jew's subconscious there's a deeply rooted terror of the pogrom. The Israeli doesn't have this. He tills a land which belongs to him and has a rifle slung on his shoulder. For centuries the uprooted Jew has inevitably hated all forms of nationalism. Nations are shadowy families from which he feels himself excluded. So he invented Communism, where the notion of class replaced that of nation. But this latest invention to have sprouted from his genius has not solved the problem, at least not for him, for the Jew is essentially outside all social classes just as he happens to be outside every nation. So he lingers on the fringe of Communism and becomes what is known as a Progressivist. The Israelis took the opposite course, but they immediately suffered from nationalist delirium.

"You see, I'm as garrulous as ever, Philippe. All this is just to tell you that I'm a Jew and not an Israeli and that Weihl is like me. That's one of the reasons I'm so attached to him."

"I'm an Israeli," said Guitte. "I'm a nationalist and I'm not under the curse. Won't you marry me, Philippe! We'll organize pogroms together and chase Weihl and old Goldschmidt with long knives down every passage in the house!"

"All right," said Philippe, "I've learnt my lesson. I'm extremely fond of you both, but just leave me in peace with my bottle of brandy."

"When are you coming to dine with us?" Guitte asked. "I'll cook you a nationalist dish, steak and French fried potatoes. I've learnt how to cook in order to seduce you all the more easily."

"You know what your father used to say," Goldschmidt went on. "'History will drive us ineluctably towards Communism. Instead of fighting it, we ought to humanize it so as to make it tolerable for the West.'"

"I know what Communism is like and I can tell you now that it isn't tolerable and can never be humanized."

Goldschmidt had some difficulty in getting up from his chair. He had asthma and panted at every step he took. One day his heart would give out and that would be the last of the garrulous, inquisitive, indulgent old man. He had always lived in the shadow of others, he had forgotten himself, and here was death suddenly reminding him that he existed.

Leaning on his daughter's arm, he shuffled slowly along the railings of the Luxembourg Gardens. He stopped to recover his breath.

"What an extraordinary fate for that Esclavier family!" he suddenly said to Guitte. "Étienne dies on his return from the U.S.S.R. where he has been received in triumph. Paul follows him into the grave a few days later after having had his brother voted out of the Socialist Party, with the result that the Communists and Socialists each bury their great man under their own Red Flag and insult each other at both funerals! Meanwhile Philippe was at death's door in a hospital at Hanoi with a wound in the stomach he had received while attacking a Vietminh village over which the same Red Flag was unfurled.

"The two dying men asked for Philippe. One of them only had Weihl on whom to bestow his 'political testament.' Paul's

bedside companion was a former president who had been involved in some shady business. But there was no one with
Philippe's mother when she died a month after her great man,
no one but old Goldschmidt. She wanted a rosary. The woman
in the religious articles shop asked me: "Is it for someone taking their first communion?' Yes, a really astonishing family!
Philippe has inherited his father's good looks, eyes as grey as
the sea off Brittany. But war and suffering have left their stamp
on his face. The raw clay has been fired in the oven. I must ask
Philippe one day why he stayed on in the army."

"I know why, because I'm an Israeli."

"You're a bit in love with Philippe, aren't you?"

"You can't walk any farther; I'm going to call a taxi."

"I warn you, the Esclaviers only admit submissive and retir-
ing women into their lives."

Alone in the drawing-room, with a glass in his hand, Philippe
Esclavier paced up and down the shelves of books: old books
bound in leather or parchment, paper-covered books whose
spines had been bleached and whose titles had faded in the
light.

When his father was still alive, the room was cluttered with
books that had just been published.

Almost all of them bore the inevitable dedication:

"To the master, Étienne Esclavier, with all my admiration . . ." "The respectful homage of a disciple . . ." "To the
guiding-light of our generation . . ."

Base flattery was mixed with sincerity.

Étienne Esclavier used to savour the new books like flowers
or fruit. He loved the smell of the paper and the fresh ink. He
would pick at the stacks at random, glance through a book
and put it down again a few minutes later, but sometimes
when his interest was roused, he carried it away clasped to his
breast like a precious discovery.

It was in this room that father and son gave full rein to their
exclusive passion. Between them they spoke a language to
which they alone held the key. The great men of the Third

Republic, the writers and artists who came to the Esclaviers, found themselves dubbed with ridiculous nicknames. Sometimes the professor would pull one of them to pieces for his son's amusement, and soon his absurdities, his vanities and falsehoods would be layed bare on the carpet. Philippe took down a book. *Marriage* by Léon Blum. The fuss it had caused on publication now seemed laughable. He remembered Léon Blum.

It was in 1936; he was thirteen years old. Étienne Esclavier, with his long silver locks nodding at every step, had marched from the Nation to the Bastille holding him by the hand to introduce him to this Popular Front which was partly of his own making.

Léon Blum, who could be gentle when he liked, had stroked little Philippe's hair, and old Jouhaux had clasped him so tightly to his "breadbasket" that he had burst into tears.

It was in this room, through this very door, that Eugen Jochim Raths had appeared.

Philippe remembered it clearly. As he himself was doing now, he had put his hand on the back of this arm-chair and, like him, he wore the badges of rank of a captain, but it was very cold in the big drawing-room.

Defeat had fallen like a black veil over Paris. Came the occupation and times were hard in the Rue de l'Université, where one was too well-bred after all to indulge in black market activities.

Paris was ruled by the Germans, and the people of Paris by the black marketeers, the B.O.F., the dairymen, the grocers and the butchers.

Étienne Esclavier had taken refuge in a magnificent isolation into which he had taken his son with him. It was easy to convince him, by pointing out the morals then in force, that this was not the moment to commit oneself. Every day he had doled him out the sleeping draught which he had baptized "detachment."

Although suspect in the eyes of the occupying forces, such was his renown that Professor Esclavier retained his chair at the Sorbonne. The students flocked to his history lectures as though they hoped these might reveal a secret message which would tell them they must fight and die.

But the professor told them nothing and the students tried to find some secret meaning in every word he uttered . . .

The German officer had arrived late in the afternoon. He was tall, slim, wore the Iron Cross and spoke perfect French.

Étienne Esclavier, looking very pale, received him standing up, and when Philippe slipped his hand into his father's he felt it trembling like that of an old man. He had no idea his father could age so rapidly and lose his self-control to such an extent.

"Don't worry," said the German, "I haven't come to arrest you. I'm Eugen Jochim Raths; I was a pupil of yours at the Sorbonne."

"I remember now," the professor replied with an effort. "Please sit down, won't you."

"Please regard this call as absolutely personal: a visit from a pupil to his master, nothing more. You used to tell us: 'The world is moving towards socialism; nationalism is dying, wars will become impossible, for the people don't want them any longer; puppets like Hitler and Mussolini will collapse in ridicule . . . ' Now, the whole German people is behind the Führer, and I mean the people, the working-classes. At the head of my squadron I crossed France from Turcoing to Bayonne in a matter of two weeks. The democracies were incapable of fighting and Europe will be rebuilt round the German nation and its legends. You were wrong, Professor."

"Possibly."

"I've got my sergeant outside on the landing with some rations. I should be glad to share them with you and continue this discussion at dinner."

Philippe had slipped away from his father.

"No. We don't want you here," he said to the German.

His father had protested:

"Be quiet, Philippe!"

And had then tried to explain:

"It's an old pupil of mine I'm receiving here, not an enemy. Please forgive him, Herr Raths."

The German had smiled:

"Young man, some boys of sixteen have already experienced the bitter taste of war and others have died with a rifle in their hands. I believe that if I were your age, if I were a Frenchman, I should not confine my fighting to a mere impoliteness. I came to tell your father that if most of us follow the Führer, I'm not one of them. In spite of their being so cruelly contradicted by the facts I still want to believe in his lessons; but I remain loyal to my country. Goodbye, Professor; goodbye, young man."

The German had put on his cap, saluted with a click of his heels and left the room.

"What came over you, Philippe?"

"I thought he was going to insult you."

"You might have got us arrested."

Then, shortly afterwards, came that evening of 17 October 1941. His father was writing, wrapped up in a heavy dressing-gown, stopping every so often to blow on his fingers. Philippe, curled up in a blanket, was trying to concentrate on a school-book. It was the *Tumulte d'Amboise*.

Antoine de Bourbon and the Prince de Condé confined them-selves to secretly encouraging all the enemies of the Guises . . . The conflict would start in their favour, without their uttering a formal challenge out loud: an equivocal attitude which reduced the opponents of the Government to the role of conspirators . . .

Philippe shut the book and threw it down on the floor.

"They're fighting in Russia, Father, thousands of young men are getting themselves killed . . . meanwhile I'm reading the *Tumulte d'Amboise*."

Bent over his lamp, Professor Esclavier raised his head.

"All that is no concern of ours, Philippe, but the *Tumulte d'Amboise* is part of your prescribed reading. In the last year you've made hardly any progress in your work. You're listen-ing too much to the echoes of the outside world."

"The Jews have been given orders to wear the yellow star. If our old friend Goldschmidt was in the occupied zone, he'd be forced to wear it, and little Guitte as well."

"The Germans are wrong, utterly wrong, but these outrages in the streets are stupid and criminal."

"You heard what Hauptmann Eugen Jochim Raths told me: 'If I were a Frenchman, I should not confine my fighting to an impoliteness.'"

"Mind will always get the better of brute strength."

"Uncle Paul . . ."

"Paul has been up to his usual tricks. Expelled from the board of education for refusing to sign something or other in favour of the marshal."

"He was quite right."

"His duty was to carry on with the education of the new generations."

Jacqueline thrust her head through the door; she was growing up extremely pretty.

"There are two gentlemen who want to see you, Papa. One of them is a former pupil of yours. They're out of breath, as though they had been running."

"Show them in."

In their old hobnailed boots and army capes dyed brown, Mourlier and Beudin looked like a couple of tramps. In spite of the cold they were drenched in sweat. Mourlier was rubbing his nose so hard that it looked as flat as a Negro's.

"It's like this," he said, "we've just brought down a Gestapo type, a Frenchman, a collaborator, right outside his house, with a revolver shot."

Beudin spoke up in his turn, but in jerky little phrases on account of his panting:

"But we only wounded him; it's the first time I've used a revolver . . . Within three hours we were traced and identified, we can't go back to where we live . . . Got to make for England and join de Gaulle . . . Mourlier said: 'Professor Esclavier's the only man who can get us out of this. We can trust him all right . . .'"

Étienne Esclavier had risen to his feet:

"I'm sorry, but I can't do anything for you."

Mourlier had given a start:

"What!"

"I don't know de Gaulle and have no wish to know him; I disapprove of violence and don't want to be mixed up in this murder."

"Murder! But wasn't it you who said: 'Those of us who prove to be so criminal as to make allies of our enemies should die; each of us has the right to be their judge and at the same time their executioner. Fascism is a crime against the soul . . . ' "

"I might have said that . . . when the war was still on. Since then there has been the armistice. I never asked you to kill men in the streets, which is liable to provoke reprisals. Furthermore, I don't know either of you. As I said before, I can't do anything for you."

"I was one of your most assiduous pupils, Professor. I attended your lectures, I read all your books and articles. Because you belonged to the S.F.I.O., I also joined that party; because you said we should fight against Fascism, I volunteered . . . and now you don't even recognize me: Mourlier, Eugène Mourlier . . ."

He repeated his name with a sort of absurd despair. Beudin chipped in:

"You wouldn't remember me, of course. I'm from the Cantal, a mechanic in a little village near Aurillac. Mourlier had taken refuge with us. He told me a lot of bunkum and I believed him and followed him to Paris. That bunkum was all yours, it seems."

He shrugged his shoulders:

"Come on, Eugène, can't you see? Your professor has simply got the wind up. We'd better be off before his windiness prompts him to call the police."

Philippe had got up, struggling to rid himself of the blanket which enveloped him. He shouted out:

"That's a lie."

"Hallo, now the kid's butting in," Beudin observed simply.

"Try and understand," the professor told them, "put your-selves in my place. I'm a man of letters. I have a book to finish; it's not up to me to meddle in these affairs. I'm too old for this sort of thing."

"There's a war on," said Mourlier.

Philippe saw his idol melting like wax. The contempt, or rather the astonishment he discerned in the faces of Mourlier and Beudin hurt him atrociously.

"We're off, Professor. All I ask is that you wait a little before summoning the police."

"I'm coming with you," said Philippe.

He put his shoes on with clumsy movements, not wishing to look at his father. He had some difficulty in putting on his lumber-jacket. The three of them went out together and, as he banged the door behind him, Philippe heard his father's heart-rending cry.

They took the métro and got out at a station at random, for they did not know where to go. The station bore the name "Gambetta." Mourlier thought this augured well; he believed in omens. Gambetta had escaped from the siege of Paris in a cap-tive balloon. They went into a café with blacked-out windows and ordered beef tea. This was one of the non-alcohol days.

A year later Professor Étienne Esclavier heard that his son had been captured by the Germans and tortured.

Philippe had been tortured for six hours, his father for sev-eral months. The professor developed a loathing for anything remotely connected with violence, brutality, armies and police forces. He forgot his cowardice; he ceased to be "that rabbit Esclavier," as he had been called by some of his colleagues who knew him well.

One day at the Sorbonne, unable to contain himself any lon-ger, he devoted a whole lecture to the subject of torture. It was extremely moving; he was once more the great inspired spokes-man of the Front Populaire and he wound up with this sen-tence which seemed incomprehensible to everyone:

"I can speak about torture, I know what it is like, I suffer torture every night of my life."

The pupils rose to their feet and applauded. Next day Professor Esclavier's course of lectures was suspended.

Goldschmidt had described this incident to Philippe, but only eight years later, when the captain had just been repatriated from Indo-China and his father was already dead. He had added:

"Towards the end of his life Étienne Esclavier used to fly into a rage whenever anyone mentioned war. He suffered a great deal from the fact that you were out in Indo-China. But what on earth came over you? Why did you stay on in the army?"

Philippe had given an answer which was not quite true, though at the same time not entirely false:

"I stayed on in the army out of disgust for what I saw on my return from deportation, later on from habit, and now because it's the life that happens to suit me."

Disgust he had certainly felt on coming back from Mathausen. He was saddled with Michel Weihl, who had nowhere to go and was as pathetic and exasperating as a lost dog. The professor had been overwhelmed at seeing his son again. He had sobbed as he hugged him in both arms, stroking his face with his fingers like a blind man. Happy and at ease, they had made all sorts of plans, one of which was to go and have a good rest at Avignon, at Uncle Paul's. Jacqueline and his mother had already gone there.

"Paul did wonders during the war," the professor had said in an off-hand, peevish tone. "But you know how stubborn he can be. He won't understand anything and does his utmost to prevent the unity of the Socialist and Communist parties. De Gaulle's got him in the palm of his hand. He has done him proud and made him a Commissaire de la Republique. But I still haven't lost all hope of convincing him . . . In two months' time, Philippe, there's going to be a special session of examinations for all those who've come back from the war or from deportation. You will present two theses. The subjects are limited and we'll help you through."

A few days later the professor had had a telephone call from the secretary of a resistance and deportees organization which was controlled by the Communists and of which he was a member.

Philippe was squatting on his haunches playing with a cat. It was marvellous, this warm, living thing. As he let himself be nibbled, as he stroked the black coat, he began to realize at last that he was free, that he could get up, go out, listen to music, smoke as many cigarettes as he liked and ask the cook to make a raspberry tart. Through the open french windows he could hear the cries of children playing in the garden.

After hanging up, his father had come back and stroked his head.

"Did they shave your head?"

"Yes, like everyone else."

"How thin you are! Not feeling too tired?"

"No, I'm all right."

"Did you suffer a great deal?"

"I can hardly remember now."

"I've just been rung up by the Association of the Republican Resistance Workers and Deportees. They're organizing a big meeting at the Salle Wagram. I have to take the chair. Many of your deportee friends will be there: Rivière, Paulien, Juderlet, Fournier . . . it was Fournier who rang me up."

"They're all the Communists of the camp."

His father appeared not to hear.

"They'd be very pleased if you came with me this evening and wore your deportee's uniform."

"I've burnt my uniform. It smelt of gas chambers and human excrement and also of all the filthy things I had to do in order to survive."

"Your friends from Mathausen asked me to remind you that if you came back alive, you owed this in part to the Communists."

Weihl had then chipped in:

"There's no problem about the deportee's uniform. The association has new ones for us to wear. I asked for the largest size for you."

"So you're also in this game, are you?"

"But I thought . . ."

"Now that the matter's settled," said the professor, "I'd like to read you the draft of my speech. The subject is falsehood. We have just finished living four years in a state of false-hood . . ."

"It isn't settled at all," said Philippe, "I'm not going and I have no wish to disguise myself. The falsehood is still continuing. I remember your talks on the wireless in 1939, Father, I also remember Mourlier and Beudin when they came to see you after firing on a Gestapo agent. I didn't want to remember any more."

"There was some misunderstanding with your friends . . ."

Philippe had locked himself up in his room. Nevertheless the professor had given his speech in the Salle Wagram. Weihl had gone there with him, wearing a deportee's uniform. Many of the audience had therefore thought that Weihl was his son. The next day he engaged him as his secretary, and a month later Philippe Esclavier embarked for Indo-China.

Philippe knew this incident had not dictated his decision, but had rather served him as a pretext. His attempt to resume his studies had not met with much success. Prolonged intellectual effort had always been repugnant to him. Philippe could be brilliant, but he lacked application and he had what Glatigny, with a slight touch of irony, called "the indolence of the well bred." Dreams and intellectual activity are incompatible, whereas action is well suited to a large measure of dreams.

Philippe had discovered that military life fits in with a certain form of laziness. The existence of an officer is divided very unequally between moments of hardship, fatigue and danger and long periods of inactivity and leisure. In those moments of supreme effort an officer can be driven, despite fear, hunger and weariness, to accomplish extraordinary feats which will turn him, but only for an instant, into someone greater, more disinterested and more dauntless than other men. During the periods of inactivity he moves with the slowness of a drowsy bear in a little enclosed world of his own. All effort is banned from it, or is anyway extremely restricted by regulation, ritual and custom; its jokes are traditional and even its malice has been codified.

With a throbbing head, Philippe staggered up to his room. He noticed the sheets had been changed and the bed clumsily remade. He recognized his sister's hand in this; some suitcases had been hidden behind a curtain.

All his personal belongings and books had disappeared; the cupboards and drawers were empty.

He realized they had not expected to see him again and that someone else had been occupying the room for some time.

Glatigny got home at two in the morning, dead drunk. He stumbled on the stairs several times. He tried to remember the last time he had been as drunk as this. Yes, it was in 1945, at the time of the liberation of Alsace. The peasants had set up wine stalls in the streets; it was that year's wine, which was still fermenting. Some girls had flung their arms round his neck.

He was so drunk that he could no longer drive his Jeep and had been obliged to stop in a little pine forest. He had lain down on the moss and the cold had woken him up. Through the branches he could see little patches of sky scattered with stars. He did not know where he had come from, where he was going or who he was, and he had enjoyed that sensation of being no one and yet being alive. A rabbit had scampered past him in the moonlight, followed by its grotesque shadow.

Glatigny had some difficulty in inserting his key in the lock; annoying hiccups kept rising in his throat.

Claude was waiting for him in her dressing gown, her ash-blonde hair scraped back from her forehead, which made her look like an old woman. She held a rosary in her hand. Always that urge of hers to repeat the obvious!

"You're drunk . . . drunk and incapable. So drunk you can't even keep on your feet. It would serve you right if I went and woke up the children so that they could see you."

"The drunken isle of the Spartans."

"What are you talking about? You make me sick. But what on earth did they do to you in Indo-China?"

"Merde!"

"We're going to have this out at once. I absolutely insist."

"Oh, balls!"

He barely had time to rush to the lavatory and be sick, and he hoped that, together with all the alcohol he had drunk, he would also get rid of his present life, his financial and domestic worries, the little countess and her roofing mania, so as to recover once more that sensation of being no one.

From that night on Claude slept in a separate room and the captain was delighted. He could now read and meditate in peace.

3

THE MULES OF THE COL
D'URQUIAGA

Lieutenant-Colonel Raspéguy spent the first month of his ninety-day leave in his native village of les Aldudes, on the Raspéguy estate, near the Col d'Urquiaga. The first days were among the best in his life.

Walking by the banks of the Nive, clambering about the mountains drenched in mist and rain, shooting in the Hayra or Irraty forest, he was reminded of the little shepherd boy he had once been—mysterious and solitary—and of the adolescent who had become an accomplished frontier-crosser and whose blood raced through his veins like a torrent. It was during the civil war and the Republicans paid a high price for arms and ammunition.

One night Franco's men had seized him and his father. They had beaten him to a jelly all night and had left him for dead out on the mountainside. A *guardia civil* had dragged the old man to the bottom of a ravine and finished him off with a musket bullet.

The Raspéguys would have worked equally well for Franco as for the Republic; they were simply smugglers who seized every opportunity to make a little money. But from that day on Pierre-Noel Raspéguy had vowed an implacable, absolute hatred against the Galician dictator.

A few days after his release from the Vietminh camps the colonel had ordered himself a car. It was waiting for him at Marseilles. It was a Régence with claret-coloured coachwork outlined in cream, masses of dazzling chromium and white-wall tires. It was equipped with a radio and with mirrors on both front fenders.

It was in rather bad taste, somewhat reminiscent of a grocer who has made his little pile, but Raspéguy did not mind that. He knew it was bound to overawe his compatriots.

The colonel had carefully calculated the time of his arrival so as to appear in front of the church just as the congregation was leaving. The men were coming down from the oak gallery by the outside staircases, their rosaries round their wrists, while the women in black mantillas emerged from the low vault, making the sign of the cross.

In a brand-new uniform, his breast adorned with all his decorations, his pipe stuck at a jaunty angle in his mouth, his bamboo swagger-stick under his arm, his red beret pulled down on one side, he stood, shoulders squared, chest thrown out, muscles flexed, in the pose which every paper in the country had popularized.

The men had hesitated an instant before recognizing him as "the great Basque condottiere."

Jean, the youngest of the Arréguy boys, was the first to cry out:

"It's Pierre Raspéguy of the Urquiaga estate, it's the colonel from Indo-China, that's him all right with an American car."

Then they had rushed towards him. Half the village was related to him on the male or the female side and they had all insisted on kissing him, so as to make it plain to the customs officials and the police that they were his kin.

They told him that his mother and brother had come to the first Mass but had gone back to the mountains immediately afterwards as one of their animals was sick.

The curé appeared—despite his age he still walked with huge strides, like a daddy-longlegs, and wore his beret pulled forward over his nose. He grasped Raspéguy by the shoulders and squeezed his brawny, root-hard arms:

"So there you are, and of course you managed to arrive at the end of Mass so as to miss the service. You haven't changed at all!"

Raspéguy heard a small boy saying in his native tongue:

"It's true, he's just as big and strong as in his pictures, and he's not at all old."

Raspéguy threw out his chest and flexed his muscles for the boy's benefit. This was the sort of praise which touched him most of all.

The men dragged him along to the village inn.

While the wine was being poured out, Escotéguy, who had been through the selection board with him, asked:

"Come on now, Pierre, tell us all about it. What was it like out there?"

What was it like out there! Explain all that to them, to these people who had scarcely ever left their valley; explain the Chinese and the Vietminh, the tall elephant grass of the Haute Région and the paddy-fields of the deltas, the mud and the dust, the fighting, the suffering, the dying, and what he and his kind were striving to find behind all that death!

"It wasn't exactly a holiday," he replied in his rasping voice, "but it got under your skin."

He peered at them through half-closed eyes.

The curé had sat down opposite him to observe him more closely. This was a Raspéguy all right, a member of that clan of shepherds who dabbled in sheep-thieving and smuggling but who never jettisoned their goods, preferring to fight and tip the customs men into a ravine, who went further than anyone else in good or in evil, who were by way of being sorcerers as well, acquainted with secrets over beasts and over men, and with a deep-rooted, violent passion for women, especially the women of others. And this one was the worst and the best of the lot, the most disconcerting, the most secretive and at the same time most garrulous, prouder and more pagan than anyone has any right to be.

But one evening, towards the end of the war, when Pierre Raspéguy had come back on a short leave, the curé had found him on his knees in the middle of the choir of the church, motionless and upright, like a knight on the day of his dubbing. He had never seen a man so handsome praying with such fervour. Lieutenant Raspéguy had just learnt that his men were fighting without him. For the rest of the time he gave every indication that he did not believe in God and feasted with the devil.

He would have to bury his roots in Basque soil, marry and settle down here. The curé had spoken to his mother and he was looking out for a wife for him. From Bayonne to Saint-Engrace, rich or poor, countess or scullery-maid, what woman would refuse to mingle her blood with that of the great colonel?

Raspéguy leant back in his chair and, with his eyes fixed on the ceiling with its smoke-blackened wooden beams festooned with clusters of red peppers that had been hung up to dry, he seemed to be searching his memory for something to tell them.

Memories he had a-plenty; they buzzed through his head like a cloud of flies over his glorious, sordid and generally gory past, that avid quest for medals and promotion, that exalting pursuit of life and of death; and it all ended with a little general fastening yet another decoration on to his breast. He loved medals; he enjoyed military pomp and splendour, but each time he felt frustrated. There was something else he wanted and he didn't know what.

What should he tell them, these peasants sitting here with their gnarled hands spread flat out on the knees of their black Sunday-best trousers? Stories about girls? They were prudish, the curé was present, and he himself found that sort of thing rather dull nowadays . . . His withdrawal through the Viet-minh lines for hundreds and hundreds of miles, and then one day the appearance of the Raspéguy battalion which had been completely written off? Even then there had been certain rats who reproached him for having abandoned his wounded, the very rats who would have found it absolutely normal for him to surrender or get all his men killed.

He knew what they were like, that headquarters rabble— bald, pot-bellied, fat-assed little men, incapable of marching half a dozen miles without melting away in their own dishwater-like sweat, with faces like Franco and the fawning manners of Spanish Jesuits.

He had thought of all that and had found nothing to tell the men of les Aldudes. He was like a bull-fighter being asked by ignorant strangers, who did not number one genuine *aficionado* among them, to describe his fight just after it is over, when he has not yet got rid of his fear, when he still feels closer to the animal he has killed in the sunshine of the arena than to these people scrutinizing him with a strange gleam in their eyes as though he was a murderer.

In any case there is no such thing as an *aficionado* of war; there are simply those who fight, and all the others.

Raspéguy drained his glass of wine and rose to his feet.

"I'll tell you some other time. I've got to go up and see my mother. You know what she's like: I may be a colonel but she'd still beat me over the head with a log if she discovered I was daw-dling in the bar instead of climbing up to see her right away."

They all laughed. As though they didn't know her—a Span-ish woman from over the border, irascible, domineering, and rapacious as well: and she had to be the woman she was if she wanted to preserve even a semblance of order in the Raspéguy household.

The colonel left his car outside the curé's house, went into the grocer's who also sold espadrilles and, sitting on a stone bench, donned a pair, surrounded by all the boys and adoles-cents of the village who drank him in with their eyes like hor-nets on a stormy day.

No, he would not speak to the old men and those of his own age, but to these youngsters who were the only ones who would understand. As he tied the laces round his ankles, he watched them and he already knew which were the three or four among them who, without knowing it, had a sense of war and adventure and who would follow him.

He could see Esclavier greeting them, with his hands in his pockets:

"Well, you little bastards. What do you think you're going to get by joining us? Something to overawe your pals and girl-friends; the red beret, the parachute badge, jumping boots? Do you know what you're really in for? Toil, sweat, blood, prob-ably death. Just get that into your heads, you nitwits. You're here to die. So if there's anyone who wants to change his mind, now's the time."

Good old Esclavier, he knew how to pile it on! Not one of them had ever stepped out of the ranks and asked to leave.

Boudin had once tried the same line, but he didn't have what it takes—out of twelve only four had remained.

That bastard Boudin—managing to go sick just at the time of Dien-Bien-Phu! He would make him pay for that. For a start, he had not given him any sign of life and had not answered one of his letters . . .

The curé came up:

"Pierre."

It was funny being called by his Christian name; it was a long time since that had happened. It forced him to remember that he had spent his childhood outside the army.

"Yes, Father."

"You ought to go and see Colonel Mestreville. He keeps talking about you as though you belonged to him."

The curé was a little jealous of this.

"Of course, I'll go and see him."

"Another thing. Here, take it! Go on, I tell you, take it . . ."

With a clumsy gesture, full of affection and brutality, he handed him his old stick, his *maquila*, with its blunted point and leather handle blackened by sweat. It was common knowledge that when he was younger, Abbot Oyamburu had gone off with the other Basque curés to fight against Franco and that his stick was the only weapon he had ever carried.

"You'll hang on to it, won't you, Pierre Raspéguy. It will remind you of your homeland, should you ever forget it."

The curé was preparing the ground.

Raspéguy slipped the leather thong round his wrist, took a firm grip on the cane before twirling it round his head, then, with his long, easy stride, started off along the path which led up into the mountains and the Hayra forest.

Half way along the road he had come across his brother Fernand with his flock; they had embraced, or rather brushed their cheeks together and slapped each other on the back and shoulders, on the knotted muscles from which a man derives his strength.

"Thanks to the money you sent," Fernand told him, "we now have a hundred sheep, fine ones too. Do you want to come and count them? Mother says you could have done better and saved a little more instead of boozing and running after the girls, that the men who have gone to America send back much more money than you did, that it's not worth being a colonel, and so on and so forth . . . Don't listen to her, Pierre. She's terribly proud of you . . . and so am I."

Their mother must have heard them. She had a sharp ear and the wind carried far that day. They found her outside the front door, short and swarthy, her scarf wound round her head, both fists on her hips. She only spoke Basque, never Spanish or French.

"So there you are, you big good-for-nothing, and you're not even a general after all the schooling and health I've given you!"

Health she had certainly given him; he was full of life; it seethed through his body and clung to him like those malignant deep-rooted weeds that cut like knives.

As for schooling, that was another matter. She had got him a job as a shepherd on another farm the day after he left school. It was lucky the owner happened to be Colonel Mestreville.

He bent down to kiss his mother, but she squirmed in his arms as though she found it distasteful; her eyes were brimming with tears.

Behind her appeared his three bashful nephews and niece with his sister-in-law: three stocky, thickset boys who were always ready for a fight, and his niece, much younger, with her big mysterious eyes; she was sucking her thumb and peering at him through her eyelashes.

Maité was the one he lifted in his arms and held up towards the sky—a sky that was forever changing, never completely blue, never completely grey, hemmed in by the mountains and which seemed to be cast in his mould, with a nature as tormented as his own.

After the meal, which they ate in silence, their noses buried in their plates, his mother said:

"Better change those fine clothes of yours, you'll only get them dirty."

She took his uniform and hung it up in a cupboard and he caught her delightedly fingering his decorations, one after another.

In the afternoon, in a fine drizzle, he went out with his brother to see the sheep, but to his surprise he found no pleasure in this. He was dreaming of other flocks, the only ones that mattered to him now: men in camouflage uniform, agile and silent, who followed him in the dark. No matter their race or the colour of their skin, he would lead them, clean-limbed, youthful and upstanding, far from this rottenness, this feebleness, this cowardice, towards a sort of brutal paradise which was only open to fighters and the pure in heart and from which would be banished all cowards, cranks, women, *guardias civiles* and anyone who served that bastard Franco.

A Spanish shepherd who had caught sight of them came down towards them; he was a friend of Fernand's; they did a little smuggling together.

Pointing with his finger, the shepherd inquired:

"Who's this big fellow?"

"It's my brother, Pierre-Noel Raspéguy, the colonel from Indo-China."

Thereupon the shepherd took off his *boina* and, holding it in his hand, gave a respectful bow. This was fine, this warmed the cockles of a man's heart even more than a tot of brandy.

In the evening Fernand left the house. He had to prepare a "crossing"; some mules being brought over from Spain. Pierre would have liked to go with him to see how it would make him feel now.

Sitting in his father's armchair, which was his own ever since the old man had died in the ravine, he dozed in front of the fire, with a *porron* of wine within easy reach. He was alone; the old woman and the children had gone to bed. Tall shadows flickered on the walls as the flames leaped in the hearth. Outside it was raining as heavily as during the last days of Dien-Bien-Phu; but here the rain was fine and icy cold.

The solitude grew heavy, unbearable. He poked the fire and sparks flew into the room. He spoke to himself, as he often did when he wanted to reassure himself.

"I've come a long way, all the same, since I won my first stripe. If there hadn't been this war, what would I have become? I would have gone to America and herded sheep in Montana, where everyone from this valley goes. I had even written to a cousin of ours out there and he had agreed to pay my passage. There were dollars to be earned in Montana; one came home rich, but old, with nothing but a few memories of flocks of sheep caught in a storm or a snowdrift."

War alone was the great adventure, cruel, poignant and heartwarming, with the shadow of death hovering over one each time a comrade fell.

"Yes, I've had to do some odd things in my time, especially at the beginning, but that was just to make a name for myself. It's hard to achieve recognition when one still stinks of the flocks one has been herding . . ."

He remembered the day clearly: the 17th December 1939, when, in a little village behind the lines, with a full company on parade, a cabinet minister had decorated him with the Military Medal and his first palm.

It was extremely cold and the men's breath formed a faint mist in front of them.

"Read out the citation . . ."

Never had the drums sounded so crisp; they shattered the icy air.

"Sergeant Pierre Raspéguy, of the 152nd Infantry Regiment . . . A warrant-officer whose courage is already legendary. His platoon commander having been killed in the course of a patrol, he assumed command, carried out his mission behind the enemy lines and brought back three prisoners . . . In the name of the President of the Republic . . ."

The drums rolled for Raspéguy, the soldiers presented arms for Sergeant Raspéguy. It was then he had felt some animal come to life within him, some little animal: his ambition, as yet no bigger than an insect but which started nibbling away at him at once . . .

Yet the thought of that patrol! The most ghastly shambles in his whole career! The men hadn't muffled their equipment properly and there was a hell of a clatter. The lieutenant had lost his way in the dark. He had actually switched on his electric torch to consult his map and compass.

It was then they had run into a German patrol, just as bogged down as themselves and commanded by an *Oberleutnant* just as doltish as the French lieutenant. They had fired at each other at random; bullets flew in all directions. It may have been the Frenchmen who killed their own lieutenant, and the Germans their *Oberleutnant*.

Eventually the six Germans that were left had raised their hands a split second before the five Frenchmen did likewise.

He, Raspéguy, had waited until it was all over; he wanted to see what the hell was going on; he hadn't fired. What was the point?

Once they had got over their surprise, the Germans were unwilling to surrender and the Frenchmen were not too keen on forcing them to behave as prisoners all over again. That was when he had made his presence felt. He had taken a firm grip on the butt of his submachine-gun: one of the first in use. He had fired a short burst and two figures in *feldgrau* had toppled over into the mud. The others had not made any more fuss. They had then quietly made their way back to the French lines, in single file, the prisoners carrying the body of the lieutenant. The party which was to have covered their withdrawal had somehow managed to fire on them instead, with the result that there were one prisoner and one Frenchman less.

Raspéguy had earned the reputation of being a killer and he hadn't denied it; it was useful in an army where everyone sat trembling with fright behind barbed-wire entanglements.

No, he did not enjoy killing; he even found it the least pleasant aspect of warfare. He would have liked to fight with cunning, simply by manœuvring, so that the boys caught in a trap should not make any fuss about surrendering—just a game, like something they played at school. But it always had to end like this: in killing.

Raspéguy took a long pull at the wine and put another log on the fire. It was still raining outside.

There was a knock on the door downstairs; he opened a window, glad at being roused from his memories.

"Who's there?"

The man was hammering with his fists; he was out of breath; it was the Spanish shepherd he had met a few hours before; his beret was streaming with rain.

"They've been cornered near here with the mules; the carabineers have blocked the pass on one side and the customs men are climbing up from the other. We're done for, *me cago en Dios.*"

"You've managed to get through, though! Wait a moment, I'll be with you."

He shook his head: "Amateurs again."

His mother and sister-in-law had got up; the children were bawling.

"Don't go," cried his mother. "I forbid you. It's not up to you."

He grabbed the curé's stick and went down to join the shepherd.

"Show me where they are."

"*Señor Coronel . . .*"

"*Coño, maldita sea la puta que te pario! Pronto!*"

The shepherd saw the stick twirling above his head and appreciated the force of the insult. He led the way.

The smugglers and their mules were bunched up together in a ravine; the pebbles kept slipping under the animals' hooves, the men kept beating them with branches.

Raspéguy seized his brother by the shoulder and spun him round. Fernand had lost his head, it wasn't the first time it had happened.

"What's the position?" he said.

"What are you doing here?"

"Never mind that. What's the position?"

"We can't cross over into Spain; there are a dozen carabineers holding the pass and a runner has just warned me that the customs men are coming up from les Aldudes in full strength . . ."

"Where are your mules bound for?"

"Spain."

"That's funny," the colonel thought, "in my day it was the otherway round, they always crossed over into France."

"Call two of your men, the youngest and most agile, and who've got a little guts. Jump to it."

Fernand dashed off into the dark and came back accompanied by two youths who had not yet been called up for military service.

"Just follow me and do what I do," the colonel briefly told them. "We're going to have to run for it . . . and listen to the bullets as they whistle over our heads. Nothing more. All clear?"

"All clear!"

"You, Fernand, when I give you the signal, scramble over the border by the quickest route, yes by the path; there'll be no one there to guard it."

"Pierre, if anything should happen to you . . ."

"In twenty years nothing has ever happened to me."

Taking the two boys with him, he set off in the direction of the pass: a little training exercise for warrant-officers, no, not even that, for corporals. It would do him good.

A hundred yards this side of the Spaniards, he found a gully which he had once used. The caribineers firing from the crest could not hit them there.

"Watch me and do what I do," he told the two boys.

He picked up some stones, dislodged some small rocks and sent them tumbling down the slope.

"*Halto!*" shouted one of the caribineers.

They could hear the bolt of his rifle as he loaded.

"Go on!" he told the boys.

"*P'aran se!*"

"Go on!"

There was a shot and a bullet whistled past, well above their heads.

"Now we're going to make a dash for it down to the left. A fifty-yard sprint as far as the trees. There's no danger. Off you go now. What's your name?"

"Manuel."

"You're Spanish?"

"Basque Spanish."

"Off you go then, Manuel."

Manuel dashed off. There were a few more shots.

"Your turn now. Who are you?"

"Jean Arréguy; I'm a cousin of yours, Mister Colonel."

"Just call me 'Colonel,' my lad. Show them you're a cousin of mine. As soon as you get there, start rolling stones down hill again. But stay there till I arrive."

The three of them drew the caribineers away in the direction of Ebañeta, which is also called Roncevaux, the place where a certain Count Roland had been soundly trounced by the Basques because he had overlooked the first rule of mountain warfare: namely, to hold the ridges when you hazard a column in a gulley. Raspéguy could never understand why they had made a legendary hero of such a bad officer.

When they were some distance away from the pass, Raspéguy called Manuel over to him:

"Can you run fast?"

"Faster than a lizard."

"Go and tell my brother they can take the mules across now."

"Yes, Colonel."

Raspéguy gave him a gentle shove with his hand and the boy dashed off into the dark.

With Jean Arréguy he went on rolling stones down the hillside and shifting his position, drawing a shot every now and then.

"What would you like to do most of all in life?" he asked his cousin all of a sudden.

"Drive a car; I've got my licence."

"Would you like to drive mine?"

"That lovely brand-new red job, Colonel?"

"Yes, and later on a Jeep. Wouldn't you like to come to the wars with me?"

"Would you take me with you? Manuel would also like to come, but he's Spanish."

"That sort of thing can be arranged. Keep rolling those stones, for heaven's sake. Come on, another sprint. You're out of breath, you ought to be in better training . . . seriously, if you want to be a paratrooper."

Behind them the mules were scuttling over the pass; the battle had been won, but this time Colonel Raspéguy wasn't given a medal but only a flea in his ear. It was enough to make one sick!

On the following day no one in the valley spoke of anything else but what had happened up on the Col d'Urquiaga and how the colonel from Indo-China had made a monkey of the carabineers. The story reached Saint-Étienne de Baigorry where Colonel Mestreville "who had been at Verdun" lived. He immediately let Raspéguy know that he was expecting him without fail on the following day "and not to crack a bottle of wine together but to do some real drinking." He had made this quite clear to one of his shepherds whom he had sent up specially from les Aldudes to the Raspéguy marches.

Raspéguy got into his car and drove off to Saint-Étienne. He stopped from time to time on the banks of the Nive to watch a trout disappear among the rocks; if the water had not been so cold he would have tried his hand at tickling. He advised Fernand to lay a net and some ground lines there one night.

Colonel Mestreville lived on the other side of the customs post, between the Col d'Ispéguy and the old Saint-Étienne bridge.

Separated from the Spaniards by a winding road over two miles long, the French customs men had an easy time of it in their barracks, more often that not in their slippers, while the carabineers froze and kicked their heels up in the mountains. When Raspéguy sounded his horn for them to lift the barrier, all the customs men came up and shook his hand; they had open merry faces and a conspiratorial manner. They, too, had heard all about it.

Raspéguy felt his temper rise. He had never tolerated familiarity from excisemen or policemen.

"I want to see your sergeant," he demanded.

"Here I am, Colonel."

The sergeant gave a clumsy salute, bringing his hand to his cap which he was wearing sideways on his head like a pumpkin.

"Last night, on the Col d'Urquiaga, in French territory quite close to my house, some Spanish carabineers fired on me while I was taking a stroll."

"But . . ."

"I was taking a stroll, I'm perfectly entitled to, aren't I?"

"Of course, Colonel."

"What were you chaps up to in the mean time, in your bed-socks, two miles away from the frontier? I'm going to have the customs post moved up to the pass."

He let the clutch in with a jerk. The customs men were no longer smiling.

Colonel Mestreville had a voice which thundered like a waterfall, the strength of an oak-tree and the stubbornness of a donkey; he always wore leather leggings with his old riding breeches, a beret which was never off his head, and played at being the old-fashioned Basque, a staunch supporter of tradition. But he was only Basque on his mother's side and was saddled with a name which betrayed his Île de France or Norman ancestry.

"Come in," he shouted to Raspéguy.

He was sitting at his desk, a narrow little table less broad than himself.

"Sit down there in front of me."

He glared furiously.

"Lieutenant-Colonel Raspéguy, since you came back on leave you've been behaving like an imbecile. No, not a word, you'll listen to me first. You don't seem to realize your position—the youngest colonel in the French army, and soon the youngest general—and what did you get up to the very night you arrived? Smuggling. You helped to get a troop of mules over the border under the nose of the carabineers. The story has now spread as far as Bayonne. Clever, isn't it? In the first place you might have come and reported to me in uniform. After all it's to me you owe your present position, and I'm your senior. I waited for you on Sunday; you preferred to go out boozing with a gang of ruffians in the village inn. If you had been caught by those *coños* of carabineers or by the customs men, you realize what a scandal there would have been. Can you imagine yourself in handcuffs?"

"You know I should never have let myself be caught . . ."

"Of course I know, you bloody fool. No Raspéguy has ever been caught, unless he was dead. Like your father, like your uncle Victor. Proud, hot-headed fools with no respect for laws or frontiers. But you happen to be a French officer. Your rank, the name you bear, your army record oblige you to behave properly. You've been made a colonel—well, then, try and behave like a colonel; and above all I don't want to hear about any woman trouble. If you ever feel that sort of urge, go and work it off in Bayonne. You ought to get married, but we'll think about that later. Concha, you blockhead, bring us some Spanish pernod. By the way, tell your brother to get me five more bottles, I'm running out. Good, now that I've had it out with you, let's get down to some drinking. First of all, let's have a look at you. Holy Virgin! Slim as a young subaltern, yet a grand officer of the Légion d'Honneur. You're only just thirty-nine, aren't you?"

"Thirty-nine last month."

"In my days it took longer, much longer, and was much harder too: and if one was commissioned from the ranks, the highest one could hope to get was captain or major . . . My God, it seems you led the carabineers a dance almost as far as Ibañeta. Your brother Fernand's lost his hand at the game; every tradition is dying out in the Basque country, even smuggling, on account of all these bloody tourists. Money destroys everything."

With his hairy fist Colonel Mestreville slowly poured some water over the sugar, which began to drip into the absinthe and turn it cloudy. In the warmth of the room the smell was faint at first, then became more pungent, like a July morning in the Basque mountains.

The two men drank in silence, the veteran of Verdun and the youngster of Dien-Bien-Phu.

"What was it like out there?" Mestreville inquired. "Did you fight as you ought to have done? I don't mean you, but the others, because, damn it all, to take such a drubbing from a handful of Annamites . . . ! I knew them myself during the first world war, they weren't worth a straw. We didn't dare use them in the front line."

"That's because they weren't fighting on their own ground or for themselves; Communism has brought quite a lot of changes too, and your Annamite quaking with fear has become a damn good soldier, one of the best infantrymen in the world."

"Look, Pierre, I remember a certain dawn attack near Douaumont, three divisions almost shoulder to shoulder to dislodge the Boches from their front line. Not many of us reached our objective. Their machine-guns mowed us down like scythes, yes, just like scythes, and felled our ranks one after the other . . . They say thirty thousand soldiers were killed or wounded that day. Did you do as much at Dien-Bien-Phu?"

Raspéguy rose to his feet. This sort of talk made him see red.

"Sheer butchery."

"What did you say?"

"Verdun! Butchery . . . useless, senseless butchery. You should have attacked in small groups, well dispersed—thirty yards between each man, lightly equipped, with hand-grenades. Figures bobbing up here and there so that there's no time to take aim. The other dopes get jumpy and begin to lose their heads . . . At Dien-Bien-Phu we were in much the same position as you were at Verdun, with artillery and trenches. We let ourselves be pinned down whereas we should have kept on the move."

Mestreville brought his fist down on the table, knocking over the glasses.

"We at least won our battles."

"When there are over a million dead, you can't call it a victory. Those million men would have sired children and I should have had them to fight with me. War's not like that any more, it's not like that at all. The soldier has become something infinitely valuable; you don't just throw him away. For our sort of war you need shrewd, cunning men who are capable of fighting far from the herd, who are full of initiative too—sort of civilians who can turn their hand to any trade, poachers, and missionaries too, who preach but keep one hand on the butt of their revolvers in case any one interrupts them . . . or happens to disagree."

"Concha, you idle brute, bring in two more glasses. Try and explain yourself more clearly, Pierre."

"It's rather difficult, but that's what I feel it should be. And then the soldiers who wage that sort of war, which is a good deal harder than yours, ought to believe in something, something worth dying for, and also in their leaders but not in the same way; they must love them, yes, love them deeply, and their love must be returned."

"What on earth do you mean, my lad?"

"The men must have their leaders under their skin; no, I don't know how to explain it, but there ought to be a sort of close communion in hardship, danger and death. Each time the least of his soldiers is killed, the leader ought to feel he has lost something of himself; it ought to hurt him until he feels like screaming. I don't believe in human cannon-fodder; I'm even against it, very much against it. A million dead! The bastards! With that lot, we could have conquered the world. I don't know what Verdun was like. But I've read some books, any number of books. I don't say what I read; that's my secret. I read and learn on the sly. A man can't discover everything on his own. Then one fine day the brass goggle with surprise at what I tell them and believe that I've thought it all out myself. It was either in Caesar, or else in Clausewitz."

"Do you mean to say you read Clausewitz?"

"On the sly, always on the sly. And I've got a captain to explain it to me, a certain Esclavier, who's very gifted at that sort of thing. We team up together. And then there's Boudin, a tubby little major who goes in for what they now call logistics, he's the mother hen of the battalion. But that's not what I wanted to talk about. I once saw a two-battalion Legion attack against a Viet position right up north of the delta, where the limestone country begins. I was to support them from the rear with my paratroops and went to see how to set about it."

Raspéguy laid the glasses, sugar-bowl and spoons out on the table; a stack of files represented the position to be taken.

"At the given signal the legionaries emerged from their trenches all at once. They began to advance, in line, step by step, as though a drum was beating out the time, a big copper drum beating out a loud death march under the heavy, overcast sky. Their ears did not hear the drum, it was in their guts that it resounded. The legionaries kept advancing at the same pace, bolt upright, without lengthening or shortening their stride. They did not even turn round when a pal fell beside them, his guts spilling out of his stomach or his head mashed to a pulp. With their submachine-guns under their arms, stopping now and then to fire a well-aimed burst, they went on step by step, a blank expression on their faces. There were quite a lot of Germans among them; they were the ones who set the pace. The Viets were firing as hard as they could, like madmen. I tried to put myself in their place; to make war, you always must put yourself in the other man's place . . . eat what they eat, sleep with their women and read their books . . . It was death advancing towards them, the icy death that inhabited the tall desperate white men with the straw-coloured hair and tall, strong, sunburnt bodies. The copper drum sounded ever more loudly in their guts. The legionaries reached their lines, impassive as ever, still moving at the same steady pace, firing their well-aimed bursts and hurling hand-grenades with mechanical precision into the trenches.

"The Viets were seized with panic; they threw down their arms and tried to take flight, but the others bowled them over like rabbits—without hatred, I'm certain; but it was something worse than hatred, this slow, inexorable advance. It was several minutes before the legionaries assumed a human expression, before a little blood came back into their cheeks, before that icy demon left them. Then some of them began to collapse—they had not even realized they had been wounded. It was splendid, that attack, quite overwhelming, but I didn't like it at all. One battalion out of the two had been wiped out. I could have done the job with ten times fewer men.

"I wouldn't have commanded those legionaries for anything in the world. I want men who are full of hope, who want to win because they're more fit, better trained and craftier, and who aren't willing to throw away their lives. Yes, I want soldiers who are frightened and who care about living or dying.

Mass hysteria is not my line. Maybe that was what Verdun was like?"

Mestreville lowered his eyes and, from his store of distorted embellished memories as a former fighter, tried to recollect what Verdun had been like.

No, it wasn't even that: a heavy human mass, bogged down in the mud and laden like mules, being driven forward—so resigned, so weary and stupefied that it raised no objection.

"Leave me now," he said to Raspéguy. "I've got to get through all this stuff. There's a whole mass of forms to fill in. It's no joke being mayor. We'll have lunch together. Help yourself to a paper or a book, or go for a walk."

Raspéguy got into his car and drove up to the Col d'Ispéguy. Seated on a rock and chewing a blade of grass, he watched the clouds twisting up the valley and being blown away in the wind. A few yards behind him stood the barrier of the Spanish customs post. He had called on the carabineers, doled some cigarettes out to them and invited them to drink from his wine-flask. He felt not the slightest resentment against them for having fired on him the night before. He merely despised them a little for letting themselves be taken in so easily. He was interested in their weapons. The Spaniards were armed with rifles which were not up to much and badly looked after; their equipment was too heavy—he could not imagine them crawling about on all fours with those heavy cartridge belts round their stomachs. Of course, it wasn't their job to make war; they were there to prevent smuggling, but Raspéguy was inclined to believe that every able-bodied man was born to fight, to bear arms and to use them against others who were also armed.

Not too keen on their job, these carabineers—Andalusians with olive complexions who could not stand the cold. They should have posted Basques here, but Franco was wary of them. The dream of a Basque nation flashed through the colonel's mind but, like the clouds in the valley, was soon dispelled.

A distant tinkling came to his ears, wafted on the rain-laden wind. When he was a shepherd, Pierre-Noel Raspéguy had been able to tell from the sound of their bells to which farm the sheep belonged. The Eskualdarry estate had the deepest-sounding bells and the Irrigoyen the shrillest, "shrill as a dried pea flicked against a crystal glass," as old Inchauspé, who made them, used to say. The secret had been handed down to him from his father who had inherited it from his grandfather, but he had not had time to divulge it to his son who had gone off to America and never come back. With him had died one of the oldest traditions in the valley. Now the bells all had the same note, and the shepherds, instead of clambering over the mountains, dancing up there, Basques of Spain and of France together, on the frontiers which they refused to recognize, to the sound of the *chistou* and the *tountoun*, then soaking themselves in wine, singing and brawling . . . instead of this, the shepherds now came down to Saint-Étienne and went to the cinema. It was even worse with the Spaniards. The Basque nation was being progressively reduced to a vague feeling of nostalgia. Raspéguy had been born on the frontier, of a mother from the Spanish side and a father from the French side. Had it not been for Colonel Mestreville, he would willingly have deserted rather than do his military service.

Each fresh medal, each promotion had bound him closer and closer to France. But he still retained something of the soldier of fortune who fights for pay and booty. He had become completely French, by free choice, when he had joined de Gaulle in England in July 1940. His country was the Army rather than France; in his mind it was impossible to dissociate the one from the other.

He was already beginning to miss the army after three days' leave. He dreamt of the regiment that he was about to command. He would take Esclavier and Boudin with him, of course, but he would also have liked to have by his side such diverse officers as Glatigny and Pinières, Marindelle and Orsini, such improbable ones as Boisfeuras, such tormented ones as Mahmoudi.

Colonel Mestreville did not work on his papers; he sat pondering on the strange destiny of Pierre Raspéguy. He had imagined him as a leader of men, a brawler, a sort of brute who forged ahead and was always lucky. A splendid thoroughbred warrior animal, who liked flaunting his medals in the midst of admiring women who were ready to give him all, and in front of jealous men.

The colonel was a leading member of the Saint-Cyrienne.*

During one of their meetings in Paris he had met General Meynier who was just back from Indo-China where he had been second-in-command in Tonkin. General Meynier was not very popular in the army, for he was said to be intelligent and had influential political connexions. He had summed up the war in Indo-China as follows:

"We're winning some battles, but we're losing the war."

He was a dry, inhuman little man, with spindly shanks, thin lips, an eyeglass and a scornful voice.

Mestreville found himself sitting next to him at the banquet which had brought the meeting to a close. Feeling rather apprehensive about the reply he might receive, he had asked:

"Do you know Major Raspéguy, General? I'm interested in his career. He comes from the village next to mine. At one time he actually worked for me as a shepherd."

Meynier had leant back slightly to get a better view of the old colonel whose sheep had once been tended by Raspéguy.

"So that wolf began his career by leading a flock! I regard Raspéguy as our best unit commander—in action, that's to say—back at base, it's rather a different matter. I'm indebted to him for the most astonishing display I've ever seen in my life. And what's more, he didn't give a damn about me, that was quite clear; but, coming from a Raspéguy, I didn't mind.

"Try and picture the Tonkinese delta during the rainy season. The paddy-fields are nothing but mud, slimy mud that clings to the soles of your boots like leeches.

"I was commanding an operation that had been taking place in that mud for several days. One morning my communications

---

*An association of former Saint-Cyr cadets whose aim is to protect the interests of army officers. It serves more or less secretly as a trades union for the only social group in France that has no right to belong to any such organization and in consequence has no one to protect it.

officers brought me a signal from Raspéguy in which he informed me directly, without bothering to go through the usual channels, that he had got a Vietminh battalion of the 320th pinned down in the village of Thu-Mat. He wanted to know if the artillery was in a position to give support and if any aircraft were available. Not a word of explanation.

"Raspéguy was ten miles forward of his previous night's position which he had left without informing anyone, but he had the Viets pinned down. I was furious with his improper conduct and lack of discipline yet at the same time delighted that this costly operation had not met with complete failure.

"I rushed off to Thu-Mat in a helicopter.

"I found Raspéguy about a mile outside the village, crouching behind an embankment between a couple of W.T. sets. In one hand he held a field telephone, in the other a ball of rice which he was munching.

"He did not even get to his feet. This wasn't insolence on his part, it was simply that he was passionately interested in what he was doing; he could not leave his post and lose contact with his men who were fighting a little farther on.

" 'When am I going to get some artillery support, sir?' he asked. 'I've kept the Viets on the move all night and they're now cornered in Thu-Mat.'

"I was anxious all the same to make him realize that the situation was, to say the least, unusual:

" 'If you had been good enough to inform me of your movements, I could have brought you up a mobile group last night. As it is, it won't be here until four o'clock this afternoon.'

" 'If I had informed you, sir, the Viets would have known about it and pulled out at once. If we wait till four o'clock, the Viets will hold out until nightfall and be in a stronger position.

" 'We could go in on our own, but it would mean a lot of casualties and I don't like the idea of that.'

" 'I've got to have that battalion, Raspéguy.'

"I stayed with him, which was the least I could do. I was the one who wanted the battalion, and he was the one who was going to get it for me. Besides, I had been fascinated by this character for some time, I'd heard a lot of good and a lot of bad about him; I was anxious to see him in action.

" 'We'll go in, then,' said Raspéguy.

"He pointed out a sort of mound in the middle of the paddy-fields, about eight hundred yards away, between us and the village. It was crowned with a mandarin's tomb.

" 'We'll have a clearer view from that hillock . . . and my radio communications will be better.'

"We slogged through the mud, getting splashed from time to time by mortar shells, and once or twice some bursts of machine-gun fire forced us to take cover behind the embankments.

"I had almost forgotten what an infantryman's war was like. Raspéguy reminded me with a vengeance. I was out of breath and stumbled at every step; he did not even look round once to see if I was following.

"He set up his W.T. behind the tomb, seemed astonished to find me there with him and immediately began moving his men into position.

"He was holding the microphone in his hand; his whole network worked on the same frequency and, over the heads of his company commanders, he addressed himself directly to his platoon officers. His rasping, captivating, passionate voice was broadcast over all the other microphones and weaved a sort of web round the battalion, with five hundred men caught in its meshes.

"He began by gently 'warming up' his paratroops who were exhausted by a whole night's march and fighting, as one holds a damp wooden bow over a fire so as not to break it before stretching it. He inspired them with his violence and strength and filled them with hope and zeal for the impending assault. A fanfare of hunting horns sounded in his voice and gave promise of a view-halloo.

" 'Hallo, Vannier. Give me your exact position, I can't see you very well . . . Right, got it, next to the little pagoda.

" 'Now listen. There's an F.M. facing you in the bamboo hedge. You must have spotted him when we drew his fire.

" 'Juve, calm down!'

"He turned to me.

" 'Juve's a second-lieutenant; he's only just joined us—in full regimental fig. He wants to try and play the hero for his first assault and he'll only get himself wiped out with his whole platoon.

" 'Now I can't deprive him of that: an assault. He'll get off to a quick start and the others won't just sit back and let him play the hero all by himself. So it's going to be quite a race. Juve is under Esclavier's orders. They're the ones who'll have the toughest job. Three hundred yards across open country before coming to grips, it won't be easy.

" 'Mercat? Mercat's an old sergeant-major, a staunch fellow. He can last the five hundred yards . . . Don't forget, Mercat, you'll pitch your mortar shells into the hedge right opposite Juve's platoon, then join up with him and stick close. Got that? Right . . . Mercat realizes I'm giving him the tail end.

" 'Shut up, Esclavier, let me speak. What's that you say? You'll wait for the signal like everyone else. You've got farther to go than the others? So what? You'll just have to move a little faster, that's all.'

"With each of his men he altered his tone, friendly, severe or ironical; but with Esclavier it was different; he spoke to him with deep affection, something akin to passion or love.

"Raspéguy turned to me and said.

" 'Esclavier's in command of the company which Juve and Mercat belong to—a thoroughbred if ever there was one.'

"Although your Raspéguy hadn't given a single conventional order, I felt his battalion was absolutely ready, his companies all in position . . . the men with their muscles flexed, ready to surge forward.

"Once more he surveyed the terrain with his hooded, falcon-like eyes, called up each of his company commanders to make sure they were under control, then gave the order to attack—'Go!'—just as the first of Mercat's mortar shells exploded in the hedge.

"Raspéguy left me and in his turn started off towards the hedge, followed by a few men from his headquarters, and I can assure you I had to summon up all my courage, all my pride, not to let myself subside into that warm mud. That damn fellow had made me forget I was fifty years old and a general.

"Within ten minutes the village had been taken and what remained of the Vietminh battalion had scattered and gone to ground in the dug-outs under the thatch huts.

"The mobile group turned up at four in the afternoon. Raspéguy's battalion then withdrew, leaving the newcomers to mop up the trenches, like a bone that the sated tiger leaves behind for the jackal to gnaw.

"The colonel in command of the mobile group jumped at this opportunity and in his report took the kudos for capturing the village."

The general drained his glass and pulled a face; the champagne was sweet and tepid and he only liked it extra-dry and well iced:

"I don't agree at all with Raspéguy's method of command. It commits one too deeply. Just because I send a private soldier to his death, I don't feel I'm first obliged to ask him into the drawing-room for coffee and listen to him talking about his mother or airing his views on the world. Units like the one commanded by your Raspéguy are liable eventually to turn into sort of sects which will no longer fight for a country or an ideal, but only for themselves, just as a monk indulges in his flaggelation in order to attain paradise. You've heard tell of the Sacred Battalion of Thebes, in which couples of men in love with each other used to chain themselves together so as to die as one? Mind you, there's nothing sexually abnormal about Raspeguy's paratroopers . . . But those chains exist and bind together the privates, N.C.O.s and officers. Raspéguy forged those chains unconsciously, I'm sure. They are made up of the hold he has over his men and of his love for them—and when I say 'love' I mean in the broadest, highest, yes, almost mystic, sense of the word. This love reaches its climax at the very moment he deliberately sends his men to their death. Perhaps that's why he insists that before going into action his troops are clean, shaved, at the top of their form and looking their best.

"It's disturbing, that sort of experience. I've given a lot of thought to Raspéguy, that bemedalled beast, a perfect tactician, as crafty as a monkey, as publicity-conscious as a film star, yet at the same time with a leaning towards metaphysics. Extremely dangerous for an army. If you asked me my advice, I would never make Raspéguy a general. I would keep him a colonel all his life, with more medals than he could possibly wear. But perhaps if he became a general, that power he has might suddenly vanish. It's happened before. Being promoted to general is a decisive step; you view the game from a different angle . . . So you had Raspéguy to guard your flocks, did you, Colonel?"

Old Colonel Mestreville had then asked the following question: "What would Napoleon have done with a man like that?"

"He'd have made him a marshal. Napoleon believed in obscure forces, in destiny, in chance. When a colonel was due to be promoted to general, he always used to ask: 'Is he a lucky man?' In other words, is he in harmony with his destiny? There's no such thing as luck any more, there's only economics and statistics, artificial economics and false statistics, which eliminates Raspéguy and everyone else like him. I can't say I'm sorry; I'm just about reaching the age of statistics."

When Raspéguy came down from the pass for luncheon, Mestreville had already poured out two more absinthes to clear his brain. He asked his former shepherd:

"Do you know General Meynier?"

A grin came over the paratroop colonel's face and his eyes sparkled with mischief:

"I remember . . . one day in Tonkin, I put on a show for him. It gave him something to think about, I hope."

"It was just a show, was it?"

"Of course. His sort don't understand anything else."

"His sort?"

"Yes, all those who only do their fighting on paper, who draw up plans and believe that a battalion strength is eight hundred men, whereas in the line you're lucky if you have half that number; who believe that soldiers can go on for ever, without being conscious of fatigue or despair, that they're nothing but machines with interchangeable gears. Those great strategists were prisoners in 1940, but they had been through Staff College. They complacently say: 'Well done, my boy,' when, on account of the stupidity and laziness of those broken-down old hacks, half of one's battalion has just been wiped out!"

"Isn't that going a bit too far?"

"No. They also tell you, like that Meynier of yours: 'Leave politics to the generals and the ministers,' whereas with the Viets politics are the concern of all ranks, right down to corporal, right down to private. Communism exists, and there's no getting away from it. We no longer wage the same sort of war as you, colonel. Nowadays it's a mixture of everything, a regular witches' brew . . . of politics and sentiment, the human soul and a man's ass, religion and the best way of cultivating rice, yes, everything, including even the breeding of black pigs. I knew an officer in Cochin-China who, by breeding black pigs, completely restored a situation which all of us regarded as lost. What gives the Communist armies their strength is that with them everyone is concerned with everything and with everyone else and that a mere corporal feels he is in some way responsible for the conduct of the war. Apart from that, the men take everything seriously, obey orders to the letter, and economize without being asked on their rations and munitions because they feel it's their own war they're waging. If ever we're given a war which we look upon as ours, then we'll win it. But away with privilege, away with the sumptuous treatment of cabinet ministers and inspecting generals on the field of battle! Everyone in the shit with the same box of rations! From now on what we need is a truly popular army commanded by leaders of its own choice. Let the victor be honoured and the vanquished thrown out or shot. We don't need staff planning, what we need is victory . . . and don't saddle a whole draft of Saint-Cyr cadets with the name of a defeat, however glorious it may be, even if it bears the name of Dien-Bien-Phu."

"You're talking like a revolutionary."

"Our only hope of getting the upper hand, whether in Algeria or elsewhere, is to have a revolutionary army which will wage revolutionary war."

"Algeria? But that will be settled in no time."

"No, I don't think so, or else I've understood nothing since I started making war. Have you noticed that in military history no regular army has ever been able to deal with a properly organized guerrilla force? If we use the regular army in Algeria, it can only end in failure. I'd like France to have two armies: one for display, with lovely guns, tanks, little soldiers, fanfares, staffs, distinguished and doddering generals, and dear little regimental officers who would be deeply concerned over their general's bowel movements or their colonel's piles: an army that would be shown for a modest fee on every fair-ground in the country.

"The other would be the real one, composed entirely of young enthusiasts in camouflage battledress, who would not be put on display but from whom impossible efforts would be demanded and to whom all sorts of tricks would be taught. That's the army in which I should like to fight."

"You're heading for a lot of trouble."

"That's as may be, but at least I shall have courted it deliberately; in fact I'm going to start courting it right away."

The peasants and shepherds of les Aldudes soon got used to seeing the colonel from Indo-China in his light blue track-suit racing up and down the goat paths. One day Jean Arréguy and Manuel, the little Spaniard, accompanied him. From then on they were always seen together, leaping through the bushes, crouching in the water holes, out on the mountainside in all weather. The two boys followed Raspeguy's example, imitated his gestures, his gait, his manner of speech and the swing of his shoulders.

Raspéguy bought the papers every morning and flew into a rage as he read the reports of the fighting going on in the Aurés and Némentchas. In Morocco the *medinas* were in revolt and in Tunisia *fellagha* bands were attacking French troops. The Viets had predicted this.

And no one mentioned him any more. He could not stand it any longer—one morning he left for Paris. The two boys joined up as paratroopers. For Manuel, this was quite a business, but Raspéguy managed to get him a false identity card.

Whereupon everyone in the valley felt that the colonel had a mighty long arm and would make a first-rate deputy on his retirement provided he was willing to go to church a little more frequently.

During the whole of his leave Lieutenant Pinières stuck to his uniform and wore his red beret and all his decorations. On the evening of his arrival at Nantes, two of his former F.T.P. colleagues, Bonfils and Donadieu, had called on him at his mother's workclothes and stationery store down by the docks. They had gone in to the back parlour, a dim little room which smelt of cooking and cats.

"We'd like to have a word with you," Bonfils had said.

He was the one who did the talking because Donadieu had a stammer. But Donadieu was more decided and therefore more dangerous. Pinières had been with him in a number of tight spots; he had admired his courage and was very fond of him.

Neither of them had shaken his hand but had brought two fingers to their forehead in a strange sort of military salute.

"We've come to warn you," said Bonfils. "We don't take very kindly to colonialist mercenaries in this part of the world but we remember what you did once . . . So if you keep your big trap shut and stop wearing those glad rags, you won't come to any harm during your leave."

"Afterwards you c-can g-go and g-get yourself b-bumped off elsewhere," Donadieu had added with an effort.

He, too, was fond of Pinières, but "What must be." This was the only sentence he could manage to bring out without stuttering and he used it frequently.

Anger had made the lieutenant lose his head. He refused to feel ashamed of what he had done with comrades he admired; he was just out of "the bag" and now that he was at home again the little pals of the Vietminh were not going to stop him doing as he saw fit. He had struck Donadieu in the Adam's apple with the side of his hand. The stutterer had collapsed in a heap of splintered chairs. Then Pinières had grabbed Bonfils by the lapels of his coat and given him a good shaking:

"Now listen to me, and you can go back and tell whoever

sent you here: I shall say what I like, I shall go on wearing my uniform, but I'll always have my gun on me. You might get me eventually but you'll pay for it; you know I'm a pretty good shot. My little chums will then come and settle up for me and there'll be some bloodshed."

Bonfils and Donadieu had gone off and Pinières had sauntered about in uniform. But he did not dare linger anywhere near the docks and had to get home before nightfall, for more than once he had caught sight of some shadowy figures behind him.

His mother began to lose her customers and wept every night. Pinières was bored; there was no one with whom he could have a drink, no one to whom he could talk about the war in Indo-China or tell the story of My-Oi and the child that hadn't been born. Bonfils and Donadieu were the only ones who might have understood.

One day he heard his mother complaining to her neighbour:

"It's because of Serge I'm unpopular in the neighbourhood. But after all I wasn't the one who sent him out to Indo-China! I'm just a poor old woman who wants to be left in peace. I've already had enough trouble with my husband; he used to drink."

Pinières wrote to Olivier Merle, who had given him his address. He received a reply by return. His comrade invited him to spend the rest of his leave at his place.

Olivier Merle no longer lived in the notary's big house but in a small cottage about ten miles outside Tours. The Loire, which had overflowed its banks, streamed past the bottom of the garden, a swirling mass of driftwood and tufts of grass.

"I'm writing a book," said Merle, as he greeted Pinières, "Yes, big stuff, the Indo-China war as seen from the civilian side. I need peace and quiet. I've also got a mistress who's married to one of the leading citizens of our worthy little town; I had to have a little place where I could meet her; hence this retreat. You'll see; the housekeeper's an excellent cook, but she uses too much cream and butter which is bad for the digestion . . . and my inspiration.

"All right, all right, I can see you know how things are . . . and there's no point in trying to pull the wool over your eyes."

"I called on your father before coming here," said Pinières. "He burst out in my face: 'Take Olivier away with you, get him out of this town before we're obliged to call in the fire brigade or the police!'

"Luckily your sister Yvette, who drove me here in your car, gave it to me straight."

Yvette had said to him:

"I'm on my brother's side. If he leaves, I'm going with him; I think he's right not to let himself be bullied. Ever since he got back he has quarrelled with his father. To begin with, he refused to read for his exams; he did not want to invest the money he had brought back from Indo-China; on the contrary, he started throwing it about and bought himself a bright red sports car; that suits me because I can use it whenever Micheline doesn't take it. Then he started an affair with Micheline Bezegue. They're as good as living together. If only they had observed 'the proprieties,' as my father would say! What proprieties, Lieutenant? Have you got any ideas on the subject?

"None of this would have mattered if it hadn't been for the incident with the secretary general of the Prefecture. Like all the other men he had his eye on Micheline and was jealous of Olivier. That evening there was a meeting at the Piverdiers. You don't know the Piverdiers, do you? Everyone was there. The secretary general was repeating a little too loudly what my father had said the evening before after a meeting of the general council: 'Indo-China and the paratroops have turned Olivier into a tramp.' Olivier overheard and gave the secretary general a shove so that he fell on to the cakes on the sideboard. There was quite a row about it!"

"Did Olivier apologize?"

"No, on the contrary, he demanded an apology, declaring that the secretary general had insulted the soldiers of Indo-China. He even said he would box his ears for him.

"The secretary general sent his apologies, in writing, to Olivier and our father returned the compliment to the secretary general. It was all rather complicated. Everyone was apologizing to everyone else. They even say that my father paid for a new suit for the secretary general who's somewhat stingy."

Pinières had burst out laughing.

"It's no laughing matter," Yvette said. "People are now saying that Olivier's a thorough bad hat, that when he's in a temper or drunk he's capable of killing, that Micheline only sticks to him because she's scared stiff and that he's living on her money. Micheline, who's absolutely mad, thinks this is all great fun and terribly exciting. Yesterday she said to her husband: 'If you don't buy me a new car, I'll tell Olivier to come and cut your throat.'

"She said this in the bar of the Metropole, in front of everyone. Some people I know believed her, or at least pretended to."

"But who do you mean by 'everyone'?"

"Well, anyone who counts in Tours, the Piverdiers, the Machalles, the Comtesse de . . ."

Yvette had embarked on a list and had hardly got to the end of it by the time the house came into sight.

"I don't think I'll ever get used to provincial life again," Olivier said to Pinières. "Something happened at Dien-Bien-Phu, a sort of break. I realized this when I got back here. That's why I want to write this book, to exorcise myself somehow, but I can't get down to it."

Yvette was often to be seen with Lieutenant Pinières, first of all walking side by side, later on holding hands, and finally with their arms round each other. That sort of thing was quick to be noticed in Tours.

It was therefore by hearsay that Maitre Merle learnt of his daughter's engagement to a certain paratroop lieutenant who still wore his red beret firmly planted on his head.

From then on Maitre Merle engaged in antimilitarism and pacifism, for he regarded the army and colonialist wars as the root of all evil.

One night Pinières heard Micheline and Olivier having an argument, which culminated in an angry outburst, a flood of tears and the noise of a car door being slammed.

The next day Olivier looked down in the mouth. He confided in Pinières:

"I haven't got a penny, and my father refuses to advance me any money. My mistress has left me because I wouldn't take

her to the Alps for winter sports—what with, for heaven's
sake? She passes me off as a killer and treats me like a pet poodle. Everyone's saying that I got knocked on the head at Dien-
Bien-Phu and now have fits of madness. They also say I pushed
Yvette into your arms to revenge myself on my family and that
I belong to a paramilitary organization which is out to overthrow the Republic—that's a good one, anyway—an invention
of the secretary general of the Prefecture.

"I'll have to get out of here while the going's good. But what
the hell am I going to do?"

"Re-enlist."

"I don't like the army. We could always go to Paris. Esclavier's there, and so are Glatigny, Marindelle and Boisfeuras . . . they wouldn't let us down."

"You don't like the army, yet when you're up against it you
immediately think of your war comrades because you know
you can count on them."

A few days later Olivier received a telegram addressed to
Lieutenant Merle and signed Raspèguy. It was a curt message:

Expecting you Paris evening January fifteenth. Contact Esclavier on arrival. Littré 28–12.

The day after that, Pinières received the same telegram
which had been forwarded to him from Nantes.

On his arrival in Paris Colonel Raspèguy had moved in with
Philippe Esclavier. He had arrived during the night. On enter-
ing the drawing-room next morning, Michel Weihl found him
in his underclothes doing setting-up exercises.

"Good morning," said Raspéguy, "one-two, one-two, in-
out . . . deep breathing, it's most important, develops your
wind, and warfare's above all a question of wind. You the
brother-in-law?"

"Yes."

"Lieutenant-Colonel Raspéguy."

He had sprung to his feet with astonishing agility. Weihl
could not help admiring his lean, muscular body, without an

ounce of fat on it. The countless scars on his torso and limbs, far from disfiguring him, on the contrary contributed to his barbaric beauty.

Raspéguy bent down, straightened up again, leapt into the air and smacked his heels.

"I used to be the best dancer in the valley," he said. "Now I daren't dance any more—the drawback of being a colonel. Philippe not up yet?"

"Philippe sleeps late when he sleeps here, Colonel."

"A man who cuts loose isn't likely to marry and an officer who gets married loses most of his value, especially in a revolutionary war."

"Fortunately we're at peace, since the signing of the armistice at Geneva."

"What about Algeria? That's the same war as in Indo-China. Haven't you read Mao-Tse-Tung? Only the Viets were much stronger than the Algerians are, which is lucky for us; otherwise, with the gang of fools who run our army, we'd soon be pushed into the sea. Come and have breakfast, I brought a ham and a demijohn of Irouléguy wine with me."

"I'll tell the maid to serve you."

"No, I like eating my breakfast in the kitchen, standing up—a habit from the time I was a shepherd—and I serve myself. Ever since I've been an officer I've never had a batman. A soldier should die for his leader and for what he represents, agreed, but there's no need for him to be a servant."

"Who's this savage?" Weihl was saying to himself. "He exudes a sort of magic, like certain tribal chieftains or Negro witch-doctors, and he talks like a revolutionary. Have you read Mao-Tse-Tung? He'll soon be questioning me on Marx."

"Perhaps you don't know, Colonel, that I'm one of the founder-members of the Fighters for Peace?"

"That's fine; peace is all very well, only we haven't achieved it yet. Now I come to think of it, I believe I signed one of your thingumyjigs, yes, the Stockholm appeal against the atomic bomb. I had got so bored with the Viets in Camp One! Besides, I really am against the atomic bomb; we're not out to destroy people, but to conquer them, to win them over. Would you care for a slice of ham?"

"I must also tell you that I'm a Jew and of German origin."

Raspéguy looked at him in amazement.

"So what? I've commanded Thais, Vietnamese, Chinese, Spanish refugees, workmen from Courbevoie and peasants from the Landes; I could just as easily command Jews if I'm given any. I'd give them the yellow star as a badge; the Nazis made it a mark of infamy, I'd make it into a banner. We would cover it in so much glory that even the Arabs, even the blacks, would be proud to fight under it.

"But first of all I'd make my Jews do two hours physical training every day; I would restore them their pride in their bodies and by the same token, their courage."

Weihl was more and more astonished. He felt that Raspéguy, in his own fashion, had the makings of a revolutionary leader and he felt almost sorry that he wasn't on his side and could not follow him. With a hollow feeling in his stomach, he shared the bread, ham and wine that Raspéguy had brought with him.

After settling the colonel into one of the spare bedrooms, Philippe Esclavier had gone out to see Mina. Percenier-Moreau was away and the captain enjoyed waking up in her apartment with its over-heavy curtains and over-soft bed, the proper setting for a kept woman. There was too much chromium plating in the bathroom, its bottles and boxes of cosmetics gave it the aspect of a beauty parlour or clinic. He could loll about in bed, in the clinging smell of perfume and love-making, read shop-girls' magazines, listen to cloying music, and enjoy at last that warrior's rest that is only to be found in the company of girls and in a certain sort of second-rate atmosphere.

When she lay in his arms, he talked to her about Souen, the little Vietnamese who had died for love of him. He expatiated on pleasure and love, the pleasure that all women can give provided they are young, beautiful and sensual, love which is unique and occurs no more than once in a lifetime. Mina would weep and beg him to stop. This was how he took his revenge on

her for the sense of appeasement she gave him. But Raspéguy
was back now, and he felt like a greyhound having his collar put
on again. He realized with rage in his heart that he also needed
a leash and a whip; he only fought well when he was chained up
and it was Raspéguy who held the chain. Free of all fetters, living in featherbed surroundings ever since his return from Indo-
China, he was frightened of becoming in a few months as flabby
as Weihl and the intellectuals of his circle. He welcomed and
feared Raspéguy's return, for he felt at one and the same time
the need to obey him and the urge to bite him.

One evening Philippe Esclavier took Raspéguy along to the
Brent Bar. It was apéritif time. The clients were talking in subdued voices, which produced a gentle buzzing sound, punctu-
ated by an occasional discordant note: dice rattling on a table
top, a glass being spilt or the shrill exclamation of a woman.
The atmosphere was compounded of good tobacco, old brandy
and expensive scent.

Edouard recognized Raspéguy at once. During the battle of
Dien-Bien-Phu several weekly magazines had had a photograph of the colonel on their cover. He went up to him:

"I should be happy, Colonel, since this is your first visit to
the Brent Bar, if you would allow me to offer you and Captain
Esclavier a whisky or a glass of champagne."

"Whisky for me," said Philippe.

Raspéguy felt the warm animal stirring within him. He was
recognized even in this Parisian bar. He turned round and
scrutinized the slightly tarnished mirrors, the red plush seats
and dark panelling. His big hooked nose seemed to inhale and
savour the various smells, hanging on to some of them and re-
jecting others.

"It's nice in here," he said to Edouard. "I'd like to have an
absinthe."

"I beg your pardon?"

"An absinthe—Spanish pernod."

"It's forbidden, Colonel."

"All the dives on the Basque coast have it. One merely asks
for 'a sugar.' "

Edouard gave a little start. The Brent Bar was not a dive and did not deal in contraband. But Raspéguy appealed to him. During the occupation he had sheltered men who had the same sort of face, who uttered strange, sometimes outlandish passwords, who came from London and handed round their last English cigarettes while asking for volunteers to help them blow up the Atlantic Wall.

"I'll settle for a whisky," said the colonel.

The barman then met Raspéguy's gaze which pierced him straight between the eyes like a harpoon.

"Do you enjoy spending your life behind this bar, serving drinks without risking anything, not even a fine for handling a little contraband? Don't you sometimes feel like closing up shop and going off to the wars, climbing a mountain or exploring a back-water of the Amazon?"

"I spent the war in the underground intelligence networks," said Edouard, "and I've stuck to my habits. I can find enough adventure here. People are inclined to talk freely to a barman, and one can pick up quite a lot of information."

"Where does that get you?"

"It's interesting to know, for instance, that everyone is fed up with the régime, everyone despises it but adapts himself to it."

"What about Algeria?"

"Not a very popular war, that one, but it won't last long."

"You're wrong, it will be extremely long and arduous. I'll bring you a banner; it's black, like a pirate's flag, with a dagger and parachute in silver. Above there's the motto: *I dare* . . . You can hang it up on the wall and all my men, their pals and girl-friends, will come and drink in here."

The colonel held out his hand and Edouard had the feeling that he, too, was enlisting under Raspéguy's black flag.

"By the way," said the colonel, "I want a room for the evening of January 15th where I can be left in peace and quiet with a few of my officers."

"We've got just what you need downstairs. Very discreet, with an exit into the courtyard."

"A plot," was Edouard's immediate thought. It was widely

believed that the officers who had come back from Indo-China were hatching something. He was overwhelmed with joy at the thought that the overthrow of the Fourth Republic would be organized at the Brent Bar, while he, Edouard, with a broad grin on his face, mixed an americano for the Under-secretary of State in the Ministry of the Interior.

Colonel Raspéguy was extremely busy between the 8th and 15th January. He paid a number of visits to the Colonial Troops Inspectorate but never took Esclavier with him. He was even received by a cabinet minister, but for once derived no sense of jubilation out of it.

Sometimes Esclavier, waiting for him at the wheel of the Régence, would see him come out fuming: "The bastards, they tried to do me in the eye again . . ."

The 15th January eventually arrived. Raspéguy had asked all the officers he had invited to come in uniform and without their wives. At seven o'clock in the evening it was like a blaze of poppies in the Brent Bar. Edouard leaned towards the Under-secretary:

"They're a nice crowd, those fellows."

"What are they doing in here?"

"I think they're celebrating someone's birthday."

"They'd be much better out in Algeria. An americano, please, Edouard."

The meeting took place in the room downstairs, round a long table made up of several smaller ones joined end to end. At one end sat Major Beudin, commonly called Boudin, with a big commercial ledger spread out in front of him. Opposite him was Raspéguy who, as he always did in battle, was breaking up his cigarettes to put into his pipe. Also present were Glatigny, Esclavier, Boisfeuras, Marindelle, Orsini, Leroy, Pinières and Merle—all of them, with the exception of Boudin, former inmates of Camp One. Raspéguy banged on the table:

"First of all, Boudin, you'll stand us all a drink."

"But . . ."

"You're far too stingy. The only reason you were late coming here was because you wanted to save the expense of a taxi."

Boudin swayed in his seat and whined:

"Look here, Colonel, that's too much!"

"As I interrogate them in turn, you'll note down the military situation of everyone who's here. We'll begin by you, since you happen to be the highest in rank. Go on, start writing: Beudin, Irinée, length of service, decorations, date of promotion, wounds—don't forget that attack of jaundice which prevented you from being with us at Dien-Bien-Phu—present situation . . ."

"You know perfectly well I've been waiting for you to be given a command before joining you."

Boudin was suffocating with indignation. For months he had been waiting for a reply to all his letters. Raspéguy had not even congratulated him on his promotion to major and yet they had been warrant-officers together in England. If it had been Esclavier, now! And here he was forcing him to record that Major Beudin, who had not been through Dien-Bien-Phu because of a liver attack, which was hardly his fault, had been "waiting for posting" for the last three months, out of loyalty to Raspéguy.

In his round bullet head, as neat and tidy as a consulting engineer's office, Boudin once again ran through his endless list of grudges against Raspéguy. But the colonel was already going on:

"Captain de Glatigny, what is your military situation?"

"My name's been sent in, Colonel. I'm being gazetted a squadron-leader in February. I've applied to be posted as a military attaché on the other side of the Iron Curtain."

He felt he had to make some excuse:

"Algeria's a rebellion which will soon be put down . . ."

"No, it isn't," said Raspéguy. "You remember what the Viets used to say in camp? The war will go on until the complete victory of Communism throughout the world. This is not the moment for an officer worthy of the name, and I saw at Dien-Bien-Phu that you are one, to go wasting time in an embassy."

"This peasant can talk like a marshal of France when he feels like it," Glatigny reflected. Claude had driven him to make that application, but he already regretted it. He felt an urge to be with his comrades, to fight at their side, far from staff offices and military and political drawing-rooms where the important commands are won by a word in the right place, a little flattery and pulling of strings. He knew that Raspéguy had managed to obtain command of a parachute regiment; he hoped to join him. He dared not admit to himself that Claude's presence was a burden to him, in spite of the clumsy efforts she was now making to draw closer to him by means of his friends. On two occasions she had entertained Guitte Goldschmidt who was said to be Esclavier's "little fiancée" and was once more on good terms with Jeanine Marindelle. But behind all these strategems Jacques detected the presence of his wife's confessor, Father de la Fargière.

"All right then, Glatigny? Good. Boudin, make a note of it: 'Waiting for a posting.' For the first time in my life I shall have a staff college graduate as my Operations officer. What about you, Esclavier?"

"I've still got three weeks' leave left."

"You can take that later. Boudin, put it down: 'Captain Esclavier is rejoining his unit, at his own request, next week.'"

"Which unit is it?"

"The 10th Parachute Regiment, at present stationed at the Camp des Pins near Algiers. Boisfeuras?"

"Yesterday I had planned to leave the army to take over the directorship of an insurance company."

"Have you handed in your resignation?"

"Not yet."

"Hang on to it then. In Algeria we're going to wage that revolutionary war which you kept dinning into my ears, and put to use what we learnt from the Viets and what you were taught by the Chinese. You'll be my Intelligence officer."

Boisfeuras had received a letter from Pasfeuro who had been in Algiers for three weeks. He remembered whole passages of it:

The rebellion is far from being kept in check; on the contrary it's spreading, since it finds fresh encouragement daily in the Government's lack of resolution and the inability of the military to organize themselves so as to deal efficiently with guerrillas. The French reject all innovations, the Moslems welcome them . . . But it's the actual climate of this war that worries me, it's amazingly similar to Indo-China. Once again we're faced with the keyword which stirs up the masses and eventually drives them to communism—"independence."

This war is already proving more brutal and savage by virtue of the violent, passionate, sexual temperament of the Arab and likewise of the Algerian Frenchman who resembles him if only in his bravado and attitude towards women . . . I haven't heard a word from Jeanine . . .

"Well, Boisfeuras?"

"I'm with you, Colonel."

"Write it down, Boudin. Now then, Marindelle. I must first of all congratulate you on your Military Cross and your promotion. But, believe me, it was quite a business getting them for you. There's a little shit in the D.P.M.A.T. who's made a note in your personal file: 'Suspected of Communism.' I've decided, for that reason, to make you the political commissar of the regiment. We'll find another name for it, of course, since it's not provided for in regulations, but that will be your job. Agreed? Make a note of it, Boudin."

"Will our wives be able to come out to Algeria, Colonel?"

"No."

"Regulations allow it."

"We're going to wage war outside all regulations. Are you really so keen on your wife coming out to Algeria?"

The question struck Marindelle like a blow in the face, No, he was not so keen on it, he'd had enough of the amorous fiction of the married couple. His love was dead. But Yves was not angry with Pasfeuro or with Jeanine. It was all over. Things would have to sort themselves out by themselves. He would have liked to leave immediately and no longer have to play this atrocious comedy. His comrades regarded him with great friendship, affection and understanding. Tears came into his eyes, he blew his nose.

"Pinières?" the colonel inquired.

"No problems at all, but I think I'm going to get married."

"That'll have to wait. Orsini?"

"I'd like to leave at once. I've lost a pile at poker. For the last week I've been living on Leroy."

"Boudin will deal with that. What about you, Leroy?"

"I'd like to leave with Orsini. I've a brother and sister-in-law in Paris; they bore me to tears; so do the movies and night clubs; I've lost my taste for girls; I sleep badly; my digestion's rotten; I get cramp in the stomach when I have one drink too many."

"You'll be in Algeria next week. You'll recover your taste for drink and girls. How about you, Merle?"

"I'm demobilized, Colonel, a civilian, a complete civilian. I've come disguised as a soldier because you asked me to, but if a policeman asked to see my papers he could arrest me for wearing uniform illegally."

"Boudin, see that he fills in a re-enlistment form before we leave."

"But . . ."

"But what?"

"I'm not at all sure I want to join the army again."

"Have you any other plans?"

"No."

"Well, then, don't waste our time. We'll have Dia as our medical officer, I've got his transfer in my pocket, and I think I'll be able to rustle up about twenty N.C.O.s of my old battalion.

"These few administrative questions being settled," Raspéguy went on, "I shall now put you in the picture about the situation. I've just been given command of the 10th Colonial Parachute Regiment, the most useless bunch of s.o.b.s in the whole French army, the rejects from every other paratroop unit. That's not all! They've just posted us three hundred reservists who mutinied so as not to leave for Algeria. Needless to say, not one of them has got his wings. You can imagine what morale is like in the Camp des Pins. To thank me for having accepted this gift, I've been allowed to take five officers of my own choice with me. I'm taking ten, you ten, and eight warrant-officers, which makes twenty. In three months from now the 10th Colonial Parachute Regiment is going to be the best unit in the French army."

"Mutineers," said Boudin, rolling his big eyes in dejection.

"Mutineers aren't as bad as all that."

"How are you going to get them under control?"

"With this."

Raspéguy drew an odd cap of camouflage material out of his pocket and put it on his head. The peak jutted out from his fore-head like a bird's beak and a puggaree hung down behind it in two folds, like the tails of a shirt.

"It's hideous," said Esclavier.

"Of course it's hideous. Do you know, it was your brother-in-law who gave me the idea. Yes, we were discussing the Jews and the yellow star. Our soldiers will not be like any others because they will be saddled with this absurd headgear. They'll be ridiculed; consequently they'll have to hold their heads high; they will rally round us and will fight all the better."

"That's pretty sound reasoning," Boisfeuras observed.

"I've bought twelve hundred of these caps."

"Who's going to pay for them?" Boudin moaned, throwing his arms into the air, "the supplies branch will never stand for this!"

"Don't worry, Boudin, it's only a matter of twenty thousand francs. It's an old stock from the Afrika Corps. I shall be flying out next week with you and Esclavier. Leroy and Orsini will follow us, then the rest of you. I want everyone to be in the Camp des Pins by 15 February."

Edouard appeared on the threshold with some bottles of champagne.

"I should like this regiment which has just come into being in the Brent Bar to be christened properly," he said. "I was hoping this was going to be a plot to send the Republic sky high. Well, nothing's perfect, but everything comes in its own good time."

"Were you eavesdropping?" Raspéguy asked him.

"We old Intelligence hands . . ."

"You're being very generous for a barman."

"I'm also the owner."

"Then who's that puppet who struts about upstairs with his hands behind his back?"

"A manager, whom I pay."

Raspéguy raised his glass:

"I drink to the great adventure which is beginning here and now. From it there may emerge a new army and a new nation. I drink to our victory, because this time, enough's enough, we can't afford any more defeats."

THE RUE DE LA BOMBE

PART THREE

THE RUE DE LA
BOMBE

THE MUTINEERS OF
VERSAILLES

Dressed in filthy old tunics, unshaven and with unkempt hair, Bucelier, Bistenave and Geoffrin were digging into some skewered meat at Manuel's, a bistro just outside the camp.

"The rosé is quite good," said Bistenave, "a little on the strong side, but still quite good. All the same, that's not a good enough reason for hanging on to Algeria."

Bucelier and Geoffrin had not yet got used to Bistenave. He was just as scruffy as any of the other reservists, but he spoke with studied elegance and smoked expensive, cork-tipped cigarettes.

"To hell with them all anyway," said Geoffrin, who felt he had to go one better.

He was the only volunteer and was anxious this shortcoming should be overlooked. Bistenave took no notice of him.

"Still no Raspéguy. He's been reported in Algiers, and also in les Pins, but so far no one's laid eyes on him."

"This morning," said Bucelier, "by the cook-house, I heard a sergeant-major whom I'd never seen before shouting his head off; he was young, decked out like a prince and clanking with medals. Must have been one of the ones Raspéguy brought out with him."

"And what was this sergeant-major of yours saying?"

"That the cook-house was filthy, the meat rotten, the wine and vegetables bought at a discount, that the whole thing stank of the black market and pay-offs and that if the men felt like burning down the barracks, he himself would provide them with matches. Then he kicked over a mess-tin of gravy because it was dirty."

The information Bistenave had managed to obtain in Algiers on Colonel Raspéguy had been extremely contradictory. Some said he was a lineshooter, a cross between a killer and a film-star, who liked to remind people he was from the working class, which flattered the men, and that he was a sergeant on the reserve in 1939, which pleased the N.C.O.s. Others, who appeared to be better informed, described him as a born leader, with few scruples, a taste for fighting and danger, a sharp mind capable of adapting itself to every situation, to every form of warfare, and backed up by a team of former prisoners from the Vietminh camps.

Up till now Bistenave had only had to exploit the adversary's faults to sow disorder all round him and to create what he was pleased to call "anarchy and revolution in the service of peace." He recalled the reservists' arrival at the barracks of Versailles. No arrangements had been made to receive them; there were no beds in the rooms, only a few palliasses, some mildewed blankets and that rancid, clinging smell of rifle oil, moth-balls and dish-water. The reservists, who resented being snatched away from their civilian way of life, their wives and their apéritifs, had boiled over with rage. An old quartermaster-sergeant with a fat paunch had confined himself to telling them in that tone of excuse and complicity which cowards readily assume:

"It's not my fault, I haven't been issued with anything else. Personally, I think it's pretty bad. If it depended on me . . . No, there are no officers here; they're all at home."

Bistenave had summed up the situation:

"This is a damned insult."

He had then thrown a palliasse out of the window; all his comrades had followed his example and in a few minutes, blankets, palliasses, "biscuits," bolsters and bedsteads lay scattered in the courtyard outside.

The military police had not dared to intervene and the "mutineers" had gone off to sleep in town.

No measures were taken against them next day. A doddery, extremely paternal old major had given them a mild telling-off, as though they were children who had raided the pantry.

Then they had been issued with old uniforms dragged out from an ordnance store which had not been in use since 1945. Boots were in short supply, so they had been allowed to keep the shoes they had been wearing on reporting to the barracks, and their high, pointed forage-caps dated from the 1939 war.

The food served in the dining-hall at lunchtime had been uneatable: a sort of greyish-coloured stew with a few bits of tainted meat floating in it; the wine had been watered down; the bread was mouldy; and there were not enough mess-tins to go round.

Bistenave had only had to give the signal and everything was reduced to a shambles; mess-tins, water-bottles, tables and benches were sent flying, while the reservists started chanting: "Down with the war in Algeria." A few of them had struck up the "International," but their comrades had not joined in the singing. Singing the "International" in an army barracks reminded them vaguely of the Commune and firing squads at dawn in the ditches of the Château de Vincennes.

A horrified duty officer had reported to the colonel:

"They're going to burn the whole place down, sir; they've mutinied and are now parading with a red flag and singing the 'International.'"

The colonel was a morose, pessimistic creature who, knowing he would never be promoted to general, delighted in catastrophes.

"What did I tell you? These youngsters—Communists, all of them. It's all the fault of that man de Gaulle who brought Thorez back. What can we do about it?"

"What if you had a word with them?"

"Are you trying to be funny? Just to be insulted by that rabble? Call the C.R.S., and quickly, before they break everything in sight. This is a job for them."

Two C.R.S. trucks had driven up in the afternoon. Wearing steel helmets and armed with submachine-guns, the police had immediately occupied the arms depot which contained nothing but a few rusty old carbines and had then surrounded the building held by the "mutineers."

Bistenave had felt that his comrades were losing heart. There

was talk of decimation, of Biribi and Tataouine. No one offered any resistance to the C.R.S.

Composing his voice, the old major had ordered the ringleaders to step forward. His appearance on the scene had
re-assured the "mutineers of Versailles," as the newspapers already called them. It was hard to imagine this old dodderer
taking severe disciplinary measures.

The reservists were herded into trucks and then transferred
on to a train which was halted in the open countryside.

There were a few juicy, revolutionary scenes in the manner
of *The Battleship Potemkin,* which Bistenave, as a follower of
avant-garde films, found much to his liking: women lying
down on the railway lines, alarm bells being rung every half-
hour, shouts, scuffles and arrests.

The sea was rough throughout the crossing and Bistenave
himself was sick. Algiers appeared early in the morning, dazzling white, with its terraced houses and modern blocks of
flats.

The reservists were expecting a state of war. They found a
port buzzing with activity, a town completely at peace.

A sentry, whose steel helmet and submachine-gun gave him a
certain warlike aspect, was good enough to tell them that there
were never any outrages in the daytime but that the previous
night, at the Clos Salembier, seven people had been killed and
twelve wounded.

"They all had their throats cut," he said, and ran his hand
across his neck by way of illustration.

As a "disciplinary measure," the three hundred mutineers of
Versailles were posted to the Camp des Pins with the paratroops of the 10th Colonial Regiment, where, they were as-
sured, "they would be put through it."

Bistenave was quickly reassured by the sloppiness and low
morale of this unit. He felt that the game was up, that the war
in Algeria was as good as lost, if the best troops in the French
army were like these flabby, loud-mouthed tramps.

He was even somewhat dismayed; but the role he had set
himself demanded that he should be the sloppiest of the lot

and that he should do his utmost to accelerate the process of decomposition. By temperament he was inclined to be a neat and tidy man.

Without ever thrusting himself forward, without running the risk of a showdown, he had become the real ring-leader of the reservists.

And while he sipped his rosé wine and munched his skewered mutton, he tried to imagine how he would set about it if he, Bistenave, were entrusted with the task of restoring order to this band of hoodlums. One must sometimes put oneself in one's adversary's place to understand him the better.

At the midday meal the food had already shown considerable improvement; in the evening it was even better. Sergeant-Major Vincenier had been joined by two colour-sergeants; they showed no interest in the men, appeared not to notice them at all and confined themselves to administrative duties.

Three parachutists and two reservists passed Captain Esclavier and Lieutenant Orsini in the main street of Staouéli. Sheepishly, they saluted them.

"You needn't salute," Esclavier told them in that dry voice of his. "I'm used to returning a soldier's salute, not an animal's. Out of the way."

On the following day Sergeant-Major Métayer, commonly called Polyphème, made his appearance. He was a legend among the paratroops, like Raspéguy, like Esclavier: an officer of the Légion d'Honneur, mentioned in dispatches seventeen times, wounded four times, he refused to accept a commission. His feats of valour were the talk of every mess, his toughness and love of a scrap were common knowledge.

Métayer was short and thickset and wore a black patch over one eye. He called the reservists out on parade and less than half of them turned up; he dismissed them all, called them out again, and three-quarters of them appeared. There was a certain amount of muttering in the ranks. He called them out on parade for the third time.

"I'm in no hurry," he said.

When they were all present, he inspected them at his leisure and everyone could see the profound disgust on his face. Then he dismissed them without further ado.

Next day a further lot of N.C.O.s and three new officers appeared and the camp was soon going full blast. But this activity had no effect on the reservists.

Bistenave managed to buttonhole Geoffrin as he rushed past him panting.

"What the hell's going on?" he asked.

"Things are moving. We're being issued with new uniforms, new jumping boots, and weapons. We're off into the mountains, it seems."

"What about us?"

"Polyphème says that the Old Man . . ."

"What old man?"

"Raspéguy is moving heaven and earth in Algiers to get rid of the lot of you; he says the 10th is not a punishment unit. I must be off."

"What's the hurry?"

"I've been waiting a whole year for a new uniform."

"Eager beavers, these volunteers," said Bucelier.

Three days later the paratroops were newly equipped and their uniforms altered; their moustaches and beards had disappeared; their hair was no more than an inch long; and all of them wore a strange cap which made their faces look leaner and gave them the appearance of young wolves.

They walked about, shoulders squared and chest thrust out, and had less and less to do with the reservists.

"Well, how's it going?" Raspéguy asked Esclavier.

The colonel had moved into a little villa on the edge of the sea. He never left the house but, with Boudin's assistance, was busy going through the personal files of every man in his new regiment.

Esclavier sat down in a wicker armchair. He looked distraught.

"These eight hundred men of the 10th—recruited from every walk of life, badly officered, badly commanded for over a year, left to their own devices for the last three months, flabby, in poor shape, no reactions; paratroops only from the point of view of brashness and swagger. Get into brawls in cafés, and more often than not get the worst of it. Yesterday evening four of them who were showing off in front of their comrades got themselves thrown out of Manuel's with a good boot in the ass—and by artillerymen!"

"Have you got their names?"

"Yes: Privat, Sapinsky, Mugnier, Verteneuve . . ."

"And the reservists?"

"A cigarette in the corner of their mouths, hands in their pockets, they're looking on at our men getting a move on: a little uneasy all the same."

"Do you know who the ringleaders are?"

"We only know of two at the moment: Bistenave and Geoffrin. Geoffrin is probably a Commie. About Bistenave, we're not so certain. But according to Polyphème he's the one who's leading them on."

"What's his profession?"

"A priest," Boudin replied, utterly aghast.

"*What* did you say?"

"Yes, a priest, that's to say he's studying for the priesthood. He hasn't yet finished his training; he's not yet ordained, I mean. Good family; his father was a quartermaster colonel; yes, he's the son of Fleur de Nave whom de Lattre pitched out of Indo-China as soon as he landed."

"Is the circus show ready for tomorrow?"

"We've set up three loudspeakers. First parade will be on the beach at eight o'clock. Boisfeuras managed to get hold of the records."

At six o'clock in the morning Bistenave was awakened with a start by the "Partisan Song" blaring from the loudspeakers:

Friend, do you hear the black flight of the ravens in the plains
Friend, do you hear the dull cry of your country in chains . . ."

He shook Bucelier.

"Listen, tell me it isn't true . . . the 'Partisan Song' . . . here . . ."

"It sounds very much like it to me," said Bucelier. "They've got a nerve, these Fascists."

"They say that Raspéguy commanded some partisans during the war," said Mougin, "and that Captain Esclavier was tortured by the Germans. So they have every right to adopt the 'Partisan Song' themselves."

"Not in this war," Bistenave drily observed.

The camp had been transformed overnight. A flagpost had been erected in the middle of it, on which fluttered the tricolour and below it a long black pennant with the motto "I dare."

"That can't be denied," said Bistenave, "he certainly dares."

"On your feet, men," blared a loudspeaker. "In ten minutes all the paratroops parade on the beach in singlet and shorts . . ."

"What about us?" said Mougin.

"They're not going to bother about lepers like us," Estreville fumed, "we're just left to rot in our filthy tents, in our tattered battledress . . ."

The "juice" arrived with slices of buttered bread and jam. The juice smelt of coffee, the bread was fresh: yet another innovation.

"Things have begun to look up since Raspéguy got here," Torlase observed. "At least there's something fit to eat."

The loudspeakers were playing regional tunes and "Sur les Quais de Paris."

At eight o'clock the regiment was drawn up in a hollow square on the beach. The sky was crystal-clear and a smell of iodine and salt was wafted in from the sea which broke in gentle waves of grey and green.

The reservists formed the fourth corner of the square. Polyphème had simply told them:

"Stand there—in line, if you can."

The warrant-officers were barking away to get their men in position and kept dressing and re-dressing the ranks. The paratroops were soon in perfect line, whereas the reservists looked like a herd of goats that had halted there at random.

"This can't go on," said Bucelier.

"You're going to get it, you know," Bistenave gently remarked.

"I don't care. What do we look like? Don't listen to him, you men."

He stepped out of the ranks and tried to draw his comrades up in line.

"Come on now, straighten up. Pull your stomachs in. You there, shift along a bit; and you, move up . . ."

Polyphème appeared behind Bucelier:

"You say, 'By the right, dress.' That's the usual word of command."

And Bucelier found himself shouting:

"By the right, dress."

"In every Commie there subconsciously lurks a military man," Bistenave thought to himself.

Raspéguy stepped inside the square, followed by Boudin and Esclavier. All three wore their medals hanging from their breast. Bistenave heard the men behind him saying:

"You see that thing Raspéguy's wearing just below the others. That's the star of a Grand Officer of the Légion d'Honneur. He's the only lieutenant-colonel who's been given it."

"All three of them have got the Resistance Medal," Bucelier drily remarked as though by way of apology.

"With that broad chest of his and lean behind, that camouflage uniform and that funny cap, the colonel looks like a tiger," the seminarist was thinking. "A cruel beast of war taking possession of his horde."

Major Boudin yelled in his Auvergne accent:

"Tenth Colonial Parachute Regiment . . . Atten . . . shun!"

The ranks stood motionless. The reservists froze more or less in a position of attention, but one after another, like tenpins being replaced. They were embarrassed and kept glancing at one another.

Raspéguy took three steps forward, saluted, then called out:

"Privat, Sapinsky, Mugnier, Verteneuve!"

The four paratroopers marched out of the ranks and came to a halt six paces in front of the colonel.

Raspéguy raised his rasping voice, which seemed to fasten on the men and hold them rooted to the spot.

"I don't like my men making trouble, brawling in bars and then being beaten up by gunners. I'm throwing you out of the regiment; go and hand in your uniforms."

White in the face, the four paratroopers about-turned.

Then the colonel began moving slowly down the ranks, stopping every so often to interrogate a man he recognized.

"Your name?"

The man gave it.

"Weren't you at Na-San?"

"Yes, sir."

"And you got scared; you went sick. There was nothing wrong with you. Go and hand in your uniform."

"And you there, what's your name? You've got a bad record. Misappropriating the regimental funds. Move off."

He came to a halt in front of a staff-sergeant.

"Raspin, you're already drunk at eight o'clock in the morning. I'm throwing you out of the regiment and at once; you're finished with the paratroops."

"I'll stop drinking, sir."

"I don't believe you: you've said that before, out in Indo-China. I'm sorry, Raspin, because you're a good soldier and you know how to fight."

"Please keep me on, sir."

Raspéguy slowly shook his head and put a friendly hand on the staff-sergeant's shoulder.

"No."

Whenever he came across a man who was too badly dressed the colonel got rid of him. But this would have meant getting rid of half the regiment. Twenty men had already been sent off to hand in their uniforms by the time he reached the reservists.

"Just like de Lattre, just as much of a bull-shitter," Bistenave said to himself.

He hated Raspéguy and this whole sinister show he had put on to "take the regiment in hand." His father had so often described what he called his "execution."

The plane had just landed at Saigon aerodrome. Troops had been brought up from the delta to welcome the new commander-in-chief. They were no better or worse dressed than the rest: jungle boots, camouflage uniform, bush hats, webbing equipment.

De Lattre stepped down from the aircraft, taking good care to show his best profile to the cameramen. He inspected the troops. He needed to make an example of someone, a victim. Suddenly he stopped and shouted out:

"How can anyone allow heroes to be so sloppily dressed! Send for the quartermaster. What's he called? Fleur de Nav! What a name!"

Quartermaster Bistenave had been sent back to France in the same aircraft and his career had been ruined. He had been in Indo-China no longer than two weeks; he had taken over his command only three days before.

That was how General de Lattre, through his love of display and theatricals, his injustices and military demagogy, had allowed the war in Indo-China to drag on for another four years.

In the eyes of the reservist Paul Bistenave, Raspéguy was made of the same sort of stuff and belonged to the same species of mankind as the marshal. The squire and the shepherd had the same thirst for glory, the same sense of pomp and splendour, the same contempt for justice.

Raspéguy, he felt sure, was the sort of man who would prolong this rotten war in Algeria. And Bistenave hated war; his Christ was the god of peace.

The colonel was now walking down the ranks of reservists and laughed as he turned to Esclavier and then to Boudin:

"Aren't they sweet, with their dear little pointed forage-caps? Upon my word, it's an absolute Bourbaki army!"

He stopped in front of Mougin because he was tall, strong and had a determined face:

"Do you like being dolled up like this?"

"No, sir."

"Well, get your hair cut, short like mine, go and have a shave and a wash, pitch your forage-cap into the sea, go and see Polyphème and tell him: 'I'm no longer a reservist but a volunteer who has joined the Tenth Parachute Regiment for the duration of my recall.' Then you'll be equipped like the others, but like the others you'll march, suffer and maybe die. You can take your choice, you and the rest of your pals . . . Bistenave and Bucelier, report to my office after parade."

That morning two-thirds of the reservists threw their forage-caps into the sea.

Bucelier faced the colonel first.

"Sit down," Raspéguy told him. "I'm told you're a Communist; I've even had an official report on you. See what they say—a dangerous ringleader. So I'm making you a sergeant since you know how to lead men."

"I'm not a member of the Communist Party, sir, but I'm a sympathizer and I'm against the war in Algeria."

"What the hell do I care? You're in it for a certain length of time. You can either stay on here where you'll have a man's life and responsibilities, a soldier's job, or you can go off and rot in some base camp where the *fellaghas* will probably come and cut your balls off without your being able to defend yourself. It's up to you."

"I'll stay on, sir."

"Go and change your uniform and report to your new captain. His name is Esclavier and you'll find him in the office next door."

Bistenave was then ushered in.

"According to my information," said Raspéguy, "you're a student-priest and a pacifist, but you've also got a sense of leadership since you've managed to create such havoc among your group of reservists. Am I right?"

"Yes, sir."

"I'm promoting you to sergeant."

"I refuse, sir."

"That's up to you, but I'm not going to put up with your low scheming and priestly hypocrisy any longer. If you persist in it, I'll beat you over the head with this stick—and it's a *maquilla* which my own priest gave me. So what's your decision?"

In Bistenave Raspéguy recognized a resolution as firm as his own.

"There's only one thing for me to do, Fleur de Nave—send you off to prison between a couple of policemen. Priests and sons of quartermaster-colonels have useful connexions. You'd soon be released, but your friends whom you've landed in the shit would stick in it for ever."

"I'd like to stay with my friends, sir. I undertake to remain absolutely neutral and obey orders, but I refuse all responsibility or to participate on your side. I undertake this in the name of Christ."

"Give me the names of two reservists whom I could make sergeants."

"Mougin and Estrevelle."

"Good. Go and report to Captain Esclavier. He adores conscientious objectors. Mougin and Estrevelle, you said?"

"Yes, sir."

"I've committed myself even more than if I'd allowed myself to be made a sergeant," the seminarist thought to himself. "But at least I'll be able to get rid of these rags and be clean again at last."

A few days later the rest of the officers arrived.

Out of the reservists, Colonel Raspéguy formed a small battalion of two companies and gave the command to Esclavier. Merle was entrusted with the first company, and Pinières with the second. Glatigny was made Operations officer. Boisfeuras was responsible for Intelligence and Marindelle was put in charge of Propaganda and Psychological Warfare.

Outwardly, the 10th Colonial Parachute Regiment was no different from any other regiment of paratroops. But its colonel and all its officers had made up their minds to establish a unit of an entirely different sort which would enable them to wage war as it should be waged in this year of grace 1956.

For two months the N.C.O.s and privates of the 10th Regiment were subjected to intensive training.

The physical training periods were succeeded by forced marches. A particularly tough and dangerous assault course was set up in the middle of the camp. Raspéguy inaugurated it by getting round it in record time. The officers followed after him. Boudin crashed on his face but limped home all the same.

In the few barrack-rooms which served as instruction halls a number of Raspéguy's favourite slogans had been pinned up:

"Whoever dies has lost." "In order to win, learn how to fight." "In battle, death sanctions every fault."

The "volunteer" reservists were subjected to the same rules and the same training as the paratroops. At the end of a month it was difficult to tell them apart.

The diary which the seminarist Bistenave kept included the following entries for the month of May 1956:

"I'm beginning to understand Colonel Raspéguy's little game.

"We are ceaselessly lectured on the subject of death, not as the final outcome of a man's life, the great step that is taken in order to cross over into the next world, but as a sort of technical misadventure due to clumsiness or lack of training . . .

"During an exercise with live ammunition two paratroopers of the third company were killed. It was their own fault; they had not followed the instructions they had been given.

"Raspéguy paraded the men of this company and delivered a funeral oration over the two bodies which were covered by a square of tent cloth. 'They died for France,' he said, 'and like a couple of donkeys. I forbid you to do as they did.' Then he strode off with his pipe in his mouth.

"Bucelier, who is a Communist, found this brutality quite normal. I'd even go so far as to say that he was fascinated by it.

"We march until we are ready to drop, in silence, our backs bent, dripping with sweat, day and night, and when we think we have reached the stage at which no further effort is possible, Raspéguy and his wolves drive us on still farther. I never thought that officers could demand so much from their men, especially of us reservists who less than two months ago were yelling at Versailles: 'Down with the war in Algeria.'

"But these officers live as we do, toil as we do, sleep and eat as we do. It only needed Sergeant-Major Polyphème to declare: 'I drink water because wine affects my legs' for there to be no more wine in anyone's water-bottle within a week. We are all becoming sober.

"In camouflage uniform and with this strange cap of ours, we are all beginning to look like one another, to have the same reactions, to use the same words, the same expressions, drawn for the most part from the radio-code. For 'yes' we say 'affirmative'; for 'no,' 'negative'; for 'all's well,' 'five five' while raising a thumb in the air. We describe such-and-such a man as 'an all good,' such-and-such another as 'an all bad.' The colonel does his utmost to prevent all contact between us and the outside world, to keep us enclosed in this strange monastery, on this wooded beach by the water's edge. He limits our leave and we know he himself doesn't ever go out.

"Various customs, or perhaps I should say rites, are now observed. Drunks are frowned upon, and so are womanizers; there is less and less talk about girls and 'painting the town red.' Is it fatigue which encourages chastity, or this atmosphere of sports stadium, country fair and church?

"With astonishing mastery and without moving from this camp, the 'wolves' are inducing us, all unconsciously, to take part in this war in Algeria to which many of us—I'm speaking for the reservists—are still opposed because they consider it unjust. The propaganda service is run by a young captain, a sort of lanky, fair-haired schoolboy who always looks as if he's preparing a practical joke or a trap. His name is Marindelle.

"The loud-speakers never cease blaring forth songs, news items, information and slogans, and these slogans sometimes have the oddest ring about them:

"We haven't come here to defend colonialism; we have nothing in common with those affluent settlers who exploit the Moslems, We are the defenders of liberty and the new order.

" 'Radio Raspéguy' lays particular emphasis on everything that can make a soldier disgusted with civilian life. The outside world is presented as vile, corrupt and degraded, power as being in the hands of a gang of small-time crooks.

"My comrades already talk about 'us' as opposed to anyone who doesn't wear our peaked cap and camouflage uniform. They are clean, neat and are becoming agile; they are pure, whereas in France there is nothing but corruption, cowardice and meanness—the 'world of sin' of our monasteries.

"Captain Marindelle has very cunningly exploited the endless inquiry into the leakages in order to discredit the government, high-level administration and a certain army.

"In the interval between a waltz and a military march the loud-speaker blares:

" 'While we were fighting out in Indo-China or languishing in Vietminh prisons, some men were being paid a fat fee for betraying us to the enemy's advantage: a collection of perverted journalists and policemen, highly-placed officials, untrustworthy generals and shady politicians.

" 'And nothing is coming out of this inquiry, no one is going to be charged with anything. Everyone belongs to this crooked gang. Comrade'—for he actually used the word comrade—'aren't you better off here with us? Here, no one will betray you, no one will lie to you.'

"I've checked up on the news items broadcast by 'Radio Raspéguy.' They are accurate and drawn from every source. *Libération* and *Le Monde* are quoted as much as *La Nation Française* and *l'Aurore*, and occasionally even our dear old *Témoignage Chrétien*.

"We live on top of each other, officers, N.C.O.s and men all together, but it's Raspéguy's 'wolves' who set the tone. They seem to be trying to canvass our opinion, as though they were waiting for us to vote them into the ranks and positions they already occupy. Once they have been elected, no one will be able to question any order they give us.

"But it's a one-sided game. These officers are not like the others; they have the maturity and 'dialectical' knowledge of mankind which they acquired in the Vietminh camps.

"The programme to which they subject us has nothing military about it. After each manœuvre, the platoons and sections get together to criticize it, and were it not for the laughter and jokes one could easily imagine oneself at a Communist self-examination session."

In the month of June Bistenave was writing:

"The 'wolves' have won; they have won our vote and if a poll were to be held to elect each of our leaders, I don't think a single officer or N.C.O. would be changed. Thus the bonds between the men and those who command them are infinitely stronger here than anywhere else.

"I was bold enough to enter into a discussion with Captain Marindelle, and I discovered that I was dealing with a mind that is open to every form of argument; he believes that only Marxist methods of war are efficient. But he tells me he believes in God.

"They are all obsessed with this word: efficiency.

"I also asked him:

"'Does this communion you maintain with your men have any other reason but efficiency and only one ultimate aim—war?'

"'No, it's because we need them. In Indo-China we experienced the solitude of mercenaries; we felt like outcasts from the nation. We don't want any more of that situation. We've got to create a popular army, thanks to which we will find ourselves in communion with the people. That's why those who've been called up, the reservists like you, are much more important to us than the volunteers who, by the very fact of enlisting, have performed more or less the act of a mercenary.'

"Any other rank can go and see Captain Marindelle and have a discussion with him. In this regiment without a priest, he plays the role of an almoner, a sort of civilian and political almoner. But the idea has suddenly flashed into my head—of course, he's the political commissar!

"To me this revolutionary experiment is fascinating and terrifying. My eighteen months' military service in a barracks on the outskirts of Paris had not prepared me for encounters like this.

"Captain Esclavier, who is in command of the two companies of reservists, has taken me on as a liaison agent, secretary and fourth at bridge. Last night I slept next to him. He shared his bedding and rations with me. I had attempted a finesse and lost.

"When we go out on manœuvres, we never know how long the exercise is going to last: a few hours, one day, or two or three days; so the usual drill is to take one's bivouac, sleeping bag and two days' rations with one. I had thought we were coming back that evening and did not want to weigh myself down.

"It was a fine, clear night and a sentry standing a few yards from us showed up as a dark patch against the sky.

"I asked this captain who has been fighting for years by Raspéguy's side if the colonel believed in God. He burst out laughing—and it's rare for this officer, who seldom sheds his reserved manner, to laugh. Captain Esclavier despises soft-hearted people, chatterboxes, and anyone who weakens and pours out his soul—but maybe darkness makes him more human. This was his reply:

" 'I also once asked Major Raspéguy whether he believed in God, and he seemed surprised. "When I've a moment to spare," he replied, "I must look into the matter." But you may be certain that Colonel Raspéguy will never have the time to look into the matter, nor will General Raspéguy . . .'

" 'What about you, Captain?'

" 'I don't believe in God, but I feel I am bound up with Christian civilization.'

"The captain addresses me as 'vous' when we're alone together, but uses the familiar 'tu' in front of my comrades.

'Esclavier gave another laugh:

"If you were to ask me what I have come out here to fight against, I would say: in the first place, excess. Sophocles says: 'Excess is the greatest crime against the gods.' I'm fighting against the savage, lawless nationalism of the Arabs because it is excessive, just as I fought against Communism, because that too was excessive.'

"I felt like asking him: 'What are you practising here if it isn't military Communism? But the Communists can at least justify their methods, their pragmatism, their contempt for individual man by an immense objective: to strip humanity of its old skin; whereas your ultimate aim is simply to win this war, nothing but this war, and, whatever you might say to the contrary, to save the privileged classes and maintain an economic, political and racial inequality. In fact, Captain, you don't really know why you're fighting—from habit, perhaps, and out of barbaric loyalty to the head of your clan who is Raspéguy.'

"But the captain had turned over and was fast asleep.

"Next morning we crossed a sort of prairie covered in wild flowers, and the captain pointed out that there were very few bees and scarcely a hive to be seen.

" 'To me,' he said, 'as to the people of the ancient world, bees are the symbol of peace, prosperity and organization. This land of Algeria has never known anything but war and anarchy, and so the bees don't come here.'

" 'The men have a strange attitude towards Captain Esclavier. They manifest a sort of jealous, fierce attachment to him. They are proud of his strength, his good looks, his courage, his medals (he's an officer of the Légion d'Honneur and a companion of the Libération—and even I am not insensible to the display of so much glory), they like to see him impeccably turned out and always on the go, but they are frightened of his sudden moods and his contempt for any form of weakness. He's the absolute prototype of the paratrooper and Raspéguy's favourite officer.

"By way of contrast, all the reservists of the first company feel like personal friends of Lieutenant Merle's. They are always happy to see him, are scared when he jumps into his Jeep, which he drives like a maniac, and would give him a word of warning if they dared.

"This lieutenant is the brother all of us have secretly dreamt about. He's as cheeky and comic as the bird that bears his name and declares at every opportunity that he doesn't like the army. He has absolutely no sense of ownership; he loses all his kit and never has any cigarettes or matches or any water in his bottle. So he borrows from everyone, with a falsely contrite air. He seems to have no sense of hierarchy. He is possibly the only one who doesn't take Raspéguy seriously, much to the colonel's secret pleasure.

"Merle is very close to Lieutenant Pinières, a sort of red-haired colossus who is convinced that there is nothing better in the world than being a paratroop officer in the best parachute regiment which is naturally the one in which he happens to be serving. To Merle, tough Esclavier is like an elder brother.

"Merle has one vice: gambling, and he 'blows' his pay at the Aletti Casino as soon as he draws it. For the rest of the time he lives on loans from Esclavier.

"Major Beudin, commonly called Boudin, who comes from Auvergne and doesn't like to see money wasted, decided this month to dole Merle out his pay in driblets of 10,000 francs. In Captain Esclavier's office I was able to witness a scene of high comedy between Merle and the major. It was like a bargain being transacted on a fairground.

"In the midst of this circus Boudin is the only one who keeps a cool head and a sense of reality; he suffers agony from all the irregularities that are committed, but he is secretly enchanted at being the only one capable of dealing with them. For Raspéguy he has the attachment of a faithful dog, and receives every kick he gets from him with something akin to pleasure. Boudin is said to be extremely courageous in battle but incapable of commanding a company.

"Major de Glatigny still preserves some of the haughtiness of a cavalry officer; in one respect he is less easy to get on with than the others, he still believes he's an officer by divine right. He goes to Mass, performs all his religious duties, but is beginning to be caught up in this crazy atmosphere.

"Raspéguy is flattered to be in command of this descendant of a great military dynasty and addresses him with false irony as 'Count' or 'Constable.'

"Major de Glatigny is the only real 'traditional' officer in the whole regiment. In spite of everything, he has preserved the sense of what a soldier may do and may not do, whereas all his colleagues are living in a dream world. He is extremely civilized and uses his influence to temper the colonel's outrageousness.

"I can never face Captain Boisfeuras without feeling slightly ill at ease.

"He is ugly, with phenomenal stamina and a rasping voice. He walks without making a sound and, like certain old college ushers, he's on to you before you can hear him coming. He's the only officer who's badly dressed, he's the jackal among the wolves. I asked Lieutenant Merle about him.

"'You know, old man,' he replied (he calls everyone 'old man') 'I owe my life to Captain Boisfeuras, and at a time when there was no love lost between us.'

"Captain Boisfeuras often goes to Algiers and is sometimes away for several days. He's the 'political' officer of our odd regiment, and his power is obviously more than that of a mere captain.

"As his chauffeur, butler, batman and bodyguard, he has a sort of Chinaman who is always behind him with a revolver on his hip. The Boisfeuras enigma stirs everyone's imagination. Some say he's a secret agent, others a politician who is lying low, others still a special envoy from the Government, and his reputation increases in proportion to the mystery surrounding him.

"Our medical officer is a magnificent Negro, Captain Dia. He addresses everyone as '*tu*,' from the colonel down. His voice resounds like a copper drum; he eats like an ogre, drinks like a wineskin; his hands are sensitive and bring relief to his patients. He overflows with humanity and love of life.

"He goes bathing at night. I noticed him one evening by the edge of the sea; he was playing on a strange little flute. Esclavier, Boisfeuras and Marindelle were with him and I fancied—for his face was visible in the moonlight—that Captain Esclavier had tears in his eyes. But a man of that stamp can't weep very often, and the moonlight may have been deceiving.

"I felt I was witnessing the celebration of a cult of some strange African or Asian divinity. The note of the flute was plaintive and was drowned by the dull roar of the sea. I had no place there, I, who am soon to be a priest of the Catholic and Roman Church.

"What curious and disturbing people these 'wolves' are! They are familiar with Sophocles, Marx and Mao-Tse-Tung, but I fancy they are burdened with painful secrets; I know that they are sometimes possessed by certain obscure forces.

"I looked at myself in the mirror just now and I was pleased and horrified at once to see that I too am beginning to look like a wolf.

"Tomorrow we are leaving the Camp des Pins, tomorrow we are embarking on this beastly war in Algeria and I'm almost relieved at the prospect.

"Dear God, help me against myself, against the others, against the temptations of the wolves!"

2

THE BLACK PANTHER

P —— was like any other little Algerian town situated in the cultivated zones: a long street with three cafés, a Moslem veterans' association, a few French shops and a larger number of Mozabite stores. The French inhabitants were called Perez or Hernandez: and the Mozabites, who never ventured outside their own front doors, were as fat and limp as slugs.

At the end of this street with its scarred and pitted surface, stood the police-station, a brand-new building with fine yellow railings and white bars across the windows.

The gateway was reinforced with sandbags, the café terraces protected against hand-grenades by iron grilles, and the entrance and exit of the town sealed off by makeshift roadblocks of spiked fences and barbed wire.

Barbed wire everywhere: round the public gardens and its bandstand where no band had played for years, along the church, the town hall and empty school, in front of the little concrete blockhouses guarded by steel-helmeted, trigger-happy sentries.

The Moslems hugged the walls and avoided running into the Christians; hatred had become a living, palpable thing, it had its own smell and habits; at night it howled in the empty streets like a famished dog.

In two months the whole area round P —— had gone over to the rebels. Settlers' farms had gone up in flames, turning darkness into daylight right up to the gates of the town; flocks had been slaughtered; men, women and children had been massacred in particularly atrocious circumstances.

Cars were machine-gunned on the roads, and buses set on fire, and one convoy every other day was the only means of communication between P—— and the rest of the world. Troops only moved about in full strength, and even then were shot at every time they emerged.

Colonel Quarterolles, the garrison commander, had been taken prisoner in 1940. He had not taken part in the war in Indo-China and he claimed to know Algeria like the back of his hand by virtue of having commanded Tunisian and Moroccan levies over a period of fifteen years. First of all, he was unwilling to admit that with a garrison two thousand strong he was held in check by a "band of thugs and murderers armed with *boukalas.*" It was only after one of his platoons that had gone out on patrol to a farm five miles outside the town had got itself wiped out that he requested the support of an operational unit.

And that was how one fine day the Raspéguy circus turned up in P—— with its trucks, its loud-speakers and its paratroops in their outlandish headgear. Colonel Quarterolles thought that these lads of twenty, with their over-tailored tunics and easy gestures, powdered like little marquises by the dust of the road, did not strike a serious note at all. He liked hefty warriors in steel helmets, clanking with heavy equipment—the old-fashioned, wine-swilling type of soldier.

Quarterolles had managed to extract the commitment from the headquarters of Area Ten in Algiers that the paratroops sent to him would be placed under his orders and that he himself would command all the operations "in person." In order to get rid of him, the Chief of Staff had promised him anything he asked.

The commander-in-chief had thought of relieving Quarterolles of his command and sending him back to France, but he feared there might be a scandal. It was only by a miracle that a scandal had so far been avoided.

At Lille the S.F.I.O. Party had just adopted a motion on Algeria requesting the Government to concentrate all their efforts on achieving a cease fire. If the newspapers had come out with a report in heavy type: "A platoon of twenty-eight reservists has been massacred outside P—— by a rebel band; three machine-guns, one 60-calibre mortar with its shells and twenty-three rifles or submachine-guns have been lost," the congress might have not only requested but demanded a cease fire as well as disciplinary measures against the army leaders who allowed the soldiers under their command to be massacred.

The only unit in reserve was the 10th Colonial Parachute Regiment which was said to be insufficiently trained and lacking in team spirit. The general had sent for Raspéguy who had reported with Esclavier by his side. They had been made to wait in a little room through which busy young officers kept passing to and fro, clacking like old hens.

A captain came to fetch them; he wore a scarlet waistcoat with brass buttons under his tunic—like a damned lackey, as Raspéguy observed.

The general was sitting at his desk, bent over a large sheet of glass with a map of Algeria spread out underneath it. His face was lifeless, his voice toneless:

"Raspéguy, I allowed you the two months you requested in order to train your regiment. Those two months are now up; are you ready?"

"Yes, sir."

"I've got a tough job for you. Do you want to hang on to your reservists?"

"Very much so."

"That's up to you. You've heard about what happened at P ——. I want those arms we lost there to be recovered. I want Si Lahcen dead or alive . . .

"Good hunting, Raspéguy! For this job you'll have an absolutely free hand. I want results and I don't give a damn what methods you use."

Raspéguy had asked:

"What's my position in relation to the colonel commanding the sector?"

"It can be whatever you like. If he gets in your way . . ."

He made a gesture with his hand as though to sweep away a troublesome fly. His handsome face with its regular Roman features remained inscrutable but Esclavier noticed that his eyes betrayed the cruel glint of a mandarin of old China, whose peace and meditation has been disturbed by an importunate intruder.

The intruder was the garrison commander.

Raspéguy had reported to Colonel Quarterolles in the pre-scribed military manner, snapping splendidly to attention, giving a smart salute, keeping his eyes fixed on some point in the middle distance. But he had no badges of rank, no decoration, no weapon, and his battledress was unbuttoned to reveal his sunburnt torso.

"I'll have to take him in hand immediately." Quarterolles had said to himself, "these former N.C.O.s always try to take the bit between their teeth."

"Look here, Colonel, I've noticed your men don't wear steel helmets. The regulations . . ."

"The regulations are all very well, Colonel, but they over-look one important point."

"What's that?"

"That we've first of all got to win. Now no one can fight properly and win while lumbering about the mountains in the month of July with a heavy helmet on his head. I've given my men orders to leave their helmets behind at the Camp des Pins, but to take two water-bottles each."

"That's your business. Tomorrow we'll mount an operation to occupy a few farms which I had to abandon for lack of per-sonnel. Today I've arranged quarters for your unit in the town. You can take over the school as your headquarters."

"No."

"Eh?"

"No. The whole regiment will camp out in the mountains to-night and we'll light some big fires so that the *fellaghas* will know that we're there. I don't like the idea of barbed wire, Col-onel; I saw too much of it out in Indo-China."

"I forbid you . . ."

Raspéguy shrugged his broad shoulders and smiled.

"Come now, Colonel, we'd better see eye to eye. Besides, it would be tiresome for you if we did not recover the weapons which you let them steal from you . . . and I feel it's not going to be very easy."

"That incident has been grossly exaggerated."

"That's to say it has been hushed up."

"But, for you and your staff, if the school won't do . . ."

"I live with my men, I march with them, I eat the same rations, I put up with the same heat and thirst. So do my staff. My compliments, Colonel."

Raspéguy saluted. The trucks disappeared in a great cloud of dust, heading for the bare mountains which were tinged mauve and blue by the clear light of the late afternoon.

In the last truck three paratroopers were singing a slow, melancholy cowboy song.

"Yet another of those tricks they brought back from Indo-China," Colonel Quarterolles said to himself, "with their don't-give-a-damn attitude, their lack of discipline, their contempt for regulations and proper channels, their line-shooting and shoulder-swinging . . . We'll see what they're like when they're on the job, those puppets."

Vesselier, the mayor, came and called on the colonel. He gesticulated with his hands while he spoke and had a pronounced colonial accent:

"Ah, Colonel. Where do they think they are off to, those fools, into the blue like that without knowing what's going on? They ought to be stationed on the farms so that the crops which haven't been burnt might at least be harvested . . ."

"And he did not even introduce me to his officers," the colonel complained. "We'll see about that tomorrow . . . Have you got any new information on the band, Mayor?"

"The band, the band . . . If it had been left to us, Colonel, the whole business would have been settled long ago. As you and I know, there's only one thing they understand, these fellows—a firm hand on the cudgel."

By nine o'clock in the evening the main street of P —— was deserted, all the shops shut, but outside on the balconies the householders sat taking the air and looking towards the mountains where the lights of the paratroops' camp blazed brightly.

On the following day Major de Glatigny and Captain Boisfeuras came and reported to Colonel Quarterolles. The colonel knew Glatigny by name. He was extremely affable.

"We should like to get in touch with your Intelligence officer," said the major.

"I'll send for him."

Presently a tubby little captain appeared; he had little boot-button eyes immersed in fat and minced as he walked. He looked stupid, narrow-minded and as obstinate as a mule.

He sank back into an arm-chair and mopped his brow.

"Moine, tell these gentlemen what you know about the Si Lahcen band."

"We estimate it's about a hundred and thirty strong, scattered across the whole range. By day they lie low in the *mechtas*, by night they're on the prowl. They have no automatic weapons . . ."

"What about the submachine-guns they captured from you?" asked Boisfeuras.

"They've got no ammunition for them."

Captain Moine was lying with complete confidence, certain of being covered and of not running any risk.

"So when they wiped out your platoon," Glatigny persisted, "the rebels had no automatic weapons? Thirty men with three machine-guns and several submachine-guns let themselves be surprised by *fellaghas* who had nothing but antiquated rifles. Is that how it was?"

"I was on leave in Algiers."

"But you held a court of inquiry on your return."

"I've been out here three years. I have my sources of information. One of these witnessed the battle. The *fellaghas* only chucked a few hand-grenades at the trucks. Our men lost their heads."

"Who were your men?"

"Reservists of an infantry regiment from the north of France."

"Who was in command?"

"A cadet who had just left school."

"And you never tried to put them in the picture or prepare them for this sort of warfare?"

"They were given two or three lectures when they landed at Algiers, at least that's what they said."

"That's all over and done with," said Quarterolles, "we can't call the poor men back to life. I'm surprised your colonel isn't here with you; we've got to make arrangements for occupying a certain number of farms. I've taken it up with the mayor; the engineers are sending up some barbed wire and a few mines."

Glatigny replied in that polite, slightly contemptuous tone which he had learnt when serving on the staff.

"The whole regiment has been out on operations since four o'clock this morning and I don't think Colonel Raspéguy is thinking for a moment of occupying any farms."

"What does he want, then?"

"The band and, above all, the weapons. For that, we need information, for nothing can be done in this sort of war without information. Who is Si Lahcen?"

"A highway robber," said Captain Moine, picking his teeth.

"Has he got any family, friends or relations who can give us any information about him?"

"We arrested his brother, but he escaped the same evening."

"So Si Lahcen must have accomplices in the town; that's only to be expected. Who are his accomplices?"

"That's a matter for the police, not the army."

Boisfeuras then brought a sheet of paper out of his pocket.

"Since you seem to be in the dark about him, Captain, I'll tell you who Si Lahcen is: a former sergeant-major in the levies, Military Medal, mentioned four times in dispatches in Indo-China. Noted by his leaders as a remarkable warrant-officer, with the makings of an officer. On his return here he sank all his savings into the transport business and bought a bus. But the civilian administrator was the undercover owner of a whole line of buses. He made things difficult for Si Lahcen, he kept imposing fines on him and one day suggested buying his bus back from him for less than it cost him. Suborned by old friends of his who had risen in revolt, unable to find a soul who could protect him against the administrator, financially ruined, Si Lahcen took to the hills and started burning all his rival's buses. One night he came down here himself and slit the administrator's throat. That's correct, isn't it?"

Flies were buzzing about the unshuttered room. The colonel

brought a handkerchief out of his pocket and mopped his brow. He had since taken over the administrator's house and did not like to be reminded of that incident.

"I want to see Colonel Raspéguy at once. He's here to carry out operations under my orders. Garrison affairs are my business and no one else's. I'd rather not know the source of your inaccurate information. I would point out, however, that you're casting aspersions on a senior official who was deeply respected in this area. I shall expect to see your commanding officer shortly. That's all, gentlemen."

They left the room. Moine followed them outside. Boisfeuras asked the captain to provide him with an interpreter.

Moine had been closely acquainted with the administrator Bernier, a short, tubby little man with bandy legs, and also knew about his political and financial dealings with the few big caids of the district and the senior public works officials. His villa on the Côte d'Azur had been completed; he was going to retire with his little pile—the sum mentioned was a hundred million, which wasn't so bad for an administrator—and he had even been awarded the Légion d'Honneur for his good and loyal services. It was about this time that Si Lahcen, clanking with medals, had come back from Indo-China and had decided to put his savings into a bus line.

"A champion, that administrator," Moine reflected. "In his day there had been no question of rebels; he had his own way of treating the natives, a way which was at once paternal and determined, but rather more determined than paternal. He was not proud and held open house. He stole as much as he could, but allowed his subordinates to do likewise. With him, there was nothing to risk; he was protected by everyone: the Socialists, the clergy, the freemasons and the settlers." It was he, Moine, who had discovered his body, his throat slit from ear to ear.

"How did the paratroops know about all this? He would give them Ahmed as an interpreter, a sly lad whom he had well in hand and who would be able to give them the information they wanted. Some hotheads maintained that Ahmed had connexions among the rebels, but the same thing was said of all the Arabs."

Once they were outside, Glatigny turned to Boisfeuras and asked:

"Where did you get that information on Si Lahcen?"

"I ran into Mahmoudi at Algiers. Si Lahcen had served under him as his sergeant-major. When he heard we were going to P —— he told me the whole story. Mahmoudi is in a bit of a fix."

"Mahmoudi is a French officer."

"But he's serving as a Moslem, under a special statute, and no one ever misses a chance of reminding him of it. I've pulled some strings to have him transferred to Germany."

"What will he do in Germany?"

"He'll wait there till we've rid Algeria of its *fellaghas*, its crooks, its civil administrators and its army of old dotards like Quarterolles and lazy bastards like that Captain Moine."

"That's a pretty tall order, my dear Boisfeuras. It will be a long time before Mahmoudi gets back from Germany."

The two officers climbed into their Jeep and left P —— with a sense of relief to rejoin their regimental base in the mountains.

Lurching over the pot-holes, with his carbine between his knees, Boisfeuras tried to concentrate on this problem: how to capture Si Lahcen's band without any information apart from a few police reports and local gossip. A band a hundred and thirty strong is bound to be seen when moving across bare, arid territory; it needs food supplies, water and ammunition. It cannot remain indefinitely in the mountains. He nudged Glatigny:

"Glatigny, what would you do in Si Lahcen's place? Don't forget that Si Lahcen has been out in Indo-China."

"In Si Lahcen's place?"

"Yes. Would you play at boy scouts out in the open in this heat when you could quite simply stay in the *mechtas* round P ——, drink cool water, listen to the radio and entertain the girls?"

"Go on," said Glatigny.

"Supposing Si Lahcen, who has seen how the Viets work, had set up an intelligence network and a good politico-military organization in the town. He would know everything: every movement of our troops, the departure times of the convoys.

While Colonel Quarterolles is forced to protect himself on all sides, he would be able to strike where he wanted, when he wanted.

"The group or section that had laid the ambush would do the job and scatter through the mountains immediately afterwards. It would have its own arms dumps; it would return next morning, mingling with the peasants coming into market. For that, all that's required is to have the population well in hand.

"Meanwhile we're rushing about the bare mountains, exhausting our men; we shall never be able to find anything."

"So, according to you, we ought to establish headquarters in P——?"

"Yes, and hold all the surrounding villages, collect information at any price and by any means, force Si Lahcen and his men to really take to the mountains, and cut them off from the population which provides them with information and feeds them. Only then will we be able to fight them on equal terms."

Colonel Raspéguy came back to camp with his men exhausted by the heat and a hard march through arid gorges, over razor-sharp stones, and along dried-up river-beds.

They had found nothing: not a trace of Si Lahcen's band, not even one of those little walls made out of a few boulders that are called *choufs* and are used by look-outs to shelter behind. But ten miles away, in the plain at the foot of the mountain, some agricultural labourers and their families had been found with their throats cut because they had stayed on in a settler's farm after he had left it.

Leaning back against the white wall of a little marabout and smoking his pipe, Raspéguy watched the shadows sweep over the plain in a series of waves which presently came and broke on his rock.

When he was a child, he used to hate coming down from the mountains. The town with its sly, worldly shopkeepers, its crowds on market days, its strident voices, its cafés and its music made him feel ill at ease.

The lights of P—— began to twinkle down below and the searchlights started sweeping the barbed-wire entanglements. The loud-speakers blared. Raspéguy had laid ambushes on every trail, at every approach which the *fellaghas* could possibly use, and had made arrangements to be notified as soon as anything happened so as to be able to be on the spot at once.

Esclavier sank down beside him and Raspéguy handed him his packet of cigarettes and flask of coffee. Then Glatigny, Marindelle and Boisfeuras came and joined them. They in their turn sat down.

A sentry could be heard loading his submachine-gun and, farther off, a man singing. The slightest noise was wafted up to them, stripped of its bare essentials in the clear air and thereby endowed with the gravity of prayer, the purity of crystal.

"It's nice up here," said Raspéguy, "it's clean and cool and we are on our own."

"But it's down below that things are happening," Boisfeuras retorted in his grating voice.

"Let's hear what you've got to say," said Raspéguy wearily.

On the following day the paratroops came back to P——.

During the siesta hour, while the whole town was sleeping, they marched through as though on parade, six deep, moving silently in their rubber-soled boots, looking straight in front of them with a blank expression in their eyes, and singing that slow, melancholy song from Indo-China which was also the song of the American Marines in the Pacific.

The Moslems crept out of their shacks and silently watched these soldiers who were not like any others, who appeared not to see them as they marched by at their slow, steady pace. And they felt vaguely apprehensive, for, like all men, they were frightened of the unusual and unknown.

Through the slits of a shutter in a Mozabite store, Si Lahcen was also watching this strange march-past.

He turned round to Ahmed:

"I'd rather they were up in the mountains but, as you see, they've come back. They're going to settle down in our midst and stir up the ant-heap until something emerges . . ."

"We could make life impossible for them in P——. This evening a couple of men can go and pitch a few hand-grenades into the two cafés on the Rue Maginot."

"You don't know what they're like, Ahmed. It's easy to see that you were never out in Indo-China with the 'lizards.' If they catch your grenade-thrower they'll hang on to him themselves, they won't hand him over to the police and the man will talk; and you won't know a thing until they come and drag you off—you, the official Intelligence interpreter—to the garrison commander himself."

Ahmed shrugged his shoulders. He did not care very much for the Kabyle Si Lahcen, with his sergeant-major attitude, his slow reactions and caution. The band he was commanding was becoming more and more like a regular company, and if it was left to him, he would dole out badges of rank and insignia, forbid looting and rape, in fact everything that endowed this war with its powerful attraction for the primitive creatures under his command.

At heart, Si Lahcen had a deep respect for the French Army and disliked being considered a bandit. He was a skinny, unprepossessing little man, but as tough and hard as a vinestock, whereas Ahmed had the indolent beauty of a desert Arab.

Ahmed was the political commissar of the area, and Si Lahcen the military leader. The rebel headquarters had not yet decided which of the two branches, political or military, had priority over the other, so that the two men often found themselves in conflict.

Si Lahcen whistled the paratroops' song between his teeth. He had often heard it out in Indo-China, when the battalions used to set off on some suicide operation from which very few of the men returned.

One day, while serving on the edge of the delta, he had witnessed the arrival of those paratroops who had been reported dead or captured for over a month. They had struggled hundreds of miles through the jungle, surrounded by Viets. They were using their rifles as crutches; many of them were barefoot, their faces were swollen by mosquito bites and the sweat had rotted the skin under their arms and between their thighs. They stank and could hardly stand upright, but they kept on singing this tune, for they knew that if they stopped they would not be able to take another step.

Sergeant-Major Si Lahcen had been proud that day to belong to the same army as them.

That battalion, he remembered now, had been commanded
by the same Raspéguy who had marched through P —— just
now, at the head of his men but wearing no badges of rank.

"Well, what do we do now?" Ahmed inquired, this time in
French. "Do we just wait to be picked up?"

"It would be best to lie low for the time being," Si Lahcen
replied pensively. "Stay up in the mountains as long as they're
in the town, come back here if they take to the mountains
again, and avoid a show-down . . ."

"No. The population's still undecided, in spite of the few ex-
amples I made. They'll veer towards the stronger side, that's
to say the one they fear the most. For the moment that's us;
but tomorrow, if we sat back and did nothing, it would be the
paratroops."

"You're coming back to those hand-grenades of yours again."

"I think I can do better than that and make your lizards lose
face once and for all."

On the following day Ahmed became the official interpreter
of the paratroops for the duration of their operation and was
attached to Captain Boisfeuras. He was issued with a cap, a
bivouac tent and a pistol. He had become a lizard himself.

Ahmed soon noticed that the sort of Chinaman who was always with the captain never took his eyes off him for a second.
On two occasions he saw him reach for his carbine, making
sure that the gesture did not pass unnoticed. It was an unconcealed warning.

The paratroops crowded the cafés and shops, and prices began to go up; there were one or two brawls between them and
the garrison troops.

Raspéguy, who had taken over the school building, had
all the barbed wire round it removed. "All it's good for is giving one a sting in the ass when one gets back after dark," he
explained.

In a class-room, which still had its desks and blackboard, he
had assembled all the leading members of the community: Caïd
Djemal and his brother, the mayor Vesselier, the representative

of the Mozabite merchants, the president of the veterans' association, and Captain Moine. Also present were Boisfeuras, Glatigny, Esclavier and Merle, whose company of reservists were quartered round the school. Ahmed attended the meeting as the official interpreter; and Caid Djemal's brother, who knew what part he played in the rebellion, kept darting little glances of admiration at him.

Raspéguy stood on the platform, a piece of chalk in his hand. The civic dignitaries and the officers were seated at the desks and had unconsciously assumed the attitude of schoolchildren, leaning on their elbows, shuffling their feet and scratching their noses.

Merle was hiding behind Esclavier's back and poring over Micheline's letter yet again.

Olivier, my love,

I've been thinking things over since you left for Algeria and I now know I love you like the most besotted little shopgirl and, as in the song, "until the end of the world."

As children we used to play at that cruel and treacherous game of hating each other, loving each other, tearing each other to shreds, making each other jealous. When you came back from Indo-China I could not help going on with the game, and besides you know how I like to shock people. I had a good time making a scarecrow out of my little Olivier at Tourangeaux.

I'm glad you left our town slamming every door behind you, glad that you're out in Algeria, earning no more than 80,000 francs a month and running the risk of getting killed, whereas my faithful spouse, "little Bezegue," gets ten times more for trailing around bars and eyeing the little barmen.

But I feel like screaming when I'm alone in my room. Olivier, I'm through. I'm going to ask for a divorce and then come out and join you. Whether as your wife or your mistress, I shall live with you and this time I'll know my place, which is that of every woman, not by the side of the man she loves but slightly behind him.

I love you and am at your orders.

MICHELINE.

Merle would have liked to read this letter out to his comrades, but Piniéres was rushing about the mountains and only the other evening he had heard Boisfeuras say to Esclavier:

"No world is more alien to women than the world of soldiers, priests and Communists, by which I mean fighting soldiers, militant Communists and evangelizing priests . . ."

Esclavier, who chased girls as though they were game but was never in love with them, had tended to agree.

They would tease him and call him a callow youth. They refused to understand, no doubt because they had never known the joy of waking up in the morning next to a beautiful young girl whom one has loved all night.

Raspéguy, who was writing something on the blackboard, reprimanded him like a schoolmaster.

"Since you're here, Merle, you may as well pay attention."

Olivier quickly stuffed the letter back in his pocket, as though he was afraid it might be confiscated. He saw Ahmed smile at him and he smiled back.

"What it boils down to is this," said Raspéguy. "Unless we can get some information, we'll never lay our hands on the band; the farms and crops will continue to be burnt down, terrorism will go on making life unbearable . . . What we need is a thread which will lead us to this band. This thread is to be found in the town. Give me one end of it and I shall soon follow it up to Si Lahcen.

"You don't know anything, Mayor? Or you, Caid Djemal, or any of you others? Are you frightened? It's as bad to fall into the habit of fear as to grow accustomed to being ill."

Captain Moine was puffing contentedly at a cigarette end. Well might the paratroops swing their shoulders and light fires all over the mountains, they could do no better than those who had been stuck in this sector for months. And they had crept back to P —— hanging their heads. The same boat as Moine's would take them back to France and they would incur the same reproaches; all the rest was play-acting.

Of course the thread which could lead them to this band existed in the town, but each time one thought one had a firm grip on it, it snapped. All was lost. Meanwhile there was nothing

more to do but drink *anisette* and have a whore sent over from
the brothel two or three times a week.

As they filed out of the class-room at the end of the meeting,
Merle found himself next to Ahmed. He invited the interpreter
to have a drink. The Moslem was a handsome, well-educated
man; he looked one straight in the eye and his laughter had the
right ring. His paratrooper's uniform suited him perfectly.

"The difficult thing about this war," said Ahmed, as he
drank his beer, "is to find that guiding thread. I've heard some
talk, however . . . But then there's always talk about something or other, we Arabs are incurable gossips!"

Merle, who had been dreaming about Micheline, suddenly
sat up.

"Yes, Lieutenant, they say there's a certain amount of dissen-
sion in the Si Lahcen band. It's only a rumour. Si Lahcen is a
Kabyle, his men are not; he treats them brutally . . . he's got a
sharp tongue . . . and his loathing for the French has sent him
off his head. They say he himself does all the throat-cutting . . .
and the other things to his prisoners."

"A dozen men belonging to his band are said to have escaped with their arms to a group of *mechtas* and are anxious
to join the French."

"Shall we follow it up, Ahmed?"

"I'm not sure how reliable this information is. This war is
tearing me in two, and I don't mind admitting it. I could never
fire on my co-religionists in spite of the atrocities they've committed; but to rally them to our side, if we promise them their
lives will be saved and they won't be molested, I'd like to do
that very much."

"Colonel Raspéguy will promise, and he'll keep his word."

Ahmed shrugged his shoulders and smiled.

"I like you very much, but you're not at all prudent. What if
I was trying to lead you into a trap? In my opinion this information is not very reliable."

"Where did you get it from?"

"A Mozabite merchant."

"Could I go and see him?"

"If you really want to; the man seemed so shady to me that I have not even mentioned this to Captain Boisfeuras."

"Could I see him tonight?"

"We could call on him together, but as it's best to be on the safe side, take a bodyguard with you to wait outside."

"How far is it?"

"Right in the town, just a short step from here. Don't forget that night is on the rebels' side, and that Si Lahcen has done me the great honour of putting a price on my head. I've already escaped two attempts on my life."

"Very well, then. Come and pick me up at the mess."

"I'd rather you did not mention this to Caption Boisfeuras. I work with him and it might annoy him. Besides, it's such a trivial thing! It's only to satisfy your curiosity. You'll find me outside the school."

Ahmed knocked at the door several times and the Mozabite, blinking his eyes, came and opened it for them. He looked scared stiff:

"I haven't done anything, gentlemen, I'm a great friend of France."

"But he also subscribes to the F.L.N.," said Ahmed, shrugging his shoulders, "put yourself in his place . . . We're not going to do you any harm, we simply want you to tell the lieutenant what you already told me."

Ahmed gave him a shove and they went inside.

Bucelier and Bistenave stood on guard outside the shop. The town was utterly silent, the stars shone brightly in a very dark sky. There was a sound of whispering on the other side of the door.

"Bucelier, I don't like it at all," Bistenave suddenly exclaimed.

"Got the wind up?"

"No, but I don't like this war, this sudden return to P —— and Merle sniffing around like a poodle that has found a bone, and Ahmed with that handsome, treacherous face of his."

"Treachery here, fifty yards from H.Q.? You must be crazy!"

Ten minutes later Merle came out again with Ahmed.

"This looks serious," he said, "and urgent."

"I don't trust that Mozabite, sir. He's got nothing to gain from this but a lot of trouble. Do think it over."

"But he's quite definite about it: eleven men with a machine-gun, ready to come over to us tonight. They'll defend themselves if they see a large force turn up, they don't trust us, but they'll give themselves up to one officer accompanied by no more than a couple of men. The Mozabite confirms what you told me about a split in the Si Lahcen band."

"Why should this Mozabite want to lead me into a trap? If he lied he'll pay for it dearly; his shop will be burnt down . . ."

"That's true. But I'm wary all the same. Besides, this group of rebels are sure to have look-outs posted and if they hear trucks approaching they'll have time to escape. Promises of this kind have often been made and then not kept. In a bulletin 'thirty dead' sounds better than thirty won over.

"This is an attempt which has got to be made alone or not at all. I'm all for dropping it. All the same, I'll go and notify Captain Boisfeuras."

Merle motioned to Bistenave and Sergeant Bucelier to come nearer.

"Look here, guys. Five miles from here there's a group of *mechtas*. We've been through there before; at the moment eleven *fellaghas* from the Si Lahcen band are hiding up there. They want to give themselves up but only to one officer accompanied by a couple of men. They won't be there after tonight, they're frightened of being wiped out and they've got look-outs posted. If we drive up in trucks, they'll make off.

"My friend Ahmed here doesn't think much of this information and believes we'll find nothing in the *mechtas*."

"Ten to one against," said Ahmed, "which isn't worth the risk."

"Can't you see the three of us coming back with our eleven rebels—the reservists teaching the professional paratroops how to wage war!"

"That," said Bucelier, "would be great fun."

In his excitement Merle had seized Bistenave by the shoulders and was shaking him:

"And without firing a shot, Curé. We'll hop into a Jeep, and if there's nothing there we'll be back in an hour. Ahmed, give us enough time to get away before you go and notify Captain Boisfeuras."

"Aren't you going to notify Captain Esclavier?" asked Bistenave, whose mouth had gone dry with apprehension.

He dared not openly protest. Bucelier would only repeat that he was afraid. Merle was pawing the ground with impatience:

"Esclavier's dining with Raspéguy at Colonel Quarterolles's. When they come out of the house we'll present arms to them with our eleven rebels, and Quarterolles will have a fit."

"It's up to you," said Ahmed. "I'll notify Captain Boisfeuras in a couple of hours. If you're careful there won't be any danger, but I'm almost certain you won't find a soul in the *mechtas*."

Ahmed sauntered off at an easy pace, but on his way home he ran into Captain Boisfeuras and his Chinaman under the yellow light of a street lamp. The captain gave him a friendly wave; Min put his hand on his revolver and held it there.

The Chinaman uttered a few words in a harsh-sounding tongue, but the captain shrugged his shoulders.

A Jeep drove off. *Inch-Allah!* The dice had started rolling and God alone knew which side they would turn up.

Lieutenant Merle had to argue at the exit of the town with a sentry who would not let him through, and for a few moments Bistenave hoped that their crazy expedition was going to end in front of the barbed-wire entanglements of the guard-post.

Merle explained that he had orders from Colonel Raspéguy to contact a patrol which was coming in with prisoners and that the matter was urgent.

The sergeant appeared on the scene.

"You've taken some prisoners, have you?"

"Yes, eleven."

"There's no denying it, sir, you're doing better than we ever did."

He helped the sentry to draw back the barrier.

The moon came up and the Jeep, with only its sidelights on, started slithering up the trail.

"I'm going to be married," said Merle, who was driving. "Yes, to an impossible girl. Got a cigarette, Bistenave? Would you light it for me, please. Thanks."

"We're mad, sir."

"Of course, that's what's such fun. Here, what about that cigarette?"

"We should have informed Captain Esclavier all the same," said Bucelier pensively.

"Look, old boy, Esclavier has done this sort of thing dozens of times and you may be sure he never informed anyone. You're really getting too regimental. It's quite simple, there are some men who want to give themselves up and we're going out to collect them."

"The night is on their side, sir."

"The night's on the side of whoever is out in it, and tonight's the finest I've ever seen. The moonlight seems to have frozen everything round us like snow . . ."

"The *mechtas*, sir . . ."

Merle switched off the engine.

"Bistenave, you come with me. Bucelier, you stay with the Jeep. I don't think it's a trap, but if anything should happen, drive back and inform Captain Esclavier. If I call for you, but only if I call, come and join us. But it'll be all right, I know; I've got a lucky charm in my pocket.

"Off we go, Bistenave. The Mozabite said the first *mechta* on the left and to knock three times. It's odd, I can't hear any dogs barking."

The dogs had had their throats slit an hour before and their bodies had been thrown into a ditch.

Bucelier saw the lieutenant, followed by the seminarist, clamber up a little ridge. He heard him knock on the door of the *mechta* with the butt of his revolver; the door opened.

At that moment a burst from a submachine-gun shattered the darkness a few yards away. He felt a jolt and a stab in the shoulder. The Jeep was rolling down the slope, he must have taken the brake off, he couldn't remember. He switched on the engine. Two, three bursts passed over his head. He switched on the lights. Warm blood was dripping on to his hand and he could feel his left arm going numb. He swerved the car round as he changed gear.

The only thing he knew was that he had to reach the First Company camp as soon as possible, warn Captain Esclavier and get everyone on his feet. If he was quick enough, the lieutenant and Bistenave could still be saved.

As he drove past the guardpost he was nearly fired on.

"What's up?" asked the sergeant.

"Quick, there's been some trouble . . . Quick, for God's sake . . . Raise the barrier. Captain Esclavier . . ."

At that moment he fainted. A glass of water thrown in his face brought him round again. He was in the infirmary, lying on a stretcher. Captain Esclavier was standing in front of him with Dia, the Negro M.O. He saw that his arm had been bandaged.

"Quick, quick . . ."

He heard the throb of the G.M.C. engines and the sound of men running about outside.

"What happened?" Esclavier inquired.

He told him.

"Oh, the silly bastards!" the captain exclaimed in great distress.

Esclavier opened the window and shouted in his ear-splitting voice:

"First Company. Ready to move off."

"I want to come with you," said Bucelier.

"He can go," Dia confirmed. "It's only a flesh wound. And I'm coming too, because I was extremely fond of Merle."

Bucelier suddenly realized they were all talking of Lieutenant Merle as though he was dead. He wanted to shout out that it wasn't true, that it couldn't be true, because no one had the right to kill Lieutenant Merle.

They found the two bodies stretched out on the ridge in front of the *mechtas,* with their throats slit, their guts ripped open and their sexual organs stuffed into their mouths. The headlights of the trucks illuminated the ghastly sight.

Second-Lieutenant Azmanian pointed out that the two bodies were turned in the direction of Mecca, like animals sacrificed in some holocaust. He had heard that at one time the Turks used to do the same thing in Armenia. He turned aside to be sick.

The reservists slowly came forward, their weapons in their hands, and formed a silent circle. They did not move but stood riveted by the scene.

Bucelier was trembling from head to foot; he no longer felt any pain in his shoulder.

"Give me your submachine-gun," he said to Mongins, "I'm going into the *mechtas*."

The men murmured:

"We're all coming with you."

Captain Esclavier appeared in the centre of the circle and never had the men seen him look so tall and redoubtable. Without a word, he unbuckled his belt and stripped off his equipment and revolver, keeping only his knife in his hand.

"Only the men," he said in his dry voice. "Don't touch the women or children, only the men, and only with knives—so that those who've got the guts can at least defend themselves."

"The *fellaghas* who did the job have gone off," Dia gently observed. "Those chaps in there don't amount to much."

Following Esclavier's example, the men were taking off their equipment, discarding their rifles, submachine-guns and grenades, keeping only their knives.

Their rage, the thirst for blood and vengeance which had seized them, was so strong that they were almost calm and detached.

They advanced slowly towards the silent *mechtas*; they felt nothing but a faint fatigue, a sort of strange hunger which drove them forward.

Esclavier broke the door down with a thrust of his shoulder. Not one of the Arabs offered any resistance.

The sun was rising by the time Raspéguy, who had been notified by Dia, turned up pensively sucking his pipe. Twenty-seven Moslem bodies were lined up together, their throats cut, their heads turned towards the West, in the direction of Rome. Flies were already buzzing around them, sipping the blood.

"What a filthy business!" he said.

Esclavier sat leaning against the trunk of an olive-tree. He was very pale, his features were drawn, and there were dark circles under his eyes, as though he had just recovered from a long illness: he was shivering a little and felt icy cold.

Raspéguy came up and approached him gently, as though he was frightened of startling him:

"Philippe . . . Philippe . . ."

"Yes, sir."

"That's not very pretty, what you've done."

"But for that, they would have massacred the lot, women and children included . . . and I wouldn't have been able to hold them back."

"I should have preferred grenades and submachine-guns, and the whole lot wiped out. Knives turn warfare into murder. And here we are doing what they do, soiling our hands like them.

"But perhaps it was necessary and we had to begin somewhere, since we were forced to come down from the heights into the plain and because we've been outraged in our manly honour by the mutilation of Merle and Fleur de Nave. It was primitive man, not the soldier, who reacted by subscribing to this holocaust.

"Call the men together, Philippe, I've got to talk to them."

Raspéguy climbed up on to a rock above the bodies. The First Company faced him, a hundred and fifty men shattered by disgust, fear and hatred of war, on the point of mutiny, ready for anything in order to forget what they had just done, and at the same time feeling closer to one another than they had ever felt before, bound together by bloodshed and horror.

Raspéguy started speaking in a low voice, staring down at his boots.

"Gentlemen . . ."

By addressing them as gentlemen he was restoring a little of their lost dignity.

"Gentlemen, you acted in the heat of anger, but myself, this morning I feel cold. After thinking it over carefully, I should have given orders for every grown man in this *douar* to be shot, and you would have been responsible for their execution. In that respect, the incident is closed."

He thrust his head forward like a falcon about to take flight and slowly glanced down the ranks in front of him.

"Because you were fond of Lieutenant Merle and little Bistenave, it's you I entrust with avenging them, because that"—he pointed to the bodies—"isn't vengeance; it's merely a reprisal. I'm giving you Si Lahcen's band. It's yours with its rifles and submachine-guns; but the next time you'll need more than your knives. That's all."

The soldiers felt as though they had been relieved of a heavy burden. They experienced a new feeling towards the colonel, in which admiration was mixed with gratitude and embarrassment.

"What do we do with the bodies?" asked Sergeant-Major Mourlier.

"Leave them there till this evening," Raspéguy replied. "They may as well be of some use."

Thus was born the cruel legend of the "lizards in caps," of the warriors with knives who were more redoubtable than the shock troops of the F.L.N. In the depths of the *douars* they began to be regarded as demons impervious to bullets, sons of Alek and Azrael, the angel of death.

"Quickly, Captain," said Min to Boisfeuras.

"What did you find out?"

"Ahmed has been to the post office and drawn out all his savings. Yesterday evening he had a long talk with Lieutenant Merle."

Ahmed lived alone in a small house on the outskirts of the town: two bare rooms. In one stood a camp bed with army sheets and blankets, in the other a table and, next to the sink, a spirit lamp.

Mash' Allah! The dice had come up badly.

The interpreter started stuffing tins of food and packets of cigarettes into a haversack. In spite of all the precautions he had taken, the job would be traced back to him in no time. He had abandoned his paratrooper's uniform for cloth trousers, a flowing shirt and a striped *jellaba*.

He bent down, lifted up a tile and drew out some documents and money, two hundred thousand francs in big blue notes.

When he raised his head again, Min stood in front of him, his revolver aimed straight at him. With the end of the barrel he motioned him to stand up and put his hands above his head. Boisfeuras came in; he took the money, the documents and papers and then sat down astride a chair.

"Now look," he said to Ahmed, "either you tell me the whole story, or Min will deal with you."

"I don't understand. I did all I could to stop Lieutenant Merle setting off in the middle of the night. I tried to notify you."

"This money from your post office savings account . . . the haversack . . . We're wasting time, Ahmed. And also these documents!"

Boisfeuras whistled in admiration; he had just glanced through a typewritten document in French and Arabic, dated from Cairo, bearing all sorts of red and blue seals, and confirming that Ahmed was the political commissar of the zone.

"I underestimated you."

Ahmed sprang forward to grab Min's revolver, but a chair came smashing down on his head.

When he came to, he found himself sitting on his bed, with his wrists tied to the metal bars with telephone wire.

"To hell with you," he calmly said to Boisfeuras, "you and your Chinaman as well. I'm not talking."

"You've got your reasons, I've got mine; I could be in your place, you could be in mine. That's fate."

"The dice rolling," Ahmed reflected.

"I'm not sentimental, but in Indo-China I saved young Merle's life and I was very fond of him. But I can forget him. Only, by cutting his throat like a dog, you've insulted us all. Unforgivable.

"We now want Si Lahcen and his band. It's become a personal matter."

"If you want Si Lahcen, go and look for him up in the mountains.

"Once again, Captain Boisfeuras, to hell with you. I'm not talking. But one day we're going to throw you out of here and chase you right back to where you came from. Then we'll give ourselves a treat with all your wives, all your daughters and your precious selves as well."

"What the hell do I care?" Boisfeuras replied, quite calmly. "I want to know how your town organization works, I want names, the whereabouts of the hide-outs and your contacts with Si Lahcen."

"No."

"What's more, I'm in a hurry. When you've had enough of Min, just let me know."

Min went out, then came back again with a sock filled with fine sand dangling from his hand. Without striking too hard, he started hammering Ahmed's head, as the Viet's had taught him, always on the same spot—but in those days it was the Vietminh who administered the blows and Min who was on the receiving end!

Ahmed endured it for four hours—three hours less than Min. That evening Boisfeuras had a complete list of the members of the political organization of P——. They were arrested forthwith. As for Si Lahcen, he had long ago taken to the hills.

Colonel Quarterolles was fuming when he called on Raspéguy.

"What the hell's going on?" he asked. "No one tells me a thing. It seems that one of your subalterns has been killed and in return you've wiped out twenty-seven *fellaghas*. You've arrested Ahmed, the interpreter, the caid and his brother . . . and all the shops are being searched. What's it all about?"

"In a week from now, Colonel, Si Lahcen's band will have ceased to exist, I'll bet you anything you like. We'll both of us be able to go back to Algiers."

"Why both of us?"

"Because no one here will have any further reason to maintain you in your command. The whole town, the whole administration, was rotten to the core and in the basement of the town hall we found three cases of ammunition earmarked for the rebels.

"Here's something else you might like to hear . . . Si Lahcen had been living here, in P ——, the whole time; Ahmed, your right-hand man, was the political leader of the rebellion; and the mayor—the worthy Vesselier—he paid the Wogs to keep their mouths shut . . .

"Our men have had to wade through all this muck and little Lieutenant Merle has had his balls cut off. It was I who brought Merle out here, he belonged to me, he was part of me.

"You killed him with your stupidity and incapacity. We're burying him tomorrow, but I forbid you to come to the funeral. If you do I'll knock you down in front of everyone."

"Well?" Dia asked Esclavier.

The captain was holding his head between his hands; he was unshaven and he and the M.O. had just polished off a half-bottle of brandy.

"Well, nothing."

"Don't you know? I've had a letter from Lescure. Guess what he's up to. During the day he follows a course of ethnology at the Sorbonne and at night he thumps a piano in a nightclub. He says he's very happy."

"Dia, what about yesterday?"

"I think you limited the damage."

"Dia!"

"You're ashamed because you let the black panther escape. It was sleeping peacefully deep inside you; it was the others that roused it, then it came and lay down again, its muzzle and claws full of blood.

"I've also got my panther, and it was growling very loudly when I saw Merle's body but it didn't escape.

"Marindelle, as you know, is never like the others; he can't believe that we've all got a panther sleeping deep down inside us. He said to me: 'Objectively speaking, the reprisal wasn't a bad job. Fear has changed sides, tongues have been loosened, our soldiers now want to fight it out. We obtained more in a day than in six months fighting, and more with twenty-seven dead than with several hundreds.'

"I don't understand the word 'objectively.'"

Esclavier pulled a copy of *Zero and the Infinite* out of his pocket.

"Look what Boisfeuras has given me to read."

He opened the book at a page which had been turned down: a quotation from the German bishop, Dietrich von Nieheim, who lived in the fourteenth century.

"When her existence is threatened, the Church is absolved of all moral commandments. Unity as an aim sanctifies every means, cunning, treachery, violence, simony, imprisonment and death. For all order exists for the purpose of the community, and the individual must be sacrificed for the general good."

"Boisfeuras had just had Ahmed shot, after dining and getting drunk with him. He even promised to look after his wife."

"Well," said Dia, "we're going to go on getting drunk together and I'm very glad it was your black panther that made you kill rather than that old bishop's maunderings. I drink, Esclavier, to your black panther and also to mine."

"What's Glatigny doing?" Esclavier suddenly asked.

"He's in church, saying his prayers."

THE LEAP OF LEUCADIA

A week after Ahmed's arrest Si Lahcen and his band were driven off the plain and forced to take refuge in the mountains. The rebels had had to abandon their dumps and their hide-outs which were no longer secure. Information became scarce and supplies were no longer available from P——— where the whole political and administrative organization of the rebellion had been decapitated.

The headmen of the *douars* came up one after another to see Si Lahcen near the cave where he had set up his headquarters. They all had the same thing to say:

"Si Lahcen, we are aware of your courage and your strength, but take your band of *moujahidines* away from our *douar*, for the French are bound to hear about it sooner or later; then they'll burn down our *mechtas*, slit our throats and shoot your men."

Si Lahcen did his best to stem their panic. He ordered some spectacular executions, but the hundred or so men and women he had shot down or butchered could not wipe out the memory of the *mechtas* of Rahlem. The only remorse he felt was when he realized this massacre had been completely useless.

Sitting near his cave, with a blanket round his shoulders to protect him from the early-morning dew, he let himself be carried away by his memories.

His best friend in Indo-China had been Sergeant Piras, a lively, skinny little chap who had worked at every kind of job and read every book. He used to wink as he rolled himself a cigarette and he kept his tobacco in a sort of round metal tin.

Each time they ran across each other in the course of an operation, Piras would wink and ask him:

"Well, Lahcen, how's your destiny?"

If Piras had not been killed during Operation Atlante, he might perhaps now be fighting against him, disguised as a lizard. He imagined holding him in the sights of his rifle while Piras, standing like an ibex on a rock, took out his tobacco tin and greedily rolled himself a cigarette.

He would fire, but to one side, in order to scare him: Piras had been his friend. He realized all of a sudden that all his friends were in this army he was fighting against, whereas his own people, on the contrary, were alien to him and some of them, like Ahmed, disgusted him. Ahmed died as he had lived, not as a soldier but as a stool-pigeon. Captured, he had given away everything he knew.

A sentry came to inform him that a liasion agent, a certain Ibrahim, had just arrived from P ——.

Ibrahim may have been fifty years old or he may have been sixty: his full beard was speckled with grey; he was dressed in European clothes, with a watch-chain stretched across his waist-coat, but on his head he wore a turban made of some sort of linen and his feet were bare. He was a wise, cruel and self-possessed man. For a long time he had been in command of the small group of killers who by night controlled P —— and the surrounding *douars*: it was a miracle he had not yet been caught when all his men had already fallen to the Frenchmen's bullets.

Ibrahim came and squatted down beside Si Lahcen and offered him a cigarette.

"What is it?" asked the rebel leader. "I told you to stay down at P —— and reorganize your group."

"Si Lahcen, there's not a single lizard left in the town. They all disappeared in the night. They're hunting you up in the mountains and they know where you are."

"Who gave me away?"

"Yesterday evening they caught three of your *moujahidines* as they were leaving a *mechta* to come and join you. One of them preferred to die, but the two others talked."

"The lookouts haven't signalled any trucks on the road."

"The lizards are making war as we do; they've marched all night and are now less than two miles from your cave. As they advance they look under every stone and behind every bush to make sure there isn't a hide-out there."

"Do you think I can still get through by way of Oued Chahir?"

"That's the route they've taken. They're there already. I almost ran into one of their patrols which had laid an ambush and was moving up the river-bed at dawn. I hid under some branches and waited; then I took off my shoes and came up here, taking great care not to dislodge any pebbles."

Si Lahcen rose to his feet and, followed by Ibrahim who was still barefoot, he inspected his position. He could not have chosen a better one. He had encamped with his band on a sort of peak overlooking a little pebbly plain as flat as a glacis, an open bit of ground hemmed in by the mountains, into which his assailants would be forced to venture.

Behind him rose a sheer cliff, on his left was the crevice up which Ibrahim had climbed and which could be easily defended with a few cases of grenades. Only his right flank was vulnerable: it formed a fairly gentle slope bristling with natural obstacles, and led towards the west. But it was a narrow approach; with his machine-gun, his three F.M.s and his mortar it would be easy for him to foil the attack of an enemy who would be unable to deploy and would therefore be obliged to advance in file.

"We'll wait for them here," Si Lahcen decided. "If they want a fight, I'll take them on."

The sun had risen; it shone straight into Ibrahim's eyes, forcing him to screw them up, which gave him the rather sly expression of an old Berri peasant. He stroked his beard:

"*Allah-i-chouf.** Let me have a rifle."

Si Lahcen had about a hundred men at his disposal, the rest of the band having failed to join him. He made each one of them—and it was a difficult task—dig into a prepared position

*Literally, "Allah sees us."

and build a little parapet of stones to protect himself. He gave orders not to fire unless certain of scoring a hit and to save ammunition, for they would have to hold out until nightfall before being able to withdraw towards the heights. He positioned the automatic weapons himself, gave each of them a definite mission, set up the mortar, then retired inside his cave. At the entrance to it he noticed a curious patch of sunlight which kept alternately appearing and vanishing.

Si Lahcen rummaged in his sack for a bar of chocolate. He pulled out a little leather case containing his Military Medal. He looked at this for several minutes. The ribbon was the same warm colour as the patch of sunlight.

Yes, he had certainly earned his medal out in Indo-China! The post overlooked the Red River. It was made of logs and the watch tower, soaring high on its stilts, looked like one of those stands which are put up in the middle of a vineyard when the grape is ripe.

The post commander was a lieutenant with a long neck and prominent Adam's apple who wore spectacles; every morning he would sadly ask:

"But why the hell don't the Viets attack? They can mop us up whenever they like."

The post was, in fact, completely isolated; it relied entirely on parachute drops; but more often than not a proportion of the containers fell into the river.

Lieutenant Barbier and Sergeant-Major Lahcen were in command of a hundred or so partisans and a dozen Europeans. The partisans had been suborned by Vietminh propaganda and were only waiting for a favourable moment to turn traitor. Wasted by fever, laid low by the damp climate, the Frenchmen were incapable of repelling a fresh attack. Lieutenant Barbier was no longer quite right in the head; he kept imagining that someone was going to murder him; at the slightest sound he would draw his revolver and fire it. He also killed all the house lizards, which bring good luck, and squashed them against the walls of his room, using his shoe as a hammer; it was a bad sign.

One night the Vietminh had landed on the bank of the river

below the post. Another group had occupied the village. At four in the morning they had attacked from both directions, while the partisans mutinied.

Lieutenant Barbier had been killed in his bed. He usually woke up at the slightest sound but this time he had not heard his murderer approaching. Lahcen and the white men who were left had taken refuge in the central block-house; they had held out for six hours against a whole Vietminh battalion.

A *dinassault** sailing up the river with its armoured barges had come to their rescue when they were down to their last hand grenade. Lahcen had received a bullet in the lung and he still remembered the pinkish froth that had clung to his lips like toothpaste; but this froth had a sickly, salty taste: the taste of his own blood.

He had been evacuated to Hanoi by helicopter. He had been operated on straightaway and three days later, in a bed with snow-white sheets, a general had come to present him with his Military Medal and announce that he had been promoted. There were flowers on the table; the nurses wiped his face whenever he was too hot. Piras had come to see him, with a bottle of brandy hidden under his coat. Hospital regulations, just like the Koran, forbade all alcohol.

Lahcen had been happy; he was properly looked after, he was equal to the other Frenchmen; he had the same rights, the same friends. He laughed at the same jokes as his comrades. On his first night out some sergeant-majors like himself, but with names like Le Guen, Portal and Duval, had got him blind drunk in a bistro and had then dragged him off to a brothel.

Today, if he was wounded, he would not be entitled to a helicopter or to a hospital, and if he was taken prisoner he would finish up with a bullet in his head fired by Le Guen, Portal or Duval, if any of them happened to be present.

To them he was nothing but a renegade, worse than a Viet. If the administrator of P —— had not brutally reminded him that

*Abbreviation of *division navale d'assaut*—a small coastal or river flotilla equipped with landing craft and flat-bottomed support vessels.

he was just a desert-rat, if he had not stolen from him, then he would have stayed on the side of the French . . . or would he?

No, on second thoughts, he would have gone over to the other side just the same, to avenge a number of other injustices, to remind the French that the Algerian also was entitled to be treated with respect.

Two bursts from a F.M. and the explosion of three grenades interrupted his soliloquy. Si Lahcen slipped the Military Medal into his pocket and ran out of the cave. A platoon of Frenchmen approaching up the crevice had been well and truly engaged.

The group leader, Mahmoud, motioned Si Lahcen to come forward and showed him, a hundred yards farther down, the bodies of two paratroopers, pathetic little mounds of camouflage cloth, and, a little farther on, the wounded W.T. operator with his set attached to his back; he was signalling to his comrades who had taken cover behind some rocks.

"Just watch, Si Lahcen," said Mahmoud, "like hunting game . . ." A paratrooper had rushed forward and was trying to drag the W.T. operator back, while his comrades opened up with all they had got to give him covering fire. The group leader calmly took aim. Hit full in the head, the lizard collapsed on top of his comrade.

"Would you like the next one?" asked Mahmoud.

Si Lahcen took up a rifle and finished off the W.T. operator. Then he turned back towards the cave. Information had just come in that on his right flank the paratroops were beginning in creep forward and were now holding the ridge overlooking the open ground.

Ibrahim came and joined him in the cave. Sitting cross-legged on the ground, he lit a cigarette, then drew his watch out of his waistcoat pocket; it was a big silver hunter which had been given him by his boss, a settler on the outskirts of P ——. He was quite fond of him but destiny had willed that the *roumi* should be inside the farmhouse with his wife and children when it was set on fire. He put the watch carefully back in his pocket.

"Ten o'clock in the morning, Si Lahcen, and it won't be

dark till ten o'clock at night; it's going to be a long wait. They will have all the time in the world to send for their aircraft and perhaps some artillery as well."

"We could have made for the heights and then dispersed, but only at dawn and you arrived too late."

Si Lahcen sent for his five group leaders and told them his plan:

"We shall hang on until nightfall, then attempt a break-out at the weakest point of the 'enemy lines' and make for the river-bed." For technical words or expressions, Si Lahcen invariably used French and he took a certain pleasure in displaying his military knowledge in front of his subordinates. "We're cut off from the mountains . . . Anyone attempting to surrender will be shot out of hand; the wounded will have to be abandoned. We may be attacked from the air, so dig in more deeply, and be quick about it . . ."

The group leaders started to embark on one of those endless discussions during which no problem is ever solved but which provides an excuse for killing time and exchanging cigarettes, noble thoughts and, occasionally, insults.

Three mortar shells landed in front of the cave, putting an end to the *chikaia*. There was a scream from a man who had been wounded. The group leaders rushed back to their men who were firing like lunatics; their bullets whined and ricocheted off the bare rocks.

Another company was now doubling across the open ground under the spasmodic and therefore rather ineffective fire of the rebel automatic weapons. Si Lahcen gave orders for the mortar to fire, but the shells fell well beyond.

From the top of the peak the long files of soldiers looked like columns of clumsy, stubborn ants as they stumbled over the obstacles or vanished behind them and reappeared again. The Tyrolean rucksack which the paratroopers wore on their backs gave them enormous thoraces and spindly little legs.

Lying flat on his stomach outside the cave, Si Lahcen kept them under observation. The leading sections presently arrived at the foot of the peak and disappeared from view.

A reconnaissance plane appeared in the sky, little bigger

than a fly and insistently buzzing like a fly. It turned and, growing larger, became a bird of prey whose savage shadow swept
the rocks. In spite of his orders, the *moujahidines* fired at it,
thereby giving away their positions. The aircraft appeared to
be hit, it dipped one wing and swooped down towards the
plain with the slow, graceful movement of a wounded sea bird.

A few minutes later two fighter planes roared over the ridge.
On their first run they dropped some bombs which burst with
an ear-shattering explosion, causing a hail of stones but no
damage. On the second run they fired rockets and four men
crouching in a hole were killed. One of them was seen to leap
into the air, his back broken, like a wild rabbit that has just received a full charge of buck-shot.

Lahcen knew they would come in again and machine-gun at
a low altitude. Only this time the aircraft would be vulnerable
to F.M. and rifle fire.

One of the planes roared over the cave, firing all its guns.
Burning-hot shell-cases rained down round Si Lahcen who
was still lying prone at the entrance.

Then there was silence. Si Lahcen crept forward under cover
of the rocks and inspected his positions. The machine-gunning
had killed two of his men and two others were seriously
wounded. The casualties had been hit in the stomach and there
was no chance of their surviving. That at least was the opinion
of Mokri, the medical officer of the band, who had studied
two years at the Algiers Faculty.

For the whole of that day the two wounded men never
stopped moaning and crying out for water; there was no mor-
phine to give them. They were disturbing the morale of the
band and suffering pointlessly, since they would have to be left
behind in any case.

Si Lahcen drew his revolver, a Lüger, the one which the administrator of P —— used to keep on his bedside table, and
deliberately, without the slightest emotion, put the two men
out of their misery. One of them just had time to curse him before his brains were blown out.

The lull lasted an hour, then the position was pounded by
the 81-calibre mortars. After a few bracketing shots they began

to find their range. One of the F.M.s and its crew of three was wiped out.

Ibrahim drew his watch out of his pocket. It was only half past one in the afternoon.

Raspéguy was crouching cross-legged by the side of his transmitter, munching some stale bread spread with the army-ration meat-paste which tasted as though it was made of sawdust and shavings. In front of him was a large-scale map in a plastic cover on which he made a number of marks in red and blue pencil as each of his companies reported their position.

Major de Glatigny, who had just been with the mortars, came and sat down beside him.

"It doesn't look so bad," said Raspéguy. "We're closing in on them and the lads are sticking it out. What are the casualties?"

"Four dead and seven wounded. The dead are all in Esclavier's unit."

"What did they get up to this time?"

"Bucelier's group advanced along a defile almost right up to the rebel position. They thought they would be able to take it on their own and pushed ahead contrary to orders. Pinières, who went to their rescue, got a splinter in his arm but he refuses to be evacuated."

"Can he manage?"

"Yes."

"Then its up to him."

"Merle's death was a great blow to him. He was engaged to be married to his sister and I think this death has put an end to the whole using."

With a gesture of his hand Raspéguy indicated that all this was of no importance and belonged to the past. His only interest now was the rebel band which was caught in the net but was going to do its utmost to escape.

The colonel bent over his map again. The shadow of his cap concealed the whole of the top of his face.

"Glatigny!"

"Yes, sir."

"You are Si Lahcen, you're surrounded with a hundred or so men on a peak, with hardly any food supplies, water or ammunition. What would you do?"

"I shouldn't let myself be pinned down on the peak. In my opinion, Si Lahcen will wait till it's dark and then attempt to break out towards the river-bed and the valley."

"That's right, that's exactly what he'd do. But in which direction?"

"On his left flank. That's the easiest for him."

"No, along the ridge on his right, so that his men won't have too much ground to cover before coming up against our force and trying to dislodge them. His last chance is a swift, fierce hand-to-hand engagement."

Raspéguy unhooked his receiver and called up:

"Blue Authority from Passavant."

"Blue Authority listening."

"Well, Esclavier?"

"I had some difficulty getting Bucelier away. They were under fire but they refused to withdraw and abandon the bodies of their four comrades."

"The band is ours; you'll have it tonight; get ready."

A W.T. operator approached at the double.

"A signal from P ——, sir, yes, from Colonel Quarterolles, it's urgent."

"Everything's urgent with him. Bring your set up here."

The operator lugged the "300" up to Raspéguy, who took up the earphones but held them out at arm's length, for Quarterolles at the other end was screaming as though he was being flayed alive:

"Send me the helicopter at once so that I can reach your position."

"The helicopter's being used exclusively for transporting the wounded, Colonel, and we've already got quite a number of wounded."

"This is an order."

"If you're so keen to get here, you can walk. That's all. Out."

And Raspéguy rang off, ordering the operator to cease all communication with P ——. Then he turned to Glatigny.

"Men have been killed and more are going to be killed because of that fellow Quarterolles, and now he wants to come swanking up here in a helicopter, give a pat on the back to our boys who've been stewing in the sun for hours, who've had no time to eat, who've got no more water in their bottles, and ask them in a fatherly fashion: 'How goes it, old boy?' when he himself has just left the lunch-table with a pint of beer inside him."

"He's still the garrison commander, sir. It's a serious business questioning the hierarchy of the army. In this particular case you're probably right! But at other times, at most times . . ."

"Jacques" (this was the first time that Raspéguy had used his Christian name, admitting him into his military family like Esclavier and Boudin), "don't you think I realize the danger? But if we want to win this war we have to shed all sorts of conventions. We are all responsible men and we stick together. What Esclavier and Boisfeuras did, which is condemned by every army regulation, has enabled us to get our hands on this band today. I don't like massacres and I don't like torture, but I feel it's you, myself, all of us, who slit those throats at Rahlem and who made Ahmed and his little friends at P —— talk."

"And God, sir?"

"Tonight Esclavier and his reservists will fight it out on equal terms with Si Lahcen's *fellaghas*. In this fight they'll settle their account with God or their conscience. Tonight they'll be making their confession to death. And we'll only intervene if they can't manage by themselves; but I know they'll hold out."

Raspéguy leant back against a rock and Glatigny had the impression he was withdrawing into himself, searching through his gory, painful and glorious memories for the strength to carry on with his war.

But Raspéguy was actually dreaming of a dark, stagnant lake, bristling with dead branches and reeds, streaked with slow-moving fish and exuding a slimy miasma. He lowered himself gently into these waters, tensing his stomach, contracting his nostrils, struggling against his fear and disgust.

The wireless began to crackle:

"Amarante calling Violettes. Send us up some more grenades; we're running short."

The hunt was on again, and the explosion of bombs and rockets echoed and re-echoed in the depths of the valleys.

Glatigny sat with his head in his hands, recalling the Méo highlands.

Night fell without a sound; there was no more firing. It seemed as though the men had forgotten their quarrel and were taking advantage of this peace and quiet to gather, friend and foe together, round a camp-fire where, relieved of their burden of anger, courage and criminal actions, they could confide in one another and talk about their homes, the ample, welcoming bodies of their wives, their barns full of crops, sheep roasting over glowing embers and the cries of children.

But all round the peak, oblivious of the magic of the night, the wireless transmitters with their little orange lights were crackling louder than crickets.

"Passavant from Blue: they're advancing on us now."

It was Esclavier's voice. Glatigny and Raspéguy remained glued to the W.T.

Esclavier had posted his men half way up the crevice, at the point where it began to open out. They did not form an unbroken line, but were scattered in twos and threes, crouching in holes or behind the rocks. They were staggered in depth over a distance of more than two hundred yards. Down in the river-bed Pinières's company stood in reserve.

It was pitch black, the moon was not due to rise for another hour.

A few pebbles had been dislodged, which had alerted the advance posts, and immediately afterwards the *fellaghas* were on top of them, yelling like madmen. The whole defile had been set ablaze, the F.M.s firing long devastating bursts, the grenades exploding with a dull thud. The mortars, meanwhile, lobbed over tracer shells which spun slowly over the gorges and ridges, transforming them into a stage décor.

Bucelier found himself next to a machine-gun. It had just jammed and the gunner was having difficulty inserting a fresh magazine. He pushed him aside to take his place and was crushed by a body bearing down on him, a body draped in a tattered *jellaba*. He felt a violent jolt in all his muscles, while a blaze of light pierced and shattered the surrounding darkness.

"They've got me, like Bistenave," Bucelier reflected.

But he felt nothing, while his head remained enveloped in the sweat-stained *jellaba*.

Then he heard some shouts, some words of command, the thundering voice of Lieutenant Pinières. Some submachine-guns were firing in short, sharp, angry bursts. He heard San-tucci shout out:

"But where the hell is Bucelier?"

He was suddenly moved to tears because they were talking about him as though he was still alive. Stupidly, he thought:

"It's good to have friends and not be dead in the midst of strangers, as in a car accident."

The body on top of him was still soft and warm, but did not move and smelt of vomit and urine. He called out and was as-tonished to hear the strange voice which was his own:

"Here, here. It's me, Bucelier."

The *fellagha's* body was dragged off him and the sergeant looked up to see some stars shining indifferently in the sky, and then the faces of his comrades above him. Hands were feeling his body, but without hurting him, unbuttoning his camouflage blouse and loosening his belt.

"But there's nothing wrong with you at all," Esclavier told him.

The captain helped him out of his hole. Bucelier was covered in blood but he was not wounded. Whereupon he burst into a loud guffaw, a nervous explosion which ended up in a sort of hiccup. Esclavier put his arm round his shoulder and held him against him, like a lost child who has just been found again.

"You're lucky, you know, Bucelier. The *fellagha* who pounced on you was mashed to a jelly by a grenade thrown by one of his own friends. You'd better get down to the river-bed; the medical orderly will give you something to drink and if you think you can manage, you can come back afterwards. It's not over yet."

"Did they break through, sir?"

"No, but they're bound to try again. They lost thirty men in the process, though."

"And us?"

"A few."

Bucelier never forgot that display of affection, when Esclavier put his arm round his shoulder.

A quarter of an hour later the *fellaghas* attempted a second break-through. This time it was Pinières's company that bore the brunt. But Si Lahcen's men failed to come to grips, and the moon which had risen illuminated the gorge and the confused fighting that ensued.

As the *fellaghas* broke off the engagement, the lieutenant caught sight of a short figure behind them silhouetted against the sky; he was firing on the runaways with a submachine-gun to try and rally them.

Pinières picked up his carbine and, standing up, with legs apart, carefully took aim and fired one, two, three shots.

Si Lahcen fell to his knees and dropped his weapon, then rolled a few yards down the slope and his hands, which had been clenched, slowly opened. Pinières searched him and drew the Military Medal out of his pocket. In his wallet there was also his pension card and his last mention in Indo-China.

"There's something wrong about this war," Pinières said to Esclavier.

A few *fellaghas* who were well dug in still put up some resistance but at dawn they were dislodged from their positions. Five or six of them surrendered, the rest preferred to die.

The regiment withdrew from the mountains towards P——, bringing its dead back with it. Information had already reached the town about the death of Si Lahcen and the destruction of his band; the population knew that it had been a tough, relentless fight and that everyone had acquitted himself well.

As the paratroops filed past, some old *chibanis*, whose sons had probably been killed by them up in the hills, waved to them; on their grey *jellabas* they were wearing all their medals.

It was not the enemy they were greeting but simply those who had had God on their side that day.

Next morning a religious and military ceremony was held in honour of the twelve men of the 10th Colonial Parachute Regiment who had been killed in the recent battle. Seven of them were reservists.

The coffins were loaded on to a G.M.C., coffins made of plain wooden planks whose thickness was laid down by Ordnance regulations, as was the diameter of the nails.

It was then Raspéguy spoke, addressing himself exclusively to the reservists.

"You fought extremely well. You have paid a high price for the right to belong to us; so any of you who wish will be allowed to go on a parachute course as soon as we get back to Algiers. Gentlemen, I am proud of you and salute you."

And standing stiffly to attention, straightening his back and squaring his shoulders, Raspéguy saluted the truck which drove off with the Ordnance coffins and the few hundred faces turned towards him, the mutineers of Versailles whose features were drawn with fatigue, but who felt happy, released by the fight from the bloody memory of Rahlem.

Then, accompanied by Major de Glatigny and Captain Boisfeuras, Raspéguy went off to take leave of Colonel Quarterolles.

"Colonel," he said, "I've got a present for you."

He produced Si Lahcen's Military Medal and put it on the desk, and also a sheet of paper folded in four and stained with rain and sweat.

"It's only a mention in dispatches from Indo-China, Colonel, but it earned Sergeant-Major Si Lahcen his medal."

Raspéguy snapped to attention and read out the rebel's citation:

"'Sergeant-Major Si Lahcen, of the Third Regiment of Algerian Light Infantry; magnificent leader of men, stalwart fighter, surrounded in a strong-point by infinitely superior forces, his officer being killed, he assumed command and although seriously wounded refused to surrender, withholding the attack for six hours until the arrival of reinforcements.'

"It's the same Si Lahcen, Colonel, that Pinières killed, while he was trying to stem the rout of his men. It would have been easier to have kept him on our side.

"Ah, I almost forgot, Mayor; I think Captain Boisfeuras has also got something for you."

"It's a receipt for a contribution to the F.L.N.," Boisfeuras sneered.

"It must be a fake," said Vesselier.

"A receipt which isn't made out in your name but in the name of Pedro Artaz, the foreman on your Bougainvillées estate. I can't see how Pedro Artaz, who earns 40,000 francs a month and has a wife and three children, manages to pay 400,000 francs every quarter out of his own pocket."

"I've also got a present," said Glatigny. "It's for Captain Moine. It's a letter from Ahmed to Si Lahcen which I found among his papers."

Puffing at an old cigarette end, Moine raised his head slightly and his little eyes betrayed the bestial hatred he felt for the handsome major who, with one foot on a chair, began to read Ahmed's letter:

Brother Lahcen,
   As far as Captain Moine is concerned, you needn't worry. He's drunk every night and owes 300,000 francs to the Mozabite, Mechaien. If he makes any fuss, we'll be able to blackmail him. But he's much too stupid, lazy and cowardly . . .

"Here, take the letter, Captain."
Without moving, Moine stretched his hand out for it.
Colonel Quarterolles tried to change the subject:
"I've drafted a number of citations, for I must admit your men behaved admirably . . ."
Raspéguy replied with exaggerated courtesy:
"Colonel, I'm in the habit of rewarding my men, both dead and alive, myself, and I don't entrust anyone else with the task."
He saluted and withdrew with his two officers. Moine tore the letter up into small pieces, then ground the pieces under his heel and suddenly raised his head.

"I hope, sir, you're going to put in a report about the conduct of Raspéguy's officers in P ——. They tortured and liquidated Ahmed instead of handing him over to the proper authorities."

"But you've done the same yourself, Moine, countless times . . ."

"Yes, but I always made out a report which was counter-signed by the police; I was quite in order."

The regiment did not go back to the Camp des Pins straight-away, but wandered all over Kabylie to support the garrison troops whenever an important operation was undertaken . . .

The "lizards" marched through cork forests, in the indigo-coloured shade of the trees. The ferns bent and crackled under their jungle boots while flies, gorged on sap and plant-juice, came and settled on them as though dead drunk after a clumsy, faltering flight.

They toiled over the burning stones of the Aurès and Nèmentchas and, with parched throats, dreamt of the fresh springs of France half-choked by watercress and wild sorrel.

They ran their tongues over the salty sweat which dripped on to their lips. They marched, they laid ambushes, they killed rebels armed with sporting rifles or submachine-guns.

On 27 July they heard that the Egyptians had nationalized the Suez Canal, which affected them scarcely at all since none of them had shares in the Company.

They went on marching or devouring the dust of the roads in open trucks. One day they were sent off to occupy a series of little oases at the foot of the Saharan Atlas where they relieved a Foreign Legion unit.

Esclavier and his two companies of reservists set up head-quarters at V ——, on the site of an old Roman camp of Cornelius Balbus. It was just outside the oasis, overlooking a broad expanse of sand-dunes.

The grove of palm-trees watered by *seguias* was cool and smelt of apricots. It was divided up into countless little gardens in which the *norias* of the wells made a gentle rattling sound. The women, unveiled, with tattooed faces, and adorned with heavy silver jewellery, smiled at the soldiers while the children, more persistent than the flies, ran after them begging for chocolate or offering them pleasures which the women of the oasis could not provide without a certain amount of danger.

The rebellion had not yet reached this area; the regiment took it easy and the officers spent their time calling on one another and showing off their palm groves with the pride and delight of owners. Raspéguy had left Boudin at Laghouat to attend to the administrative questions and supplies.

One evening almost all the officers had dropped in on Esclavier who, having taken over the legionaries' furniture, had the most comfortable mess. It boasted a refrigerator, a few fans and, on a whitewashed wall, a primitive fresco depicting the Battle of Camerone.

Glatigny had brought a gazelle which he had shot from his Jeep, Boisfeuras a case of whisky which he had ordered from Algiers, and Boudin had sent up a small barrel of Mascara wine. They had decided to make a night of it and had started drinking systematically to get drunk as quickly as possible; through drink they contrived to come to grips with the painful, unwelcome memories that dogged their footsteps, to grapple with them, and exhaust themselves in the effort so as to wake up in the morning with a splitting headache and their minds at rest.

They drank first of all to Merle and all the others who were dead, then to themselves, to whom the same thing might happen any day, to Si Lahcen whom they had had to kill, and to Colonel Quarterolles, Moine and Vesselier whom they would very much have liked to shoot. But as they got more and more drunk they began to forget Algeria and France and presently all of them were talking or dreaming of Indo-China.

At the same moment all the officers and warrant-officers of the French Army, all those who had known Tonkin or Cochin-China, the Haute-Région, Cambodia or Laos, whether sitting in the mess, lying in ambush or sleeping in a tent, were likewise aggravating their yellow infection by picking at the thin scabs that covered it.

Esclavier had never been able to bear drunken conversation for long and so went out into the cool, blue desert night. He wandered about the ruins of the Roman camp until he came to the edge of the plateau. Sitting down on the base of a broken column, he contemplated the infinite expanse of the sky and the dunes; he felt a shiver down his spine which was perhaps nothing more than the cold night air. To reassure himself, he ran his fingers over the column and touched the inscription that he had deciphered on the morning of his arrival: *Titus Caius Germanicus centurio III^a Legio Augusta.*

Twenty centuries earlier a Roman centurion had dreamt by this column and peered into the depths of the desert on the lookout for the arrival of the Numidians. He had stayed behind there to guard the *limes* of the Empire, while Rome decayed, the barbarians camped at her gates and the wives and daughters of the senators went out at nightfall to fornicate with them.

The centurions of Africa used to light bonfires on the slopes of the Saharan Atlas to make the Numidians think that the legions were still up there on guard. But one day the Numidians heard they were no more than a handful and they slaughtered them, while their comrades who had fled to Rome elected a new Caesar in order to forget their cowardice.

The centurion Philippe Esclavier of the 10th Parachute Regiment tried to think why he, too, had lit bonfires in order to contain the barbarians and save the West. "We centurions," he reflected, "are the last defenders of man's innocence against all those who want to enslave it in the name of original sin, against the Communists who refuse to have their children christened, never accept the conversion of an adult and are always ready to question it, but also against certain Christians who only think of faults and forget about redemption."

Philippe heard the yapping of a jackal in the distance and, closer at hand, the song his comrades were bawling out, as they rapped on their plates with their knives and forks . . .

He thought of the Communists; he could not help feeling a certain respect for them, as the centurion Titus Caius Germanicus had felt for the nomads prowling round his desert camp. The Communists were frank enough to say what they wanted: the entire world. They fought fairly and no quarter or pity could be expected. Did Titus Caius also know he would have his throat cut?

But Philippe felt hatred and disgust welling up against the people back in Paris who were rejoicing in advance at their defeat, all those sons of Masoch who were already getting pleasure out of it.

Titus Caius must have thought the same about the progressivists of Rome. The barbarians, like the Communists of the twentieth century, had needed those traitors to open the city gate to them. But they despised them and on the day of their victory they had decided forthwith to exterminate them.

A strange thought crossed the captain's mind: "Perhaps we could prevent the empire from collapsing by transforming ourselves into barbarians, by becoming males disgusted with all these females, by turning into Communists."

As he rummaged in his pocket for a cigarette, Esclavier came upon a letter from the incestuous Guitte who refused to remain his sister by adoption. He had given her money and clothes, as he would to a real sister; he had even paid the instalments on her small car. She had spread it abroad that it was perfectly normal for him to keep her since she was his mistress and was living with him.

Old Goldschmidt, who had heard these rumours, had given his daughter a severe reprimand in front of the captain. She had merely shrugged her shoulders and said:

"It was only to help Philippe. He's frightened of giving me a bad reputation; now that I've got one, what's he waiting for?"

Guitte had waited a few minutes, and since he had made no move, she had left the room; he had not seen her again before his departure. But she had just written to say that she had got a lover, which suited her down to the ground.

Mina kept sending him postcards from the Côte d'Azur where she had gone on holiday. They were photographs of grand hotels, naked girls on the beach, parasols and pedal-boats, regattas and water-ski championships. Philippe stuck them up in the mess; the second-lieutenants and cadets of the reserve came and brooded on these holiday pictures for hours on end.

How paltry everything suddenly seemed in the middle of this African night!

He heard a great crash; back there in the mess a table had collapsed.

Marindelle came out and joined Esclavier.

"They're dead drunk," he told him. "Dia made a bet he could jump over the table and landed right on top of it. Pinières has passed out in a corner of the room, stripped to the waist and covered in bandages. Glatigny is sitting back in his chair quietly smoking his pipe, while Boisfeuras is practising knife-throwing against the door."

"And Raspéguy?"

"He hasn't opened his mouth but keeps eating, drinking and cutting up his bread with his penknife. He's not very keen on these systematic binges. He thinks they're a waste of time, effort and breath."

"What about you, Yves?"

"I'm rather fed up."

"Your wife?"

"I don't love her any longer but I've got to get her out of my system; it'll take some time. There's some talk about the French and British intervening in Egypt. You know we're rather well in with G.H.Q. Algiers since that business at P ——."

"I'm not very proud of that . . . We say we come out here to protect the Algerians against the barbarism of the F.L.N., and my men and I then go and behave like Ahmed's or Si Lahcen's thugs."

"We came out here to win, you know, and for no other reason. It's thanks to the example you set at Rahlem that we wiped out the best organized band in Algeria, thereby saving the lives of hundreds, maybe thousands, of men, women and children."

"When I went into the *mechtas* with a knife in my hand, I didn't think of that. I should like to be in a war which wasn't a civil war, a good clean war where there are only friends and enemies and no traitors, spies or collaborators, a war in which blood doesn't mingle with shit . . ."

Raspéguy came up behind them.

"It's not a bad spot," he said. "We might have stayed here a little longer, but in a week's time we're going back to Algiers. We've just been posted to the general reserve."

"What does that mean, sir?" Esclavier inquired.

Raspéguy put a hand on each of the captains' shoulders, leaning heavily on them.

"It means we'll be the first to enter Cairo."

Two weeks later the 10th Colonial Parachute Regiment got back to its quarters in the Camp des Pins.

Before the reservists, who had just completed their six months' stint, were demobilized, Raspéguy insisted on putting any of them who wished through a parachute course. All the reservists who had taken part in the Rahlem business volunteered.

"I don't see how we can very well do anything else," said Bucelier.

He couldn't explain exactly why, but he felt it had to be done. Five or six soldiers who had been put off by the rigours of the training or the fear of breaking a leg just when they were on the point of going home, tried to get out of it. But their comrades did not give them a moment's peace until they too decided to jump.

One evening, at eighteen-hundred hours, during the daily Press conference at Government House, the Press Information captain of Area Ten announced that "the mutineers of Versailles" were going to do a parachute jump at the Camp des Pins a few days before being demobbed and that they had all volunteered for it. The journalists had been invited by Lieutenant-Colonel Raspéguy who was in command of the unit to which they belonged.

The spokesman who was at the meeting thereupon button-holed Villèle, his favorite butt.

"You'll be writing this up in that rag of yours, won't you, Mr. Villèle—that some reservists, Communists, have asked to do a parachute jump before leaving Algeria?"

"I'll see," said Villèle. "I'm going out there and if it's true I'll certainly write about it."

He turned to Pasfeuro:

"Coming?"

They descended the broad stairs of the forum as far as the war memorial and went into a café where they ordered two anisettes.

"Had you heard about this story?" Villèle asked. "You know the whole Raspéguy outfit pretty well, don't you?"

He gave a slight sneer.

"Especially that fellow Marindelle."

"Some day, my fine friend, I'm going to bash your face in if you don't keep off that subject. No, I hadn't heard."

"Shall we go and have a look?"

"You said you were going anyway, do you need me as well?"

"No . . . but I think it'll be a good story. You could give me a lift . . . Let's meet outside the Aletti."

"Why don't you hire a car like everyone else?"

"I'm never in Algiers more than a few days at a time. Please let me pay for your drink."

Villèle could not help wondering what Pasfeuro's reaction would be if he knew that he put the cost of a car down on his expenses although the one he always used was borrowed from a friend. He had even managed to get hold of some blank Europe-Cars receipt forms.

In front of two or three generals, a handful of colonels and a dozen journalists, two hundred reservists led by Captain Esclavier launched themselves for the seventh time into the blue. Their parachutes floated in the air for a few moments. Pulling on their rigging-lines, they landed without mishap and received their brand-new paratrooper's badge from the hands of Colonel Raspéguy.

Then they marched back to their quarters and prepared for their departure. Bucelier, who had signed on again because he was now frightened of going back to France, watched them with a lump in his throat.

The rest of them were quits; they had done their jumps. But he wasn't yet, at least he thought not.

Colonel Raspéguy, Esclavier and Pinières went down to the docks to watch the reservists as they embarked on the *Sidi Brahim*; they remained there until the last moment when the liner cast off. While waiting for them at the bar of the Aletti, Pasfeuro, Villèle, Marindelle and Boisfeuras proceeded to get drunk.

It was after the fifth whisky that Boisfeuras mentioned the leap of Leucadia.

"I once knew an Englishman out in Burma," he said, "a crazy sort of chap who dropped into us one morning with some containers of gasoline meant for another unit which, unlike us, did at least have one or two vehicles. He was a specialist, but on Ancient Greece. Though he didn't have a clue about the Far East, he knew a great deal about Greece and her esoteric customs. All he could do was talk and I often used to listen to him.

"One evening, while the mosquitoes were busy eating us alive and we were trying to force a stew of monkey down our throats, he asked me:

"'Do you know the origin of the parachute? I thought not. And I don't suppose you've heard of the island of Leucadia in Greece, either, have you?'"

"He was a bit of a bore when he assumed his professional tone after whining all day:

"'Well, it was at Leucadia that the parachute was born. At Leucadia there's a white cliff dedicated to Apollo—Leucadia from *leukos*, the Greek for "white," as of course you know—a hundred and fifty feet high, from the top of which, in an extremely remote age, probably the proto-historical—that's to say some time between prehistory and history—they used to hurl people into the sea as a sacrifice to the Sun-god. They were either youths or young girls who had been charged with all the crimes of the community, like the scapegoat in Leviticus.

"'At a later date the priests of Apollo used to look for volunteers among incurable invalids, criminals or victims of unrequited love, all of whom were much the same thing in the eyes of the Ancients. The unloved is a culprit, don't forget.'"

Marindelle almost upset his glass. "The unloved is a culprit!"

But Boisfeuras, punctuating his story with little sniggers, parodying the voice of the archaeologist-paratrooper, went on with his tale:

"'They say that Sappho threw herself off the leap of Leucadia in a moment of despair. But which Sappho? There were two, one was a courtesan, the other a poetess. A woman who writes can't ever love, so it must have been the courtesan who did the leap.

"'Whoever survived the leap of Leucadia was cleansed of his sins and was certain to obtain his heart's desire.

"'The priests humanized the leap, posted boats down below to retrieve those who had jumped from the cliff. But there came a time when no one was willing to take such a risk any longer; in the course of its development, civilization eliminates heroism. Those who were unlucky in love were more discreet or else were made to look ridiculous.

"'So in place of those who wanted to redeem their faults, the priests themselves volunteered to jump, for a certain fee. They trained seriously, did gymnastics, strengthed their muscles, exercised their reflexes, and learnt how to fall. To delay their drop they fastened feathers, live birds and God knows what else on to themselves . . . in other words, the parachute.

"'I knew all this when I dropped, and that's probably why I sprained my ankle. I was always the scapegoat up at Oxford; now I'm at peace at last.'"

Boisfeuras drained his glass, ordered another round and proposed this strange toast:

"I drink to the leap of Leucadia which Esclavier's two hundred reservists performed today to cleanse themselves of a fault which they thought they had committed."

"What fault?" Pasfeuro asked.

"Didn't you ever hear about the *mechtas* of Rahlem?"

"No," said Villèle.

He almost asked for further details, but his instinct warned him not to; this evening he was being barely tolerated.

"By the way," Boisfeuras went on, "I forgot to tell you what became of that English fellow. The gods felt that he had not cleansed himself sufficiently of his faults, or else those of Oxford University were too heavy by half. On his next jump he did a 'Roman candle' and smashed himself to bits."

4

THE PASSIONS OF ALGIERS

Leaning over a balustrade festooned with mauve bougainvil-laea, Glatigny and Esclavier stood and looked at Algiers. They had just got up and, barefoot and in dressing-gowns, were waiting for Mahmoud to bring them breakfast out on the terrace. Étienne Vincent, an old friend of Glatigny's, had asked them to stay at this villa of his in the Balcon de Saint-Raphael for as long as they remained in Algiers.

Glatigny admired the white city rising in regular tiers above the bay where two cargo boats, reduced to minute proportions, described two long parallel furrows in the early morning sea which was as smooth and grey as silk. In a soft voice, without turning round, he said:

"A sailor friend of mine once told me that on the heights of Algiers the early morning air had a peculiar quality, unique in the world, a mixture of brine, tar, pine, virgin oil and flowers. I like Algiers, but with a slight feeling of uneasiness. It's a disconcerting town which has always surprised me with its reactions. The French of Algiers, well, you've only got to look at the Vincents . . . They've got five thousand acres of vineyards and are considered one of the wealthiest settler families in the Mitidja. Étienne, of course, is rather inclined to judge people by the number of vines or orange trees they own and Juliette's snobbery is the sort you find in the wealthy, provincial middle class . . ."

"I've never seen you as lyrical as this before, Jacques. The air of Algiers . . . ?"

Esclavier inhaled the sea breeze in order to get a whiff of the brine, tar, pine and virgin oil that Glatigny had mentioned, but the air of Algiers seemed anything but intoxicating. He found it rather insipid.

"Étienne Vincent was with me in Italy," the major went on. "He was wounded on the Garigliano, and it's a miracle he's still alive. He belonged to the Cherchell draft, all of whose cadets were killed or wounded, a draft of Algerian Frenchmen and refugees from France. Étienne loves his land with the ferocity of a Cevennes peasant, his town like a burgher of the Middle Ages, prepared at a moment's notice to take his pike and helmet and mount guard on the ramparts, and France with the ingenuousness of a *sans-culotte* . . .

"Philippe, don't hang back, surrender to the charms of this town."

"No," said Esclavier. "I'm a child of the Mediterranean. I love the sun, indolence, idle chatter and well-upholstered girls. I've a certain taste for jurisprudence and rhetoric, for café-life and the Republic, lay schooling and great principles. I'm certainly descended from the garrulous and demagogic Greeks and the high functionaries of Rome, but I don't like Algiers."

"Here you've got the sea and the sun. The people are handsome, young and athletic, the girls long-limbed and sunburnt, the boys manly and muscular."

"Yes, but they talk . . . and what an accent, the most common I've ever heard . . ."

"You've also got, as in the south of France, outdoor cafés with belote-players and freemasons endlessly preparing for the elections . . . but also *yaouleds*, cigarette-sellers and bootblacks . . . those pilfering sparrows of the Algiers pavements. The smell of the Mediterranean is somewhat stronger than on the other side of the sea. It's the smell of the Barbary Coast which is already apparent in Spain: a mixture of amber and billy-goat."

Esclavier shook his head.

"You'll never win me over to Algiers. It's a puritan town, puritan in the Spanish way. The girls are attractive, but they're all far too keen on preserving their virginity, because that's a currency which is still in circulation among the Barbary pirates. Money seems to be the only standard of values with these recently established parvenus. I find the complacency and ostentation of these vulgarians even more unbearable than the Arab attitude. Their talk based on sexual comparisons, their conception of honour which is limited to the loins, the perpetual affirmation of their virility . . . everything about them puts me off."

"Philippe, you're nothing but a fake Parisian Latin, a great big *bourgeois* purist. You can't see the funny side of the tribulations of a Bab-el-Oued family going off for a Sunday picnic on the beach, complete with stove, pots and provisions, followed by all their children, grandparents, cousins and maiden aunts. It's a real circus. The small talk is comic and almost always rather racy. The *pataoueds* switch from anger to laughter, from insults—and God knows they're pretty fluent in that respect—to hugs and kisses, from tears to practical jokes, and always with the deepest conviction. France, as we felt on our return from Indo-China, is becoming a vast cemetery haunted by extremely distinguished dead. In Algiers people are at least alive. I sometimes feel sorry I wasn't born in a little street in Bab-el-Oued. I should have had a magnificently raucous and ragged childhood even though I might have appeared somewhat vulgar and circumscribed to you in later years."

"Didn't you have enough sunshine and squalor as a child?"

"None at all; my parents were well-bred, terribly well-bred, and utterly boring."

Mahmoud arrived, shuffling in his slippers. He carried a big copper tray laden with heavy bunches of black Mitidja grapes, oranges and grapefruit from the Chelif plain, pears as yellow as farm-house butter and apples as red as a schoolboy's cheeks, which had just been plucked in the garden of the villa.

The light was now a trifle sharper but the atmosphere still retained the limpid quality of dawn. Washing flapped on the roof-tops; an Arab merchant ambled past with his donkey, shouting his wares.

"I like Algiers," Glatigny said once again. "I feel completely at home in this town, in absolute harmony with it; I could never agree to our giving it up."

"Nor could I . . . because we've no longer the right to give it up, but I feel that on principle, not by inclination. I don't like Algiers."

Étienne Vincent came out and joined them a few minutes later. He limped and in spite of his sunburnt complexion, his broad shoulders and the determined expression he attempted to assume, one could tell that some mysterious mainspring had broken inside him. He had been drinking heavily for the last three months and his eyes were extremely bloodshot.

The settler was frightened, he was ceaselessly haunted by this fear of his, which he could no longer exorcize by going off and fighting.

He sank back into a basket-chair.

"A bomb exploded last night at the Clos Salembier; there was a lot of damage. There were some hand-grenades thrown in the Boulevard du Télemly, and some revolver shots on the Rampe Bugeaud; a farm was set on fire at Maillot . . . The *fellaghas* dragged off all the Europeans who were there: men, women and children. They were found a little farther off and they had all been treated in the same way . . ."

He described this series of horrors and catastrophes in a toneless, monotonous voice and his hands on the arms of his chair—beautiful, nervous, muscular hands—were trembling slightly.

"It's simple being a soldier," he exclaimed all of a sudden, "it's very simple, and I only wish I could join up again."

He refused a cup of coffee and stalked off. Glatigny realized he had gone to have a swig of brandy in his bedroom.

"You know, Philippe, Étienne was one of the bravest men I've ever known . . . What are your plans for today?"

"I've got to go back to camp; a lot of junk to deal with . . . Then I'll go and bathe at the Club des Pins."

"Do you know the private beach there is the most exclusive spot in Algiers? It was quite a job to persuade the members to allow mere paratroop officers to come and lie on their sand."

"Are those gentlemen really so anxious about their wives, so frightened of being cuckolded?"

Glatigny slowly filled his pipe, lit it and took a couple of puffs. The care he took to perform the simplest gesture with a certain gravity and complete lack of haste was inclined to get on Philippe's nerves. As the captain left the terrace, Glatigny's mocking voice made him turn round:

"The French in Algiers aren't cuckolded any more than we are, Philippe, but they make more of a song and dance about it. Don't forget dinner tonight; the whole of Algiers will be there."

Lying in the sun on the beach of the Club des Pins, with his eyes shut, Philippe Esclavier found himself in an intermediary state between waking and sleeping. The sound of the surf, the cries of children at play, the rustle of the wind in the pinewood mingled with the incoherent images of his dreams and served as an accompanying sound-track to them, endowing each one with a reality of its own.

Here was Étienne Vincent, in evening clothes, with a rifle in his hand, commanding a patrol in a cork forest in Grande Kabylie. He took an enormous bottle of brandy out of his pocket and said that Algeria had better be drunk while it was still in good condition. Glatigny refused the bottle which Vincent offered him but Esclavier, out of politeness and because he didn't like Algiers, felt obliged to accept it. The brandy was as sticky and cloying as blood . . .

A woman's voice close at hand dispelled this disjointed image.

"He's sleeping like a dog."

It was a pleasant, gentle voice, which seemed to settle on him like a butterfly. Cautiously, another voice inquired:

"Who is he? I've never seen him in the club."

"He's a *Frangaoui*. You can see, he's as white as an aspirin tablet. He's also got a scar on his stomach, another on his chest . . . How thin he is . . . He's an officer . . ."

"You're cheating; you saw the identity bracelet on his wrist."

"I didn't see anything, but I'm a psychologist."

Esclavier half opened his eyes and saw two young women sitting on beach towels and rubbing sun-tan oil into their skin.

One was dark, tall and slender, with a slightly boyish manner. She looked about twenty-eight, thirty at the most. The other was an ash-blonde and, when she sat up, he compared her body which was bursting with vitality to a wooden bow, supple and at the same time firm. She was the one who had referred to him as an aspirin tablet. Her friend's name was Isabelle. They went on with their conversation:

"Isabelle, are you going to come tonight? Bert will be there . . ."

"Bert's a bore. He mopes and always looks as though he's about to ask my husband for permission to make a pass at me. I feel like hitting him at times . . . No, I'm dining with the Vincents up at the Balcon de Saint-Raphael. Haven't you been asked?"

"I don't belong to the vineyard nobility, as you do . . ."

"Juliette Vincent told me there's going to be a count there, the genuine article, crusades and all the rest of it . . . He's a paratroop major . . . You know, those paratroops with the funny caps . . ."

Amused by this, Esclavier came over and knelt down beside the two young women. They looked scandalized.

"Major Glatigny," he said, "is the father of five children, a good Christian and faithful husband. Let me introduce myself: Captain Philippe Esclavier of the Tenth Parachute Regiment, the ones with the funny caps. I'm also staying with the Vincents. If I look like an aspirin tablet it's because we didn't have much time for sun-bathing up in the mountains. I'm a bachelor and have no moral sense . . ."

"Captain," Isabelle retorted, trying to make her voice sound as dry as she could, for she found the big paratrooper far from unattractive, "Captain, here in Algeria we're not used to being accosted by strangers on the beach. It's just not done."

"I know, I'm just a filthy *Frangaoui* . . ."

"But since you're a friend of the Vincents, don't go on kneeling there like that as though you were on your mark for a hundred yards' sprint. Come and sit down."

The dark-haired Elizabeth lit a cigarette with a gold lighter she took out of her bag. "Men have no sense at all," she was thinking. "They fall for Isabelle who turns love into a sterile,

disappointing game; she's frigid and therefore provocative."
Elizabeth, when she felt like it, could be warm, gentle and ma-
ternal with these hard and tender, saturnine and innocent
child-men who were just back from the wars and would shortly
be leaving again.

She would have liked to entertain the captain in the spare
bedroom which she reserved for her guests and her lovers in
her old Moorish house overlooking the ravine of the Femme
Sauvage.

At a loose end, Glatigny strolled down to the Rue Michelet to
have a drink in the Bar des Facultés. He wanted to behave like
a selfish old bachelor and forget his wife and children for once.
He planned to lunch afterwards at La Pêcherie on grilled red
mullet and fried squid.

As he walked down the little lanes and stairways, he felt
happy and vaguely uneasy, as though he was playing truant;
he almost bought some flowers from an old Arab crouching by
his basket—but to whom would he have given them? A girl-
friend of his had once told him that Saint-Exupéry, on certain
evenings in Les Halles, when he was drunk, used to buy up
armfuls of flowers and solemnly decorate the dustbins with
them. But Saint-Exupéry didn't have any children and he wasn't
married to Claude.

He sat outside on the terrace of the Bar des Facultés and ordered an anisette, which was served with black, oily olives and
little pieces of cheese. A lovely young girl, a brunette with the
dark eyes and velvet skin of certain Andalusian women, carrying a beach bag in her hand, was jostled by a young man. The
bag fell on the ground. Instead of picking it up and apologizing, the young man spat like an angry cat:

"You Moorish whore, get back to the Kasbah."

Then he rushed off to rejoin a skinny, dried-up European
girl with straw-coloured hair drawn back in a pony-tail.

Glatigny rose to his feet, picked up the bag and handed it
back to the young brunette. She gazed at him with eyes burning with hatred.

"Didn't you hear, Major? I'm only a Moor, a Moorish whore."
The words came bubbling out of her mouth.

"I apologize for that little idiot. Please, don't take it to heart.
Here, come and sit with me."

The girl hugged her bag tightly, as though she was frightened it would be snatched away.

"You, a paratroop major, are asking a little Moorish whore
to sit at your table?"

"Please."

She looked at him, hesitated, then sat down next to him, but
ostentatiously moved her chair away from his. She ordered an
orange juice and began to look a little more composed.

"That student who jostled me," she said, "has failed his
first-year medical exams twice. He's a fool. I started at the
same time as he did and now I'm in my third year . . ."

"My name's Jacques de Glatigny," the major gently told her.

"And I'm Aicha . . ."

She almost gave her surname, but suddenly stopped.

"I'm also from a 'big tent.'"

The expression brought a smile to the major's lips but it appealed to him. To him racialism and exaggerated nationalism
were due to the middle class and parvenus and he felt close to
"big tent" people, no matter what their country, their religion
or the colour of their skin, for in them he found the same reactions as his own. Aicha was twirling the stem of her glass between her fingers and gazing at it pensively.

"They say," she said, "that the lizards have caused a lot of
bloodshed up in the mountains."

"It's a painful, unfortunate war . . ."

"Mere repression, that's all, with guns, tanks and aircraft
against bared breasts. The revolutionaries of 1789 wouldn't be
very proud of you."

"You know, Aicha, those revolutionaries of 1789 went to a
lot of trouble over my family, but only in order to cut their
heads off. Would you like a cigarette?"

She took one, but he could see she was not used to smoking.
Her lips made the paper wet, the tobacco came apart between
her teeth, and she kept coughing.

Aicha was as beautiful as the fruit they had had for breakfast that morning up at the Balcon de Saint-Raphael, highly coloured and luscious, with firm, youthful breasts and naturally scarlet lips. He pictured her firm, sunburnt thighs under her light dress and was ashamed of the thought.

"I must be off," she suddenly said.

She assumed a saucy manner which did not suit her at all.

"Would you go so far as to see me home?"

"Of course."

"I live in the Kasbah."

He settled the bill and took her by the arm; her skin was soft and downy. He hailed a taxi.

"Rue Bab-Azoum," she told the driver, "yes, that's right, at the entrance to the Kasbah."

The driver, who was a European, pulled a face.

Just before they arrived, a patrol stopped the taxi. Aicha hugged her bag tightly. Seeing Glatigny, the sergeant saluted and waved them on.

The entrance to the Kasbah was sealed off by a network of barbed-wire entanglements and guarded by steel-helmeted Zouaves with their fingers on the triggers of their submachineguns. They had the tense expression and drawn features of men who are frightened.

Glatigny stepped through a gap in the barrier, still holding Aicha by the arm.

"Is the lady with you, sir?" asked a fat captain in a uniform that was too tight for him. His eyes were alert but his voice was friendly.

"Yes, Captain."

He waved the young girl on, but stopped Glatigny.

"I'm sorry, sir, but you can't go any farther. You're not armed, I should have to detail a patrol to escort you . . ."

Aicha turned round with a mischievous grin on her face.

"I should like to see you again," said Glatigny.

"Tomorrow, at the same time, at the same place, Major Jacques de Glatigny . . . And thank you for my bag."

She started off up a stairway, her skirt swirling round her thighs.

The Zouave captain, who was bored, tried to start up a conversation. He said to Glatigny:

"There are still a few Europeans and quite a number of Jews living in the Kasbah. I wonder how long it'll last . . ."

So the captain thought Aicha was Jewish or European. Glatigny saw no reason to disillusion him. He asked:

"It's as bad as that, is it?"

The captain threw up his arms:

"Even worse. We've got absolutely no control over the hundred thousand Arabs in the Kasbah. We need a platoon escort just to move a few yards . . . So, like rabbits in a hutch, we've wired them in. It's dotty. We're simply mounting guard over the F.L.N. headquarters. Yes, sir, that's what it has come to."

Glatigny did not enjoy his red mullet and squid, and the rosé wine seemed to taste of vinegar.

Aicha went up the stairs at a run, putting to flight the cats which were feeding on the refuse outside some heavy, studded doorways with brass knockers. The ruins of an old *moucharabieh* overhung the lane; behind a little window with iron grilles a curtain was raised, then lowered again. But Aicha knew she was now out of danger. Since March French law had ceased to apply in the Kasbah. The Front was in complete control. All the stool-pigeons had been liquidated or were working for the F.L.N.: the last M.N.A. dissident had been killed the previous day and the police inspectors behind their sandbags received no more callers. The police were waiting in terror for the killer gangs which would one day come and cut their throats.

Aicha was proud to belong to this organization, to be a militant working for the cause, instead of wasting her time over pointless studies. Later on she would take them up again, when the green and white flag fluttered above Algiers.

At the corner of the Rue de la Bombe and the Rue Marmol she came across the whore Fatimah leaning against a wall. Fatimah was wearing the heavy silver ear-rings of a tribal girl, a yellow scarf and a fluffy white sweater; she had the attractive, brittle face of a girl who has seen a lot of life.

Fatimah gave her a friendly wink and murmured:

"God be with you, sister Aicha."

Fatimah was aware of the young girl's role and dangerous work; she too belonged to the Front, like everyone, like the whole of Algeria. Its members addressed one another as brother and sister. And Aicha's heart swelled with pride, she felt she was doing something really worthwhile. She stopped for a moment to stroke a child whose head was covered in ringworm, who stared at her in astonishment.

At 22 Rue de la Bombe, she knocked three times, paused, then knocked twice again. She wondered what the paratroop major would have said if she had told him:

"In my bag I've got the wherewithal to blow Algiers and its rich modern quarters sky-high and I'm going to 22 Rue de la Bombe, where there are some men who will know how to use it."

An old woman with hennaed hands opened the door. She looked at the young girl with disdain. Old Zuleika still observed the laws of Islam and considered Aicha a shameless wench for not wearing a veil and for dressing like a European woman.

But Aicha knew that once the Front had conquered the settlers, it would make every woman shed the veil, forbid polygamy, and put men and women on equal terms, as in the West.

The major had treated her like a lady, he had picked up her bag for her, the bag containing the detonators that the Communist woman had just handed over to her; he had opened the door of the taxi for her and had bowed as he said goodbye. The major had a slim, distinguished figure and his eyes were gentle and full of tenderness . . .

"Well, don't stand there gaping," Zuleika shouted in her strident Arabic, "come in."

She went down a series of passages, up some stairs and across an outdoor terrace, then up some more stairs and down some more passages, where men and women whistled or signalled to one another as she passed. The whole of Amar's bodyguard was in position. So it was he who was waiting for her.

The old woman still led the way. She was extremely quick on her feet in spite of her advanced age. She was said to be the mother of Youssef the Knife. As though that dirty dog could ever have had a mother!

Zuleika opened a door adorned with a partly obliterated black hand of Fatmah. In the little room beyond stood Youssef the Knife and one of his henchmen; they were both armed with Mat submachine-guns which they had seized from some French soldiers they had killed.

"Come in, little sister," said Youssef.

He motioned to her with a hand loaded with heavy rings. He was trying to behave like a man of the world and was puffing at a long cigarette-holder, but he still looked like the pimp he was.

"Did you get the stuff?"

"Yes," she said, "it's in my bag. The European woman gave it to me."

Youssef's cold, cruel little eyes surveyed her from head to foot, pausing at the buttons and zip-fasteners of her dress, delving into her breasts and between her thighs. He ran the tip of his long, obscene tongue over his lips, while his acolyte gave an inane snigger.

Aicha handed the bag over to Youssef; he put it down on the table and seized her by the arm exactly as the major had done, but this contact repelled the young girl whereas she hadn't minded the officer's touch at all.

"Leave me alone," she said. "Where is brother Amar?"

She could hear how unsteady her voice sounded.

"You'll be seeing him. Aren't you touchy, my little gazelle? The daughter of Caid Abd el Kader ben Mahmoudi doesn't like being touched, at least she doesn't like being touched by Youssef because Youssef was born in the gutter. Is that it?"

He shook her, while his acolyte smirked all the more inanely. Aicha suddenly felt weak, defenceless and infinitely vulnerable, and Youssef embraced her more closely. The pimp's lips brushed her hair.

The young girl shuddered with disgust and tried to snatch

her arm away. Amar came into the room; he was a frail, nat-
tily dressed little man. He wore gold-rimmed spectacles and
his hands were as chubby as a child's. He looked fragile and
disarming. His voice was soft and gentle.

"Take your hands off her, Youssef."

"It was only in fun, brother Amar."

"Take your hands off her and don't ever do that again, otherwise the Front will have to get rid of you."

Youssef took a step back; his strength and virility were of no
avail against this little man who, they said, had never touched
a woman and for over ten years had been hunted by the police.
If he was expelled from the Front, Youssef knew he would
die . . . perhaps even before being told he had been expelled . . .
like Lou Costello, the mobsman who controlled all the girls in
the Kasbah, all the *tchic-tchic* players and kif-sellers. He was
known as Costello because he was so tubby, like the American
comedian, but his real name was Rafai and he was a killer
whom everyone feared. A machine-gun burst through his body
had taught him he was no longer the master.

Youssef was in France at the time because of some trouble
over a woman. On his return he had been summoned to this
very room. He had been ordered to put his hands up and, "to
purge himself," had been forced to swallow a big bowl of salt.
Then Amar had told him about Costello's death and demanded
that he work for the Front with the rest of his gang.

Amar had spoken in his usual gentle voice, while behind
him one of his henchmen had prepared a garrot with which to
strangle the pimp in the event of his refusing the offer.

Youssef had that little strumpet Aicha in his blood; she
came and inflamed it in his dreams, but he was still keener on
saving his skin.

"Come along, sister Aicha," said Amar.

He was the one who had suggested that they call one another brother and sister. Youssef thought the whole thing was
ridiculous but never dared to laugh about it.

Amar led Aicha across a passage into a slightly cleaner room
which had just been freshly whitewashed. Its only furniture

was a wooden table, a camp bed, and two wicker chairs. On the table stood a portable typewriter, on one of the walls hung the F.L.N. flag.

Amar made Aicha sit down on the bed and the young girl embarked on her report, while he paced to and fro with astonishing litheness, making no more noise than a cat: a habit he had developed in the cell in which he had spent five years.

When Aicha started talking about the group of the Algerian Communist Party with whom she had made contact, Amar asked her for detailed information and made her describe every one of its members. He was wary of them because they were mostly Europeans or Jews who had proved their efficiency and had a doctrine and methods which had been put to the test in the rest of the world. Amar was a nationalist, "a Maurras type of nationalist," as he had once been told by his cell companion at Lambèze, a former lieutenant in the L.V.F. As a Moslem, Amar had a deep aversion to renegades and pimps but he was already making use of the Algerian underworld and was quite prepared to co-operate with the Communists. He needed bombs and the Communists alone knew how to make them . . . so far. When they had served their purpose he would get rid of them in the same way as those who had joined the Tlemcen guerrilla band: Guerrale, Laban, Maillot, Bonalem . . .

"Let's take them one by one, Aicha," he said. "What's this man Percevielle like? Do you know if he takes kif, or drinks, or has a weakness for women?

"You say they're willing to take on two of our men in their workshops and teach them how to make explosives? What do they want in return? To belong to the Front? We could only accept them on an individual basis, provided they're prepared to resign from the A.C.P. We'll see about that . . .

"Tell me, do you ever see your brother, Captain Mahmoudi? He's serving in Germany at the moment? Give me his address, will you. No, don't be frightened, we don't wish him any harm . . . None at all . . . Rather the reverse, in fact. We regard him as one of us. Not everything that France has done out here has been entirely useless; she's provided us with some very fine soldiers . . . Like your brother . . ."

The Vincents had invited about twenty guests to dinner, all people of quality, at least they thought so.

Juliette Vincent counted them off on her fingers, wrinkling her brow as a rebellious fly kept buzzing just above it. Four army men: the general commanding the sub-division and his chief of staff—the general was paying court to her slightly more than mere politeness demanded—Jacques de Glatigny, for whom she had had a soft spot ever since 1945, and his friend Captain Esclavier; a professor of geology from the Faculty who was just back from the Sahara where, so everyone said, he had made some wonderful discoveries . . . anyway he was all the rage that month; and his wife whom she had never seen, whom no one had ever seen. There are women like that, whom no one ever sees anywhere. That accounted for six of the guests—the foreigners, so to speak.

Then came the Algerians, those who were exclusively from Algiers and did not own a country estate handed down to them by their ancestors. First of all, Dr. Yves Mercier with his wife and Geneviève, his sister-in-law, who was reputed to be his mistress; the three of them were always asked out together. After that, Bonfils and Maladieu, two big Public Works contractors who were established on both sides of the Mediterranean and dealt in millions. They had important political connexions and were lavish with their inside information. Bonfils had married a girl from the upper-crust of Algiers whose first husband had been killed in Italy. Dear little Yvonne still made a great show of being a war widow. She was also worth about fifteen hundred acres of the finest land. Maladieu was coming with a young actress who had a leading role in the company which was presenting *Bal de Voleurs* at the Grand Theatre—"My God, what have I done with the tickets?" she suddenly thought—Maître Buffier and his two daughters. People were saying that since he became a widower, the lawyer sought consolation among his youngest secretaries; his daughters, Monette and Loulou, were very much in the swim; they were to be seen at every ball, at every surprise party. They were both looking for husbands, preferably from metropolitan France. Juliette already knew that the two Buffier sisters would throw themselves at Glatigny and Esclavier. When they discovered the major was married they would quarrel over the captain. Loulou would get him, as usual, and Monette would come and weep on her shoulder. Juliette had a certain affection for poor little Monette. At one time, in order to hang on to a possible fiancé, she had surrendered to him entirely, which had been unwise and useless. Luckily only a few close friends knew about this.

Then Isabelle Pélissier, her husband and their follower. That was what Juliette called Bert, "a follower." The Vincents, the Pélissiers, the Bardins and the Kelbers belonged to the same clan: the big settler overlords of the Mitidja and the Chelif. Isabelle was a Kelber and Juliette a Bardin.

Things weren't going very well between Paul and Isabelle; yet they were childhood friends. What a curious girl, that Isabelle, Juliette reflected. She was considered flighty and flirtatious and whenever she disappeared for several months from Algiers, every one thought she was having an affair. But in point of fact she had gone off to stay with old grandpa Pélissier on his farm which he had sworn never to leave again.

Before the troubles the old man used to spend six months of the year in France; since November 1954 he had not set foot in Algiers.

"Whatever happens," he had said, "I shall only leave the farm as a corpse—having died from old age" (he was eighty years old) "or because the *fellaghas* have killed me or because we have lost Algeria and I have put a bullet through my head."

They said he still drank a litre of rosé wine at breakfast.

There would be no one from Government House at the dinner. The Vincents had fallen out with the Resident Minister.

Isabelle was the first to arrive, in a very simple grey dress.

"It suits you perfectly," Juliette told her, as she kissed her on the cheek.

Isabelle knew that the compliment was sincere for it was slightly tinged with envy.

"I've come to help you receive your guests," she said. "Let's see your table plan. You've put me next to old Colonel Puysange. He gives me the creeps; he's as lecherous as an old curé. No, put me here, that's right, next to this Captain Esclavier."

"But what about Monette?"

"Give her Bert."

"Captain Esclavier is bald and bloated and suffers from B.O."

"Liar. He's tall and slim, with lovely grey eyes. He's brash and very sure of himself."

Out in the garden, as the sun went down, iced champagne was served by Arab servants. They were dressed in the traditional uniform: red leather slippers, baggy trousers, and short tunics with gilt buttons.

While paying his usual subaltern's compliments to Juliette, the general automatically kept an eye on Monette and Loulou Buffier, who made their skirts swirl every time they moved so as to display their golden legs.

The general was uneasy. He had just heard that on the 10th of August a big meeting of the rebel leaders had been held in the Soumann Valley, that it had taken place quite openly and that the Kabyles and the hard core of the interior had got the better of the Arabs and the politicians from outside. Open warfare was now inevitable, irregular, guerrilla warfare which would now be conducted by the most intelligent of the Algerians. Furthermore, they would be able to rely financially and politically on the 200,000 Kabyles who were employed in France.

The general asked for some more champagne. It was dry and chilled, exactly as he liked it. The Vincents certainly did their guests well, they kept the best table in Algiers. He decided to forget his worries.

Colonel Puysange had joined Glatigny and Esclavier who were chatting to Isabelle and her husband. He seized the major by the arm in a friendly manner.

"Glad to see you again, my dear Glatigny. What news of Claude? And how are your five children?"

He was warning Isabelle, if she did not know it already, that

Glatigny was the father of a large family. Every woman, he thought, had a horror of that buck-rabbit sort of man.

Ever since he arrived in Algiers, Puysange had had his eye on Isabelle and kept weaving intricate webs all round her.

Glatigny introduced Esclavier to him.

"Delighted to know you, Captain. Your name's familiar to me, of course. It's a great name in our Republic . . ."

Isabelle looked at the captain with renewed interest. Puysange was a pain in the neck. He turned to Isabelle, fully aware of her passionate nationalism and attachment to the land of Algeria:

"This name may mean nothing to you, madame: the Dreyfus case, the Front Populaire of 1936, the Fighters for Peace, the Stockholm Appeal. Of course, the captain's absolutely on the other side, since he's out here with us."

Esclavier went white in the face.

"You seem to have forgotten my family's activity during the Resistance, sir, not to mention the part played by my Uncle Paul, General de Gaulle's delegate. Our Resident Minister was one of his closest friends. I hardly dare call on him as he's anxious to take me into his military department whereas, by temperament, I prefer to be in action . . . in the mountains."

Glatigny appreciated this passage of arms. Esclavier had just scored a direct hit. Puysange had been doing all he could to join the Minister's military department, and his horror of combat and campaigning was a legend in the army.

The professor of geology came and joined them. The lenses of his spectacles were like magnifying glasses, behind which his eyes seemed to swim like a couple of fish in an aquarium. He was extremely thin, with the coppery red complexion produced by the Sahara, he wore thick winter clothes and one of his shoe-laces was undone. He asked the captain:

"You're the son of Professor Étienne Esclavier, are you? I'm delighted!"

He seized Philippe's hand and started shaking it with an energy which one would never have suspected in such a skeleton.

Seeing that things were not turning out as he expected, Puysange stumped back towards his general. But the innocent pleasure which this worthy man felt at the good dinner which was about to be served in the loveliest surroundings in Algiers, made him all the more exasperated. He decided to ruin his evening for him and leaned towards him.

"I almost forgot, General. The commander-in-chief wants a detailed report on the situation in Algeria for the Ministry of Defence. He'd like you to let him have it by Monday morning."

"Hell!" said the general. "There goes my Sunday . . . The situation . . . well . . . you know it as well as I do, Puysange . . ."

"The Minister needs it for a question to be put before the Assembly . . . This report, without disguising the known facts, must be on the optimistic side . . ."

The consommé au madère was served.

Paul Pelissier was watching his wife, the other Isabelle, the woman she suddenly became when she wanted to appeal to a stranger: her eyes were sparkling, her skin looked brilliant, her voice sounded warmer. He himself was only entitled to her withdrawn expression, her inert and unresponsive body. For the last six months they had been sleeping in separate rooms.

He noticed Bert who was also looking at her, who was suffering as he was but who had not had the luck to hold her at least once or twice in his arms, the luck or the disappointment.

Isabelle was trying to seduce the captain who was sitting next to her; she was displaying all her charms but would certainly get rid of him before he ever became her lover. There were moments when Paul was glad that his wife was frigid.

His neighbour was Monette. He knew the little idiot had gone to bed with Tremagier in the hope that he would marry her. He felt an urge to be unpleasant:

"Well, Monette, have you heard from Albert recently?"

The young girl blushed and hung her head.

On the other side of her, Bonfils and Maladieu were discussing business across the little actress who was sitting between them. He lent an ear. Maldieu was talking about the plans for a new building project out at El Biar. Paul was interested in this; if the project materialized, the land he owned would increase its value threefold.

Real estate and dealings on the stock exchange fascinated him as much as gambling, whereas he had never been interested in vines and citrus fruits. The settler's days were numbered. Isabelle still felt deeply attached to the land, but then she was just a sentimentalist. Paul regarded himself as someone up-to-date, a man of the times, with an international outlook equal to that of a New York broker accustomed to luxury hotels. Summer on the Côte d'Azur or in the Balearics, winter in Switzerland. He had a certain prediliction for that country, with its stable finances, and he was far from insensible to the respect its inhabitants showed for money . . . He had spent three months in a sanatorium there and retained a pleasant memory of that period of aseptic semi-consciousness.

When he had left for the sanatorium, old Pélissier had said to Paul's father:

"Only one grandson you've been capable of giving me, and he's turned out unsound."

Paul could not understand why his grandfather had such a passion for Isabelle. In moments of doubt and defiance, when he had drunk too much and his wife had denied him his rights, he imagined there was a vast plot hatched against him and made a show of sniffing at his food as though it was poisoned.

Glatigny was exchanging small talk with Loulou Bouffier. The young girl found the major distinguished and intelligent and was sorry he was married. Another pointless dinner, she thought. She turned her attention to Captain Esclavier, but Isabelle had appropriated him completely. That little bitch had an astonishing talent for keeping the man in whom she was interested apart from everyone else round him. Paul was bursting with jealousy and Bert could not bring himself to eat—it was very funny and served them right! Hallo, there was Monette wiping her eyes with a handkerchief. Still thinking of Tremagier, the little fool! In strict confidence she had told him she had not even enjoyed it, which really was the limit! The professor of geology was gulping his soup rather noisily. Every now and then he would stop, with his spoon in mid-air, and declare that there was oil in the Sahara.

Glatigny was thinking about Aicha. He tried to imagine her

at this dinner, violent and rebellious, reminding them all of the tragedy being enacted in Algeria; she would have been the loveliest woman present apart from that strange Isabelle who was leaning over towards Esclavier and arguing with him, her cheeks aflame.

"No," Esclavier was saying to Isabelle. "The only reason I'm here is to do my duty as an officer and I try to do it as best I can. In Indo-China, I sold my soul: out here, I'm simply doing a job."

"Out here, you're in France, Captain. My grandfather came from Alsace. He was driven from his home by the Germans in 1870, and he was given a settler's plot. My name's Kelber and our village in Alsace is called Wintzeheim. They also make wine there. My grandfather brought some vine plants with him when he left, with five hundred gold francs as his total assets.

"No, don't look at my husband; he's not one of us, he's from Algiers. His grandfather and mine were close friends. He came from Touraine with his vine plants. I do so wish I could make you understand . . .

"Would you like to come with me tomorrow to our estate in the Mitidja? We'll go and see old Pélissier; my own grandfather is dead, but Julien Pélissier is so like him . . . that I feel I'm his grand-daughter. We'll leave at dawn, as soon as the road is open."

To Esclavier, Isabelle had suddenly stopped being that flirtatious, winsome girl with the magnificent body whom he would have liked to hold in a long embrace; she was beginning to assume a proper shape and existence in these surroundings which had no attraction for him.

Going to look at some vineyards in the company of a French colonial Egeria did not appeal to him in the least. Nevertheless he accepted the invitation in the hope that the drive would bring them closer together and offer certain opportunities which he would be able to exploit.

"I'll come and fetch you at seven o'clock," Isabelle went on. "Bring a weapon with you."

"A dramatic outlook on life peculiar to the Mediterranean races," thought Philippe.

Vincent, who had drunk a great deal, left the table before his guests. Everyone pretended not to notice. Maladieu was speaking with brutal lyricism about Algiers where buildings were going up like mushrooms. One could tell that, as far as this particular businessman was concerned, the development of the Algerian capital was not only a sound speculation but an adventure which suited his sanguine nature.

The little actress was charming and silly; she recited some poems and everyone applauded. The general left; he looked very worried. Puysange asked Esclavier and Glatigny to lunch with him next day at the Saint-Georges. They were glad to be able to refuse, Esclavier on the grounds of a previous engagement with Isabelle Pélissier and Glatigny because of urgent matters that required his attention.

The geologist was still talking about oil, anticlinals and grapholithic sandstone. Everyone nodded his head very wisely.

Lieutenant Pinières was dining alone in the Brasserie de la Lorraine. He had been trying to write to Merle's sister, but had torn up several rough drafts one after the other. It was all over. What answer could there be to the young girl's declaration:

"I loved Olivier so much that I could not bear the idea of having his best friend always with me . . ."

Pinières had toyed with several ready-made phrases, such as: "Life must go on" and "Nothing lasts for ever" but on paper they looked pointless and odious.

Pinières could not bear his dreadful solitude any longer. He ordered a double brandy and decided to visit the clandestine brothel where he had been told he could find a Vietnamese girl . . . Tomorrow he would seek refuge with Dia who would take him out deep-sea fishing, which was the doctor's latest passion. Then they would have some fish soup and get so drunk they would have to crawl on all fours up the grey sandy beach.

"Don't you know how to eat with chopsticks?" Marindelle asked Christiane. "It's quite simple; you hold one of them steady and use the other as a lever. No, hold them a little higher up . . . Now then, let's try again."

They were in a little Vietnamese restaurant which had just opened at the top of the Boulevard Saint-Saens.

The only other people in the room were half-a-dozen Nungs in black berets belonging to the commander-in-chief's personal bodyguard, two colonial infantry sergeants, and a half-caste.

Christiane Bellinger abandoned her chopsticks and used a spoon to eat her rice. She was surprised and secretly delighted with her adventure: this impromptu dinner with a young paratroop captain.

Because he was five years younger than she was, he had appeared to her as a sad young lad at a loose end, with great curiosity and a lively mind. She was astonished when he had told her he was a professional soldier and had been in the army since the age of nineteen.

At the Prado Museum, in a little cubbyhole next to the Saharan gallery, she had been busy taking a plaster caste of a neolithic skull which she had discovered herself at Gardhaia. She was just wiping her hands clean on her old white smock when the captain had bashfully come in, with his red beret in his hand.

"Could you tell me where the guide has gone, please, madame? I can't find anyone in the museum, even to pay for my ticket."

She had laughed:

"Are you as anxious as all that to pay for your ticket?"

"No, but I'm looking for a catalogue with some information on those primitive paintings discovered in the Sahara . . ."

"They're only copies, the originals are at Tassili des Ajjer."

"I don't even know where Tassili des Ajjer is. You see how badly I need a catalogue, or a guide!"

Thus it was that Christiane Bellinger, a lecturer in ethnology at the Faculty of Algiers, after washing her hands and taking off her smock, had acted as the young captain's guide for the entire afternoon.

Never had she had such an attentive and passionately interested pupil; the conscientious, unassuming Christiane had shone as a result. She had launched into the boldest comparisons, conjuring up the history of the dark ages of the Maghreb, with as much dash as the worthy Maître E. F. Gautier. The captain had asked her out to dinner. He was now the one who was doing the talking, as he initiated her into the mysteries of Vietnamese cooking, telling her about the Far East, about that war in Indo-China whose complexity she had never realized, about the Vietminh for whom he unmistakably displayed a certain sympathy.

When he saw her home afterwards, Christiane asked him in for a drink. It was only as she opened the heavy studded door of her old Arab house that she remembered that men meant nothing to her, that she had decided to do without them and organize her entire life round her work. But the captain was more of a child than a man, with that odd tuft of fair hair on the top of his head.

"I shan't go," Raspéguy said to himself.

Boudin was contentedly smoking his pipe, buried in a rickety old armchair with a detective novel in his hand.

"What do you think of women?" the colonel asked him all of a sudden.

Boudin peered over the top of his book in surprise:

"I haven't really thought of them much . . ."

And he returned to his book. Raspéguy looked out of the window at the sea and the crowd of bathers on the beach. An Arab went past, carrying a sort of jerrycan containing ice-cream.

"Ices . . . Ices . . . Cold as snow . . . Fifty francs."

"Right, I'll go, but in civvies," the colonel decided. "And I'll tell her that if she won't sleep with me tonight, she can go and get stuffed elsewhere: a dirty little slut of a Mahonnaise who can't see a pair of pants without . . .

"If Esclavier or Glatigny got to hear about this, I'd look pretty silly. With Boudin, there's no danger; he's not sharp enough."

The colonel went into his room to change; when he came back Boudin was still reading.

"Going out?" asked the major.

"Yes, I thought I'd go into town, see what's on at the movies, maybe spend the night at the hotel."

"See you tomorrow, then."

"See you tomorrow."

Boudin dashed into his room to don his walking-out uniform. The colonel, he was certain, was off to see his little slut of a Mahonnaise.

This evening Boudin was going to dine at the Ambassade d'Auvergne, have a good solid meal of sausages and cabbage, and all his compatriots would listen to him religiously and count his medals. They had asked him to bring the colonel along, but the dinner would then lose all its spice, for Raspéguy would be the centre of attraction.

Concha was seventeen, with dark curls and the rounded forehead of a young kid. Her red skirt set off her slender waist, and her blouse her firm young breasts. The merest suspicion of a moustache emphasized her full lips which were thickly coated with dark red lipstick.

The whole of Bab-el-Oued was hanging out of the windows waiting for the promised arrival of the colonel with whom she went out. Paulette, her friend and best enemy, was standing beside her outside the Martinezes' house to see "if the colonel was true." Concha stamped her foot.

"*Mira*, I keep telling you. It's a colonel he is, I've even seen his badges, five bars on each of his shoulders."

"You've seen them?"

"Well, nearly. You are a beast! The paratrooper came and spoke to him in his Jeep and he called him colonel."

"That's a good one! He's probably only the driver, your colonel."

"Colonel, I tell you, even though his name is Raspéguy, and he's going to arrive in full uniform."

"Raspéguy, that's not a French name!"

"Not French? It's as French as Lopes, isn't it?"

Paulette's surname was Lopes, but her christian name made her intransigent in matters of origin.

The big black car came gliding up the slope and drew up in

front of the two girls. Furious that a little slut could get under his skin to such an extent, Raspéguy slammed on the brakes. He opened the door and leant out:

"Are you coming?"

"Why didn't you put on your uniform?"

"Maneate un poco," he shouted to her in Spanish.

With her hands on her hips, Paulette gave a snort of triumph.

"You see, he's only the driver . . . a Spaniard from Oran who wants people to think he comes from France."

"Never mind, you've never driven in a car like this!"

Concha bundled into the car, furious at having lost face, while the old women leaning out of all the windows shrieked with laughter and slapped their thighs.

"Where shall we go?" asked Raspéguy.

"It's all the same to me. I've got to get back early."

"You told me you were free this evening?"

"With a colonel, yes, but not with a driver."

The colonel switched off the engine and took his officer's identity card out of his pocket.

"Can you read? No! You can see the photograph, though. Now either you get out at once or else you stay with me. *Pronto, puta de chica* . . . make up your mind about it."

"What a way to talk to me!"

She threw him a sidelong glance and sat back in her seat.

"I'll stay."

"What good does it do me, your being a colonel, if the others don't know it," Concha presently said, pouting as the car streaked along the coastal road. "Don't drive so fast, you're going to kill me, you great brute."

But she was proud of the colonel's contempt for the rules of the road and whenever he passed a car, hooting furiously, she gave a saucy little wave; once or twice she also put her tongue out but that was only because she thought she had recognized some merchants from her neighbourhood.

The young girl's presence inflamed Raspéguy's blood and sent shivers up his spine. He had booked a room in a small seaside hotel and carefully set his trap. The owner, a Maltese, whom he had gone to see in uniform in order to impress him, had proved extremely understanding.

As he drove along he fondled Concha's breast. She allowed him to do so for a few minutes, then suddenly scratched his hand.

"You're for it tonight, my girl," he said to himself, "or else I've forgotten all my Latin."

Then he realized he couldn't very well forget all his Latin since he had never learnt any in the first place, and put his foot down on the accelerator.

First of all they went for a bathe and Concha admired the colonel's powerful physique, his long muscles without an ounce of fat on them.

"He's a handsome man," she thought, "but there isn't a single hair on his body."

Hairiness was very popular in the Martinez family, who regarded it as a sign of virility.

"*Frangaouis,*" Odette had told her, "are not so quick off the mark as our men . . . but they're much more cunning."

She made up her mind to be extremely careful. She had already been close to disaster more than once. Men's desire disturbed her most of all at night, when "her blood boiled" at the thought of their caresses.

Raspéguy swam far out to sea until his head was nothing but a black dot, and when he came back she could see his diaphragm expand and contract as he panted for breath.

"Well I never!" she said. "I thought you were going to drown yourself."

"What would you have done?"

"Hitch-hiked back."

With their apéritifs they ate some skewered meat. Calmer after his long swim, Raspéguy watched the Sunday-afternoon Algerian crowd. Its vitality, its mixture of child-like innocence and vulgarity, appealed to him, but he thought the men made too many gestures with their hands when they talked and that in that respect they resembled the Arabs. A number of sturdy, handsome young men walked past their table and ogled Concha, but they were not the sort who would ever join up in a parachute regiment and Raspéguy felt almost inclined to tell them so.

"Listen," said Concha, "after dinner let's go out dancing or to a movie. I've got to be back by midnight because of the curfew."

"I've got a pass."

"I haven't."

Bowing from the waist, the manager ushered them into the restaurant.

"There's not a table left, sir," he said, "they've all been booked; but if you would like to go upstairs you could have dinner in one of the small rooms with a balcony looking over the sea. They're used as bedrooms during the week, but on Saturdays and Sundays we serve meals up there."

"Let's go somewhere else," said Concha.

"No."

She looked askance at the colonel but her woman's intuition, which in her case took the place of intelligence, told her that he would not yield an inch and would rather leave her stranded on the road.

A small table was laid out on the balcony. Concha noticed the bed with its white coverlet in the corner of the room and the towels hanging by the side of the wash-stand.

While they were eating Raspéguy made no attempt to kiss her or fondle her. He showered her with little attentions, but his cruel eyes never left her and followed each of her gestures, her slightest movement; they were as cold and fascinating as the eyes of a reptile.

Concha began to feel drowsy.

At the end of the meal the colonel ordered champagne. It was the first time she had ever drunk champagne. It tickled her nose and she would have laughed out loud if she had not felt so frightened and if she had not at the same time derived such pleasure from her fear. She was both hoping and dreading that something might happen.

The colonel got up and locked the door; he moved with dangerous deliberation, without making a sound.

"No," she said, "the curfew . . ."

He still had not touched her and yet she felt her whole body was being caressed and ready to surrender.

He picked her up in his arms and, just as he was putting her down on the bed, she summoned up all her strength and aimed a kick at his groin. She struggled valiantly for several minutes, remembering the story she had been taught at school about Mr. Séguin's nanny-goat, but she soon realized that the nanny-goat had always wanted to be eaten by the wolf and so, like the nanny-goat, she surrendered with a sigh of relief.

Raspéguy did not bring Concha home until the following evening. The whole neighbourhood realized what had happened. Out of bravado, just as she was leaving her lover, she bent down and kissed him. She shrugged her shoulders as she saw all the familiar faces leaning out of the windows.

"Those lads smirking there, little do they know that none of them's as strong as my colonel, for all the hairs on their chest!"

For several years now, Concha had had a detailed knowledge of the sexual possibilities of men. At Bab-el-Oued these were discussed by the women with the same passion as football matches were discussed by their husbands.

To avenge the honour of the Martinezes, her mother gave her a sound drubbing with a broom-handle, though without hurting her at all, but Concha, who knew what was expected of her, promptly began screaming at the top of her voice that she was being murdered, which gave all the neighbours an excuse for gathering en masse out on the landing.

When they began to protest rather too loudly, Angelina Martinez came out and gave them to understand that her daughter was a little tart and that if she wanted to kill her she was perfectly entitled to do so.

Then she rounded on Montserrat Lopez and, since both of them were fairly articulate, there was a slam-bang brawl which echoed and re-echoed through the sonorous cul-de-sac which was Bab-el-Oued.

"Anyway my daughter needn't feel ashamed," said Angelina, "because as least if she does go whoring, it's with a colonel, yes, a genuine colonel. My son Lucien went to check up. Colonel

Raspéguy, he's called, he's in command of the ones with the funny caps; whereas your daughter goes out every night and gets tumbled by the soldiers in the guard-post and by some who aren't even sergeants!"

"My daughter! A lieutenant asked her to marry him, but she didn't want to . . ."

Meanwhile old Martinez had not even budged from his armchair; as a good Spaniard, he felt that a man worthy of the name had no business interfering in women's affairs.

He simply said to his daughter:

"Now that the damage is done, do whatever your colonel wants, anything, you understand, anything, like a *puta*, to hang on to him. That was how your mother married me."

Then he relapsed into silence and appeared to take no more interest in the matter.

"How much farther is it?" Esclavier asked.

They had been driving for fifteen miles through a flat, monotonous countryside, between vines laden with grapes ready to be picked for the vintage. The sun was hot and dazzling. At rare intervals they passed vast corrugated iron sheds and huge farmhouses roofed with red tiles that looked like factories.

Several times they had to pull over to the side of the road to make room for convoys of armoured cars.

"Here we are," said Isabelle.

She turned off to the left and through a big wooden archway which bore the freshly-printed inscription: "Domaine Pélissier."

The car skirted some sheds and outhouses behind which a company of infantry was encamped with its tents and vehicles, crossed a sweet-scented orange-grove and drew up in front of a long, low, freshly-whitewashed house with a veranda running all round it.

An enormously tall old man appeared, walking on two sticks. He had a rubicund complexion and white whiskers growing on his chin, out of his nostrils and out of his ears.

He appeared to be in a fury of rage and began by barking:

"Where's Paul? He didn't come with you. Come here and give me a kiss."

Esclavier saw that as the old man put his arms round the young woman, his eyes shone as though brimming with tears.

"Who's this fellow?"

He pointed at the captain with his stick.

"I've brought him here, grandfather, so that you can tell him why we want to stay on in Algeria, because he doesn't understand. He's dirty *Frangaoui* who has done a lot of fighting . . . for the Chinese . . . But he doesn't care for our war at all."

"Come here," said the old man. "Come on, I'm not going to eat you. You're like my other grandson, the real one who was killed in Italy, tall and lean, all bone and muscle. You've got the Légion d'Honneur, I see, but what's that, yes, the green one?"

"The Croix de la Libération."

"So you were with de Gaulle? I was all for Pétain and Giraud myself, because they at least were gentlemen and your de Gaulle was just a politico who brought the Communists back. But you fought, which was the right thing to do."

In the drawing-room with its tall shutters, through which the sun's rays filtered, shimmering with dust, they were given some iced rosé wine whose sharpness disguised its strength.

"I made this wine myself," the old man told them, "the best rosé in the Mitidja. I sell it in bottles with my own trademark, I don't export it to France to strengthen our anaemic wines.

"Would you like to know why I want to stay on here in Algeria? For the sake of this wine and a number of other things. When I brought the first plants out here, it was a pale little Anjou. Look what the soil of Algeria has done for it; it has given it some of its own fire."

"That's true," said Esclavier, "but perhaps your wine is lacking in subtlety and tact . . ."

"We've had enough of subtlety and tact; what we need is strength and justice.

"Is he your lover?" he suddenly asked Isabelle. "No? Yet I told you to get yourself one. Our women must choose their husbands or lovers from among the men who are capable of protecting us."

"I told you, grandfather, this one doesn't want to protect us."

"I never said anything of the sort," Esclavier protested.

He was beginning to like this old man for his violence, his outspokenness and absolute contempt for convention.

"Well then, what did you say?" the old man barked. "Women always understand the men they're in love with either too well or not well enough."

Isabelle tried to fight back.

"I'm not in love with anyone."

"Yet this is the first officer you've ever brought to see me. And I must say, you haven't made a bad choice. When the war's over he can leave the army and move in here with you."

"What about Paul?"

"Paul will get what he deserves: a kick in the ass."

As they went into lunch, Isabelle took Esclavier by the arm and held him back for a moment.

"You must forgive him, Philippe . . . The troubles have gone to his head a bit."

The captain was dimly aware she had called him by his christian name. After the long drive in the sun in an open car, the wine had made him slightly fuddled and his reflexes were slow—"all velvety" as his mother used to say. It was not often he thought of her.

The meal consisted of fried courgettes and a highly spiced couscous, washed down by the same rosé wine which went to the head and caused a pleasant torpor in the limbs.

After venting his anger on Algiers, Paris, the Republic, the other settlers and these idiotic Moslems who were going to lose everything in their rebellion, the old man fell fast asleep at the table.

Two Arab servants came and helped him to his feet and gently guided him up to his bedroom.

"They worship him," said Isabelle. "He curses them, tells them to go off and join the *fellaghas* and leave him alone, but they all know how much he loves them. He has built houses and an infirmary for them, and given them plots of land; he pays them much more than the other settlers, which has caused him quite a lot of trouble. At one moment they even spread the rumour that he was helping the Nationalists."

"What's the Arabic for 'Independence'?"

"*Istiqlal.*"

"That's a very strong word, like your grandfather's wine, it's stronger than gratitude . . . I say, I'm falling asleep in my chair . . ."

"There's a bed made up for you."

"What about you?"

"I'm going to drive round the farm in the Jeep. As a child, I used to play in the orange-groves . . . with the boy who was killed in Italy. Paul used to hide behind a tree and watch us."

Philippe lay down fully dressed on his bed in a room full of books, sporting trophies and club pennants.

On the opposite wall, in a lemon-wood frame, hung a picture of a cadet in uniform. He was twenty years old, with a dimple in his left cheek, and seemed to be contemplating him with a conspiratorial smile. Philippe dropped off to sleep and the young cadet's smile accompanied him.

When he woke up, Isabelle was sitting beside him. She handed the captain a glass of iced water.

"You've slept for two hours," she said.

He noticed she had changed her clothes; she was no longer wearing the light printed dress in which she had started out from Algiers but a coarse linen shirt, a pair of old jeans and desert boots, and from her leather belt hung a revolver in a highly polished leather holster.

"I don't like women playing at soldiers," he said.

"I've no wish to be raped and have my throat cut a few yards from home without being able to defend myself. What my grandfather was too upset to say is that we want to hold on to this land because we were born here and made it what it is. We've got as much right to it as the settlers of the Far West who drew up in their covered wagons on a river bank where there was nothing but a handful of Indians. They built their huts and began tilling the soil. Only the American settlers killed the Indians, whereas we've looked after the Arabs.

"It would be mad, unjust, unthinkable to drive us out of this territory which we were the first to cultivate since the Romans, out of these houses which we have built . . .

"What on earth have we ever done to you, you people from France?

"In 1943 and 1944 we came to fight for you. At that time we loved France more than you can possibly imagine, while our brothers and fiancés were being killed in the mud of Italy, the beaches of Provence and the forests of the Vosges.

"Why do you want to desert us?"

She had become very emotional, wringing her hands in front of the captain, and there were tears on her cheeks which she did not even wipe away.

Esclavier took her hand and drew her gently towards him. He was moved to see how the elegant little doll, the flirt of the Club des Pins, was transformed into a "Passionaria" of the land of Algeria.

Isabelle came and lay down beside him. He unfastened her belt and tossed it into a corner of the room together with the weapon hanging from it.

Later on, when Isabelle tried to recall in detail how it had all happened, she could not remember a thing, only a wave which came rolling in from afar, towered above her, broke over her and swamped her, dragging her under in a turmoil of sand and gold.

At another moment she saw herself as the land of Algeria. The warrior bending over her was fertilizing this land with his strength and by this union she became part of him for ever.

It was the first time she had found any pleasure in the act and when the wave receded, leaving her insert on the shore, when she saw Philippe lying beside her, naked but by no means shameless and repellent as every other man's body had seemed to her hitherto, she felt that no harm could come to her ever again, that Algeria was saved and all the dangers dispelled.

She stroked his scars and his wounds, timidly at first with the tips of her fingers, then she kissed them.

In the evening they walked hand in hand through the orange groves. Old Pélissier accompanied them in his wheelchair.

"I've managed to make Philippe understand," she told him.
He ran his hand through his whiskers.

"It must have been quite a job, you made so much noise about it. Do you really think he understood just because you rubbed yourself up against him like a cat in heat . . . Well, anyway, he's now got something worth protecting in Algeria."

"What?"

"You."

Esclavier and Isabelle spent the night on the estate. The wave came and bowled Isabelle over again and Philippe no longer made any attempt to fight against this passion which was creeping over him.

In the middle of the night a servant came and woke them up. They went outside; there was a red glow in the sky; the neighbouring farm had been set on fire.

The Murcier estate was one of the oldest in the area; it had been founded a few years after the conquest by one of Bugeaud's officers who had been demobilized on the spot.

Leaning on his sticks and sniffing the air, old Pélissier went on cursing without a pause. Eventually he had a stroke and had to be put to bed. Isabelle decided to stay behind on the farm and Philippe drove back to Algiers by himself in the young woman's car. Before leaving her, he said:

"I'd like you to meet Dia."

"Who's Dia?"

"A Negro, our medical officer. To some of us, especially to me, he's an extremely important person. If I ever had the urge to go to confession like a good Christian, Dia would be the man I'd choose as my father confessor."

"Meaning?"

"That maybe I'm in love with you, maybe I'm genuinely in love, but I should very much like Dia to tell me so."

Captain Boisfeuras had arranged to meet Chief Inspector Poiston in a bar next door to the Mauretania. He had known the inspector in Saigon, when he was dealing with the Chinese community there.

"They're a bit wary of me," said the inspector, "because I

come from Indo-China, but at least I know my job and I don't deceive myself . . . Algiers is in the hands of the rebels. We've got the names of all the leaders of the F.L.N. We know where they're hiding out, but we can't put a finger on them.

"The laws in force in Algeria are the same as in France; they prevent us from taking any action. The police are busy watching one another and every man is ready to denounce his rival if he commits the slightest irregularity. There's only one solution . . . in my opinion. Let the paratroops loose in the Kasbah, a whole division of them. We'd keep them informed and they could pull off all the jobs that are forbidden to us. But it's urgent."

"We're due to leave for Cyprus."

"This is hardly the moment!"

"The Resident Minister says that a French division in Egypt would be worth four in North Africa."

"But when you get back here, the *fellagha* flag will be flying over Government House and the Resident will have been strung up to a lamp-post unless he manages to get away in time. Things are moving quickly. Have you heard of the autonomous zone of Algiers?"

"No."

"Well, imagine Saigon entirely in the hands of the Vietminh. apart from a few residential quarters, with Ho-Chi-Minh, Giap, Ta-Quan-Bu and all the rest of them firmly established in the town . . . Because, I may as well tell you, the leaders of the rebellion are already in Algiers . . . They've just come in from Kabylie . . ."

"Put them inside."

"Algeria can go to hell, so long as our rivalries continue. I'd better be off, Captain; it's rather frowned on to be seen talking to the army . . . But hurry up and come back from Egypt before everything is drenched in blood."

5

MR. ARCINADE EMERGES
FROM THE SHADOWS

During the month of September and the beginning of October there were several events which preoccupied the French of Algiers. For the initiates of the Yacht Club there was the surprise party which Isabelle Pélissier gave in honour of Captain Esclavier so that no one should fail to know that he was her lover. Bab-el-Oued, with the tactlessness, open-mindedness and good humour that were typical of this quarter, focused a sharp eye on the liaison between Concha Martinez and her paratroop colonel. The only thing that took temporary priority over this affair was the match between Racing Universitaire Algérois and Saint-Eugène; but from then on Bab-el-Oued became deeply attached to the colonel, it made him its hero at the same time as its adopted son and forced his name down the throat of the prudish, upper-class quarters of Algiers.

There also appeared, in what it is now customary to call the "fashionable circles," a mysterious Mr. Arcinade. He was smooth and sociable, he loved sweet cakes, knew all the ins and outs of the Algerian question and appeared to have inside information on Parisian politics. Boisfeuras, who met him several times, could never make up his mind if he was a double agent, a police informer or a sincere patriot whose mind had been somewhat disturbed by reading too many thrillers and spy-stories.

But "Force A" which was due to land in Egypt, which had been standing by since 22 September and whose existence was now an open secret, had soon ceased to be of any interest to local society.

Every morning the people of Algiers would open their shutters, put their noses out to sniff the sea air and notice that the
fifteen merchant ships that had been requisitioned for the
transport of the troops were still in the harbour. Whereupon
they would go off to their various occupations, shrugging their
shoulders.

The taxi-driver Jules Pasdeuras, who kept his vehicle in the
rank at the foot of the Rampe Bugeaud and held court in the Bar
des Amis, summed the situation up twice daily in what was possibly a rather coarse manner, but at the time there was no one in
Algiers who did not share his opinion:

"The Egyptian expedition? My ass!"

The phrase was accompanied by a magnificent gesture of
derision. In a short time no one ever referred to Force A except
as the "My Ass Expedition."

It was only after the arrival at the Saint-Georges Hotel of
two hundred civilian pilots, who were due to convoy the paratroops to Cyprus, that the people of Algiers began to take the
matter a little more seriously.

On the other hand, with the exception of a few rare initiates
of the rebellion, no one knew that a certain Khadder, who until
then had fulfilled a very secondary role as a medical orderly up
in the mountains, had just been posted to the autonomous zone
of Algiers. Thanks to a government grant, he had previously
received a sound education in the Faculty of Science. He had
stooping shoulders and a whining voice and never stopped
complaining of the pain he suffered from one of his vertebrae
which had been displaced as a result of a fall; he harped on it
continuously, like an old hypochondriac on his health or a general on his one and only victory, and thereby earned the nickname among his fellow-students of "Khadder the Vertebra."

Khadder's mind sometimes used to wander, he would forget
where he was, what experiment was under way and which of
his friends was with him. Mireau, who was his neighbour at
the laboratory, would then give him a good kick in the behind.

"A boot in the ass is the poor man's electric shock treatment," he would bitterly observe.

Mireau was working his way through college and was reputed

to have once shown leanings towards the Algerian Communist Party.

Pasfeuro had been recalled to Paris "for consultations." The director of his paper, a man of considerable presence and with any amount of decorations, liked to endow his correspondents' movements with the importance of a diplomatic posting. The Minister for Foreign Affairs having sent for his ambassadors and experts to question them on the possible repercussions of the Suez Expedition in the Middle East and the rest of the world, he promptly followed suit by summoning all his permanent representatives to the *Quotidien* head office. The ambassadors got the best part of their information from the *Quotidien* correspondents, who in their turn got it from the unofficial military and commercial attachés, the fake consuls and "box-wallahs" who were extremely well informed but with whom their Excellencies would never associate.

The two meetings took place on the same day, at the same time, one on the left bank of the river, the other on the right. The director of the *Quotidien* and the Minister for Foreign Affairs both had a "contact" in the rival establishment. They were both waiting, the latter to take a decision, the former to orientate the policy of his paper and cull the sensational news items which could not fail to emerge from these meetings.

Villèle had greater freedom of movement, the managing board of his paper having decided once and for all to stick by the opposition until such time as they were invited to take up the reins of office. To these uncomplicated souls, Paris was France; Jewish banking, the École Normale, Polytechnique and the 16th *arrondissement* were Paris; the cafés of Saint-Germain-des-Près were a school for thinkers, and progressivism a political ideal. Young, brilliant and well dressed, they had just the right amount of insolence, caddishness and cynicism to maintain the illusion.

Villèle, who was in Algiers, was therefore able to witness what later came to be called the "El Biar scandal." He was the one who described it to Pasfeuro, in a report which was accurate enough in detail despite the somewhat "sneering" interpretation he gave it.

Pasfeuro had seen Jeanine in Paris and resumed his liaison with her. His director had congratulated him on "his very remarkable work in Algeria." He had all at once forgotten to ask for the increase in salary that he had been promised for some time.

Reclining in a deck-chair in the garden of the Hotel Saint-Georges just as night was beginning to fall, drowsy and yawning with happiness, he was listening inattentively to his companion's account. The name of Marindelle roused him from his torpor.

"Imagine," Villèle told him, "one of those grand penthouse apartments, with a terrace all round it adorned with flower-pots, succulent plants, dwarf palm-trees and olcanders; big French windows overlooking the Bay of Algiers with all its twinkling lights; thick carpets, deep sofas, first-rate drinks. That big oaf Esclavier certainly knows how to choose his mistresses. Apart from the professional interest he arouses, I'm beginning to have quite a soft spot for him.

"I had met him the evening before in the Aletti bar and he had asked me to come ... What an excellent introduction Indo-China is for all those army people! No matter what you write about them, provided you've once set foot in Viet-Nam you're absolved, you're one of the family.

"The official reason for the party was not, of course, because Captain Philippe Esclavier had given Isabelle Pélissier joy when she had always believed herself to be frigid. No, it was in honour of the officers of the Tenth Parachute Regiment who were just off to capture Cairo. Her husband was there: a narrow-chested little squirt, but not without intelligence. If I were the captain or his lady-love I'd be a bit more careful ...

"The accepted hierarchy of Algiers was completely upside-down for once. Your cousin, Marindelle, for instance, had brought ..."

"What's that?"

"Ah, I thought that would wake you up! Marindelle turned up with a somewhat mature woman, a lecturer in Saharan ethnology at the Faculty. Neither he nor she left any room for doubt about the kind of relationship that united them. There was something incestuous about their liaison. Oedipus and his mother . . . Does that suit your book?"

"What a bastard you are!"

"Do you know, the role of the utter, out-and-out bastard is becoming more and more difficult to keep up in this dull, hypocritical, tolerant world of ours?

"The paratroops arrived in their camouflage uniform, with their sleeves rolled up and their collars undone. The Algerines were all in black ties, silk shirts and white shantung dinner-jackets; the women, for the most part, in cocktail dresses by the leading Paris designers.

"The local dignitaries made a big fuss of the mercenaries whom they badly needed in order to bring to heel the Arab League which was threatening their privileges. You remember *Salammbo*, the dinner at Megara, in Hamilcar's garden. I kept thinking about it all the time . . . 'The more they drank the more the mercenaries remembered the injustice of Carthage. Their efforts, viewed through a haze of drink, seemed prodigious and too poorly rewarded. They showed one another their wounds, they recounted their battles . . . Whereupon they felt alone and abandoned in spite of the crowd, and were suddenly afraid of the great city slumbering beneath them in the shadows, with its flights of stairs, its tall dark houses and its obscure gods who were even fiercer than the people themselves . . . '"

"Do you know Flaubert by heart?"

"Yes, I could quote whole chapters at the age of fifteen. I had stolen the book from a stall; it was *Salammbo*—just imagine, if instead of *Salammbo* I had taken *Les Mystères de Paris*—and all at once I was forced to go to work for the *Quotidien* . . . Colonel Raspéguy turned up with a little tart from Bab-el-Oued, a luscious little piece, dressed up to kill, as common as they make them and stinking to high heaven of skewered meat and pimento. He believes in direct action, that chap. He noticed straightaway that the fine ladies of Algiers were rather discreetly made up, so he turned to his little marmoset who was plastered in red, blue and black, took her by the scruff of the neck, locked her up in the bathroom and gave her a good scrubbing. When she came back she was bright red, as through she had just been sand-papered. She was fuming and never opened her mouth for the rest of the evening except to say 'shit' each time a worthy gentleman offered her a glass of champagne or something to eat . . .

"At first the various groups kept apart. The paratroopers discussed the war, the settlers wine and citrus fruit, the business men money, the women clothes or the latest diet: and all of them, as they sipped their whisky or champagne, kept whispering about Isabelle and her paratrooper and casting sidelong glances at Paul Pélissier to see what attitude they should adopt towards the adulterous wife and her lover. For rarely have I seen two people proclaim so openly that they were in love and sleeping together. They left in their wake a warm, provocative aura of sex.

"Dia, the Negro, turned up a little later with his little chum Boisfeuras, that disturbing character with the grating voice. They looked as if they had already had a drink or two. They were followed by a big red-haired lieutenant with a set expression who distinguished himself by tripping over the edge of a mat. He measured his length on the floor, thereby provoking a caustic comment from Raspéguy:

" 'When you can't hold more than a quart, Pinières, it's best not to drink a barrel.'

"Dia gulped down a tumbler of neat whisky, gave a belch of satisfaction and affection, then put his arms round Esclavier and Isabelle and hugged them to his breast. Dia's got the same sort of voice as Paul Robeson, rich, deep and melodious, a voice made for seducing women, children and slaves . . . which speaks to the heart and the guts. All the guests who were out on the terrace came inside again; that voice attracted them like wasps to a honey-pot.

" 'Philippe,' he said to the captain, 'I'm glad you're in love with a woman who's so like you, who's your own sort, a real live woman . . . this time. What's your name?'

" 'Isabelle.'

" 'Isabelle, this evening there's something we've got to do;

we've got to kill your little rival; she's already died once, you know. Don't be too frightened of her; she was a girl with plaits and a fibre helmet on her head. Little Souen, we all loved her, she was our Indo-China war, she was the one we had come to protect, although we didn't know it, against the very people with whom she was fighting. We loved her like a little something outside time and space. Souen wasn't lively like Isabelle. Indo-China wasn't as real as Algeria . . . It was a place apart, where we lived by ourselves, in a war which we had invented for ourselves, where we crept away to die like those sick or wounded elephants who struggle off on their own feet to their secret burial grounds. With you, Isabelle, it's much more simple. You've become Philippe's girl so that he can come with his friends to protect your home . . . '

" 'The nigger's dead drunk!' Paul Pélissier cried out in a shrill voice. 'How dare he address my wife as "*tu*"! He'd better get out of here . . . he's raving mad . . . '

"Whereupon Raspéguy seized the husband by the arm.

" 'If you like, we can all go with him. With our nigger, we'll go off and leave El Biar, Algiers, Algeria, the Sahara; we'll leave you to deal with your Arabs whom you claim to know so well. But if it hadn't been for us they would have thrown the whole lot of you into the sea ages ago.'

"At that moment, I promise you, everyone found it quite normal that Isabelle should be Esclavier's mistress and even that she should advertise the fact, everyone, even her husband . . . What really shocked poor little Paul Pélissier was that Dia had addressed his wife by the familiar '*tu*' and put his arms round her. As the evening wore on, and the glasses were emptied and refilled, the mercenaries began talking about the war, the Resistance, the prison-camps and Indo-China. I discovered a great deal about them that night.

"I now realize they're a simple, rather pathetic lot, anxious to be loved and delighting in contempt for their country, capable of energy, tenacity and courage, but also inclined to abandon everything for a girl's smile or the prospect of a good adventure. They revealed themselves to me in their true light: vain and disinterested, thirsty for knowledge but averse to instruction, sick at heart at being unable to follow a big, un-just and generous leader and being forced to attribute their reason for fighting to some political or economic theory . . . to take the place of the leader they haven't been able to find.

"Those 'reprobates' who paid Isabelle the homage of their tales of bloodshed, their savage or nostalgic songs, their distant loves, their mad dreams of conquest, who tore off their medals and ornamental armour to cast them at her feet, were pathetic and at the same time exasperating. In Indo-China they had become adults, and suddenly, because they were about to be launched against Egypt in a good old war of re-conquest, they were once more transformed into the preten-tious, unbearable warriors they had been before.

"It was an absurd, heroic nightmare: Ubu turned hero. I could imagine that little fool Isabelle, while they were setting fire to the mosques and palaces of Cairo, licking her lips with the satisfaction of a well-fed cat.

"Do you know what I thought, Pasfeuro? For God's sake lis-ten, because it's serious . . . much more serious than your senti-mental problems. Those paratroops are all free and unattached, they're on the look-out for a master. And the only ones capable of producing this master who would know how to break them and at the same time cover them with glory, inflict on them the discipline they're longing for and give them back the admira-tion of the people which they feel they are being denied, are the Communists. That night they were passing through a phase of infantilism, the last in their lives perhaps. While they were fondling the girls, breaking the furniture and draining their glasses, while the Negro, banging on a copper pot he had discovered in the kitchen, kept urging them on before the hor-rified eyes of the men 'responsible' for those ladies who were now transformed into spectators and stood rooted to the spot, I was thinking of that story in *Salammbo* and of the orders the Senate of Carthage gave to Hamilcar to herd the mercenaries into a deep ravine and there exterminate them. Because one day those cohorts of yours will have to be exterminated, and a *bourgeois* government will have to take the responsibility for doing so.

"Pasfeuro, you can stand me a double whisky. I've just told you an extremely interesting story."

"You told it me, because neither of us could use it as copy because no one would understand it . . . You don't happen to know the name of that girl who was with Yves Marindelle, do you?"

Paul Pélissier met Arcinade the day after the "scandal," at the house of some mutual friends. He was still somewhat fuddled from the night before; and his injured feelings and wounded vanity made him feel as though he had just been flayed alive.

Mr. Arcinade knew how to soothe wounds of this sort. His stout little body was carefully ensconced in the depths of a big arm-chair, and in his hand he was warming a glass of brandy.

"My dear fellow," he said to Paul, "I've heard so much about you, your illustrious family which has been established here ever since the conquest of this land of Algeria from which they want to drive us out, and the influence you have in certain circles; that's why I wanted to meet you. You're no doubt aware of the vast plot which is threatening Algeria . . . a plot with countless ramifications . . . I know, you're thinking at once of the left wing, the Communists . . . No, that aspect of the plot isn't serious. There's another side to it, an infinitely more pernicious side, which has gained ground with the middle class, among business circles and even part of the army . . ."

"Really?"

"Do you know Colonel Puysange? Only the other day he was telling me how uneasy he felt about it. A number of officers, including some of the best, contracted the virus out in Indo-China. Some of them didn't even wait for Indo-China. You know Captain Esclavier, I believe?"

A hot flush rose into Paul's cheeks, but Arcinade appeared not to notice it.

"A splendid war record, undoubtedly . . . but with de Gaulle and in the Resistance, which gives it a certain . . . political character . . . Above all there's his family which has been associated for ages with international Communism. Captain Marindelle and Major de Glatigny appear to belong, like him,

to an organization which is, shall we say"—he gave a scornful, superior pout—"liberal. Colonel Raspéguy takes a special
pride in his working-class origin. Those aren't the sort of
defenders we need in Algeria. We need tough men with conviction, real soldiers of Christ and of France, who are settlers,
merchants, labourers or officers by day . . . but at night-time
are handy with a knife or submachine-gun . . . These men
should be organized by specialists provided with arms, the latest technique and proper support, in Paris as much as in Algeria, in the army as well as the civilian population . . . But
because these men are honest and sincere, they're sometimes
short of money . . ."

Paul gave a slight start. He had a reputation for "tight-
fistedness" in spite of his great wealth. With his finger-nail Arcinade traced a heart surmounted by a cross on the table-top.

"That's the sign of Charles de Foucauld," he said, "but it's
also the sign of the Chouans."

And in a piping voice, which recalled the noise of frogs on
certain summer evenings, the astonishing Mr. Arcinade suddenly burst into the Chouans' song.

> Your remains will be flung to the waves,
> And pledged to dishonour your names,
> We've one honour alone in the world,
> And that is to follow Our Lord.
> The Bluecoats, while leading the dance,
> Will lap up the blood of our heart,
> We have only one heart in the world,
> And that is the heart of Our Lord.

"I hope we shall meet again, my dear Pélissier, and very
soon. I must ask you to keep all this to yourself, of course. By
the way, did you know Captain Esclavier was a freemason?
Quite a senior one, too . . . like our commander-in-chief and
our resident minister."

As he made his way home, Paul decided to see no more of
this madman with his mealy-mouthed manner. The sound

peasant sense he had inherited from his ancestors put him on his guard, but he had to admit that what Arcinade had to say was extremely disturbing and he seemed to be well informed.

As he got into his car, he whistled the Chouans' song between his teeth:

> The Bluecoats, while leading the dance,
> Will lap up the blood of our heart . . .

The Bluecoats, that meant Esclavier . . . And all the suppressed romanticism of a rickety child rose to his lips.

On 20 October the paratroops of the 10th Regiment received orders to embark in the aircraft which were to fly them to Cyprus.

Colonel Raspéguy, in full uniform, with his badges of rank on his shoulders, and with two armed guards sitting behind him, drove up in his Jeep to say goodbye to Concha.

The whole of Bab-el-Oued was leaning out of the windows. The washing flapped in the blazing Mediterranean sun.

He kissed the young girl, gave her a pat on the behind and went off to capture Cairo amid the frenzied applause of a crowd in which Spaniards, Maltese, Arabs and Mahonnais rubbed shoulders with a handful of "Frenchmen by extraction."

On 5 November, at six o'clock in the morning, the paratroops of the 10th Regiment were dropped just south of Port Said so as to seize the bridge over which the road and railway line led to Cairo. This bridge lay across a subsidiary canal connecting the Suez Canal to the Lake of Manzaleh, and the dropping zone consisted of a narrow strip of sand between two stretches of water.

The aircraft dropped them from a height of 400 feet, the minimum safety height being 350. They had to slow down to 125 miles an hour, thereby providing a splendid target for the Egyptian anti-aircraft batteries.

Anti-aircraft batteries which were massed round the bridge, opened up as soon as the first plane appeared in the sky, thereby revealing the position of their quick-firing cannon, twin

pom-poms and heavy machine-guns. The aircraft had only
dropped equipment: a couple of Jeeps and a recoilless 106 mm.
gun, which had landed in the canal. In the still water the white
parachutes looked like gigantic water-lilies that had just burst
into bloom. The paratroops had jumped behind a smoke-screen
and most of them managed to land on the strip of sand. Casualties were less heavy than had been anticipated.

Esclavier and his men had made for the company's lock-
chambers so as to approach the bridge from the rear. To achieve
their objective, they had been obliged to cross a thicket held by
the *fedayin*, Nasser's suicide squads. Each of these *fedayin*, concealed behind a tree, was equipped with a regular miniature
arsenal: submachine-gun, rifles and bazookas. They opened up
on the French with all they had got, but without causing much
damage, for their fire was hopelessly inaccurate and the paratroops knew how to make the best use of the slightest irregularity
in the ground. Seeing that the paratroops, far from retreating,
were continuing to advance, they suddenly broke off the engagement, abandoning a position from which it would have been
difficult to shift them, together with their arms, uniforms and all
their ammunition. While pursuing them, the paratroops crossed
the bridge and actually went two hundred yards beyond it. The
road to Cairo was open to them. But the other companies, who
were having a harder time of it under heavy artillery fire, took
several hours to catch up with them.

Glatigny doubled across the platform of the bridge which
was once again being swept by machine-gun fire and flung
himself into Esclavier's fox-hole just as a mortar shell burst behind him.

"First of all," he said, "many congratulations. Raspéguy
asked me to tell you not to overreach yourself. We're at the
apex of the entire Allied force . . . for this time, at last, we've
got an ally, which hasn't happened to us since 1945. This is
real war, Philippe, and it does one good."

"Yes, real war, with Cairo as the final objective."

"Do you know what Cairo means in Arabic? *El Qahirah*,
the Victorious."

"We'll behave like Napoleon," Esclavier grinned. "We'll loot the museum. My father once told me it's one of the richest in the world and the worst arranged: a real Ali Baba's cave . . . The gold of Tutankhamen!"

"We haven't got there yet."

"What's stopping us? A few bands of poor *fellahin* who don't know what they're meant to be defending, some theatrical warriors festooned with ammunition belts, who take to their heels at the very first shot—in other words, nothing. We'll live in the Semiramis, on the banks of the Nile, we'll climb the pyramids and go and visit the Valley of the Kings. We've at last escaped from that prison called Algeria . . ."

Another salvo of mortar shells burst near their fox-hole, raising a cloud of dust. But their only reaction was to laugh, because they had taken Cairo.

Pinières and fifty of his paratroops took the *fedayin* barracks of Port Fuad by storm. They killed or captured a hundred and fifty of them and collected enough arms and ammunition to equip an entire regiment.

"A fine war," he said, mopping his brow.

Captain Marindelle and Lieutenant Orsini, with a truckload of paratroops, forged ahead without orders down the El Kantara road and got to within a few miles of the town. There they were machine-gunned rather half-heartedly by some regular regiments who were rapidly retreating in the belief that the Israelis were already in the Egyptian capital. They took so many prisoners that they had to release them again, merely taking the precaution of removing their trousers.

Raspéguy established contact with the one-eyed general who was circling over them in his flying headquarters, a Dakota.

"The Suez road is free," the colonel reported. "One of my units is just outside Kantara. What are we waiting for? Shall I go ahead?"

"We're expecting orders at any minute."

The Dakota went on circling over the company's workshops, then suddenly made off in a northerly direction towards the sea and Cyprus.

"What the hell's going on?" Raspéguy inquired, feeling suddenly uneasy.

It was the pilot who replied:

"Nothing. We're going to refuel."

A brief signal now came over the air: "The Franco-British troops are advancing on Suez." All the strategists were making calculations on their maps: the tanks moved at sixteen miles an hour, but the French AMXs could do over sixty. Ismailia would be taken in the course of the night and Ismailia was just under a hundred miles from Cairo. The rout of the Egyptian Army was gaining momentum. Raspéguy was fuming with impatience. He was frightened another unit might go through ahead of him.

Next morning the navy started unloading the trucks, Jeeps and heavy material at Port Said and Port Fuad. Seething with rage, Raspéguy saw the vehicles of Fossey-François's and Conan's regiments being taken off first and then those of Bigeard's, and it was not until the evening that he at last got hold of his "rolling stock."

At ten o'clock that night the general in command of the parachute division sent him an urgent summons.

"Everyone ready to move off for Cairo in an hour's time," he barked. "No stores, no supplies, just weapons and ammunition. We'll pick up what we need on the way."

The general was boorish, not to say uncouth, but Raspéguy who did not like him at all—did he ever like anyone commanding him?—was willing to admit that "he had guts."

"Sit down," the general told him.

He handed him a glass and a bottle of whisky.

"Have a drink. No, a bigger one than that, for heaven's sake!"

He was suddenly addressing Raspéguy as "*tu,*" which made the colonel realize that things were going badly.

"Now listen and don't blow up . . . because I feel like blowing up myself. I've just received the order to cease fire. We're pulling out."

"But we've already won!"

"Eden has been forced to give in, Guy Mollet tried to save

the situation but without much conviction. We haven't won, we've lost. An ultimatum from the Russians, threats from the Americans. I don't know what's happening with the Russians, but it seems Hungary is up in arms."

"I don't give a damn about Hungary. Supposing we hadn't received this order, we'd now be advancing on Cairo . . ."

"Do you think that hasn't crossed my mind as well? But we'd have to be covered, anyway as far as the French command is concerned."

"That could be done."

"I'm afraid not. Our commander-in-chief is a graduate of the staff college, unlike you or me. He wages war with maps, statistics and sand-tables. He can't believe that four parachute regiments on their own can send a whole tin-pot army packing . . .

"So get this into your head, Raspéguy: I forbid you to move an inch. But if you want to get drunk with your officers . . . I can send you a truck-load of whisky. There's no shortage."

"What's in store for us after this?"

"Algeria again, though the solution to Algeria is probably to be found here . . ."

"Algeria, that shit-house!"

"Yes, we're condemned to that shit-house again. Do you know the garrison of Port Said has just surrendered?"

"It's a bad business, sir, giving up like this when victory was within our grasp . . . and we badly need a victory. It's specially bad for our men. They thought they had escaped from prison. Now they're going to be taken back to their cells under police escort . . ."

The paratroops of the 10th Regiment embarked on 14 November, a few hours before the arrival of the U.N. police, ninety Danish soldiers in blue caps. They had skin and hair the colour of butter, weapons which they had never used except on exercises, and complexions as clear as their consciences.

On 20 November the Regiment disembarked at Algiers in the dark. Colonel Raspéguy had arranged for them to be sent off at once into the mountains for he felt he had to take his men in hand again. A *fellagha* band had just been reported in the Blidian Atlas. On the very next day the lizards set off in pursuit of it.

On Saturday, 30 September, at five o'clock in the afternoon, while the streets were swarming with people, a bomb exploded in the milk bar on the corner of the Rue d'Isly and the Place Bugeaud, just opposite the flat which the commander-in-chief occupied in the headquarters building of Number Ten Area.

At the same time, in the cafeteria in the Rue Michelet, a second bomb went off. This one was made of the same primitive explosive as the first: "schneiderite," manufactured from potassium chloride. The two bombs killed three people and injured forty-six. The casualties included a number of children who had their legs blown off.

At the cafeteria some medical orderlies had just laid a child, screaming with pain, on a stretcher; they were about to close the doors of the ambulance when one of them noticed he had left the child's foot and shoe on the pavement. He threw both under the stretcher and, leaning against a tree, promptly vomited. He was called Maleski. Regularly once a week, at the Swiss Restaurant, he used to take a nurse, with whom he occasionally spent the night, out to dinner. He was a happy man and until that day had never been assailed by any political, moral or sentimental problem.

The fuse of another bomb placed in the main hall of the air terminal failed to function. It consisted of an alarm-clock connected to an electric battery, and contained the same explosive as the cafeteria and milk bar bombs: schneiderite.

On 5 October yet another bomb exploded in the Algiers-Tablat bus, killing nine Moslem passengers . . .

Horror reigned in Algiers, to the sound of wailing ambulance sirens and in the midst of shattered shop windows and pools of blood hastily sprinkled with sawdust.

Stretched to breaking-point, the nerves of the Algerines quivered at every rumour, at the most improbable report. But sometimes these very same men appeared to be unaffected by the most atrocious sights and, as they drank their anisette, would raise their glass to the next grenade of which they themselves might be the victims. Then they would work themselves into a frenzy over a conversation about football.

Horror was succeeded by fear and hatred. Moslems began to be beaten up without rhyme or reason, simply because they had a parcel in their hands or because they had "a nasty expression on their face." Europeans got rid of their old Arab servants and *fatmahs* who had been part of the family for twenty years.

"You can't trust any of them," they would say. "One fine day we'll wake up to find our throats cut and our children poisoned."

Then they would quote the story of the baker who had been murdered by his assistant. The two men had worked together every night for over ten years; they had become close friends and were to be seen every morning emerging covered in flour from their bake-house. They would go and have lunch in a bistro on the other side of the street, taking their newly baked bread with them and ordering some ham to go with it.

Within a few days Bab-el-Oued witnessed a distinct rift between the Moslems on the one hand and the Jews and Europeans on the other. This was exactly what the F.L.N. wanted: to divide that ill-defined zone and split up its inhabitants who tended to resemble one another more and more, for they had so many things in common: a certain nonchalance, love of gossip, contempt for women, jealousy, irresponsibility and inclination to day-dream.

Villèle and Pasfeuro spent every night at the *Écho d'Alger* offices, where there was a W.T. tuned in on the police transmitter's wave-length. They listened in to the calls and were thus able to ascertain the number of the outrages and the place where they had occurred. In November they averaged more than five a day and accounted for two hundred deaths.

In the early days the journalists would rush to the spot at once, by car, motor-cycle or taxi. There they would see a few bodies lying on the pavement and covered in an old blanket, some wounded being taken off to the Maillot Hospital, or the impotent rage of a man with a face distorted by hatred and misery; there they would hear a woman screaming as she went

for the police or ambulance men with her claws. The Jewesses
and Spanish women were the most uncontrolled of the lot.

Very soon the journalists could no longer bear to photograph these horrors, listen to these screams, and be taken to
task as though it was they who were arming the terrorists.

Pasfeuro and Villèle had again attended a Government
House Press conference. The spokesman had given a garbled
version of the outrages and minimized the number of casualties; more often than not the outrages were modestly referred
to as "incidents." He had announced the arrest of several terrorists "whose identity could not be revealed," promised that
measures would be taken against them and reported the anni-
hilation of a sizeable *fellagha* band in the Collo Peninsula,
where a considerable amount of weapons had been seized.

Villèle had given a knowing smile and Pasfeuro had shrugged
his shoulders in despair, which had succeeded in unleashing
the spokesman's anger:

"Are you again questioning the accuracy of my information?"

"Naturally," Villèle calmly replied, rising to his feet.

"Come and see me in my office with Pasfeuro. We must
thrash this out together once and for all."

Their colleagues on the local Press watched the two bad
boys enter the headmaster's study with the satisfaction of
goody-goodies who were beyond reproach.

As soon as he was alone with the two special correspondents, the spokesman changed his tune. He sank back into an
arm-chair, his head lolling limply against the head-rest.

"Out with it," he said wearily.

"To begin with," said Villèle, "the outrages have caused seventeen victims and not six, not one arrest has been made, and
the Government has no disciplinary measures in view . . ."

"Secondly," Pasfeuro chipped in, "we got the worst of it in
the Collo skirmish: fifteen dead and twenty-two wounded. The
arms that were seized amounted to two sporting rifles. But
what about the arms that were lost? They haven't been mentioned in any report."

The spokesman rose to his feet and started pacing up and
down the thick office carpet, peering at the two confederates

through his eyelashes, which were as curved and long as a woman's; he had confused and tricked them so often that he was now reduced to treating them with a certain amount of frankness and honesty.

A minor civil servant who had embarked on his career in the wake of the Resident Minister, the spokesman had allowed himself to be carried away by the Algerian tragedy and, with all the resources of a nimble mind, with all the unscrupulousness of a pupil of Machiavelli who has pledged himself to a cause, he had set about defending Algeria inch by inch.

"All right," he said, "there's no point in deceiving you; your information's quite correct. But what good would it do to make it public at this stage? It would only add to the general alarm. We're on the brink of a catastrophe; anything could happen within the next few days. The crowd may get completely out of hand, Europeans and Moslems may start killing each other. But we can't do a thing, our hands are tied by your friends, Villèle: they need the loss of Algeria in order to seize power . . . no matter if the whole of Algiers goes up in flames."

"You're exaggerating, Mr. Spokesman, we only want to save what can still be saved, by coming to terms with certain valid elements of the F.L.N."

The telephone started ringing.

"What the hell does this bastard want, I wonder?"

Since living in the company of army men he had assumed a coarse manner of speech which he felt was demanded of him.

He lifted the receiver.

"Hallo? Oh, it's you, Vivier . . . What's that? Froger has just been killed? Where? On the steps of the Main Post Office . . . Serious? I should damn well think so. We're in for it now, Vivier. No, it's up to you to notify the chief. You're the head of security, after all . . ."

Without waiting a moment longer, the two journalists dashed out of the room and raced down the marble stairs of Government House.

Amédée Froger, the President of the Interfederation of the Mayors of Algeria, had by virtue of his qualities and shortcomings become the standard-bearer of all the settlers. The

F.L.N. had struck the Europeans right between the eyes. The repercussions were bound to be violent.

At eleven o'clock that night Pasfeuro, who had just filed his copy, joined Villèle in the Press Club, the only place that kept open after curfew. This tunnel, obscured by cigarette smoke, was a seething mass of journalists, police officials, pimps and informers, drug-pedlars, secret service agents, professional prostitutes and amateur tarts, the latter, like the former, on the look-out for a greenhorn who was drunk enough to see them home.

"Well," Villèle inquired, "what's the latest?"

"The funeral's fixed for tomorrow, 28 December. The New Year's getting off to a good start!"

"It will see the independence of Algeria, that's inevitable. History, like a river, always flows in the same direction."

"Balls!" said Pasfeuro. "Utter and complete balls, this irreversibility of history . . . Your little Commie chums were clever to appropriate destiny for themselves. What strength it gives them!"

"Do you think Algeria can be saved? Can't you see that it's rotten to the core? It appears sound enough, but that's merely a façade which is going to be blown down in the gale of the general strike which Cairo and Tunis are threatening before the U.N.O. debate.

"We've got the same number of officials at Government House, rather more than last year in fact, and they all keep sending one another memoranda and publishing reports; but the machine's working in a void, no one reads the things, no one acts on them. Meanwhile four hundred thousand soldiers are standing by, waiting to be able to go home."

"You're exaggerating, the army holds the hinterland."

"Perhaps, but it doesn't control a single town; its sphere of action ceases at the gates. And in the towns, what do you find? A few old flatfoots entangled in their peacetime regulations, who have got no information and are only too anxious to save their skins. The rebellion, like a worm, has insinuated itself into this defenceless fruit and devoured it from the inside.

"The F.L.N. is master of the towns, starting with Algiers

itself: it has therefore won. Remember Morocco; the revolt there started in the *medinas*, after which the hinterland followed suit."

"Why not put the army into the towns?"

"Out of the question, it's illegal."

"But legality now merely serves to protect a band of terrorists and assassins. The whole of Algiers is controlled by a few hundred killers, as you know perfectly well."

"Those who are in favour of withdrawing from Algeria are very keen on the legal aspect. Legality is only interesting when it's useful to us and is on our side."

"You talk like Louis Veuillot, my dear Villèle: 'The liberty which you demand from us in the name of your principles, we deny you in the name of ours.'"

A tart came and sat down at their table; her fair hair fell over her face, her breasts drooped and she smelt of drink.

Villèle gave her a smack on the behind with the palm of his hand:

"You see, Pasfeuro, I'm going off to sleep with her. More often than not one sleeps with whatever comes to hand."

He rose to his feet and rested both fists on the wine-stained table-cloth:

"And perhaps it's for the same reason that I sleep with the flow of history."

Amédée Froger's funeral gave rise to several incidents of violence, in the course of which a number of Moslems, who had nothing to do with the killing or with the F.L.N., were clubbed to death, knifed or shot by a raving mob. This sort of pogrom was commonly referred to as a "rat hunt."

At seven in the evening Pasfeuro was standing outside the Aletti with Parston, one of his American colleagues, when the mob emerged from the Rue de la Liberté and the Rue Colonna d'Ornano, and swept up the little lanes and stairways towards the Rue d'Isly.

By the tobacconist's stall on the other side of the street, an old Arab stood watching this milling crowd in amazement, wondering what mysterious reason there could possibly be behind it. Pasfeuro distinctly saw a man run up to the Arab and brain him with a heavy iron bar.

He dashed across the street, forcing a way through the crowd with his elbows, and began to pick the old man up. He was already dead, his skull bashed in, and the journalist withdrew his hands which were now covered in blood. But he could see a policeman who had witnessed the murder taking to his heels.

Pasfeuro straightened up slowly and his rage was so intense that he was trembling from head to foot.

"Some day I'm going to do in one of those bastards," he said to the American who had come across and joined him.

Parston was an old hand who had been in every war and every revolution. He took Pasfeuro by the arm.

"It wasn't a man who killed the Arab," he said, "it was the mob. The mob's a strange sort of beast which lashes out at random and then doesn't remember a thing; it has a taste for murder, arson and plunder. The man who struck him down was probably a nice young chap who loves his mother and looks after his cats. I've studied the mob for a long time . . . Leave well alone . . . and come and wash your hands."

"I hate the beast, I'd like to shoot it dead . . ."

"Everyone hates the mob, but everyone belongs to it."

They went back to the Cintra and spent the rest of the night drinking. To calm Pasfeuro down, Parston treated him to a description of all the horrors he had witnessed in the last twenty years. He now talked about the mob as though it was some monstrous, mythical hydra, like the one whose heads and arms were chopped off by Hercules only to sprout anew immediately afterwards.

Pasfeuro then remembered the policeman he had seen taking to his heels; there was no more law and order, the hydra was prowling about Algiers in complete freedom. The F.L.N. would soon be able to put its men into the streets and launch the Kasbah against the European quarters.

Day by day armed commandos coming from the Wilaya IV were infiltrating in small groups into the Kasbah or going to ground in the suburbs of Algiers.

On their side, the Europeans were buying weapons and grenades regardless of the cost. Mr. Arcinade suddenly assumed great importance; one day all the walls appeared daubed with his emblem: a red heart surmounted by a cross.

The first meeting of the anti-terrorist commando he had created was held on the very evening of Amédée Froger's gory funeral, at Telemmi, in a rented flat occupied by Puydebois, a little settler from Blida. Puydebois, a violent, tough, outspoken man with a thickset, powerful frame, close-cropped hair and a blue chin which he had to shave several times a day, kept saying over and over again:

"We've got to choose between a suitcase and a coffin. My choice is a coffin, but it had better be a big one because I plan to take quite a number with me."

Paul Pélissier had come accompanied by Bert. He had been driven to action by a variety of sentiments. The desire to surprise his wife and win her back from Esclavier was mingled with the need "to do something," and not feel so isolated and therefore so unhappy in the midst of this town which was collapsing in anarchy and bloodshed. Now that he carried a weapon he had the sensation of being at last the man of exception born in revolution and conspiracy.

Bert followed Paul as he had always done. He was a placid, handsome, rich young man, but there was no life in those 176 lb. of healthy flesh, in that beautiful statuesque head, no desire, not even the most commonplace envy, nothing but Paul to whom he had belonged since his childhood.

The medical orderly Maleski had been brought by Malavielle, a Government House employee recruited by Arcinade.

There was only one thing in the world that Malavielle feared: not being "in the thick of things." He loved mystery as other men love sport, gambling or women, with passion, and suffered for the very reason that there was no mystery in the sort of life he led: the life of an exemplary minor official who boarded in a H.L.M. with his unassuming little wife and three over-well behaved little children.

Maleski could not dismiss from his mind the vision of the cafeteria, the ambulance and the injured child. He had haunting nightmares and hallucinations; women filled him with horror; he could no longer stomach a mouthful of meat or a single glass of wine. His hatred of the "rats" was akin to that of a teetotaller bent on preserving his chastity; it was cold and implacable, it manifested itself neither in word nor gesture, it verged on madness.

The student Adruguez was not quite sure how he came to be there. One falls into conversation with a stranger in a café one evening, one drinks a few anisettes, one accepts an invitation to dinner and one finds oneself involved in a plot. Since it was not the first time this sort of thing had happened to him, he was not unduly impressed.

Arcinade took up his position in front of a table on which lay a Bible and a revolver. He was in shirt-sleeves, with his collar open at the neck, chubby and glistening with high-quality sweat.

"Gentlemen," he said, "we are on the brink of defeat. Tomorrow Algeria will cease to be French . . . unless we act promptly and decisively! Our organization already numbers hundreds of adherents, there is no lack of volunteers for printing pamphlets, bill-sticking, and collecting information; but that's not enough; we now need men for killing."

"As usual," Adruguez said to himself, "we've got to kill, but whom? No one seems to agree on that score . . . there's nothing but a lot of talk about rat-hunts and submachine-guns. If you're not in the thick of things, there's not a chance of getting a girl. Nowadays you've got to pack a pistol before you're entitled to give them a smack on the behind."

"Terror," Arcinade went on, "must be answered by terror, outrage by outrage. That's what you all think, isn't it, Puydebois, isn't it, Maleski?"

He raised his voice and thumped the table.

"Well, that's not the solution! First and foremost, we've got to be efficient. It's not enough to throw a few bombs of our own, what we've got to find out is who is throwing them. We've got to do the work which the police are incapable of doing and the army isn't allowed to do: counter-terrorism.

"You, whom I've chosen for your devotion to the country,

for your high moral qualities, your courage and self-denial, this evening I bring you . . ."

He thumped the table again.

". . . the support of several important leaders of our army. We're going to act in conjunction with the Secret G.H.Q."

Adruguez şat up in his seat. This time things looked rather more serious than usual.

Arcinade believed implicitly in this Secret G.H.Q., a myth he had fondly cherished ever since he had been in touch with one of the countless clandestine organizations that flourished at Vichy during the occupation, for this deceiver of others succeeded also in deceiving himself.

He had met Colonel Puysange on three separate occasions and had spoken to him in guarded terms of "certain steps he was planning to take." The least the colonel had been able to do was to "lend him the support of G.H.Q."

Nothing more had been needed for Arcinade, who was always inclined to read between the lines, to imagine some vast collusion between his own organization and this great G.H.Q. of which Puysange could be none other than the Algiers representative.

"Before going any further, my friends, I'm going to ask you to take an oath on this Bible, as I shall now do in front of you."

Arcinade squared his shoulders and, with a great show of emotion and sincerity, pledged himself as follows:

"In the name of Christ, in the name of France, so that Algeria shall remain French, I swear to fight to the death, to keep my activity secret, to carry out every order I am given, no matter what it may be. If I betray my oath, I shall expect to be executed like a traitor."

The new adherents repeated the oath one after another, Puydebois quivering with emotion, Bert without understanding a word, Malavielle with delight, Maleski with the sombre conviction of someone possessed reciting a formula of exorcism, and Paul Pélissier with such deep anxiety that he stuttered from the effort.

Eugène Adruguez spoke in a strong, clear voice which impressed everyone; he did not believe in the oath for a moment.

"Now as far as action is concerned," said Arcinade, "our friend Malavielle has a most important announcement to make."

"It's like this," said Malavielle. "I've been keeping him under observation for the last three weeks and I now know that he's one of the main leaders of the rebellion."

"Who?" Puydebois asked.

"Ben Chihani, the cloth merchant in the Boulevard Laferrière."

"Let's be serious about this," said Adruguez, who was twenty years old. "All Chihani thinks about is money; no doubt he contributes a little to the rebellion, like any other Moslem merchant . . ."

"I'm certain of what I'm saying," said Malavielle. "I've got information."

He was not certain of anything at all, but since he went past Chihani's shop every day, the idea occurred to him to suspect this self-satisfied little fellow who was doing good business and stood in his doorway rubbing his hands together with pleasure.

"Then off we go," said Puydebois. "We'll take him to some quiet spot, beat him up and make him talk. That little bastard earns all his money from European customers."

Arcinade chipped in.

"This first operation must be organized with great care and I must first of all refer it to . . . you know who. Any volunteers?"

"Me," said Puydebois, "and besides, I've got a car."

"Me too," said Maleski.

Malavielle could not do otherwise than volunteer as well.

Adruguez, who had not taken this expedition against the cloth merchant seriously for a single moment, did not even see fit to warn him.

He was indebted to him. Chihani had lent some money to his mother when she became a widow.

Four days later, as Adruguez walked past Chihani's shop, he did not see him in his doorway. He went inside; his son Lucien was at the cashier's desk and he looked rather odd.

"Where's your father?" Adruguez inquired, "there's something I want to ask him."

The young man came up to the student and, after glancing round the shop, whispered in his ear:

"He's disappeared, he hasn't been seen for the last two days. We know it's neither the F.L.N. nor the French police."

"Who can it be, then?"

"He received a telephone call about some business or other. This was the day before yesterday, at ten o'clock in the morning; that's the last we heard of him. If you could possibly find out . . ."

"But how do you know it's not the F.L.N.?"

Lucien Chihani suddenly looked extremely ill at ease.

"Because . . . because there's nothing they could hold against us on any score whatsoever."

It was not until the evening that Adruguez learnt the truth, when he managed to get hold of Arcinade. The little man was quite beside himself. Fate had willed that Chihani should be the treasurer of the whole of the autonomous zone of Algiers, entrusted by the rebels with the handling of funds exceeding a hundred and fifty million francs. Chihani knew most of the F.L.N. leaders and even the whereabouts of some of their hideouts, not to mention the whole politic-administrative organization.

After being dipped head first in a water tank by Puydebois, he had confessed everything.

"We must hand him over to the police at once," Adruguez exclaimed.

Arcinade threw his little arms up in the air:

"Too late. He had a weak heart. Maybe we held him under too long and his heart gave out during the night. Maleski did all he could to revive him."

"Couldn't the information have been invented by the others?"

"No, Chihani told us about an arms dump in his villa in the Parc de Galland. We found twelve submachine-guns there and twenty million francs."

"Twenty million!"

"Yes," said Arcinade, modestly lowering his eyes. "Puydebois took the body off in his car and pitched it into a disused well near his farm."

"I'm going out of my mind," Adruguez said to himself, "I'm living in an absolute mad-house . . . What are you going to do now, Mr. Arcinade?"

"I've seen Colonel Puysange. The paratroops are moving into Algiers in two days' time. He has advised me to have a word with the Intelligence officer of one of the regiments, a certain Captain Boisfeuras. I've arranged to meet him tonight."

The decision to throw a parachute division of four regiments, which in fact amounted to four big battalions—five thousand men at the most—into Algiers had been discussed on 15 January at a dramatic meeting held in the big council chamber at Government House and attended by the members of the civil and military cabinets, the chiefs of police and the representatives of the commander-in-chief and of the Prefect of Algiers.

The Resident Minister was in Paris at the time. He was notified by telephone of the outcome of the meeting and that evening he obtained the President's permission to adopt the measure "with all the risks it might entail." The general commanding the division was forthwith invested "for the duration of the emergency" with full civil and military powers.

The régime was playing its last card in this affair. It threw it down on the table because it was reduced to this extremity, but with ill grace, as though it already realized that by taking such a decision it was condemning itself to death.

Villèle, in his turn, was summoned to Paris. His "boss" asked him what he thought of the paratroops.

"There's a lot of good and a lot of bad in them," he replied. "They're dangerous because they go to any lengths and nothing will hold them back. They've assimilated the Marxist conception of enlisting the masses and, like the Communists, they are beyond the conventional notion of good and evil."

He was then asked for his opinion on the 10th Colonial Parachute Regiment, its C.O. and its officers. He replied:

"It's the regiment which will do best in this new form of

warfare. One could almost say it was formed specifically with that aim in view."

The boss produced a file dealing with the massacre in the *mechtas* of Rahlem.

"We're building up a file on tortures and measures of oppression."

"What about the F.L.N.s?"

"We're not interested in them. What should we do about this file?"

"Wait and see."

"Do you think you can stay on in Algiers without running too many risks."

"Yes. The paratroops will look after me, because they feel the need to convince me, to win me over to their side. They're like the Communists, they don't yet consider me 'irrecuperable.'"

"What chance have they got of succeeding?"

"Hardly any. The paratroops know nothing about the rebellion and its organization or about Algerian mentality. The police and the civil administration will do everything in their power to put a spoke in their wheel; from jealousy, because they can't allow others to succeed where they themselves have failed. The rest of the army is envious of the airborne units and they all fall into rival camps according to whether they wear red, green or blue berets or forage caps."

"Would you be able to meet any 'political heads' of the rebellion?"

"No. You sometimes forget that I come from Algiers and that my mother, brother and sisters might be blown up by a bomb any day."

"When you meddle in politics, it's best to rise above that sort of contingency."

"That's easy, when you've got your whole family living in the Avenue Foch."

"I thought you had fallen out with yours?"

"You can't keep that sort of thing up at a time like this."

"Mr. Michel Esclavier wants to see you."

"He can go and take a running jump at himself!"

"He's a great friend of the firm, and for the first time we've got him in our clutches. He doesn't want his name to be compromised in the business of the *mechtas* of Rahlem on account of his brother-in-law."

"It's not his name!"

"Just as Villèle isn't your name. He is anxious to cover up for Captain Esclavier. You seem rather jumpy and aggressive . . . The air of Algiers perhaps? When are you going back?"

"Tomorrow."

"Go and have a rest, then come and dine with us this evening. It should be quite an interesting party . . ."

"I already know who's going to be there: an academician, three ambassadors, a few past, present and future ministers, some business tycoons and a title or two, an American Communist, an official from a people's democracy who has just chosen freedom, a Dominican, some conscientious objectors, a syndicalist and a film star . . . An interesting party! I'd rather go and join that idiot Pasfeuro."

"What are Pasfeuro's views on the situation?"

"He doesn't have any. He's nothing but a journalist who reacts to every event and passes on his reactions to five hundred thousand readers. An idiotic, devoted hack."

"Are you thinking of leaving us?"

"No, because you're on the winning side."

"You occasionally forget that I'm the one who made you."

"I've served you well."

"If there was any fighting in Algiers, would you go out into the streets?"

"I'd take to my heels, hoping that everything would go up in smoke, that there would be nothing left of the town . . . because, sir, I love Algiers. You once told me that a man who is attached to something, no matter what, a town, a woman, a country or an idea, can never have a great destiny."

"I love my country, my wife and my children."

"A country which is merely a reflection of yourself, your wife because she's nothing but your shadow, your children because you cannot imagine they could ever be different from you."

"I'm also fond of you, Villèle."

"A contradictory emotion but an understandable one. You need a man on this paper who stands up to you, but only up to a certain point, merely as a stimulant, like a cup of coffee."

"One day I'm going to make you a director."

"I certainly hope so."

"Do come and have dinner this evening."

"What's the name of that actress of yours?"

"Evelyn Forain. She's free and unattached."

"On the down grade?"

"On the contrary, a rising star."

"Good, then I'll come."

The boss signed an expense voucher for Villèle. It was for double the amount he was usually given.

Villèle sneered:

"The four hundred thousand francs of Judas."

On 20 January, the chief of staff of the division summoned all the regimental Intelligence officers to Algiers.

Boisfeuras and Marindelle took part in this strange conventicle, at which a dozen officers received orders to clean up Algiers as rapidly as possible, foil the strike, unearth the terrorist networks, take the whole organization of the town in hand and to do it in such a way as "to avoid too many casualties."

"How does a town of seven hundred thousand inhabitants work?" Marindelle naïvely inquired.

"I've no idea," the colonel replied with a shrug of his shoulders. "We were not taught that sort of thing at staff college."

"Have we got any information on the rebellion, the way it's organized, the names of its leaders?" a captain in a red beret inquired.

"Very little. Algiers is established as an autonomous zone, with a civil and military governor whose names we don't know, tribunals, armed groups, a bomb network, committees and even, so they say, hospitals. You will be given a little pamphlet on the rebellion which I've had roneotyped for your benefit, the same pamphlet that's handed out to the foreign journalists who come to Algeria. That's all the police is willing to let us have."

"How will the town be divided up?" Boisfeuras asked.

"In four sectors, one to each regiment. The Tenth, for instance, will have in its sector the west part of the Kasbah on the water-front, including Bab-el-Oued, of course."

There was a burst of laughter, for the whole division knew about Raspéguy's adventure.

"What about orders?" an elderly captain inquired.

"No written orders. Do as you see fit. You'll be covered by the general, you've got his word for this."

"That's pretty meagre, the word of a brigadier-general in a matter of this importance," a young major observed. "What about the Government?"

"It's the Government that has given you the order to occupy Algiers and to act in such a way as to . . ."

"A written order?"

"We're not here to discuss points of procedure but to fight. We've got to do this job irrespective of all legality and conventional method. The strike must be foiled, otherwise the F.L.N. will be able to show U.N. that they're in control of Algiers. If we don't achieve some rapid results against terrorism, the Europeans will come out into the streets, there will be massacres, and once again everyone will say that France is unable to maintain order in Algeria, that she must therefore be relieved, the problem put on an international footing and U.N. observers sent in, which will be tantamount to the victory of the F.L.N."

"It still means," the major went on, "that we're now being asked to do a police job, after being forced to act as schoolmasters and wet-nurses. It's extremely unpleasant."

"Yes, but you've all been trained in operational intelligence. Look upon this Algiers business as a battle that you've got to win at any price, the most important of your battles, even though it isn't normal campaigning. The stakes are even higher than at Dien-Bien-Phu.

"The regiments will enter Algiers after dark on 24 January. The population must wake up in the morning to a new town of which you will be the masters. The surprise, the shock, must be as violent for the Moslems as for the Europeans.

You've got the right to requisition, you can enter any house, by day or by night, without a search warrant."

"Who gives us this right?" Boisfeuras asked.

"You take it upon yourselves. The general will see all unit commanders at midnight on the 24th. Good hunting, gentlemen."

Boisfeuras parted from Marindelle, who had decided to spend the night at Christiane Bellinger's, and went to report to Colonel Puysange who had sent for him.

Boisfeuras was one of the few paratroop officers who was on good terms with him. The man did not inspire the captain with aversion despite his twisted mind, his love of intrigue, his lack of scruples, good faith and honour, his monstrous thirst for power which he could only quench in the shadow of his seniors in rank, which made him sly and at the same time embittered. Boisfeuras felt a certain attraction for people who, in the image of his father, pursued great aims by devious paths, the disciples of Machiavelli, Ignatius Loyola, Lenin and Stalin.

That day Puysange had assumed his expression of a sphinx with half-closed eyes. He was the initiate of great mysteries and was anxious to appear so.

"My dear Captain," he said, "You're being launched on an adventure in which there's every chance of coming to grief. You know the deep regard I feel for Colonel Raspéguy, the finest soldier in the French Army, and for you yourself and your friends . . . So I've decided to come to your assistance by providing you with one of the keys of Algiers, which will enable you, while the others are marking time, to get a move on. This key is called Mr. Arcinade. He'll be waiting for you at eight o'clock this evening at the Aletti bar; he'll be wearing a grey suit and be ostentatiously reading *Nouvelle France*. From now on, my friend, it's up to you!"

After the captain had left, Puysange allowed himself to smile as he drummed with his fingers on the glass slab covering his desk. He had got himself out of an embarrassing situation extremely cleverly, by ridding himself of that madman Arcinade, and at the same time he was settling an old score with Raspéguy by foisting him on to the colonel together with the cloth-merchant's corpse.

After an hour's conversation with Arcinade, Boisfeuras came to the conclusion that the man ought to be locked up and that Puysange, once again, had indulged in a manœuvre for which he could see no rhyme or reason. Arcinade maintained that the principal leader of the rebellion, Si Millial, was living in Algiers under the name of Amar, as well as Abbane, Krim Belkhacem, Ben M'Hidi and Dalhab Saad, his heads of the interior, and that he, Arcinade, had got hold of twenty million francs belonging to the rebels, not to mention the plan of the whole financial organization of the autonomous zone.

He had taken this plan out of his pocket, together with a list of the names of the merchants who were acting as cashiers.

"Money matters," said Arcinade, "have always been the weak point of the F.L.N. Many of the collectors made off with the dough, so Chihani had decided to split the merchants up into groups of ten; having received the subscriptions from nine of them, the collector would then hand the funds over to the tenth, which avoided leaving large sums of money in the hands of young cut-throats . . ."

"If this crackpot story is true . . ." Boisfeuras suddenly reflected.

He pocketed the papers and asked Arcinade to assemble his team of "activists" on the following evening and also to bring the funds he had unearthed with him.

The word "activist" had a genuine revolutionary ring; Arcinade seized on it at once. He had discovered a new word with a certain amount of consistence, on to which he could fasten, as though they were so many coloured balloons, his most extravagant fantasies.

After leaving him, Boisfeuras rang up Inspector Poiston and asked:

"Which branch of the police handles the confidential information in connexion with the rebellion, in other words the rebels' card index system?"

"The D.S.T.," Poiston replied, "but nothing would persuade them to make it available, least of all to you."

"Where's the card index kept?"

"State Police Headquarters, third floor of the Prefecture, Room 417. Is that all you want to know? You'd better be quick about it, the card index is liable to be moved at any moment."

"Thanks for the information, Poiston."

"But I haven't given you any information!"

On the evening of 20 January, Marindelle had called on Christiane Bellinger. He did not have time to let her know he was coming and found her in company with a Moslem friend, whom she introduced to him by the name of Amar. She had known him, she told him, for a long time, for he had been her guide on her first expedition to the Mzab. He had managed to get her into certain Ibadite circles and into Melika, the holy city, and had introduced her to an old *cof* official who had given her valuable information on the Immamate of Tiaret in the tenth century.

Christiane seemed restless and uneasy; she kept launching into technical terms and historical references to make Amar's presence there more plausible.

At first the captain wondered if she slept with this Arab when he was away, but quickly realized this was highly improbable. With Christiane, Marindelle had found peace and happiness, the pleasure of long conversations, and affection too; all that Jeanine had been unable to give him. Christiane was not the sort of woman to conceal from him that she had another liaison if such was the case. She had frankly admitted far more embarrassing things to him, in particular the passion she had once had for one of her young female pupils, of which she had never been completely cured.

Amar seemed a rather odd little chap, with eyes that sparkled with intelligence, a broad forehead above a rather commonplace face, and chubby little hands like a child's.

"I'm very pleased to meet you, Captain," he said in his gentle voice, "Christiane has often spoken to me about you and your experiences out in Indo-China.

"Christiane's a little uneasy because she thinks I'm not quite in order; I once spent five years in prison at Lambèse for . . . let's call it nationalism . . . and there's a rumour that you paratroops are soon going to be masters of Algiers, that you're going to be invested with every power, including therefore the powers of the police.

"Don't worry, though, my growing pains are over and there's nothing that can be held against me now."

"You'll stay to dinner, won't you, Yves?" Christiane asked. "We've all become rather on edge in Algiers. All this shooting in the streets, these bombs and searches . . . You see, I even ask you if you'll stay to dinner when this house is just as much yours as mine! I've asked Amar to move in here. Up to now he's been living in the Kasbah, where he's exposed to all sorts of troubles. He's like me, he has nothing to do with this war."

After dinner Marindelle had a long conversation with Amar.

The uneasy atmosphere had lifted; Christiane had put Mozart's Horn Concerto on the gramophone, which reminded Yves of their first awkward embraces. Amar sat with his eyes closed, puffing at his cigarette.

"How long were you a prisoner?" he asked the captain.

"Four years."

"I was inside for five. What did you think about all that time? What enabled you . . . how shall I put it? . . . to remain yourself?"

"I made the best of it. The Vietminh taught me a number of things . . . among others, that the old world was doomed."

"It's doomed in Algeria just as much as in the Far East. Why are you fighting to preserve it?"

"My friend Boisfeuras would say: 'To give the lie to History.' History is on the side of the Nationalists, as it's on the side of the Communists. Anyone who tries to turn man into a submissive robot is travelling with the flow of History. What I'm fighting against in Algeria is this mechanization of man."

"If I were a rebel, I would say I was fighting for much the same reason. At one time I fought so that we Moslems should become French. It was a great mistake. It's in themselves, in their history, that nations must seek their reasons for existing."

"And when they haven't any history?"

"They must invent it."

"France is an offspring of Rome, but she's not ashamed of it."

"Algeria will also be an offspring of France. But the time has come to divorce, and one of the parents refuses to divorce, in the name of the past, in the name of moral rights, because her settlers cultivated the fallow land, built towns and apartment houses. The Vietminh must have taught you that History is ungrateful."

"The Nationalists are going rather too far to obtain this divorce: outrages, arson, bombs, the massacre of children . . . culminating in Communism. If you think that History . . ."

"The weak have to use whatever weapons are at hand. The bomb may be the weapon of faith, and the just man (it was a Frenchman from Algeria who said this) may be the one who throws the bomb to destroy a tyranny, even if that bomb kills some innocent victims. If you granted us independence, perhaps we would come back to you."

"You're divided among yourselves by different languages and customs; the people of the mountains hate those of the plain . . . If we left you to your own devices, you'd be at each other's throats. You're not a nation."

"I know. I've also said, like Ferhat Abbas: 'I've looked for Algeria in books and cemeteries and I never found her.' But since then you've filled our cemeteries sufficiently to create a history for us."

"Do you believe the Algerian people will benefit from independence?"

"It's too late to think about that. The Algerian people have been too scarred by war, their existence has been too disturbed to turn the clock back at this stage. You yourselves are creating Algeria through this war, by uniting all the races, Berbers, Arabs, Kabyles and Chaouias. The rebels should be almost grateful to you for the violent measures of repression you have taken."

"And the million French?"

"Why do you think that we, who number eight million, should be forced to become like them, which they have always refused to allow in any case?"

"Very soon all men will be alike all over the world."

"What interests us is today and not tomorrow."

"And you, Christiane, what do you think?" Marindelle asked.

"All I want is peace," she said, "and that the masses should have the right to account for themselves."

"It's always a mere handful of men who account for the masses, and nothing great, alas, has ever emerged from peace, neither a nation—as Amar has just pointed out—nor a great work. Peace has always been the reign of mediocrities, and pacifism the bleating of a herd of sheep which allow themselves to be led to the slaughter-house without defending themselves."

"I never pictured you as an apostle of war, Yves, but then I keep forgetting you're an officer."

"You've just said," Amar went on, "that it's always a mere handful of men who account for the masses; that's true. But these men still have to follow the basic direction of the masses. The handful of men that make up the F.L.N., either here or in Cairo, are moving, in my opinion, in that direction."

"The side who'll win, my dear Amar, is the one who'll take the masses in hand: us . . . I'm referring to our own little army out here, which is numerically inferior to the *fellaghas'* or to you."

"I'm not a rebel. Can you see an impractical little intellectual like me at the head of a rebellion? But let's pretend, for the sake of argument; let's assume I am a rebel, a leader of the rebellion."

Amar's eyes sparkled with mischief. He went on:

"There's only one word for me: *Istiqlal,* independence. It's a deep, fine-sounding word and rings in the ears of the poor *fellahin* more loudly than poverty, social security or free medical assistance. We Algerians, steeped as we are in Islam, are in greater need of dreams and dignity than practical care. And you? What word have you got to offer? If it's better than mine, then you've won."

"We haven't any, but we're now going to start thinking seriously of one. Thanks for the advice."

"Not at all, but you won't be able to find it, for this word is unique and belongs to us. Let's go on pretending, if you don't mind, Captain. You're just back from Egypt, I gather?"

"Yes."

"You were beaten by the Egyptians."

"Yet they ran pretty fast at the sight of us, leaving their weapons and sometimes their trousers behind."

"That bunch of runaways, that tin-pot army incapable of using the arms which the Russians had given them, those officers with splendid moustaches who stripped down to their under-pants so as to run all the faster, nevertheless defeated you—you, the paratroops, who are said to be the finest force in the whole of free Europe—and they defeated you by taking to their heels! The whole world rose up against France and England, the Russians and Americans alike, because in Egypt you tried to play a game that is no longer in current usage. You've been allowed to play that game again in Algeria, but it won't last much longer. Maybe within the next few days the general strike will ring the death knoll of French imperialism in the Maghreb."

"If we break that strike . . ."

"We'll start another one later, until the whole world supports us against you."

"Is there no means of coming to an understanding?"

"Get out of the country, embark your soldiers as you did in Port Said. We'll protect your settlers provided they observe our laws."

"Get out of the country, leaving a million hostages behind . . ."

"The four hundred thousand Moslems living in France would also be hostages."

"What régime would you like to establish in Algeria?"

"A democracy which wouldn't have the blemishes of yours, with an infinitely stronger executive body, a collective administration operating within the framework of all the leading elements . . ."

"As I said before, the final outcome is bound to be Communism. Perhaps we are defending an out-of-date system, but your revolution is also out of date; it's middle-class, and if it wants to succeed it will have to employ the only methods which are up to date, that is Communist methods—your collective administration is one example of this—unless your military get the upper hand . . ."

"We shall know how to protect ourselves against our military as well as against your Communists. But let's stop this game. I'm only an unimportant little man called Amar. I'm going up to bed."

"Just one more question: I'd like to know if you're still a Moslem."

"The only aspect of Islam that I've retained is a belief in *baraka*, that beneficent force which is enjoyed by those who have a destiny unlike that of others."

Later on, when they were in bed, Yves Marindelle asked Christiane:

"I'm fascinated by Amar; he plays the role of the rebel leader with absolute conviction, he seems to be abreast of international politics. Where does he come from? What's his background?"

"A police interrogation already?"

"There's no need to be so touchy; I'm merely doing my duty to the best of my ability. I'd like to help Amar if he's in any trouble, provided of course you give me your word that he's not a member of the F.L.N."

"Amar is from the Ksour Mountains and his family, who are extremely rich, send him enough money to live on. He reads and studies a great deal; his only interest in politics is theoretical. But it's quite possible he sympathizes with the F.L.N.

"Yves, let's forget the whole business, Amar and bombs and all the rest of it. Hold me in your arms. I'd be miserable if anything happened to separate us . . ."

It was on the night of the 25th that Boisfeuras managed to get hold of the card index system of the D.S.T. He had had to overcome Raspéguy's scruples, but won him over by maintaining that if the 10th Parachute Regiment did not do the job, another regiment would pull it off and get all the credit. Escorted by a dozen paratroopers in battle dress, he went and "requested" the collaboration of the heads of that police branch, which in fact, acted as an intelligence service.

"If we refuse to let you have this card index system, what will happen?" asked the director of the D.S.T.

"We shall be forced to conclude that you're covering up for the rebels, that you are their accomplices; by the same token we might be forced to regard you as traitors and, in order to avoid any scandal . . ."

He drew his attention to the submachine-guns.

". . . wipe you out."

"I submit in the face of force."

"Please, let's say in the face of reason."

Boisfeuras took the card index system away with him and promptly sent back a letter signed by Raspéguy, thanking the D.S.T. for having so promptly displayed such a spirit of co-operation with the units responsible for the security of Algiers.

On 26 January, when they woke up in the morning, the people of Algiers discovered they were living in a new town.

6

RUE DE LA BOMBE

When Pasfeuro and Villèle tried, in their articles, to explain the paratroops' success in the battle of Algiers and the failure of the strike, the reason they gave was the over-confidence of the F.L.N. Believing that victory was in sight, it had omitted to take the usual precautions of clandestine activity, in particular the security measure of keeping the various cells and networks apart. In evidence they quoted the arrest of Si Millial, followed by that of Ben M'Hidi and the hasty flight of all the members of the C.C.E.* who had settled in Algiers as though the town was already the seat of government of the Algerian Republic.

In actual fact, the audacity with which Boisfeuras had seized the card index system from the D.S.T., his contacts with Arcinade, the burlesque turn which fate had taken and the speed which the paratroops displayed were the factors which determined their success. This speed resulted both from the paratroopers' ignorance of police methods and their habit of always relying on surprise for the successful conduct of an operation.

The 10th Parachute Regiment had established its headquarters at the gates of the Kasbah, in an old Arab palace which had long been abandoned. During the night the paratroops installed a field telephone network and an electric light system operating on a portable power plant. In the middle of the town they therefore still had the impression of campaigning "in the field," of remaining soldiers and not being transformed into policemen.

*Comité de Co-ordination et d'Exécution, the clandestine-rebel government created at the Soumman Congress.

The companies were billeted within the unit perimeter, the men living in the outhouses or in requisitioned villas. Boisfeuras and Marindelle had moved into a big empty room opening on to a gallery on the first floor which encircled the patio. The roof was flaking and the sky-blue paint on the walls had turned a dirty grey as a result of the damp.

In the basement of the old palace, which was used by a neighbouring school as a store-room, they had found some tables, desks and a big blackboard on its wooden stand. Since they did not have a stick of furniture themselves, and their own stores had not yet arrived, they appropriated this makeshift material.

Boisfeuras had brought in the D.S.T. card index system, a massive cabinet of polished wood with a stout lock. He broke it open with his knife; the cabinet contained a hundred and fifty cards.

At three o'clock in the morning Sergeant Bucelier came and brought the two captains some coffee, which they laced with two small bottles of rum they had extracted from some ration boxes.

The power plant droning away below them faltered every now and then and the naked bulbs hanging on their lengths of wire would begin to dim; once or twice they went out altogether.

Because of the cold they wore blue duffel-coats over their uniform. Every now and then, to warm themselves up, they would stride up and down the room slapping their thighs, looking like two Grands Meaulnes against this schoolroom background.

Boisfeuras started going through the cards. The same names kept cropping up: Mohammed abd el Kassem, Ahmed ben Djaouli, Youssef ben Kichrani . . . Most of them had no address; a few of them lived in the streets and lanes of the Kasbah, the shanty-towns of the Clos Salembier or the Ravine of the Femme Sauvage.

The records mentioned that Mohammed abd el Kassem had belonged to the Étoile Nord-Africaine, then to the U.M.D.A.; that Djaouli was a member of the M.T.L.D., after having first joined the P.P.A.

All these initials and descriptive signs of anti-French activity meant nothing to the captain who was completely ignorant of the political history of Algeria.

Marindelle glanced through the pamphlet which had been distributed to the intelligence officers of the parachute units. It was marked in red with the word: "Confidential," and in its content and layout resembled one of those brochures that are handed out to tourists on arrival at an airport or frontier.

Bucelier sat on his bench reading an old magazine which had a fascinating article on the love life of some minor royalty.

At five in the morning, utterly worn out, they fell asleep at their desks, their heads pillowed in their arms.

They were woken up with a start by Raspéguy's voice:

"Nothing has been done about the tap water, I see. Everyone is dozing in this regiment, as though we were at ease."

The colonel was already washed and shaved; he had just doubled round the old palace to get some exercise. He was longing for immediate action but, like his officers, did not know in which direction to expend his energy.

He began thumbing through the card index system, glancing at the names inscribed in regulation block capitals by some conscientious clerk.

"All this stinks of rebels," he said. "Is this what you pinched from the flatfoots, Boisfeuras? Well, when are we going to act on it? You've at least got some addresses. Get moving; the strike's in two days' time and in this box we may have the names of the men who are organizing it."

"There's nothing in it," said Boisfeuras, "but the usual informers' statements, out-of-date political stuff, no reliable evidence, nothing but hearsay . . . So-and-so is *said* to have done this or that . . . So-and-so is *said* to be in such-and-such a place . . ."

Raspéguy flared up impatiently:

"Get to work! These men may have been marked down rightly or wrongly but among them there's bound to be a few who haven't got a clean conscience. We'll round them up and have a little talk . . ."

"The curfew's been lifted for the last two hours, sir,"

Marindelle pointed out, "the birds will have flown and as soon as we round up the first one the Arab grape-vine will sound the alarm. We've got to arrest the whole lot or else none at all. We could let the other regiments have the addresses of the ones living outside our sector."

"To hell with that! We've got the cards and we're going to hang on to them."

"The curfew starts at midnight," Boisfeuras observed. "Five minutes past midnight would be a good time to begin the operation since, legally, our birds will think they're safe from a police search at that hour."

"We must think this out carefully," said Raspéguy. "Bucelier, move over to the blackboard! And take that expression off your face, haven't you ever seen a blackboard before? The captain will read you out the names on the cards and you'll write them down in chalk; Marindelle, you'll pin-point the addresses on the town map. We'll divide the suspects up into areas, one area to each company. We should be able to have the whole lot in the bag in less than half an hour. I want all company commanders to report to me at thirteen hundred hours. I'll go and warn them now in any case and see how they're settling down."

Raspéguy strode off, happy to escape from the schoolroom atmosphere; he had spent most of his childhood playing truant.

He drove through Bab-el-Oued in his Jeep as though he owned the district and hooted loudly as he went past the "*casa de los Martinez.*" A shutter opened and Concha, not yet properly awake, with her young breasts escaping from her blouse, appeared at the window.

"I must try and find a minute or two this afternoon," he reflected.

Then, on second thoughts, he said to himself:

"But why shouldn't I go and visit her at home? I'm the boss of Bab-el-Oued now."

Boisfeuras was busy reading out the cards and Bucelier, who was fed up with this job, did his best to make the chalk grate as he inscribed the names on the blackboard.

"Hallo," Boisfeuras suddenly exclaimed, "here's a good one, filled in on both sides, and with far less hearsay evidence than usual:

> Si Millial, belonging to a big family in the Ksour, university graduate, studied at the Sorbonne, has always taken an active part in nationalist movements. During the war made contacts with the German and Italian services, then, after the landing, with the American O.S.S. Arrested while working for this organization and sentenced to only five years' imprisonment for collaborating with the enemy, the Americans having intervened in his favour.
>
> In 1948, almost immediately after his release, attended the Youth Congress at Prague, where he spoke against the crimes of French colonialism. Later reported in Iraq, Syria, the Lebanon and Cairo.
>
> Still owns a flat in Paris, on the Quai Blériot. Large private income, but insufficient to account for his standard of living and travelling.
>
> Appears to have risen to the leadership of the F.L.N. extremely quickly, although there has been no trace of him since 1 November 1954, the date of the outbreak of the rebellion.

The name Si Millial rang a bell in Boisfeuras's mind. He remembered now: that madman Arcinade had mentioned him.

The captain turned the card over, paused for a moment, then handed it to Marindelle.

"Any interest to you?"

The bottom line was underlined in red:

> When in Algiers, Si Millial is said to live at 12, Passage des Dames, the address of Christiane Bellinger, a lecturer at the Faculty; she is believed to be his mistress.

Marindelle had gone as white as a sheet and the card trembled in his fingers. This card was one of the few which bore an official identity photograph, full and side face, taken in the prison at Lambèse. Amar had hardly changed at all since then, but the set expression gave no hint of his lively intelligence or charm.

Chalk in hand, Bucelier waited impatiently.

"Leave me this card," said Marindelle. "I'll deal with this case myself."

Boisfeuras took up another card and began reading out:

"Arouche, dentist, 117 Rue Michelet . . . M.T.L.D. . . ."

At five minutes past midnight about twenty Jeeps set out from the 10th Regiment barracks and drove straight into the deserted city, each with three armed men on board. Each team had been given a name, an address, and in some cases a photograph.

At the company commanders' meeting Raspéguy had made himself quite clear:

"Cast your nets wide, round them all up, and if any of them don't like it . . ."

He made a sweeping gesture with his hand.

"No rough stuff, mind you, but I don't want any escapes . . ."

With a serious air Esclavier inquired:

"What if they ask to see our search warrants?"

Raspéguy turned on him:

"This is no time for joking. We're at war."

Major de Glatigny had tried to have as little as possible to do with this operation, which he assumed to be necessary but which he found extremely unpleasant on account of its police-like aspect.

Boudin had had to leave for France at short notice, his mother having fallen seriously ill. Glatigny had taken his place and his new duties enabled him to confine himself to billeting and supplies and to communications between the various companies.

As the first Jeeps started off, he was lying on his camp-bed smoking a stubby pipe. He tried to remember if military regulations, which provided for every eventuality, had envisaged that a regiment in a French town, in peace-time, without a state of emergency being proclaimed, without an official proclamation being made by the Government, could be invested with all civil and military powers, including those of every branch of the police . . . No, that had never been foreseen.

The arrival of Marindelle interrupted his thoughts.

"Well, how far have you got?" he inquired, unconsciously emphasizing that he was not whole-heartedly with them.

Marindelle was looking rather odd. His expression aged him, suddenly revealing that he was over thirty and had suffered a great deal of hardship.

"Jacques, I want to ask you a favour."

"Go ahead."

"A personal favour . . . I want you to come with me on a search."

"You can have my Jeep and my driver. I don't see what use I could be myself."

"I want you to come with me to Christiane Bellinger's. That's where Si Millial, one of the leaders of the rebellion, is hiding out."

Glatigny leaped to his feet.

"What! It's not possible! Police rumours . . . You can't trust those chaps an inch. Don't forget, you were listed as a Communist. I only know Christiane slightly, but all the same I could see that she's a very gentle, warm-hearted girl. Now Si Millial is the man who has organized terrorism and brought it to a fine art."

"I've met this Si Millial at her house. He quoted Camus to me—*Les Justes*—and yesterday I shook his hand as though he was a friend—that hand which is responsible for every bomb that's exploded in Algiers. We listened to the gramophone. He likes Mozart as much as I do."

"But Christiane doesn't know his real identity, surely?"

"Yes, she does. She reproaches me for being a policeman, but consents to his massacring women and children. The Communists are quite right to treat their intellectuals like calves, to castrate them and fatten them up, because they know their fine principles will allow them to be as foul as they like, without giving them the slightest twinge of conscience."

"Don't get so worked up about it."

"Jeanine was a dirty little strumpet, and now this girl has led me up the garden path with her humanistic attitude, while the bombs were going off all the time. She's made me an accomplice of the terrorists."

"All right. I'll come with you."

That was another of those eventualities that had not been catered for in army regulations.

Marindelle and Glatigny went to Christiane's house with an escort of two paratroopers. There was a light on in the drawing-room.

Marindelle posted the two men on either side of the entrance, with orders to fire on anyone who tried to come out, then he opened the heavy studded door with the key that Christiane had given him.

The drawing-room light shone out on to the staircase, illuminating the blue-patterned tiles. Christiane's voice called out:

"Is that you, Yves?"

"Yes, I've brought a friend of mine with me. I've told him about Amar and he'd like to meet him."

Amar was sitting in an arm-chair thumbing through an art book which he held in his chubby hands. A glass of whisky stood on a table by his side.

He looked up, smiled at Marindelle and rose to his feet.

"Nice to see you again, Captain."

All of a sudden he noticed that the two officers were in battle order; their caps, which they had not taken off, made their faces leaner than ever; each had a revolver and a knife hanging from his webbing belt.

"I'm glad to find you're still here, Si Millial," said Marindelle. "For a moment I was afraid you might have changed your address."

Amar glanced at the window . . . then at the door. The window had a grille on it; by the door stood the major with his hand on his holster.

He had been caught in the hide-out which he believed to be invulnerable. His lucky star, his *baraka*, had let him down again. But his nimble mind had been trained by long years of clandestine living to react properly to the most unexpected situations.

"It remains to be proved, Captain, that I'm Si Millial"—he glanced at his wrist-watch—"I must remind you that it's now half past twelve and the law forbids you to make a search at this time of night. However, out of regard for Christiane, I am willing to prove my identity."

He sat down again, but Glatigny noticed he kept glancing at the telephone. He locked the drawing-room door from the inside and came and stood by the receiver.

"Yves, I find your manners intolerable, and your friend's too," Christiane exclaimed. "I thought you were too intelligent to be jealous. Si Millial . . ."

She had no time to correct herself and went scarlet in the face.

Si Millial rose to his feet, stretched out his stubby little arms and in a calm, almost amused voice declared:

"I've made two mistakes, gentlemen. I've confided in a woman and I've slept in a bed. Let me telephone my lawyer, Maître Boumendjel, then you can bring in the policemen who are with you."

He moved towards the telephone, but Glatigny intercepted him.

"Those aren't policemen at the door, sir, they're paratroopers; you're not being detained, you're a prisoner of war and you are not entitled to a lawyer."

"What are you going to do with me?"

"Interrogate you," said Marindelle, "until no more bombs go off in Algiers, until the strike has failed, until the last terrorist in your network has been wiped out."

Christiane kept glancing alternately at Marindelle and Si Millial.

"Amar, these men are mad. You told me you belonged to a political party, but surely you, a man of peace, an enemy of violence, have never had anything to do with bombs?"

"My right hand, my dear Christiane, does not know what my left is doing. I make war as best I can. If I were in the position of the French, I wouldn't need bombs, but I've no other means at my disposal. What difference do you see in the pilot who drops cans of napalm on a *mechta* from the safety of his aircraft and a terrorist who places a bomb in the Coq Hardi? The terrorist requires far more courage. You're a woman and too tenderhearted; you are open-minded but without conviction, and besides . . . you're not one of us.

"Gentlemen, I'm at your disposal."

Marindelle summoned one of the paratroopers who came and handcuffed Si Millial. He stretched out his hands and turned to Glatigny.

"I didn't know you handcuffed prisoners of war?"

"Yes, when they're not in uniform."

Marindelle was the last to leave. He collected a suitcase with a few clothes and a briefcase stuffed with documents from Si Millial's room. He put the key down on the chest of drawers, then marched out without a word. Christiane made no attempt to hold him back. Yet she had been pregnant for the last week.

Glatigny and Marindelle brought their prisoner back to the dilapidated old palace which served as their regimental headquarters. They made him sit down on a camp-bed in a corner of Glatigny's office.

The major then settled down in front of his small square table. He unscrewed the cap of his fountain-pen and took out a clean sheet of paper. He felt ill at ease and could not decide how to begin the interrogation.

"Your name?" he asked.

Si Millial appeared indifferent, almost amused, as he sat there with his manacled hands in front of him. This was not his first interrogation, nor the first time he had had handcuffs round his wrists. Like an earnest pupil, he replied:

"Amar Si Millial, but also Ben Larba, Abderhamane . . . I've used at least a dozen names in the last five years. But thousands of Algerians also know me by the name of 'Big Brother.'"

Glatigny put down his pen. He suddenly remembered the Vietminh political commissar who had interrogated him for the first time in the tunnel which served as an air-raid shelter. He had had the same reactions as him: the fountain-pen, the sheet of paper . . .

"Are your handcuffs bothering you, Si Millial?"

"A little."

Glatigny went over and unfastened the steel bracelets which he then tossed into a corner of the room.

"As you can imagine, Si Millial, we don't find this sort of work particularly pleasant. We would much rather be fighting you on equal terms up in the mountains; but you've forced us to wage this sort of war."

"I agree, Major, your conception of military honour must be a bit of a disadvantage in this sort of . . . work, as you call it. Why don't you hand me over to the police?"

Once again Glatigny was reminded of the Vietminh, who had also been sarcastic about military honour, as displayed by colonial officers.

"Stick to the rules of the game, Major. Send for my lawyer, and the police inspector of this area and his constables, to draw up a warrant for my arrest, for we're not in a state of emergency. Then your conscience will be at rest and you will have observed your code of military honour."

"No," Marindelle burst out. "Our *bourgeois* conception of honour, we left behind us in Indo-China in Camp One. We're now out to win, and we're in much too much of a hurry to saddle ourselves with such ridiculous conventions. Our diffidence, our indecision, our pangs of conscience are the best weapons you could use against us; but they won't work any longer."

A long silence ensued; the lamps began to dim, faded away to a few red filaments, and then went out completely. Marindelle spoke up again in a more confident tone:

"Si Millial, we want to know who's responsible for the general strike. We've got to have his name."

"My honour as a soldier prevents me from replying. In our army I've got the rank of colonel."

A rectangle of dark blue sky appeared through a shattered pane in the window. A Jeep drove off outside. The signallers repairing the power plant could be heard cursing the "useless bloody contraption."

The rasping voice of Boisfeuras came to their ears:

"Well, have you got it going? Bring in some lamps."

The harsh light of the hurricane lamp that Boisfeuras was carrying drew closer, casting flickering shadows on the walls; presently, enclosed in this circle of light, they settled by the side of the bed, so close together that they were almost touching.

"Well, Marindelle," Boisfeuras observed, "I see you found the bird in his nest. This is Si Millial, isn't it? Why haven't you tied him up? With all these light failures, he could make a break for it. Have you searched him? What about his luggage?"

Marindelle showed him the briefcase and the suitcase on the table.

"Get up, Si Millial," said Boisfeuras. "Come on, on your feet! Take off your jacket, your tie and belt and shoes. Bucelier, take all this stuff away and put it in my office. Don't forget the briefcase or the suitcase."

Si Millial now looked ridiculous, as he stood there in the shaft of light holding his trousers up with both hands.

"The address of the letter-box? Come on, be quick about it!"

"I'm a colonel, I'm entitled to my rights."

"Out in Malaya, Si Millial, I once picked up a Japanese and stripped him down to his under-pants. He also told me he was a general. I had it inscribed on his tomb: 'General Tokoto Mahuri, War Criminal.'

"Well, are you going to come clean?"

Si Millial was disconcerted by this forthright, brutal treatment; until then he had held all the cards; but Boisfeuras brought him back to the harsh reality of his position: that of a terrorist without any safeguard.

"Are you going to come clean or not?"

He tried to parry the blow by bluffing:

"Everyone knows I've been arrested by now. My letter-box is blown."

"No one knows yet."

"What about the woman?" Boisfeuras suddenly asked, turning to Marindelle. "Did you bring her with you?"

"She won't talk," said Marindelle.

"I'll take your word for it; after all, you know her better

than I do. We've got to act quickly, we've only twenty-four hours left. Your letter-box, Si Millial?"

Glatigny tried to intervene. He was surprised and disturbed by this new side to his character that Boisfeuras was revealing.

"Why not go through his papers and belongings? Perhaps you'll find the address you need among them."

"Leave this to me; I know how to deal with this sort of business. And Si Millial is by no means a beginner; before starting up on his own he had already worked for several intelligence services, it didn't matter which, provided they were operating against us."

He sneered:

"But I suppose you're not too keen on what we've now got to do, Glatigny. Afraid of getting your hands dirty, perhaps? This man in our clutches is an unexpected stroke of luck. Perhaps he'll be able to prevent our having to fight in the streets. But it's no good putting him behind glass, in a shop-window. This is Si Millial, the bomb man. Come on, Marindelle!"

The power plant suddenly started up again and the lights came back. They dragged Si Millial off in his stockinged feet, still holding up his trousers with his hands.

In the "schoolroom" stood Min.

"The address of the letter-box?" Boisfeuras asked once again.

Si Millial slowly shook his head and Min took a step towards him.

Marindelle had opened the window and was taking deep breaths of the cool night air. He knew it had to come to this, that this was the ghastly law of the new type of war. But he had to get accustomed to it, to harden himself and shed all those deeply ingrained, out-of-date notions which make for the greatness of Western man but at the same time prevent him from protecting himself.

"22, Rue de la Bombe," Boisfeuras eventually informed him. "Marindelle, take a couple of Jeeps and drive like hell. We've only an hour left before the curfew ends."

The patio began to overflow with prisoners. Some were in pyjamas under their overcoats and, still half asleep, kept rubbing their eyes. Others with a searchlight trained on them, were lined up against a wall with their hands in the air, expecting to be shot at any moment.

Raspéguy, with a pipe in his mouth, stood leaning over the gallery on the first floor, wondering what he was going to do with this lamentable mob. He longed to escape with his men into the mountains, leave this job to others who were qualified to do it, inhale the damp morning air into his lungs and experience once more the sadness and intense delight of days of victory. Today was only a day of arrests.

"We've got Si Millial, sir," said Marindelle, as he went past him.

"Who the hell's that?"

"A rebel colonel, maybe the chief one."

"Good God, where is he?"

"In Boisfeuras's office."

Raspéguy found Si Millial tied to a bench. Min stood by the side of Boisfeuras's desk, connecting the field telephone up again.

The colonel sat down on the bench next to the prisoner and gave him a light-hearted slap on the thigh.

"So you're Colonel Si Millial, are you?"

Si Millial was beginning to lose heart; he felt as though he was being drawn and quartered so as to reveal his innermost secrets. A breach had been made in his courage and he feared it was bound to grow wider.

He wanted to reply, however, and reassert himself under that label of colonel which was the only thing that was likely to impress these army men. He replied with a certain self-satisfaction.

"Yes, I'm a colonel, because with us there are no generals!"

"A good thing too," Raspéguy replied. "If only we could do without them! What's your command?"

"Thousands of men, hundreds of thousands, an entire nation which is up in arms against the oppressor."

"I see, just as I'm at the head of the entire French Army. But try and be a little more specific."

"I'm the military leader of the Committee of Co-ordination and Execution, our government in other words."

Raspéguy gave a whistle of admiration. He turned to Boisfeuras, who was making notes in red pencil on Si Millial's papers, and asked:

"What did you get out of him?"

"He's a hard nut; he wouldn't give away a thing. Only an address: 22 Rue de la Bombe. I've sent Marindelle over there."

Boisfeuras suddenly leapt to his feet in excitement and tapped the papers:

"There's the whole plan of the strike in here, Si Millial's contacts in France, a letter from the Afro-Asiatic Group written on paper with a U.N. heading . . . We caught him just in time!"

Raspéguy looked at Si Millial with renewed interest.

"Well, I must say, you've got some important connexions!"

Si Millial was shivering with cold. Raspéguy called for Bucelier:

"Give him back his coat and his shoes, and let him have a drink of 'juice.'"

Si Millial put his clothes on and tied up his shoe-laces.

"I also know you, Colonel," he declared, "at least by repute. In their brutality and efficiency, your methods are rather like ours. After Rahlem we wanted to liquidate you, for we considered you infinitely more dangerous than a lot of generals and politicians."

Raspéguy bridled and offered Si Millial a cigarette.

"No, thanks," he said, "I only smoke American tobacco."

Raspéguy sent Bucelier off for a packet of Virginia cigarettes.

"Philip Morris," Si Millial specified, "and a box of matches, I forgot my lighter."

Boisfeuras had stopped examining the papers. He now knew who Si Millial was; the "colonel" was exaggerating his military rank, a courtesy title bestowed on him by the group of Kabyle chieftains after the Soumman meeting. His political power, however, was considerable, especially outside Algeria.

He was on intimate terms with several politicians who had played, and perhaps would soon be playing again, an extremely important role. He had numerous acquaintances among intellectual circles in Paris, also among the Catholics, and even among certain figures reputed to be of the "centre," who represented high finance and heavy industry and who found that the war in Algeria was costing them far too much.

Si Millial would obviously have to be handed over to the judicial authorities. But at a time when certain sections of public opinion were prepared to come to terms with the F.L.N., a prisoner of such importance would immediately be transferred to Paris where his detention would soon be changed to open arrest; he would then be able to renew all his contacts.

Si Millial was *par excellence* a "qualified spokesman." His charm and moderation, which served to conceal his energy and harsh realism (his papers contained ample proof that he was the instigator of terrorism), made him at this moment the most dangerous man in the whole rebellion; he was the one who would be approached if there was a question of coming to terms.

Boisfeuras felt that for the moment he held the fate of Algeria in his hands. Destiny was giving him the dice to throw, but he would not have them in his hand much longer.

In a few hours his prisoner would be taken away from him; he had to act quickly. Si Millial would not talk, would not tell him anything more than he had found in his papers; he decided he would have to disappear.

Boisfeuras already saw Raspéguy in that attitude which all his officers knew only too well, making a naïf and effective show of his charm. A soldier of fortune, he had inherited from the smuggler-peasants of his Basque mountains the taste for extravagant gestures occasionally accompanied by somewhat sordid bargaining. To him Si Millial was a prize which was well worth its ransom of glory, like a Spanish infanta captured by a Barbary pirate. He would surrender his prisoner in exchange for honours and Press publicity and would keep a jealous eye on his state of health.

Boisfeuras, brought up among realists like the Chinese, was blind to the beauty of a gesture and had no professional ambition. As far as he was concerned, Si Millial was merely part of the over-all picture he had painted for himself of the destiny of France. In the eyes of this *émigré* Frenchman, Algeria was the ball and chain which kept France fettered to her role of a great power and obliged her to behave with more nobility and generosity than a nation of complacent *bourgeois* shopkeepers like Switzerland.

Si Millial was in a position to give France an opportunity of ridding herself of her ball and chain; he could be the man of independence. That was why Boisfeuras decided he would have to die.

"We'll have to keep Si Millial's arrest a secret, sir," he told Raspéguy. "There's still quite a lot I want to ask him."

"Of course! Of course! Just imagine how the other regiments are going to take this; Bigeard will have a stroke and 'Prosper' won't get over it in a hurry. Give him anything he wants; take good care of him. I'm counting on you."

He shook hands with Si Millial and gave him a hearty slap on the back.

"See you soon; we must have a long talk together some day. There'll be plenty of time."

Raspéguy stalked out, rubbing his hands together.

"You've still got some questions to ask me, Captain Boisfeuras?" Si Millial inquired.

"No, no more questions."

Si Millial then realized that he was going to die. This captain who was looking at him, with his head propped up in his hands, had decided his fate.

In his place he would have done the same and, for a few moments, he felt a strange respect for him, for, of all these officers, he was the closest to himself. Boisfeuras belonged to his own just and efficient world, just with a justice which thinks nothing of men being slaughtered, women being raped or farms being burnt to the ground. At the same time Si Millial pitied that other self of his, which would continue to live without friends, without women, in the chilly solitude of men who make and unmake history.

Si Millial suddenly felt utterly weary; he hoped it would be over quickly and painlessly. He regretted all that he had never known, all that was the common lot of other men: jasmine, women's affection, the laughter of children, the click of checkers in a Moorish café smelling of mint.

Boisfeuras said something in Chinese to Min—just a few brief words—then turned to Si Millial:

"Min will show you to your cell. Good-bye, Si Millial."

"Good-bye, Captain Boisfeuras. Your nights are going to be very long from now on . . . as mine have been."

Min took Si Millial by the arm and escorted him outside. Boisfeuras looked at his watch: seven o'clock in the morning. Marindelle was not yet back: he could sleep for an hour.

He lay down on a bench and fell sound asleep at once.

Marindelle came back from 22 Rue de la Bombe with one male prisoner and three females: a whore by the name of Fatimah, an old hag, a woman with hennaed hands called Zoullika, and her daughter Aicha. More difficult to handle than an angry cat, this Aicha had insulted, bitten and scratched the soldiers escorting her. Oddly enough, for a Kasbah girl, she was wearing European clothes; her dress was simple, elegant and in good taste; she wore none of that heavy silver jewellery affected by women of the people, but only a small gold wrist-watch.

The man was Youssef the Knife, with his fingers loaded with heavy rings. An old offender, he had come quietly; but he protested violently when he was separated from Aicha to whom he claimed to be engaged.

Marindelle had found nothing in the Rue de la Bombe except a few pamphlets, two knives which at a pinch could be considered lethal weapons, and a miniature F.L.N. flag which could be found in every other house in the Kasbah.

He woke Boisfeuras who was still asleep on his bench.

"A wild-goose chase," he said. "At Si Millial's address I picked up a pimp, his old beldame of a mother, and a couple of tarts. Nothing else. One of the tarts, the youngest, at least has the advantage of being extremely pretty."

"Let's begin with her, then," said Boisfeuras somewhat wearily.

A big paratrooper with a moustache dragged Aicha into the office.

"Captain," she said to Boisfeuras, "your men have been trying to rape me in the courtyard outside."

The paratrooper shrugged his shoulders:

"She planted her claws in my cheek, so I gave her a good slap. She's a holy terror, this bird!"

"Well," Aicha inquired, "are you going to let me go? I haven't done anything."

Boisfeuras considered her for a moment. The way she had immediately addressed him as "Captain" revealed that she was a well-bred woman who was used to the society of officers.

He seized her by the arm and took off her wrist-watch.

"I'll make you a present of it," she said scornfully, "but please let me go."

Boisfeuras examined the gold watch-case.

"Since when do little tarts from the Kasbah have Cartier watches?"

Aicha went scarlet in the face.

"I found it."

"Good heavens," Marindelle exclaimed, "she was having me on! Bucelier, bring this lady's fiancé in."

Youssef sauntered up to the deck, with a broad grin on his face, looking very pleased with himself.

"Take your fiancée in your arms," Marindelle told him, "and give her a kiss."

The two captains watched Aicha twist away from him in disgust as the pimp brought his lips to her mouth.

"That'll do," said Boisfeuras.

Youssef was taken away.

"Right. Now we've had enough of your nonsense. What's your name?"

"Aicha."

"Where do you live?"

"22 Rue de la Bombe."

"Do you know Si Millial?"

"Which Si Millial?" she retorted arrogantly, her eyes glinting with hatred, her lips quivering.

Boisfeuras seized her by the shoulders and started to shake her.

"Leave me alone," she screamed, "or I'll complain to your superior officer, Major Jacques de Glatigny. He's a friend of mine."

"Marindelle, go and fetch Glatigny."

The major arrived a few minutes later. He still had some lather below one ear; he had been shaving and had just had time to wipe his face. He caught sight of Aicha.

"What on earth are you doing here?"

"Ask the captain."

"I found her in the Rue de la Bombe," said Marindelle, "at the address of Si Millial's letter-box. Do you know this bird?"

"Yes."

"You'd better deal with her, then," said Boisfeuras, "she's a dirty little liar. She was trying to pass herself off as a Kasbah girl."

"She's a third-year medical student," Glatigny quietly observed. "Aicha, come into my office."

"Don't let her get away with it, Glatigny, I'm certain she knows Si Millial."

Aicha followed the major out of the room, after casting a defiant glance at Boisfeuras.

"I never knew Glatigny had connexions of that sort," Marindelle observed dreamily.

Boisfeuras sneered:

"Now he's in it up to the neck! None of us will be able to get off until we're on an equal footing with the *fellaghas*, as covered with mud and blood as they are. Then we shall be able to fight them; and in the process we'll lose our souls, if we really have souls, so that back in France some jokers can go on airing their views with a clean conscience.

"Bring that pimp of a Youssef here, Marindelle; I'm certain we'll be able to talk turkey with him."

"Sit down, Aicha," said Glatigny. "I think there must be some mistake; a girl from a big tent doesn't get involved with a certain class of people. What were you doing in the Kasbah?"

"I live there; you saw me home there youself. Are you going to torture me to make me confess?"

"I beg your pardon?"

"To make me confess that I know Si Millial?"

"Don't talk rubbish. I'll see that you're escorted home presently . . . as soon as you've given me your real address."

"22 Rue de la Bombe."

Bucelier knocked at the door and came in.

"The young lady," he said, "forgot her watch. Seems this little job is worth hundreds of thousands of francs, sir. At least, that's what Captain Boisfeuras says."

He clicked his heels and went out. Glatigny handed the watch back to Aicha who put it back on her wrist.

"If it hadn't been for you," she said, "that Captain Boisfeuras would have stolen it from me."

"I very much doubt it. He's extremely rich, you know, but he's not interested in money; he prefers to be out here with us. Come along now, Aicha, let's get this over. Your address?"

"22 Rue de la Bombe."

"I know that a girl like you can't possibly be involved in all these bomb outrages and terrorism, with a lot of fanatics, pimps and drug-addicts."

"Naturally, because a man like you, Major de Glatigny, can't imagine using a knife or a bomb."

"In 1943, in Savoie, I killed a Gestapo colonel, in his bed and with a knife. It was an unpleasant experience, but I did it. Women shouldn't have any part to play in war."

"What about Joan of Arc? If she had known about bombs, she would have used them against the English."

Aicha looked lovelier than ever to the major, even more attractive than when he had first met her: a luscious fruit which he would have liked to cut open to quench his thirst. He could not take his eyes off the young breasts which swelled beneath her blouse. He remembered the softness of her skin.

He got up, came and sat down beside her on the camp-bed and took her arm; he felt he was on fire.

"Come along now, Aicha, be reasonable and let's have done with this. At least tell me your name; our job's unpleasant enough as it is."

"Then why don't you leave us and go home?"

"This is our home, just as much as it is yours. If you like, we could have dinner together this evening and forget all this unpleasantness. Now then, your name and address."

"Captain Boisfeuras wanted to find out if I knew Si Millial

and, to do so, he would have tortured me. What you want is to sleep with me in order to ask me afterwards if I know Si Millial. The secrets of the bedchamber . . . a well-known police method!"

Anger brought the blood rushing to Glatigny's cheeks.

"I'm an army officer, not a policeman. I'm married, a Catholic, and faithful to my wife. I only want to get you out of this mess in which your thoughtlessness and silly pride have landed you."

"I live with a friend, a European woman, Christiane Bellinger, a lecturer at the Algiers Faculty. You can ring her up if you like."

Glatigny rose to his feet. He had gone as white as a sheet.

"We arrested Si Millial at Christiane Bellinger's last night. He would only have given the address of this hide-out to someone utterly reliable and close to him."

Boisfeuras came in.

"Youssef the Knife came clean at once," he said, "an old habit with him. He's just an underling, but not her. Your little girl-friend, Glatigny, is one of the chief organizers of terrorism in Algiers. I think you'd better hand her back to me; this is getting serious, she must certainly know the whereabouts of the bomb dumps and workshops. You're liable to get your hands dirty; mine already are . . ."

Aicha felt overwhelmed with fear each time the captain with the rasping voice came near her. He frightened her even more than Youssef; there was nothing to Youssef, he simply wanted to sleep with her; but in Boisfeuras Aicha felt she inspired nothing but a purely professional interest.

With a look of entreaty in her eyes she turned to the major:

"No, I'm staying with you!"

"Boisfeuras," said the major, "I've been behaving like a fool. I think it would be better if you took her off my hands."

Aicha became furious:

"Major de Glatigny leaves the dirty work he daren't do himself to others; but all the same he was the one who helped me carry my bag and got me through the road-blocks."

She suddenly realized, but too late, that she had gone much too far.

"What were you carrying in that bag?" the major asked in a toneless voice.

He slapped her across the face twice and repeated the question:

"What were you carrying in that bag?"

"Detonators."

Boisfeuras gave a sarcastic chuckle:

"I see you can manage all right. I'll leave her to you."

He strode off, swinging his shoulders slightly. Glatigny felt he was beginning to hate him for that chuckle of his.

Aicha crouched on the camp-bed, weeping. Her rage was mingled with a strange feeling of impotence, the same sensation she had felt when Youssef had embraced her in the house in the Rue de la Bombe before Amar intervened.

She cast a sidelong glance at the major who was sitting back in his chair; she hated him as she had never hated a man before and hoped he would strike her again, that he would cease being that puppet with the bloodless face, mechanical gestures and toneless voice who was saying:

"Go on. Who were the detonators for?"

She insulted him first in French and then in Arabic and, since he still did not react, she scrambled to her feet and came and spat in his face.

He struck her in the face and the gold signet-ring on his finger scored her cheek. She fastened her claws into him and they tumbled on to the narrow bed together.

For the first time Glatigny experienced the fury of desire, a raging torrent which swept away his beliefs, his honour and his faith like so many floating corpses.

The girl went on struggling but more and more feebly. He crushed his mouth against her burning lips, against her cheek streaked with blood and tears. He squeezed her swelling breasts and her thighs now opening to receive him.

Aicha gave a loud scream and clumsily returned his kisses.

"I love you and hate you," she said to him a little later on. "You've raped me and I've given myself to you; you are my master and I shall kill you; you hurt me terribly and I want you to start all over again."

"I've got to go off to a meeting," he said, "I'll be back soon."

"Don't go. I'll tell you everything I know, everything, the whereabouts of the bomb dump and the address of Khadder the Vertebra who makes them."

"I'll get back as soon as I can."

"Don't go. The dump is in the Rue de la Bombe. It's behind a cupboard . . ."

"Draw me a plan."

She got up half naked and made a rough sketch of the dump on a clean sheet of paper.

He took her again, in a welter of torn clothing, blood and tears, and to his horror he heard himself saying he loved her.

It was then she told him her name: Aicha ben Mahmoudi ben Tletla, the daughter of Caid Tletla, a former lieutenant-colonel in the French Army, the sister of Captain Mahmoudi who had been taken prisoner by the Vietminh in Indo-China. It was her brother who, on his return, had bought her the watch.

Glatigny went back into the "schoolroom." He flung the sketch of the bomb dump down on Boisfeuras's desk.

"Send some men over. The bombs are there."

"What shall we do with the girl?"

"Aicha's never planted a bomb herself, and she's Mahmoudi's sister."

"Have you known this for long?"

"No, I've only just found out, but the job was already done."

"What if you had known?"

"It wouldn't have altered a thing. I can't help thinking I must have been born with that girl in my blood. I'm an utter swine."

"Like me."

"Far worse. I see myself as a dirty little bastard who can only think of his loins."

"My father used to say that in love one must stake one's soul in the same way as one stakes one's life in war, and if he had known about the war we're fighting now, he would have added: one's honour."

"I've lost my honour and I've lost my soul, but at least it might lead to something! Go and collect the bombs. There are twenty-seven all ready to be planted."

As he went out Glatigny ran into Dia who was wandering about with his hands in his pockets.

"There are some things here I don't like," he said in his deep voice. "It's not very pretty, men in their shirt-tails with their hands in the air, and women in tears."

"And bombs exploding, is that pretty?"

"No, that isn't pretty either. I'd like to get away from here."

"Look, Dia. I want to make a confession."

"There are plenty of priests in Algiers, in white robes, in black robes, and even some in uniform who swear like troopers and dream of a holy war."

"You're the only one who will understand, Dia."

"Come along to the infirmary; I've got some brandy there; come and make your confession to the bottle."

Seated on a packing-case which had not yet been opened, in a sort of cellar lit by a large skylight enclosed in a grille, Jacques de Glatigny described what had just happened to him.

"Dia, in my dishonour I experienced the greatest pleasure in my life."

"Only pleasure?"

"No, the greatest joy as well. All the time I was wallowing in horror, fanfares were sounding in my head. All my past life collapsed like a wooden fence devoured by termites. There was nothing left but this girl next to me. A huge void, a desert, and this girl held tight in my arms, this monstrous love . . ."

"Have another drink. What about her?"

"Everything collapsed for her as well: the Front, the independence of Algeria . . . she betrayed her friends to me, she's in the same desert as I am."

"You know, that's not a bad story! It's rather like what happened to Esclavier in the hospital at Camp One. All this hatred, the screams of women and children disembowelled by the bombs, and of men being killed and tortured, the even greater despair experienced by the torturers, all this has once again given birth to love."

"A strange sort of love, Dia, which reeks of fire and brimstone, which reminds me of some obscene stories I once read in my adolescence . . ."

"No, get that idea out of your head. Don't you see that this is yet another victory for life, life in all its sexual greatness and serenity, which doesn't give a damn for man's beastliness, thoughtlessness or stupidity . . ."

"I happen to be married."

"Which doesn't give a damn if a man is married or fights his fellow man, which doesn't give a damn for causes and independence, races and hatred, because the destiny of man is love and all the rest is worthless.

"I don't care for cold, calculating minds, but when something so magnificently spontaneous as your adventure occurs, then I'm reassured and I drink and I feel warm and comfortable."

"But Aicha is Mahmoudi's sister!"

"All the better! When you and Mahmoudi were slogging side by side along the tracks of the Haute Région, that merry, openhearted god already knew that one day he would bind you a little closer together by a virgin's tears. I think he loves us all, that round-bellied god, who is always willing to stretch out a helping hand to prevent us from sinking into despair. By the way, I've just had a letter from Lescure. He's marrying the cousin who used to tease him so much. He must have hooked her like a fine silver fish with a little tune on his flute."

"Dia, you're the only one who can save us. This girl, Aicha, I want you to look after her, because of Mahmoudi and because of me. We can't ever release her now."

"Because she wouldn't want it, and nor would you."

"Maybe. She's a third-year medical student."

"I'll take her on. I'll make her look after her own people, and like that, by being good and generous with them, she'll forget that, for having earned the right to love, she was forced to be disloyal to them. Then I'll tell her about Mahmoudi and his friend Merle, and she'll understand that since he was one of us, she is as well. Go and fetch her. This evening we'll all eat together and she'll have the place of honour. She's entitled to it; she's Mahmoudi's sister."

"Will Boisfeuras be coming?"

"I don't think so; he needs to be alone, all alone to do what he has to do or thinks that he has to do. He'll be leaving us soon, and so will Marindelle if he goes on feeling so miserable."

The briefing that evening at divisional headquarters was a triumph for Colonel Raspéguy. He had discovered a dump of twenty-seven bombs, arrested one of the leaders of the rebellion and captured all his documents.

The general wanted Si Millial transferred forthwith to G.H.Q. Raspéguy telephoned to Boisfeuras:

"The general wants Si Millial to be brought here at once; I want our bird here within the next ten minutes. See that he's well guarded."

"It's too late, sir."

"What? Did he get away?"

"No, he's just cut his wrists in his cell with a piece of glass."

"Couldn't you have stopped him?"

"Min was meant to be keeping an eye on him."

"A pity," said the general, "they would have been glad to see him in Paris. What about the strike, Raspéguy?"

"I think Boisfeuras has a plan in mind."

"He sometimes has extremely odd plans in mind, that Boisfeuras of yours!"

Since his return Esclavier had spent almost every night with Isabelle in a small flat in the Bouzareah which she had borrowed from a girl-friend. He was just going off to join her there, when Boisfeuras rang him up:

"Among the men you rounded up," he asked, "is there anyone called Arouche, a dentist, 117 Rue Michelet?"

"Yes, but of no interest to us; I'm planning to release him tomorrow morning, with apologies: a completely assimilated Kabyle, who studied in France and whose clients are all European."

"Arouche is responsible for the bomb network of Algiers. At least all the information that's just this moment come in leads me to think so. Tomorrow morning, at the moment the general strike is declared, fifteen bombs are due to go off in various European shops in the town. These bombs mustn't go off whatever happens, and Arouche knows exactly where they've been planted."

"Well, what shall I do with him? Bring him along to you?"

"No, I've got the strike to attend to; you'll have to deal with him yourself."

"How?"

"That's your business."

Esclavier repeated his question:

"How?"

And his knuckles turned white as his grip tightened on the telephone.

Boisfeuras had rung off.

In the villa where Esclavier was living, there was no heating and it was bitterly cold. He lit a cigarette and coughed; he had been smoking a lot to allay the anxiety amounting almost to fear which he had felt ever since the first Jeeps of his company had driven off to round up the suspects.

Esclavier shouted for a runner and told him to bring in Arouche.

He had installed his office in the small drawing-room of the villa. There were seats and arm-chairs upholstered in white, an upright piano and, on the chimney-piece opposite, an ornamental brass clock supported by dolphins. Its hands now pointed to a quarter past nine.

There had been the same sort of clock at Rennes, in the office of the Gestapo chief, with the same ridiculous design, the same gilt face, the same Roman figure in black. Perhaps it was this clock which made Esclavier feel so apprehensive.

Arouche was pushed into the room by the runner. He had a thin, pale face, deep-set eyes, and a camel-hair overcoat over his clothes. He had not had time to put on a tie, but had buttoned up his shirt collar.

When he talked his lips curled back, revealing snow-white teeth as pointed as those of certain primitive African tribes.

"So you've decided to release me at last, Captain. That won't stop me bringing a charge against your arbitrary conduct."

"Where are the bombs, Arouche?"

"*Doctor* Arouche. What did you say?"

Esclavier noticed this reaction of vanity but reminded himself that many dentists in France had it as well.

"The fifteen bombs which are due to go off at nine o'clock tomorrow morning in the European shops which will have just opened up for the day, where are they?"

Arouche gave a little start as though he had been pricked, then pulled himself together.

"You must be confusing me with someone else. There are many Arouches in Kabylie."

"But only one Arouche who's a dentist at 117 Rue Michelet."

The telephone rang. It was Boisfeuras again.

"This time," he said, "it's certain. He's a short little fellow, narrow face, he has a scar on his jaw, the little finger of his left hand is deformed; thirty years old at the most."

"That's him all right."

"While you're about it, ask him about a certain Khadder the Vertebra. And don't forget: the bombs are due to go off tomorrow morning, just when all the clients who haven't been able to shop at their usual retailers' are pouring into the food departments of the Prisunic and Monoprix. You must make him tell you in which shops they've been planted and for what time they've been set. As soon as we have the information, I'll send along four bomb disposal squads; they're already standing by."

Esclavier put down the receiver.

"Arouche, some squads are standing by to dispose of the bombs; out with it now, and be quick about it. After that we'll talk about a certain Khadder the Vertebra."

Arouche had risen to his feet and was twisting his hands to prevent himself from shouting out his hatred in the paratrooper's face.

"Have you finished squirming about?" the captain asked him drily. "I'm in a hurry."

Arouche sneered:

"A girl waiting for you?"

"Exactly, a woman."

"While Algeria is going up in flames, that's all you can think about—fornicating like a pig. But tomorrow, the whole of Algiers is going up, and maybe your girl-friend with it."

Esclavier had to make an effort to master his anger and not strike the little dentist in the face.

"The bombs?"

"No. I'm the only one who knows. You may as well go off and join her now. Your bomb disposal squads can spend all night searching the shops of Algiers, they won't find a thing. You can kill me, torture me, I'll die with pleasure in your hands, because tomorrow . . ."

"I could easily make you talk . . ."

The clock struck ten, emitting a faint tinkling sound like an old music box.

". . . But I shan't make you, Doctor Arouche; it's against all my principles. You have your reasons for fighting, I have mine, but that has nothing to do with bombs which go off and kill women and children.

"Once you have talked, I'll hand you over to the police; you can then settle matters with them, but you can call your lawyer beforehand and I'll see to it personally that nothing irregular occurs."

"No."

Arouche ran his fingers over his scar in the hope that it would revive the hatred that gave him his strength. He remembered the punch in the face which had sent him flying and the subsequent kick that had broken his jaw.

It was on his return from Paris. Back there, there had been a few girls in his life but he had never been able to keep them for long; for there came a day when he could not help calling them whores—in many cases they were whores, but they didn't like being reminded of the fact.

In Paris he used to see a lot of the French students from Algeria, who treated him more or less as one of themselves. He had changed his Moslem name of Ahmad to Pierre; were not his ancestors Christians at the time of Saint Augustine?

Algerines together, they formed a united front against the *Frangaouis*, whose lack of virility they derided—this enabled them to forget their own idleness.

On his return to Algiers Arouche had moved into a European quarter of the town; he had found his old Paris friends again but did not realize their relationship was now on a different footing.

One evening, after a professional dinner, he had gone out with them to a night-club; he had then—not without encouragement—made a rather too obvious pass at the sister of one of his friends. The friend had promptly flown off the handle:

"What the hell does this nigger think he's doing? He's forgetting himself!"

He had then been beaten up in public and thrown out. Ever since that day hatred had replaced every other sentiment in his heart.

He knew he would not talk. He could see that the paratrooper, in spite of his lean, handsome face, was a weakling, full of contradictions, a phrase-spinning type.

Let him go on spinning phrases to his heart's content! In the meantime the minutes were ticking by. The captain would never find the bombs which were cunningly concealed in packing-cases containing tinned food and had already been planted in the shops thanks to the co-operation of a delivery boy. They were timed to go off at half past nine.

Esclavier weighed his words carefully, racking his brains to find some argument based on reason and humanity which might appeal to this motionless, unshakable body sitting in the white-upholstered arm-chair.

In spite of himself, all he could produce were his father's threadbare theories on non-violence. His words sounded false, his phrases trailed away into the void, for they found no echo.

The captain noticed the imperceptible gesture Arouche made to glance at the clock and his expression of relief when it struck eleven; all he wanted was to gain time.

Esclavier tried another tack.

"Arouche," he said all of a sudden, and in a dry tone of voice, "I was tortured once myself. I know what it's like, and I know that one talks, for everyone talks in the end . . ."

And, while Arouche kept his eyes on the clock, he embarked on this confession which was so painful to him that the sweat broke out on his forehead and he found himself panting for breath:

"It was in 1943, Arouche. I was dropping for the third time into the occupied zone; the Germans were waiting for me down below. Before I could even get out of my parachute harness and draw my revolver, I was caught, with a pair of handcuffs round my wrists."

Arouche glanced at him, with an almost amused expression, then switched his gaze back to the clock.

"It's not so much the beating-up that's hard to bear, Arouche; it's the waiting for it and not knowing what the pain will be like. The Gestapo man was dressed in black; he had a smooth, shiny face and wore steel-rimmed spectacles. He kept looking at his hands pensively, as though they reminded him of some unpleasant memory. It wasn't he who frightened me, but something behind him, a clock like this one here. What frightened me was what was going to happen.

"He asked me who I was and what rank I held; he knew everything about my mission, which was to blow up the powerhouse of a factory, but what interested him far more was the names of the people I had to warn in case of an accident, the recovery team . . . 'To some extent or other,' he told me, 'everyone talks over here; and the proof is that we've got you in our hands. I'll give you half an hour to think it over.'

"After that, Arouche, I kept watching the clock, as you're watching it now, with its chubby Tritons blowing on their trumpets and the minute-hand starting on its course. Would you like a cigarette, Arouche? The German offered me one before leaving me alone in the room.

"The instructions we had been given in London were quite simple: to hold our tongue long enough for the networks to be able to take the necessary security measures. This length of time was never precisely defined.

"So, as I watched the clock, I kept trying to persuade myself that I wouldn't talk, that I would rather be mutilated for life than admit that if anything misfired I was to go to a certain bookshop in the Rue Guynemer at Vannes and ask for the rare edition that Mr. Duval had ordered.

"I pictured the owner of the bookshop as an old white-haired lady who had nothing more to expect out of life . . . whereas I was only twenty years old. How old are you, Arouche?"

Arouche shrugged his shoulders without replying, unable to take his eyes off the clock.

"The German displayed no emotion, neither hatred nor pity, nor even a trace of interest. He actually told me:

"'I don't think the information you've got will have the slightest effect on the eventual outcome of the war, whichever side wins, but what you'll suffer will mark you for the rest of your life.'

"He came back half an hour later; he sat down at his desk and, like the good, conscientious official that he was, he checked his wrist-watch by the clock."

Automatically Esclavier pushed back his cuff and likewise checked his wrist-watch by the clock. It was now a quarter to twelve.

"Then the German pressed a bell and three men in civilian clothes came in; one of them was a Frenchman. They dragged me out of the room."

Esclavier had risen to his feet and was pacing round the Kabyle.

"It's the first blow that hurts. It takes you by surprise, you're not expecting it, you think it won't be possible to stand another. Then, just as you're beginning to persuade yourself that the pain is just bearable, the second blow comes down and shatters your resistance, all the little illusions you've so carefully built up.

"It's then you begin waiting for the third blow, which does not come right away; your wincing, throbbing flesh prays to get it over as quickly as possible until the moment comes when it begins to hope that there won't be a third blow, and that's the very moment it comes.

"And this goes on, Arouche, hour after hour, with men who have got all the time in the world, who stop every now and then for a drink or a snack. You tell yourself: now they're going to leave me in peace for ten minutes, for a quarter of an hour. But suddenly one of them gets up and gives you another wallop, still chewing on a piece of sausage he has just popped into his mouth.

"I held out, Arouche, up to the moment they began thumping me over the head with a sock filled with sand; I felt as though my skull was coming apart, that my brain was being bared: a wretched, quivering jelly.

"I gave them the address of the bookshop in the Rue Guynemer; I told them everything I knew. After the war I spent six months on garrison duty not far from Vannes, in the Meucon camp. I never dared go near the Rue Guynemer or ask about the bookshop there. What if the old lady had been a young girl of twenty!

"You know why I didn't hold out, Arouche? For the same reasons that you're going to talk. I didn't have a sufficient motive, nothing but vague ideas and theories: peace among nations, anti-Fascism, high principles and all that sort of nonsense, meanwhile taking care not to catch a cold in the head and to avoid sitting in a draught; I also felt a certain amount of resentment and scorn for my father. But that's not enough to turn a man into a martyr.

"All you've got, Arouche, is hatred, and what a petty little hatred it is! You've never been able to have the sort of girl you wanted—a European girl—isn't that it? I realized that just now. That's not a good enough reason to blow up a whole town and massacre women and children.

"You won't hold out; and you'll know as I do what it feels like to be a coward and to be saddled with that cowardice all your life.

"Come on now: where are the bombs?"

Arouche still kept silent, but Esclavier could now see how fragile the dentist's courage and resolution were. Out in Indo-China he had once known a Viet who had refused to talk. He had had the impression that the man had withdrawn into himself and was sealed off by a trapdoor in some mysterious refuge where he no longer felt, heard or saw a thing.

Arouche did not have such a refuge. The twelve strokes of midnight issued with a gentle tinkling sound from the clock.

"Arouche, the bombs?"

Once again Esclavier felt like a coward because he was incapable of making another man go through what he had been through himself. He would have to ask Bordier and Malfaison to deal with the dentist.

The telephone rang—no doubt Boisfeuras was getting impatient. It was Isabelle, with a sob in her voice:

"Philippe, they've killed grandfather and his three servants, set fire to the farm and destroyed the vines. I want to get out there at once, but because of the curfew . . . Oh, Philippe!"

She burst into tears. After a short silence she went on:

"He was so fond of them! Come and join me as soon as you can. Yes, I'll be waiting at the Bouzareah."

It was not until dawn that Esclavier reached his mistress's flat. The news of the murder of old Pélissier had made him see red, and what he dreaded most of all he had managed to accomplish all by himself, without having to appeal to his N.C.O.s.

By the time the dentist was carried off on a stretcher, in the early hours of the morning, he had confessed everything; none of the fifteen bombs went off.

But when Philippe tried to make love to Isabelle, he found he was incapable. The young woman had been too involved in his mind with the ghastly hours he had just spent and a little of that horror still clung to her. And since there was no one else he loved or desired, he suddenly discovered the inferno of love in which all those who cannot quench their desire have to live.

Philippe stroked Isabelle's hair and went and lay down on the other bed; he felt he wanted to die.

The general strike broke out on 28 January. During the morning it was almost universal. Following the instructions of Radio Tunis, the inhabitants of the Arab quarters who had laid in enough foodstocks for a week did not set foot outside. The streets were empty, the shops closed.

The Zouaves strutted about the Kasbah in full-dress uniform and distributed sweets to the children whose numbers gradually increased until they swarmed around the soldiers like flies. Other units were busy driving these children off to school in trucks.

A large number of Moslem school-teachers followed them; out of a sense of solidarity or because they were frightened, a few Frenchmen went on strike. They were replaced by soldiers and were meanwhile set to work emptying the garbage cans.

The 10th Parachute Regiment was entrusted with the task of opening up the shops. Its squads hooked the metal shutters on to the rear of their trucks and tore them down bodily. Some of these shops were looted, but none of the owners came and protested, for the looted shops all belonged to F.L.N. subscription-collectors. Boisfeuras had carefully compiled his list from the documents Arcinade had provided.

Marindelle no longer slept at night. His past life stuck in his gullet until it almost choked him. That evening, while in the room next door Aicha and Glatigny kept embracing and recoiling, loving and hating each other, he tried to imagine the bonds that linked them together and the motives which had driven the young girl to go even farther in her submission to her lover, farther even than Glatigny wanted. It was she who had asked to attend the parade of suspects. Sitting at a school desk, with her head concealed in a coarse hessian sack which had been pierced with two holes for her to see through, she had picked out the members of the F.L.N. organization from among the men who were marched past for identification.

Aicha was consumed by a fire, the fire of her love, and she was feeding it with everything in her past life that had been of any importance. When she had nothing more left, she would plunge into the flames herself.

This state of mind could be traced to her inordinate and passionate nature, but still more to her spirit of rebellion against the social system in which she had lived. Even in a sophisticated family like Caid Tletla's some traces of a nomad, warrior society still survived, and a woman, even if she wore Paris dresses, was regarded solely as a source of pleasure and as booty.

For the first time in her life Aicha felt she was being treated as an equal by a man who was at once her lover and her enemy. She had just discovered that dignity had the lean face of Glatigny, his slightly pursed mouth and his frequently sad eyes.

Through the medium of Aicha Marindelle realized what

immense power lay in this spirit of rebellion which had been stored up for centuries by millions of women. There was enough explosive there to blow the whole of the Maghreb sky-high. The Algerian F.L.N., like the Tunisian Neo-Destour and the Moroccan Istiqlal, had been frightened of it and had not dared touch it, even in their struggle for independence.

How could one awaken the Moslem women, how could one make them feel that their emancipation might come from us? Certainly not by treating them to feminist lectures . . . At this point an idea occurred to the captain which most of his comrades found extremely odd, not to say unpleasant. On the following morning he had a number of women and young girls rounded up in the Kasbah; he filled three trucks with them and drove them off to a wash-house. There he made them scrub away at the paratroopers' sweat-stained vests and pants. These women had been hauled off without any of their menfolk raising a finger to protect them. They thereby lost their prestige as warriors, which suddenly reduced the ancestral submission of their wives and daughters to nothing. Bent all morning over their washing, these women felt as though they were submitting to being raped over and over again by the soldiers whose garments they were purifying.

When they came back to the Kasbah without having been molested, when these strong young men had helped them out of the trucks with a courtesy which they were rather inclined to exaggerate (more often than not their fiancés or husbands were old, decrepit and ill-mannered), some of them thought of abandoning the veil, and others that they might take on a lover who was not a Moslem.

Algiers became a paratroop city. It got used to living to the silent, stealthy tread of patrols in camouflage uniform who, with a blank expression on their faces and a finger on the trigger of their guns, paced up and down the narrow lanes and stairways.

The paratroops did not mingle with the local population; they lived on their own, outside the town and its customs, like occupants from another planet. They answered no questions, refused the wine and sandwiches that people offered them. They broke the strike, they destroyed the bomb network, but even the best-informed journalists could not tell "what was going on."

Si Millial was the brains behind the strike. Once he had vanished, the entire organization he had built up fell to the ground. The paratroops were able to penetrate the rebellion at various levels. Some of the former F.L.N. followed them through fear, because they had given away their comrades and could find no justification for this except in the victory of the paratroops; others, the greater number, because they always veered towards the stronger side, those who were able to protect them.

Within the framework of the 10th Parachute Regiment each company began to assume an autonomous existence, thereby escaping to a certain extent from the colonel's control.

Esclavier became the specialist in bomb networks and Lieutenant Pinières dealt with the Communist groups who were assisting the rebels by providing them with explosives.

One morning in February Pinières laid hands on the schneiderite factory, which was installed in an isolated villa on the seashore. There were four Europeans there, including a chemical engineer called Percevielle, and a single Arab, Khadder the Vertebra.

So as to avoid all complications, Pinières used the schneiderite to blow up the villa with all its occupants.

On 28 March Raspéguy applied for an interview with the general, which was forthwith granted. The 10th Parachute Regiment had covered itself with glory in the battle of Algiers and its colonel had become the most popular figure in the paratroop units.

The general began by congratulating Raspéguy on his promotion to full colonel.

Raspéguy puffed pensively at his pipe.

"This is certainly the first time I've felt no pleasure at being promoted, sir, maybe because this isn't the proper way to earn promotion."

"You've saved Algeria."

"And I've lost my regiment. We need a little fresh air. We've fallen into bad habits. The lads are drinking too much in order to forget what they've been forced to do. We've achieved better results than the others because we've wallowed in the shit more than they have. So we ought to be dragged out of it before the others: the process of disintoxication will be longer. Come on, sir, we've done our job, we've got our hands good and dirty, please let us go."

"I still need you here."

"Boisfeuras isn't the only one I'm worried about, sir. Marindelle blows all his pay in the Aletti casino in a single night and you know all about Glatigny and that Moslem girl of his. I don't know what's happened to Esclavier, but there's something wrong with him as well."

"Reinforcements are needed for the Némentchas."

"We're all set to go."

"Perhaps it would be better after all if you left Algiers, while there's still this little matter to be settled . . ."

"There's still some little matter to be settled?"

"It's nothing, don't worry."

While the 10th Regiment was taking to the mountains again, fifty-two Algerian officers signed a letter addressed to the President of the Republic, which they submitted to him direct, without going through the usual channels.

Sir,

In the face of the events which have disturbed our country for several years, we are anxious to remain true to our word, as officers, and to the ideal of Franco-Algerian friendship to which we pledge our lives.

If we have hitherto concealed the resentment and anxiety we feel, it is because, on the one hand, we were bound by our very education to the country we were serving and, on the other, because we had hoped that our sacrifices would sooner or later serve the cause of Franco-Algerian friendship.

Today this hope is replaced by the deep conviction that the present turn of events is actually opposed to that ideal. Our position as Algerian officers is rendered untenable by the ruthless struggle which divides our French comrades and our blood-brothers.

If we appeal to you, who represent the French nation, it is certainly not to break with our past as soldiers in the service of France, nor is it to sever the bonds of friendship, comradeship and fraternity by which we are attached to her and also to her military traditions, but out of hostility towards a policy which, if we were to condone it, would transform this attachment into a betrayal of the Algerian people who turn to us for support and of France who needs and will continue to need us.*

Captain Mahmoudi, having been charged as one of the instigators of this manœuvre, was first put under close arrest in Germany and then transferred to the Cherche-Midi prison in Paris.

It was from this prison that he wrote a long letter to Olivier Merle to try and justify the attitude he had been driven to adopt.

The letter was returned to him, with the following observation in red ink:

Lieutenant Merle has been killed in action.

While they were marching over the grey crags of the Némentchas in bitter wind and driving snow, the officers of the 10th Parachute Regiment heard that legal proceedings were being instituted against a certain number of them. The charges were brought against an anonymous X—on the grounds of excessive cruelty, and the officers in question were only to be cross-examined as "witnesses"—a pure formality which was part of the usual legal procedure.

At the evening halt, Glatigny, Boisfeuras, Esclavier, Pinières and Marindelle gathered round a camp-fire. The flame-coloured smoke rose twisting into the dark sky. Every so often the wind would blow it back into the officers' faces; whereupon they all coughed and their eyes began to water.

*This letter was published *verbatim* in *L'Affaire des Officiers Algeriens* by Abdelkade Rahmani (Editions du Seuil).

Raspéguy emerged from the blizzard, with his *maquila* in his hand. His oil-skin ground-sheet and Balaclava helmet made him look like a shepherd from his homeland in winter dress.

He squatted down by the fire and accepted a little coffee in an empty cigarette tin.

"What were you talking about?" he asked. "Those subpoenas you've received? I've also got one in my pocket. But what's a bit of paper worth when we've got guns in our hands? And yet 'they' told us to use every means at our disposal to win that battle of Algiers. Luckily we went about it fairly gently, but if we had taken them at their word! Now that they're no longer shitting themselves with fear, they send us these little bits of paper. Each time any cabinet ministers or deputies visited our H.Q. I used to say to them: 'This is on the side . . . We're doing this job because your government has ordered us to, but it repels and disgusts us.' Some of them pretended not to understand or to think that I was making a huge joke. Others would answer with a sanctimonious little gesture: 'It's for the sake of France.' And now these same bastards, are trying to haul us into court. Hold tight on to your guns, then no one will come and bother us."

There was a short silence, then Esclavier burst out in a fury which startled them all:

"Let Rome beware of the anger of the legions."

Lashed by the squalls of rain and melting snow, with their faces all but hidden in their Balaclavas, the centurions of Africa brooded on their bitterness and despair. Under their streaming ground-sheets they clutched their weapons. A more than usually violent squall put the fire out and they found themselves in the dark. Boisfeuras's rasping voice then made itself heard:

"Now we know there's only one thing left for us to do: abandon the whole damned issue."

Then Glatigny remembered. It was springtime at Sarlat College. The windows of the class-room looked out on to the golden dust rising in the courtyard. Surrendering to the confusion and poetic anguish of his adolescence, he sat there daydreaming. The voice of Father Mornelier, the professor of

Latin and Roman history, rose a note or two higher to indicate that the lesson was over. Glatigny had given a start, abruptly awakened from his gentle torpor; he had retained nothing but a clear recollection of this final sentence:

"A large number of the centurions of the Proconsulate of Africa abandoned the legions and came back to Rome. They became the Praetorian Guards of the Caesars until the day they adopted the custom of nominating them and then electing them from among themselves. That was the beginning of the end of Rome . . ."

There was a burst from a submachine-gun in one of the advance posts. A sentry had fired at a shadow or a noise: a tree bending in the wind, a *fellagha*, or some animal or other.